Freedom Fire

Elizabeth Evelyn Allen

WARNER BOOKS

A Warner Communications Company

WARNER BOOKS EDITION

Warner Books, Inc.
666 Fifth Avenue
New York, NY 10103

 A Warner Communications Company

Printed in the United States of America

First Printing: September, 1986

10 9 8 7 6 5 4 3 2 1

"What do you feel for me, Rebecca?"

"I don't want to be dependent on any man, Philip, not even you."

Hurt by her uncompromising candor, he reciprocated hotly, "Then you should have married someone like Roger Tupton. He'd have allowed you to support yourself and him too. Why didn't you just leave Hartford with him when you had the chance? Stoneham said the strutting cockerel looked smitten enough. Obviously you don't give a damn about me."

Rebecca's eyes were oddly intent as she looked at her husband. "Roger hasn't been smitten by anyone but himself since he first looked into a mirror. The only emotions I feel for him are hatred and contempt and—fear. You're also wrong about what I feel for you."

"What do you feel for me, Rebecca?"

"I want you to—" Her voice dwindled off into silence; she couldn't articulate the difficult words.

"Make love to you?" Philip asked gently.

Her "yes" was almost inaudible, but Philip heard it and rose swiftly to his feet, reaching out with both hands to pull her toward him. He lifted her up, his arms encircled her and he kissed her deeply this time. Slowly he unbuttoned her robe and pushed it to the floor—and laid her gently on the rumpled bed...

Also by
Elizabeth Evelyn Allen

The Lady Anne
Rebel

Published by
WARNER BOOKS

CHAPTER
1

FROM her hiding place in the stone wall of the library at Langley Hall, Rebecca Rayburn listened to Stanton Tupton as he confronted her Uncle Jonathan.

"Where is she, Jonathan?" Tupton demanded in a bellicose voice that reached even into the recess where the frightened girl was crouching.

"I have no idea," Jonathan responded calmly. "Have you searched her father's newspaper office?"

"You know damn well it's been shut down since Jeremy left town a month ago."

"Then I'm afraid I can't help you, Stanton. I no longer regulate Rebecca's activities. She could have left town already for all I know."

"That she hasn't," Tupton snapped. "She's still here in Falmouth, and by God, that's where she's going to stay and fulfill the contract Jeremy Rayburn made for her."

"Rebecca doesn't want to marry your son," Jonathan protested mildly.

"She had her chance to say so last Sunday when the

1

minister made the announcement in church, but she didn't say one damned word until after the service.''

''My niece has always been shy about speaking out in public; and in this case, she was taken completely by surprise. Until you showed her Jeremy's letter, she didn't believe her father could be so callous as to force her to marry a man she detests.''

''The devil you say! She was as smitten as the other girls in town when Roger first returned from England.''

''That was four years ago when she was sixteen; and what small infatuation she may have felt for a few weeks did not survive his rudeness to her. I advise you to forget Jeremy's promise, Stanton; my niece isn't going to marry your son.''

Tupton's voice rasped harshly as he responded to the blunt candor of Jonathan's advice. ''Willing or unwilling, the disobedient jade will be wed on the same day I locate her. And I advise you not to attempt smuggling her aboard the unwelcome ship that arrived in port today. The captain may be another of your British friends, but this is a patriot town and our word is law here.''

''Then there's nothing more to be said. Since your man has completed the search of my home, I ask that you leave.''

When Tupton came to make a second search of Langley Hall three days later, Rebecca scarcely reached the hidey-hole in time. Accompanied by six of the men he'd organized into the Falmouth chapter of the Sons of Liberty, Stanton shoved his way past the housekeeper and ordered the others to search the three-story structure from the attic down. His unwilling host this time, however, was not Jonathan Langley, but Captain Silas Keane, the one man in the port town whom the vast Tupton clan could not intimidate. Seated in the library, the New England ship-owner awaited Tupton with sardonic anticipation.

''You know why we're here, Silas,'' Tupton advised as he strode into the room. ''Rebecca Rayburn is not your concern, so don't be fool enough to hide her as her traitorous uncle did.''

''Two years ago when Jonathan Langley kept this town

from meeting the same fate as York, you and your brothers were damned grateful to him," Silas admonished pointedly.

Listening tensely from the concealed closet, Rebecca shuddered at the mention of York, the small village south of Falmouth. There, in the worst massacre in New England history, her mother had been killed and her sister Abigail kidnapped. Rebecca closed her eyes tightly to shut out the bitter memory.

"What the devil are you talking about?" Tupton demanded.

"Your short memory, Stanton. Before you malign Jonathan, remember that it was he who persuaded the British to give us extra muskets and enough lead for bullets to protect Falmouth after you'd riled the Indians by stealing still more of their lands."

"The local Indians wouldn't have dared attack Falmouth!"

"That's what the York farmers believed in 'sixty-nine when they stole Abenaki land."

"They were a pack of fools! But I didn't come here today to talk ancient history. I'm here to locate a fugitive and to uphold the law."

"What law? You're never going to persuade Becky to marry that reluctant lummox of yours after he refused her three years ago when Jeremy first proposed the match."

"She'll have no say in the matter. Legally she's still under her father's control."

Silas's burst of laughter held genuine amusement. "Becky hasn't been under her father's control for years. And she's a better reporter than he ever was. Folks around here didn't give a damn about his dull rehashes of Sam Adam's drumbeating, but they liked her stories about ordinary people just as they had her mother's."

"That's a pack of nonsense! Rebecca's worked under Jeremy's supervision for six years."

"Only because he needed her to keep the *Clarion* from bankruptcy. When she wasn't tramping over the country-side gathering stories, she was doing the dirty job of ink devil or setting type when Ezra Jenkins was too drunk to tell an *e* from an *o*. No matter how good Jeremy is at soldiering, he's no newspaperman."

"You're wrong there, Keane. He was born to the trade.

His New York brothers publish the best of the weeklies and run a thriving book business as well."

In the darkness of her cramped quarters, Rebecca nodded in silent agreement. Her New York uncles also paid good money for contributions, she mused, smiling in memory as she strained to hear Silas's response.

"They were smart enough to ship Jeremy two hundred miles from their own newspaper twenty-five years ago. Everyone knows it was Audrey Langley who supported him for eighteen of those years."

Reminded of the reason for his intrusive visit, Stanton Tupton reverted abruptly to the pressing business at hand. "There won't be any problem in the future. Roger has agreed to continue backing the *Clarion* when Jeremy returns."

"Damned generous of him, but a little premature considering that he doesn't have control of Rebecca's money yet. Just as a matter of interest, Tupton, why didn't your son marry her three years ago?"

"Because she was the dowdiest girl in town and too involved with those heathen Indians. What decent white man could forget that she'd buried one of those murdering savages alongside her own mother?"

"That 'murdering savage' was a boy no older than she was, and he hadn't had time to murder anyone. It was his first raid. He spared Rebecca's life because he admired that odd-colored hair of hers. If he hadn't hesitated, Will Davis might never have shot him."

"Well, the fact remains that afterward she became a heroine to the whole damned Abenaki tribe without a thought for her own reputation."

"She drew a picture of the boy for his grandfather; and if you recall, it was her kindness to that Indian boy that helped secure the release of the hostages, including her sister."

"Abigail and her Indian papoose were hardly worth the effort. My family and I didn't appreciate her disgracing our name."

"I'll be damned," Silas blurted with a chuckle. "I'd forgotten that Jeremy's first wife was another of your

nieces. But the so-called disgrace was of your own manu-
facture. If you'd bothered to count the months, you'd have
known that her child was born five months after the
massacre that claimed her husband's life. Old Henry Davis
publicly admitted the grandchild was his quick enough.
Incidentally, Abigail sold him all her York property.''

Again Rebecca smiled in recognition of Silas Keane's
purpose in raking up old scandals; he wanted Stanton
Tupton's nose rubbed in the manure of his own bigotry.
She listened with appreciative glee to the explosion.

"The devil she did! I put in a claim for that worthless
property years ago.''

"On what grounds?''

"Abigail is a relative after all, and when Jeremy's new
wife refused to have her, I did offer to take her into my
home.''

"According to Abigail, you offered her a job as a
servant so she could earn her board and room with hard
work. Obviously she preferred Jonathan's more generous
offer. As for Jeremy's third wife, enough said the better.
Now, she really did drag the Tupton name through the dirt.
She married Jeremy a month after the massacre and presented
him with a daughter four months later.''

"She's birthed two sons since and made him a good
wife,'' Stanton blustered defensively before returning to
the more important topic of money. "Who handled the sale
of the York property?''

"Jonathan hired a Boston lawyer. You might inform
Jeremy of the sale when he returns from wherever it is he's
taken our two hundred rustic soldiers.''

"He won't be back for months; he's joining the Vermont militia.''

"Ethan Allen's bailiwick? You damn fools are determined to start a war regardless of how the rest of the
country feels.''

"The colonies are all up in arms, Keane, as well you
should be.''

"Hogwash! You've never been out of Massachusetts
long enough to know a damn thing about the other colonies. If old King George came calling to the South, most

of the people there would fall on their faces in greeting. The Quakers divide Pennsylvania in half, and New York's more Tory than Whig.''

Stanton Tupton's voice became plaintively aggrieved. ''Obviously we've all been mistaken about your sympathies, Keane. You're as much a loyalist as Jonathan Langley.''

''I'm a realist. As for Jonathan, he's dealt as fairly with colonials as he has the British; but at any rate, you won't be bothered with him in the future. He isn't returning to Falmouth; he'll be making a home in New York for his new family. By this time he and Abigail will be married.''

''Langley married my niece?''

''And adopted her son.''

''So he decided to secure her inheritance for himself.''

''He's already a wealthy man—a damn sight wealthier than I am at the moment. Before he sailed for New York two days ago, Jonathan sold me the Langley Import and Shipping Company lock, stock, barrel, and ship—plus this stone barn of a house. So if you've finished your trespassing in my home, you can call off your bloodhounds and get out. If Becky were hiding here, they'd have found her by now.''

Still positive that he'd been hoodwinked, despite his failure to locate her during either of the two thorough searches of the suspect house, Tupton blustered threateningly before he and his men finally departed.

''Very well, Keane, we'll leave; but we'll be watching you and your son when he returns with his ship.''

''Philip won't submit tamely to being bullied,'' Silas warned.

''Be damned to him, the law's on our side! We'll impound the *Falmouth Star* if he tries to smuggle the girl aboard; and if he attempts to spirit her out of town any other way, he'll be arrested. I have men posted on every road and trail, even the ones leading to the Abenaki villages.''

Until she overheard that threat, Rebecca had considered her entrapment only a temporary inconvenience. Both Silas Keane and Jonathan Langley had been confident that Philip would have no trouble getting her safely to New

York. Not only was Philip one of New England's most successful smugglers, he was highly respected by Falmouth residents for his courage both on land and at sea. Rebecca, however, wondered if Philip would be willing to defy his fellow patriots and accept the responsibility for her safety. The answer she received when he arrived at Langley Hall four days after Tupton's final visit was discouraging and insulting. Because Silas's lookouts had reported that his son was under escort when he approached the house, Rebecca fled again into the safety of the stone cubicle. From that refuge she overheard the words Philip bellowed at his father.

"What the hell is going on? I damn near had to use force to get rid of the thugs who followed me here, and there's another two rebel idiots posted aboard my ship. How the devil did you become Cottontop's guardian angel?"

"I didn't. I reserved that right for you. Did Stanton tell you why she needed your protection?"

"Only that her father insisted she marry that ass Roger Tupton. Christ, even Jeremy should have had better sense than to force her to do something against her will. She can be as stubborn as a mule."

"I don't understand his reasons either, except that he seems to have an affinity for the whole Tupton clan. Odd thing, though, is the timing. Roger never displayed a lick of interest in her until after Jeremy left town."

"Why didn't Jonathan try smuggling her aboard the British ship with him?"

"You know the answer to that fool question. The drum-beaters in town who'd decided he was a loyalist traitor would have been rougher on him than they'd dare be on us. Why the reluctance this time, son? Seems to me, you were quick to volunteer your services to her during the Indian scandal a few years ago."

"The last time I took her to their village, I wanted to leave her there. With that tongue of hers, I was the one who needed protection."

As Rebecca emerged from the closet, she repressed her amusement, which threatened to erupt into giggles. She'd forgotten how angry he'd been on that occasion.

"Hello, Philip," she greeted him primly. "You deserved the scolding I gave you. I was eighteen, and you kept treating me like a hoyden brat while you bragged about your paragon of a mistress."

"Scolding, hell! You threatened to print a story about Paulette in the *Clarion*," he charged accusingly.

"Well, I didn't," Rebecca reminded him. "Although I still think everyone in town would enjoy reading about her exquisite taste in dresses, her beautifully groomed hair, and her flawless manners."

"I told you about Paulette in hopes that you'd do something to improve your own appearance, but you still look like someone's chimney-sweep kitchen slavey. It might cure pretty-boy Roger of his greed if I did let him marry you. Don't you ever brush your hair, Cottontop?"

"That's enough, Philip," Silas interrupted sharply. "Becky's hair isn't the problem; getting her to New York is—and the sooner the better. You've a few other commitments that won't wait. Do you think you can smuggle her aboard without those jackals knowing?"

"Are the other ships loaded and ready?"

"Will be by morning, but you still haven't said how you're planning to get Becky out of here."

"Before dawn tomorrow I'll take her aboard while those two guards are sleeping off the rum the ship's cook will start serving them tonight. How many trunks are you taking, Cottontop?"

"Four."

"Packed?"

"They have been for a week."

"Better dig out your leather Indian britches and boots; it'll be cold that early in the morning."

As familiar with the dangers of winter weather as Philip, Rebecca obeyed his instructions readily enough, adding a heavy linsey-woolsey skirt and an oversized fur-lined coat that had belonged to her uncle. She was dressed and ready when he arrived with eight of his crew for the silent trip down Munjoy hill to the waiting *Falmouth Star*. A hundred feet along the path, Philip whispered a low-pitched warning to her; the dock ahead was alive with lantern-armed men. Instantly, he signaled his crew to follow him, grabbed Rebecca's arm, and propelled her toward a clump of underbrush dimly visible in the gray light of wintry dawn. "Don't make a sound and don't budge from this spot until I come for you," he whispered tersely before he and his men disappeared from her sight.

Too frightened to protest, she watched the activity on the dock with straining eyes, trembling with renewed fear when Silas and Philip strode up the gangplank closely followed by Roger and Stanton Tupton. As her tension eased, she studied Roger and Philip with an objectivity she'd never before applied to either one. At twenty-nine, she reflected, Roger Tupton was more conventionally handsome, a well-built man a few inches over average height, whose expensively tailored clothes and carefully groomed hair just missed being dandified. His wellborn Canadian mother had insisted that her only child complete his education in England; his return three years later had been a social event that Rebecca had duly reported for the *Clarion.* She hadn't attended any of the parties as a guest, however, just written about them; but she was attracted to him. Her infatuation ended abruptly one afternoon in the *Clarion* printing room several months later when Roger shared a bottle of rum with Ezra Jenkins, and Rebecca learned his acquired refinement was only a shallow pretense. From the alcove next to her father's office, where she'd been writing copy, she cringed as she overheard him refer to her drunkenly as the "albino squaw," the "moon maiden who wasn't," and speculate about her "Indian lover." Rebecca had fled from the building without his knowing she'd heard, but from that day to this one she'd hated him. Angrily, she vowed she would attempt to swim the icy waters of Casco Bay before she'd consent to become the wife of Roger Tupton.

Philip Keane, she realized, was a different kind of man altogether. For the last ten of his thirty years he had been Falmouth's most elusive bachelor. Not handsome by conventional English standards, since his face clearly bore the stamp of the Indian blood he'd inherited from his Algonkin great-grandmother, he looked more like a Caribbean buccaneer than a Maine seafarer. Darker skinned than Roger, he was a tall sinewy man with a shock of black hair that framed his hawklike features. But his eyes were the vivid blue of an Irish grandmother—bold eyes which mirrored his volatile moods, from fiery temper to insolent humor.

Since he'd spent most of his time at sea or in places other than Falmouth, Rebecca's memories of Philip were concentrated on the weeks when he had provided her protection as they traveled to and from the Abenaki village at two-year intervals. On the last such journey she had tried to change his good-natured condescension to a more personal interest. Frustrated when her unskilled attempts at flirting had not worked, she'd teased him with childish impudence about the beautiful French-Canadian woman who'd taken up residence in Falmouth a month earlier. Philip had become angry at her; and she'd learned that although he was a bachelor, he wasn't an available one. His mistress, Paulette Burnell, had a firm hold on his affections. But even so, those weeks Rebecca had spent with him had been the most exciting ones of her restricted life.

Suddenly, from her hiding place, Rebecca noticed a spurt of activity on the deck of the *Falmouth Star*. She gasped in dismay as she heard Philip shout a barrage of orders to his crew, grab his father's arm, and dash down the gangplank. Minutes later the longboats were lowered and alert crewmen clambered up the lines to unfurl the sails. As the brig came alive with motion, the Tupton father and son were forced to jump onto the dock.

Rebecca was tempted to accost the four men striding toward Langley Hall, until she remembered Philip's warning. Alternating between the conviction she'd been forgotten and the fearful certainty she'd be captured, she convulsed in terror when a hand was clamped over her mouth and a terse voice whispered into her ear, "We'll have to crawl out of here, Cottontop, so shut up and concentrate on speed. My father will take care of your trunks."

With her bulky wool skirt rolled up, she was able to follow the path Philip left behind him as he moved rapidly through the underbrush. Indian style, he used his elbows to propel himself along the ground and through the occasional patches of week-old snow, and Rebecca struggled to follow his example. When they reached the protection of the scrub pine that fringed an uninhabited cove a mile from the dock, Philip stood up cautiously before he pulled his sodden companion to her feet and massaged her frozen hands.

"Start stripping pine needles for a flooring while I rig us some overhead protection," he ordered sharply. "It'll be dark before my crew can bring a boat ashore to look for us. Stop shivering, Cottontop, and get to work; it's going to be a long, cold afternoon."

The shelter was half finished when Philip dropped to his knees and covered Rebecca's mouth with a pitch-smeared hand. Silently he pointed toward the northern end of the beach, where two men were studying the trackless shoreline. Rebecca sucked in her breath sharply as she recognized the taller of the men. It was Roger Tupton. He'd shed the elegant frock coat and buff-colored pantaloons he'd worn earlier in the day. Now in practical leather buckskins, he looked like a frontiersman with hatchet strapped to his waist and a flintlock musket in his hands. It was, however, the distinctive fur hat snugged low over his forehead that triggered Rebecca's memory and sent a shudder down her spine.

"He means to trail us," Philip whispered in astonishment. "God knows why, but that strutting peacock must really want you."

Oblivious to the insult, Rebecca stared fixedly at Roger as her mind traveled back to a day two months earlier. She'd been returning from an outlying farm where the goodwife had just birthed twins, and was using the well-worn forest trail to avoid the chill winds of the open field when she heard the voices of several men, some of them Indian, a short distance from the trail. Needing more news for an indifferent issue of the *Clarion,* she'd approached the group cautiously and concealed herself in the undergrowth surrounding a small clearing. She recognized none of the white men seated cross-legged around the small campfire, but the three whose faces she could see spoke the Indian language with British accents. The fourth white man was seated with his back toward her, but his accent was colonial Maine and his well-cut buckskins and hat were identical to the ones Roger was now wearing, especially the hat. The fact that none of the Indians were from the familiar Maine tribes had frightened Rebecca into a cautious retreat from the disquieting scene. But as soon as she reached the safety of the dingy *Clarion* printing room, she'd rapidly sketched what she'd seen in the forest.

Ezra Jenkins had snorted with disbelief at her drawing of one of the Indians. "Ain't been a Huron around here since the French used them to kill off settlers fifteen years ago. But why in tarnation would those British bastards be talking to Injuns at all? Reckon you'd best tell your father, Becky; him and those lads he's training are all the pertection we got jest in case them Injuns are being riled up for an attack."

That talk with her father had been the last one she'd had with the temperamental, self-centered man who'd never made the slightest attempt to understand her. Jeremy Rayburn had studied the charcoal sketch carefully and subjected her to a thorough inquisition about any fragments of conversation she'd overheard.

"Not a word of this to anyone," he'd cautioned her sternly. "There would be the devil to pay if the enemy or any of the damned Tories in this town knew you'd seen that unholy meeting. It's too bad you didn't recognize the fourth man; he'll be the real villain if he's American."

Rebecca remembered her father's words now as she stared at Roger's departing back. He'd been the fourth man, and she'd never suspected him—not even after the *Clarion* had been delivered a week later, and Roger had dropped by the office and demanded to know when she'd visited the Watkins's farm. Angered by his harsh tone of voice, she'd forgotten her father's warning and answered the question. He'd stared at her with a grim intensity, then just walked away!

"Philip," Rebecca hissed tensely to the man crouched by her side, "we can't stay here. Roger'll be back with reinforcements."

She was so frantic that Philip felt compelled to do as she asked. Moving as silently as Indians, they walked single file through the thickets of trees that bordered the shoreline, scrambled over icy bluffs, and clawed their way through brambled underbrush. Three miles south, Philip sat down heavily on a barren rock and glared at her.

"Why the devil did you panic back there, Cottontop? Roger Tupton may not be your choice of husband, but he's not a savage monster. Your senseless fear may have cost us two days of waiting for my crew to reach us with the *Star*. Just where are you proposing we find food and shelter?"

"Roger may not be a monster, but he's not the idle fop he pretends to be," Rebecca snapped, "and he's no patriot either. It's not my money he's after, it's my silence." Tensely, she repeated the story about the clandestine meeting in the forest and her father's reaction.

"I'll be damned," Philip whistled quietly. "I thought he looked out of character today. Are you sure he's the man?"

"Positive."

"In that case, he could be dangerous; you'd be much more silent with a bullet in your head. No wonder Stanton is so anxious to get you under his own control. It's the only way he can protect his son's reputation. Catch your breath, Cottontop. We've a long walk ahead of us. Do you know the fishing village of Saco?"

"No. Do you think there's an inn there where we might stay?"

"Something much safer. One of my marines has a house there, and his wife's a close-mouthed woman."

The house proved to be a one-room log cabin with a dirt floor, and Mrs. Purdy merely grunted a greeting as she admitted the exhausted couple. But nothing had ever felt better to Rebecca than the warmth of the fire, and no dinner had ever been more appreciated than the dried-fish stew they ate in the silent company of three curious children.

Philip left immediately after the meal to locate a neighboring fisherman willing to remove his boat out of drydock long enough to take Philip out to intercept the *Falmouth*

Star. Rebecca had another plan. "Mrs. Purdy," she asked, "is there a church in the village?"

"Aye," the woman replied cautiously, "there's a sma' one about a mile yonder, but it ain't a regular faith. It's a Scot kirk, mum. Most of the folk hereabout are Scots too."

"It'll do," Rebecca announced with satisfaction. When Philip returned, tired and discouraged, she had a speech prepared. "Marry me, Philip," she told him. "It'll only be for a year, just until I'm twenty-one." She blushed furiously. "Just a name-only marriage, then we can get it annulled. I'll be of age and no one can force me to marry Roger."

Though Rebecca didn't expect Philip to be pleased, his rude reply still hurt.

"I promised Jonathan six years ago that I'd try to keep you out of trouble," he sighed tiredly, "but I sure as hell never expected to have to marry you."

"You needn't bother, Philip Keane," she replied hotly. "There must be someone else who—"

"Simmer down, Cottontop, we don't have enough time to look. Two armed Tuptons rode into the village an hour ago, and one of them is the other man we saw on the beach today. I imagine Roger will be lurking around before morning. You stay here while I fetch the minister and a couple of fishermen for witnesses. But for God's sake, do something about your hair while I'm gone."

Long before she finished untangling the snarled mop of hair she'd hated all of her life, tears were streaming from Rebecca's eyes. While her mother had been alive, she'd insisted Rebecca's pale blonde hair be strenuously brushed each day until the unruly curls formed a bearable halo around the intense, vividly colored young face.

"Your Grandmother Langley was an Icelandic girl with hair just like yours," Audrey had explained patiently. "She was a beautiful pale blonde lady with blue eyes and a pink complexion like mine."

"Then why don't I look like her?" the rebellious nine-year-old had demanded.

"Because, missy, you inherited your father's darker skin

and brown eyes.'' But her mother had frowned in understanding even as she scolded. In a town where the few
towheaded infants became dark blonde or brown-haired
six-year-olds, Rebecca's permanent combination of silvery
pale hair, vivid brown eyes, and a light tan complexion
often invited unkind comment.

After her mother's death, Rebecca had ceased the daily
agony of repeated brushings, combing her hair instead
with a few painful yanks each morning and shoving the
unruly curls into an ink-stained mobcap for her working
day at her father's shop. On more formal occasions she'd
worn a large stiff-brimmed bonnet that covered her offensive hair and screened her face as well. Over the years her
clothing had acquired a thrown-together appearance. She
owned only several well-tailored garments her Uncle Jonathan
had brought her from London which Jeremy Rayburn had
insisted she save to wear during their trips to Boston.
Since most of the women in Jeremy's wide circle of
friends there wore their hair heavily powdered or donned
white wigs, Rebecca's unusual coloring attracted little
attention.

Dismally depressed as she attempted to groom her hair
with Mrs. Purdy's worn brush, Rebecca gazed down at her
bramble-shredded brown skirt lumped over mud-stained
leather trousers and winced. Philip had a right to be
ashamed of her, even as a name-only bride; she looked as
seedy as a Jone Tawdry from the most remote of frontier
settlements. Only the sight of the untidy minister garbed in
a suit as ancient as the curled piece of yellowed parchment
he'd used for the marriage certificate restored her humor.
Like everything else about this unique day, the document
with the names Rebecca Langley Rayburn and Philip
Yancy Keane written unevenly across the page above the
crude X's of the two fishermen and the embellished signature of a Scot pastor seemed most appropriate.

Following the brief, unsentimental ceremony, Philip
suggested she pay for the service. She laughed aloud as
she dug into the pocket of her skirt and extracted one of
the six gold sovereigns she'd earned from the Rayburn
Publishers of New York for the stories she'd submitted.

Embarrassed by the munificence of the amount—a gold sovereign translated into an impressive one pound sterling—the minister solemnly promised to share the fortune with Goodwife Purdy and departed.

During the first three days after the wedding, Philip and the two fishermen searched the nearby coastal waters for the *Star* without success. On the fourth afternoon one of the Saco men reported back at the cabin with the news that Captain Keane had located his ship and was safely aboard, heading back to Casco Bay for the remainder of his fleet. Rebecca was ordered to remain hidden until her husband returned in two or three days.

That night a northeastern howler swept down from Canada, dumping its violence and snow on coastal New England without regard for human safety. Worried about their husbands trapped at sea by the vicious weather, both women kept vigil before the cabin's foot-square window. During a lull in the snow Rebecca spotted the shapes of three men approaching the cabin, and for one heart-pounding moment she thought one of them might be Philip.

"Them's outsiders," Elva Purdy whispered sharply. "You git to the loft; the young 'uns'll know what to do. Move, girl. That kind won't abide waitin' outside."

Following the three children scrambling up the crude ladder, Rebecca emerged through a hole into a small loft, three feet in height at the center.

"Lay on yer stumick, mum, and stick yer nose agin' that chink in the daubin'. We hid Paw here onct whin they 'uz after him," the older lad whispered.

Obeying the ten-year-old's instructions without argument, she felt the thin straw ticking thrown over her and the pressure of three wiry bodies using her as their pillow. The children were coughing artfully by the time their mother opened the door. Only Mrs. Purdy's high-pitched voice was audible in the loft.

"Never heered of anyone by that name, misters, so's you ain't got any call bein' here. All my young 'uns are down with the croup, and I ain't got no time fer durn fool nonsense. Do what you come fer and git out."

Rebecca held her breath when she heard one man laboriously climb the ladder, but she reckoned without the sharp wits of the oldest child. In between coughs, he gasped, "Best not come any closer, mister. This here's no ordinary croup, it's the whoopin' kind, and that kind ain't good even fer old folks."

Long after the men had hastily departed and the household was back to normal, Elva Purdy explained laconically, "Psaw, Miz Keane, my man 'us in smugglin' long afore he j'ined the cap'n. Don't you be worryin' none about the fisherfolk neither. They hate the Nosy Parkers from Falmouth and Boston 'most as much as they do the limeys who come here lookin' fer rum. But them three today will be back; they 'uz fooled all right, but they know you're somewheres around."

After the search, Rebecca and the children became fast friends. She entertained them as she had her nephew Willy during the winter months at Langley Hall. On the stretched-out deer hide that covered still other chinks in the mud daubing sandwiched between the logs, she drew the faces of the three children, using slender pieces of charcoal from the fireplace.

"Where'd you learn a stunt like that, Miz Keane?" Elva Purdy asked in wonderment.

"From my uncle partly, but mostly from my mother. She studied art in New York before she married and moved to South Carolina."

"You ain't no southerner, Miz Keane. You sound pure Maine t'me."

"My mother married a Falmouth man—my father—after her first family died during a yellow fever epidemic." Until she'd located Audrey Rayburn's trunks in the attic at Langley Hall a year after the York massacre, Rebecca hadn't known about her mother's prior marriage or about her two half brothers who had died. But then, she hadn't really known her mother either—at least not as a person until she'd read the diaries and stories carefully preserved in those trunks. The perceptive humor of her mother's writing had fascinated the girl. Several years later on the advice of a Boston bookseller, Rebecca had added some

paragraphs of her own to the stories left by the dead
woman and sent them to New York under the pseudonym
of Eb Burns, a fanciful derivation from her own name. To
her delight she'd reaped a harvest of six gold sovereigns,
which she'd kept hidden until she'd run away from Langley Hall. Now she was Mrs. Philip Keane, the temporary
wife of an arrogant sea captain whose knowledge of
women was limited to an expensive French mistress.
Rebecca smiled ruefully as she considered her first purchase with those gold coins; she had, in effect, purchased
herself a husband.

In the meantime the days of hiding passed swiftly
enough in a snowbound cabin as the three alert children
and a still-young housewife settled to learning the alphabet
and numbers Rebecca painstakingly taught them. In return
she acquired some valuable training in the art of duplicity.
The second time the Tupton cousins arrived to search the
Purdy home, they approached from the rear; and the only
warning they gave was one muffled curse seconds before
they pounded on the barred door. At a gesture from their
mother the younger Purdys clambered up the ladder, Rebecca
behind them. Swiftly the older lad rubbed dirt on his
brother's and sister's faces until their eyes were reddened
with stinging tears and they were coughing in earnest as
they settled down on the untidy bed covering their frightened guest.

As effective as their performance was in discouraging
the one man who poked his head into the loft, it was Elva
Purdy's shrieking tirade that ended the Tuptons' interest in
her home. From the moment she opened the door, she
shouted angry imprecations and accusations, drowning out
all attempts to interrupt. Even as the frustrated men retreated
across the snowy fields, her shrill voice continued berating
them; but she was smiling when she closed and barred the
cabin door.

"Ain't nothin' like a talkative woman to send a man
skedaddlin'," she chuckled.

Three days later the *Falmouth Star* dropped anchor in
Saco Harbor, but it was not Philip who arrived at the
Purdy cabin to release his imprisoned wife. A six-man

contingent of his crew appeared, led by the venerable ship's cook, Jed Daws, who'd known Rebecca since her toddler days, when she'd been allowed to play on what had then been her uncle's ship. Before Rebecca accompanied her old friend to the waiting long boat, she quietly gave Elva Purdy two gold sovereigns.

"Where's Philip?" she demanded.

"Cap'n's ashore with the rest of the crew," Jed responded promptly, "but that's the only one of your durn fool questions I'm supposed to answer."

"Are my trunks aboard?"

"Reckon so, and the Cap'n says you're to have a bath. Them Injun britches of yourn look like you've been wallowing in mud."

"That and sleeping with a thousand unfriendly insects for almost two weeks," she complained. "Why didn't Philip come to the cabin?"

"He needed to talk to the folks hereabout and didn't want you interferin'."

"Does he know that some of the Tuptons are still here?"

"Couldn't miss seein' them since they was on the dock waitin'. But they ain't all that important anymore, Becky."

"Why not? Just what's become more important all of a sudden?"

"Durn limeys, that's what. They was layin' in wait off Casco Bay when we left, and we played hide 'n' seek with them the whole way here."

"Where's the rest of the Keane fleet?"

"Old Silas is stickin' it out in Falmouth with his ships, but we'll be meetin' up with our ten somewheres in the Nantucket below the Cape."

"That's not the most direct route to New York," Rebecca exclaimed.

"Nope, it sure ain't."

"But it is the way to New Bedford, isn't it?" she thought aloud. "What happened in Falmouth, Jed?"

"Work 'uz what happened, Becky. Cargo was changed, and the *Star* was stripped down to a durn merchantman."

"Were there any members of the Massachusetts congress in town?"

"That's a durn fool question."

"No, it isn't. Six months ago the congress named New Bedford as the training center for the colony's marines."

"Jest how'd you be knowin' that, Becky?"

"My father was a member of the defense committee, and I attended the meetings with him. Has the Keane fleet joined the Massachusetts navy?"

"Ain't fer me to say, and I wouldn't be pesterin' the cap'n with questions if I 'uz you. He's been madder 'n a caged bobcat all week."

Rebecca sighed in resignation. "Did he tell you he married me?"

"Nope, but I figured you comin' aboard must be the reason he ordered that fancy Frenchie of his off the *Star*. She sure raised a ruckus about comin' with him, and he ain't one to like female strings tying him down."

While Rebecca spent the next hours scrubbing the accumulated filth from herself and from her worn leather clothing, she contemplated the increasing complexities in her life. When she rejoined the bald-headed, wizened cook in his galley, she readily accepted the mug of rum-laced coffee he offered her. As the night temperatures plummeted, she and Jed huddled near the galley stove for warmth while eating the unappetizing food he called Yankee hash and imbibing several more pots of coffee and rum. She was giggling quite happily when her old friend escorted her back to the master's cabin, opened the door for her, and departed wordlessly with the lantern. Stumbling awkwardly around in the dark before she located the bunk, she removed only her cloak, dress, and shoes before tumbling into the warm haven; her only reaction to the irritated grunt from the man already ensconced there was another burst of giggles. Eight nights of sleeping with three wriggling children in a bug-infested loft had dulled her sensibilities enough for her to be unselective in choice of bedfellows. Snuggling against the warm back of her name-only husband, she burrowed down beneath the covers and fell asleep instantly.

By the time that name-only husband shook her awake early the next morning, Rebecca's wayward humor had vanished without leaving a trace. She watched him balefully as he seated himself at the chart table on the far side of the cabin, disapproval stamped on his features.

"If you want me to get dressed, Philip," she reproached him tartly, "you'll please do me the courtesy of leaving."

"A little late for modesty, isn't it, Cottontop? Especially after you crawled into my bed last night without the slightest hint of maidenly reticence," he countered.

"Where was it I was supposed to sleep?" she demanded. "This was the cabin Jed ordered my trunks placed in."

"He'd been told to quarter you in the mate's cabin. You didn't by any chance tell that old reprobate we were married, did you?"

"I wasn't aware it was supposed to be a secret. Didn't you tell anybody in Falmouth?" she asked curiously.

"My father, and he wasn't exactly overjoyed. Was our marriage what you and my ship's cook were celebrating last night when you two consumed that bottle of uncut rum?"

"Hardly. Jed was merely being sympathetic."

"Next time he'll do it with watered wine or I'll have him keelhauled. Just as a matter of interest, where'd you learn to drink like a shore-leave sailor and still wake up with your wits reasonably intact?"

Rebecca shrugged resentfully. "Ezra Jenkins didn't like to drink alone."

"Well, I hope you're equally adept at making coffee."

"If I hadn't been," she snapped, "the *Clarion* would never have been printed."

"Good, because that's what you're going to be doing for the next hour. It'll take Jed the rest of the day to come to."

"Then tell John Sugs to take over; he's a better cook anyway."

"So my top marine is another of your old friends. Just don't try any of your tricks on him. Now put on some warm clothing, Cottontop; you've got work to do, and it's colder than billy-be-damned outside. I'll give you fifteen minutes of privacy, and if you're not up by then, I'll dress you myself.''

Shivering with cold as she cracked the film of ice formed overnight in the water bucket, Rebecca sped through the ritual of washing before she pulled on the best of her wool dresses, this one the color of new-hulled chestnuts with only one small disfiguring spot of ink. She'd just finished a vigorous brushing of her hair when Philip strode into the cabin, ignoring her very presentable appearance as he jammed a sailor's stocking cap over her head and forced her arms into one of his own heavy wool coats.

"You're not dressing for a party, Cottontop. That bath you took last night used up every drop of galley water, so now you can fetch two buckets of it from the rain barrel on deck. You can screech all those angry words at me after I've had some coffee."

With her jaw held grimly shut, Rebecca climbed the short companionway to the aft deck lugging the heavy oaken buckets. The scene that greeted her was breathtakingly beautiful, a rare winter day on the North Atlantic coast when the water appeared a sparkling blue in the slanted morning sunrise. From a small seaward island a flock of gulls soared skyward as if they too rejoiced in the glory of the cloudless day. Caught up in the serenity of the peaceful scene, Rebecca forgot her anger, but when she turned her eyes shoreward, she froze in terror. Fifty feet away from the *Star* was a longboat full of men—not the ship's returning crew, but men who were rowing Roger and Stanton Tupton toward her with swift efficiency. As she turned to flee back to the companionway, she heard Philip's low-pitched voice, "Stand just where you are, Cottontop. I want them to see you."

CHAPTER
2

NUMBLY aware that Philip and the safety of the companionway were fifteen long feet away, Rebecca felt as defenseless as a chicken on the chopping block. Still clutching the empty buckets as if they afforded her some slight protection, she watched tensely as two grim-faced men climbed over the taffrail and strode toward her determinedly. Roger Tupton reached her first and gripped one of her arms with fingers that dug into her flesh with a cruel pressure. Both of the heavy buckets clattered to the deck as Rebecca tried to pull away, but her captor's only reaction was to yank her closer to him as he forced her toward the railing.

"That's far enough, Tupton," Philip called out harshly, stepping from the concealment of the hatchway.

Swiftly, Roger dropped Rebecca's arm and reached for the pistol holstered beneath his heavy beaver coat, but before he could turn around to level the weapon at the ship's captain, Philip's voice rang out again, this time addressed to the father.

"Stanton, if you value your son's life, advise him to put that gun away. I wouldn't like his blood staining my deck."

Having already ascertained that there were no crewmen in sight and that Philip was unarmed, the older man responded with a blustering authority, "We're not here to do violence, Keane. We're here on legal business, to take this runaway girl into lawful custody."

"Aboard my ship, I'm the only law, Tupton."

"Don't be a fool! You've got only three men aboard to back you up; the rest of your crew are sleeping drunkenly ashore on the floor of the rum shack. My son and I have six armed men with us, so there's really no contest. Come along, Rebecca, you've caused me enough trouble."

"I'm not leaving, Mr. Tupton," Rebecca shouted with a sudden fury, "and I'm not marrying your son."

"You should have said so when the preacher made the announcement from the pulpit, but you didn't say a word," Stanton reminded her calmly. "Moreover, your father's instructions are clear, and I mean to see them carried out. While he's away on our country's business, he wants you under our protection."

"There's no way you can force me into marriage, not now. I'm already—"

"Relax, Cottontop. You're not going to be forced into anything," Philip interrupted her smoothly. "If our visitors will take the time to look up into the rigging, they'll find Jed Daws and John Sugs there with rifles, and both of them are experienced sharpshooters. And if they'd care to glance shoreward, they'll see my 'drunken' crew and a dozen local fishermen watching them. Stanton, I've been waiting an hour for you to make this move because I wanted to talk to you and your son privately. Until I deliver Rebecca to her uncle in New York, she'll remain with me. I'd advise you to leave peaceably without delay. Since you boarded my ship illegally, I could order both of you shot or thrown into the water, where you'd drown in five minutes at the current temperature. In either case I'd be within the law. If you're still thinking your six men will come to your rescue, look over the railing. There's been a rifle trained on them from a gun port since you and your son climbed aboard."

As Philip spoke, Rebecca moved unsteadily to his side, watching with a satisfied malice as the two Tuptons glanced uneasily at the riggings and the shore. They had already reached the railing when Philip issued a final warning.

"An additional word of caution, Roger; until you started this insanity, Rebecca didn't have a notion in hell that you were the fourth white man at that powwow of imported

Indians; and she hadn't overheard a word of what was said. Whatever your purpose was in consorting with the enemy, you'd be wise to avoid being caught in the middle. In a civil war as bloody as this one will be, no one can play a double game and hope to survive."

Shocked by Philip's final pronouncement and by the grim conviction expressed by his tone of voice, Rebecca didn't bother to contradict him about having understood some of what had been said at that forest meeting. Compared to the threat of war—a bloody civil war, Philip had called it—Roger Tupton was only a minor irritation.

"What makes you so sure?" she asked later as she and her preoccupied husband ate breakfast.

"That there'll be a war? It's already started as far as I'm concerned."

"Because a British ship followed you here?"

"Jed talks too much. Cottontop, why didn't you speak out in church when Stanton made the announcement about you and Roger?"

"I didn't believe it at first, and then I was afraid people would laugh at me if I tried to say anything in public."

"You weren't shy with the Indians, not even that first time in their village."

"That was different; they didn't treat me with contempt."

"But most of the people in Falmouth did? You have to admit, Cottontop, that you earned some of that criticism," Philip chided her lightly. "You spent almost as much time on the waterfront as the busiest doxy in town."

"If the *Clarion* hadn't carried the news about incoming cargoes, shippers like your father and my uncle would have been out of business. And stop trying to change the subject, Philip. Why didn't you warn me the Tuptons were coming this morning?"

"I thought you'd panic if you knew ahead of time."

"Why didn't you just tell them that you'd already married me?"

"For the same reason I didn't have the certificate recorded in Falmouth. The fewer people who know about our marriage, the better chance we'll have for an annulment in a year's time."

"Then why did you even bother?"

"It was the only protection I could give you at the time. Believe it or not, Cottontop, I do care about your safety. That's why I staged that reception this morning. I wanted to make sure that Stanton knew about his son's involvement with British agents, and I wanted to frighten Roger enough to leave you alone."

As unconvinced by Philip's explanation as she was unsure of her own feelings, Rebecca persisted with questions she realized instinctively he was trying to avoid. "What happens if we can't get an annulment?"

"Then we're both in trouble. I don't believe that a sailor has the right to marry anyone until he's permanently beached. He isn't home long enough to raise his children. Until I was thirteen, I rarely saw my father. But on that visit home, he handed me a seaman's outfit and informed my mother that I was joining his crew. He never once asked if she minded or if the sea was what I wanted as a life's work. She died of loneliness the next year."

"Some wives live aboard ship with their husbands."

"Not many of them, Cottontop, especially after they begin a family. Besides, it's an unfair practice for the crew. A woman aboard ship can play havoc with the men's morale."

"Is that why you refused to bring Paulette with you? Jed told me she asked you."

Philip's eyes narrowed to angry slits as he glared at the composed face opposite his. "One woman aboard ship is bad enough luck; with two of you, we'd have sunk before we rounded Cape Cod," he snapped. Looking sourly over at her trunks and untidy parcels of luggage piled against the bulkhead, he added caustically, "You may sink us yet with all that junk."

"Since I seem to irritate you with my presence," she responded evenly, although she was seething with resentment at his blunt honesty, "you can transfer me and my *junk* to another ship and be relieved of any responsibility for an unwanted wife. I can find my own way to New York from New Bedford."

"Christ, Jed even told you about New Bedford! Did he also mention our purpose there?"

"He didn't have to. I know all about New Bedford, including the fact that there may be British soldiers stationed there."

Philip's eyes were still narrowed, but in speculation now rather than anger. "Where'd you hear that, Cottontop?"

"From one of the letters that arrived at the *Clarion* office after Jeremy had already left. It seemed only logical to me. Why would the British take control of Boston and leave the port of New Bedford completely free? Especially if they'd learned of the defense committee's plans? If I were you, I wouldn't sail into that harbor with a fleet of privateers. You don't have enough men or guns aboard the *Star* to ward off a well-armed packet boat, much less a ship-of-line."

"You know too damn much for your own good, Cottontop. Until we reach port, I'm keeping you locked in this cabin so you don't demoralize what crew I do have," Philip growled.

To Rebecca's chagrin, he removed the ship's chart and a few of his essential sea garments from the cabin and left without even a hint of apology. Within an hour she felt the ship begin to move seaward, and for two days through the rolling trip around Cape Cod into the calmer waters of Nantucket Sound she saw no one except the taciturn John Sugs, who treated her as he had when she was a child.

"Best eat your dinner, Becky. You know I ain't about to answer those durn fool questions of yourn. Ain't none of this your business."

More amused than irritated by the blunt refusal, Rebecca refrained from mentioning what she'd already learned by looking out of the windows at the aft of the cabin. Early that morning she'd watched as the ten companion ships of the *Star* had dropped anchor off one of the Elizabeth Islands south of Cape Cod and due east of Buzzards Bay. At least, she reflected wryly, Philip had the sense not to expose his entire fleet to danger.

When she received a brusque note from Philip warning her that there might be a boarding and reminding her curtly to brush her hair, her earlier complacency dissipated. He hadn't even noticed that her hair had been thoroughly brushed and groomed during every one of the fourteen days of their marriage. With a deliberate malice she donned the dark red wool dress and its matching pelisse that Jeremy had allowed her to wear only on special occasions in Boston, and carefully tied the small complimentary bonnet over the pale curls that cascaded neatly down her back.

Childishly disappointed that it was not Philip who unlocked the cabin door, but rather John Sugs accompanied by a pair of red-coated British soldiers, Rebecca reacted in anger and announced that she was leaving the ship and would be staying at a New Bedford inn.

"Not unless you have official permission," one of the soldiers stated laconically, but the younger Englishman smiled at her with a flattering interest.

During her escorted walk along the embarcadero where the *Falmouth Star* was snugged to the wharf between two whalers, Rebecca saw only her husband's back as he strode some fifty feet ahead flanked by another pair of vigilant soldiers.

Even when they were both deposited in the same office to face the same uniformed inquisitor, Philip's only greeting for her was a scowl of annoyance. But Rebecca was far too interested in the British officer to pay attention to a disapproving husband. The man's insignia identified him as a captain of a British ship-of-line, yet she had seen no such vessel anchored in the harbor. She listened with some trepidation as Philip took the offensive.

"I want to know why my ship has been searched," he demanded.

"We're checking the cargoes of all colonial ships," the Englishman responded blandly. "But in your case we were particularly interested in the possibility of contraband arms, Captain Keane. Our finding nothing unusual aboard does not completely satisfy our interest in your father's company. Where are the other ships that left Falmouth with you a week ago?"

Rebecca observed that her husband's jaw was harshly set as he answered tersely, "Scattered over the Atlantic on their individual merchant routes."

A faint smile greeted this response. "And is New Bedford your particular merchant route?"

"Only for the potatoes and jerked venison. My main business here is buying new rigging for the *Falmouth Star* and additional crew members. Are there any more questions?''

"No questions, Captain Keane, but rather a relayed command. The crown insists that the ships your father acquired when he bought out Jonathan Langley be used to fulfill the contracts Langley made for cross-Atlantic trade with the mother country."

In the silence that followed this announcement, Rebecca could sense the growing tension between the two men. Remembering the advice Elva Purdy had given her about talkative women, she exploded into speech.

"That's just not fair, Captain Sinclair," she declared vigorously. "My Uncle Jonathan sold out because he couldn't make a profit carrying English cargoes. The rebels wouldn't buy anything, not even the dishes and wool cloth they needed. And you know good and well they kept most of the loyalists away too. Eventually, he had to reship all of that unsold merchandise to New York or to the southern colonies where, thank goodness, folks aren't as political as they are in Massachusetts. But he lost money, and I'm as positive as I can be that Silas Keane is too shrewd a merchant to make the same mistake."

"What's your name, young lady?" Captain Sinclair interrupted in exasperation.

Her smile was vapidly broad as she answered, "It's Rebecca, Captain Sinclair, Rebecca Langley, and that's what I want to talk to you about. Captain Keane was supposed to be taking me to New York to join my Uncle Jonathan there, and I'm most frightfully eager to arrive before he begins to worry about me. But now that Captain Keane is going to be here in New Bedford for goodness knows how long, I wonder if you might be able to help me arrange faster transportation. There's a terribly important reason why I want to rejoin my uncle. You see, I wasn't allowed to leave Falmouth with him and my sister because I had an annoying problem with a man who was under the delusion that I'd agreed to marry him. Have you ever heard of a Falmouth family named Tupton, Captain Sinclair?"

"No, Miss Langley," the naval officer responded curtly,

"and I'm not in the business of arranging transportation for civilians."

"Well, you needn't glare at me as if I've done something wrong, Captain. I'm sure you never threatened to kidnap your wife as Roger Tupton threatened me. Since I'm a stranger in town, the least you can do is recommend an inn where I'll be safe."

"There's not a spare bed to be found in either New Bedford or Dartmouth; so until I permit Captain Keane to leave, you'll have to remain aboard his ship. Both settlements are full of country riffraff who've been drifting in all winter, young men mostly and not the kind an unchaperoned young lady could associate with safely."

"Then will you kindly allow Captain Keane to go about his business of refitting his ship, although goodness knows, the *Falmouth Star* rarely needed repairs when my uncle owned it. But if you keep him here talking all day about English contracts that he doesn't know a thing about, I never will get to New York."

There was no mistaking the Englishman's irritation as he rose abruptly from his chair and ordered her to wait in the corridor while he finished his business with Captain Keane. Listening through the closed door minutes later, Rebecca giggled silently as she overheard the Britisher fervently bless the naval code that forbade women aboard English warships.

"Your Miss Langley would make a bottle of rum a daily necessity within the limited confines of a ship," he blustered. "Does she always talk that much?"

"She can be equally annoying in other ways," the American growled in response. "There have been times I've needed two bottles to put up with her."

"What the devil did you think you were doing in there?" Philip demanded after he'd been dismissed and had all but dragged her away from the building.

"I was preventing you from losing your temper and being charged with treason by Captain Sinclair," she retorted tartly.

Philip halted abruptly and glared down at her. "How did you know his name?"

"I asked one of the soldiers who took me there. People like Captain Sinclair expect social inferiors like us to know their names."

Momentarily silenced, Philip resumed walking at a more normal pace. "Where'd you learn the kind of deceit you were using with Sinclair?" he asked as casually as a slowly receding anger would permit.

"From Jonathan. He made friends of every British officer who visited Falmouth by talking about the things they wanted to hear. You know as well as I do that half of his ships were as illegally engaged as yours, but the only ones he ever mentioned to the English were the six that sailed cross-Atlantic between Falmouth and Liverpool. That's why the British believes he's a dependable loyalist."

"You sounded like one yourself, Cottontop."

Rebecca shrugged impatiently. "I'm as much a loyalist as I am a rebel, Philip. I think that Massachusetts laws are just as restrictive as English ones. And I'll wager you that Sam Adams and John Hancock and John Adams and Thomas Jefferson and the other politicians who're starting this war won't fight in a single battle themselves. The only things they'll get into a fight about will be who gets the most important positions in the new government."

"Your father will be fighting," Philip reminded her.

"My father will be fighting because he believes in fairy tales and myths," she snapped stridently.

Smothering a smile at her vehemence, Philip murmured, "Whatever happened to your claim that you hated to speak out in public?" The answer he received to this frivolous question an hour later disturbed him far more than had her behavior with Captain Sinclair.

At a modest inn inconspicuously located on the one commercial street in New Bedford where Philip had been told to make contact with the patriot authorities, he was led immediately by a nervous innkeeper to a private dining room. To Philip's annoyance, the two men waiting there recognized Rebecca and greeted her warmly before they paid any attention to him.

"What in the world are you doing here, Rebecca?" the

older man demanded. "Your father said he'd arranged for
you to be married."

"My father forgot to ask me if I approved of his
choice," she explained calmly and proceeded to introduce
Philip to the men she identified as members of the Massachusetts defense committee. "Do you want me to wait in
the public room while you discuss your business with
Captain Keane?" she inquired with the same composed
self-assurance she'd displayed since she'd entered the room.

"Lord, no," the younger of the committeemen assured
her. "You can save us considerable trouble if you'll act as
our secretary as you did when your father attended the
meetings. The others should be along shortly. In the
meantime I suggest the landlord serve us food and drink to
allay any suspicions on the part of soldiers watching this
establishment. I suspect Captain Keane has already met the
officious British devil who took over New Bedford a
month ago."

Philip nodded grimly. "Miss Rayburn and I were both
interviewed by Captain Sinclair."

"Good lord," the older man protested, "what did he
want with you, Rebecca? I hope he didn't ask you any
questions about your father's present whereabouts."

Before she could articulate a denial, Philip answered for
her. "Your Captain Sinclair met a Miss Langley this
morning, and I very much doubt he'll want to meet with
her again."

Any further discussion of a personal nature was ended
by the furtive arrival of the six men who made up the rest
of the local contingent of the defense committee. During
the meal that followed, Philip spent his time in a silent
appraisal of the girl he'd married. This was not the
skittish, unkempt hoyden he'd known in Falmouth. This
was a woman whose eyes—really beautiful brown ones, he
realized with shock—watched the activity around her with
an alert attention. Even in the dark red outfit, which did
little to enhance her vivid coloring, Philip recognized the
incipient beauty of her face.

Uneasily he recalled his own sluggish awakening the
morning after she'd crawled into his bed four nights ago.

He'd wanted her then, but only because of the pressure her sleeping body had exerted against him. The fine silky texture of her hair had alerted him to the identity of his bedfellow and driven him to make a hasty retreat. In the excitement of baiting the trap for the Tuptons, he'd forgotten the momentary attraction he'd felt for her; and he'd carefully avoided any chance for a repetition of what would have been the worst of all situations for him—a consummated marriage. As matters now stood, the name-only convenience was as much a protection for him as for Rebecca. It had already spared him another unwelcome intrusion into his freedom.

Two years ago, when Paulette Burnell had left the home he'd maintained for her in Quebec for the previous five years and followed him to Falmouth, he'd realized that his infatuation for the beautiful, older Frenchwoman had become little more than a tolerant companionship. Increasingly, he'd resisted her attempts to make the alliance permanent by reminding her that she still had a husband even though he'd deserted her in Canada and returned to France. But two weeks ago when Philip had come back to Falmouth from Saco, she'd renewed her insistence on marriage with a determination that had made him grateful he was no longer available. Having gone to her Falmouth home with the vague intention of telling her about Rebecca, he'd found himself back in Paulette's bed. It was considerably later in that warm cocoon that she'd reopened the old argument.

"*Chéri*, while you were rescuing that foolish girl from the Tupton *cochon*, I received a letter from my old priest in Quebec. He agreed with me that my husband could well be dead, since no one has heard from him in ten years. He was also sympathetic about my desire to marry you. It has been a long time, *chéri*, and we are *très agréable* together, *n'est-ce pas*? We could be married just as you wanted when we first discovered our love for each other."

Shaken out of a pleasant euphoria, Philip had left the bed hastily and sought the doubtful warmth of a dying fire. "I'm no longer twenty-two, Paulette," he'd told her harshly, "and I no longer want the responsibility of the permanency of marriage.'' He didn't even remember Rebecca until after he'd reached the safety of his ship.

Despite the continuing violence of the storm, he'd driven himself and his men hard for the next five days, provisioning the Keane fleet for the war that was inevitable. Under the concealing cover of a blinding snow, they'd emptied the warehouses of ammunition, installing all of the cannon aboard the ships Silas Keane would operate in the deadly waters between Falmouth and Halifax where a British fleet was already assembled. In the presence of the four members of the provisional congress of Massachusetts, both Philip and his father had pledged their fleets to the defense of the war-ready colony; and Philip had promised to report to New Bedford for additional armament and men.

On the eve of his departure, Philip was writing a cowardly farewell to Paulette when she appeared on the dock with a carriage full of trunks and parcels.

''I have decided to go with you this time, *chéri*,'' she announced with a determined finality. ''This *cochon* town is now an impossibility for me. We will find us a more civilized city where it will not be so necessary for us to marry, since you are so opposed.''

Philip experienced a twinge of guilt when he recalled the scene that followed her ultimatum. She had pleaded tearfully at first and then angrily when he'd adamantly refused to allow her to board the *Falmouth Star*. Silas had intervened finally and promised to delay his own departure long enough to arrange overland transportation to Boston or New York for her. Relieved to be freed of at least one of the women with whom he'd become foolishly involved, Philip had sailed with the outgoing tide the next morning.

But now he was confronted by the second one, whose hold over him could prove the more deadly. How in the devil had he been deluded enough to believe Rebecca hopelessly unattractive? With an abrupt understanding, he recalled how she'd looked in the library at Langley Hall the night before he'd brought her to Saco. She'd been wearing a soiled mobcap of the type that made all women look like grotesque children, and her aproned dress had made her appear as shapeless as the plump housekeeper. Yet today the damned girl was gracefully slim, and her face bore no trace of its usual disfiguring suspicion. Philip was sharply aroused from his contemplation by a man exasperated at having to repeat his question.

"I asked you how many marines and additional crew you will be needing, Captain Keane." The speaker was a ferret-faced merchant whose life was already dedicated to the revolution that had yet to begin, but whose fortune was still obviously uncommitted as he presented his bill for the outfitting of the men to the two provisional congressmen.

Having dealt with the same type of blunt Yankee businessmen for a dozen years, Philip responded with an equal brevity. "Five hundred and fifty marines, half that number of able seamen, and fifty officer-caliber recruits. In addition, I'll need twenty cannon each for eleven ships and a long rifle for every marine."

The younger congressman frowned heavily. "It'll take a month to fill that order, maybe longer. Every man and piece of equipment will have to be smuggled out to your fleet past Sinclair's shore patrol, and you'll have to remain here in port under Sinclair's personal surveillance. He's no fool, Captain Keane; he'll demand to know the reasons for such a long layover."

"He already knows and has granted me permission to replace my ship's rigging for the accommodation of more sail, providing Mr. Coxton agrees to do the job."

"Aye, lad," the leather-garbed shipwright responded promptly, "some months ago your father notified me about the specified changes. I'll handle your *Falmouth Star* myself, but it'll take some doing to smuggle my work crews and the needed material to your fleet. Dan'l," Coxton addressed the older congressman abruptly, "will your defense committee bear the cost of paying some of the local whaling captains to undertake the smuggling for me?"

"The money's available, Coxton," the congressman replied readily, "and Miss Rayburn has agreed to write up the bills all of you gentlemen will be submitting. So I suggest we get to work."

For the next two hours the voices of the New Bedford merchants were the only sounds accompanying the scratching of Rebecca's quill as she recorded the charges and costs. No one thought to ask if her fingers were cramped as she wrote the lists of cannon, shot, and rifles; food, rum, and water barrels; lamps, flags, and charts. When she'd finished, the nine men present solemnly signed the bill that would be presented first to the provisional Massachusetts congress and eventually to the embryo Continental one. Rebecca's own signature was never elicited.

The only personal note injected into the sordidly commercial considerations of war was the frequent contemplative glances Rebecca received from the Connecticut armorer, Henry Cravens, who was supplying the long rifles. At the end of the meeting he offered her his personal escort overland to New York, an offer Philip declined peremptorily.

"Miss Rayburn has been entrusted into my care until I deliver her safely to her uncle. I cannot delegate that responsibility."

Nor did he! Once aboard the *Falmouth Star* after a brisk walk from the inn, he opened the door to the master's cabin and waited until Rebecca was inside before he locked the door. Proceeding to the galley, he instructed Jed Daws and John Sugs to see to her needs during the weeks in port.

"Becky ain't goin' to be happy about bein' locked in again, Cap'n," Jed remonstrated.

"No, but she'll be safer. The men we'll be taking on as crew could be a damned randy lot since they've been holed up in hiding for a month or more; and there'll be outside workmen crawling over this ship every day. I'll see she takes a walk onshore if she becomes too bored."

The reception Rebecca had received at the inn still rankled Philip's sense of the appropriate. She wasn't even a patriot, yet every man there had trusted her, and one fool had acted downright smitten. Philip's eyes narrowed in anger as he remembered her deliberate duplicity—talkative as a magpie with a dangerous British officer and as mute as a church mouse with the Americans. Whatever had possessed Jeremy Rayburn to let a slip of a girl take part in so many secret negotiations? If she were a loyalist in reality, she could be a threat to his own safety. Frowning heavily, Philip turned his attention to the immediate problems of ship alterations as the supply wagons began appearing on the dock.

For the remainder of that day and the next, he was too preoccupied with the engrossing challenge of increasing the speed of a staid commercial brig with a more efficient rigging of sails to worry much about an irksome personal problem. But on the third morning that problem became a major one when Captain Brian Sinclair boarded the *Falmouth Star* and demanded to see Miss Langley. A startled and apprehensive Philip led the British officer to her cabin, hoping she'd be in no fit condition to receive an unwelcome guest. Once inside, however, he scarcely noticed her well-groomed appearance; he was too busy staring at the interior of the cabin, which had been altered beyond his recognition. Every foot of flat wall surface was covered with black-and-white drawings of human faces. Philip stared at them in consternation, recognizing most of the subjects instantly: a sardonic representation of the disapproving minister who'd married them, a humorous caricature of Jed Daws, and a romanticized sketch of a Saco fisherman. On the most prominent spot on the bulkhead opposite the door was a detailed and highly flattering likeness of Captain Sinclair himself.

The Englishman's opening question was a purely rhetorical one delivered with a biting sarcasm. "Did you believe me stupid enough not to investigate the lie you told me about your name, Miss Rayburn? A simple interrogation of my officers revealed that Jonathan Langley is not your father as you implied, but rather the brother-in-law of Jeremy Rayburn, whose name appears on several lists of suspect colonists. One of the officers even recognized you from the description I gave him, and his subsequent testimony proved very enlightening."

Philip's pulse rate increased alarmingly as he glared at the composed face of the damned woman who may well have destroyed all of his carefully laid plans with her idiot chatter. Her indifferent shrug in response to Sinclair's accusation only increased the American's premonition of peril.

"It's a name I prefer, Captain Sinclair," she murmured easily. "My mother was a Langley, and I haven't lived at father's home since before her death. He and I do not agree on many subjects, and I preferred my uncle as a guardian. I imagine you were also told that my father owns the *Falmouth Clarion*, which in the past has featured a number of incendiary editorials. I can assure you that my own contributions to the newspaper had nothing to do with politics. Here you are glaring at me as if I were some kind of criminal because I choose to use a less controversial name. However, I don't want you to think that I'm a rebellious daughter. It was my father who requested that I live with my uncle since his new wife objected to a grown stepdaughter. Does this explanation answer your question, Captain Sinclair?"

"To an extent, Miss Rayburn," the discomfited man replied noncommittally, "except for the reasons you're a lone woman aboard a ship captained by a man who is himself not above suspicion."

Rebecca's voice became several degrees more emotionally intense. "I told you the reason, Captain. My father agreed to a marriage for me that I did not want, but the man was an aggressive boor who would not accept my refusal. I'm quite certain that you never placed your wife into such an unhappy position, and I can only be grateful that Captain Keane rescued me. I know nothing evil about his reputation, and he works very hard to keep mine unblemished. I am kept locked in this cabin with only the ship's cook to tend my needs, and Jed Daws could not possibly be a threat to anyone. That's his picture behind you."

Captain Sinclair, however, was far more interested in the one he'd discovered of himself. "When did you draw this, Miss Rayburn—or if you prefer, Miss Langley?"

"Right after I met you."

"What is it you use?"

"Pieces of native graphite from the Barrowdale mines in

Cumberland. My uncle always brought me boxfuls when he returned from England."

"Would you sell me this sketch, Miss Langley? You were right about my being married; and since I haven't been home in two years, I would like my wife to be reminded at least of how I look."

"You may have it, Captain Sinclair, but it won't ship well at all because graphite smears easily. Oil paints are the only ones that can survive ocean travel, and I don't have any of those with me."

"If I located some, would you be able to complete a picture before Captain Keane leaves?"

"It never takes me long because I'm not a real artist. About the only thing I can promise is that it will last better and look something like you."

"Fair enough. I'll arrange for you to be escorted to my office every morning. I'll be too busy to pose formally, but your memory seems more than adequate. I apologize for my earlier distrust, Miss Langley."

That night Philip joined Rebecca in the cabin for dinner and took her for a walk afterward, but the evening was not an unqualified success. The first unpleasant moment occurred when he noticed another drawing added to the original collection. Under the caption "Pinch-penny Patriots" were caricatures of eight vulturelike faces, crudely sketched but still recognizable as the men who'd been at the inn.

Furiously Philip tore the offending picture into small pieces. "If your English friend had seen that damned thing, he'd have hunted those men down and accused them of treason against the crown."

"He'd never have found them," Rebecca scoffed. "Their kind can always find safe holes to hide in. Only men like you and my father will be killed in this war, never the schemers who started it."

Frowning now with concern rather than anger, Philip put his hands on her tense shoulders and shook her gently. "You're too bitter, Cottontop. Those are all good men who take real chances with their lives. What I'm worried about is your becoming involved with that Englishman. It's as if you're trying to give aid and comfort to the enemy.''

"Is that what you call it, Philip?" Rebecca asked in astonishment. "I thought it was merely diversionary tactics. While Captain Sinclair is in his office having his picture painted, he can't be watching you so closely.''

Regarding her with increased speculation, Philip shook his head. "There was no way you could have predicted his discovering your real name.''

"Why not? Jonathan brought hundreds of British officers to America, and some of them met me at Langley Hall. Any one of them could have told him about me, or about Jeremy for that matter.''

"Why did you draw his picture?''

"He has an easy face to draw.''

"How did you know he had a wife?''

"Don't you notice anything, Philip? There was a framed cameo of a woman on his desk, and most men don't display pictures of their mistresses in public.''

Reminded of a bothersome fact in his own life, Philip was silent during the unimaginative supper of red-flannel hash and stewed parsnips until Jed Daws served the coffee and Philip discovered that Rebecca's coffee contained rum. Silently he poured the contents of her mug into the slop bucket and ordered Jed to bring her nothing stronger than watered wine in the future.

"What I do or drink, Philip Keane," she stated firmly without any outward display of emotion, "is none of your business. I appreciate all you've done for me, but I can take care of myself.''

"Not with men like that Connecticut fool who leered at you as if you were up for public auction, you can't. Come on, Cottontop, let's go for that walk I promised you. Maybe the fresh air will improve your disposition.''

"Maybe it would, but only if I can go by myself.''

"Not a chance, not with your ability for getting into trouble.''

The walk, an ill-advised venture on the unpaved, snow-clogged streets of the village, ended a scant half hour after it began, when they were both struck by a heavy sheet of snow sliding from the steep roof of a building. Damp and chilled by the time they reached the *Star,* they hustled to the only warm spot aboard, the ship's galley, where the cook stove still radiated heat. Aware of Rebecca's continuing resentment, Philip attempted a conciliatory conversation.

"Why haven't you drawn any sketches of me, Cottontop?"

"I've tried," she admitted, "but they weren't any good. They never are—not with people I—not with someone like you. And you needn't scowl; I know you're as good-looking as all the women in your life have said you were. It's just that—"

"Just what?" he prompted with a cutting sarcasm. "That I'm not as interesting or as easily deceived as your elegant Captain Sinclair? I'll admit I could never be as exciting as a half-grown savage Indian who called you a moon maiden before he died happily in your arms."

Rebecca let her breath out slowly. "Like everyone else in Falmouth, you can believe what you want to about what happened in York. It was stupid of me to think that you were different from the others."

Philip caught her arm before she'd taken two steps toward the darkened companionway. "I'm sorry, Cottontop," he apologized, "I had no right to say what I did."

"Why not? It's what you're thinking. Don't worry about it; almost everyone else believed what Tom Skaggs told them."

"You're wrong, Cottontop. I never thought you were to blame. That's why I volunteered to take you to the Indian village that first time and every other time. But you never did deny that bastard's accusations."

"It wouldn't have done any good; even my father believed him. The only men who didn't were your father and Jonathan, and both of them advised me not to waste my breath denying the rumors. So I followed their advice. Would you like me to tell you about that night? I suppose you've earned the right to know."

"Only if you want to, Cottontop."

"Stop being so condescending, Philip. I'm no longer a frightened fourteen-year-old girl. My mother and I had been living in York for six months ever since my sister had

married William Davis. We lived on a farm on the outskirts of town while Abigail and her husband remained in
the big Davis house. Because my mother was very ill, we
didn't have many visitors except my sister, Abigail. During that whole time only one person from Falmouth ever
came there. That was Mark Stoneham, who came in
Jonathan's place because my uncle was stranded in England
with ship repairs. My father never came, and I didn't know
why until afterward. To tell you the truth, I didn't miss
him because Captain Stoneham was a good friend of my
mother, and his visits never upset her. But he wasn't there
when the Indians attacked.

"That night our housekeeper, Annie Skaggs, and I
finished the dishes and went to bed. As he did every
evening, Tom Skaggs had already gone to the outdoor root
cellar where he drank his nightly supply of hard apple
cider or rum or whatever else he could get his hands on. I
didn't even wake up until I was being dragged through the
house. All I could see was some terrifying giant until he
shoved me into a snowdrift outside and I saw his face in
the bright moonlight. Then I heard another Indian shouting
a word that sounded like *ne-oma*. I don't know where the
first Indian went because it was the second one who knelt
down beside me. I was too numb with fear to open my
eyes until he began to stroke my hair and repeat *ne-oma*
over and over. When I finally did look at him, I realized
that he was no older than I was and that he didn't mean me
any harm. He kept pointing to a curved piece of bone
strung on a leather thong around his neck. It was in the
shape of a new moon. When he smiled at me, I stopped
being afraid.

"I heard a gun explode somewhere close to us, and that
beautiful young Indian stopped smiling and fell on top of
me; but he didn't die for a long time. He just lay there
without making a sound except for that one word. I put my
arms around him because it seemed unfair for someone so
young to be dying without anyone to comfort him. After a
while he simply stopped breathing. I moved him then and
went back into the house. I remember pulling on an old
beaver coat and boots—I guess they were Tom's—and

getting a kitchen knife from the cupboard before I walked to my mother's room. She—she was already dead, but I didn't want anyone to see her looking like that. I wiped the blood from her face and wrapped her in a clean sheet. I took another sheet outside and wrapped it around the Indian boy.

"You know the rest. I cleared the snow from the ground and buried both of their bodies under the rocks that I dug out of the snow. I didn't remember Annie until I was finished. She'd been killed in the same way as my mother, so I buried her too. I marked my mother's grave with her beautiful old Bible and Annie's with the one from the parlor. I put the bone carving on top of the young Indian's; and for some reason, I cut a lock of my hair and placed it underneath that curved piece of bone. After that I returned to the house for two fur rugs so I wouldn't freeze and sat down by those three graves. Tom Skaggs didn't say a word to me when he crawled out of the cellar; he just stared at me like a drunken ox. I didn't realize then that he'd watched me the whole time through the gun slots of the stone wall that extended a few feet aboveground. Sometime during the next hour he must have left because the following day when other people arrived in York, they said that Tom was the only survivor other than myself—the hero who'd ridden our horse for help, but not soon enough. I learned then that eighty people had been murdered and a hundred others kidnapped; but not until I was taken to Falmouth did anyone tell me that my sister Abigail was a hostage or that William Davis had been killed right after he'd shot the young Indian who'd been kneeling beside me. It was another week before Hannah Tupton told me what else Tom Skaggs had reported.

"I hadn't seen any of the violence that night, and I mourned for the Indian boy almost as much as I did for my mother, perhaps even more so. I'd known that she was dying for a long time, and I was relieved that she'd been spared another month of suffering. But he was just about my own age. It was six months before I saw those graves again. Jonathan had put a wrought-iron fence around them and planted flowers, and there was an Indian totem from the boy's grandfather. I learned from Jonathan that the word *ne-oma* meant moon maiden and that the young Indian's special sign had been the new moon.

"Do you know something ironic, Philip? I didn't hate the Abenaki for what they'd done. We'd pushed their ancestors from their tribal lands a century before, and now we were trying to steal even more of their land."

"I wish you'd told me six years ago, Cottontop."

"I didn't know what the word *rape* meant then; and by the time I learned, I no longer cared what people thought. So don't waste your pity! I told you the truth because you've taken care of me in spite of your irritation. But even if you hadn't, I'd have survived. I know you weren't happy about marrying me, but when this year is over I'll take care of myself without asking you for any more favors."

She fled from the galley, leaving Philip alone with his thoughts, not at all sure his marrying Rebecca had been such a one-sided favor after all.

CHAPTER
3

AS Rebecca had predicted, the hours Captain Sinclair spent with her provided the American conspirators with the opportunity to smuggle the weapons and men to the fleet waiting off the Elizabeth Islands. Two mornings after the dinner she and Philip had shared, a British soldier escorted Miss Langley to the military headquarters where Captain Sinclair waited with an adequate supply of paint and an impressively mounted canvas. For a month the routine established that morning was maintained with few daily exceptions. At the end of four hours of work in the office, Rebecca's escort soldier carried the canvas back to the ship, where she continued the painstaking task of creating the painting she'd promised. To Philip Keane's increasing annoyance, she concentrated on her efforts with a single-minded intensity. Irritably he retaliated by avoiding her completely until the day she failed to return to the *Star.*

His furious search for her in New Bedford culminated at the Bedford Arms, where only the ranking British officers were quartered. In the private dining room a celebration was in progress, a party attended by a half-dozen uniformed Englishmen and one glowing American girl. In the place of honor on the polished table was the completed portrait. Not even the rude arrival of a Yankee captain of doubtful loyalty could dim the spirit of the occasion. The picture was a success and the commanding officer more than satisfied with it.

Rebecca had struggled to achieve an honest portrayal of Sinclair's rugged face, this time with graying hair and wind-roughened complexion. Centered in front of the red of a British flag and the cloudy blue-grey of open sky, the face was that of a sailor who loved the sea; but in one lower corner against the dark blue of his uniform was a faithful reproduction of the small cameo of Mrs. Sinclair. That one touch had eliminated the last of Brian Sinclair's distrust of the young artist, and he'd talked freely to her about his hatred for a policeman's job and of his conviction that a long and bitter struggle lay ahead. Rebecca made no attempt at denial; his gloomy prediction reflected her own fears.

"What about you, young lady?" he asked gently.

"I can only hope that I'll still have friends on both sides after it's over," she responded with a bleak honesty.

Whatever her motives had been in her brash introduction to this stern man, she now valued the gruff friendship he offered. Never before had she cared about the reception of any of her carelessly sketched drawings, but she'd worried about and shed tears of frustration over this oil painting. At the end of her month-long ordeal, she basked in the praise she was receiving from educated men who'd actually seen the work of the famous artists she'd only read about.

Philip's rude entry into the room destroyed much of her sense of triumph, and she was grateful for Sinclair's diplomatic explanation. "I believe our Miss Langley had earned our congratulations, Captain Keane. She's done something I didn't believe she could, and I'm grateful to her for a temporary respite from my weightier problems. But your presence here reminds me of one of my more pressing ones. I'm granting you permission for the trial runs you requested to test your new sails, since I'll be aboard to see for myself if the change of rigging has been worth the effort. Is tomorrow morning agreeable?"

Forced to respond with an equal civility, Philip nodded his compliance and remained long enough to drink a glass of port, exchanging a few guarded pleasantries with men he already considered enemies. His only comment to Rebecca on the walk back to the ship was a regretful observation. "You're right, Cottontop, about most of the decent men who'll be fighting this war. They don't believe it any more necessary than I do."

Alone in the cabin all the next day, Rebecca slumped in the apathy of anticlimax, as indifferent to the uneven movements of the ship as she was to the muffled sounds of the other occupants. In spite of her protests, Sinclair had insisted on paying her ten sovereigns for the painting; but the money held little meaning for her. Even the prospect of finally acquiring the large amount her mother had left her did little to dissipate her depression. In a few days she'd be reunited with her uncle and her sister, but the New York home they'd all occupy together would belong to Abigail. Rebecca would be merely a tolerated interloper. As people-shy and unassuming as Abigail had become since her release by the Indians, her younger sister was certain that there'd be no room for anyone other than her husband and son in Abigail's newly won world of respectability.

As she always had during the emotional crises of the past five years, Rebecca reread her mother's journals, the fifteen slender volumes begun by a seventeen-year-old girl burdened with the responsibility of a younger brother after their parents had died. Uncomplaining, Audrey Langley had remained steadfast in her resolve for five years, teaching her brother and sharing her art lessons with him. She'd also retained a quiet sense of humor and triumphed over her isolation from a social life of her own. She'd recorded her impressions of the limited people around her—the quarrelsome servants, the avaricious tradespeople who tried to cheat her, and the parsimonious guardian who doled out the money her parents had left behind. And she'd imparted her own philosophical resignation to her brother Jonathan. At thirteen he'd been apprenticed to their uncle in Falmouth, Maine, to begin learning seamanship and shipping. Without her beloved Jonathan to care for, the twenty-two-year-old Audrey had married a middle-aged widower and moved to his small plantation in South Carolina to raise the last two children of his existing family and to bear him two sons of her own.

Throughout those ten years, she'd maintained her diaries, and her humor had gentled as her happiness increased. But suddenly the writing had become starkly brief as she fought to stem the tragic spread of yellow fever among her family members. First a beloved stepdaughter succumbed, then a son and husband, and finally her remaining son. Generously the older, surviving stepchildren had shared their inheritance with the quiet woman they'd learned to love, but it was her brother, Jonathan, who supplied enough healing balm to encourage her to start writing again. Audrey found the picturesque individuals of Falmouth a never-ending inspiration for her stories, which soon became the favorite contributions in the dreary, small-town *Falmouth Clarion*. When she was thirty-six she married the paper's owner, a widower ten years her junior. Within months his withdrawn little girl, Abigail, had come to adore her new stepmother.

Never in those last seven volumes could Rebecca find any trace of complaint against Jeremy Rayburn, even

though it was Audrey's money that now supported the
family and her efforts that produced the *Clarion* on a
weekly basis. She was almost forty when she gave birth to
Rebecca, the same year her husband, a captain in the
Maine militia, joined the British forces for a seven-year
tour of duty in the French-Indian war. Taking her oddly
colored infant and her pretty stepdaughter with her to the
Clarion office, Audrey continued to produce a newspaper
that earned money; but it was her investments in property
and in her brother's shipping firm that built her fortune.

Until Rebecca had read the journals, she'd jealously
considered her mother's favorite child to be Abigail. During those years of Rebecca's early childhood, when her
father was far away, people often made unkind remarks
about the origin of her unusual combination of dark eyes and
pale hair. Somehow Audrey had deflected the hurt and used
it to encourage her daughter to be resilient. She'd also
carefully fostered the child's talent, publishing Rebecca's
childishly perceptive doggerel in the *Clarion* without correc-
tion and guiding the strong young hands in early art lessons.

Rebecca had wept in the attic of her uncle's nome when
she'd read about her mother's unabated joy in raising her.
During those emotional hours, Rebecca had relived her
own childhood as she recalled her mother's tolerance of
her stubborn drive to operate the balky press after Ezra
Jenkins set the type. Never once had Rebecca been scolded
about her ink-soaked aprons or ink-spotted frocks, and
never had her mother compared her untidiness with Abigail's
immaculate neatness.

Very little in her life had changed after her father
returned in 1763, because he now spent most of his time in
Boston, leaving Audrey with the same responsibilities
she'd carried for the previous eight years. Gradually,
though, Audrey's journals had become more guarded in
personal revelations and more bitingly satiric about the
uglier people she was forced to contend with. Old Hannah
Tupton, whose hatred for Jeremy's second wife had increased with the years, was no longer described as a
garrulous old woman who boasted endlessly about an

inglorious past. Audrey now called her a witch with a broken broomstick.

Hannah was the matriarch of the Tupton family, the mother of eight sons, none of whom welcomed her into their own homes. Instead, she'd lived with Jeremy Rayburn ever since he'd married his first wife, Jobina Tupton. A sly old woman who flattered Jeremy while avoiding an open rupture with his second wife, Hannah concentrated her malice on a terrified Abigail and an often impudent Rebecca. Her imperfectly remembered stories of her own childhood in Salem during the infamous witch trials of 1691 were embroidered with dark threats of her abilities to recognize evil. When Audrey died, the old woman persuaded Jeremy to allow Rebecca to live with her Uncle Jonathan. Since he'd now married another of her granddaughters, Hannah wanted no reminders of his second marriage to an outsider. However, when she learned that Audrey Rayburn had left her considerable estate one-third to Abigail and two-thirds to Rebecca, Hannah incited her sons to contest that will when Jeremy refused to do so. Rebecca recalled with a vindictive satisfaction that their efforts had been ignominiously routed by the incorruptible Boston lawyer who'd written the document.

It was these pages about Hannah Tupton that formed the basis of the first story Rebecca submitted to the Rayburn Publishers in New York, a humorous tale she'd appropriately entitled "Grandma Witch." The second, more successful contribution had been named "Puritan Pirates" and dealt with the acquisitiveness of Hannah's sons. Having belatedly discovered that Audrey Rayburn was a wealthy woman whose investments flourished, the Tupton men had schemed to divest her of a part of that wealth. Rebecca had vented her own comic spleen in the exaggerations she'd added to that story. A third story, which Audrey herself had entitled "Hog Wallow, the Five-Month Pond," was a satire about New England prudery. Because they'd waded in a pond used by pigs, pristine young girls produced babies as plump as piglets five months later after hastily arranged marriages. Rebecca had hated that story because

it revealed the extent of her mother's unhappiness and her
father's infidelity.

Oddly, though, Audrey's final volume expressed no
regrets or recriminations. More than any of the others,
those pages written in York had guided Rebecca's development during the past five years. The short fragmentary
paragraphs had preached the gentle humor of forgiveness
and had enabled the daughter to tolerate her father. Gradually,
Rebecca had learned that his feet of clay were buried deep
in a personal insecurity that had prevented him from
maturing beyond the need for recognition. Until Jeremy
had earned that recognition honestly when he proved to be
the only competent military leader in Falmouth, Rebecca
had often shielded him from public scorn.

With a sad finality she returned the last of her mother's
diaries to the chest; there were no signposts left in them to
guide her own insecure future. Except for Silas Keane's
gruff friendship, she had nothing left in the town that'd
been her girlhood home. Even her tenuous ties to Philip
Keane were about to be severed. He'd be moving into the
active violence of war while she'd become another of
the women left behind. Morosely, she wondered how the
wives like Mrs. Sinclair survived without seeing their
husbands for years on end.

The realization that she wasn't really a wife did little to
relieve the uneasiness she felt at the prospect. Although
Philip had studiously avoided any emotional attachment,
Rebecca knew that he was not unaware of her. Frequently
as she'd left or returned to the ship during the stay in New
Bedford, she'd seen him watching her with a brooding
look that had accelerated her own heartbeat and aroused a
forlorn hope that he would not abandon her completely
after he'd deposited her in New York.

As her thoughts dwindled away, she became aware that
the ship was no longer moving and that the rhythmic
cadence of marching feet indicated that Captain Sinclair
and his inspection officers were leaving the *Falmouth Star.*
Until the morning tide the ship would remain peacefully
attached to land, still ostensibly a cargo ship and not the
battle-ready privateer it would soon become. For Rebecca

there was an infinite sadness in the thought that a ship that had served its owners faithfully for a decade must now face perils more dangerous than the unpredictable sea. She'd never heard cannon fire, but the sound of muskets had always made her muscles twitch nervously. If the *Star* were ever trapped at sea by even the smallest of the British ships-of-line, it would face the destructive power of forty or more cannons. There would be no survival for the modest brig or for any of its crew.

Jerking at the sound of the heavy bronze key being inserted into the cabin's door for the first time since early morning, Rebecca hastily smoothed her hair and skirt. Not since her wedding night had she been uncaring about her appearance, and all day long she'd expected company. Disappointed that her visitor was only Jed Daws, she accepted the bottle of Madeira wine he handed her without enthusiasm.

"The limey cap'n left this for you, Becky. Sez you ain't to forgit him. The rest of us sure ain't likely to after what he put us through today. Poked into every box and barrel aboard with that durn stick of his. 'Pears as if,'' the old man chuckled, "someone took liberty with British stocks ashore sometime last night. A wagonload of muskets was missin' and thirty cannon. That limey 'uz sure riled when he didn't find any of that contraband aboard.

"And Cap'n Keane knew jest how to add to that rile. Kept the *Star* at half her old speed even. Fust off, the rest of us 'uz slow to ketch on; but when the riggin' lads did, the sails jest flapped in the wind, and we 'uz dead slow gettin' back.

"Cap'n sez he's havin' supper with you tonight, Becky, so don't you be sippin' that wine afore he gits here, and don't you be usin' any deviltry on him neither. I know he's a mite harsh on you, but he 'uz durn worried about you yesterday.''

"No, he wasn't, Jed. He was just angry as he always is when he's around me. Will we be sailing for New York tomorrow?''

"Nope. It'll be New London first to finish the job of gittin' the fleet ready.'' Just before he left the cabin, Jed became more sharply critical. "Becky, if you don't mind my sayin' so, that dress you're wearin' ain't exactly company. 'Pears to me, you dressed a heap sight better for the limey cap'n, and Cap'n Keane ain't one to overlook a thing like that."

Rebecca sighed in agreement; the month of dressing for the "limey cap'n" had completed the destruction of much of her meager wardrobe. Except for the red outfit she was saving for New York, she had only one presentable dress left, a black gown that had been her mother's but that Jonathan had ruled too mature for a young girl. However, Jed was right about the gray linsey-woolsey she had on; in addition to two ink spots, it was disfigured by several recent smears of oil paint. Before she donned the doubtful black dress, she attempted to arrange her hair into the elegant style her mother had worn, but the mass of pale curls was too unruly to be so easily disciplined. Brushing it with exasperation, she wondered if she'd ever find the courage to purchase a wig. She also wondered if she'd be able to endure the tight bodice of a dress that had been made for a woman without Rebecca's breadth of shoulders and breast. Uneasily she tried to stretch the silk fabric to cover what she realized was an immodest expanse of bare neckline. Just as she was contemplating a prudential change back into the security of the dull linsey-woolsey, Jed's voice sounded outside the door.

"Got my hands full, Becky. Best open the hatch afore I drop yer dinner."

Hurrying to help her old friend settle the laden tray on the table, Rebecca wasn't aware of the quieter entrance of her husband until he stood in front of her. For an awkward moment she stared at him with her mouth open. He was dressed as she'd never seen him before in slim buff colored breeches, a white ruffled shirt, and a blue superfine frock coat. Unfortunately, the pleasant effect of his sartorial elegance was of short duration since his greeting held its usual sour note of disapproval.

"If you'd worn that dress yesterday for your English friends, Cottontop, you'd have been recruited for other things besides painting pretty pictures. My God, you look like a—''

''Obviously you don't know waterfront bawds very well, Philip Keane,'' she flared in an angry retort. ''The ones in Falmouth wore red skirts and smeared white lead all over their faces.''

''In that outfit you wouldn't have to work the waterfront, Cottontop. You'd qualify for one of the best houses on Manhattan. Where'd you get the dress?''

''It was one of my mother's,'' she admitted sullenly, ''but if it annoys you, I'll change into something that won't.''

''Simmer down, Cottontop. I didn't mean to start an argument. Besides, I much prefer the dress to your Indian britches. In fact, you look very beautiful tonight.''

Alerted by the odd change in his voice and by the sudden smile that softened his features, Rebecca became nervously wary as she watched him fill her pewter cup with the Madeira wine. She was all too uncomfortably aware of the speeded-up pounding of her own heart.

''Is this some kind of celebration?'' she asked cautiously.

''At least the dinner is special, Cottontop. I had John Sugs fetch it from Sinclair's own inn. I decided that you and I had earned something more than ship's fare tonight.''

Self-consciously Rebecca toyed with the food Philip heaped on her plate, and her taste buds tingled at the sight of the thick slice of ham and the honeyed yams. But regretfully she knew that the seams of her black silk would burst open if she consumed too much of it. As she sipped her wine, her sense of caution increased steadily; in the past Philip had objected strenuously to her drinking anything alcoholic, but tonight he was keeping her cup full.

''Are you celebrating your eagerness to go to war, Philip, or your relief that in a few days you'll no longer have to worry about me?'' she inquired circumspectly when he laid down his fork.

''Neither one, Cottontop. Only a fool looks forward to a battle at sea, and I expect to be worrying about you for the rest of my life.''

''Why should you? Once I reach New York—''

"You'll still be my wife. Our marriage isn't going to be annulled because I've changed my mind."

"But why?"

"Damned if I know, Cottontop. I've spent the past four weeks asking myself the same question."

"What did you finally decide, Philip? That a marriage such as ours would give you greater protection from your mistresses, both present and future?"

"One mistress only, Cottontop, and she's no longer in Falmouth."

"Neither are you."

"That's right, I'm here with you; and I don't know where Paulette is."

"Then I don't understand. What happened to your conviction that sailors had to be free men?"

"This sailor now prefers being married to you and living with you aboard ship and on land. Is the idea so hard to accept, Cottontop?"

Her rigid control destroyed, Rebecca stared at him in shock. "You mean a real marriage?" she gasped.

"What the devil did you think I was talking about?"

"I wouldn't know, since you haven't bothered to talk to me about anything for several weeks. And then without warning you come here tonight and—" Her voice trailed off into an agitated whisper.

"I came here tonight to propose marriage, a real marriage this time. I think I'd have been more successful if I'd just crawled into your bed a long time ago."

"But you didn't," she reminded him reasonably. "The first morning I was aboard, you shot out of bed like a bee-stung cat."

"I thought you were asleep," Philip admitted with an annoyed frown. "But that's a fairly accurate description of how I felt that morning. I wish now I'd stayed as I wanted to and saved myself some uncomfortable nights."

Conveying none of her inner agitation, Rebecca's voice remained calmly impersonal. "If it's merely a more comfortable bed you want, I'll gladly move to a smaller cabin."

"No, you won't, Cottontop. There's a full complement of men aboard now, so you and I will be sharing this one."

Studying her averted face, which revealed little of her thoughts, Philip experienced a frustrating anger at his own ineptitude. He'd anticipated some reluctance on her part, but certainly not the articulate resistance he'd received and certainly not such an accurate analysis of his past behavior. His avoidance of her had been a deliberate attempt to convince himself that he wanted no part of a talented, intelligent, self-possessed wife; but his arguments had failed miserably. Watching her leave his ship each day had been an irritating torment; she was legally his wife, but she'd paid more attention to a damned Englishman than she had to her husband. Since the first day in New Bedford he'd been aware of her elusive, unusual beauty—the sudden smile she'd flash at the enemy soldier who'd been her attentive daily escort, the impish grin she gave Jed when he rushed to help her up the gangplank, and the poise she'd displayed with a roomful of fawning British officers. It had been their elegant uniforms that had caused him to dress more formally tonight, but she'd outdone him with a gown that had made his already jangled nerves throb. Despite his disapproval of the unexpected décolletage of her dress, he'd hoped that her intentions were the same as his own until she'd begun her skillful counteroffensive. How the devil was he to make love to a defensive girl who had good reason to distrust men?

Suddenly Philip cursed himself silently for being a forgetful dolt. It'd been a long time since he'd played at love with village girls who had to be coaxed to allow even innocent kisses. Standing up, he pulled Rebecca purposefully to her feet, wrapped his arms around her, and kissed her gently, ridiculously pleased that she was trembling. Making no attempt to prolong the kiss, he continued to hold her.

"You're supposed to put your arms around a man when he kisses you, Cottontop," he murmured, bracing himself for the provocative question of "why?" Instead, he received an insultingly prosaic response.

"This dress will split wide open if I raise my arms,

Philip." Before he could judicially suggest that she remove it, she added matter-of-factly, "It's been suffocating me for an hour. If you'll turn your back for a minute, I'll take it off. I would have a long time ago if you hadn't been so critical."

So much for the trembling, blushing bride, he reflected with exasperated humor as he slipped off his coat, which had also proved an uncomfortable choice of costume. His amusement increased when he turned to find his wife staring ruefully down at her white petticoat and chemise with distaste; both garments were marked with permanent spots of ink.

"I don't suppose I can walk around New York in clothes like these," she said, trying vainly to control the tremor in her voice. "I guess I've always looked like a chimney sweep, haven't I?" Stop rambling like a fluttery fool, she scolded herself sharply. He's just offered you what you've always wanted. But the hard core of defensive distrust would not yield its hold on her consciousness.

"Before I answer your question, Cottontop, I'd like your answer to mine."

"About marriage? I will as soon as I find out why."

"I was about to demonstrate when I was interrupted by an overly tight gown."

"I should never have tried to be someone I'm not. Do you mind if I eat my supper now? Jed was too busy to bring me anything but coffee today."

Smiling with a helpless resignation, Philip refilled the wine cups and watched the slender girl devour all of the ample portions of food on her plate and drink her wine with dispatch.

"If you eat like that all the time, Cottontop, you'll soon find the rest of your clothes too tight."

"My mother was very thin when she wore that dress, and she wasn't as tall as I am. She was different from me in other ways too. That's why I don't think the kind of marriage you're talking about is a good idea."

"Women can enjoy love as much as a man, Cottontop," he murmured.

"I don't have any schoolgirl illusions about love or

marriage. Jonathan and my sister have been lovers for the past three years, and Abigail is the kind of woman who likes to talk about herself. I also have no illusions about you, Philip; you've been committed to someone else for a long time.''

''Who told you that?'' he demanded.

''The person who should know. Paulette Burnell also likes to talk to another woman. She and I became friends of a sort after the last time you took me to the Indian camp. Philip, I couldn't stand a marriage like my mother's. She put up with my father's roving ways for a long time without making any complaint. I don't plan to complain either, but my marriage will end the day my husband is unfaithful to me. My conduct then will become more than a match for his. I think you'll be much happier with Paulette.''

Philip stared at her in stunned silence, a dull flush of anger staining his tanned cheeks. He'd just been issued a flamboyant ultimatum by an arrogant chit who until an hour ago had never even been kissed by a man.

''It's too bad,'' he taunted her, ''that you didn't acquire part of your remarkable education from men. You might have learned that a jealous wife is seldom attractive enough to entice all those lovers you so optimistically expect to find waiting for you. But you're right about our marriage; we'll keep it just the way it is permanently. Unfortunately, we still have to share this cabin; so if you're through with your eating and drinking, you can put the dishes outside the door and blow out the lights. I want to get some sleep and I don't believe in wasting whale oil.''

Completing his tirade as he strode toward the door, Philip shouted one final order. ''You have fifteen minutes, madam, to make your own preparations for bed.'' Had he glanced toward Rebecca, he might have paused. Her face was ashen and her brown eyes suspiciously bright. Only after he'd slammed the door did she force herself into frenzied activity, pulling on her dark red ensemble and fur-lined boots and hurriedly rebrushing her tousled hair. Pausing only long enough to wash her hands and face, she checked the hoard of gold sovereigns in her reticule, hastily deposited the dishes outside the door, and extinguished the three lanterns.

In the companionway she encountered only Jed Daws, who allowed her to pass without articulating any words other than "Cap'n said you weren't to—" before she disappeared up the short flight of stairs. The deck, however, proved a more formidable obstacle for the fleeing girl; the gangplank had been raised, and the five sailors leaning over the land-side taffrail were strangers to her. Having learned much about the seamier aspect of waterfront life during her years in Falmouth, Rebecca sighed with realistic acceptance and walked toward the men.

"Gentlemen," she ordered in a voice she hoped was brassy enough, "I have concluded my business with Captain Keane. Will you be so kind as to replace the gangplank." Had she been the businesswoman she claimed to be, she could have served additional customers that night, judging by the avid looks she received as the men hastened to obey. She was three hundred feet along the cobbled embarcadero before she stopped shaking and remembered Captain Sinclair's boast that his curfew had rendered New Bedford streets as safe as church aisles. But that curfew also limited the traffic in and out of the modest inn where she and Philip had met the Americans. She knocked three times before the cautious innkeeper opened the door and shone a lantern on her face.

"Miss Rayburn," he gasped as he pulled her into the smoke-filled public room where resident guests were socializing.

"Is Mr. Cravens still here?" she asked breathlessly.

Glancing fearfully around to determine if she'd been overheard, the innkeeper shook his head. "None of your friends are," he whispered urgently. "But some of the men who are could be loyalists."

"They won't bother me," she assured him. "Can you arrange transportation for me to New York?"

"The coaches were stopped weeks ago, Miss Rayburn. Only way out of town now is on horseback or aboard a ship. I thought Captain Keane got clearance to leave port."

"The *Falmouth Star* sailed an hour ago on a mission

that Captain Keane decided was too dangerous for a woman,'' Rebecca lied glibly. "May I stay here until I can find passage on another ship?"

"The only room that isn't full is the kitchen, Miss Rayburn," he mumbled in distress, "but it's no place for a lady like yourself."

"The kitchen will be excellent," she whispered, recalling with relief that the kitchens of public inns always had rear doors. She'd scarcely introduced herself to the landlord's wife and accepted the proffered mug of hot rum punch when she heard the distant front entry doors being pounded imperiously. Silently her hostess nodded to the weathered door at the end of the pantry and retrieved the mug her flustered young guest was still holding. As she hustled Rebecca toward the door, the woman asserted conspiratorially, "Knowed Philip Keane for a dozen or more years, and he sure ain't one to let a pretty girl git away. But if you're so goldurned agin seein' him, best you hide in the stable out back. Reckon the one broken-down old nag the British overlooked won't mind company tonight."

Clutching her skirts in one hand and her reticule in the other, Rebecca fled through the door the landlady held open for her and into strong arms that easily subdued her thrashing attempt to free herself. A callused hand over her mouth prevented her terrified outcry, and a swiftly applied piece of cloth effectively stopped any subsequent ones. As ignominiously as a hempen sack of grain, she was hoisted to a man's shoulder and bounced at a stomach-jarring pace along the garbage-clogged alley at the rear of the inn.

Her heart was pounding painfully by the time her abductor stopped running and dumped her unceremoniously on her feet. As she tried to pull away from his restraining hand, he jerked her sharply toward him and pulled the cloth from her head. Gulping in the cool air in gasping breaths, Rebecca tried to focus her eyes, but the darkness in the narrow street seemed impenetrable. Without warning the man bent his head and kissed her, not with the savagery of a waterfront lout but with a slow, insidious warmth, and his arms tightened around her until she felt crushed and boneless. When he finally removed his lips from hers, she heard the familiar voice of Philip Keane.

"You don't learn much from experience, do you, Cottontop? I told you earlier that you were supposed to return a man's embrace. And if you ask why, I'm going to gag you again."

"I thought that was you at the front of the inn," she mumbled shakily as her breath steadied.

"That was John Sugs. He followed you in your mad dash for freedom while Jed gave me the warning. I know you won't believe that anything could happen to the fair-haired darling of the British commandant in this town, but there are lawless thugs here who don't give a damn for anyone's authority. Now shut up and walk faster than you ever have during your wayward life."

Breathless again by the time they reached the ship, Rebecca braced herself mentally for the tongue-lashing she expected from Philip and for the leering grins from the sailors who'd helped her escape. Instead, the darkened deck was alive with muffled activity as the men stowed the gangplank and cast off the great hawsers to release the *Falmouth Star* from moorage. As the ship floated free, the only sounds were the rhythmic strokes of the oarsmen in the longboats that pulled the parent vessel into the open port. Held firmly by Philip's arm about her waist, she listened to the added whispering sounds of men high up on the great masts, releasing the lines that'd kept the sails reefed.

She saw the lights of a second ship before Philip did, and nudged him sharply. "Your friend Sinclair planned to follow us tomorrow," he explained. "But if we're lucky all of our ships will be in open sea before dawn, and he'll need a fleet to locate us then. It isn't the first time we've run at night to avoid capture, Cottontop."

Before the British ship faded into the distance, the *Star* was under way and wind driven, her longboats pulled aboard by straining sailors as the oarsmen clambered up the rope netting. Inexperienced though she was about a ship's operation, Rebecca realized the extent of expert seamanship required for the silent flight in the dark dead of night.

"When did you plan this, Philip?" she asked quietly.

"Four nights ago when my scout reported finding a British ship-of-line in Fairhaven waters. It anchored just outside New Bedford Harbor late this afternoon. We managed to leave about six hours earlier than Captain Sinclair expected us to."

Using shaded lanterns now to monitor the ship's instruments, he issued ever-changing orders to the helmsman as the *Star* was navigated into the channels bordering the Elizabeth Islands. Not until the first light of dawn did Philip turn the ship's command over to his first mate. In the eastern distance Rebecca could see the silhouettes of other ships and beyond them nothing but ocean. Despite her avowed political neutrality, she experienced a keen pride in the night's accomplishment.

Philip was silent as he led her into the disputed cabin, and Rebecca voiced no complaint as he stripped off his seaman's uniform and climbed into the wide berth. Stiff with cold, she removed her outer garments and lay down tiredly beside him. His only greeting was a sleepy grunt and an arm placed heavily across her waist. She wasn't aware that she was smiling as she fell asleep. Hours later when Philip's hand ceased being an inert weight and became a muscular force that pulled her relaxed body firmly against his own, Rebecca sleepily remembered the lesson in the art of kissing and put her arms around her husband.

During the next few moments, she discovered that her claims of being enlightened beyond schoolgirl ignorance were woefully unfounded. His strong, agile fingers expertly untied the drawstrings of her petticoats and pantalets, easing the loose chemise and other garments over her hips without seeming to break his concentration on a kiss that was both gentle and comforting. Even when those same expert fingers began caressing her shoulders and back, Rebecca remained quiescently unaroused, enjoying the unaccustomed sensation of physical closeness to another human being. The shocks began slowly when those gentle lips left hers and traveled downward to her chin, her neck, and finally to one breast, where they paused to encircle the nipple and massage it softly.

Seeking a purchase for her hands, which fluttered in an uncontrolled agitation, she clutched his head; and her fingers encountered the crisp satin of the dark hair she'd so often admired. She gasped in shock as the heat within her burst like a flood over her consciousness, forcing her body to move awkwardly in response, ignoring the mental control she tried desperately to regain. As Philip returned his lips to hers, his hands moved swiftly from breast to thigh, urgently nudging her legs apart and invading the most secret areas of her person with those questing fingers. Without warning the seductive caresses ceased as his body pinned her firmly on her back.

Rebecca sucked in her breath with a painful catch when she felt that part of the masculine anatomy she'd only dimly guessed about before enter her body like a fiery brand. Her involuntary cry of distress was silenced when Philip paused long enough to murmur consolingly, "It'll never hurt again, fondling, only the first time. Relax now and enjoy the pleasure."

How could anyone have relaxed during the tumult that followed the pain? Her body responded to Philip's powerful surge of passion with an emotional violence of its own. Yet when he collapsed on top of her with a sigh of contentment that sounded very like the deep-throated purring of a cat, Rebecca stiffened with a resentful discontent. Abigail had been entirely euphoric in her description of the beautiful fire that united hers and Jonathan's souls, yet the fire that still burned in Rebecca's loins was a nagging reminder that Philip obviously felt more united than she did. Still holding her possessively close to him, he told her confidently, "With a few more lessons, you'll get over being afraid. If I didn't have a ship to run, we wouldn't leave this bed for another six hours. It took you a long time to learn to kiss me properly, but I think you're going to master the important skills more quickly."

Since it was the longest speech he'd ever made to her other than undeserved reprimands, Rebecca was intrigued.

She was also very tempted to discover whether or not he might be right. After using her newly acquired aptitude for kissing, she pressed close to him and murmured, "Must you leave right now, Philip?"

His response was a salacious grin as he threw off the covers and slapped her lightly on her slender derriere. Hoisting himself swiftly out of bed, he leaned over to return her kiss.

"Sorry, my impatient young temptress, I have a ship and a half-trained crew depending on me."

"May I join you on deck then?"

"No, sweetheart, the crew doesn't need another reminder that there's a lusty woman aboard any more than they need a captain whose mind wouldn't be on his work."

"Philip, I refuse to remain a prisoner in the cabin another day."

"Don't blame me, Cottontop, it's your own fault. Until I can convince the new crew members that you're my wife and not the brazen doxy you pretended to be last night, you wouldn't be safe even in your Indian britches."

His smile broadened as he fastened his leather trousers. "Of course," he added, "I could hang the sheet you're lying on from the mainsail yardarm to let them know that you're only a beginner."

Sharply reminded of an unpleasant reality in her changed status, Rebecca grimaced. "If you don't mind, I'd rather just throw it out the window."

"But I do mind, Cottontop; linen sheets are a luxury aboard a working privateer. Besides, Jed would be sorely disappointed in me. He's been calling me a damn fool since Saco and insisting that underneath those ugly dresses of yours was a beautiful woman."

Noting the insecurity mirrored on her face, Philip sat down on the side of the bunk and gently pushed aside the protective blanket she was clutching. "Jed will never know how beautiful," he murmured as his arms encircled her. "I wasn't a complete fool, Cottontop, only a coward. I'm still afraid to ask whether or not you have any regrets."

Rebecca's doubts vanished in a flood of joy. It didn't

matter that her husband's avowal omitted any mention of love or that her initiation into marriage had fallen short of her own expectations or that she faced another lonely period of isolation. Putting her arms around his neck, she kissed him and shook her head. "No regrets, Philip." But as he headed once more for the door, she amended her earlier declaration. "I'll have even fewer if you remember occasionally between here and New London that you're married too."

Events, however, in the form of a capriciously violent storm and a captured French privateer combined to reduce the marriage of Philip and Rebecca Keane once again to a name-only basis. The storm which struck with little warning three hours into Philip's watch could not have occurred at a more unfortunate time for the Keane fleet. Crewed by a mixture of men who had not yet welded themselves into a smoothly functioning unit and handicapped by complicated new rigging which the sailors were just learning to operate, the eleven ships were driven off course and separated into three groups.

Being the least laden of the vessels, the *Falmouth Star* weathered the four days of gale-force winds and sheeting rain without any structural damage. A veteran of sixteen years in western Atlantic waters from Maine to the Caribbean, Philip was a cautious captain who left little to chance. Except for brief periods of rest and necessary changes into dry clothing, he did not leave his command post during the crucial four days the storm lasted. Rebecca saw him only twice because she, too, was recruited as a crew member shortly after the storm began. While the sturdy Maine-built brig withstood the fury of the wind, some of its men were not so fortunate. Jed Daws was the first victim, his leg broken when he was hurtled down the companionway after delivering food to the cockpit; and several of the riggers were injured when Philip ordered the sails reefed.

While the two veteran seamen assigned to the hospital area midship were competent enough to handle the initial doctoring, the maintenance of wounded men on a ship bucketing through mountainous troughs of angry sea was beyond their exhausted capabilities. However awkward Rebecca proved during her first stint of nursing, her services were welcomed with gratitude, especially by her old friend, Jed Daws. Under the direction of the laconic John Sugs, she undertook the task of carrying the rations of cold food to the injured men.

The thick green soup she brought to them had become a mass of unappetizing lumps, and the rock-hard rounds of unleavened bread normally wrapped in oilskin cloths had quickly mildewed when exposed to the damp air. With little regard for the ship's budgeted allotments of rum, she and John Sugs lavishly quadrupled the daily amount for the wounded men and tripled it for the hard-pressed sailors still on duty.

Never leaving the *Star*'s interior throughout the entirety of the ordeal, she remained unaware of the enormity of the work necessary to maintain a ship under the onslaught of the storm. Whenever a line snapped under pressure, splicers were forced aloft to make repairs before the damage spread. Despite the prudential reefing of the larger sails, the coarse linen canvas of the ones essential for navigational control suffered frequent rending tears, necessitating immediate replacement. Thus by the third day, the number of injured reefers had increased to twenty, with varying degrees of lacerated hands. Second in number, but more seriously hurt, were the carpenters on whose vigilance the safety of the ship depended. Their job—to secure hatch covers that'd jarred loose, reinforce weakened masts, and batten the hull timbers that split open—was hard work even in calm weather; but during a storm it was fraught with danger. Three of these men remained unconscious for two days.

When the ship finally ceased its wallowing and steadied to the sedate rhythm of calmer waters, Rebecca was summoned to the master's cabin to tend still another patient. The sight of the haggard, unshaven man huddled asleep on the bunk terrified her. His closed eyes seemed sunken in a face lined with exhaustion, and his body shook with convulsive shivers. Removing only her soiled dress, her leather pants, and boots, she climbed into bed beside him and wrapped her arms around him. Gradually, as her body warmed his, Philip relaxed and his breathing deepened into heavy sleep.

Unnumbered hours later Rebecca was awakened by a persistent knocking on the door. When Philip didn't stir, she climbed groggily out of bed, pulled on the least complicated of her shabby dresses, and cautiously stepped out into the companionway. There she was confronted by the second mate, a humorless New Bedford man who'd twice attempted to stop John Sugs's liberal dispensation of rum during the storm. Glaring at her in sour disapproval, he demanded to see the captain.

"Unless it's an emergency," she responded testily, "I'm not going to disturb him."

"That's not up to you, woman," he sputtered. "The captain asked to be notified when we sighted another of our ships, and notify him I will. Stand aside."

Instantly, Rebecca's sleepy irritation was replaced by the icy composure she'd developed after earlier encounters with other boorish prigs. "My name is Mrs. Keane, not *woman,* Mr. Milford," she snapped, "and henceforth you will address me as such. What ship was sighted and how far away?"

Something in the unwavering directness of her brown eyes inhibited the man's impulse to call her a waterfront tart who'd consorted with the enemy. An uncompromising upbringing in a harsh moralistic home had taught Jesse Milford that women who were not under the supervision of husbands or father were subject to the sins of the flesh. Moreover, this particular woman had openly associated with an arrogant British officer and moved on and off the *Falmouth Star* without a hint of female chaperonage. Still, there was an educated precision to her speech that even a naive man could not credit to a working drab. Choosing the more prudent path, he answered her grudgingly.

"It's the *Langley* and her captain's on his way here now."

"That'll be Mark Stoneman, Mr. Milford. He's captained the *Langley* since it was commissioned into my uncle's fleet. Until we know what he has to report, we'll let my husband continue his sleep."

An hour later Rebecca thankfully relinquished the authority she'd assumed. Mark Stoneham's report piled horror on horror and presented a problem far beyond her limited capacities. Throughout the storm the three Stoneham brothers' ships and the one commanded by George Peckham had remained together somewhere southeast of the *Falmouth Star*. While none of the brigs had escaped damage completely, they were in a reasonably navigable condition when they emerged into calmer waters just after dawn. Suddenly the lead ship, *Vixen,* was fired upon without warning, its main and mizzenmasts destroyed by expertly aimed cannons. So swiftly had the attack been executed, Captain Matthew Stoneham had insufficient time to reorganize his already exhausted crew, and none of the companion ships were close enough to retaliate. Their captains had watched in helpless frustration as the *Vixen* was taken in tow and its colonial crew replaced by a British one.

"But that's piracy," Rebecca gasped.

"It's war, Cottontop," Philip's voice sounded behind her.

"I thought you were asleep," she mumbled in embarrassment.

"I was until I heard men boarding my ship. Did you note the make of the enemy, Mark?"

"Aye, Philip, it's a French-built privateer, a square-rigged four-master, carrying as much canvas as a ship-of-line. I'm thinking it also carries as many cannon. Smartly captained too. He kept us from seeing the *Vixen* long enough to complete the transfer of crews."

"Could you read the ship's name?"

"Aye, we could when she headed north. It was the *Antilles Reine.*"

"My God, that's one of Jean Falconet's devil ships. How in hell did the British ever capture her?"

"Could be the owners joined the enemy."

"No, the Falconets have been preying on British shipping for a decade or more. Any sign of redcoats or marines aboard?"

"I don't think so, but the cannoneers are deadly shots."

"What would be your guess about her destination, Mark?"

"North to Halifax. She was too heavily loaded to risk the mid-Atlantic in winter, especially with a tow."

"Good. It'll give us a chance to try out the new rigging."

Rebecca watched in dismay as her husband's face sharpened in intensity, reminding her of the only wolverine she'd ever seen. With untried crews, rigging, and cannon, he confidently expected to overtake a larger ship that had an eight-hour lead, forty expertly manned cannon, and a pirate for a captain.

By the time Philip and Mark Stoneham had completed their planning, fifty of Philip's veteran crew had been exchanged for the storm-wounded from the three sister ships. Because it was virtually unarmed, the *Falmouth Star* would proceed to New London under the command of George Peckham while Philip took the lead attack position aboard the *Casco Bay*. Resigned to another separation, Rebecca knew that any attempt to dissuade Philip would be futile. She shared not one jot of the excitement that radiated from him like steam escaping from a boiling pot. His eyes glinted with anticipation as he loaded his pistols and buckled on a serviceable cutlass without a hint of nervous trembling.

Remembering the rumors she'd heard in Falmouth that Philip had served time as a privateer in the employ of the Caribbean British authorities, she fervently hoped he was as experienced as he seemed. But even so, in this new role her husband had become a stranger to her. His hurried farewell kiss drew little from her but hopeless regret, and his final half-joking advice that she avoid trouble in New London received only the faintest of smiles from her. She was, she reflected gloomily, a war widow before she'd really become a wife.

CHAPTER
4

JUST how much a stranger her husband was became apparent to Rebecca during her first dinner with George Peckham, who'd served as Philip's first mate for eight years before he'd earned a ship of his own. An uncomplicated man in his early thirties, Peckham answered her probing questions about Philip's career at sea with an enthusiastic candor.

"Don't worry about him, Mrs. Keane; the captain knows as much about surprise attack as the outlaw who captured the *Vixen*. The British hired only the best to privateer against the Spanish and French smugglers."

"How long did he work for the British?" she asked quietly.

"He held a letter of marque for five years until the limeys rescinded it on suspicion of smuggling and of returning slave cargoes to Africa. Silas Keane organized those return voyages, but it was Philip who learned how to attack without damaging the target ship or its cargo."

During her subsequent two dinners with the affable George Peckham, Rebecca learned many additional facets of her husband's complicated life, a life which seemed to hold little room for a wife. According to Peckham's circumspect allusions, Philip had been a popular guest with the social hostesses both in French and English colonies from Martinique to Quebec. Judging by the embarrassed manner with which Peckham stopped talking about one protracted shore leave in Martinique, Rebecca knew that at least one of those French hostesses had competed with Paulette Burnell for the title of mistress. Already insecure in her role as wife, she was unable to suppress jealousy that eroded her confidence still further and aroused the stubborn defiance that had sustained her throughout a troubled past. Another small, alienating wedge for the young wife was the discovery that her husband had mastered the foreign languages of French and Spanish while she was still struggling with her native English.

It bothered her too that Philip had not given her a wedding wing. Without a ring, a marriage certificate, or a husband, no respectable innkeeper would give her lodging. She had already decided that when the ship docked in New London, she'd not spend another night aboard. Since the wives of drapers in colonial port cities were usually expert seamstresses, she would locate the most obliging such couple in New London and request board and room in addition to a complete new wardrobe. As an employee of the Keane Company, George Peckham would be obliged to pay the bill from the company money in the ship's strongbox. As she recalled the frivolous and expensive dresses Paulette Burnell had always worn, Rebecca experienced no compunction at the thought that Philip Keane would be buying the clothing for still another woman, this one his wife. If pretty dresses could achieve the miracle of winning a reluctant husband's admiration and constancy, she vowed to choose only the most beautiful fabrics and the most flattering styles.

Had Rebecca not offered to help with the demanding task of preparing the bedridden wounded for transfer to land, she'd have been on deck when the *Falmouth Star* sailed into the mouth of the deep-water Thames River leading into the finest harbor in the thirteen colonies. Had she been on the bridge, she'd have seen the odd circumstance which caused George Peckham to order the two flags which the *Star* had flown for a decade—the Cross of St. George and the Union Jack—replaced by the Pine Tree flag of Massachusetts. Of the scores of schooners, frigates, brigantines, and sloops already at anchor in the wide expanse of water, not one was flying a British flag.

With excited anticipation, the captain ordered the long-boats carrying towlines into the water for the long pull to the unloading wharf. By the time the hard, exacting work of docking the ship was complete, every man on deck was aware that the traffic and activity along the entirety of the spread-out New London waterfront, familiarly known as "the beach," exceeded the normal many times over. Moreover, the faces of the three port officials who rushed up the gangplank to intercept the captain on the bridge were exceedingly grim.

Preoccupied with the immediate goal of avoiding Captain Peckham's attention and leaving the ship unnoticed, Rebecca waited nervously belowdecks, oblivious to the anxious activity of the men above. Neatly clad in her red cloak and dress, she carried only one small piece of hand luggage as she stood quietly beside Jed Daws's litter. In common with the other nonambulatory wounded, Jed had been sedated with laudanum to deaden the pain of being jostled up the narrow companionway on the way to a land-based infirmary, in this case an embarcadero warehouse emptied to accommodate the hundreds of storm-wounded sailors already under treatment there.

Once off the ship Rebecca was forced to continue the charade of accompanying the wounded by the peremptory order of the second mate, Jesse Milford, who'd been placed in charge of the assignment. "You'll wait with the men until I decide what to do with you," he barked at her sourly.

Rebecca nodded mutely and watched while the men were settled in an area cleared for them. But as soon as the offensive officer's attention was claimed by the presiding doctor, she left the gloomy building through a rear door, walked swiftly down a narrow alley, and emerged on the commercial street where the domestic shops were located. It took her less than half an hour to locate a draper who displayed a cautious enthusiasm for her proposal. Handing him a sealed letter addressed to Captain George Peckham aboard the *Falmouth Star*, Rebecca smothered a smile as the rotund merchant walked out of his shop at a pace that belied his girth and age.

Left behind with his wife and two daughters, Rebecca wasted no time in choosing from the excellent array of luxury fabrics, gloves, shoes, and bonnets brought to New London by French privateers.

Listening to the women's chatter, Rebecca selected the finest of the silks, velvets, muslins, and lawn, ignoring the drab bolts of homespun, fustian, twills, and huckaback. Upon his return an hour later, the draper beamed broadly at her accumulated choices and ordered his wife to prepare the guest room for Miss Rayburn. Rebecca winced slightly at the reminder of the deception she'd practiced in using her maiden name, but quickly regained her conviction that it had been a logical decision. Until Philip arrived in New London to claim her as his bride, her life would be far less restricted.

By early afternoon her enthusiasm for new clothing had waned considerably. The hours of conversation with women whose interests were limited to flounces, collars, and panniers had driven Rebecca back into the street, headed toward the business establishment she'd thought to avoid. Only once had she met Eldin Cooper, the editor-owner of the *New London Times,* but her father had forced her to read the dozens of letters the man had sent to the *Falmouth Clarion* in his capacity as a member of the Committee of Correspondence. Like Jeremy's own contributions, Cooper's philosophy had been drearily repetitious and predictable.

Locating the dusty newspaper office on a side street less frequented than the main commercial area, Rebecca pushed open the weather-beaten door and introduced herself to the harried man seated behind an untidy desk. From his blank expression she realized that he did not remember the eighteen-year-old girl who'd recorded a four-hour discussion among members of the New England Mutual Defense Committee two years earlier. However, Mr. Cooper quickly proved more knowledgeable about her father's current activities than she was.

"It's finally come, Rachel, the great day your father and I have anticipated for ten years. If only my health were better, I'd be at his side in the next battle for independence."

Ignoring the misnomer of Rachel, Rebecca asked sharply, "What did you mean by 'next'?"

The editor's pale blue eyes beamed at her with a

condescending pity. "With a journalist for a father, particularly a journalist so dedicated to the cause, I'd have thought you'd be more alert than most of the ladies. The war began two days ago in Lexington, my dear, with the courageous stand of seventy-seven of our patriotic minutemen against seven hundred ruthless British regulars. Eight of our men gave their lives, but their names will go down in history, their names and the date, April 19, 1775. I was just completing the rest of the story when you interrupted. You may read what I've already written."

With a presentiment of doom, Rebecca learned about the brief skirmish at Lexington and the subsequent sustained battle at Concord in which a larger group of militia forced the British to retreat to Boston. Cynically, she noted that Eldin Cooper's article had not named a one of the Americans killed in either village.

"Is my father going to Boston?" she asked heavily.

"No, my dear," the editor assured her, "your father will be on a far more important mission under the command of Ethan Allen, an expedition, I'm happy to report, that is being financed wholly by Connecticut war funds. I'm sorry that I'm not at liberty to tell you more; in fact, I must leave you now. A few hours ago a Maine ship arrived in port with an astounding tale of a battle at sea, and I must locate someone who knows the particulars."

"I know them, Mr. Cooper, I was aboard that ship."

"What a dreadful experience for a young girl!"

Rebecca heard the sincere distress in his voice and shook her head in astonishment. This innocuous-looking zealot could send half-trained fifteen-year-old boys into suicidal battle, yet he was genuinely shocked at the idea of a twenty-year-old woman facing even limited danger. Abruptly recalling her reason for visiting this enigmatical journalist, she challenged him boldly.

"It wasn't at all dreadful for me, Mr. Cooper; but it is an exciting news story, and I would like to write it for your paper."

"Come now, Rachel, news-writing is a skill that takes years to master."

"I know, I've been writing news for six years in my father's paper."

"Jeremy actually published your stories?"

"Have you ever read the half of the *Falmouth Clarion* that wasn't devoted to Samuel Adams?"

"Domestic trivialities hold little interest for me. The question is whether or not you can write a coherent report about something important."

An hour later Rebecca handed him a completed story far more coherent than his own, and for good measure, a second article about Philip's escape from New Bedford.

"Extraordinary!" Eldin Cooper murmured in reaction. "You do have a flair for words. I cannot pay you much and I certainly won't permit you to do the actual reporting, but it would make my work easier if you organized my notes for a few hours each day."

Jubilant over her success, Rebecca hurried to the infirmary to report the news to the only genuine friend she had in New London. She found Jed Daws and the other Keane employees in a state of sullen rebellion.

"The durn gruel they give us ain't fittin' fer hogs, Becky," the old man complained bitterly. "And we 'uz the only ones in this whole durn place what didn't git a drop of rum."

"What were the other men served?" she asked sharply.

"Meat stew, that's what. Buckets of it from the Londonderry Inn, and rum, double the ration if you ask me. The other captains pay fer it, but that durn second mate said he'd have to git the cap'n's say-so to do the same fer us."

Refraining from voicing her own opinion of Jesse Milford, Rebecca promised equal treatment for the injured Keane crewmen. Escorted by two riggers whose bandaged hands did not inhibit their walking and by the young marine who'd been left in charge, she headed for the kitchen of the Londonderry Inn, her mind in a whirl of angry speculation. Whereas George Peckham could not refuse to pay her personal bills, he would most likely hesitate to override the decisions of another ship's officer. And if the parsimonious, vindictive Milford learned of her interference, her own freedom could be jeopardized. It cost every one of her gold sovereigns to pay for one week's supply of food and rum for the men, but the gratitude she received the next day more than compensated for her loss.

Rebecca's estimation of Captain Peckham's probable reaction was an accurate one. Had he been reminded of his promise to Philip Keane to keep a close watch over Philip's wife, he'd have been horrified at the extent of her activities in New London and would most certainly have insisted she return to the ship. He realized that he'd failed miserably in this assignment the day the recaptured French privateer *Antilles Reine* with the damaged *Vixen* in tow arrived in New London, and Peckham received a note from his employer.

"Please continue your supervision of my wife until Matthew Stoneham is free to take over the job," Philip had written. "She tends to be undisciplined, so don't be fooled by her innocent looks or glib explanations. And don't tell her that I'm after other prizes. She's quite capable of stirring up a hornet's nest once she learns that the war she considers unnecessary has already begun with a vengeance. As much as she needs lessoning, I don't want her bedeviled by the local minutemen."

Cursing the belated warning, Peckham hastily left the essential work of converting the *Falmouth Star* into a thirty-cannon privateer and ordered a longboat lowered. He was aboard the *Reine* when it was pulled into dockage and the British prisoners of war were turned over to a waiting contingent of Connecticut militia. As the battle-injured Americans and the half-starved survivors of the original French crew were being carried ashore, Peckham noticed an odd reception committee forming on the cobble-paved parade area. Seated beside a packing crate was a woman dressed in the same color red outfit Mrs. Keane had been wearing when last he'd seen her seventeen days earlier. Hovering close to her was a rumpled-looking gentleman with a tricorn hat pulled over lank, unpowdered hair; and engaged in asking her questions from a few feet away was a trio of well-dressed New London officials.

Increasingly certain that the woman was Rebecca Keane,

Peckham nervously held his peace until Matthew Stoneham joined him at the rail.

"What the hell is Becky doing down there?" Stoneham demanded. "Philip said he'd given you orders that she wasn't to leave your ship."

Peckham nodded miserably. "She left without my permission, but I thought she'd be safe enough in a private home ashore."

Shaking his head and chuckling, Stoneham commiserated with his unhappy companion. "I've known Becky most of her life, and she's never asked anyone's permission as far as I remember. I imagine she's hired herself out to work on the local newspapers; but if I were you, I wouldn't try scolding her in public. She's not quite the lady her mother was. Tell you what, George. I'll take care of the minx if you'll supervise unloading the cargo of this floating arsenal. There's enough small arms and ammunition aboard to supply a regiment."

Relieved to be rid of an irksome problem he no longer felt capable of handling, Peckham nodded his agreement and watched as the more capable Stoneham strode toward the waiting group of Connecticut officials.

Pointedly ignoring Rebecca, who was busy writing down the words Eldin Cooper dictated, Matthew Stoneham addressed the men briskly, "Gentlemen, I have better than a thousand British muskets for sale and enough powder for a year's supply. Are you interested?"

"That's why we're here, Captain Stoneham. The officer you sent ashore earlier informed us about your cargo, but at the moment we're more interested in that remarkable ship. She looks to be almost the size of a ship-of-line frigate," one official commented.

"Fifteen feet shorter and narrower in the beam, but she carries the same number of cannon. She's a new French design, and we're hoping shc's faster on the tack and in general speed. According to her former French crew—those poor devils who were locked in the hold to starve to death a month ago—one of the Antilles sister ships demasted a man-of-war and would have captured it, had not two other Britishers intervened."

"Was that when she was captured, Captain Stoneham?" another of the officials asked.

"No, the entire Antilles fleet—the *Reine,* the *Grande Dame,* and *L'Aventure*—were taken by stealth and trickery while they were riding at anchor in the Spanish port of Havana, Cuba. While most of their crews were asleep belowdeck, the three ships were boarded simultaneously by hordes of scum released from British prisons for that purpose. One of the prisoners you watched being taken into custody is a man named Tom Granger, a one-time officer in the Royal Navy who became a privateer. Three years ago he was sentenced to fifteen years on the charge of piracy. While I was a prisoner aboard his ship, he boasted that an informer from Saint-Domingue had told him exactly where Jean Falconet's fleet would be that night. Granger insisted, though, that the death of Falconet's son, Antoine, aboard the *Reine* was an unfortunate accident; but after he'd surrendered to Philip Keane, he admitted that one of the other French captains had been deliberately murdered.

"When they left Cuba, Granger and the other two pirate leaders, also released from British prisons, sailed the ships to Nassau, where they were given additional assignments. First, they were to transport munitions from the armory on New Providence Island to Halifax; and second, they were to capture or destroy the entire Keane fleet."

"Did he tell you why the Keane fleet was singled out?" Eldin Cooper demanded to know.

"He didn't have to. It's the only American fleet in a position to disrupt the shipping lane between England and Halifax. But Tom Granger also had a personal grudge to settle. Silas Keane had been a government witness at Granger's trial."

"That I can understand," Cooper persisted, "but what seems impossible is the speed with which this Granger located his assigned target. Given the size of the Atlantic Ocean and the storm, it could only have been a chance meeting."

"Not if the intelligence was accurate enough," Stoneham snapped, "and Granger claimed it was. He said he'd been informed that our ships were en route from New Bedford to New York, so he positioned the *Reine* and her two sister ships across the coastal shipping lane west of Long Island. Had New York been our destination, they'd have intercepted us. Since unluckily we were blown south of our course to New London, the result was the same.''

The third official, a thoughtful man who'd listened intently to the dramatic narration, took over the questioning with a deceptively mild authority. ''Just how was it that the British in New Bedford were told anything about the destination of an American ship?''

Casting a baleful look at her old friend, Matthew Stoneham, Rebecca laid her quill aside and faced the inquisitor. ''Mr. Wyndom,'' she admitted calmly, ''I was the one who informed the British commandant about New York.''

''You, Miss Rayburn?'' Wyndom asked. ''I'd be very interested in knowing how the daughter of one of our most prominent patriots became friends with an enemy captain.''

''I was not at war with Captain Sinclair,'' she retorted crisply. ''I was merely the artist he employed to paint his picture.''

''Perhaps I can explain,'' Cooper intervened hastily. ''Rebecca told me about her activity in New Bedford. Captain Keane needed a diversion in order to smuggle nine hundred men and quantities of munitions out to his fleet in the Elizabeth Islands. Rebecca supplied that diversion by offering to paint Sinclair's portrait. I believe she used her uncle's name rather than Rayburn to aid in the deception.''

Regretting her bad judgment in having confided in the garrulous editor, Rebecca waited for the inevitable suspicion of her uncle's loyalties to be aired.

''That would be Jonathan Langley,'' Wyndom asserted on cue. ''Was this Captain Sinclair a friend of your uncle's, Miss Rayburn?''

''No,'' she responded curtly, ''but like you, Captain Sinclair kept accurate records of the political sympathies of well-known colonials.''

''Miss Rayburn, did your uncle tell you his reasons for

selling his ships at a time when his country needed him to aid in its defense?''

With her composure once again intact, Rebecca's perverse sense of humor surfaced. ''Jonathan recently married a widow almost half his age,'' she explained with a spurious innocence, adding softly, ''A very pretty, rich young woman. Like most older captains, I imagine my uncle was afraid to leave her alone while he was at sea.''

It was Matthew Stoneham's laconic Maine drawl that broke the awkward silence following Rebecca's subtle impudence. ''Gentlemen, I think we have more important matters to discuss than Jonathan Langley. Just what arrangements have you made for the payment of the cargo? Silas Keane insists on monies rather than promissory notes.''

''Connecticut doesn't deal in promissory notes, Captain; however, since our militia is otherwise engaged, you will have to deliver the arms to Hartford yourself. The other members of the Committee of Inspection will want to check the weapons. I'd advise you to take sufficient protection with you. The interior of our colony is cursed with a large number of militant loyalists imported last year from New York. One additional condition; Miss Rayburn is to accompany you. I'm certain her New Bedford experience will prove of considerable interest.''

''They didn't even ask about the battle,'' Rebecca complained cynically as she and Matthew watched the officials stride off, followed obsequiously by Eldin Cooper.

''It wasn't much of a battle, Becky. Granger was so confident, he was running with lights on both the *Reine* and the *Vixen*. I'd been allowed to remain on deck, but even I didn't see our ships approaching an hour before dawn. At first light they were in position, the *Langley* and the *Maine* pacing within rifle range on the port and starboard sides of the *Reine* while the *Casco Bay* tacked back and forth in front. When the British officer on watch refused to strike the colors, our marines opened fire. Granger was forced to surrender within minutes after he arrived on deck; none of his cannoneers had been able to reach their posts.''

"And now Philip and your brothers have gone after the other two," Rebecca said dully, her heart plummeting in disappointment and renewed fear.

"Not alone, Becky, four others of the fleet were in good enough shape to join in the hunt. Enough of war news, young lady. I'm interested in something a good deal more puzzling. Why aren't you using your married name?"

"Did Philip tell you why he married me?"

"He mentioned something about protecting you from the Tuptons, but what has that to do with your—"

"I don't need protection here, and Philip seems to be too busy to remember he has a wife. Matthew, why *did* my uncle sell out to Silas?"

"For a good reason, Becky. He had contracts with the British which could have forced him to work for them. Jonathan's not a loyalist, and I think I can convince the Hartford people that it was the only way he could keep his fleet out of British hands. In the meantime, young lady, you'd better get packed. Even if Mr. Wyndom hadn't suggested your going to Hartford with me, I'd have taken you anyway. Philip insisted on my keeping an eye on you, and I intend doing a better job than George Peckham did. I won't be taken in by your pussy-sweet shenanigans."

"I can take care of myself, Matthew Stoneham," she boasted tartly. "I'll go to Hartford with you because I don't want anyone to lose the prize money. But after I've answered all the questions about my father and my uncle and Captain Sinclair, I just want to be left alone."

Eight days later in Hartford, Rebecca was humbly grateful that Matthew had ignored her protestations and imperturbably carried out his assignment as guardian. The day before their wagon train arrived in the colony's capital, the news of the first patriot victory had been broadcast throughout the town. On May 10, 1775, Ethan Allen had defeated the British at Fort Ticonderoga and captured an arsenal of heavy field equipment. Greeted upon arrival by Thomas Green, the publisher of the *Hartford Courant* and another longtime friend of her father, Miss Rebecca Rayburn was introduced as a heroine for her part in Captain Keane's escape from New Bedford. As the daughter of one of the heroes of Ticonderoga, she was invited to attend the celebration balls hosted by the elite families of the prosperous city. At each of the parties Matthew Stoneham had been her quietly unobtrusive escort.

At first he had been vaguely disturbed by the continued use of her maiden name, but gradually his enjoyment at watching her gloom replaced by a developing self-confidence had eliminated his objection. In Falmouth he'd often pitied the shabbily dressed girl who'd never attracted an iota of attention from the young men. However, there was nothing to pity about her now. She'd discovered that her unusual combination of pale blonde hair and dark brown eyes created a unique beauty. In either of the two party dresses that'd been completed in time for the trip, Matthew smiled with amusement, she was a radiant siren who could prove irresistible to men far more knowledgeable about women than Philip Keane. Usually a tolerant man, Matthew was suddenly and intensely irritated with a husband who preferred a jaded French mistress to a sparkling young wife.

In a jubilant mood Rebecca had chosen to wear the more daring of the two gowns for what was to be her last party in Hartford. It was a vivid coral-pink silk that not even the soft candlelight of Thomas Green's ballroom could dim. Tightly girdled around her slender waist, the dress belled out with elegant panniers over a gracefully full skirt; but it was the low-cut, softly shawled neckline that made the delicate gown distinctively different. Glowing with delight at the flattering attention she'd received from every partner throughout the evening of dancing, Rebecca was just completing the minuet when she glanced up from the concluding curtsy to discover with a cold shock that her former partner had been replaced by a grim-faced Roger Tupton. Forced to accept the hand he offered to help her rise from the awkward position, she tried unsuccessfully to break the contact once she was securely on her feet.

"I've explained the situation to your host, Rebecca," Roger asserted tersely, "and he agreed that my claim was valid and that you had failed to meet your obligations to your father and to me. Are you going to come quietly or do I drag you across this dance floor? My friends are waiting for us just outside the door, and they'll gladly help me if you prove obstreperous."

Rebecca's playful mood of make-believe had vanished, replaced by an angry defiance. "I'm not going anyplace with you, Roger. Unlike your lickspittles outside, my friends are right here in this room."

"What friends? Philip Keane is at sea, and none of the people in Hartford know you well enough to fight for your so-called honor."

Forcing herself to relax, she studied the face of the man she'd admired as a young girl. He'd called her insulting names in the past, but never had he been as crude as he was this night.

"I thought when you attended college in England, you might acquire some manners; but you're the same bully you always were. If you don't release my arm, I'm going to call for help."

"Since I've already announced to the older man that I'm your husband-to-be, no one would pay any attention to you."

"You're months too late, Roger. I married Philip Keane in Saco," she asserted flatly.

"You're a poor liar, Rebecca. We were there, remember? And we went through every scrap of paper in the one church in Saco."

"Did you talk to the minister?"

"We didn't have to. One of the fishermen told us that the man maintains a second parish in Kennebunk and hadn't been in Saco for weeks. As I said before, you're a poor liar. I've followed you from New Bedford to New London and to Hartford, and you've been Miss Rayburn in all three towns. Crawling into bed with a man like Philip Keane does not make you a legal wife, Rebecca, only a temporary mistress. His permanent one lives in Falmouth, and he reports to her regularly."

Although she winced at the blunt reminder, her voice remained expressionless. "Regardless of Paulette Burnell, Philip and I are married; and the certificate has been officially registered in Boston."

A flicker of doubt momentarily clouded Roger's eyes

before his jaw hardened with obstinate resolution. "I wouldn't put too much faith in Boston records if I were you. A marriage certificate without hometown witnesses isn't all that permanent."

Recalling her uncle's sardonic comments about Tupton wealth being based on trickery and deceit, Rebecca wondered how much of that money had been gained through forged or altered records. But the Tuptons hadn't succeeded in changing a single clause of her mother's will, she remembered suddenly.

"That's an empty threat, Roger," she taunted him. "The city clerks of Boston wouldn't allow a Tupton near their records, not after your Uncle Sidney made such a fool of himself over my mother's will. Well, you won't be any more successful in getting your hands on that money than he was. Jonathan wouldn't give you a shilling of it."

"You're being ridiculous. You don't even know where Jonathan Langley is, but I do."

Something about the smile that accompanied this boast frightened Rebecca. She'd known since Saco that Roger Tupton could be ruthless, and he appeared even more self-confident now.

How could he know anything about Jonathan's whereabouts? And how had he located her or known where she'd been since Saco? Motivated by a growing fear, she exerted her strength in a sudden lunge to break free from the arm that gripped her waist tightly, but Roger's smile only broadened as he propelled her out of the ballroom and into the entry hall. Rebecca's voice was shrill with terror now when she called out the name of Matthew Stoneham, and never had any sound been as welcome as his Maine accent coming from the shadows near the heavy oaken door.

"Right here, Becky. I've been waiting ever since Mr. Tupton made his little speech to our host about your being his runaway bride. Didn't want to embarrass his folks by calling him a liar or worse in front of strangers who're already riled up about loyalist sympathizers. If I were you, Roger, I'd leave here before someone becomes curious about those three men who're waiting outside."

"I'm leaving, Stoneham," the younger man responded

harshly, "but I'm taking Rebecca with me. Her father wants her decently married, not playing fast and loose with an irresponsible libertine. I doubt anyone here would believe her story about a secret wedding in Saco."

"It doesn't matter what they believe, it's what I know that counts. Now let go of her and get out of here. Until her husband returns, I'm responsible for her safety, and I don't take foolish chances, as you seem inclined to do."

"The devil you don't, Captain! It's taken me three months to locate Rebecca, and I'm not letting her go on the say-so of an unarmed old man."

Matthew Stoneham smiled with an amused confidence. "I may be unarmed, Tupton, but the six Massachusetts marines on patrol outside are spoiling for a good fight. Philip Keane saved their lives two weeks ago, and in defense of his wife they might not be particularly civilized."

For several seconds Roger stood his ground without relaxing his hold on Rebecca, but she could feel the increasing tension in his muscular body. With an abrupt burst of speed, he shoved past the veteran ship's captain and yanked the door open. For a brief moment his face mirrored both shock and savage fury as he faced two of Stoneham's marines, their pistols drawn and aimed. Rebecca was shaking with relief when Roger relaxed his hold on her and smiled with a semblance of the charm that had once captivated her.

"Your moon-maiden luck seems to be holding, Rebecca, but not forever. Next time I'll take Captain Stoneham's advice and be more careful." Before she could react, he bent his head and kissed her lightly on her trembling lips. Smiling recklessly now, he left her side and strode swiftly toward the street.

Rebecca stood motionless where he'd left her, a cynical smile gradually replacing her look of stunned surprise. "If he'd done that four years ago, I'd probably have married him," she murmured to Matthew. "I'll be eternally grateful that he despised me then."

"He's become a dangerous man, Becky. I thought for a minute that he'd try to use the pistol he'd concealed under his fancy coat or the hunting knife hidden in his boot."

"How did you know he'd be here tonight?"

"I didn't. To tell the truth I didn't recognize him until I heard him talking to Mr. Green and the other men. These marine lads were ordered here to guard the chest of prize money, not a flighty young woman with husband problems. I trust you've had your fill of flirting because we're leaving Hartford within the hour. Best you change that pretty dance frock for some warmer clothing; it's bound to be an uncomfortable boat ride down the Connecticut River, especially at night."

The adjective *uncomfortable* was an ironic understatement, as Rebecca discovered within the first minutes of boarding. Built to protect both the crew and cargo from frequent musket attacks by British custom agents or cutthroat freebooters who often hid in the dense shrubbery along the banks, the sturdy boat was as much a floating fort as the ancient Viking ships and just as lacking in civilized amenities. In the crude cabin ventilated only by musket ports which allowed the defenders to return fire with reasonable security, there were a built-in chart table and two sets of three-tier bunks. There were also six sleeping men, four in the narrow upper bunks and two huddled on the crowded floor. Too tired to care about propriety, Rebecca climbed fully clothed into one of the lower cubicles and drifted into uneasy slumber. Not until morning did she learn that there were twenty-four men aboard the small craft, all of them preoccupied with a mission that had nothing to do with her safety or that of her husband's chest of prize money.

"I didn't realize there'd be any danger involved," Matthew Stoneham told her quietly after he'd shaken her awake, "but we were followed by another boat last night."

"Roger wouldn't dare attack," she exclaimed scornfully, "not against your marines."

"Keep your voice down, Becky," he scolded her sharply. "Sound carries a long way over water. At the moment we're anchored behind a river island, waiting for the enemy boat to pass our position."

"What enemy, Matthew? There's no British in Connecticut."

"In this case, loyalist spies who followed the men we're protecting from Ticonderoga. The Hartford people asked me to provide armed escort to a pair of couriers who're carrying captured documents to New London. I thought the river would be the safest route, but obviously I was wrong. Downriver there're two more boats waiting for us and a hundred or more armed men lying in ambush along the shore."

"What documents could be that important, Matthew?" she asked hollowly.

"Maps, Becky, maps of the location and contents of every British arsenal from Boston to the Caribbean. Like Massachusetts, Connecticut plans to defend itself regardless of the action taken by the other colonies. Its defense committees have already chosen twenty privateers to strip those armories bare; my undertaking this escort mission will give the Keane fleet an equal chance to compete."

"But how can we now, Matthew? We'll be ambushed and sunk."

"Not if we run the blockade at night using old smuggling tricks. Best put these heavy moccasins on, Becky; you'll not be going with us."

"Why not?" she demanded.

"Because, lass, I work for your husband and father-in-law, and they'd order me keelhauled if I took you into battle. Besides, the men will fight better without a woman aboard. One of the couriers knows the trail on the opposite side of the river, so you'll be walking the twelve miles between here and Middletown."

Rebecca's first impression of her guide was that of a rawboned frontiersman a year or so younger than herself. It took her a minute longer to discover that Simon Parrish was angrier about the ignominious assignment than she was.

"Ever walked twelve miles before?" he drawled with an insulting skepticism.

Recalling the harrowing fifteen-mile hike to Saco with Philip, Rebecca nodded curtly. "Many times, Mr. Parrish," she boasted, "but usually with more congenial companionship."

"This isn't a pleasure jaunt into the woods, mistress. We'll be traveling mostly at night through enemy territory, and there won't be any social conversation to keep you entertained. You'll do exactly what I tell you without any argument, and you'll let me do whatever talking is necessary. Furthermore, we won't be stopping for food or rest. Is that understood?"

Rebecca made no effort to answer the peremptory demands, since the young courier had already turned away from her and rejoined his partner. Her affronted expression, however, was of such intensity that a watchful Matthew Stoneham moved swiftly to her side in an effort to assuage her outrage.

"Don't pay any attention to young Parrish's manner, Becky. He's been fighting this war a long time, and both he and his fellow courier—incidentally, Seth Parrish is his older brother—have been under a British sentence of death for the past three years. Do what he says, Becky; he knows more than you do about avoiding trouble."

Hours later, had she not been so terrified, she would have disagreed sharply with Matthew's evaluation of her young escort. From the moment she and Simon were put ashore on the north bank of the Connecticut River, he maintained a pace that left her breathless. Hampered by the full skirt and cloak of her red outfit and by the oversize moccasins tied to her feet, Rebecca moved clumsily over the uneven trail, tripping over half-buried stones, protruding roots, and once over a muscular coil that slithered quickly into the underbrush. Twice she was unable to prevent a fall, and each time Simon was forced to stop and help her regain her feet. For three miles she endured the hardships without complaint until a small rock embedded in the sole of one moccasin became too painful to walk on. Plopping down on a fallen log, she was removing the offending pebble when an exasperated Simon broke his own rule of silence.

"What the devil do you think you're doing?" he hissed.

"I'm massaging my ruined feet back to life," she snapped, "and I intend to remain right here until I catch my breath."

Instantly, Simon's caution reasserted itself. "Not here," he whispered tersely. "We're too exposed. Wait until I find us a safer hiding place."

His warning was minutes too late. Fifty feet from the fallen log, three musket-armed men emerged silently from the underbrush and walked toward the stricken pair. Rebecca watched in dismay as Simon's hand reached for his hunting knife. Forgetting all about her sore feet, she stood up and unceremoniously shoved him aside as she faced the three strangers. Her voice was shrill with strain, and she used the first name she could remember.

"Jed Daws, stop acting like a lubbering dolt before you cut yourself with that silly knife. Perhaps these gentlemen can help us find our way to the nearest farmhouse. Goodness knows we've been lost for the last hour. I'm Rebecca Langley," she proclaimed loudly, "and this is my cousin, Jed Daws. Six miles or more back on the road from Hartford our horse went lame and we had to leave the wagon with a farmer who told us we'd be safer on the river trail. But I think he was just a frightened bumpkin who sees Indians behind every hayrick. You're the first people we've seen in hours, and I'm so tired of this twisty path I could drop in my tracks. If you can convince this stubborn country cousin of mine that we won't be attacked by ruffians or highwaymen, we just might be able to reach Middletown in time for me to take the public coach. I can't wait to leave this dreadful colony where everyone talks about nothing except war, and get home to New Bedford. So if you can tell us how to reach the road, at least I won't have to spend the night by this awful river where I just know there're all kinds of crawly snakes and—"

For a frantic moment Rebecca believed that she'd have to continue the inanities until she ran out of words, but abruptly a voice as crisply accented as Captain Sinclair's interrupted her monologue.

"Where's your luggage, young lady?"

"Exactly where my cousin made me leave it—in the wagon. If he hadn't chosen the worst horse on the farm—"

Again she was stopped midsentence. "Where in New Bedford do you live, Miss Langley?"

Not daring to hesitate, Rebecca named the inn which lodged Captain Sinclair and the other British officers. "At the New Bedford Arms. My father owns and operates it," she responded glibly.

The spokesman's eyes narrowed speculatively as he studied the articulate young woman facing him. "You don't sound like an innkeeper's daughter, Miss Langley," he challenged her thoughtfully. "And you don't look like a barmaid trained to wait on tables, even in an establishment as respectable as the New Bedford Arms."

Rebecca kept her features expressionless as she absorbed the fact that this Englishman knew about a particular inn in a remote Massachusetts town. Forcing her voice to retain the young loquacity she'd affected earlier, she bubbled with an enthusiastic denial.

"My goodness, I should hope not. My father sent me to Boston years ago where I attended a simply awful school for young ladies, and he would never let me do a bit of work around the inn because he didn't—"

"When did you leave your father's inn?"

"About five weeks ago, when he sent me to visit my Aunt Lucinda—that's Jed's mother. I was supposed to stay all summer because my father said he needed my room to house some more of the officers stationed in New Bedford."

"What officers?"

"British ones, of course. New Bedford has been under their control for months. But the only one my father would let me talk to was Captain Brian Sinclair because he was older and had a wife in England whom he wrote to all the time. He used to tell me how he hated not being aboard his ship and how he wished that the rebel colonials would settle down so he could return to his home."

Momentarily, the Englishman's harsh features relaxed and he nodded almost pleasantly. "All right, Miss Langley, I want you and your cousin to get off this trail and back on the main road. You'll find it quite safe for the next eight miles; and if you ask for shelter at any of the farmhouses along the way and tell them that Major Welford has given you safe conduct, they'll put you up for the night."

Rebecca's farewell was an ungraceful bob of her bonneted

head; her knees were shaking too badly to risk a curtsy. Forcing herself to walk sedately after Simon, who'd already started to push through the underbrush in the direction indicated by a wave of the Englishman's musket, she willed herself to smile back at the three men rather than to rush away in a blind panic. But once on the dusty roadway Simon had to hustle to keep up with her. Not even when she and Philip had been eluding the Tuptons had she been as frightened. No longer did the war seem like a remote philosophical tilting at windmills; it had become a very real threat to her own physical safety. Until long after dark she plodded steadily on, ignoring her thirst and hunger, tensely aware that even though she wasn't an enemy, she was in enemy territory. When Simon pulled up short on the outskirts of Middletown and spoke in a normal tone of voice, she jerked nervously.

"You can relax now," he announced. "This is a Yankee town where we'll be safe until the others arrive to pick us up. If you don't mind eating in an old-fashioned country inn, we can get us some supper." Rebecca wouldn't have minded had the wayside inn been a biblical den of iniquity as long as it served warm rum and hot food. She was dozing peacefully from a repletion of both when Captain Stoneham located his two landlubbers.

Awakening late the next morning in her bunk aboard the riverboat, she learned that the sturdy craft had rammed one of the enemy vessels anchored athwart the river and left the second one befouled with snags of fallen trees uprooted by winter storms. Protected by the height of freeboard timbers, the oarsmen had been able to maintain enough speed to avoid any damage by shore snipers before reaching the safety of patriot-controlled waters.

Stoneham smiled in self-deprecation at Rebecca's lavish praise. "An old trick learned during my misspent youth as a smuggler's apprentice, and nothing compared to the courage you displayed onshore. Simon told me you didn't stop talking until the Englishman backed down. I don't think I'm going to tell Philip what else young Parrish said."

"What?" Rebecca demanded suspiciously.

"That you were the slickest liar he'd ever met and would make a better courier than he is."

"Those lies may have saved us both from being shot!"

"According to Simon, there's no doubt of it. If I'd known the enemy was patrolling that side of the river, I'd have kept you aboard; but I thought he was skilled enough to protect you."

Rebecca shrugged impatiently. "If Simon had been alone, he'd have never been caught; I was the one who broke the rules. Matthew, how did the enemy"—she corrected herself hastily—"how did an English agent learn about any of us being on the river?"

"Britain has spent years preparing for this war, and the capture of Ticonderoga with its arsenal and the maps showing the locations of the other arsenals was a bitter blow. I imagine they ordered their spies from miles around to prevent those maps from reaching New London."

"The rebels employ spies too," she murmured absently, unaware of the odd look on her old friend's face.

"We rebels intend to win this war, Becky," he said gently, "by whatever means we can; otherwise we'll all be hanged as traitors."

A sudden poignant memory of Philip Keane's vividly handsome face made Rebecca shudder with a piercing dread.

CHAPTER
5

BY the time the small river craft had reached the safety of New London Harbor, Rebecca's fear for her husband's life was greatly intensified. During a brief stopover in New Haven at the mouth of the Connecticut River, the captain of a dry-docked merchantman had informed Matthew Stoneham that a large British fleet under the command of Admiral Lord Richard Howe had left Halifax and was sailing southward into New England waters.

"Ships like mine don't stand a chance against royal frigates," the embittered mariner complained. "Only the fastest of our privateers can avoid being trapped once those cursed ships-of-line string out into fighting formation."

"Do you know what Howe intends to do?" Matthew demanded.

"No, but with that number of ships he could blockade every one of our ports from New York to Boston. If you're planning on taking that river tub of yours past the sixty miles of coast to New London, better do it at night. Rumor has it that there's more than a hundred ships in port there, all of them scrambling for more cannon and supplies so they can clear harbor before the British get this far south. Maybe the hotheads in Congress figure they can fight a land war and win, but every one of our ships is sure as hell at deadly risk."

Having remembered those grim words throughout the tense voyage in the coastal waters north of New Haven, Rebecca was distressed once the small craft reached New London, and she learned that her husband's ship was not among the battle-damaged brigs now anchored near the *Antilles Reine*. George Peckham was relieved to see her, but she heard only snatches of news before she was whisked aboard the *Reine* and installed in the large and elegantly furnished master's quarters. At her protest that she'd prefer to remain ashore, Matthew shook his head.

"Not with that Tupton scoundrel still in the area."

Although she was willing to admit that particular danger existed, she was furious when Peckham added, "Your husband was very positive about where he wanted you domiciled until he returned, Mrs. Keane."

"My husband wrote to you?"

"Aye, on official business that Matt and I must attend to. Good day, mistress."

Angered by the abrupt dismissal and by the necessity of obeying a husband whom she hadn't seen in over a month and who hadn't been considerate enough to write to her directly, Rebecca wandered aimlessly through the connecting cabins, impressed despite her gloom by the efficient graciousness of the accommodations. In the sleeping quarters the bed was large and comfortably mattressed while the necessaries room was sectioned off and equipped with a burnished copper bathtub, a civilized commode instead of a chamber pot, and a washstand with the unaccustomed luxury of a mirror behind it. Reminded that she'd lived in the same soiled red dress for five days, she was about to leave the cabin in search of hot water when Jed Daws knocked briefly on the mahogany door before he entered the large outer cabin.

Hobbling capably on his half-mended leg with the aid of a crutch, Jed grinned at her and deposited a bottle of rum on the table before he beckoned to the two figures standing outside. Rebecca stared in amazement at the exotic pair who entered the cabin bearing steaming bowls of food. Even though they were dressed in the loose canvas breeches and striped jerseys of common seamen, they bore little resemblance to any men she'd ever seen before. Their skin was golden brown in color, their large eyes velvet brown, shades darker than her own, and their closely cropped bristly hair jet black. But it was the enigmatic look of pride in their faces that captivated the artist in Rebecca.

On only one other occasion had she studied the faces of Negroes when a damaged slave ship had landed in Boston for repairs. It had been one of the few times she'd admired her father. "Poor devils," he'd muttered angrily. "Slavery's one of the worst curses England has placed on the colonies." Rebecca rarely contradicted Jeremy and so had not pointed out that in this case it'd been a pro-independence Boston merchant who'd brought this particular shipload of the curse to America. Instead, she'd studied the spiritless, apathetic faces of the men and women chained together and shivering in the wind-blown chill. The magnificent men who now set her table looked nothing like those poor creatures. In response to her inquiring look, Jed explained as he poured two mugs of rum.

"Thought they might perk up your interest, Becky. Them two's mulatto brothers from Saint-Domingue—Leon and Louis, who 'uz cabin boys to the Frenchie cap'n. Best cooks I ever had helpin' me, and I've heered they're devil sword fighters when it comes to boardin' an enemy ship."

"Are they slaves, Jed?"

"Nope, the Frenchie cap'n took a likin' to them and freed them. When Cap'n Keane rescued them from the limeys, they asked t' be his cabin boys. That's how come they're waitin' on you."

"Will Philip be taking over this ship?"

"It's already his."

"When will he and Mark Stoneham be coming back?"

"Don't rightly know about the cap'n, but Mark Stoneham won't be comin' back ever. The *Langley* 'uz sunk, Becky, but that wasn't when Mark 'uz kilt. The bastard limey cap'n ordered the lifeboats fired on afore Cap'n Keane and Luke Stoneham could git their ships into position. Luke brought the *Maine* here when it 'uz shot up. It 'uz him who give us the news about his brother."

Rebecca felt a cold horror engulf her. Tragedy at sea had always been a part of her life, but never before had she heard of such a breach of maritime law except by pirates. Mark Stoneham had been a good friend of her mother's, a big bluff man who'd always been unfailingly kind to a rebellious little girl. She remembered his anger of a few weeks ago after Matthew had been captured; his eagerness to fight had cost him his ship and his life.

"What about Philip?" she mumbled hollowly.

"Luke said he didn't know how the cap'n done it, but he took the *Casco Bay* in close an' him and the marines boarded the limey and took it over. The bastard what ordered the firin' won't be facin' the hangman's noose; his body 'uz the first one pitched overboard."

"Is my husband all right?"

"Right as rain. Soon as he got control, he ordered his own gunners to fire the limey's cannons at the other ship.

Took a half hour to git the colors struck, but the prize weren't damaged all that much. While Luke came here, the cap'n took the rest of the fleet and the two limeys to his paw in Falmouth.''

At Rebecca's cry of dismay, Jed's grin broadened. ''Leastwise you didn't shout hooray when you heered he'd be late gettin' here. Time you was settled down anyways; you've been gallivantin' around long enough. Besides, there's something I'm wantin' you t' do fer me and some of the lads what knowed him. Mark Stoneham 'uz a fair cap'n with his crew, and we'd like Matthew and Luke t' know that. Reckon you can set the words down better 'n any of us.''

Of the twenty men who contributed to the letter Rebecca wrote that afternoon and the next day, only three could sign their names. The others stood by in awkward embarrassment as she recorded their separate memories of Mark Stoneham. Touched by the sincerity of these uneducated seamen whose harsh lives at sea should have brutalized them, she added her own praise for the lonely man who had taken the time to visit her mother when she was sick. As a final contribution to the tribute, Rebecca added the last piece of art her mother had painted three months before her death—a china cameo of Mark Stoneham's pleasantly rugged, weather-beaten face. Impulsively, she wrote a second letter to Matthew thanking him for his recent protection of her and for his long-ago kindnesses. Had she not been so self-centered after her mother's death, she reflected sadly, she could have also thanked Mark while he was alive.

Despite her momentary gloom, Rebecca quickly adjusted to shipboard life; for the better part of a week she enjoyed the luxury of a daily bath and the excellent meals served by the politely friendly mulattoes. But the novelty of her own activity quickly palled as she watched the speeded-up work of preparation going on aboard the *Reine* and the nearby *Maine*. Even Jed was too busy to spend much time with her, and the second mate, Jesse Milford, remained antagonistic. His restrictions and prohibitions ended any desire Rebecca may have developed for a life at sea with her husband. With a dry disapproval Milford informed her that it was not seemly for her to associate with the crew or to distract the men's attention from work by drawing their pictures and giving them ideas above their station. Neither did he deem it seemly for her to eat at the officers' table and mix with them. On the day her new wardrobe was delivered personally by the New London draper, Milford was rudely critical; but it was his adamant refusal to allow her to accompany Simon Parrish ashore that ended her two weeks of unwilling obedience to his domination.

Simon had come to ask her help in describing the Major Welford they'd met on the trail. A company of Connecticut militia, he told her, was being organized to clean out the enemy stronghold in central Connecticut; and the commanders wanted to talk to her. Before she could respond, Jesse Milford asserted unpleasantly, "Since she's forbidden to leave the ship, your militiamen will have to come aboard to speak with her." Having delivered his ultimatum, the second mate strode away, leaving Simon Parrish embarrassed and Rebecca outraged.

Twenty minutes later two leather-clad figures climbed down the Jacob's ladder to the rowboat tied below. The taller wore the traditional buckskins of the frontiersman, while the shorter climber appeared misshapenly bulky in loose Indian breeches, fur-lined boots, and an oversized leather coat. Not until they reached a small beach farther inland along the Thames River did Rebecca remove the coat and lower the skirt of her durable red dress to cover the unsightly trousers. She also removed her sketch pad, graphite sticks, and a hairbrush. For the first time since she'd known him, Simon burst into laughter. But his amusement turned into admiration when she began to sketch a face she'd seen for only a few minutes weeks before.

Unlike Simon, who'd been watching all three of the armed men on that trail, Rebecca had concentrated on the one spokesman; and his face had been distinctive enough for her to remember the separate features, particularly the prominent nose and deep-set eyes. From time to time as she worked, she asked her companion questions about the details she'd overlooked. Simon's descriptions of the musket and hunting knife were flawless, as was his estimation of Major Welford's weight and height. He had even noticed the hilt of a second knife protruding above the man's soft leather boots. By the time she finished, both were satisfied with the accuracy of the sketch their combined memories had produced.

"That should do the trick," Simon exclaimed with satisfaction.

"What trick?" she asked gingerly.

"His capture and execution as a spy. He's nothing but a bloody English agent who's terrorized the countryside for more than a year, and each month more and more cutthroat loyalists from New York have joined him. Come on, Rebecca, the militia's waiting for us about a mile from here."

Because her father had trained a similar group in Falmouth, the scene was depressingly familiar to Rebecca. The two hundred men assembled were the same mixture of grizzled veterans and farm boys, many of whom had yet to feel the touch of a shaving knife on their downy cheeks. Like Jeremy, the older man who greeted them had a look of guarded fanaticism and expressed the same enthusiastic faith in the efficacy of war. His questions were also like Jeremy's in their demanding thoroughness.

In addition to the sketch, which he handed to the other officers, he asked for a detailed account of the confrontation and of every landmark along the road. While Simon remembered the general area with a professional soldier's eye—the mileage, the condition of the road, and the possible spots for ambush—Rebecca recalled oddities she hadn't been aware of noticing. Until darkness had reduced everything to vague silhouettes on that frightening night, she'd seen a field of horses that were too slender to be heavy draft animals, a small army of farmhands lounging around one barn, and a windowless stone structure unlike any farmhouse she'd ever seen.

"That's it!" the militia leader exclaimed triumphantly at this final description. "That's the enemy arsenal we knew they had hidden somewhere. You two did a good job of reconnaissance.''

It was late afternoon before Rebecca and Simon were allowed to leave. Her fingers ached from drawing every remembered detail while Simon had spent hours patiently studying and correcting the company's maps of the designated area. Rebecca's mood was unsettled as she waved farewell. She now fervently hoped this unbalanced militia of old men and young boys would win their fight against the British interlopers, and such a partisan bias was definitely not that of a neutral observer. Depressed by her own thoughts, she turned toward her silent companion. ''Are you going with them?''

His response was a curt nod.

''Why?'' she persisted.

He shrugged impatiently at her intrusive question and replied tersely, ''They need me.''

''But why do you continue risking your life for a war that doesn't make much sense?'' For a moment Rebecca thought he didn't intend to answer, but he was merely flexing his often unused vocal cords to denounce an enemy he had real reason to hate.

''It does to me. Four years ago when New York and Vermont were feuding over boundaries, an English court awarded our farm to a New York loyalist. My father and oldest brother were killed defending that farm, which my family had owned for fifty years. Those murderers were never punished because the English courts said the law was on their side. We'll never have any real justice in this country as long as the government is three thousand miles away.''

Envious of someone her own age whose convictions were so much more confident and positive, Rebecca changed the subject to the less controversial one of wilderness survival. Again Simon surprised her with such an articulate description of his adventures in outrunning Indians and in eluding British authorities that she almost forgot to tell him to leave her at the New London docks rather than rowing her back to the *Reine*.

"I'll be staying with friends in town," she said casually. "You can return to the soldiers back there."

"Not until I see you safely to your friends' home," he insisted with a quiet stubbornness. "The docks are not a safe place for a woman."

Rebecca's sigh of resignation was cut short as she stared in dismay at the small procession of men striding toward her: four ships' captains and a glowering second mate; but the most furious face was that of her husband.

"We were about to notify the militia to help us locate you," Philip shouted at her in exasperation from ten feet away.

"Had you done so, you would have found me," she retorted with a composure that belied her inner agitation. "Simon and I had business with them."

"I've heard all I care to about the business you've been conducting for the past six weeks," Philip berated her. "Just for once I'd hoped you'd have the sense to stay out of trouble."

Aroused to a belated chivalry by the angry words, Simon protested, "You can't blame her for being ashore today. I insisted she accompany me."

Flashing her escort a grateful smile, Rebecca demurred smoothly, "Captain Keane knows better than to blame anyone else for my shortcomings, Simon. I want to thank you for an exciting day and to wish you Godspeed and good luck in your undertaking."

Although he realized he'd been dismissed, Simon was unwilling to leave before he was assured of Rebecca's safety; but after hearing Matthew Stoneham's quiet explanation that the man in question was her husband who had just cause to be angry, he left with an embarrassed haste. During this byplay, Rebecca had stepped into one of the longboats and asked the grinning sailors to row her to the *Reine*. A harsh counterorder of "Not without me" warned her that her action had not gone unobserved. Seated woodenly in the bow of the craft while Philip glared at her from the aft, she refrained from attempting any conversation. With her swimming ability limited to six strokes in a shallow tidal pool, she was well aware of the danger in stimulating her husband's already aroused temper. She was also acutely aware that her own temper was bubbling to the surface.

When she reached the comparative safety of the *Reine*'s deck, she learned that half the crew had been pressed into a search for her; and their relieved smiles only added to her chagrin. She listened silently as Philip ordered the hot water for two baths and a dinner sufficient for twelve guests to be served in his cabin. She listened even more silently to his angry castigation once they were alone in that cabin.

"If we hadn't wasted the day searching for you, we'd have been finished with the business long ago. Now we'll be pushed for time since we have to clear port in three days." Philip paused to glare at her. "Aren't you going to ask why? Or was that the reason for your inane escapade today? To avoid having to explain to me why you've refused to use my name and why you let that ass Tupton kiss you at a public dance? You knew I'd be here today."

Goaded beyond her endurance, Rebecca shouted back at him, "I haven't known where you've been for six weeks."

"I sent word last night as soon as we anchored."

"Not to me, you didn't."

"No, to Mr. Milford."

"Mr. Milford didn't tell me last night or this morning when he ordered me to remain aboard without a word of explanation. If you were in port last night, why didn't you just come yourself?"

"Because I was tired, damn it! And you still haven't answered my question. Why aren't you using your married name?"

"Who'd believe me? Roger didn't, and your nasty Mr. Milford never has." Shrugging coldly, she turned to open the door and admit the sober-faced mulattoes with the first of the bathwater. From the open doorway she murmured with a casual politeness, "While you're taking your bath, Philip, I'll arrange with Jed for my own supper."

Philip's eyes were narrowed into slits as he grabbed her arm and propelled her urgently into the bedroom. "You're going to play hostess tonight, if only to prove I didn't administer the beating you damn well deserve.''

For the hour it took to prepare, he was unrelentingly tyrannical: he locked the door and pocketed the key, warned her she had only fifteen minutes for bathing, and selected the dress he told her she'd be wearing. It was this selection that restored her humor; the black satin gown was the least modest one in her new wardrobe, the result of a defiant impulse on her part to teach her forgetful husband not to take her for granted. Since that day in the draper's shop, she'd learned far more than the minuet and reel; she'd learned that she was attractive to men. The round of parties in Hartford had been extremely educational for a girl who'd never danced or flirted before. When Philip emerged from his own bath, she was ready for him with her pale curls gleaming in a well-brushed cascade, held off her face by the two pearl-encrusted clips that had belonged to her mother. Not even his muttered exclamation, ''My God, didn't you order anything less revealing?'' could weaken her newfound confidence.

Throughout the dinner, which was more a business meeting than a social event, she was graciously attentive to the eight captains and the four Connecticut defense officials without once interrupting the war-oriented conversation. She was equally attentive when Philip spoke, and her face remained pleasantly composed even though his news was grim.

''Since Admiral Howe has taken over Boston Harbor, the coastal waters of Massachusetts will be too dangerous for us; and he's not the only one we have to worry about. A damned English corsair named Henry Mowat is operating his fleet outside of Falmouth Harbor, and he's already captured two of my father's brigs. In order to help my father overcome Mowat's superior cannon power, I gave him one of the Antilles frigates.''

''What are your own plans, Captain Keane?'' the defense committeeman Wyndom asked.

''I've returned the third Antilles frigate to its former captain, Edmond Falconet. He will join my fleet in raiding enemy arsenals in the Caribbean and preying on British merchantmen. If New London remains an open port, we'll bring the captured contraband here for distribution to the militia in Massachusetts. But a word of caution, gentlemen. From now on the Keane fleets operate in secrecy. There'll be no public announcements of our arrival or departure. My father is certain that an enemy spy operating out of Falmouth is responsible for the loss of the two brigs.''

The introduction of the subject of spies abruptly turned Wyndom's attention to Rebecca. After giving Philip a slightly exaggerated account of her part in the incident on the Connecticut River and a flattering description of the aid she rendered to the militia earlier in this day, Wyndom leaned forward and addressed Rebecca directly.

"Mrs. Keane, ever since I heard about your meeting with Major Welford, I've been puzzled. Just why did the beggar allow you and Parrish to escape his trap? For more than a year our agents have been unable to learn his name or to get a glimpse of him. Yet he revealed himself to you and let you walk away. Why?''

Rebecca was smiling as she stood up. "Mr. Wyndom, a very wise lady once told me that men are always eager to be rid of a talkative woman. Good night, gentlemen, I'll leave you to your wine and business.'' Noting the flush on Philip's face with satisfaction, she allowed Matthew Stoneham to escort her to the door of the connecting room.

"Luke and I appreciated the picture of my brother, Becky,'' he said softly. "It helped ease the sadness. Mark was a good man, but I don't want you to fret your husband about his death. Luke said that Philip risked his own ship trying to save Mark's life. You just use that pretty charm of yours to get your man to relax during these next few days. He's had more than enough to face lately, and he was half wild until you showed up today.''

Pondering the kindly meant advice as she prepared for bed, Rebecca admitted that Philip had just cause for his anger. Had the situation been reversed, had he spent a day in the woods with another woman, the fur would have flown in the opposite direction. Thoughtfully, she stored her dress in its sea chest and wondered if it had accomplished its intended purpose. It had proved a sensation for several of the other men, but Philip had largely ignored her until she left the table. Then he'd merely glared at her with his blue eyes glinting anger. The only time he'd looked pleasant throughout the entire dinner was during the discussion of his beloved ships and the challenge of testing the *Reine* against British frigates. Philip had been right months ago when he'd told her a sailor didn't need a wife, particularly not a wife such as herself.

Smiling as she snuggled down beneath the covers, Rebecca remembered with feline satisfaction that he'd been angriest about Roger Tupton's kiss and the use of her maiden name. He'd also glowered at Simon Parrish when that surprising young man had defended her on the docks today. Perhaps with a few more reminders that Rebecca Rayburn Keane was not a spiritless wife who could be left safely behind whenever he decided to roam, Philip might yet become a husband, however unwilling.

She was deeply asleep when he joined her hours later. Had she known that his last wakeful thoughts as he lay beside her dwelt long and darkly on her alone to the exclusion of ships and charts and battle plans, she'd have been pleased. Awakening in a happy frame of mind, Rebecca impulsively kissed the cheek of the man still slumbering heavily and eased herself from the bed. Briefly tempted to crawl back in again until she remembered the effect her unbrushed hair had on Philip's temper, she fled silently into the necessaries room. Neatly groomed and clad in a concealing green wool bedrobe when she emerged, she padded noiselessly to the door of the cabin, hoping to find Louis and Leon waiting to serve her morning coffee. In the next second her pleasant anticipation was replaced by a blind fury—the door was locked and the key missing! Forgotten was her earlier good mood as she whirled around only to bump violently into the rock-hard body of her husband whose one hand moved to grip her waist while his other dangled the missing key before her temper-hot eyes.

"Are you planning to scratch my eyes out, Cottontop, or are you going to kiss me again?"

Rebecca hated the flush that suffused her face. "You were playing possum!" she muttered.

"I serve you fair notice, my sweet, that I'm not a man who can sleep through a morning kiss delivered by a tempting woman, especially one who's been rubbing her nicely rounded backside against me all night."

"I did no such thing," she gasped.

"Yes, you did, Cottontop. You were as restless as a caged bobcat."

"Why didn't you just wake me up?"

"If I had, I'd have spanked you before I made love to you. That was some show you put on last night. Half the men there couldn't keep their attention on business."

"You seemed to have no trouble doing so," she snapped.

"Is that what you think, Cottontop? If you'd been sitting on my lap, you'd have known why I didn't dare stand up."

For a second she stared at him without understanding until his laughter triggered a shocked embarrassment. "You still don't know much about men, sweetheart," he chided her gently.

"And you don't know much about me," she flared in a sharp retort.

"I learned more than I needed to know after the others left last night. Matt Stoneham roasted my ears about your heroics on the riverbank and about your other conquests in Hartford. He said you needed to be convinced that you're a married woman."

"What I do is no one's business but my own!"

"You're wrong, Cottontop. What you did for my men is very much my business. Jed told me how you fed them in the infirmary. As a matter of record, where'd you get the money?"

"It was my own mostly."

"You had only three sovereigns when we left Saco."

"Well, I had thirteen when we left New Bedford."

"From Sinclair?"

"Yes."

"And the rest of the money?"

"From Mr. Cooper and indirectly from you. The draper

agreed that he'd overcharged me for my wardrobe. Are you satisfied now?''

"Very satisfied, Cottontop, and very grateful."

"Good. If you'll open this door, I can have my breakfast and you can go back to sleep."

Looking down at her flushed, angry face, he cursed himself for being a fool. How in the devil had he put himself into a position where a girl ten years his junior could twist him inside out? He'd only wanted to make love to her this morning, but as always her defensive independence had set his tongue in motion, and he had yet to win one verbal battle with her. Ironically he hadn't really been suspicious of her actions, only jealous. The threat she'd made about fidelity in marriage had worked its poison deep into his consciousness. Watching the effect she'd had on the other men last night had convinced him that she was more than capable of carrying out the threat. She was the most stubbornly disciplined woman he'd ever known, and twice he'd been damn fool enough to be unfaithful to her.

The first time it hadn't really mattered because he'd still been uncommitted, but even so he'd felt guilty; not guilty enough to tell Paulette the truth or to make a final break with his longtime mistress, just vaguely uneasy about a towheaded girl hiding in a cabin fifteen miles away. But during the last stopover in Falmouth after two brutal clashes at sea, he'd reverted to type—a tired sailor on shore leave in search of a woman's body and the release of animal urges—nothing more.

Philip had known Paulette was still in town the first day; she'd always had an uncanny knack of knowing exactly when his ship docked. He'd received her letter while he was still on the bridge giving orders for the unloading of the wounded men. For five days he'd ignored her summons, tense days of hard work and of concern for his father, who was still at sea. Upon his return Silas had compounded his son's problems with the demoralizing news of the capture of two Keane ships during a battle with a flotilla of Henry Mowat's privateers. That night Philip visited Paulette after convincing himself that he owed her the courtesy of an explanation and enough money to take her wherever she wanted to go. Three days later he carried out his initial intention, but he'd spent those seventy-two hours drinking recklessly and wallowing in bed with a woman he hadn't loved in five years.

He'd staggered away with Paulette's shrill recriminations still ringing in his ears, almost blotting out the calm promise of the young wife he'd just betrayed: "My marriage ends the day a husband is unfaithful to me."

Adding a parental castigation to Philip's own self-contempt, Silas Keane further aroused his son's temper without easing the turmoil. "Good thing you're not serious about your marriage to Becky Rayburn, son. She's a damn sight too good for you, and she's independent enough to pay you back in kind and lead you a merry chase to hell and back. Why the devil did you return to that French leech who's bled you dry for eight years? My God, any waterfront slut would have served your purpose better, and I was hoping you'd have learned that lesson after the last time. Becky may not be what I'd have chosen for a sailor's wife; but if you'd taken the time to notice, you'd have found her a damn entertaining minx who'd have made you a better wife than you deserve. Now you have a serious problem in deciding what to do with her, since you've made yourself legally responsible. Her Uncle Jonathan is not in New York and won't be until this ruckus is finished."

"Where the devil is he?"

"London. The British merchantman that he and Abigail sailed on was rerouted a day out at sea."

"How did you find out?"

"Jonathan sent word to some Canadian friends, and they relayed the message to me. All of Becky's money is in an English bank, and neither it nor her uncle will be allowed to leave."

"Why didn't you tell me this four days ago when you arrived in port?"

"Wanted to see what you'd do about the Burnell woman, and you did exactly what I hoped you wouldn't. So now you'll have to supply Becky with a home, even after you get that annulment."

"There won't be an annulment."

"I thought that might be what was churning your gut. Did she agree or did you force her?"

"She agreed."

"Then God help you."

During the frantic search yesterday, Philip had been driven as much by his father's warning as by the fear that Rebecca might be in real danger. When she'd been located unharmed and unrepentant, he'd been intimidated by her cool flippancy. She was all the woman his father had claimed, and she would slip out of his life without a backward glance if he couldn't regain her affection. Smiling down at her, he shook her stiffly resistant body gently.

"I'll open the door for you if you'll order my breakfast too, Cottontop. I meant it when I said I was grateful to you about the men. From now on I'll make sure you have an ample supply of money, and there'll be no more locked doors. You're probably safer aboard my ship than I am."

When he emerged from the bedroom freshly shaved and clad in a full-sleeved, open-collared white shirt atop his black breeches and boots, Rebecca giggled in greeting as she poured his coffee.

"You look like a pirate."

"I am a pirate, Cottontop, who's decided to take you to the beautiful Caribbean where we'll live happily ever after."

"Where I'll more likely die of rum addiction and boredom," she countered. "I don't even like bananas."

"There's a wonderful variety of food there and European imports you never saw in Maine. Since I'll be working in the area—"

"You mean fighting!"

"Not if I can outrun the British, I won't be."

"Are you serious, Philip?"

"Dead serious, sweetheart. It'll solve most of our problems." He'd been frowning at himself in the mirror when he'd made the decision. In French-speaking Saint-Domingue Rebecca would be constrained to be more circumspect during his absences, and Paulette would be severely handicapped in her threat to locate him. Such a move would also postpone the need to tell Rebecca about Jonathan and her money.

Puzzled by his obvious enthusiasm, Rebecca asked cautiously, "What problems?"

"This one mainly, Cottontop." Swiftly he leaned over and kissed her lightly on the lips. "We're both still shy about marriage, sweet, so I want you with me until we learn to trust each other. Are any of your new dresses suitable for a day in New London in the company of your husband? Have you one that isn't quite as enticing as the black thing you wore last night? I don't need the excitement of another riot today."

"Philip Keane," she scoffed, "during the weeks I spent walking around in New London, I received a few winks from harmless old men, a number of rude remarks from people who resented a woman working on a newspaper, and some flattering nonsense from the injured sailors. But never did I start anything resembling a riot. So you'll be perfectly safe. Did you mean it when you said you'd lend me some money?"

"You're my wife, Cottontop, and I mean to support you. I'll supply whatever funds you need."

"I only want a few pounds, but as a loan, not a gift. I have my own money, or I will have as soon as I see Jonathan. I don't want to be dependent on any man, Philip, not even you."

Hurt by her uncompromising candor, he reciprocated hotly, "Then you should have married someone like Roger Tupton. He'd have allowed you to support yourself and him too. Why didn't you just leave Hartford with him when you had the chance? Stoneham said the strutting cockerel looked smitten enough. Obviously you don't give a damn about me."

Rebecca's eyes were oddly intent as she looked at her husband. "Roger hasn't been smitten by anyone but himself since he first looked into a mirror. The only emotions I feel for him are hatred and contempt and—fear. You're also wrong about what I feel for you."

"What do you feel for me, Cottontop?"

"I want you to—" Her voice dwindled off into silence; she couldn't articulate the difficult words.

"Make love to you?" Philip asked gently. "Even though you didn't enjoy it the first time?"

"I told you I had no regrets," she muttered.

"Would you care to demonstrate?"

Her yes was almost inaudible, but Philip heard it and rose swiftly to his feet, reaching out with both hands to pull her toward him. He didn't kiss her until they were in the bedroom with the door closed. Then he did, a light caress which lasted only until he sat on the edge of the bed to remove his boots. Caught up in the emotional tension, Rebecca knelt mutely and helped him with the task. When he lifted her up, his arms encircled her and he kissed her again, deeply this time but without the impatience of mounting passion. Slowly he unbuttoned her robe and pushed it to the floor before he laid her gently on the rumpled bed. Neither of them spoke as he undressed and joined her, the tempo of his lovemaking still deliberately slow and cautious.

The light caresses, though, were having an effect on Rebecca that his more aggressive ardor had failed to produce. During her incomplete initiation weeks before, she'd been too ignorant and too reluctant to participate properly; but this time her inhibitions were replaced by the awakening urges of her own body. More confident about her physical attractiveness, she responded with an un-abashed sensuality, moving her slim body sinuously as Philip's caresses moved from her nipple-taut breasts to the throbbingly moist passage above her inner thighs. She heard his grunt of satisfaction as he positioned himself atop her, and she welcomed him with a soft urgency, matching his driving thrusts with an equal strength and gasping when she experienced her first brief thrill of ecstasy.

Her usually analytical mind was a welter of confused impressions as the tumult quieted—a half-humorous ad-mission that Abigail had not exaggerated unduly, an inar-ticulate gratitude to Philip, who still held her closely to him, and a tremulous exultation in her own fulfillment.

She was still euphorically dazed long minutes later when he shook her gently and smiled lazily down at her.

"Any complaints this time, Cottontop?"

Challenged by the complacent undertone in his voice and by the involuntary reminder that his experience was considerably greater than her own, she shrugged imperceptibly. "No," she murmured, "but then, I don't have much basis for comparison. What about you?" The softly taunting question had an instant effect; Philip's smile faded, and his expression became one of guarded speculation as he moved abruptly away from her.

Regretting the impulse that had destroyed their happy rapport, Rebecca rolled swiftly over until she was on top of him, put her arms around his neck, and kissed him with a recently acquired thoroughness. At his lack of response she lifted her head and spoke with a mock severity.

"When a woman kisses a man, he is supposed to put his arms around her and kiss her back."

His smile returned full force, a predatory, baiting smile of conquest as his hands gripped her hips and pushed her down on the bed with their position reversed.

"There's another rule you're about to learn, Cottontop. When a woman issues the kind of invitation you just did, she'd better expect more than a kiss. My father was right; you're not only a fast learner, you're getting to be an impudent temptress."

Rebecca's giggle was cut short by an assault on her senses that destroyed her mental control and drove her relentlessly toward a climax. She writhed beneath his caresses, which were no longer gentle, and her fingers bit deep into his muscular back in a frenzied encouragement. When he gripped her straining body to keep her uncontrolled thrusting in concert with his own, she struggled to escape his restraint. But there was no doubt about the rolling, shocking, overwhelming waves of ecstacy that swept over them simultaneously, leaving them breathless with exhaustion.

Goaded by the unpleasant knowledge of a dozen appointments waiting for him in New London, Philip was the first to recover mobility, rushing his relaxed, smiling wife through a cold breakfast and sitting on the edge of the small bathtub to limit her dawdling. At the sight of her slender, pliant body, though, he surrendered to the temptation of indulging the pleasant lassitude he felt. Her skin coloring, he noted with pride, was as unusual as her hair—a muted ivory instead of pink and white; and her arms and legs were sleekly muscled rather than softly plump. Lazily he reached down and caressed a firm young breast, only to have his own body react powerfully. Smiling sheepishly, he pulled her out of the water and wrapped a length of linen toweling around her before he engulfed her in his arms.

"I've changed my mind about taking you into town today, Cottontop. I wouldn't be able to keep my mind on work."

Instantly, Rebecca's own eyes opened accusingly wide. "Why not?" she protested. "I wouldn't distract you. I wouldn't even need to stay with you."

"But you do distract me, Cottontop, more than you realize," he admonished her lightly, holding her close enough to make an explanation unnecessary. As he watched her face flush with embarrassed chagrin, he regarded her with amusement. "That's the second time today you've blushed, sweetheart. I'd have thought that by now you'd have learned that men can't hide their emotions as well as women."

While Rebecca's responsive smile was still tremulous, her wits had regained their customary aplomb. "If you recall," she murmured, "I'm a very slow learner. I always have to practice something to do it right." Putting her arms around his neck, she kissed him with an impressive skill and demanded softly, "See what I mean?"

Philip's eyes glinted appreciatively as he returned her salutation; but a moment later he sucked in his breath sharply when she began to move her hips against his with a slow, sensuous insinuation. My God, he thought, she's only a beginner; but already she's more enticing than any woman I've ever known. Tightening his hold on her, he moved toward the bed, thankful that he'd postponed dressing. He didn't want anything to shatter the fragile bond of trust she'd extended to him in her first overture of love.

Unaware that her capricious gesture had aroused such a lofty sentiment, Rebecca welcomed her husband into bed with an irreverent giggle. "I'm not the only one who blushes," she teased.

"You took me by surprise," he acknowledged, a predatory smile replacing the gentler emotion. She was the entertaining minx his father had called her, Philip decided; but she was also a woman whose awakening passion held the promise of sensual abandon. Slowly he began the ritual of seduction.

Arising an hour later to keep his appointment with Jesse Milford, Philip regarded his sleeping wife with satisfaction; his instinct had been right. She was innocently wanton and completely desirable. Impulsively, he bent down and shook her awake. Why should he be separated from her unnecessarily? "Wake up, Cottontop, I'll need your help in identifying some of my crew," he informed her.

Half joking when he'd issued the order, Philip quickly learned that Rebecca's weeks aboard the *Reine* had not been wasted. She had explored the magnificent ship from prow to stern, and she knew almost as much about storage and supplies as the dour second mate. She knew the names and personalities of the crew considerably better; and not even Milford's disapproving comments inhibited her friendly greetings to the men she'd nursed during the storm and those whose faces she'd sketched.

While he studied Matt Stoneham's and George Peckham's reports about the *Reine*'s battle readiness, Rebecca transcribed the names of the crew and the marines into a newly purchased ship's roster. Watching her work, Philip occasionally found his own concentration wavering. Even in the worn red dress he'd once considered unattractive, she was still an enticing temptation.

"Do you still want to go into town with me tomorrow?" he asked during one of his periods of inattention, a little miffed when she only nodded her response without looking up from the columns she was copying.

"It'll mean an early start," he persisted stubbornly.

Setting her quill aside, Rebecca smiled at him with an

impish confidence. "I'll be ready before you are," she boasted.

"Oh, no, you won't, sleepyhead!" he contradicted her. "I had to pry you out of bed twice today."

Twelve hours later, when she finished dressing fifteen minutes before he did, Philip grinned his approval with a frustrated admiration. She was as unpredictable as the temperamental sea, and she looked as innocently untouched as a bride in a full-skirted summery dress modest enough for a protected schoolgirl. Manlike, he didn't realize that the delicate lace which softened the neckline and flounced over the elbows was costly Valenciennes or that the tiny brown flowers on the finely woven muslin had been embroidered by expert Frenchwomen. All he saw was that the creamy color blended with her hair and that the wide brown sash girdling her waist and the tiny bonnet perched over her well-brushed curls matched her eyes.

Philip wasn't the only man in the shore party to appreciate the cool elegance of her costume. The oarsmen who knew her smiled respectfully, and the short, swarthy French captain, Edmond Falconet, helped her aboard the longboat with a flattering gallantry. Philip watched his chameleon wife with a warm humor; not a hint of blush or starry-eyed daze marred the alert and pleasantly composed expression on her face. The only indication he had of her personal awareness of him was the pressure of her body leaning almost imperceptibly into his as they sat side by side on the wooden bench. On display for the first time as a husband, Philip found her presence distracting him from his fierce attention to all things concerning ships.

Despite her calm appearance, Rebecca was in a state of impatient anticipation. She'd achieved a goal of sorts and had every intention of attaining the trophy she'd promised herself. Since Philip had generously tucked ten pounds into her reticule, the only thing that might prevent her private business transaction would be his insistence that he accompany her. To her dismay she learned that he wanted her to accompany him on his tour of a New London business world vastly different from her own. It was a world of ship chandlers, mapmakers, and wine merchants;

of rooms at the better inns reserved for naval officers; of port officials and the weather-beaten captains of coastal packet ships that carried the news from Falmouth to Savannah. In this exclusive and vital world of men, women were tolerated only as decorative listeners.

For several hours Rebecca was obligingly silent, even during the walks from one place to the next, since Philip and Captain Falconet were engrossed in planning a coordinated departure. But after the dinner in the private dining room at the Londonderry Inn, she decided she'd been a nonparticipant long enough.

"Philip, I have some shopping to do," she murmured during a lull in the general conversation. "When would you like me to meet you on the dock?"

He was shaking his head before she'd completed the first part of her declaration. "I'll go with you as soon as I complete my business," he promised firmly. "I don't want you on the streets alone."

Years of experience with her father at similar all-male meetings had taught her that such promises were rarely kept; men had a way of equating importance with their own self-interests. However, she'd also learned that they disliked compromising their dignity by arguing with women in public.

"I won't be alone," she wheedled. "There'll be other people, and you'd just be bored in a draper's shop."

Surprisingly, Philip returned her smile and acquiesced, escorting her to the entrance of the inn; but his smile had not been as trusting as Rebecca had thought. As she turned to leave him, he signaled to the three marines who'd been in discreet attendance throughout the day and told them to follow her.

"She'll be all right, Cap'n," John Sugs insisted. "None of the folks we asked recollected seein' anyone who looked like Tupton, and he ain't an easy man to overlook. Not bein' a sailor, he'd stand out like a durn beacon in this town—him and his pack of bullies. But we'll keep an eye on her anyways. Seems like womenfolk just got to git their fill of shopping afore they're willin' to settle down."

Rebecca's targeted shop today had nothing to do with

clothing; she wanted a wedding ring, the lack of which made the title of Mrs. Keane seem like the defensive claim of a wayward girl. Three doors down from the newspaper office on a back street, she'd located the small, untidy shop of a silversmith who'd been skeptical when she'd ordered a plain gold ring. As he looked up from his worktable and recognized her, he smiled with sportive good humor.

"Did you find yourself a husband, young lady?"

"I've had one for some time," she replied primly, "a sailor who's been at sea for the past month."

"They're an elusive lot, all right. A local lad or one of the foreigners?"

Enjoying the freedom of a verbal duel after hours of enforced muteness, Rebecca returned the smile. "A Maine lad," she admitted demurely, "who still has a thing or two to learn about the requirements of marriage."

"You have enough money for the ring? As I told you before, I've always found credit a bothersome thing."

"I have the money, providing you've inscribed the initials I requested."

"All but your—er—husband's middle initial. As far as I know, there's no given name beginning with Y. You sure you even know his name, miss?"

Rebecca studied the man silently before she responded to his taunt. "You've a very limited mind, sir. My husband's name is Yancy. However, I'll take the ring without that initial, and I'll subtract one shilling from the price," she murmured as she studied the unimpressive band with the letters PK and RLR neatly engraved on the inside. Reminding herself that two days of lovemaking did not automatically transform a novice bride into a successful wife, she tried to repress the warm glow she felt at the sight of those initials united on the simple ring. But the happy glow resurfaced when she remembered that Philip was taking her with him on this next voyage. Perhaps there would be time enough to make him forget the more experienced Paulettes of the world.

Tucking the ring and the remainder of the ten pounds into her reticule, Rebecca left the shop, frowning at the silversmith's final witticism that he hoped her husband didn't have a wife in every port. So intent was she on returning to the shop with Philip to administer a much-needed reprimand, she walked blindly into the wiry body of John Sugs, who'd been waiting impatiently for her to emerge. Like Jed Daws, the veteran marine had known her too long to be intimidated by her irritated denunciation that she didn't need a bodyguard.

"Don't git your dander up, Becky. Cap'n just wanted you safe, and it was a good thing we was watching out for you. Feller named Cooper says you was to look him up soon as you got your shoppin' done. You know him?"

"Yes, I know him, John. Did he say what he wanted?"

"Reckon so. Says he's got a letter from your paw."

Rebecca sighed in resignation, quite certain that the message would be another of Jeremy's moralistic rebukes about filial obedience.

"Is Mr. Cooper in his office, John?"

"Yup. My two mates are watchin' him, and I plan to go in with you. Got a thing or two to say about a paw that'd turn you over to scum like Tupton anyways."

In the cluttered office Eldin Cooper appeared typically disheveled and disorganized. But Rebecca knew him well enough to realize that the flustered editor was more upset than usual. His reproachful greeting confirmed her suspicions.

"If you'd confided in me a few weeks ago, Rebecca, I might have been able to prevent this embarrassing situation you've gotten yourself into. Yesterday I was accosted by a man who claimed he was your husband. I recognized Captain Keane, of course, but I found it hard to believe that he was telling the truth—and I told him so. I told him that you'd used the name of Rayburn while you were working for me."

Rebecca groaned inwardly; she'd sworn Matthew Stoneham and George Peckham to secrecy about the use of her maiden name, but she'd forgotten the garrulous Mr. Cooper.

"May I see the letter from my father?" she asked curtly.

"I don't have it, Rebecca. It was shown to me by a New York man who claimed to have met your father at Ticonderoga."

"Did he give his name?"

"No, he claimed that he was on a secret mission. I was suspicious naturally—"

"What did he look like?"

"Very foreign to New England—powdered wig, satin coat, white breeches, and silver-buckled shoes. As I said, I was suspicious; but the letter was in your father's handwriting, and it claimed that you were supposed to marry a man named Roger Tupton. Jeremy was afraid that you might need protection from some group of traitors you'd overheard talking."

"My father was a trusting fool, Mr. Cooper," Rebecca exploded tersely, "and you have been hoodwinked. Roger Tupton was one of those—" Her voice trailed off as her eyes fastened on the man's figure entering the office silently through the door leading from the print room. For a moment she didn't recognize the elegant apparition as a man she'd known most of her life. The powdered wig was ornately curled, the coat was a brilliant cerise satin that dazzled her eyes, and the heeled shoes added two inches to his height. But the face was Roger Tupton's and as threatening as the two cocked pistols he held in his hands.

"I've been waiting for you to show up for three days, Rebecca," he announced quietly. "From my room at the inn overlooking the harbor I watched the reunion with your pirate lover and your arrival back on the dock today. It was a simple matter to have a confederate follow you until you left the Londonderry Inn alone. Then, with Mr. Cooper's willing help, I took over the pursuit."

Roger's voice became menacingly sharp when John Sugs lunged forward. "Rebecca, tell your watchdog that I'll kill him if he moves again."

Not a man to back away from danger, Sugs's response was equally threatening. "There're three of us, Tupton, and you've got only two bullets in those fancy guns of yours. One or two of us will live long enough to slit your gullet."

"Unlike you, Sugs, I don't take foolish chances. My confederate is outside the window with his two pistols leveled on the occupants of this room. But I didn't come here to commit violence, only to reclaim what is mine. Rebecca, remember my telling you that records could be corrected? Boston is now entirely under British control, and my friends have promised to perform that minor service for me. Why not save the lives of your reckless friends and the useful Mr. Cooper, and accompany me quietly to the chaise I have waiting outside the rear door.''

The sick thudding of her heart which had destroyed her ability to move or speak while Roger was talking stilled long enough for Rebecca to put her hand on John Sugs's arm and shake her head. Clutching her reticule as if the frivolous little purse could somehow protect her, she walked through the print room on trembling legs, her face a frozen mask of despair as Roger kept his pistols trained on the helpless marines until she stepped out into the dirt-paved alley. Her one desperate hope to scream for help was crushed when a third man waiting there wrapped his arm around her throat and covered her mouth with his hand before he dragged her to the waiting carriage. Her last conscious thought before she fainted from a blow on her head was that Roger had lied. It wasn't a chaise; it was an open curricle with two strong horses instead of one. That realization demolished what small amount of courage she had salvaged and numbed her senses into a deep unconsciousness as she was shoved into the cramped space on the floor of the cab.

CHAPTER
6

TWENTY minutes after a flamboyantly dressed man had driven a well-sprung curricle through the outskirts of New London on the river road leading to the northern reaches of the Long Island Sound, the alarm was sounded. While John Sugs raced to warn Philip Keane, the youngest of the three marines ran along the route taken by the fugitive and persisted in the futile pursuit until he was certain of the direction of the flight.

In his terse report to Philip, Sugs made no attempt to deny the fact that he'd been caught off guard. "Until he opened his mouth, I didn't know the barstard; he was done up like one of the fancies of Baltimore or Charles Town. But them guns of his was real enough; and when he threatened us, Becky jest walked out like she was being led to slaughter. Then the other barstard come to the door and took over with his two guns while Tupton run out through the shop and got into the rig. We got jest one quick look at Becky on the floor afore he drove off. The other two was still holding guns on us until they reached their horses and rode off in the opposite direction."

Handicapped by an incoming tide which prevented any effective movements of his ships down the Thames River, Philip experienced the frustration of a man forced to fight out of his element. Since none of the men who'd been with him when Sugs brought the news were local, there were no horses immediately available. But even if there'd been a stable full, no one had much hope of overtaking a swift curricle drawn by two powerful carriage horses since none of the mariners were expert horsemen.

In less than an hour, Eldin Cooper, furious at being tricked, had enlisted six New London residents to join the hunt on horseback and located a Conestoga wagon for the seamen. Seated beside the driver of the wagon, Philip gripped his pistols with knuckle-whitened fists, cursing himself for his failure to protect one slender woman from danger. His ugly mood was compounded by the hopeless conviction that Rebecca would be lost to him. Roger Tupton had only to get her aboard a British ship headed for London, show a sufficiently bribed captain the letter from Jeremy, and request an immediate wedding. Philip's jaw tightened when he considered the result of such a fraudulent ceremony. Roger could claim Rebecca's fortune as his right in London and do what he wanted with a defenseless woman. Only if he were foolish enough to return to America could he be brought to justice. Philip's mood darkened steadily with each passing mile.

Rebecca, however, had won her freedom before the search party left New London. Minutes outside the town during the wild ride, she had awakened with an aching head to find her hands tied to an iron railing on the carriage. Throughout the first minutes of returning consciousness, her eyes had been blinded by the slanted rays of the late afternoon sun striking against the dazzling satin of Roger's coat as he leaned forward to whip the lathering horses to a greater speed. Fancifully, the red color and the savage look of determination on the man's face reminded her of the whispered tales of messengers from hell conveying damned souls to eternal doom—in this case, to her doom. But not even the devil himself, Rebecca decided as her courage revived, was going to destroy her.

"Where are you taking me, Roger?" she asked with a voice that sounded more like a croak.

"My father has a ship waiting at the mouth of the river."

Shaken by the realization that she'd have the father to contend with as well as the son, she continued her questioning. "To go where?"

"To Boston first and then to England."

"Why England?"

"Because that's where your uncle and your money are."

"My uncle's in New York," she shouted defensively.

"No, he's not. That's what I tried to tell you in Hartford. The ship he took from Falmouth was rerouted."

It was the absolute assurance in Roger's voice that released the bonds of terror which had held Rebecca's mind captive. The Tuptons might be powerful men in New England, but they were mere colonials without the power to turn a British ship around in midocean. And never would Stanton Tupton spend the amount of money necessary to bribe a ship's captain to change course! Someone else had issued the order, someone with more at stake than a reluctant bride. She paused as the words "or a reluctant bridegroom" formed themselves in her mind. Roger hadn't wanted to marry her until after she'd seen that meeting in the forest, and he hadn't really been worried about himself. His family could always shield him with a contrived explanation, particularly in a town they controlled. It was the identity of the three Englishmen in the sketch she'd drawn that he must have been ordered to protect. They were the important men, the ones who were organizing the savagery of frontier warfare and whose anonymity had to be preserved if they were to succeed. Roger had been told to marry her and to take her to England, not by his greedy father, but by the English agents in charge of gaining the cooperation of the Iroquois nation.

As casually as she could manage, she asked the next question. "Did your English friends see the sketch I'd drawn of them, Roger?"

The startled fury of the look he bent on her was the only answer she needed. "At Saco, when Philip told your father about your activities, did you tell him you were only acting as a spy for the Sons of Liberty?" she persisted.

Again he remained silent, his face reflecting a curious mixture of stubbornness and fear as she continued with a relentless curiosity. "Why, Roger? Why would you agree to arouse the Indians to war when half of your family's wealth is based on tribal land stolen from the Algonkins?"

"The Algonkins aren't the ones who'll be fighting with the English," he shouted at her. "Our allies will be the six Iroquois tribes, the only real warriors among all the American savages. If it hadn't been for your interference, I'd be working with the greatest Indian leader in New York, a Seneca named Red Jacket. He trusted me more than he did the others at that meeting. Now I probably won't get the chance to fight at all."

"Is the rest of your family as loyalist as you are, Roger?" she asked quietly.

It was as if she'd opened a vent in a boiling caldron; the words poured from the impassioned man like escaping steam. He labeled his relatives shortsighted fools for having chosen the wrong side; he praised what he called British invulnerability; and he boasted about the power and wealth he would attain once the rebellion was crushed.

Rebecca didn't interrupt the violent catharsis even when he told her that her money would be used to attain those goals for him; she'd already learned what she wanted to know. Roger was the only avowed loyalist among the Tuptons, and his political choice had not met with their approval. Nor would they dare approve of his forcing her into a fraudulent marriage and exposing themselves to the vindictive fury of Silas Keane, not if they knew she was already married to his son. Silas might not approve of her as his daughter-in-law, but he was too proud to allow anyone who'd hurt a member of his family to go unpunished.

Engrossed in her own hopeful rationalizations, she failed to notice the small assemblage of men and horses waiting ahead by the roadside until Roger pulled the curricle to a jarring stop and leaned toward her long enough to whisper a terse warning.

"If you value your safety, Rebecca, you won't say a word to these men. They wouldn't hesitate to kill you if you made them angry."

She nodded mutely in agreement because the threat was not an idle one. The man standing apart from his three companions and staring at her with a brooding speculation was one of the British agents she had sketched. Fearfully she interpreted his facial expression: if she were dead, her silence would be permanent. Returning the agent's contemplative expression, Rebecca felt the same desperate bravado with which she'd outfaced Major Welford well up within her, but her breathing was tortuous until Roger returned to the carriage and untied her hands.

"There's a boat waiting for us on the beach," he advised her harshly. "My friend knows you recognized him, so you'd best act like a willing bride-to-be. He wasn't too happy about my having to tie your hands on the ride here.''

"I wasn't too happy either," she muttered as she accepted the arm he offered. Not until they were down the embankment and walking along the sandy expanse did she look back in time to see the horsemen and the curricle moving away in a southerly direction. Any relief she may have felt was quickly dissipated, however; the expression on Roger's face was too similar to that of the British agent for a lasting reassurance of safety. Moreover, the small rowboat with one nervous oarsman was too flimsy to withstand even the slightest physical violence. Grimly Rebecca held on to her reticule and stared anxiously out over the expanse of water; Stanton Tupton was her only hope.

Fifty feet away from the small sloop, she saw three of the older Tupton brothers somberly watching the approaching rowboat. Just before she clambered up the Jacob's ladder ahead of Roger, she intercepted the scowl of disapproval on Stanton's face as he glared at his son's garish clothing. Hoping that disapproval would make her own petition more acceptable, Rebecca was shouting her complaint even as she ran toward the trio of men.

"Mr. Tupton, your son abducted me an hour ago and has held me prisoner ever since. If you are his confederate in his insane scheme to force me into marriage and take me to England, I accuse you of being equally stupid. Philip Keane and I were married in Saco more than four months ago."

"I don't believe it, Rebecca," Stanton said heavily. "If it were true, Philip Keane would have said so the morning we boarded his ship. But neither of you said anything about a marriage then."

"No, we didn't," she admitted desperately. "We wanted to make sure you couldn't destroy the certificate before it was safely filed. It was recorded in Boston ten days later by Daniel Wharton and Proctor Sedgwick. Last week in Hartford, when your son threatened to kidnap me the first time, both Matthew Stoneham and I told him that the two congressmen had already fi—''

"That's a lie," Roger interrupted loudly. "At that party you were still using the name of Rayburn, just as you did in New Bedford and New London."

It was Sidney Tupton, the oldest of Hannah's eight sons and the father of Jeremy's third wife, who asked impatiently, "Is that true, Rebecca?"

"Part of it is. I used the name of Langley in New Bedford because the British captain there was suspicious of Philip, but he approved of my uncle. In New London and Hartford the editors of the local newspapers were friends of my father, and I wanted to tell Jeremy myself. I won't have to now because Philip announced it all over New London when he arrived in port."

Gripping her arm with a vicious anger, Roger shouted, "That's another of her lies, Uncle Sidney. I talked to the editor in New London today, and he doesn't believe what Keane told him any more than I do."

"You didn't *talk* to Mr. Cooper, Roger Tupton; you threatened him with a gun all the time one of your men was hitting me on the head and shoving me into that curricle." Rebecca's voice was no longer shrill with fear; she'd seen the flickers of doubt in the eyes of Sidney and Miles Tupton and the growing anger in Stanton's.

"Let go of her, Roger," his father ordered sharply. "I'll determine whether or not she's telling the truth."

"Then don't be a fool, Father. Look at her hands. She isn't wearing a wedding ring, and she wasn't wearing one today when she left the editor's office with me."

Jerking her arm free of her restraint, Rebecca took a triumphant breath before she spoke. "Oh, yes, I was, but you didn't tie my hands tight enough. When I woke up I managed to slip my ring off my finger and into my purse. I didn't want it thrown into someone's cornfield. Look for yourself, Mr. Tupton," she cried.

Slowly Stanton reached his hand out and accepted the brown silk pouch she shoved at him. Awkwardly, he loosened the cord ties and groped inside until his fingers located the small gold circlet. He was silent as he peered at the inscribed initials, but his face was taut with a barely controlled rage as he handed her the ring and turned to face his son.

"Did Matt Stoneham tell you she and Philip were married?"

Roger shrugged uncomfortably. He hadn't expected anyone to listen to her, and he hadn't expected her to produce a ring. The lying bitch hadn't been wearing it earlier! Why the devil hadn't he gagged her and told his father that she was still unwilling? They all knew she was and they hadn't said a word in protest, but now—now he'd have to tell his father at least part of the truth.

"May I speak to you privately, Father?" he asked tersely.

"Answer the question!"

"How would Stoneham know any more about it than we do? He wasn't even in Saco."

"Was there anyone else in the office today other than Rebecca and the editor?"

"There were three marines."

"Keane's men?"

"I suppose so. At least John Sugs used to work for Langley."

"Then we can expect a lynch mob the size of an army if we try to return Rebecca to New London," Stanton said thoughtfully. "I don't suppose one of you—" he added, looking hopefully at his brothers.

Rebecca interrupted the angry refusals with a mounting fear. "I'll be safer alone," she declared shakily, "provided you make sure Roger stays aboard this ship."

"You're probably right," Stanton agreed heavily. "I'll see that my son doesn't disturb you again. I'm sorry about the misunderstanding, Rebecca, but you must understand my concern about you. I promised your father that I would—"

She didn't wait to hear the remainder of the defensive apology, and she didn't see the two uncles grab Roger's arms to prevent his following her across the deck and down the rope ladder into the rowboat where the lone oarsman still waited. A hundred yards from the sloop she discovered that she'd left her purse behind, but the providential miracle of the unadorned gold wedding ring was securely on her finger. Suppressing the hysterical urge to laugh, Rebecca focused her attention on the muscular seaman, praying that he not slacken his speed. When he landed her at the same stretch of beach she'd left an hour before, he grinned at her and spoke for the first time.

"They're a rum lot, missus; and if it weren't my father's ship, I'd be hoping your Captain Keane would send the pack of them to the bottom of the sea."

Before she could do more than heartily agree with him, he'd shoved the boat back into the water and resumed his methodical rowing. Shivering in the chill of approaching evening, Rebecca looked around at the desolation of the windswept coast and clambered up the embankment to the level stretch of empty road. Predictably, it was Simon Parrish's advice that guided her footsteps. "When you're not sure whether the territory is enemy or friend, you're safer on the roads at night," he'd warned her. "But stay alert enough to dive for cover if you hear anyone approaching."

The nagging fear that the grim quartet of Englishmen might return to seek her out or that Roger Tupton might be allowed to follow her speeded up her steps along the dusty road. Other, more demoralizing realizations added to her sense of urgency. The only security left in her life was a marriage that could still prove impermanent. No longer did she have the alternative choice of New York and the protection of Jonathan and her own money. She was a pauper now, dependent on the generosity of a husband in whatever place he decided to leave her when he returned to sea; and he'd chosen an alien world far removed from the familiar colonial life she'd known. Suddenly she understood why—Philip knew that her uncle had been taken to England! He'd just spent several weeks with his father, and Silas Keane was the one man in New England Jonathan would have notified. Despondently, she trudged on, her pride in being able to take care of herself shattered and the warm memory of Philip's lovemaking weakened by the corrosive doubt that she was still little more than a bothersome responsibility to him.

Just after dark she heard the sounds of horses and churning wheels approaching from the east, and she fled blindly into the thick underbrush by the side of the road. It was the wrong direction for a search party from New London, but it was the right direction for the Englishmen should they have turned around. Her heart was pounding with a smothering intensity as she huddled behind the dense brambles and watched the bobbing pinpoints of lanterns approach. Only as the caravan passed did her fear-attuned ears detect the rumbling sounds of four wheels instead of two and the thundering hooves of more horses than the Englishmen had with them. But her mind remained too paralyzed to formulate a logical explanation until the travelers were far in the distance.

Shakily she resumed her harrowing walk, too demoralized and exhausted to do any more than concentrate on the mechanics of moving forward. What had been a forty-minute ride with whip-driven horses seemed an endless journey to a tired pedestrian. Eventually, though, her numbed feet left the dirt road and trod upon the harder surface of cobbled streets, and she could see the flickering lights of New London. At the Londonderry Inn she located the townsmen who'd joined the search for her, and gratefully accepted the mug of hot rum one of the astonished men pushed into her hand. She was slumped over the table and asleep before she'd consumed a third of it.

Alarmed by the suddenness of her collapse, the guilt-ridden Eldin Cooper insisted on summoning a doctor to examine her. Until that grumpily annoyed medic pronounced her fit enough except for a lump on the head and induced the sleeping woman to swallow a deadening, cure-all potion, none of the civilian volunteers thought to intercept the Keane fleet, which had left the harbor immediately upon Philip's return from the futile search. That she'd not be reunited with her husband was the first news Rebecca received upon awakening late the next day in a small overcrowded room at the Cooper home. With a heavy heart she listened to the editor's dramatic description of the search for her and of Philip's sworn determination to board every ship in nearby coastal waters until he rescued her.

If only she'd had the courage to remain on the road last night, she despaired, she'd be with him now and he wouldn't be risking his life for her. Rebecca closed her eyes to prevent Eldin Cooper seeing the tears that threatened to spill over her cheeks before he left the room. It wasn't fair, she mourned, to have her happiness destroyed so soon, to be forced to sleep alone again without the warmth and joy of Philip's arms around her. Not for hours could she think of anything other than the remembered intimacy of the brief days and nights they'd spent together, the passion they'd shared, and the possessive look in Philip's eyes when he'd reached out for her.

But eventually the practical considerations of survival pushed these golden memories aside. Never had Rebecca been in such a precarious financial situation; she was stranded in a town without friends and without money. Her one dress had been inexpertly laundered and mended by the overworked Mrs. Cooper, her dainty shoes were beyond repair, and her lovely new bonnet had disappeared sometime during the wild ride with Roger. For the first time in her life she understood how impoverished her childhood would have been had not her mother defied convention and become a successful businesswoman.

The Coopers were typical of the genteel poor in every New England town, accepted by the wealthier residents because of education and position, but too underpaid to maintain any but a Spartan home of watered soup and thin-sliced bread. Appalled by the prospect of being a financial burden on a family so ill-equipped to bear it, Rebecca left the Cooper home the following morning and returned to the Londonderry Inn. Wiser now about the politics of innkeeping in a privateer's port than she'd been during her earlier stay in New London, she approached the innkeeper in the public room where a dozen privateer officers were dining. She requested suitable lodging until she could contact either her husband or her father-in-law and the loan of sufficient money to purchase a basic wardrobe.

Resisting the temptation to tell her to go to a money lender, Oliver Hamden groaned inwardly and acquiesced. His business, present and future, depended on the good will of men like the ones who were watching him and the brazen young woman asking for help. As a group, Hamden knew from long experience, they tended to be temperamentally fraternal about any real or imagined slight to one of their own. Moreover, the Keanes, both father and son, were too powerful in the privateering world for a mere innkeeper to insult. An even shrewder calculation broadened his jolly smile still more; an unchaperoned and pretty woman could be a highly decorative attraction in his business rooms.

Rebecca was thoughtful as she walked to the familiar draper's shop to order what would have to be a very limited but flexible wardrobe. The innkeeper's generosity, she reasoned practically, would extend to no more than an inexpensive outfit or two and a month's lodging. Choosing the plain fabrics she'd scorned before, she ordered a brown wool pelisse with just enough fur trim to avoid drabness and two fustian cloth dresses for winter, bright-colored cotton calico and cambric for summer frocks, and stout leather shoes to replace the ruined slippers tied to her feet with cord. She wouldn't be elegantly dressed, she reflected dismally, but at least she'd be decently clad in whichever of the four locations proved possible.

The first one she ruled out sorrowfully. Philip's description of a home somewhere in the vast Caribbean had been too nebulous even for an experienced traveler to locate. Her second choice of England was equally impractical; even if she could book passage on an English ship, she could never earn enough money to pay the fare. Of the remaining two, she much preferred the potential excitement of New York and the two uncles she'd never met to the dull familiarity and limitations of Falmouth with a father-in-law who might very well resent her intrusion into his life. But even for these last two, more modest destinations, she'd have to earn sufficient travel funds while she was in New London. There was nothing modestly ladylike in the employment she chose to pursue.

On her way back to the inn, she stopped by the print shop for the supply of heavy paper and the box of the Cumberbund graphite she'd used when she worked there. Thus encumbered with her art supplies and a hairbrush and cambric nightclothes borrowed from the draper's wife, she moved into the cubicle room assigned her near the servants' quarters. The only features that made the niggardly accommodation acceptable were a small window for ventilation, a door that could be secured against unwelcome intrusion with a sturdy oak bar, and a close proximity to the kitchen, where she could eat her meals away from the parsimonious scrutiny of the proprietor. Oliver Hamden's jolly smile was rarely seen in the working areas of his establishment. Rebecca did not, however, avoid the public rooms; and during the first of her working sessions there, the landlord discovered he'd been correct in his assumption that she'd prove to be an attraction—albeit not entirely in the way he had intended.

Selecting a corner table, she began a sketch of the innkeeper himself, a flattering one that made his smile a genuinely merry one and omitted the disfigurement of sagging jowls. After signing the finished work with the uninitialed name *Keane*, she laid it faceup on the table and rapidly sketched the face of the floridly handsome sea captain who was watching her with more than a passing interest. Those two men were her first customers. When the elegantly garbed ship's officer had approached her table with a determined stride, Oliver Hamden had bustled over and pointedly introduced the Portuguese Captain Oliveira to Mrs. Philip Keane. Shrugging philosophically, the foreigner flashed her a toothy smile before he drew the landlord aside for a more private conference. Rebecca's face remained composed and expressionless as she overheard a business arrangement made for some unseen lady's presence in the captain's bed. With an inward humor, she wondered if the obliging tart would make more money for a night's work than an aspiring artist. Four hours later Rebecca decided in her own favor; six gold sovereigns weighed down the pocket of her embroidered muslin dress.

For ten days her business venture flourished until she'd

accumulated a hoard of money equivalent in value to seventy-one pounds sterling. But on the eleventh day a packet ship raced into New London Harbor with news that destroyed all semblance of peaceful pursuits for the townspeople and privateers alike. Two days earlier, on June 17, a battle had been fought in Boston, a clash of arms that would be forever mislabeled in history books because the first reports sent out by the defeated New England militia incorrectly identified the location as Bunker rather than Breed's Hill.

Rebecca was still in her room when the oldest of Eldin Cooper's six children delivered an urgent message from his father requesting her help. Mystified but not overly eager to return to the print shop, she unwillingly accompanied the messenger through the rear door of the printing room and heard the shaken voice of the editor reading the dispatches to a silent crowd gathered in the street. She learned the reason for their anxious attention when she began writing the story; out of the one thousand colonial militiamen, eight hundred from Massachusetts and two hundred from Connecticut, four hundred and fifty had been killed, wounded, or captured. Some of the listed casualties had been from New London.

When Cooper asked the packet ship captain whether or not the militia would continue the war, the man's response earned a rousing cheer from all but a handful of listeners. "My God, they've only begun. They're sixteen thousand strong with more joining each day, and they've proved they can outfight the damned enemy. Even the patriots of New York will come forward now, and they'll be signing up by the thousands when they learn that New York City is next on the British invasion list."

Rebecca sighed in unhappy resignation; her four options had been reduced to one—an ignominious return to Falmouth. She had no desire to be any closer to the war than she'd been this day, writing the account of a futile battle that had decided nothing. The idea of being trapped in a British-held New York where another Bunker Hill could take place appalled her. As soon as the crowd dispersed, she asked the packet captain if he would take her as a passenger on his return trip to Maine. Only the mention of her relationship to Silas Keane secured his reluctant consent, but he'd accept only a fraction of what she offered to pay for passage.

"It wouldn't be right," he insisted, "to take a profit from a man who's already risking more than most in this war."

Surprisingly, Rebecca found that Oliver Hamden, innkeeper, was also momentarily infused with a patriotic fervor; he charged her very little for board and room and persuaded the draper to pare his prices for her scanty new wardrobe to a minimum. She paid her remaining debt in New London by giving each of the Cooper children a sovereign.

Early the following morning she left the town that had sheltered her for two months while she'd waited for her future to begin. In all that time she'd seen her husband for not quite two complete days, and the future she'd longed for seemed more uncertain than ever. Stored belowdeck in a four-by-six-foot cabin were two oilskin bundles that contained all of her worldly possessions—a scant supply of paper and graphite, a few garments, and thirty pounds left over from the money she'd earned. As the small ship plowed northward from the mouth of the Thames River, she regretted her decision not to take chances in New York. Manhattan was not an isolated, insular town like Falmouth; it was a challenging city where she could have found employment, even if her uncles had refused to accept her. Like Boston, it would have offered her an escape from the boredom of small-town stagnation. Unfortunately, it was also a loyalist center that the British planned to occupy, according to the packet captain, and Rebecca wanted no part of being under the control of loyalists like Roger Tupton or Englishmen like the Indian agents.

Four months later on a cool October morning, she learned that her decision had been as faulty as the rumor that prompted it and that the British military leaders were no more predictable than any other governmental officials. It wasn't the logical choice of New York, with its sympathetic population and vast resources, that was the British target; it was the unimportant rebel town of Falmouth. And their intention was not to occupy, it was to destroy!

During the time she'd been back in her old home, she'd become accustomed to solitude because Silas Keane was there only at irregular intervals. When she'd first arrived in late June, her father-in-law had greeted her with a laconic affection and put her to work. As a consequence, she'd learned more about wartime privateering than she really wanted to know. Since acquiring the French-built frigate the *Antilles Belle Dame*, Silas had lived up to his earlier reputation and become a very real threat to the British sea-lanes that connected the impregnable port of Halifax to England and Boston. With his fleet of eight well-armed vessels, all of which were swifter and more maneuverable than the ponderous English merchantmen, he'd stripped the cargoes from more than two dozen victims.

Two weeks before the British attack on the town, Silas prepared his ships for one final ocean search before winter storms made such voyages unprofitable, while Rebecca helped the warehousemen inventory the bountiful pillage already stored in the Keane warehouses. The muskets and powder would be transported overland before the winter snow began and delivered to the American army besieging Boston, but the sale of civilian goods to merchants and shopkeepers would be delayed until Silas returned.

From the stone parapet that formed an observation platform on the third story of Langley Hall, Rebecca watched his fleet leave eleven days after it had sailed into Casco Bay. From that same vantage point three days later she watched another fleet sail in. When she heard the cannons boom, she was preparing to take her morning walk up Munjoy's hill. Racing up the stairs to the parapet, she was in time to see the first of the violent attack. As she watched in horror, the four British warships, spaced apart in the traditional line of attack, concentrated their fire power on an anchored schooner until it listed crazily at its moorings. With methodical precision the attacking fleet maneuvered past ship after anchored ship, from merchant brigantines to whaler sloops, and repeated the deadly havoc until the harbor was cluttered with burning or sinking hulks. .

Gripped by fear, Rebecca witnessed the wanton destruction without moving until her fear turned into stark terror. Anchoring itself in a straight line broadside to the docks, the English flotilla commenced the deadly cannon fire again, this time aimed at the buildings in the town. When she felt the stone walls of Langley Hall shudder as they were struck repeatedly, her terror lost its paralyzing hold and her mind began to function coherently. Rushing first to her bedroom, she pulled the homespun counterpane from her bed and tossed her hard-earned clothing into the makeshift bundle. Her second stop was the library, where she emptied the contents of Silas Keane's strongbox on top of her jumbled garments. In the pantry at the rear of the house, she located a sack of jerked venison and another of parched corn—two winter staples stored year-long in most Maine homes—and added the food to her survival hoard. Dragging the unwieldy bundle behind her, she left the house through the back door and struggled up the hill until she reached the shelter of the first stand of trees.

Pausing to look back one last time, she saw the beginning of the final phase of the assault. Longboats full of armed men were pulling away from their ships and heading for shore. She didn't wait to see the end of the grim drama. Still dragging the heavy pack, she struggled awkwardly to the top of the bluff and then proceeded ever deeper into the forest that had been a familiar playground during her childhood. Breathless and disheveled half an hour later, she stopped beside the small creek and looked around for a safe hiding place.

"Underbrush is the best," Simon Parrish had told her during his informative lecture on wilderness existence. "Most folks look for caves, but caves generally have resident critters; and it's easy to be trapped if someone's in pursuit. Underbrush has more than one way out."

Close to the creek, she crawled through an opening in the shrubbery at the base of a clump of poplar aspens and pulled the bundle in after her, remembering Simon's instructions to reach out and rearrange the thick carpet of fallen leaves. She could hear the intermittent sound of cannon fire only dimly now, and the crackling noises of burning buildings not at all. Only the acrid odor of smoke invaded her sanctuary as she rested with her back against the smooth bole of one of the sheltering trees. Throughout that long day and night, she napped in uneasy snatches, awakening each time with a pounding heart to listen nervously for the sounds of other humans. Toward dawn, after the wind had eliminated most of the smoke, she slept more soundly; but not until midmorning did she risk a furtive walk to a rock promontory that overlooked the harbor. The British ships were gone, leaving only a few still-floating hulls of their victims to mark their passing.

Why Falmouth? How had such an unimportant town earned the grim fate of total destruction? Boston citizens had been more rebellious, yet their city had been spared. New London harbored ten times the number of privateers, yet it remained untouched. And how had the British known that Falmouth was momentarily undefended? Had the Keane fleet been in the harbor, that small a number of attackers would themselves have been defeated. Silas Keane never allowed his ships to be undefended, even while they were riding at anchor. Recalling Philip's grim announcement four months ago that someone in Falmouth kept the British informed about the departure times of the Keane fleet, Rebecca wondered if that same spy had reported this last departure. It couldn't be Roger Tupton, she decided, since Silas had made certain he wasn't in town. Still, she reflected thoughtfully, it would be interesting to see if the Tupton properties had been spared.

They hadn't been, she discovered as she viewed the burned-out ruins of the town from the slope of Munjoy's hill. Every one of the four hundred homes and shops had been reduced to blackened ruins, every one of the once sturdy warehouses along the embarcadero had been leveled to piles of rubble. Looking down on Langley Hall, Rebecca experienced a brief, abortive hope that it had survived. The thick granite walls were still intact, but the timbered roof was caved in and the three-story interior had become a gaping black hole. Fifty feet to its rear, she could see the stone spring house which had supplied almost a century of tenants with cool water. Praying that the marauders had not destroyed the spring itself, she dragged her bundle down the remaining slope and looked inside. The water was still bubbling gently, but the racks that had contained slabs of bacon, hams, eggs, and rounds of cheese were empty. Rebecca hoped that the common seamen who'd committed the theft had been allotted a share of the bounty by the ships' officers.

Recalled to the practicalities of her own immediate future, she contemplated the contents of the heavy load she'd dragged to safety and back—the remains of the jerky and parched corn, her clothing and small hoard of sovereigns, and what might well be the remnants of Silas Keane's fortune. Removing only the food and her hairbrush, she once again relied on the advice Simon Parrish had given her about hiding caches of supplies from both animal and human predators. With a sharp piece of stone she dug a pit in the sandy soil near the spring house, lined it with slabs of shale that littered the ground, and carefully placed the wrapped bundle inside, covering it first with shale, then sand, and finally with larger rocks to mark the location.

With that essential chore completed, she began to take stock of the equipment still remaining in the spring house. Four of the wood buckets had been smashed, but three were still intact; the rolls of discarded canvas sails were still suspended from the rafters, but not one of the dozen barrels of rum Silas kept stored there had escaped plunder. The weeks of waiting for his return, she reflected glumly, were going to seem much longer.

How wrong she was about that prediction, she admitted readily within days; the memories of that October would become some of the most treasured. As soon as the shock had worn off for the townspeople who'd been able to salvage even less than she had, the resilient character forged by pioneer hardships and snowbound winters reasserted itself. Family groups began the long treks to Cape Elizabeth and other Maine communities where they had relatives or friends, even while the ruins of their homes were still smoldering. For those who chose to remain behind, particularly the Keane warehousemen and the families of the crews aboard the Keane ships, the challenges of survival were met with a spirited communal effort. Because Langley Hall offered the best protection from the increasingly cold nights, both men and women worked to clear out the burned debris and to scrub the stone floor. The canvas sails from the spring house and later from the fishing boat that arrived from the outer islands were stretched across the opening to form a makeshift roof, and the hay donated by area farmers whose property had escaped both burning and pillage was mounded into narrow beds for the women and children. Huge cast-iron cooking pots were recovered from the ruins and used to prepare the communal meals of fish stew, that simmered over the fires in all three of the stone fireplaces.

Those weeks of sharing the warmth of the fires with people who had become her friends were the happiest Rebecca had spent since she'd been separated from Philip. No longer did she lie awake at night worrying about his safety and wondering if he remembered her. The hard work of cleaning fish, chopping kindling, and helping the children root out potatoes and parsnips from ruined gardens brought her to bed eager for sleep. Companionably surrounded by women who were also separated from their husbands, Rebecca began to believe that her own marriage might become as permanent as theirs.

Only twice during those three weeks was Rebecca reminded of the problems connected with her past and future. When the Tupton caravan of wagons was readied for departure to the Cape Elizabeth homes of two other Tupton brothers, Sidney Tupton sought her out to make a blunt request.

"We have decided," he informed her stiffly, "that your father's family is more your responsibility than ours. Since you will be establishing a home in New York, they will remain with you until Jeremy returns."

Rebecca stared at him in consternation. She'd seen her young sister and younger brothers only a few times, and then only at a distance. Her stepmother and Hannah she'd avoided assiduously since leaving her father's home at fourteen. The idea of being saddled with their care and support infuriated her.

"Your nephew Roger," she snapped acidly, "made certain I'd be unable to establish a home of any kind in America when his British friends rerouted my money to England. I am now completely dependent on the charity of my husband and his father."

"You have two uncles in New York," Sidney persisted stubbornly.

"So does my father's new family," she reminded him.

"You're a hard woman, Rebecca Rayburn. Not many daughters would refuse to help their brothers and sisters in time of trouble."

"Mr. Tupton, you have not supplied a home for your mother in thirty years or for your daughter in the last ten."

"Seven," he amended sharply.

"Seven and a half," she countered with a malicious smile. "But you'll have to now because I doubt that Silas Keane would allow a Tupton or a Rayburn other than myself aboard his ships. He still feels strongly about my father's gullibility and even stronger about Roger's attempt to kidnap me with your full approval."

"I kept Roger from following you that day."

"Only because you were afraid of what Silas and Philip would do to the lot of you. But I imagine that you still regret the fact that Roger no longer has access to my money."

"I am not responsible for my nephew."

"And I am not responsible for my father's family nor for your mother and daughter," she countered and walked stiffly back into the protective shell of Langley Hall.

So much for my past, she reflected with a bitter satisfaction. But on the occasion which involved her future, Rebecca was not as philosophical nor as self-assured. Seated on the floor in front of one of the fireplaces the night before Silas Keane returned to view the ruins of his waterfront holdings, she was a silent audience to a conversation that placed another threatening cloud over her already insecure marriage.

The two men, the foreman of the Keane warehouses and

an aggressive captain of the Sons of Liberty, had been asked a question about the suspected identity of the British agents who'd betrayed the town.

"Can't be any doubt about who they were," the captain replied promptly. "The trouble started when they arrived here in 'seventy-three. After the woman left four months ago, the bastard who posed as her servant carried on. Two days before the cursed Henry Mowat sailed here aboard his damned sloop *Canceau,* we searched the Frenchwoman's house and finally located what we'd missed on the previous five searches: a hidden observation room that overlooked the harbor! It'd been built after she moved in, with its entrance concealed in a closet. In it we found a telescope and signaling devices and enough paraphernalia to prove the spy was a naval officer of considerable experience, but the bastard himself had gotten away.

"We figure that some of the information he sent out came from Madame herself. She could have learned enough from young Keane whenever he was in port to have known exactly what was stored in all our waterfront warehouses. Before the devils burned us down, they stole everything of value—including the muskets our militia was counting on."

"I know Silas suspected her," the warehouseman volunteered. "Leastwise he began tryin' eight months ago to git her out of town. Heard him yellin' at her once in a warehouse office, but she 'uz a cocky one—told the old man he didn't own his son, and cool as you please, she jest walked away with a smile plastered on her face. How come you didn't arrest the pair of them soon as you suspicioned they was the guilty ones?"

"Didn't want to rile Philip Keane until we had proof," the captain retorted sharply. "She'd been his fancy woman a long time, and none of us wanted to tangle with his temper until we were sure. Now, of course, I'm damned sorry we didn't."

Rebecca had remained motionless throughout the entirety of the dialogue, her expressionless face averted from the glow of the fire, her mind seething with a sick tabulation of the weeks and months. Paulette Burnell had been in town both times Philip had returned; and Rebecca knew with a dread certainty that he'd been unfaithful to her. Oddly enough, no one in the group seemed to remember that she was Philip's wife. She'd been just Becky to them for three long weeks, and they'd accepted her as one of their own kind rather than as a member of their employers' family.

Quietly she stood up, walked through the rear entrance, and climbed the crude ladder that led to the stone parapet which was manned by a sentinel watcher during the daylight hours. But at ten o'clock on this blustery November night it was deserted. Wrapped in her grimy brown cloak and braced against the chest-high wall, Rebecca breathed deeply in a futile attempt to ease the hurt. She'd known from the beginning that Philip was not a man who could be easily possessed, but she'd believed him when he'd told her that Paulette was no longer a part of his life. She tried to recall his facial expression on the rare occasions he'd been an attentive husband to her, but another man's image flashed across her mental vision instead—the strong face of Captain Brian Sinclair. Two thousand miles and two years away from his wife, the Englishman was a more faithful husband than Philip might ever be.

Reluctant to return to the crowded sleeping quarters below and to the people who'd become her friends, Rebecca remained on the parapet all night, sleeping finally after physical exhaustion brought oblivion. Awakened by the late dawning of a pallid sun, she was the first to see the welcome sight of a dozen familiar silhouettes of the returning Keane fleet and four other Falmouth privateers. The fisherfolk whose craft had escaped Mowat's demolition had accomplished what they'd promised; they'd located and given warning to the men aboard the larger ships.

Her gloomy mood dissipated by the prospect of rescue, Rebecca climbed down the ladder to arouse the others; but she was waiting on the beach long before they joined her. In the lead longboat of the thirty pulling away from the hastily anchored privateers, Silas Keane was bellowing orders and questions long before he stepped ashore.

"There's an offshore storm brewing to the north, so we

have to be out of here within the hour. Each of you can bring only a few of your essentials aboard and nothing more. Becky,'' he shouted to her personally, "how much water's left in our cistern?"

"It's three-quarters full," she yelled back.

"That'll be ten barrels a ship. You supervise the filling, girl, while we get everyone aboard, twenty-five to each of the smaller ships and the rest to my big one."

Rebecca was grinning as she rushed to do his bidding. She'd expected her gruff father-in-law to rail against the "bloody limeys" for an hour before he consented to allow "blasted landlubbers" and "dratted females" aboard his sacrosanct ships. Recalling his greeting the day she'd returned to Falmouth, she laughed aloud.

"Don't just stand there, girl," he'd grunted. "You know this old barn better than I do, so make yourself useful. You're family now." Her laughter bubbled up at the thought of her buried hoard. She might yet be able to surprise the laconic Silas Keane.

Waiting until the water crews had finished before she dug her bundle out of its sandy hiding place, she watched the expression on his face as he checked the contents. He was smiling with undisguised satisfaction.

"Knew you'd have the gumption to keep your wits about you. There's fifteen thousand pounds here that'll keep the Keane afloat for another ten years, and there's the deeds to all our ships and properties. It'll take more than the damned British to defeat us now. Welcome aboard, girl."

During the turbulent voyage southward just ahead of the advancing storm, when many of the "blasted landlubbers" became seasick and the "dratted women and children" seemed everywhere underfoot, Rebecca remembered these words of praise with a warm glow. She also appreciated Silas's insistence that she use his sleeping quarters, share his meals, and join him on the quarterdeck, where the other passengers were denied entry. Just how much a part of his family she'd become she discovered when she offered to ask her New York uncles for asylum.

"The Keanes take care of their own, Becky," he promised her. "We're going to locate Philip at Saint-Domingue and get you settled in your own home. Not permanent, though. I couldn't stand living where only ten percent of the people are free—and most of that ten percent are mincing French fops. It'll be back to Falmouth for the three of us when this war's over."

In New York the refugees were greeted by a jubilant committee of the Sons of Liberty who'd begun their own war against the British three months earlier by seizing the enemy arsenal and two ships. Now they were eager to secure the added protection of well-armed privateers and a thousand New Englanders who hated the English as much as they did. Accepting the generosity offered them, the four independent privateer captains readily agreed to use New York as their home port, and more than half the Falmouth residents disembarked when they were promised employment and shelter. But Silas refused even the added inducement of free warehouse space, and his workers elected to remain with him.

"Can't be defended," Silas muttered privately to Becky. "The limeys can pick this city off like a ripe plum whenever they want. All they'd have to do is land on Long Island or Staten Island and blockade the Hudson River. There are not enough armed men or ships in the thirteen colonies to stop them. Don't trust the people here either. Most of them can't make up their minds which side they're on, and I've never approved of some of the scum that call themselves Sons of Liberty. It's one thing to start a riot and form a gang of bullies, it's another to fight in a war against veteran soldiers. Their kind won't win this war; only men like your father and the lads he trained will stand up to be counted when the real fighting begins."

Rebecca looked at her father-in-law with deep respect and nodded, adding silently to his sentiments: And men like the Keanes and the Stonehams and the Parrishes. Remembering the confident courage Philip had displayed on the night he left the *Falmouth Star* with Mark Stoneham to rescue the *Vixen,* she felt a surge of pride that erased the bitterness of recrimination and left only a longing to be with her husband.

CHAPTER
7

FORTY years at sea had provided Silas Keane with a remarkable knowledge of colonial waters and port cities. As much as he distrusted New York Harbor and the people of Manhattan, he approved of Baltimore. "It's a port the enemy can never take," he informed Rebecca, "and it's a smuggler's and privateer's paradise run by merchants who've ignored British laws for a dozen years. But they're fair men, Becky, who pay top prices for our cargoes and then supply us with enough tobacco to turn a profit in any of a dozen Caribbean ports. Don't be fooled by the peacock clothes they wear; they're brave men who'll defend their city by land and sea. They don't cotton much to slavery either; most of the Negroes you'll be seeing there are free men."

Intrigued by Silas's description, Rebecca found Baltimore to be still another kind of paradise. Its shops contained an array of products she'd never seen displayed before—art supplies and artifacts, magnificent and costly furniture, and beautiful ready-made gowns designed for women whose own seamstresses were unskilled.

"Booty," Silas explained with a chuckle. "Almost every European merchantman headed for the Caribbean saves cargo space for the chests of frocks and nonsense ordered by the rich colonial wives on the islands. Our ships just

reroute them to wealthy American women who'd sell their
souls for anything made in Paris. I prefer sensible clothes
like the ones you're wearing myself, but you'll be needing
a dozen or more of the fancies where you'll be going.
Can't have you looking like a New England Puritan in
Port-au-Prince. Well, come on, girl, I owe you that at
least. If you hadn't saved my money in Falmouth, I'd be in
a beggar's position now.''

Increasingly aware that she looked shabbily unattractive
on Baltimore streets, where the women all seemed fashion-
ably gowned, Rebecca didn't protest Silas's generous offer.
She quickly discovered in the first shop, however, that her
father-in-law was both knowledgeable and opinionated
about color and style. Autocratically he ruled out the
youthful pastels and whites, approving of only three of the
eight dresses she tried on in that shop, all of them more
sophisticated than any of the ones she'd ordered made in
New London. In the second shop he turned Rebecca over
to the proprietress after giving the shrewd women orders to
outfit his daughter-in-law from the skin out with a wardrobe suitable for the tropics. Returning four hours later,
Silas escorted Rebecca to one other establishment, one that
specialized in expensive wear. Three already selected ball
gowns were waiting for her in the discreetly elegant
dressing room. Silas's lean, weather-beaten face reflected a
satisfied, confident humor when she appeared before him
in the first one, a Spanish-style black lace.

''Jonathan always claimed that you had a little witch in
you, girl,'' he asserted. ''Do Philip good to learn that his
wife's more than just a pretty woman. Maybe now, he'll
stop acting like a damn fool!''

Because of reports that the British were patrolling the
Florida Straits, Silas chose the longer eastern route around
the Bahamas and through the Windward Passage, which
delayed their arrival at Port-au-Prince for more than a
week. As they sailed past the large emerald-green island of
Saint-Domingue, Rebecca learned that the elongated eastern portion belonged to Spain and that the French colony
occupied only the western third. However, Port-au-Prince,
its capital city, was one of the most magnificent harbors in

the Caribbean, protected on both the north and the south by two long peninsulas that jutted westward. Within the port itself Silas and his fleet captains anchored near the other Keane ships already snugged up to the stone docks in front of a spread-out warehouse bearing the newly painted legend *Falconet et Keane*.

Frowning heavily as he noted the name, Silas confided his fears to Rebecca. "Don't like the idea of Philip being mixed up with this pack of vultures. They may be fighting in the same war, but they'll be fighting for their own gain, not for Americans. The privateers here are descendants of some of the most notorious pirates who ever plagued the West Indies. Damn, I don't like my name connected with theirs, and I'd give a pretty penny to know if any of the prize cargoes Philip's taken in the past four months ever reached an American port. Profit's one thing, but the fleet was sent here to help build the colonial arsenal. Becky, you best stay aboard while I locate that son of mine and scout out the lay of the land."

Grateful that he didn't expect any verbal response from her, Rebecca nodded mutely. Five months of separation from Philip had badly strained her confidence in a marriage that had never really had time to begin, and her husband's failure to be here to greet her, however unrealistic her expectations had been, completed the demoralization. As she stared listlessly out of the windows of the cabin, which seemed airless in the sweltering heat of the tropical island, she felt completely homeless and alone. The sense of family she'd developed with Silas Keane during the recent weeks would become only another memory when he returned to Baltimore.

Picking up her sketch pad and several pieces of graphite, she walked restlessly to the deck, where a slight breeze cooled her overheated skin and wafted heavy, unfamiliar scents past her sensitive nose.

"What's that smell?" she asked a young sailor lounging at the rail near her.

"Them's what you git in all these places, Miz Keane, burned cane being boiled into sugar or rum. Al'ays makes me sick at first afore I git used to it. Whenever I git down here, I sure do miss home."

"You're not from Falmouth, are you?"

"No, ma'am. Where I come from, we call you people *downlanders*. My town's Bagaduce on the Penobscot. Ain't big enough to rile the British like you Falmouthers done, so I reckon we'll be left alone. Wonder why the limeys are pickin' on New England towns where there really ain't much worth stealin' and leavin' a hellhole like this 'un go untouched. Reckon I won't be earnin' enough money in my whole life to be buyin' anything like one of them painted sedan chairs; but the rich folk here got passels of them and carriages to boot. Jest look at them peacocks struttin' around yonder, Miz Keane. Wonder what in thunderation they're gittin' ready to do?"

For some minutes Rebecca had been watching the assemblage of ornate carriages and gold-embossed sedan chairs crowding in front of the warehouses bearing her husband's and the Falconets' names. Fascinated, she stared at the men and women dismounting from their expensive conveyances, assisted by Negro servitors exotically uniformed in varying liveries. But it was the costumes of their white masters and mistresses that caught Rebecca's attention. All of them—men and women alike—wore elaborate wigs and high-heeled shoes that forced them to walk like mincing marionettes. The coats of the satin-clad men reached to the knees with a wide-skirted fullness that looked grotesquely effeminate, while the bell-like silhouettes of the panniered women's dresses seemed like layers of unnecessary material competing for exposure.

Intrigued by the inappropriate apparel in a climate that had rendered her own lightweight lawn frock damp with perspiration, Rebecca began to sketch one of the women standing apart from the others. Atop a two-foot-high wig she wore a hat with feathery plumes that extended still farther upward, feathers that matched the vivid purple of the beruffled bodice and wide panniers, the bright pink of the draped overskirt, and the pale lavender of the full underskirt. Even in the elegant evening gowns Silas had purchased for her in Baltimore, Rebecca mused wryly, she'd look like an underpaid governess compared to these women. Abruptly, her attention was averted from her half-finished sketch by the startled exclamation of the young sailor.

"Gawd, it's a blinkin' slave auction!"

Too far away to hear the voice of the auctioneer, Rebecca watched in mute horror as twenty men and thirty women in livery far simpler than that worn by the French servants were pushed one by one onto the viewing platform. Most of them stood quietly with resigned dignity as the potential shoppers haggled for their possession. As each sale was completed, the hapless slave was led off by one of the auctioneer's burly helpers and deposited near the sedan chair or the carriage of his new owner. An hour after the sale had begun, there were only six Frenchmen left clustered expectantly in front of the viewing stage.

Rebecca gasped as two young girls were led onto the platform, one of them a golden brown and the other almost white. There was no doubt about the colors of their skin, since most of it was exposed; each young body was shielded from complete exposure by only a brief length of cloth. As the darker skinned girl was led off by a plump, periwigged man too old even to be her father, the piece of graphite in Rebecca's hand snapped into small pieces and her lips articulated the words "The goddamned old lecher. I hope she castrates him with dull scissors."

"Becky, you oughtn't t' be here," the familiar voice of Jed Daws sounded from a dozen feet away. "Soon's he knowed what 'uz goin' t' happen, Cap'n Silas sent me and John Sugs here to keep you out of sight 'cause what you jest seen ain't the half of it. There's slaver scum in this port who don't give a durn what a pretty woman is as long as they kin peddle her in the next port-of-call."

Rebecca's eyes were peppery with anger as she swung around to face her old friend. "Jed, did my husband have anything to do with that slave sale?"

"Nary a bit. None of us knowed about them until the Frenchie's ship was unloaded after him and the cap'n left on the Frenchie's gig t' go to one of the durn Falconets' plantations somewheres west of here. Them poor devils was stole by the Frenchie's crew whin we raided Jamaica. While we 'uz lootin' the arsenal outside the limey town of

Kingston, he sent some of his men to rob the rich folk in the town itself. Those 'uz all trained house servants, Becky; and there's another hunnert of them hid in the warehouse that the Frenchie plans to smuggle into Savannah."

"Why isn't my husband here, Jed?"

"Don't reckon he ever expected to see you agin. I tried t' tell him you 'uz a slippery one who'd git away jest like Silas says you done, but the cap'n warn't listenin' to the likes of me. He 'uz listenin' to the durn Frenchie who convinced him that you 'uz lost fer good. That 'uz after three weeks of lookin' fer and boardin' four limey ships out of Boston. Well, the fancy Frenchie, he boards one by hisself and reports back with the danged lie that the limey cap'n says you 'uz long gone, and that you didn't kick up any fuss when you and that Tupton scum sailed for England. After that the cap'n brought us here and worked us worse than slaveys until the other cap'ns told him to let up or they'd toss him overboard."

"Has it been dangerous, Jed?"

"It ain't been no picnic, Becky, but we 'uz in only one fight until Jamaica, and that was bad. If we'd knowed the bastards had burned Falmouth, reckon we'd have torched Kingston. But the cap'n ain't like the Frenchie; he plays 'cording to rules. We 'uz sent to git arms an' that's jest what we done. Reckon we'd best git you packed, Becky, so's we kin take you ashore soon's Cap'n Silas sends word."

"I'm not going ashore, not after what I saw today."

"I got my orders and there ain't no other place. Most likely you'll be stayin' at old Jean Falconet's house jest outside of town, and that's durn near a palace."

"I won't do it, Jed. I'm not going to be dumped on strangers like a moldy sack of potatoes."

"You'll be put where Cap'n Silas says, and the Falconets sure won't be mistreatin' you. They're too durned grateful to the Keanes."

Rebecca knew that her protests would be in vain when she made them, but this day had been the culmination of five months of uncertainty. Resignedly, she smiled at Jed; it wasn't fair to burden him with her problems.

"Could we take the trunks I left aboard the *Reine* too?"

"Ain't aboard anymore. Cap'n put them ashore when we got here, but I'll bring 'em to you soon's you're settled. Now let's git that packin' done."

It was afternoon before Rebecca was rowed ashore and her three trunks lashed aboard an enclosed barouche ornately embossed with the name *Falconet*. Jed had guessed correctly about the location of what was to be her next unasked-for prison. Cynically, she wondered if her Uncle Jonathan ever worried about the niece he'd left penniless and dependent upon the charity of other people on the eve of war.

Silas Keane's thoughts were equally gloomy as he sweltered in a poorly sprung wagon being jostled along a rutted road leading to another Falconet stronghold thirty-five miles west of Port-au-Prince. The island was the same damned inferno it'd been twenty years ago, Silas reflected sourly, and Jean Falconet was the same charming scoundrel he'd been when he captained his own fleet of privateers or slavers, whichever activity was more profitable at the time. To give the man his due, Silas admitted grudgingly, Jean had been no worse than a hundred others the New Englander had met; and today he hadn't hesitated a minute in offering Becky a home and sending a competent servant to fetch her. But Jean Falconet had been damned reluctant when Silas had announced that he was going to fetch Philip himself.

"*Non, mon ami*, for a white stranger to travel on Saint-Domingue is too dangerous."

"When wasn't it, Jean? You've had escaped slaves on this cursed island for a century, first from the Spanish and then from you French."

"It's not just the escaped ones anymore, *mon vieux*."

"Your own people attack?"

"Not openly, and not when they're guarded, but *mon Dieu*, they're so many of them. Half of mine were intended for sale in your colonies until the Royal African Company of Jamaica decided the cursed *Anglais* had the monopoly and bottled us up."

"Then why in hell did your son steal another two hundred in the Jamaica raid?"

"Because the English have the finest trained servants in the New World, and your southern colonials, *mon ami*, will pay handsomely for them. That is the only way we'll survive, even with your Philip's generous return of one of our ships. With your war preventing the legitimate sale of our coffee and cocoa, how else can we obtain the income to support ourselves? Meanwhile, allow me to send a message to your son."

"Don't have the time to waste, Jean. I want to get those guns and powder to America before the British close this port with a damned blockade. I'm taking twelve marines with me so I'll be safe enough. One additional word of caution about my daughter-in-law, Jean; best leave her alone until my son gets here."

"*La petite* is shy then, *mon ami*?"

Despite the odd note of relief in his genial host's inflection, that innocuous question provided the only humorous moment in Silas Keane's disturbing day. The idea of anyone mistaking Becky for a shy woman amused him. That she could keep her mouth shut he knew for a fact, but she certainly wasn't a timid flutterer. When he'd been dickering with Benjamin Maitland about buying a Baltimore embarcadero warehouse, she'd held her peace until the skeptical man had started to walk away. And then she'd said in that dulcet voice of hers, "Silas, tell Mr. Maitland about the cargoes of arms that Philip will be bringing to Baltimore from the British arsenals in the Caribbean. Of course if Mr. Maitland is not in sympathy with the war that New Englanders are fighting, I can understand his refusal to sell you the warehouse."

Silas smiled sardonically when he remembered the speed with which Maitland had signed the sales contract without another dicker. But for the next three weeks Silas had worried about fulfilling the promise that her sly comment had implied. During his four months in the Caribbean, Philip hadn't returned to American ports with any cargoes, much less the needed munitions. Yet today Silas had seen enough muskets and powder stored in the Port-au-Prince warehouse that now bore his son's name to start a small war. He'd also seen something that bothered him a good deal more. He'd seen huddled groups of stolen slaves hidden in the warehouse awaiting their fate. Although both Luke and Matthew Stoneham had assured him that none of the Americans had taken part in the theft of these house servants in Jamaica, Silas was still furious with his son for becoming involved with slavery in any form.

Hatred of the practices of slavery and indenturing had always been the most powerful moral influence in Silas Keane's life, a legacy of a Scot grandfather who'd been an indentured servant. For six years the young emigrant had been the property of a Virginian planter until he'd earned his freedom. Embittered by the experience, Douglas Keane had fled to the northernmost American colony, married an Algonkin woman, and slowly acquired a fishing fleet. Now, fifty years later, the proud Keane heritage of freedom was being threatened by a son who had often baffled his father but never played him false before.

The miserable ride ended just after dark before the locked gates of another walled compound, and Silas bellowed furiously at the armed Negro guards who refused him entry until they had their master's permission. Profusely apologetic despite his shock at seeing a man he believed to be a thousand safe miles away, Captain Edmond Falconet suavely ordered his servants to provide for the twelve weary marines and ushered Silas into a drawing room that affronted the blunt New Englander with its opulent display of wealth.

"Where's my son, Captain?" Silas demanded.

"Philip prefers his own house whenever he visits me," the Frenchman explained. "I'll send a servant to summon him."

"Not necessary. Just tell your servant to point the way and I'll go myself."

"This is Saint-Domingue, Captain Keane, not your sterile New England. At night we have any number of unpleasant scorpions that inhabit our walks. If you insist, I'll accompany you."

It required the services of six barefoot slaves to protect

two boot-clad mariners the short distance from the mansion to the small house five hundred feet away. When a startled Philip met them at the door, Silas realized with a cynical surety that a seventh servant, scorpions or no, had been sent on ahead to warn him. His temper shortened by a long day of unaccustomed strain, Silas exploded into angry speech.

"Why the hell have you delayed getting those arms back to the colonies?"

As always with his father, Philip's own temper was quick to surface. "Because I was too damned busy stealing them. What the devil are you doing down here?"

"You might say I was driven out of Maine by the British. Two months ago Henry Mowat sank every ship left in Casco Bay and burned the town after stealing everything from our warehouses."

"My God, why?"

"It's an interesting story, son, but one I prefer to tell you in private. Will you be ready to return to Port-au-Prince with me tomorrow morning?"

Momentarily, Philip hesitated and then responded with a shrug. "No! What work there is to do has already been assigned to the other captains. I'm going to stay here and rest for a week or more."

In the constrained silence that followed Philip's refusal, Silas looked around the graciously decorated parlor, his face mirroring his disapproval of both it and his son. Attempting to ease the uncomfortable tension, Edmond Falconet cleared his throat, but before he could speak, a pleasantly accented, distinctly feminine voice interrupted.

"Philip, *cher,* where are your manners? Your papa is tired after such a terrible ride, and you do not offer him wine or dinner. Monsieur Keane, I am Annette Gironde."

"Annette is my cousin, Captain Keane," Edmond explained. "After her husband was killed, she joined her plantation to that of the Falconets and now helps to manage the combined estates. She also frequently acts as my hostess."

Silas's only response to the introduction was a curt nod as he studied her face with an ill-concealed contempt. She was what he'd expected her to be, a handsome woman in her midthirties with the unmistakable poise of a determined and disciplined courtesan. Turning toward his son, whose eyes were narrowed in an embarrassed consternation, Silas spoke scornfully.

"I'll say this for you, Philip, you're remarkably consistent and predictable. You're also a bloody damn fool. Captain Falconet, if you'll have one of your people show me where my men are bunked, I'll join them for the night; and we'll all be gone by morning. But one more thing you and my son should know; I've already ordered my men to clear the warehouses of all such matériel as might be needed by the colonies."

Edmond's studied politeness vanished and his dark eyes snapped with arousing temper. "One moment, Captain, part of that matériel is mine, and Philip has agreed to sell some of the arms to the planters of Saint-Domingue for the protection of this colony. There are a dozen other arsenals we plan to raid for the use of your American armies."

"As I said before, my son is a damn fool. He forgets that the Keane company is no longer working exclusively for itself. We have been commissioned by the Massachusetts congress to capture weapons, and half of our crews and most of our marines signed up to fight for the independence of America, not to keep thirty thousand Frenchmen safe from their half million slaves on this damned island. Concerning your profits, sir, I'm quite certain that the income from the sale of the slaves you stole from Jamaica will prove more than your one-eighth share of the prize monies."

"Those slaves are my own enterprise; they have nothing to do with Philip's and my partnership."

"Was that the agreement, son?" Silas demanded.

The anger expressed in Philip's eyes was no longer directed at his father or the Frenchwoman; it was now centered on his new partner. "No, it was not. Our only agreed-upon target was the arsenal itself."

Edmond's shrug was accompanied by a bland smile. "I saw no reason to pass up the opportunity for additional gain, *mon ami*. Besides, I employed extra men for that part of the operation. My regular crew and I were with you when we raided the fort that night.''

"Where I lost twenty men to your one," Philip said thoughtfully.

"So? My men are more experienced in that kind of battle. I didn't tell you about the slaves because I know your prejudice against the practice. But it is the basis for the culture and the economy of this colony, and as such, a necessary part of our lives."

Paying little attention to Falconet's explanation, Silas concentrated on his son. "Four of your captains, Philip, complained to me about having to obey a split command during that raid; and they requested my permission to make Baltimore their home port. They want their crews reunited with their families and away from this demoralizing atmosphere. Can't say I blame them. Well, I'll let you and your partners settle your differences while I get some sleep. Good night, madam."

As the gruff New Englander attempted to brush past her stiffly wide skirts, Annette Gironde reached out with a feminine gesture of supplication and placed a restraining hand on his arm.

"Monsieur, this argument is ridiculous and very unfair to Philip. In the three months since I met him, this is the first time he has relaxed enough to forget the war. Surely you do not begrudge him some little recreation?"

"Madam, did my son inform you that he already has a wife?"

Taken aback by the abrupt rudeness of the question, Annette withdrew her hand and replied with a defensive dignity, "Edmond informed me all about the unfortunate girl, *monsieur,* but she is now reunited with the man who'd been her intended husband before Philip interfered."

"Did Captain Falconet also tell you that Rebecca was kidnapped by that man at the point of a gun?"

Annette's shrug contained the merest hint of insolence. "Sometimes perhaps force is necessary to convince a woman, monsieur. I'm certain that in England she has found enough diversion to forget her impulsive mistake. And since her marriage to Philip was not performed in the

Church of England or by a Catholic priest, it can undoubtedly be annulled.''

Silas's laughter was a short bark of scornful amusement. ''I'd not depend too heavily on that priest, madam. My son may be a fool, but he's not the gullible simpleton you seem to think.''

Without waiting for any response to his final thrust of sardonic humor, Silas strode from the room and house, took a lantern from one of the servants, and walked toward the rear of Falconet's home. He located his men in the barrackslike wing that projected from the main structure, joined them for a meal of sweetened pork and uncut rum, and slept in exhaustion on a straw mat for eight hours. In the early morning Philip was waiting by the wagon when Silas and his marines emerged from the barracks without alerting any of the house servants.

''I'm going with you,'' the younger man announced grimly.

''Thought you might,'' his father grunted as he climbed aboard the ugly contrivance.

''You were damned rude last night,'' Philip rasped.

''Wasn't sure you noticed, what with your new mistress spreading all that soothing oil around. She sounded a degree or two more conniving than your last one. As a point of interest, son, how much did you contribute to that remarkable theory she proposed about an annulment?''

''Not a damned word. I've never told her anything about Rebecca.''

''Then she was well coached by someone else before she made herself so available. Did you really think it was an old Caribbean custom for a female relative with the brass and looks of that one to be lent as a temporary bedfellow to a visiting sea captain?''

''I thought Annette was old enough to run her own life; she's been married twice before.''

''I'll wager you found out differently after I left last night.''

''Something like that. She admitted that her second husband had made an arrangement when her first was still in prison. But, my God, why me? I swear I never gave her any encouragement, and I hadn't expected to see her again. But there she was at Edmond's plantation waiting for me. How the devil did you know her intentions?''

"Experience, son. I've dealt with scoundrels like Jean Falconet for forty years. He and most of the other island-raised captains—whether they be English, Dutch, Spanish, or French—are just a notch above flying the Jolly Roger. And why not? Their fathers and grandfathers were the best in the business of piracy. In your case the answer's simple. The Falconets are down to their scuppers, overloaded with raw slaves they can't sell and undersupplied with ships. They need our fleet and our reputation to help them recoup. By tying you up in a marriage to one of their own women, they'd have the wedge they wanted. Tell me, did old Jean offer you any choices other than that overaged madam?''

"He introduced me to his two daughters, but compared to Rebecca they seemed like giggling idiots.''

"Compared to Becky, most young girls are.''

"Since when did you change your mind about her? I remember your telling me she wouldn't be a good wife for a sailor.''

"I said she was the wrong choice for you because you don't have the sense to appreciate her. What happens if you find her?''

"I'll kill the bastard who took her away.''

"That wasn't the question, son.''

"It'll be up to Rebecca. I don't think she really wants to be married to me.''

"What about you?''

"Until Edmond convinced me of the impossibility, I almost sailed to England to search for her.''

"And you thought she'd be in England because that same friend told you so, right? Do you still think you can trust the Falconets?''

"My God, she could still be in Boston.''

"At least you're not entirely stupid. Now let's get back to our ships and get out of here.''

Philip shook his head. ''No, I'll have to stay if I'm to locate any of those other arsenals. The Connecticut maps are useless. Without Edmond, I wouldn't find a one of them. He and his father have access to a network of Spanish and French fishing boats whose crews keep them informed about the movements of the British fleets, and they know where the arsenals are hidden because they've raided them before. I'd have been trapped in Jamaica if Edmond hadn't known a way through the swamps. You'll have to honor the commitments I made with the Falconets if we want their help in the future. I don't like the slavery thing any more than you do, and the sign can come down if you object to it; but if we want to take full cargoes of arms home, we'll need Edmond's help on Trinidad, Tobago, and the other British colonies.''

"Will you be able to avoid any more entanglements with that woman?''

"Yes, I told her there was no chance for marriage. What was it you wanted to tell me about Falmouth?''

"It was your Madam Burnell and that servant of hers that kept the British informed.''

"My God!''

"Mostly the servant. He was a naval officer of some kind.''

"I knew she had a manservant, but I never saw him. Are you sure about them?''

"Wouldn't say so if I weren't.''

"The bitch! The goddamned bitch.''

"It happens, son. I imagine she was paid to cooperate since she didn't have the brains or loyalty to be a spy without the promise of money. Fortunately, the Keanes will survive because we had some mighty good help when the British sacked the town. Becky saved all the deeds to our ships and property in addition to fifteen thousand pounds in gold. She's waiting for you in Port-au-Prince. You panicked too soon at New London. You should have remembered that Roger couldn't have pulled a stunt like that without the help of his father. And while Stanton's a scoundrel, he's no bumpkin and he's not a traitor like his son. As soon as he learned Becky was already married, he put her ashore and skedaddled. Someday I'll take him to task about putting a lone woman ashore at night, but in the meantime I'm glad to see you smiling. I thought last night I'd be taking her back to Baltimore without telling you."

"You would have, wouldn't you?"

"That's right, son, and you're going to be toeing a mighty fine line if she consents to remain here with you. We'll give the Falconets their twenty percent as long as old Jean promises to keep his son and that Gironde woman away from Becky. But if you play fast and loose, I'll be the one to get that annulment for her. Becky's not one damn bit happy about you or this devil's island at the moment."

Confined in still another narrowly circumscribed prison, Rebecca had spent her first day in Port-au-Prince in hopeless rebellion against her unseen jailers. There'd been only one passenger waiting for her in the Falconet coach, a slender woman with closely cropped African hair and a complexion only a shade darker than Rebecca's own. She'd greeted the newcomer in excellent, liquid English.

"I am Akhoi, Madame Keane. I will be your housekeeper while you're visiting L'Émeraude."

Relieved that she would not be completely isolated by a language barrier, Rebecca exclaimed inanely, "You're not French!"

The ironic inflection of the reply was accompanied by a blankly unfathomable look. "No, madame, I am quadroon African and octoroon Arawak Indian. I was born on Jamaica."

"Then you're English!"

"I am a slave, madame."

Embarrassed into silence by the bleak declaration, Rebecca lifted the heavy curtains that obscured all view of the passing scenery, only to have a well-cared-for hand reach over and lower the blue velvet drapery.

"It is not yet safe, madame," Akhoi warned without any change in her musical inflection. Fifteen minutes later, in the same pleasantly indifferent voice, the housekeeper opened the curtains of all four windows and murmured, "Welcome to Saint-Domingue, Madame Keane. Did you know that the good saint's followers were called Black Friars? Ironic, isn't it?"

Everywhere on the crowded, narrow street outside the carriage, Rebecca saw unsmiling Negro people watching her with eyes that held the same enigmatic look as Akhoi's. Not even when the watchers were shoved out of the way by the Falconet guards running alongside the barouche did their expressions change, and Rebecca began to experience the fanciful sensation of being the only living person in a netherworld of the almost dead. The heat in the enclosed carriage threatened to smother her.

Abruptly Akhoi leaned over and held a small vial to the American woman's nose. "It was perhaps unkind of me, madame. I merely wanted you to appreciate the beauty of Émeraude more. The people on these streets are no longer slaves. They were freed after they'd been injured or had become too old to work and could not be sold."

Revived by the perfumed ammonia, Rebecca accepted the challenge of the provocative words. "I have two friends aboard the *Reine* who vow they will never set foot in Saint-Domingue again. Now I understand why. They were freed by their French captain before he was killed."

"I know your mulatto friends very well, madame. Theirs is an interesting story. Antoine Falconet freed Louis and Leon because they were his half brothers. You may look out of the windows safely now, madame, we're about to enter the grounds of L'Émeraude."

Shaken by Akhoi's casually uttered revelation that it had been a brother rather than the guilty father who'd ended the slavery of her mulatto friends, Rebecca stared at the verdantly green trees and lawns of the luxurious estate with a vague antipathy. She gasped in shocked surprise at the sight of the huge colonnaded baroque building just ahead. "It looks like a painting of a French chateau," she murmured dryly.

"I believe it is the copy of one, madame. The owners on this island are very proud of their French heritage."

"I thought most of their ancestors were pirates."

"That word is no longer used on Saint-Domingue, especially since the most successful of them were forgiven by the King of France and appointed governors of this and other colonies. Fortunately, madame, you will be spared the ordeal of being a guest in that house. While you're at Émeraude, you'll live in the house your husband uses whenever he remains ashore in Port-au-Prince.''

Silenced by the reminder that she'd soon be seeing her husband after a long separation, Rebecca felt numb. How little she really understood of the man she'd married! The only Philip Keane she knew was a blunt Maine seaman, not a man who could live on an estate like this one and associate with the overdressed fops she'd seen at the slave auction. How could he have become partners with a man who'd kept two of his own sons in slavery?

Even the small house Akhoi led her into affronted Rebecca with its satin and brocade elegance, because behind the profusion of flowering trees and shrubs that surrounded the exquisite stone structure, she'd glimpsed the ugly dirt-floored slave shacks. And inside the carved mahogany clothes press in the bedroom, she found some men's clothing which she fervently hoped were not Philip's. One of the coats was a gold satin, and she shuddered as she remembered Roger Tupton's cerise one.

Her sense of disoriented imprisonment was heightened hours later when the trunks she'd left aboard the *Reine* were delivered by blue-liveried Falconet slaves rather than by Jed Daws and John Sugs. When she opened them, she gasped in dismay. The only dress that remained of the beautiful ones she'd had made in New London was the black satin she'd worn at the dinner party Philip had hosted on the night he'd returned. As she watched Akhoi hang up the Baltimore dresses, Rebecca felt as if some of her own individuality had been destroyed. Those gowns had been created for other women, but the New London ones had been her own; she'd chosen the fabrics, the designs, and the bonnets to match.

The next morning after a lonely, restless night, she defiantly donned an ancient work shirt and a simple drawstring peasant skirt, omitting both pantaloons and petticoats but feeling comfortable for the first time since landing on this hot, humid, decadent island. Noting with satisfaction that Akhoi had also discarded her primly buttoned dress and was wearing a woven black skirt and a white blouse similar to her own, Rebecca settled down with her sketch pad and graphite. A prison was, after all, only a state of mind.

She made several sketches of Akhoi whose face did not seem to change expression, but each drawing had revealed a different facet of what Rebecca realized was a very complex personality. Not by a flicker of an eyelid did the housekeeper evince any interest in the artwork until Rebecca completed a sketch of the fat, good-natured cook.

After studying the portrait with a critical concentration, Akhoi finally nodded her approval. "It is too bad, madame, that you do not work in oils. The French people here are enamored of immortalizing their faces for the doubtful benefit of their great-great-grandchildren."

Rebecca smiled as she recalled Brian Sinclair's rugged face. "I was once paid for doing a portrait in oils," she admitted, "but I prefer sketching. Nobody bothers to save sketches beyond a few weeks. Akhoi, would any of your immortal Frenchmen mind if I escaped from here for a while and went for a walk?"

"It is allowed, madame, providing I go with you."

"Even L'Émeraude isn't safe?"

"You will be safe enough. It is merely that some of my people are superstitious and I wouldn't want them frightened."

"By me?"

"By the color of your hair. If I am with you, they will know that you're a—that you're not like the other white women here. Many of the slaves cling to their ancient beliefs as a protection against the religion our owner demands we accept. In Africa, demons are often thought to have white hair."

"Someday," Rebecca groaned, "I'm going to shave it off and buy myself a wig."

"You won't like it, madame. Wigs are very uncomfortable. I was forced to wear one for ten years to conceal my African heritage."

More intrigued than ever with her strange companion, Rebecca longed to ask questions; but she knew instinctively that she'd be rebuffed. Throughout the walk, though, as Akhoi identified the different crops as sugarcane, indigo plants, coffee shrubs, and cacao trees, Rebecca paid far more attention to the attitude of the field hands toward her guide than she did to the lesson in botany. Men and women alike stopped their work and waited respectfully until Akhoi had passed them, but the most interesting reactions came from two whip-armed overseers, one white and one mulatto. Each man backed away from the light-skinned slave woman in wide-eyed fear. When Rebecca asked for an explanation, Akhoi smiled derisively.

"In spite of the prevailing conceit that the lords of creation are logical creatures, white blood does not guarantee immunity from superstition. They're afraid that I might hasten their well-deserved doom with magical incantations and curses."

Near the completion of the walk, while they were still a hundred feet away from the guest house, Akhoi became the formal servant once again. "If Madame will excuse me, I have duties to perform for the Falconets." She disappeared into the concealing shrubbery without waiting for the younger woman's permission or response.

Inside the parlor of the house Rebecca found her husband staring at the sketches of Akhoi. "Hello, Philip," she mumbled breathlessly and braced herself as his expression changed from glad recognition to the more familiar one of frowning disapproval of her inappropriate attire.

"I thought my father bought you some decent dresses, Cottontop," he scolded.

"He did, but it's too hot to wear them when I'm alone."

Frowning more heavily as he nodded toward the drawings, he demanded brusquely, "Is this the servant the Falconets assigned to be your maid?"

"Akhoi? No, she's the housekeeper."

"I'll ask Jean to send you someone else."

"Why? Akhoi is the only one who speaks English." We sound like casual acquaintances, Rebecca thought with an icy hurt, but then perhaps that's all we really are to each other. He even looks different, much thinner and—she paused in her unhappy reflections to grope for words that would describe the more subtle changes she noted—more defensive than ever and oddly nervous. With a heavy sense of failure, she wished she'd remained in Baltimore or anyplace other than where he was.

"Where's your father, Philip?"

"At the docks. Why?"

"I'd like to return to Baltimore with him."

"Aren't you forgetting something, Cottontop? You're married to me, remember? I'm sorry about the past months and all the danger you've faced. If I could turn the clock back to that day in New London, I would. I've cursed myself a hundred times for letting you go off by yourself when I knew that criminal might be lurking around. Did he hurt you?"

"No, it was his friend who hit me over the head. Roger was too busy boasting about his glorious future once the British had quelled the minor rebellion."

"Rebecca, why did you lie to me about where you'd be that day? You didn't go near the shops where you'd have been safe. Instead, you went to a deserted end of town. Why?"

"I went to a silversmith to pay for a wedding ring I'd ordered. For some reason that day I thought I should have one, and it was fortunate I did. It was that ring that convinced Stanton Tupton that I was unavailable for Roger."

For a moment Philip stared at her before he made any response to her announcement. "I haven't been much of a husband, have I, Cottontop?"

"No, but then you never wanted to be one at all, so it's understandable. You look tired, Philip. Why don't I order you a bath while I repack my clothes?"

"You're not leaving Saint-Domingue, Cottontop, at least not until I do. There's still the same war going on."

Rebecca was struggling to keep her breathing under control, to keep the rage that was building within her from breaking through its restraints. "Philip," she countered tensely, "the last time I was left stranded in a strange town, dependent upon the charity of strangers, I was able to earn enough money to return to Falmouth. But here that would be very difficult for me. I'd rather take my chances in a battle at sea than walk alone through the streets of this city.''

"You won't be allowed near this city, Cottontop, unless I'm there to protect you; and you're an honored guest here at L'Émeraude, not an unwelcome burden. At dinner tonight you'll meet the Falconets and some of their friends, and you'll find they're not the monsters you're imagining them to be. Maybe by the time our fleet leaves in a week or more, you'll find I'm not such a monster either.'' His voice softened suddenly. "Have you thought about me at all, fondling?''

"I tried not to think about you. Wondering where you were and what you were doing wasn't a good idea. I didn't know if you were still alive. And now that I'm here, you're going away again.'' Fearful that she was admitting more than she intended, Rebecca tried to be matter-of-fact. "When do you think you'll return from your next trip?''

"How the devil should I know?'' he answered irritably, annoyed by the direction the conversation had taken. "The Jamaica raid was scheduled to last only ten days, but we were there for three weeks, one of them spent hiding in a swamp. Damn it, Cottontop, I hate this part of the world as much as you obviously do; but it's where I have to be for the next six months. And I'd like you to stay here with me.''

Rebecca took a deep, trembling breath and blurted, "Why didn't you say so in the first place instead of asking all those stupid questions and glaring at me as if I were some snaggle-toothed fishwife?''

"Damned if I know, fondling. You have a talent for upsetting me.'' But even as he put his arms around her, a final criticism exploded from his lips. "My God, you're not wearing a damned thing underneath.''

"No, I'm not,'' she muttered in a choked voice and tried vainly to pull away. She was shaking too badly for coherent thought, and not until he began to kiss her did she even realize that his hands were not steady and that he was breathing as erratically as she was.

Between kisses Philip made one more attempt at explanation. "It's just that I worry about you, Cottontop. I've never felt responsible for any of the—'' He stopped talking abruptly; he'd almost said "the others." In a slurred voice he rushed to alter his words: ''—anyone except my crew before you came along.''

Desperately needing the safety of distance to rebuild his shaken self-confidence, he gently pushed Rebecca away. "Sweetheart, you said something about a bath a few minutes ago. Could you order one for me now? I feel as if I've been locked in a sweatbox for a week.''

Her instantaneous response to his request made him cringe; she couldn't wait to get away from him. But he didn't dare attempt another embrace and risk exposure of something far more offensive than perspiration. When his father had first told him about her escape from Roger, he'd experienced a surge of emotion so intense he'd forgotten everything else until he learned she was staying at Émeraude. How the devil was he to keep her from learning that Paulette had not been his only mistake? If his father had told him last night that Rebecca was here, the final indignity would never have occurred. But it had! Even after he'd learned that Annette Gironde was not merely an accommodating mistress, but an ambitious woman set on marriage regardless of the methods used in its achievement, he'd still gone to bed with her. And not until he held the unscented body of his wife in his arms did he remember the cloying perfume the Frenchwoman used.

A second, more sordid memory also added to his burden of guilt. For the first two months after New London, anger and a devastating sense of loss had been his only emotions until a delegation of fleet captains and ship's officers reminded him sharply that all of the crews needed shore leave and rest. Philip had spent that layover in Port-au-Prince as the guest of Jean Falconet, and he hadn't refused the additional hospitality of the services of a skilled mulatto woman slave. It hadn't been Akhoi, although she too had been tacitly available; but it'd been the light-skinned Akhoi who'd brought the other woman to Philip each night he'd stayed in this same guest cottage.

If Rebecca were only more experienced and less emotionally prejudiced, she'd realize that the mulatto woman

had meant nothing to him other than a temporary bed
partner at a time when he'd never expected to see his wife
again. But with a heavy heart he realized that not even a
tolerant wife would understand his involvement with Annette
Gironde, nor would she believe that the Frenchwoman
meant no more to him than the mulatto had. He'd never
really been attracted to her; he'd merely drifted into the
relationship to fill the void in his own life. Although he'd
met her casually at the Falconets' parties, not until the day
at the warehouse had he become her escort.

In the company of a dozen social leaders including
Madame Falconet, Annette had attended the advertised
sale of women's clothing taken from captured English
merchantmen. While Philip had been overseeing the more
important auction of stores of wines and spirits, Annette
had asked his opinion about a dress she contemplated
purchasing. Indifferently at first, he'd glanced at the black
satin gown she held up for his inspection, and had almost
given his approval until the gleam of the fabric triggered
his memory. It was the dress Rebecca had worn aboard the
Reine. To his consternation, he discovered that his wife's
trunks of clothing, which he'd stored in the warehouse
when he could no longer stand the sight of them in his
cabin, had been mistakenly included in the auction. The
black satin was the lone survivor of the dozen new frocks.
Although Annette had been understanding of his anger,
she'd been practical about the destructibility of silk fabrics
in the tropics.

"It is just as well the others have been sold," she
reproached him as she folded the dress and returned it to
the trunk. "Now you will have less to remind you that you
no longer have a wife. When my Emile was killed, I wept;
but I've learned it is better to forget and go on living."
Philip had quickly learned that he was included in her
philosophical acceptance of fate. At her insistence he'd
accompanied her to a dinner party that same night and to
an expensive tailor's the next day to purchase what she
called the "basic accouterments of civilized society"—two
satin suits and a powdered wig that made him look
undistinguishable from the olive-skinned Frenchmen.

For the next month he'd taken his fleet out of harbor on only two brief sorties against enemy shipping and had spent the remainder of the time attending the constant rounds of card and dinner parties in Annette's company. However, not until he'd returned from a third, more disastrous mission, had he become her lover. With the help of a Spanish fisherman, the Keane fleet had overtaken and surrounded a flotilla of four English ships, one of which proved to be a small warship on escort duty. Although the outcome of the brief battle was never in doubt, thirty Americans had been killed and two of the old Langley brigs damaged before the British naval captain surrendered. Because one of the enemy ships had been a slaver bound for Jamaica, Philip ordered all four vessels confiscated and their passengers and crews turned over to the Spanish authorities on De Piños Island south of Cuba. Despite the enormity of the financial gain, he'd been so depressed when he'd returned to Port-au-Prince that he had accepted Annette's consolation without any sense of guilt or betrayal. And last night even after he learned that her generosity had long strings attached, his anger had quickly cooled to cynical amusement. Until this morning he'd still considered himself above the general depravity that prevailed on this island colony.

When he and his father had arrived at L'Émeraude, they'd been greeted by the owner himself, who announced that he'd arranged a dinner party to introduce *la petite* Madame Keane to a select group of his island friends. Silas had refused the invitation brusquely, but Philip had been constrained to accept for himself and Rebecca when Jean Falconet smilingly informed him that Edmond and Annette would not be present. Until that moment Philip hadn't realized that his private life had become a subject of public gossip.

It had been easier for him to salve his conscience with condescension when he'd first seen Rebecca. Because her hair was windblown and her clothes more casual than a servant's, he'd been carpingly critical, scolding her about one unimportant thing after another until she'd retaliated in that damnably composed voice of hers and announced she was returning to America. Even when he'd kissed her, she'd seemed poised for flight, as if she couldn't wait to get away from him. Damn, if he could have made love to her then, perhaps he might have overcome her stiff resistance; but he hadn't dared, not with the scent of another woman still on his body and in his nostrils.

Viciously he scrubbed himself in the privacy of the bathhouse and then donned the elegant clothing that had become his usual attire at parties during the past months. When he emerged from the room just before the dinner hour, he was fully garbed in satin—blue coat, flowered waistcoat, and ivory pantaloons—with a powdered wig covering his own dark hair. He found his wife waiting for him in the parlor, and as usual he'd underestimated her. She'd make every other woman at the party seem overdressed and artificial. Her black lace dress was devoid of flowers, panniers, drapes, and ruffles; but it made her look more desirable than any woman he'd seen on this island. And that beautiful, pale hair of hers was as simply groomed as a child's, and as alluring as a shower of precious metals.

"You've grown even more beautiful, Cottontop," he murmured in appreciation as he guided her along the stone-paved path.

The subtle irony of her response made him wince. "So have you, Philip."

Smothering a rueful chuckle, he reflected with an odd pride, She's always been able to make me feel like a fool, even when she was a fuzzy-haired girl in ugly Indian britches. Taking a firm grip on her arm, he turned around and headed them back to the small house.

"I've decided that one beauty in the family is enough. If you'll help me polish my boots, I'll go as myself tonight."

Rebecca was giggling as she polished the supple black leather boots and watched him change into a slim-fitting black suit. "It's not a total loss, Philip," she murmured. "You can always use the wig as a nightcap."

"I prefer the bed warmer that kept me from freezing to death the night after the storm," he bantered lightly.

"I wasn't sure you'd noticed."

"I noticed, Cottontop; and if you weren't the guest of honor at this party, I'd demonstrate my gratitude."

Half an hour late in arriving at the ornate villa, Rebecca and Philip were greeted by Jean Falconet, who'd worried that the young American woman might prove too shy to come. Instead, it was the usually urbane Captain Keane who appeared ill at ease as he escorted his wife past the twenty other guests hiding their amused disapproval of the black-clad pair behind suddenly busy fans and wineglasses. Hurrying across the floor to prevent a social disaster, Jean pulled up short when he overheard his guest of honor's *sotto voce* comments to her husband. "Now I know how Lady Godiva felt when she rode through Coventry. A person doesn't need to understand French to know what that bandy-legged old man with the monocle glued to his eye is thinking. He bought himself a twelve-year-old slave girl yesterday."

Even while he arranged a broad smile of welcome on his shrewd face, Jean Falconet was undergoing a dismayed reaction. Madame Keane was not the shy girl he'd expected, and unfortunately she was as beautiful as she was daring. One look at Philip's face reaffirmed what the older man had already concluded. Not for a moment had the American captain been serious about Annette Gironde, not with a wife like this. With a delayed gallantry, Jean offered Rebecca his arm and led her rapidly away from the vicinity of his own daughters, whose giggling whispers were embarrassingly gauche and insulting.

The Frenchman's problems with this ill-considered dinner, however, were just beginning. Five minutes after he'd succeeded in seating the twenty-four people around the long, lavish table, his seven-foot Negro majordomo, resplendent in a blue and gold uniform, delivered an urgent message to his master. Ordering the dinner to continue without him, Falconet left the room hurriedly and walked toward the distant foyer in another part of the vast chalet. His opening remark to the three people awaiting him was a sharp reprimand. "Edmond," he addressed his son, "I sent a message to Léogane that you and Annette were not to come tonight."

"Talk to Annette," the younger Falconet disclaimed indifferently. "She was upset when Philip left without an

explanation this morning. Is what Captain Keane told us at
the docks true? That Philip's wife is your guest at
Émeraude?''

Bristling defensively, Silas Keane responded to the questions, ''I'm neither a liar nor a fool, Captain. I left
Rebecca here with your father in the mistaken belief that
she'd be safe. That was before I learned of the plot you
and the madam cleverly hatched concerning Philip's future. Jean, your son lied when he claimed some Englishmen
informed him that Becky had gone to England willingly;
and since then he and your niece have obtained some
ignorant priest's promise for an annulment. Obviously
none of them know scat about Massachusetts law or about
my son's and my hatred of blackmail, polite or otherwise.''

Again Edmond's reaction was an eloquent shrug. ''I told
the lie to prevent Philip from endangering all of our ships; it
was the only way to stop him from sailing into Boston
Harbor and challenging the entire British fleet there. As for
the so-called plot, Captain Keane, our consulting the priest
was a mere formality after your son became Annette's—close
friend so readily. I was certain that he'd prefer the society on
Saint-Domingue once he realized that his wife was such a
flighty girl. That day she was presumably kidnapped was not
the first time he'd had to look for her. She'd spent the day
before in the company of still another man, and she'd never
used her married name in New London.''

''Didn't say that Becky can't be irritating at times, Captain. She's been earning her own living since she was a slip
of a girl, and she's developed some downright annoying
notions of her own. But the fact remains that she's married to
my son and is going to stay married, if I have my say.''

During this interchange the person most affected by its
content had listened imperturbably, confidently elegant in a
gown even the blunt New Englander recognized as expensively refined. Having smuggled more than one bolt of
costly fabric into America, he knew that the apricot silk
kincob woven that heavily with gold and silver threads had
been made to order for the woman wearing it. Grudgingly
he admitted that Madame Gironde was attractive enough to
have turned a less susceptible head than Philip's, but he

was equally certain that without a maid clever enough to apply cosmetics artfully, the Frenchwoman would look the calculating thirty-eight he suspected she was. He watched her closely as she turned toward her older relative.

"Uncle Jean," she railed lightly with the same placating charm she'd used on Silas the night before, "I have no intention of acting like *une femme jalouse*. I merely told this ridiculously defensive papa that the choice is not his to make. Philip is a grown man who has never mentioned this problem wife to me. I think he has forgotten all about her. Edmond was perhaps foolish to say she was in England, but you were even more foolish, Uncle, to introduce her to our friends without consulting me. Now it will be difficult to avoid scandal." Without waiting for a response from either man, she addressed Silas in the businesslike tones of a woman accustomed to issuing orders.

"Monsieur Keane, tell your son that I wish to see him now. Tell him also that if he performs this courtesy, I will not insist on being introduced to his wife tonight."

Long years of meeting the challenges of the sea, a mistress far more demanding and dangerous than the Frenchwoman now threatening him with subtle blackmail, had given Silas a ruthless courage. "Madam," he warned her bluntly, "you can do what you damn well please; but before you interfere again in my son's life, I think you should hear what I have to say. This afternoon I spoke to a local privateer who'd already petitioned my son to join the Keane fleet. In return for my approval, he revealed some interesting facts about both of your late husbands. Before Emile Gironde joined the Falconets as a business partner, he'd amassed a fortune as a slaver. The problem was that he rarely went to Africa for his cargoes; he stole them from other ships on the open sea, and according to my informant he didn't care what flag the ship was flying. Several times he was accused of piracy, but because he left no witnesses and sold the captured ships to other slavers as unscrupulous as himself, he was never convicted.

"Your first husband, a renegade Englishman named Sidney Hudson, wasn't as fortunate; he was given a fifteen-year sentence for piracy. But two years ago he was

pardoned by the British Admiralty and issued letters of
marque that allowed him to return to his old profession.
By a curious coincidence, his first assignment after being
released in the company of two other pardoned pirates was
the capture of the Falconet fleet in Havana, where both
your second husband and Antoine Falconet were murdered.
Just how Hudson knew where the fleet was that night is
still a mystery, since he didn't live long enough to reveal
the name of his informant. He was killed and thrown into
the sea, as he deserved to be, after he'd ordered his scurvy
men to fire on a captain and crew who'd taken to open
boats when their ship was sunk. If Hudson had escaped,
my son and I would still be looking for him.

"Now, Madame Gironde, I'm not accusing you of
having taken part in the criminal activities of either man,
but I am advising you not to contact their old slaver friends
with regard to my daughter-in-law. Jean can tell you that in
the past I've sunk more than one pirate with less provoca-
tion; and, madam, I wouldn't give a damn whether my
enemy was man or woman.

"Jean," Silas said, turning to his host, "I gained some
additional information today that makes it imperative that
Becky leave your home tonight. Since Gironde's death
your niece has lent you large sums of money on several
occasions; so I concluded—correctly, as it turns out—that
she'd not be denied entrance into your home. Therefore
I've instructed the bank to locate more secure accommodations. But there is one favor you can do for me. Yesterday
you provided Becky with an English-speaking housekeeper. I want to purchase that woman's freedom, if she'll
agree to work for me in the same capacity."

Throughout Silas Keane's lengthy castigation of his
niece, Jean Falconet had experienced a curious ambivalence. While nothing that'd been said surprised him, the
New Englander's undercurrent of suspicion about Annette's
possible culpability in the murder of Antoine and Gironde
disturbed the older Falconet. Emile had been a fat, un-
couth *cochon* of a man whom any wife would have wanted
dead, and Antoine had been foolish enough to accuse his
cousin of being more vicious than Gironde. It could be that

she'd conspired with her first husband upon his release from prison to rid herself of the two men, as Silas had implied. God knows she had a ruthlessness about her that intimidated everyone in the family including himself, although the plan to ensnare Philip Keane had originated with him. But now, with the arrival of the wife, such a solution to his financial problems was impossible, despite Annette's stubborn refusal to admit defeat.

Frowning heavily, Jean realized that his only recourse was to play the toady to the implacable American awaiting an answer to the request for a slave. But alas for his peace of mind, that particular slave was the only one of his ten thousand that the Frenchman feared. For six years prior to his death, Akhoi had been Antoine's mistress, a dangerously well educated woman whom his foolish son had freed and made his heir. Only by bribing the authorities had Jean been able to reactivate her slave status and thus keep the money in the family. There was a second, more deadly reason he feared the light-skinned slave. She was reputed to be a conjure woman, a *sorcière* who'd already played havoc with the other Falconet slaves. As relieved as Jean would be to get her off his property, she would be even more dangerous to him as a free woman in the small colony. Tactfully, he phrased his refusal.

"Akhoi is not for sale, *mon ami,* but I have others who'd be more appropriate."

"Not interested in the others. According to what you said yesterday, this one has run her own home and is smart enough to look out for Becky in a strange city. She has another characteristic that suits her for the job; she's mostly white so she'd fit in better at home if she wants to stay with us."

Jean sighed in resignation, making only one stipulation as he agreed to the sale. "If you promise to take Akhoi away from Saint-Domingue when your daughter-in-law leaves, I'll prepare the freedom papers."

"Good. Now we'll complete the rest of our negotiations so there'll be no future misunderstanding. Captain Falconet, since my son informs me that you're necessary for the successful completion of our assignment down here, I'll agree to the percentage he offered you. But only a fourth of the arms you've already captured will be sold to your island friends, and none of the future stores will be made available to them. However, if you cooperate to the fullest extent with my son, I'll offer you a greater benefit. You can keep half of the ships that are taken, providing you promise to postpone your slaving activities until after our temporary partnership is dissolved. Are we in agreement?"

Both Jean and Edmond nodded vigorously; neither man had expected such generosity. Silas had shrewdly gauged their financial need and given them sufficient incentive to keep their female relative under better control, although he seriously doubted that Annette Gironde would submit to any man's domination. Brusquely he returned his attention to her, noting with satisfaction that her face was now set in angry lines that reduced her beauty considerably and revealed the underlying cupidity.

"You were right about my son being old enough to know his own mind, madam, so I'll deliver your message to him. Keep in mind, though, that I'll be the one to hunt you down if you harm my daughter-in-law."

CHAPTER
8

HAVING been assigned the seat of honor on her host's right, Rebecca was left stranded by Jean's abrupt departure. Directly across the wide table from her was the man with the monocle, who soon abandoned his obvious attempts to catch her averted eyes and concentrated his attention instead on his own dinner partner, a plump middle-aged woman whose rapid French was punctuated with girlish giggling. The man on her right, Rebecca thought, might have made an interesting companion had either of them spoken the other's language, but even thus handicapped he'd made an effort at kindly meant instruction.

When she'd first been seated, she'd been dismayed by the array of cutlery, dishes, and glasses spread out on the three-foot length of table in front of her. She had no idea of the intended purpose for the six knives, forks, and spoons; and the profusion of crystal glasses sparkling in the soft candlelight was equally intimidating. Scarcely able to see down to the far end of the table, where Madame Falconet had risen to undertake her husband's duties, Rebecca had no idea that the speech and proposed toast was for her until she reached for the nearest wineglass. Her companion gently touched her hand and shook his head almost imperceptibly. Smiling at him gratefully, she survived the uncomfortable moment when the men around the table all stood and motioned toward her with their wineglasses. That was the last time during the two-hour ordeal that she met her husband's eyes, but Philip was not smiling at her. Instead, he was scowling as his eyes shifted to her helpful dinner partner. Although she was unaware of the cause of his disapproval, Rebecca was neither surprised nor overawed; except for a few moments during their ten-month marriage, he'd never approved of her.

She survived the first course of the dinner by following the smiling instructions of the Frenchman, using the cutlery and glass he did and dabbing her lips delicately with her napkin. But shortly after the plates bearing the remains of the spicy shrimp concoction had been removed, her companions' attention was claimed by his other dinner partner. Rebecca continued to follow his lead, but without much interest in the food or wines that were placed before her in rapid succession. Instead, she began to study the faces of the other diners, particularly the two animated women flanking Philip and vying competitively for his attention. Rebecca could understand why; he was the best-looking man in the room. He had adjusted to this artificial life so easily, she reflected with a dull sense of withdrawal as she watched his lips form the French words almost as rapidly as the two women's. He doesn't even see the injustice of having twenty-four liveried slave footmen stand behind the pampered guests or notice that their black faces had become expressionlessly inhuman. They moved with mechanical precision between the table and the room-long sideboard kept filled with ever-changing plates of food by a small army of equally blank-faced women servants. How could the son of Silas Keane have accepted the cruel practice of slavery so easily?

Her first awareness of the man who'd moved from his place somewhere near the other end of the table to fill the vacancy left by their host was a firm grip on her arm and an amused question.

"Do you remember me, Rebecca Keane?"

Startled by the abruptness of his approach, she stared at his smiling, sun-wizened face for a moment before she burst into laughter. She remembered him very well; he'd been the only ship's captain she'd sketched at the Londonderry Inn who'd revealed a sense of humor when she'd given him a full head of curly hair instead of a balding pate. Although the dignified wig altered his appearance, his face held the same merry, irreverent expression it had at the inn. He'd been her frequent audience there, making bold and occasionally bawdy suggestions about the beautification of her subsequent models.

"I didn't realize that anyone like you would be allowed in this colony, Captain Riccard," she murmured between giggles. "The others seem to take themselves so seriously."

"They are sanctimonious peacocks, aren't they?" he retorted promptly with a wide grin. "I tried to bribe old Jean to let me be your dinner partner, but he'd reserved that pleasure for himself. When I spoke to him, he was suffering from the delusion that you were a shy young thing who needed his sponsorship. I didn't disillusion him, but you should have seen his face when you swung into the room in your so-beautiful black dress and your lovely hair unfettered by one of these hideous pretenses.''

"Where were you when Monsieur Falconet paraded me around like a two-headed chicken?" she demanded.

Leaning toward her, Captain Riccard whispered in the same theatrical hiss he'd often used at the inn when his comment was particularly outrageous, "I was watching old Gilette." He paused to indicate the man seated opposite her. "His eyes almost popped out of his head when he saw you. You should feel very flattered; our estimable representative of King Louis's royal *trésorerie* usually prefers his ladies under the age of fifteen."

The dinner courses came and went without Rebecca's noticing what she ate; it was the first time in months that she'd had occasion to laugh. Patrice Riccard was a font of information about the dinner guests—most of it humorously derogatory—and he was a tireless raconteur who kept her well entertained with trivialities until the third untouched dessert had been removed. Then he leaned forward again and became more personal.

"I have a confession to make to you, Rebecca. It is my wife who sent me here to beg a favor. She is jealous of the picture you drew of me and would like you to paint an equally flattering one of her. You have my permission to overcharge her as much as you like, since it is her own money she is so eager to spend."

"I'm not a professional artist," Rebecca protested laughingly.

"So much the better. She would die of shame if you were clever enough to paint her as she really is. It would be a kindness if you would grant her wish, and in return she might be able to convince your husband that this Émeraude is not where you should stay while you're in Port-au-Prince."

Surprised by his abrupt seriousness, Rebecca replied impulsively, "I'm afraid that would take a miracle, Captain Riccard. My husband seems to have become very fond of this medieval horror and of the people who own it."

"Then it is good you have come in time to rescue him from their clutches."

"I'll be lucky if I can rescue myself."

"Rescue yourself from what, Cottontop?" Philip asked harshly as he clamped his hands on her shoulders. With a guilty start, Rebecca looked down the table to discover that only she and Riccard were still seated. "My wife," Philip continued rudely, "has developed quite a penchant for needing to be rescued."

Instantly, the mercurial Frenchman reverted to humor and was regaling the angry husband with an amusing account of Londonderry Inn when Madame Falconet insisted that Rebecca join the exodus of women from the room. Twenty minutes later Silas located his son standing alone on the terrace, glaring into his crystal goblet as if the expensive brandy were a bitter dose of calomel tonic.

"Why didn't you tell me how my wife earned her living in New London?" he rasped angrily at his father.

"What the devil are you talking about?"

"According to that damned charlatan Riccard, she made a fool of herself by sitting in the public room at Londonderry Inn like some barmaid, drawing a picture of anyone who'd pay her."

"What's wrong with that?"

"My God, she doesn't have any sense. The Londonderry Inn attracts men who have only one use for women."

"Becky has more sense than you do, son; she was safe enough at the Londonderry. Old Hamden wouldn't have allowed any of his patrons to insult her. Only thing she told me about her activities there was that she reckoned she'd outearned the tarts who'd gone to bed with those sea captains who paid her to draw their pictures. My God, she's a sly puss." Silas chuckled with a mirth he hadn't felt for months.

"It's not funny," Philip raged. "You should have seen her tonight. First, she let one man flirt with her; and then when that damned Riccard left his own seat and took Jean Falconet's at the end of the table, the two of them laughed and whispered throughout the entire meal. Not once did she even look in my direction."

"Don't blame her. It should have been you who rescued her from the pack of French-speaking fops after Jean left the table. As it is, I'm grateful that Riccard had the sense you didn't. He's a good man, and he'll be joining our fleet the next time out."

"You hired him and his ship without consulting me?"

"That's right, son. He did me a favor today that just might save us all some heavy trouble, and he's a more experienced man in these waters than most of our captains."

"I don't like the man, but at the moment he's not my problem. My irresponsible wife is. What the devil am I going to do with her?"

Silas scowled in disapproval of his son before he answered the irritable question. "Shoe's on the other foot, Philip. Question should be what Becky's going to do with you when that French barracuda of yours lights into her. The woman's waiting for you in the entry."

"What the hell is she doing here? Falconet said—"

"That madam does what she pleases around the Falconets. It's her money that's kept them afloat. You couldn't have picked a worse one, son; both of her husbands were slaver scum and she could be worse. Leastwise she's used to getting her own way."

"Not this time she won't, but Rebecca can't stay here even tonight."

"Knew that as soon as I did the investigating you should have."

"Is that why you said you wouldn't be here tonight?"

"Wouldn't be here now if that pair hadn't arrived by boat three hours ago. I don't think the Falconets will give us any more trouble, but there's no way I can shut that woman up. Don't suppose you can either, but you'd better try before Becky gets curious. She's not one to overlook a second damn-fool stunt."

Philip groaned, "She found out about Paulette?"

"Trouble with you, son, you've been spoiled by women all of your life, beginning with your mother. Even as a half-grown sprout, you played fast and loose in a town where a dozen busybodies kept score. I was damned relieved when you finally moved your playground to Quebec so I wouldn't get a full accounting whenever I was in port. Then during an impulsive moment, you marry a bright girl like Becky and expect her to be deaf, dumb, and blind. Of course she heard about your last flings with your old mistress, and you'll be lucky if she doesn't hear about your shenanigans with this new one. I certainly heard about the affair from three of the people I've talked to. Best get started, son. It's not going to get any easier to tell your madam that you've decided to salvage your marriage. I'll take care of Becky."

The obligatory ladies' hour spent in a sitting room adjoining the large *salon de nécessité* was a lesson in patient endurance for Rebecca, with only one moment of pathetic comedy to lighten her boredom. In one of the six cubicles sheltering the commodes, two maids crowded in with a plump Frenchwoman and held the voluminous skirts high off the floor as their mistress squatted down to use the convenience. Cynically, the New England woman wondered what other demeaning tasks the Negro slaves were asked to perform. Certainly a variety of activities were taking place in front of the mirrors—maids unfastening dresses and loosening tight stays, removing wigs and toweling the heads of the perspiring guests, repowdering damp faces and retouching smeared makeup, and rearranging the complicated layers of skirts.

In the sitting room another half-dozen maids were lined up along the walls waving huge palmetto fans in a steady rhythmic pattern, their muscles straining as they maintained the pace. But it was the variety of fans which the Frenchwomen held in front of their faces as they engaged in *tête-à-têtes* with their neighbors that fascinated Rebecca. These expensive ornaments had nothing in common with the more useful palmettos; they were symbols of comparative wealth. Two were costly painted masks with openings for the eyes which allowed the owners to view their competition from concealment, one was made of frothy Argentan lace, another glittered with chips of precious gems, while the others gleamed with mother-of-pearl and delicately lacquered pictures. Her empty hands folded tensely on her lap, Rebecca felt much like a female

Gulliver from Jonathan Swift's fantasy of strange worlds as she composed her features into an agreeable expression and waited for the ordeal to end. She watched her alert hostess silently direct the two maids assigned the task of keeping the long-stemmed glasses full of Madeira wine, reflecting thoughtfully that she'd enjoyed the ritual at the Abenaki village in Maine far more. During their periods of regulated separation from their men, the Indian women harvested the communal crops of butternut squash, pole beans, and corn. Rebecca had enjoyed the company of those women and the hard work; but these idle, pampered Frenchwomen alienated her to the point of total negation.

Silas, not Philip, was waiting for her when the women filed out of their sanctuary, and Rebecca smiled with a tremulous relief at his blunt greeting. "Come on, girl, you and I are getting out of here."

"It won't take me long to pack."

"Housekeeper's already doing it. I'll be bringing your trunks along to you after you and Philip leave."

"For where?"

"His ship. You'll be living there until I locate another home for you."

"Not one like this, I hope."

"No. It'll be your own house this time."

Aware of her father-in-law's preoccupation, Rebecca was silent as he led her through the lantern-lit gardens to the carriage waiting on the broad driveway near the cottage. Fifty feet in the distance she could see a cluster of white-trousered seamen standing near a wagon being loaded by a procession of Negro slaves moving in and out of the small house. Dutifully, she climbed into the dark interior of the carriage and settled on the seat already faintly dampened by the moist tropical air of a port city. Not since the night she'd spent with Simon Parrish on the Connecticut road had she felt so nervous. Away from the glitter of the ballroom, this opulent, decadent estate with its thousands of slaves seemed fraught with unseen danger; and she wondered if any of the Falconets dared walk around their property without armed guards. Rebecca jerked convulsively when the carriage door opened and both her husband and father-in-law joined her.

"The loading's finished so we'll all be leaving together," Silas announced cheerfully; but Philip remained broodingly silent even while he put his arms around his shivering wife. Although he grunted noncommittally when his father announced that he'd ordered the *Reine* towed five-hundred yards from shore and agreed readily enough to the suggestion that he and Rebecca remain out of Port-au-Prince, Philip did not speak directly to his wife until they were aboard, watching her luggage being hoisted onto the deck. Throughout the carriage and boat rides he'd kept his arm tightly around her waist, a gesture she'd considered a mark of affection until she tried to pull away as they stood near the companionway to the aft cabins. When his arm tightened more firmly, she stood where she was and waited until her trunks were stored and the deck cleared of all but the officer and crew on watch.

"Where did you learn to flirt the way you were doing tonight?" Philip asked her suddenly. "Before Riccard took over, you were all but holding hands with the man sitting next to you."

Because Philip had scowled so grimly when Riccard had told him about New London, Rebecca had expected to be scolded about her unique business enterprise five months earlier, but never about the kindly man who'd helped her at the dinner party tonight.

"That poor man," she exploded.

"That poor man, Cottontop, has been challenged to a dozen duels for seducing other men's wives."

Recalling the repugnant old man with the monocle who had ogled her so intently, Rebecca burst into laughter. She really was a backwoods innocent when it came to judging men! Between burst of giggles, she denied her husband's implied accusation. "My honor won't be needing any defense, Philip. The only seduction he performed upon me was to point out which fork to use and what wine to drink. And the only thing Captain Riccard asked me to do was to paint a picture of Madame Riccard."

"You can't blame me for being angry, Cottontop; you glanced at me only one time during that entire dinner."

"How would you know? You were so busy entertaining those two French tabby cats, you wouldn't have felt anything if I'd thrown a dart at you. So you can let go of me now and tell me what cabin I'm to use."

"What do you mean what cabin? You'll be with me. You are still my wife, regardless of your adventures with other men."

"I've been your wife for the past eight hours, six of which you spent ignoring me." No longer softened by laughter, her voice rose steadily in volume as she continued, "As for our marriage, I've seen you less than one month in ten; so as soon as I earn enough money, I'm getting out of your life and going to England." With a sudden swift lunge, she broke free of his restraining arm and ran toward the forward companionway leading to the crew's quarters.

Philip overtook her ten feet from the entrance and imprisoned her once again, using both arms this time. "You fool! You damned little fool!" he muttered before he kissed her with an ungentle harshness rooted more in anger than in passion. Had she resisted him, that anger might have turned into violence because he had no defenses against the jealousy that had inflamed him at dinner. Still too upset about his wife to be diplomatic to a discarded mistress, he'd told Annette bluntly that she'd never been anything more to him than a temporary companion. Her vengeful taunt that she'd make certain his wife would be equally temporary had added a bitter certainty to his anger. Rebecca was already planning to leave him, and she'd gained a self-confident resiliency that convinced him that her next flight would be a permanent one.

Seconds into the punishing kiss he discovered that she'd also become more boldly passionate as she wrapped her slender arms about his neck and returned the pressure with a soft warmth. The desire that he'd denied himself for those long, traumatic hours since he'd first seen her in the cottage exploded into throbbing life, blotting out his anger and guilt. Breaking off the kiss, he lifted her easily into his arms and carried her swiftly back across the deck, down the companionway steps, through the larger cabin, and into the bedroom before he stood her on her feet and resumed the interrupted kiss. With a speed that threatened the survival of the delicate black lace, his agile fingers undid buttons, hooks, and ties.

"If you don't want your dress ruined, you'd better finish the job," he muttered thickly and stepped away from her to remove his own clothing. For just a moment as she knelt to pull off his boots that she had polished earlier, Philip relaxed his tense impatience. As he looked down at her loosened hair frosted silver by the pallid glow of the soft light streaming in through the opened transom windows, his slender wife seemed ethereal—a moon maiden the Indian boy had called her. In bed, however, a few minutes later there was nothing unearthly or remote about her. Despite her newly acquired sophistication, he'd half expected a return to virginal reluctance, but she was passionately receptive to his caresses, even those far more intimate than he used with her before. But as she reciprocated with caresses of her own which were disturbingly effective if not entirely expert, the jealous speculation that had plagued him throughout the dinner party intensified. Just how innocent had those sketching sessions at the Londonderry been? And who else had she charmed with that challenging boldness of hers?

Experimentally, he forced her lips apart and invaded her mouth with his tongue, his suspicions subsiding slightly as she tensed in surprise and her eyes opened wide. Reassured that it was her first time for such an innovation, but oddly relieved that she had not rejected it, he relaxed in enjoyment of her increasing sensuality. In contrast to her trembling vibrancy, his mistresses and the mulatto had been merely skilled professionals. Philip closed his eyes and unleashed the self-control he'd tried to maintain.

It was a reunion that left both of them breathless and drenched in perspiration. Philip had intended it to be a skillful seduction that would entice a reluctant and elusive bride into becoming a resident wife; but tropical heat and a lengthy abstention on Rebecca's part had all but obliterated his initial intentions. At some point during the foreplay he'd lost all awareness of her relative inexperience and responded to her eager invitation with hands and lips that explored her firm young body with a possessive thoroughness. The act itself was an explosion of ecstasy that shook them both with its mutual intensity.

"This should have been our greeting earlier today, Cottontop," he murmured as he rolled to his side still holding her in his arms. "From now on when I return to port, we don't say a word to each other until afterward."

"Who'd have anything to talk about then?" she mumbled with a muted giggle, and promptly fell asleep.

Vaguely discontent with her lack of sentimentality, Philip remembered that he'd yet to win a declaration of love from her. Such avowals had virtually flowed from the lips of the two older Frenchwomen, even while one was betraying him with treason and the other plotting a permanent entrapment. But not Cottontop, he reflected ruefully; she never relaxed her defensive guard long enough for him to know how she really felt.

As if she were attuned to his disturbed thoughts, Rebecca moved restlessly in her sleep, and her hand shifted position on his chest, exposing her narrow gold wedding band in the pale moonlight. Gazing at that inexpensive symbol with a dawning comprehension, Philip realized that she'd already come to terms with a marriage that had yet to offer her much security or happiness. Even knowing about Paulette, she'd still returned to him; and even though she'd threatened to leave him just minutes before he'd made love to her, she'd returned his passion in full measure. His last waking thought was a vow to be worthy of her love and trust.

Long past dawn the next morning, when he awakened and reached out for her, that admirable sentiment was replaced first by fear and then by anger. His elusive wife was neither by his side nor in either cabin! After pulling on the short canvas trousers he often wore aboard in tropical waters, he raced first to the galley and then, at Jed's suggestion, to the aft section of the deck. She was standing with her hands on the heavy oak taffrail, staring out toward the distant Gonâve Island. As silently as an Indian he crossed the deck and bracketed her against the rail with his arms, smiling at her when she spun around to face him.

"I thought I told you a long time ago that I want you by my side when I wake up in the morning," he scolded lightly.

Wrapping her arms around his neck, Rebecca stretched up and kissed him. "You also once told me that you weren't the kind of man who could sleep through a kiss delivered by a pretty woman. But this morning all you did was roll over and mutter in your sleep."

"Next time just keep on kissing me until I do wake up. It'll save my having to dress before I can even look for you. And one more word of warning, fondling; you'd better damn well be wearing more than a thin blouse and skirt when you go walking alone on this ship."

Impudently, she tweaked one of the black curls on his bare chest and scoffed, "Compared to you, I'm overdressed."

Grinning down at her upturned face, he once more picked her up and carried her into the bedroom cabin. When he released her, she discovered that he'd already unfastened her skirt. Peeling off her white blouse, she stepped out of the circle of printed calico and smiled at her husband with impish mockery.

"You're a prude, Philip Keane. Women have as much right as men to be comfortable when it's this hot. I don't imagine the native Indians ever wore much of anything."

"If I'd known three years ago that underneath all that ink you were a forest nymph, I'd have taken you then and saved myself a peck of trouble."

Rebecca's lips curled in a derisive smile. "Three years ago if I'd so much as winked at you, you'd have outrun every Indian in camp just to get as far away from me as you could. And even yesterday you didn't have the slightest idea of what you were going to do with me."

Grinning back at her with a predatory gleam in his eyes, Philip pulled her down onto the rumpled bed. "I do now, Cottontop," he promised her and proceeded with a demonstration that left no doubt about his intention. Fired by her uninhibited lack of modesty, he caressed her pliant body until she responded with seductive overtures as arousing as his own. Rebecca had embarked on a campaign of her own.

While Philip slept that morning, Rebecca had faced an unpleasant fact. Either she must become an exciting bed partner who could make him forget women like Paulette Burnell or resign herself to the unpleasant fate of being an ignored wife. It was one thing, she'd reflected unhappily, to threaten to be unfaithful herself; but it was quite another for her to earn the social forgiveness that a man would. Her husband had considered himself quite justified in accusing her of misconduct without evidence while he himself consorted openly with his mistress. She had one week to change the social system for Philip and herself; if she failed, she would be the one to end their marriage. Unfortunately, since she had no book of instruction in the art of husband captivation and seduction, she would have to improvise her own techniques.

That at least some of her caresses succeeded she knew instantly when he responded and followed her lead until their mutual passion obliterated all deliberate seduction. Together they drove their bodies toward the elusive goal of ecstasy until they lay panting on the warm bed in the aftermath of the drawn-out climax. And when Philip held her tightly pressed against him during the long moments it took their heartbeats to return to a slowed-down normal, she felt wonderfully content.

Throughout the silent breakfast that followed, neither of them paid much attention to the exotic mixture of fried pork and bananas that Jed served them. Neither of them made any attempt to share reactions with the other or to interrupt those reactions with trivial conversation. Jed finally galvanized them into speech as he was clearing the table.

"We lowered the sail gig like you told us, Cap'n. You still plannin' on takin' Becky out?"

"I am as soon as you stow our lunch aboard. We'll be heading for Gonâve Island."

"Then you'll be a durn fool, Cap'n, takin' Becky off this ship lookin' like she does. There's more than one cutthroat sailor out there who'd slit your gullet t' git a chance at her," the old man warned bluntly. "Ain't enough wind today fer you t' stay ahead of a longboat bein' rowed by the murderous scum."

Speculatively, Philip studied his wife's face and admitted the truth of Jed's shrewd observation. Despite the composure of her features, there was an underlying glow that any randy, woman-hungry sailor could recognize even from the deck of a ship.

"Best you take me and four marines along fer safety, Cap'n," the persistent cook continued. "From what I heered ashore there're three slavers anchored out there and a half-dozen other ships flyin' furrin flags."

One look at her husband's face warned Rebecca that he was going to follow Jed's advice, and the prospect of chaperons ended her enthusiasm. "Jonathan used to take Abigail and me out in his gig," she asserted with an innocent smile, "and we were safe enough because he made us wear seamen's clothes. You remember, Jed," she added sweetly, "I borrowed your mackintosh whenever it was cold."

"This ain't Casco Bay, Becky, and you ain't a little girl anymore."

"That's why I'll look more like a member of the crew," she insisted glibly, "especially if you bring me a big enough one of those striped jerseys and a hat to cover my hair. But the pants and sandals will have to fit me."

Half an hour later the disgruntled cook returned with an armful of clothing and insisted on remaining with the cap'n while she retired to the bedroom. To her dismay even the smallest of the sandals were uncomfortably large and her pantalets were too long for the ugly, wide-legged canvas britches. With a grimace of distaste she removed the underpants, secured the sandals with lengths of heavy cord, and solved the third problem by lacing a camisole tightly over her breasts before donning the largest of the jerseys. But not until Philip had braided her hair into a flat pigtail hanging down her back and jammed the low-crowned, wide-brimmed hat over her forehead did he approve the costume. Jed grunted his satisfaction only after he'd removed the red triangular scarf from around his own neck and tied it around hers.

As she followed her identically dressed husband across the deck and down the Jacob's ladder, Rebecca smothered a triumphant giggle; the three men holystoning the wood deck had not even glanced up as she passed them, and the sailor who helped Philip cast off gave her only a bored glance of nonrecognition. Her successful disguise, however, did not inhibit her as she snuggled next to her husband throughout the three-hour trip to the emerald-green island that was nestled equidistant between the two long peninsulas of Saint-Domingue. More confident than she'd ever been before of her power to attract the temperamental man she'd married, she was emboldened enough to caress him liberally as he operated the tiller.

It was a rude shock for her to learn upon landing in a small cove that her distraction had not pleased him in spite of the fact that his attention had been more on her than on the sail billowing from the small mast. As Philip lowered himself into the waist-deep water to tie the line around a rock jutting seaward from the sandy beach, he ordered her brusquely to carry the tarp and picnic supplies ashore. Returning to the boat before she'd complied, he helped her into the water and piled her arms high with the folded canvas, the food Jed had prepared, the small jug of rum punch, and, for good measure, the boat's water cask. Thus burdened, she struggled toward the beach while he followed, carrying two pistols and his sword. After dumping her load on the dry sand, she spun around to face her unchivalrous husband only to be told to spread the tarp in the shade of the mangrove trees.

"And put the water cask in the pool at the roots of the trees. Both of our tempers will need cooling by the time we return from reconnaissance," he added curtly.

Feeling the same humiliating resentment she had on the day she'd crawled after him during their escape from Falmouth, Rebecca followed his instructions with a sullen anger and then plopped down on the stained canvas.

"I'm not going anyplace until you tell me what it is I'm supposed to have done wrong," she announced coldly.

"Just this, Cottontop; you seem to have lost every shred of modesty. A man is supposed to do the pursuing, not the woman."

Averting her eyes as the flush of embarrassment stained her cheeks, she muttered, "It'll never happen again."

"I'm not really angry, fondling. It was just that you—that you distracted me when I was trying to concentrate on sailing. Now let's find out if this place is safe."

It was the odd hesitation in his voice that ended Rebecca's momentary mortification; the reason he gave was not the real cause of his anger. But whatever the cause, there was no escaping the conclusion that her carefully planned campaign had failed in its purpose. She still had much to learn about men in general and about her husband in particular. The lessons began immediately with a silent walk around a wide perimeter of the beach, through a mangrove swamp, and up a small hill overlooking a verdant inland valley. In lead position Philip carried only his sword, but both pistols were held firmly by the rope belt around his waist. Back on the beach Rebecca broke the tense silence.

"I didn't know the Indians here were dangerous."

"They aren't. The Spanish killed most of the Caribs; and what Arawaks are left, hide from us. Escaped slaves are the ones who're deadly, Cottontop; they're more savage than the wildest Hurons who ever took to the warpath. I don't know whether there are any on this island, but there are thousands in the mountains of Saint-Domingue. That's why the planters have to maintain small armies of guards; they're not even safe from the freed slaves."

"The ones I saw my first day here didn't even look human."

"Most of those in Port-au-Prince use a drug in order to stand the misery of their lives. They chew the leaves of the coca tree to forget their troubles, and wind up as derelicts. I've lost more than one good seaman that way."

"The same cocoa we drink?" Rebecca asked in horror.

"No, those beans come from the cacao tree; it's the coca leaves that are narcotic. Come on, I want you to see what those leaves look like so you'll never be tricked or tempted.''

During that second walk, Rebecca was shown the eight-foot coca shrub and the forty-foot cacao tree; she sampled the sweet fruit of the mangrove tree and had her hands slapped when she reached for the large, ripe berries hanging from another tree not ten feet away.

"That's the manchineel," Philip warned her sharply. "It's the deadliest fruit in the Caribbean. The Indians used to tip their arrows in the manzanilla poison to kill their enemies."

"I wouldn't eat anything that grows in this place," she declared in disgust.

"Oh, yes, you will, Cottontop," he assured her good-naturedly, his earlier sour humor forgotten. "If I can locate my favorite fruit, you'll have a dinner tonight you'll never forget."

What seemed like a thousand trees later, her elated husband pointed to a densely foliaged tree that looked like all the others to a tired and deflated Rebecca. Its only claim to distinction was green fruit instead of red or yellow—melon-sized, pear-shaped, scaly green fruit.

"Hold the bottom of your shirt up, Cottontop; we're going to need a sack to carry them in," Philip directed as he began picking the largest ones.

He used the communal *we*, but Rebecca was the one who carried the dozen drupes back to the beach, her hands aching from the strain of suspending the hem of her jersey in front of her like some primitive animal mother with a pouch full of heavy, burdensome young.

"The Indians called them *ahuacatl*," Philip informed her companionably, "but the Spanish word is *aguacate*. You eat them raw with fish or fruit. Come on, let's store them on the boat. You look as if you could stand a little cooling off."

With her jaw clenched tightly shut to prevent the flow of angry words that bubbled in her mouth, she plowed through the water and stood mutinously still until Philip had carefully placed the ugly fruit into a lashed-down container aboard. However, his next condescending, inequitable, and tutorial action ended her mute acceptance of his authority. When she poured herself a mug of the rum punch, he smilingly removed it from her hands and diluted the contents with water. Although he repeated the process for himself, she calculated cynically that hers was three times more watered down.

The hot words that had been forming for hours tumbled out. "Stop treating me like an idiot child, Philip Keane. I can take care of myself, even on these cursed islands; and I don't need you to tell me what to drink or what to do. So you can forget any more instructions you have planned for me today; as far as I'm concerned, school is out!"

"Only one more lesson, Cottontop," he responded with a glint of humor. "I want you to learn how to load, fire, and clean these pistols. They'll be added protection for you while I'm at sea."

"I refuse to be left behind again."

"It has to be that way, fondling. I wouldn't be able to keep my mind on business if you were aboard."

"Why not? You didn't have any trouble yesterday, and you've treated me like a member of your crew today. It seems to me that—"

"Shut up, Cottontop, and pay attention. Guns are very complicated—"

"Shut up yourself, Philip. My father made me practice with one of those ugly things until I hit the target more often than he did."

"If you know so much about guns, why didn't you try to grab Roger's when he was busy controlling a team of horses?"

"Roger didn't trust me any more than you do. He tied my hands to a railing."

Grinning down at his irate wife, Philip admonished her lightly, "He'd have done better to keep your tongue from wagging. You say some outrageous things when you're angry. Of course I trust you, Cottontop. Just to show you how much, I'm going to let you stand guard while I catch the other half of our dinner. And while I'm gone, you can drink all the rum punch you like."

Still smiling with an amusement that infuriated her, he

laid the pistols and sword by her side and ran lightly to the water's edge, where he stripped off his clothing and draped the garments carefully over a dry rock. For the better part of an hour he swam lazily across the shallow water, diving at irregular intervals to bring up a sea creature Rebecca recognized as lobster. After each successful dive, he swam to the boat to deposit his catch. Satisfied when the number of lobsters equalled that of the *aguacates,* Philip waded to shore and returned to the picnic tarp.

Standing a few feet away with a pistol in each hand, Rebecca turned alertly toward her husband and said quietly, "The birds stopped making noise a few minutes ago. I think we should leave."

Philip stooped swiftly to pick up his sword before he grabbed her arm and propelled her swiftly toward the water. "Get aboard and raise the sail. And for God's sake, keep those pistols dry." With one swift stroke of his sword, the line was severed and the sail gig floated clear of the land.

Two hundred feet offshore he spotted the intruders— shadowy, dark-skinned men who blended with the multiple-rooted mangrove trees as they stared out at the fleeing white couple.

"Take the tiller," Philip ordered tersely. "I want to make sure they don't have a canoe hidden somewhere or try to follow us by swimming. With this little wind they might overtake us, and then I'd have to use the pistols to discourage them. When did you first notice the bird thing, Cottontop?"

"Just when you started out of the water, but before that I'd heard other sounds. They're not as quiet as Indians."

"My God, why didn't you get to the boat?"

"If I'd run, they might have come out of hiding sooner. I wasn't sure I could warn you in time because you weren't always close enough to the boat."

"Were you terrified, sweetheart?"

"Yes, but at the time I really didn't think they'd hurt me."

"They'd have killed both of us to get the boat. In calm weather this gig could sail twenty of them to freedom."

"Where could runaway slaves ever be free?" she demanded scornfully.

"On any of a hundred uninhabited islands or in South America or Florida."

"Well, those pathetic wretches didn't steal your boat, and they're not pursuing us. So you can take your tiller back now."

Having been on his knees resting the pistols on the boat's gunwale in tense expectation of attack, Philip had been too preoccupied to remember that in addition to the picnic paraphernalia, he'd also left his clothing on the beach. He discovered the lack in the most painful of ways when he sat down on the sun-hot helmsman's bench next to his wife. His cursing leap upward rocked the frail craft so violently Rebecca was forced to exert all of her strength to maintain even a minimal control of the tiller. Once more on his knees, Philip reached up swiftly to lend his strength in steadying the pitching boat.

As soon as the emergency was past, Rebecca relinquished her hold and peeled off the striped jersey she was wearing. "Slit the neck opening bigger and use it as a skirt," she suggested. "I'll handle the boat for a few more minutes. And you needn't worry about my proving an embarrass-ment; the undergarment I have on is no more revealing than the evening gown I wore last night."

The final part of her declaration had been in response to her husband's frown when she'd removed the shirt. Recalling the remark he'd made earlier about her lack of modesty, she watched stoically as he yanked the mutilated garment over his naked hips before rejoining her on the bench. Quite obviously he considered modesty necessary only for her; and just as obviously he had no intention of relaxing his vigilance concerning her attire or her education.

"I'll return it before we reach port," he temporized stiffly. "That thing you have on is as tempting as nothing at all. In the meantime I want you to be able to handle this boat in any emergency. You were too slow in tacking into the wind back there at the beach, and you're fighting the tiller rather than guiding it. Didn't Jonathan teach you anything about navigation?"

"It wasn't necessary in Casco Bay," she replied wearily.

"It's always necessary, Cottontop. If it'd been foggy when you got us away from the beach, you could have started off in the wrong direction. That's why I want you to learn how to read a mariner's compass."

For almost three hours Rebecca endured his calm, persistent instruction until the long, graceful hull of the *Reine* hove into view, and Philip took control. Still fifty feet away he bellowed out orders for Louis and Leon to fetch some replacement clothing; and not until Rebecca was clad in another outsized jersey was she allowed to clamber up the Jacob's ladder. The last sound she heard before she reached the sanctuary of the empty cabin was her husband's voice arranging to have the gig's equipment replaced and the lobsters and *aguacates* prepared for dinner. Rebecca shut off the sound with a violent slam of the heavy oak door and stared about the large outer cabin with an angry distaste. There was no place in this masculine world for her; and if she remained, she could expect little else than repetitions of the disastrous day she'd just spent in her husband's company. He was a temperamental despot whose unpredictable moods vacillated without warning from passion to anger to condescending contempt; and unless she could reach England and the independence that her own money could provide, she would be miserable under his fluctuating domination.

Thoughtfully, she rummaged through the oldest of her trunks and removed two of the sketch pads and the box of graphite she'd purchased in Baltimore and the remainder of her gold sovereigns, a slender hoard that totaled under thirty pounds. From another trunk she dug out the canvas duffel bag she'd used aboard the *Falmouth Star* and carefully tucked the articles inside. England was no longer the impossible goal it'd been in New London; according to the information Philip had revealed today, Port-au-Prince was four sailing days away from the British crown colony of Jamaica. Another two days of navigational instructions, Rebecca reasoned, should be sufficient for her to make the voyage successfully, providing she could locate the right chart.

When she first opened the chart locker, she stared in dismay at the profusion of stored maps; but like all of Philip's possessions, they were arranged in impeccable order. Within minutes she'd located the well-marked Jamaica chart and was so intent on copying it that she didn't hear Jed knock or enter the room until he spoke.

"What in tarnation you doin', Becky? Cap'n would skin you alive if he caught you messin' with them things."

"No, he wouldn't," she disclaimed with a glib mendacity. "It's his idea that I learn to navigate that damned boat of his."

The old man chuckled with an understanding sympathy. "Cap'n can be a mite overbearin' once he makes up his mind, but you won't be needin' charts. He wouldn't risk takin' the gig outside of protected waters."

"Why not?"

"Them's enemy shippin' lanes out there, so you best put that map away. Anyways, you got other things to do right now. Cap'n sent me to tell you that dinner's goin' to be in the officers' quarters in an hour. His paw and some other cap'ns come aboard about ten minutes ago, so I reckoned you'd be wantin' a bath afore you dressed."

In no mood to face a discerning father-in-law whose shrewd eyes would instantly detect the extent of discord between his son and herself, Rebecca shook her head. "Tell the captain that I'm too sunburned and tired to see anyone, and I won't be wanting what you're serving them for dinner."

"Cap'n ain't used t' havin' his orders disobeyed, Becky."

"Then don't tell him until the last minute."

Reluctantly, Jed left the cabin, returning shortly with a tray of fruit and cheese while two crewmen filled the bathtub with hot water. Long before the appointed dinner hour, Rebecca was in bed and sound asleep; her exhaustion had not been merely a manufactured excuse. She didn't stir when her irritated husband strode into the cabin, only to leave silently a few minutes later. Awakened by the ruddy sunlight of late dawn, she lay quietly by his side, her anger of the day before quiescently subdued and her plans for a quixotic escape momentarily in abeyance.

In retrospect, yesterday's misadventure seemed more humorous than traumatic. She'd failed to take into account the fact that her bizarre costume had made her look like a cross between an ungainly zebra and a street urchin. No wonder Philip hadn't even tried to kiss her. But he'd been just as funny in his attempt to sound like a church elder, especially since his attitude toward religious propriety was more irreverent than her own. She chuckled aloud when she thought of what a pair of improper fools they must have appeared leaping through the water to reach the safety of the boat. Still giggling, she jerked only slightly when Philip's arm reached out for her and he murmured sleepily, "What's so amusing, Cottontop?"

"People and their illusions."

"Mine or yours?"

"In general."

"I don't believe that."

"Mine then."

"Which one of yours?"

"That you'd finally begun to take me seriously."

"What makes you think I don't?"

Rebecca shrugged restlessly and inched away from him; he was beginning to sound disturbingly familiar. "The way you treated me yesterday," she replied vaguely.

"Because I didn't make love to you on the beach?"

"As things turned out, it was just as well you didn't. At least one of us still had clothing when we left."

"I'm sorry about the way I treated you, but I was upset. You've changed, Cottontop, and I'd like to know why and how."

Startled by the accusation, she propped herself up on one elbow and stared at him. "You mean because I tried to flirt with you on the way there?" she asked in amazement.

Equally aroused, he glared back at her. "It wasn't the intention I objected to, it was the way you did it. When I left New London, you were damned close to being an innocent; but you aren't anymore. Between then and now you've learned a hell of a lot about men and what—what attracts them. Just how well *did* you know those captains you sketched while you were on display at a public inn?"

No longer ignorant about the cause of his anger, Rebecca felt an icy fury of her own begin to form. "I know that most of them were married men," she countered with a deliberate insolence.

"Most of them were hardened privateers who were damn well used to taking what they want," he lashed back, "so you can stop acting like a naive schoolgirl."

Pushing herself out of the bed, she walked swiftly toward the necessaries room, not even bothering to face her furious husband when she responded to his taunt in a flat voice devoid of emotion. "I stopped being naive about married privateers some months ago, Philip."

When she emerged from the washroom, she was dressed in a seaman's garb, carrying a small bundle of towels which contained her hairbrush and a bar of soap. In the main cabin she quickly shoved a few other essentials into her duffel and left without a backward glance.

Cursing himself for having opened the Pandora's box of his own infidelities, Philip was sitting moodily at the dining table a half hour later while an officious Jed poured his coffee.

"Becky goin' to be wantin' her breakfast too, Cap'n?"

"My wife is someplace about the ship, Jed. I'll be looking for her in a few minutes."

"What's she doin' wanderin' about alone?"

"God knows!"

"Cap'n, if you don't mind my sayin' so, you got a durn poor way of takin' care of her."

"I'm fully aware of my shortcomings."

Philip had been grimly conscious of his own stupidity since she'd flung those damnable words at him, leaving him no doubt about their meaning. And he had no one to blame but himself! Why hadn't he taken his own advice and made love to her without his usual preliminary criticism? Yesterday he'd acted the fool simply because she'd been uninhibited enough to take the initiative, to addle his senses until he felt like a drunken sailor on shore leave. He'd wanted to break every rule of sensible seamanship and drop the sail in the middle of a busy ship's channel and satisfy the wild desire she'd aroused in him. Instead, he'd rebuilt his own defensive barriers; it had gone against his grain to be dominated by a slip of a girl who could tempt him to the point of stupidity. And he'd turned that resentment into suspicion and, eventually this morning, into an open accusation.

Philip moved restlessly in his chair. Why the hell was he so jealous? He didn't really believe that she'd made good her threat, but damn, every man she met seemed to succumb to that wide-eyed charm of hers. In the past his father had called her an amusing irritation, but now he championed her like a protective mother hen. Even that posturing ass Riccard had rushed to her defense with unstinting praise for her talent and courage. She'd always had that courage, Philip reflected uneasily; yesterday she'd remained calm in a dangerous emergency that would have sent most women screaming hysterically into the water. Why hadn't he had the sense to praise her rather than lecturing her as if she were some half-witted cabin boy? Jed's precipitous return ended Philip's gloomy self-castigation with a shattering finality.

"What in tarnation is Becky doing out in the gig alone, Cap'n?" the old man shouted.

Galvanized into action, Philip swore all the time he was ordering a longboat lowered, his hands gripping the rail as he watched the light craft being maneuvered with a fair degree of competence around the ships at anchor some two hundred yards away. Christ, she was heading for open water rather than the docks! The men would have to row double time if they were to overtake her; but a dozen of them lined up with zealous determination and Jed was already seated on the coxswain's bench. It took half an hour of gut-straining labor for the heavily laden boat to catch up with the lighter, wind-driven craft and another few minutes of expert seamanship before Philip could board the gig and join his fugitive wife. After listening with a silent fury to Rebecca's apology to the crew, he told Jed to triple the rum allotment for the rowers before he took control of the sailboat.

"Where the devil did you think you were going?" he asked quietly.

"Jamaica."

"In God's name, why Jamaica?"

"To locate a ship headed for England."

"If you wanted to get away from me, you could have gone to my father."

"It's not your father's problem."

"When did you decide on Jamaica?"

"I thought about it last night, but I didn't decide until this morning."

"Just because we had an argument?"

"You don't argue, Philip; you criticize and you pass unfounded judgments, but you never argue."

His eyes sparked with an angry glint when she moved abruptly to a forward bench and sat down with her back toward him. "If you try shifting position again without giving me warning, Cottontop, we could both be overboard. And unless you're a damn good swimmer, you'd never reach the shore. Can you swim at all?"

"No."

"Good. For once you can't run away. Just how were you planning to reach Jamaica?"

"I borrowed your chart with the compass markings on it."

"What else besides the boat and the chart did you borrow?"

"Your pistols and four bottles of wine."

"Anything else useful in that bag of yours?"

"Only my hairbrush and some soap."

"No food?"

"The fruit and cheese Jed brought me last night. With the sea biscuits and water already aboard, I'd have survived."

"No, you wouldn't have. The minute you went to sleep, you'd have drifted off course and eventually washed ashore on some island as barren as the one just ahead. That's where we'll be staying until you promise never to try another damn fool stunt like this one."

Rebecca watched in mutinous silence as Philip nosed the craft into a rocky inlet of a small island half a mile off the southern peninsula of Saint-Domingue. But she didn't refuse his order to help him unload the boat and construct a makeshift tent with the boat's oars and sail in the lee of a rocky bluff, nor did she protest aloud his announcement of an investigative walk around the bleak island. On the debris-strewn beach which extended only on the channel side, they located a stand of stunted mangrove trees and one small rivulet of fresh water winding down from the craggy bluffs which occupied most of the island's surface.

"I hope you like fish," Philip commented dryly, "because that's going to be our main diet. You'll find some hooks and a pole lashed to the bow of the boat, but you have to dig in the sand for your bait. I'll hustle up some driftwood while you catch our breakfast."

Relieved to escape from his disapproving domination, Rebecca spent the next two hours in an increasing state of excitement, catching an assortment of fish more vividly colored than any she'd seen in Falmouth. Twice she'd gone into the water to subdue one of her captured quarry. After the last such effort, she looked up to see her husband observing her.

"I think the fish looks better than you do, Cottontop," he taunted her with a broad smile.

Flushing with renewed anger, Rebecca dropped the fish at his feet and walked huffily back to camp.

"Get out of those wet clothes," he called after her. "You'll find my jersey inside the tent."

She obeyed him only because her own soaking jersey dragged somewhere below her knees and the coarse canvas britches chafed her tender skin. Remembering his frequent insults about her hair, she brushed it with a savage vigor until her scalp tingled. When she emerged from the shelter to spread her own garments over dry rocks, she noted with satisfaction that Philip watched her with more appreciative eyes while they ate the fish he'd cooked on spitting sticks over the small fire.

"What kind of fish were they?" she asked curiously, instantly regretting the impulse. His laughter was neither flattering nor grateful.

"A mess of throwbacks mainly. I kept the bonefish for bait, but the shipjack, snook, and cobia were undersized and bony. Later I'll show you how to get a better catch when you're shore fishing, but right now we're going to wash up. In the tropics the odor of fish can smother you. Come on, Cottontop, you've rested long enough. I'll race you to the water."

Ten feet from the foamy edge he turned around to shout at her, "Take that shirt off, Cottontop. Didn't anyone ever teach you to remove your clothing before taking a bath?"

That it wasn't to be a traditional bath, by any stretch of the imagination, Rebecca discovered as Philip propelled her forcibly toward deep water, where he released his supporting hands. Gasping in terror when she surfaced, she swam desperately toward shore, surpassing her six-stroke limit by a dozen or more flailing motions of her arms. Grinning at his screaming wife, Philip dragged her backward once more into deep water; but the third time she eluded his grasp and raced through the shallow water, across the sand, and into the tent.

"Don't you dare!" she shrieked as she heard him pounding after her. But this time his intentions were not another dunking in the warm water. Tackling her from behind, he absorbed the weight of her body with his own muscular strength as they fell together onto the packed sand, and he kissed her before she had time to protest. His attack with his hands and lips on her sensibilities was expertly thorough, overcoming the restraints she'd placed on her own participation. Long before he claimed her sun-warmed body, she'd forgotten her resolve to remain unresponsive and concentrated blindly on the searing need for fulfillment. She was panting with physical and emotional exhaustion when he collapsed on top of her, breathing as if he too had been running uphill.

There was nothing she could say in her own defense; she'd been as passionately unrestrained as the immoral adventuress he had accused her of being. Twice she'd experienced the exquisite pleasure-pain of ecstasy before he'd reached his climax, and she'd been as shameless as an animal in heat. Fervently she hoped he'd not remember her fingers digging into his back and buttocks, her lips seeking his with a mindless sensuality throughout. When he moved onto his side, she glanced apprehensively at his face, expecting to see a reoccurrence of his earlier suspicious disapproval. Instead, he was smiling as he caressed her face and gently closed her eyes.

The sound that startled her awake was a change in the rhythmic pattern of the surrounding sea. For a moment she listened contentedly until the memory of the twenty-foot bores of her native Maine helped her identify the altered pattern as incoming tide. Shaking Philip awake, she whispered urgently, "The water will cover us if we stay here."

"No, it won't, sweetheart," he murmured sleepily. "Tides don't change more than a foot or two here, but it's time to get up anyway if I'm going to catch the supper I promised. Lord, I feel like a porcupine with all this sand."

They worked separately during the late afternoon hours because it took longer for Rebecca to rinse the sand from her hair. While Philip busied himself with the task of tying multiple hooks to the fishing line and casting it far out into deeper water, she rearranged their sleeping quarters. The tent itself was much smaller when she finished, but it now had a canvas floor. Indian style, she scooped out a pit in the nearby sand and surrounded it with flat rocks before she started a fire to toast the unappetizing sea biscuits. Rummaging in the boat to seek out additional equipment, she located two dirty drinking mugs and a long metal rod that would serve as a more permanent cooking spit than wooden sticks.

When Philip returned to camp with two fish, each one larger than the four of Rebecca's combined, he ignored the improvements she'd made and concentrated his attention on that one metal rod.

"Where did you find it, Cottontop?" he demanded.

"In the cracks of the floorboards aboard the gig. What is it?"

"You don't know as much about guns as you claimed if you can't recognize a ramrod."

"It's too long for a musket."

"But not for an American rifle. One of the marines claimed to have lost his rod during the Jamaica raid."

"How could a soldier reload fast enough with that long a barrel?"

"It's difficult, but the long gun is three times more accurate at three times the distance. It's a weapon that'll give us the edge over anything the enemy has, especially for our marines. The man who lost that ramrod is in for a reprimand."

Sorry that she'd ever found the thing, since Philip's attention was now far removed from her, Rebecca hung the fish over the fire and handed her frowning husband a mug of wine. But not until long after they'd finished eating did he notice the other improvements. In a world of his own, he talked about his life at sea—the intense excitement of mastering a ship during a storm and the black fury he'd felt when Mark Stoneham and sixty other good men were brutally murdered. As the rising moon cast its soft light over the lonely scene, Rebecca listened to her husband describe other events in his life at sea—his first voyage as a captain at the age of twenty, his embarrassment and fear when a Spanish privateer had stripped his small brig of cargo and supplies, and his own determined mastery of both smuggling and privateering.

As fascinated as she was by his revelations, Rebecca realized with a gloomy foreboding that she'd been worried about the wrong mistress. Philip Keane belonged to the sea, and even the most exciting of women would hold his interest only when he was ashore, away from the turbulent challenges of trackless expanses of saltwater.

CHAPTER
9

DURING the next four days the ramrod remained suspended over the fire pit, and Philip limited his conversation about the sea to fishing and swimming. But for Rebecca that innocuous rod had become a symbol of the future pattern of her married life. In the short weeks between months-long voyages, he would be her ardent lover, provided, of course, that Paulette or some other mistress did not prove more appealing, and provided that his beloved ships did not demand his total attention even while in port.

There was a second niggling concern about those inevitable separations that also bothered her. Slipped into his daily conversational offerings were subtle directives about the do's and don'ts of her life while he was at sea. She was to limit her activities to the home and her social contacts to the people he deemed safe. Despite her growing competence in swimming, she wasn't to go into the water without him; and she could use the gig only if she wore her sailor clothes, was accompanied by a guard, and remained within the confines of the harbor. Despite her irritation with his overprotective domination, Rebecca held her peace, unwilling to endanger the pleasant harmony of their relationship.

Philip was a sensuous, virile man with volatile emotions never far beneath the surface; and that driving passion was now concentrated exclusively on her. An expert lover, he reached for her compulsively during those nights and days on the barren island, aroused equally by the sight of her nudity—often necessitated by a lack of sufficient clothing—and by the inadvertent brush of her body as they slept in the limited space within the small tent. Even his bantering condescension in casual conversation now reflected a gratifyingly warm possessiveness, and he was no longer reluctant to display the growing emotional attachment he felt for her. On the last morning of their spartan isolation from the chaotic world of Port-au-Prince, Rebecca was giddily happy that she'd managed not to provoke any argument with him. Although he still avoided saying "I love you," he came very close to admitting a permanent commitment.

"I'll miss you, sweetheart, when you aren't by my side when I wake up in the morning," he told her quietly. "If we survive the war and you're willing, I'll want you with me all the time."

Rebecca forgot all of her earlier unhappy speculations about the future as she responded to his sentimental mood with the pent-up fierceness of her developing love for him. Clinging to him as he caressed her with a tenderness he'd never before displayed, she knew without words that the idyll was finished and that his soft endearments were his way of saying good-bye. The knowledge that this special time together was almost over lent a poignancy to their passion and its fulfillment and to the reluctant separation of their perspiring bodies. As if neither partner wanted to destroy the fragile bond, they were silent during a brief swim and an insipid breakfast of watered wine and hard-dried sea biscuits. While Rebecca was brushing her hair into the hated flat queue, the more familiar normalcy began to resurface. Frowning as he polished the blackened fire spit with handfuls of sand, Philip smiled only after he'd restored the ramrod back into an efficient piece of military equipment. As she watched him, Rebecca also smiled, but her expression held a note of self-derision; she may have captivated a domineering husband but she hadn't a hope of holding the interest of the privateer-patriot Captain Philip Keane.

At the moment of their departure a bit of the magic returned briefly when he put his arm around her waist and told her to take control of the boat. "This time it's my turn to distract you, Cottontop," he murmured lightly, asking more seriously a few minutes later, "Any more doubts about us?"

Turning around to kiss him lightly on his cheek, Rebecca shook her head; she couldn't bring herself to admit that she hated the thought of another separation from him. An hour later their future took on an even grimmer aspect when Rebecca recognized a Dutch brig headed eastward under full sail.

"That's the same ship that passed our island late yesterday, Philip. I thought you said that a good mariner returns to port only when his mission is completed."

"Cort Luden wouldn't be returning, at least not at that speed, unless there was good cause. Better let me take over, Cottontop; we'll need more speed if we're to find out what the reason is."

Under Philip's expert handling, the gig seemed to leap through the water; but even so the sleek Dutch ship increased its lead until Rebecca could hardly make out the orange, blue, and white of its Holland flag. In the harbor itself there was no need to question Captain Luden about the seriousness of the news he'd brought. Muster flags were flying from the masts of every privateer in port, and the bay was dotted with longboats returning the crews to their ships. Braced high on the rigging of the sailing vessels, seamen were already unfurling the sails while lookouts trained their telescopes westward.

"Are the British coming to burn the city?" she asked, the memory of the attack on Falmouth so vivid that she gripped her husband's arm.

Intent on maneuvering the gig alongside the *Reine*, he shook off her restraint and replied irritably, "Don't be a fool! It'd be an act of war against France for British ships-of-line to enter these waters without permission, but they'd sure as hell sink our fleet anyplace they could find us. Ahoy!" he shouted to the man lowering the rope ladder. "What's going on, and where is my father's ship?"

"Damned good thing you decided to return, son," Silas Keane shouted back. "We were about to pull anchor without you. A flotilla of British ships is blockading the entry, and two of them are flying the Union on jack staff. The others are privateers and armed merchantmen."

"How many all told, and what's their position?" Philip demanded.

"According to the fishermen who warned us last night, there were ten concentrated on the southern route and two patrolling the north. Your officers have already been briefed; so if that sailor sitting next to you is Becky, best kiss her good-bye. You've got work to do."

"Where's your ship?"

"At anchor in front of Becky's new home. I'll take her

there while you finish organizing here. We rendezvous in three hours six miles due north.''

As it had been on the day Philip had left her to rescue the *Vixen*, his farewell was cheerfully businesslike; and the fire that gleamed in his eyes had little to do with her. Rather, it was the thought of battle that dominated his senses.

"Don't worry about me, Cottontop; just make certain that you stay out of trouble.'' He kissed her thoroughly enough and smiled at her; but when he climbed the rope ladder, he was carrying the ramrod carefully in his hand.

First things first, Rebecca reflected with a bittersweet envy. Until he accomplished this mission, he wouldn't remember her or the passion they'd shared, while she'd have little else to think about. She watched as father and son talked briefly on the deck before Silas climbed down to join her aboard the gig. She wondered painfully if Philip would take the time to wave to her and smiled with a burning relief when he leaned over the railing. But his farewell words were only ones of additional instruction.

"Make sure you wear those sailor clothes whenever you take the boat out, Cottontop!'' he reminded her.

For the first time in days she didn't edit the response that flooded past her lips. "I prefer to use the more basic outfit I wore on the island,'' she shouted sweetly, and for a moment her husband's eyes did glow with the memory of her nudity.

Laughing down at her upturned face, he warned her jokingly, "You do that and I'll lock you in a windowless room the next time I leave port.''

Silas, too, understood the import of the threat and chuckled as he oared the boat into the path of the wind. "Glad to hear you're still impudent enough to give him what-for whenever he gets on his high horse. What'd he do that made you take off like a scalded cat five days ago?''

"He judged me by his own standards,'' she replied bluntly.

"Get him to change his mind?"

Grinning at her father-in-law, Rebecca shook her head. "Not entirely, but at least he'll be more cautious about asking those same questions." Abruptly she interrupted her chain of thought and demanded, "Where are you taking me? We passed Port-au-Prince minutes ago."

"Five miles north, Becky. Figured it'd be far enough away to discourage the buzzards. A place called El Abrigo. Built by a pair of Spanish pirates a century ago and used by the first French governor as a garrison."

"It sounds like a prison!"

"More like a fortress, but your quarters are passably comfortable and you won't be lonely. Jed Daws is beached because of that leg of his, and Jesse Milford took a bullet in the elbow during the Jamaica thing."

Shuddering at the memory of the second mate, Rebecca protested, "Milford's a nasty prude, Silas!"

"Don't care for Bible spouters either, but he's the shrewdest cargo appraiser in the company and mean-minded enough to keep the Falconets from claiming more 'n their share. But there'll be thirty or forty other lads who were injured at the same time, and I've hired you a housekeeper—same one you had at Émeraude."

"Akhoi? But she's a—"

"Not anymore. The damned old pirate was asking a thousand pounds for her until I convinced him two hundred was a more reasonable sum."

"You gave her freedom papers in return for work?"

"Nope, she gets a salary. Don't believe in indenture any more 'n I do slavery. She's a hard woman, Becky; but according to her, you two got along; and she's smart enough to keep the Falconets and their breed away from you. The Riccards, though, are different—never been slavers or slave owners; so they'll be coming to see you and likely to be asking you to teach them English since they'll be moving to Baltimore same time as you and Philip."

"Mrs. Riccard wants me to paint her picture."

"Do it, girl, and charge her the limit. Don't be underestimating your value. The ones you drew of the housekeeper are better 'n most of the pretentious claptrap hanging on people's walls. Look yonder, Becky. There's where you'll be living."

Rebecca stared at the two-storied granite structure surrounded by a high wall that extended to the water's edge. Repelled by the iron-barred windows and by the row of cannon on the parapet facing the sea, she asked, "Are those cannon just antique ornaments or real?"

"The best I could find. They'll blow anything out of the water for twelve hundred yards. The British aren't going to burn me down again."

"Philip doesn't believe they would attack a French colony."

"Not with their ships-of-line, but old King George would wink at any of his prison-scum privateers who could put us out of commission, French territorial waters or not. Happens the governor here agreed with me, so we got a year's free rent for the price of those cannons."

"Silas, how did the British know the Keane fleet was in Port-au-Prince?"

"Logical place to suspect after the Jamaica raid but nothing for you to worry about. We'll use the northern route and slip past their blockade at night. But even if the lot of them attack, we could most likely outgun all but the two damned ships-of-line."

Rebecca was silent as Silas nosed the boat alongside the stone pier jutting out from the fortress that was to be her home. At the seaward end of the long pier was the third Antilles ship, its crew lined up along the rails awaiting their captain's return. Suddenly the war seemed very real again.

"Best get inside, Becky, and stow those tears. Didn't think a girl like you would have any use for that female nonsense. Nothing's going to happen to the Keanes this trip, and Philip'll be back within the month. Between now and then you've got a job to do making this pile of rocks

into a home for him. Jed's waiting to show you around the
place, so you'd best get going.''

Mumbling a few words, Rebecca kissed his leathery
cheek and fled toward the wide entrance where Jed was
standing. That entrance provided her first shock. Once
she and her old friend were inside the tunnel wide
enough for a wagon, a heavy iron portcullis dropped
into place behind them. At the sound of her startled
gasp, Jed burst into a delighted chortle and reached
over to the side of the stone wall to show her the release
mechanism.

"Whole thing's built like a Spanish fort,'' he boasted.
"Nobody kin come in without our say-so, and there ain't a
better place for a layover in the whole durn Caribbean.
Other gate like this 'un is landside so we got two ways of
goin' to town if we've a mind to. But it's more 'n jest
comfortable quarters. Cap'n Silas fixed it to hold off any
ship that attacks, and we got enough rifles to man the gun
ports along the land-side wall.''

"How many men are here, Jed?''

"Fifty all told, countin' the twenty cannoneers Cap'n
Silas left behind. But we sure ain't crowded fer space.
More 'n three hunnert crew can berth belowdecks, and
twenty officers above. Right now there's only Milford up
there and that fancy housekeeper of yourn. She's a crack-
er, Becky. Seen to everything right off soon as Cap'n Silas
told her what he wanted, so's your rooms are plain durn
elegant. And she don't take any sass from old Milford
either; fixed up our quarters almost as good even while he
'uz bellowin' about cost.''

During the half-hour tour of the facilities, Rebecca
began to understand Jed's enthusiasm. Topping the wide
stone walls of the fortress were enough open storage
cisterns to supply sun-warmed rain water for the tiled
bathtubs in both the crew and officer quarters. The original
Spanish builders had also commandeered enough brown
tiles to make the smooth floors appear invitingly cool.
Even the huge, stone-paved muster court, lined with storage and cook sheds, had been rendered attractive with
verdant shade trees in the several garden areas. As Jed had

promised, the three rooms she would occupy were gracious; and even the unglazed, barred windows blended with airy Spanish decor of dark-beamed ceilings and whitewashed walls. But it was the six-foot-long, blue-tiled tub in the necessaries room and the roofed terrace overlooking a patio garden that ended her lingering sense of imprisonment; and not until Jed guided her from the terrace up the steep stone stairs to the watchtower did her earlier mood of desolation return.

In the distance she watched as the Keane fleet assembled into flotilla formation; and with an added anxiety, she noted that the *Reine* was in lead position. The long days until Philip returned would seem like a lifetime, she thought despairingly as she stared out over the bright, marine-blue water until the ships disappeared from her view.

Back in her apartment she bathed listlessly and donned the cotton skirt and blouse that had been laid out on the bed without even noting their newness and delicate elegance until Akhoi explained.

"Captain Keane instructed me to purchase additional clothing for you, madame; and I remembered you enjoyed more freedom than most ladies."

Quizzically Rebecca surveyed the stiff gray dress and white apron the ex-slave was wearing. "I thought you did too, Akhoi," she said dryly.

"I wasn't sure what your wishes would be, madame."

"For you to have as much freedom as I do."

A sardonic smile flitted briefly over Akhoi's face as she glanced at the barred windows.

"Did my father-in-law ask you to guard me?" Rebecca demanded.

"He wanted you safe."

"There're fifty men stationed below who'll see to our safety. What I want is a friend."

Again a cynical smile briefly touched the housekeeper's lips, but her words were woodenly servile. "Perhaps as I learn more about freedom, madame, I'll also learn about friendship."

Although the refusal was delicately phrased, Rebecca

winced; however, she noticed with satisfaction that Akhoi was wearing a loose blouse and skirt as she served dinner. Immediately after the solitary meal, though, the housekeeper disappeared, leaving the lonely American with only unhappy reflections for company. As Rebecca remembered the uninterrupted days and nights with Philip on the small island that now seemed idyllic, she dreaded the thought of sleeping alone on the large, ornately Spanish bed in the next room. It hadn't taken long, she mused uneasily, for her self-sufficiency to crumble—for her to miss her temperamental husband with an emptiness akin to pain.

Rebecca didn't hear Akhoi's silent approach until the woman spoke softly in the darkness of the terrace. "Madame, it is not good for you to brood about things you cannot change. Captain Keane suggested I tell you something about myself so that you won't feel quite so exiled in a strange place."

"More likely what Silas told you," Rebecca countered with a flippant cynicism, "was to keep me from moping around the house like a castrated old tomcat."

Only a quiet chuckle greeted this retort as the younger woman added more seriously, "I would enjoy hearing about your life, Akhoi."

"I hope not, madame. It is not a story for enjoyment. By the time I was fourteen, I'd been sold three times and forced to live under a variety of alien circumstances. I was twelve when the wife of the Jamaican planter who owned me sold me to the proprietor of a Kingston sporting palace. I had become an embarrassment to the woman because I resembled her husband too closely. My mulatto mother had been his mistress for twenty years.

"At the palace my training as a whore was begun on the first night, when the proprietor himself took me to bed. Three days later, with my hair shaved and my head covered by a hideous brown wig, I was made available to the white clientele. Within weeks I was sold to a wealthy businessman as a replacement for his aging mistress-slave, who'd been demoted to the position of housekeeper. Although the man was old and not too demanding, I still became pregnant and presented him with a son who was too white to be raised as a slave. Unlike the French, Englishmen are curiously prejudiced about their white-skinned children being sold into bondage. Instead, my owner gave our child to a Dutch sea captain who lived eight thousand miles away in the East Indies. But the coloring of that child attracted the attention of the English merchant who became my fourth owner. I hated the man on sight and didn't learn for three months that he was the one who'd purchased me from the Jamaican businessman.

"In the company of a tutor who was hired to give me a basic education in return for his passage to England, I was taken to New Providence, where I was given the last name of Hutchins and outfitted with a small wardrobe of very plain dresses. One day the tutor and I were ordered to board a ship in the Nassau harbor. To my horror the merchant was waiting for me, and several days later he and I were married by the captain, who'd been told that I was the daughter of an English colonist. Ten years later I learned that the ceremony had been a charade on the part of my husband; he already had a wife whom he'd deserted when she proved barren. The only reason he'd insisted on the wedding was to prevent my running away. In England it is more difficult for a woman to escape her husband's domination than it is for a slave to elude his master's.

"Unlike his legal wife, I was not barren. Within four years I had produced two sons white enough to satisfy their exacting father, whose obsession for heirs had nothing to do with love. His merchant partner had four sons, and my 'husband' was afraid they would inherit his share of the business if he had none of his own. But I was allowed no part in their rearing. That task was assigned to a governess-nurse, and I saw my sons only in her presence.

"We lived in a gloomy, isolated estate far from Bristol, and for ten years I was a prisoner there with only one diversion. I became an avid scholar, largely because the improvident tutor was allowed to work there as an overseer to run the estate during my 'husband's' frequent and lengthy voyages abroad. During one of those absences, I gave birth to a third child, and he arrived home six months later to discover that he had sired a daughter who could not pass as white. That discovery ended my stay in England. I learned then that my marriage was a sham and that I was still a slave.

"Within the week I was en route to France with a broker who specialized in the sale of exotic merchandise. My sons remained with their father, my daughter was given to a family of coloreds in London, and I was once again sold, this time to a French privateer and ex-slaver. Atonine Falconet installed me in his Port-au-Prince home as his *placée* and generously placed few restrictions on my activities. Until his death I was given more freedom than most of the wives of the wealthy Frenchmen in that city. A major part of that freedom I retained even during my enforced stay at Émeraude."

Akhoi paused a moment before she continued the stark narrative. "This much I told Captain Keane before he purchased me from Jean Falconet and ended my thirty-four-years of slavery. However, I did not risk telling him the rest; I was afraid that he would consider me an unfit servant for the daughter-in-law he so obviously admires. But you, madame, have already guessed some of it. From the day my daughter was spurned by her father, I have considered myself a Negro rather than the white woman I so desperately tried to become for all of those unhappy years. I began to study Negro histroy and religion and— and black magic. I changed my name to Akhoi, one of the African words for woman; and in Port-au-Prince I contacted a hungan, a voodoo priest, and eventually became a mambo, a priestess. Are you shocked, madame?"

Rebecca's voice exploded with a pent-up anger. "If I knew enough voodoo, I'd put a curse on all of those men, Akhoi; and I'd dip the pins in manzanilla poison."

The housekeeper's soft laughter was unrestrained. "I would have preferred the more African method of tying them down in the path of soldier ants."

As silently as she'd arrived on the terrace, Akhoi left; and Rebecca spent a restless night. At first her thoughts revolved around the empty space next to her on the large bed; she missed the comfort of Philip lying beside her. But gradually her mind reverted to Akhoi's history, and she awoke at dawn in a state of urgent excitement. Rebecca knew that what she'd heard was a shocking revelation of a custom as cruel and savage as a Salem witch hunt. A practice that was tolerated by society because the practitioners were wealthy men who claimed the female victims as their property by right of legal slavery! Before the room was light enough for writing, Rebecca was washed and dressed, her imagination fired by the title "Mama Mambo" and by a plot that extended beyond Akhoi's experience into a darkly humorous area of a sorcerer's revenge.

That day and the following two she wrote with a single-minded concentration until she'd completed the story. For the first time in all the years she'd written careless news stories or rewritten her mother's or Eldin Cooper's work, Rebecca was exactingly critical about this first story that had really inspired her. Seeking out the only educated person among her currently limited companions, she asked Akhoi for help. The housekeeper forced Rebecca to rewrite each painful paragraph until the story acquired a cohesive clarity. It was then that Akhoi revealed the final ironic chapter of her personal saga.

"When I received the news of Antoine's death, I learned that the freedom he had allowed me was real. Although he never told me, he had filed official papers naming me a free woman and the heir to his estate. But a month after I'd been given those papers, the governor of Saint-Domingue summoned me to his office and announced that Antoine had acted illegally in granting my freedom. I was once again a slave and my inheritance was awarded to Jean Falconet."

"Did Silas know that the governor wasn't to be trusted?"

Akhoi smiled with a sardonic amusement as she answered Rebecca's tense question. "Captain Keane made quite certain that both the governor and Jean Falconet would prove entirely trustworthy in this instance, providing, of course, that I leave the island when you do."

"Why should you have to do anything you don't want to?"

"It was the only way Monsieur Falconet would agree to the sale."

"Why should he care as long as he made money selling you?"

"Because I know that Antoine's death was planned by another member of the Falconet family."

"Who?"

"His niece, Emile Gironde's widow."

"But I thought—"

"Captain Gironde's death was also deliberate. Did your husband tell you the names of the British pirates who stole the Falconet fleet in Havana?"

"I only heard the name of one of them, a man named Granger."

"He was the leader, but it was Madame Gironde's first husband who committed the murders with madame's assistance. At least she was in Havana that night."

"How do you know that, Akhoi?"

"I have many friends in these islands."

Alerted by the odd inflection in the housekeeper's phrasing, Rebecca asked cautiously, "Why are you telling me this?"

"Annette Gironde is a resourceful woman. When she learned that her first husband had been killed during the battle with your husband's fleet, she decided that Philip Keane would make an admirable substitute."

Rebecca sucked in her breath sharply; she didn't need to ask the painful question of whether or not her errant husband had been with his new mistress on the day of her own arrival in Port-au-Prince. Intuitively, Akhoi understood the American woman's agitation.

"Your husband was the intended victim, not the pursuer," she said gently. "And he was very relieved to escape the trap Madame Gironde and Jean Falconet had set for him. But it was your father-in-law who made certain that neither of them would dare threaten your safety."

"By hiring you," Rebecca sighed dejectedly.

"Your Silas is more thorough than that, madame. He hired a man the white people on this island have good reason to fear—all of the white people and one very black slave owner."

"I didn't know that Negroes ever—"

"The African who owns Jean-Jacques Dessalines comes from a long line of slave traders. His specialty was buying the prisoners taken during tribal warfare from the victorious chieftains. Eighteen years ago he acquired the nine-year-old son of a defeated chief, but he lived to regret that acquisition. Six years ago when Jean-Jacques escaped, his owner was forced to hire white soldiers as bodyguards because he could no longer trust any of his Negro slaves. The French military leaders also fear my friend because they know that someday he will organize the thousands of other escaped slaves into an avenging army."

"How did Silas meet such a man?"

"Quite easily. Jean-Jacques was using the dungeons of El Abrigo as his headquarters. That's why I suggested this place to your father-in-law."

Uneasy about living near a man who sounded as savage as the dark, shadowy figures she'd seen on Gonâve Island, Rebecca asked cautiously, "Where is he now?"

"He and seven of his men are still here. Tonight I will bring him to meet you after your Mr. Milford has retired. His story, madame, is far more important than my sordid life. I would very much like the white world to know of him before he fulfills his destiny."

Oddly enough, very little of what was said during that interview behind closed doors in Rebecca's living room was ever used in the short biography she wrote of Jean-Jacques Dessalines. He had not requested the interview with the strange foreign woman out of curiosity; he wanted to know about the revolution being waged by the American colonies. More precisely, he wanted to know how it had been engineered.

From the moment he had strode from the balcony into the dimly lighted room, Rebecca had no difficulty in accepting his claim of royal birth. His black eyes shone with a fanatical arrogance, and he exhibited none of the servile humility of a beaten man, although his naked back bore evidence of earlier whippings. In speech, too, he revealed a demanding, imperious personality, although she understood few words of his African-French patois. That he'd already learned much about the American revolution was apparent in his opening questions about Samuel Adams. Not even Akhoi's muted translation could suppress Dessalines' intensity of purpose or his shrewd understanding of the propaganda techniques Adams had used in his ten-year struggle to arouse thirteen disunited colonies to rebellion. Although Rebecca was convinced that only through revolution could the half-million slaves on Saint-Domingue free themselves, she hated the thought of the violence such a revolt would unleash. She also became increasingly tired of having to repeat the details of the political exaggerations the American patriots had used, of the secretive training of rebel militias, of the theft of guns from British armories, and of the hit-and-run tactics her father and the other militia leaders had taught their men.

Two hours later, after Jean-Jacques Dessalines had departed as abruptly as he'd arrived, Rebecca asked Akhoi why the Negro leader had asked those questions of her rather than the sailors and cannoneers. The housekeeper's laughter reflected a genuine amusement.

"Your father-in-law told Jean-Jacques that you'd know better than anyone, that your unconventional work on your father's newspaper had given you a remarkable fund of knowledge. He was right. For a person who doesn't believe in revolution, you know everything that is needed to start one."

During the following month, Rebecca's life became more unconventional than it had ever been in Falmouth, and her knowledge of revolution progressed from theory to active participation. Three days after Dessalines' visit to her apartment, a Colonel Auxier arrived with his troop of French soldiers and demanded the right to search El Abrigo for what he described as a band of murderous runaway slaves. Long before the deliberately slow American guards had opened the heavy iron portcullis facing the dusty road, the Negro leader and his seven men had hidden in the massive clothespress in Rebecca's bedroom while her hastily removed wardrobe was jammed back into trunks. Although she had neither chosen the hiding place nor given her consent for its use, Rebecca watched the search from the privacy of her own balcony with an

amused contempt for Jesse Milford. As usual the second
mate was obsequiously attentive to anyone with more
authority than his own, in this case, a shrewd Frenchman
who easily recognized the insolent game the other American seamen were playing with the unpopular and insensitive Milford. The superficial search ended without any
official notice being taken of the upper-floor quarters,
much to Milford's disappointment, but none of the conspirators were fooled by Colonel Auxier's bland farewell.

To Rebecca's shock, she was included in the subsequent
preparations. As the only person authorized to use the
captain's sailing gig and at Jed's curious insistence that she
was the most competent sailor, she was cajoled into taking
Jed and Akhoi on long jaunts around the harbor for the two
days after the French colonel's visit. On both occasions
she was intensely irritated and nervous when her companions delayed the return to El Abrigo until long after dark
on one pretext after another, despite her protest that she
lacked the skill to operate the boat at night. Not until the
third day did she learn the reason for their erratic behavior.
Then her nervousness turned to stark terror.

The long, tension-filled day began at dawn with a
second visit by Colonel Auxier, a visit that had been
prearranged with Jesse Milford, who helped by raising the
iron gate and dismissing the guards. Only the fury of the
aroused Americans prevented the capture of Dessalines
and his men. Grabbing whatever makeshift weapons they
could find, forty of the cannoneers and seamen swarmed
into the court and held the French soldiers at bay until Jed
could spirit the Negroes once again into Rebecca's bedroom. Jed arrived back in the court barely in time to
prevent a pitched battle, since the furious colonel had
finally ordered his men to discharge their muskets at the
attacking Americans, who were armed only with the lesser
weapons of barrel staves and knives.

"Hold it, lads," the cook shouted to his friends. "These
ain't the bastard limeys we 'uz expectin'. They're the
Frenchies come to pertect us from them murderin' slaves. I
reckon it won't do no harm to let them look around a
piece."

Auxier's "look around" was a thorough search, even into hidden passages the inquisitive Jed had not yet discovered. At Jesse Milford's carping insistence, the colonel and two of his men finally invaded the only uninvestigated footage of the intricate fortress—Rebecca's personal apartment. She greeted them from behind the barricaded door of the necessaries room with the calm announcement that she was taking a bath. When she emerged long minutes later, only the apologetic French officer and a watchful Akhoi remained in the living room.

Without a quiver of inflection the housekeeper translated the colonel's opening announcement that he and his men would remain at El Abrigo until the savages were captured and executed. Rebecca listened to his bland explanation that he was concerned for her safety with a frightened expression on her face that was only partly simulated; the half hour she'd spent locked in a small room with eight fierce slaves poised for battle had been a harrowing experience. It wasn't until Auxier focused on the exploits of Jean-Jacques Dessalines that she regained her customary poise. Two nights earlier while she'd been concentrating on guiding the sailboat safely back to El Abrigo, a band of Negroes had robbed the arsenal of Colonel Auxier's own garrison in Port-au-Prince, escaping with both muskets and ammunition.

"Dessalines is the only slave on Saint-Domingue with the animal cunning to have dared such a raid," the Frenchman declared. "And El Abrigo is the only place where he might find misguided foreigners to shelter him."

At this blunt insinuation Rebecca exploded into a defensive tirade which Akhoi quickly stopped attempting to translate because there was no need. Realizing belatedly that he had blundered politically, Auxier was still attempting to mumble an apology as he fled from the room, leaving Rebecca breathless and Akhoi amused. The housekeeper's amusement, however, was ended by a furtive knock on the door and by the sober look on Jed Daws's face when he sidled into the room.

"Becky," he asked softly, "d' you recollect that beach you 'n the cap'n found on Gonâve Island? Reckon you'd best be studyin' this chart 'cause you 'n me 'n Akhoi here'll be takin' Jean and his lads there soon as it's dark enough t' git away.''

Rebecca got no farther in her shocked protest than, "Jed, I don't know the vague—" before he shushed her with the reassurance that all she need do was maintain a simple compass heading, and changed the subject to one of more immediate import.

"That durn fool Milford is raisin' all kinds of Cain, Becky, and the Frenchies are as skittish as caged cats. Best you and me git down there while Akhoi gits Jean and his mates outta here. Reckon it's time fer some of them same diversionary tactics you pulled on the old limey in New Bedford.''

Rebecca began her tactics with a malicious order to the parsimonious Milford to serve "their guests" all the wine they wanted from the "Captain's private stocks," and she thoughtfully sent two of the burliest American cannoneers to help the furious second mate carry the bottles. Her secondary action was a fulsome apology to Colonel Auxier for having lost her temper earlier and a request that she be allowed to sketch the faces of his men for her "collection." Three hours later, her fingers cramped into claws, she completed the last of the flattering graphite drawings of the twelve French soldiers before she joined their commanding officer for the dinner Jed placed before them, a meal considerably better than the usual fare Jesse Milford had allowed to be served at El Abrigo. Oddly enough, she enjoyed the Frenchman's companionship despite the language barrier and was sipping her fifth glass of wine when a disapproving Akhoi interrupted the impromptu celebration. Had Rebecca understood the rapidly delivered French dialogue, she'd have learned that she often overindulged in spiritous libations and that Akhoi was more keeper than housekeeper. Only when Colonel Auxier escorted her solicitously to her apartment did Rebecca realize that her sobriety was in question. Her response was a giggle of approval when Akhoi led the French officer into the bedroom. As Rebecca knew it would be, the door to the necessaries room was wide open, and the room itself was innocently empty.

Fortunately for the eight apprehensive fugitives huddled on the floorboards of the small sailboat and for the half-dozen conspirators who had spirited them safely out of El Abrigo, Rebecca's light-hearted self-confidence lasted for the four hours it took to guide the overloaded craft safely to the beach where she and Philip had picnicked weeks before. Having memorized the sequence of compass headings, she blithely instructed a nervous Jed to watch the instrument while she manned the tiller; but only rarely during the outward voyage did she ask for his concurrence about the direction. Only on the homeward-bound trip, after Jean-Jacques and his relieved followers had waded ashore on Gonâve Island, did she discover her successful navigation had been entirely her own doing. Not only had the veteran cook lacked sufficient light to read the compass, he lacked the educational skill to read at all. With only the uncertain moon to guide her, she sailed blindly eastward, landing a mile south of the fortress just as dawn was breaking. By the time she'd jockeyed the small boat to its customary place alongside the dock, both the French soldiers and American seamen in the fort were awake, leaving the weary travelers no alternative but to scale the twelve-foot wall on the swaying rope ladders hastily lowered by their confederates who'd remained on watch throughout the long night.

Three more times during the fortnight that Colonel Auxier remained at El Abrigo, Rebecca made the round trip to the beach and back without arousing his suspicions unduly. Unwittingly, Jesse Milford aided in the enterprise by reassuring the Frenchman that Madame Keane was allowed the privilege of sailing to Port-au-Prince, providing she was accompanied by Jed and Akhoi. A mile offshore on each of those three excursions, the sailboat took a longboat and the four Americans who manned it under tow until Jean Dessalines' embryo fleet numbered three boats, each one liberated by the Americans from the rows of shore boats lined up along the docks of Port-au-Prince. The food and supplies packed into those longboats, however, had been more conventionally obtained, according to Jed Daws.

"We figured them poor devils don't stand a chance without our help," he explained to Rebecca, "so we used our wages t' git this food t' start them out with." The pledge of help also extended to expert instruction in the use of the stolen French rifles and in the synchronized rowing of the longboats. On the occasion of their last arrival at the beach, they were met by a jubilant Jean Dessalines, who refused any future help. He had already conducted his own "liberating" raid on Saint-Domingue and now claimed a membership of fifty runaway slaves in his army.

It was just as well that the American conspirators' participation in the incipient revolution was at an end. Upon their return to El Abrigo they discovered that Auxier had extended his investigation beyond the narrow confines of the fortress. He'd spent a busy day in Port-au-Prince learning that the innocuously cooperative housekeeper had been the notorious slave mistress of Antoine Falconet and was now reputed to be the most powerful voodoo mambo on the island. During his conference with the city's prefect of police, he'd also learned about the missing boats and about the disastrous raid on the warehouse of one of the biggest plantations. What galled the proud French officer the most was his own gullibility. Except for the officious Milford, who'd made the initial report of suspected intruders at the fortress, Auxier had excused only three people from the suspicion of complicity—the young and problem-prone Madame Keane, the good-natured Jed Daws, who'd been so helpful during the frequent searches, and the housekeeper, who'd seemed a well-adjusted servant until Auxier had learned the truth of her identity.

Yet these three were the only ones who could have engineered the successful escape of Jean Dessalines and his murderous followers. They were the only ones with access to the cursed sailboat! Just how they'd managed, Auxier did not know; but he did know that he could not accuse the housekeeper or the cook without involving the innocent-looking Madame Keane. And such an involvement was too great a risk for a mere colonel to take! At the moment, the safety of Saint-Domingue was somewhat dependent upon the Keane fleet continuing its use of Port-au-Prince as a base of operations, since the French admiralty had refused to send any warships for colonial defense. To insult the wife of the younger Captain Keane by making charges he could not prove could end his own military career as well as endanger the colony.

With a cynical frustration, Colonel Auxier took the only punitive action possible under the circumstances. Before withdrawing his twelve men from the fortress, he issued an order that Akhoi and all the Americans except Jesse Milford were restricted to El Abrigo until the return of the Keane fleet.

For Rebecca the restriction was a welcome relief from tension; for weeks she'd been unable to concentrate on her interrupted writing or on the nagging doubts she once again had about her own future. She had not forgotten Akhoi's warning about Annette Gironde or about Philip's tendency toward infidelity. At the housekeeper's unrelenting insistence, she completed the biography of Jean-Jacques Dessalines and the story of the American sailors' generous contributions toward a revolution not their own before she turned her attention to the more biting tales of a buccaneer with a mistress in every port and a vengeful wife who reciprocated in kind. In yet another burst of sardonic comedy she created a fantasy in which the characters were a trio of mask fans like the ones she'd seen the women use at the Falconet party.

As Akhoi's critical approval of the literary output increased, Rebecca's sense of entrapment diminished. Each time she signed a story with the pseudonym of Eb Burns, her confidence in her ability to survive alone increased. The Rayburn Publishers had paid for earlier contributions that lacked the originality of her current productions; eventually they might pay her enough to free her from financial dependence upon the Keanes. Since the failure of her one foolish attempt to reach England, she had accepted the possibility that she might never gain control of her inheritance. Thus the need to secure an alternative income was imperative. Although she had as yet no plans for leaving the errant husband she loved, her resolve never to become a neglected wife had strengthened with each added day of separation.

The exuberant return of Patrice Riccard provided Rebecca with the means of sending the ten completed stories to her uncles in New York and of earning an even more substantial amount of money while she remained a virtual prisoner in El Abrigo. The raids on Trinidad and Tobago had yielded the needed cannon and ammunition, but the capture of a dozen English merchantmen had guaranteed a rich profit for all the partners. A veteran opportunist, Riccard had followed Silas Keane's example and purchased a home in Baltimore, a city he'd found a delightful contrast to the oppressive Port-au-Prince. Relieved that he'd been spared the onerous task of delivering the military supplies to the American army in Massachusetts, the Frenchman had readily agreed to convoy the Falconet share of the captured ships and booty to Saint-Domingue and to keep Rebecca entertained until her husband returned.

Having learned to deal successfully with women during his varied career, even to the extent of cozening the overly plump heiress he'd married into contented domesticity, Riccard anticipated no trouble from the lively girl whose talent and wit he already admired. But even if she'd been a dull provincial clod, he'd still have exerted all of his considerable charm in enticing her to join the whirl of holiday parties in Port-au-Prince. Rebecca Keane was an important part in the felicitous new life he was preparing for himself and his family in America. Since continuing good relations with her father-in-law were essential to those plans, Riccard was eager to prove his diplomacy in a situation he realized might prove delicate.

That Philip Keane was less than an exemplary husband, the Frenchman knew all too well. He'd watched the cleverly baited entrapment of the dashing young man with cynicism; Annette Gironde was a ruthless woman who'd dominated her late, unlamented husbands and could well prove vengeful to a relatively naive young girl. Moreover, the protective older Keane had hinted broadly about earlier peccadilloes committed by his roving son. Riccard himself professed no moral scruples against discreet infidelities—

the nature of men being what it was—but he firmly believed that such affairs should be conducted only with women who played the game according to established rules.

Armed with the comforting assurance that Madame Gironde had left the city days before the Keane fleet had sailed a month earlier, Riccard visited El Abrigo the day after his return. Expecting to find a lonely young woman eager for news of her husband, he was shocked to learn that Rebecca was already more informed than he was. Because Riccard considered it wise never to reveal an iota of his business affairs to his wife, he was appalled that Silas Keane had no such reticence with his daughter-in-law. In a letter which had been in a packet Riccard had delivered to Jesse Milford a day before, Silas had written a detailed account of the action at Tobago and Trinidad, of the capture of several small enemy fleets of merchantmen, and of the plans for a proposed raid on New Providence. He'd also requested an urgent account of everything she knew about the two newly appointed commanders of the American military, a Virginia planter named George Washington and a Rhode Island fleet merchant named Esek Hopkins. She was on the second page of writing about the first man when Riccard arrived. Her greeting was a blunt demand.

"Will the raid on New Providence be more dangerous than the last ones, Captain Riccard?"

Too startled to exercise his usual evasive diplomacy, he blurted his response, "That is none of your business."

"It is now, and I know it's more important than the others because it involves both the commander of the Continental army and the commodore of the fleet. Silas wants to know what information I have about these men."

"You know them?"

"My father has followed Washington's career for twenty years, and my uncle did business with Esek Hopkins. According to my father, Washington is an overrated show-off and slave owner who knows more about horse racing than he does about organizing and training a militia."

"You believe someone like your father would have been a better choice?"

"Good heavens, no! Jeremy hates the South almost as much as he does England. At least Mr. Washington will be popular with all of the colonies, and he is willing to spend his own money."

Keenly impressed by her analysis, Riccard asked about the leadership qualities of the naval man who would be responsible for the safety of the Keane fleet. Her answer confirmed his own suspicions.

"Esek Hopkins? My uncle Jonathan called him a vulture who did more profiteering than fighting during the French-Indian War. It was my uncle who had to take the risks the one time they combined their fleets. If I were Silas, I wouldn't trust him."

Riccard nodded in agreement. "According to Baltimore people, he refused a congressional assignment to drive Lord Dunsmore's fleet out of Chesapeake Bay. The word *coward* was mentioned more than once by the privateers who claimed that he was made commodore only because his brother was head of the naval affairs in your congress."

"Why would Silas and Philip ever agree to fight under such a man? They've had more experience than he has, and neither of them is a coward."

Smiling with a secret relief at her vehemence, since it was the first time she'd mentioned her husband's name, Riccard shook his head. "They both refused the honor of sailing with the unpopular commodore, but your husband agreed to secure a beachhead on New Providence and engage the small British army there while Hopkins conducts the actual raid on the arsenal."

"Did my reckless husband also agree to fight the British Navy stationed at Nassau so that Esek Hopkins would be doubly safe?"

"That particular British fleet has been dispersed into small patrol units throughout the Caribbean."

"Like the one that was waiting for you outside of Saint-Domingue waters?"

Wondering how much more Silas had revealed to his daughter-in-law, Riccard nodded cautiously; but even so her next blunt remark shocked him.

"I have been told that it was Madame Gironde who informed the British when the Keane fleet would be leaving Port-au-Prince on that voyage."

Once again the Frenchman's diplomacy deserted him. "Who told you about Annette Gironde?" he asked sharply.

"My housekeeper, and don't look so shocked. I'm certain you know all about Akhoi, Captain Riccard, just as you know all about my husband and Madame Gironde. Tell me, do you agree that she aided her first husband in the murder of Antoine Falconet and Emile Gironde?"

Silently cursing Silas Keane in his choice of companions of this pertinacious girl, Riccard reluctantly admitted that he'd been among those who'd suspected the beautiful widow. "But," he added hastily, "she is not a threat to you, Rebecca, and it is not good for you to brood about things that are no longer of importance."

"I'm not brooding, Captain, so you can spare me your sympathy. I knew my husband for years before I married him; and if Silas has asked you to keep me entertained until Philip decides to return, you can relax. I have no intention of supplying the *pièce de résistance* at another party." After studying the oddly hurt expression on her companion's face, she smiled with an apologetic impudence. "I couldn't leave El Abrigo even if I wanted to, Patrice Riccard. For some reason that he didn't bother to explain, your Colonel Auxier ordered me not to leave this prison. That's the reason I'd like you to do a small service for me without informing my husband or his father. After you've delivered this letter to Silas, I want you to send some nonsense I've been writing to my uncles in New York."

Realizing that he was being artfully manipulated, Riccard gallantly accepted the commission; but he spent a busy three hours upon his return to the city. When Auxier informed him that someone at El Abrigo had aided in the escape of a band of dangerous fugitives, the veteran privateer smiled with an appreciative cynicism. Madame Keane was a most challenging young woman!

Early in the afternoon of the following day, he escorted his plump wife into Rebecca's apartment and blandly reminded his unwilling hostess of her promise to paint Leoné's portrait.

"It will pay you better than nonsense written to New York uncles," he told her slyly, "and it will help me forget the name of Dessalines when I see your husband."

Rebecca's muttered accusation of "Blackmail!" was greeted by another sardonic smile of amusement. Within the week Riccard had cajoled her into painting five additional portraits of Leoné's friends, vain women who had not flinched when he'd mentioned prices double the one his wife was paying.

Satisfied that he'd fulfilled his promise to keep the restless young *Américaine* entertained and out of trouble, but grimly hopeful that her *imbécile* of a husband would return before she found new mischief, Captain Riccard hoisted sail for Baltimore. Two days out, when he was nearing the Florida coast, he remembered her probing questions about Annette Gironde and doubled the number of lookouts. In such an insane, disorganized kind of war, it was merely prudent to take added precautions. Since meeting Rebecca Keane, Riccard had lost some of his comfortable conviction that the only warfare women were capable of waging was in the salon or boudoir.

CHAPTER
10

GLARING at the six unfinished portraits that littered the once gracious room, Rebecca experienced an overwhelming revulsion for every aspect of her present life. Despite the growing facility of her painting, which could earn her a living in any community where there were idle wealthy people, she realized that such a parasitic existence would lack any real purpose. It would also be incredibly dull! The idea of creating a lifetime of untruthful memorials to vain women appalled her. Even the worst issues of the *Falmouth Clarion* had given her more satisfaction than did the best of these flattering portraits; yet she knew she could never support herself as well with writing. Even if her uncles paid two pounds for each story rather than one, she'd still earn only twenty pounds for the work she'd just submitted, ten stories that had taken her a month to write. She was being paid twenty times that sum for these six paintings.

In this stultifying world where the weather rarely varied, Rebecca missed the changing seasons of New England, and she missed the freedom of movement she'd enjoyed in Falmouth, and the stimulation of argumentative conversations with the cantankerous, democratic people who'd lived there. Except for the early morning hours she spent walking on the beach or fishing with Jed and others of the restless Americans penned up in the fortress, her only relief from boredom was the uninspired concentration of applying colorful oil paint to the sketches she'd drawn of the women who visited her apartment on a daily schedule.

As the weeks of separation from her husband extended beyond the second month, the burning memories of their few days together faded, replaced by doubts and soured by a sense of futility. At best, their marriage would never be anything but brief physical reunions and long intervals of lonely waiting. In her present mood of detached objectivity, she wasn't certain that she wanted the emotional involvement of another fleeting period of readjustment to a demandingly temperamental man.

Three of the portraits were completed and she was working industriously on a fourth the morning Jed burst into her living room with the news that the three Antilles frigates and Captain Riccard's brig were two hours sailing time from Port-au-Prince.

"We 'uz 'sposed t' git eight hours warning," the old man complained, "but the durn Frenchies at the northern outpost semaphored that the ships 'uz foreign on account of the new flags they 'uz flyin' fore and aft. Them flags is red-and-white striped and I reckon that's what we'll be salutin' from now on. Old Milford's already took twenty men into port to git things ready and there's another fifteen leavin' any minute, so you best be puttin' that paintbrush away. Cap'n'll be expectin' t' see you fust off when he ties up."

Continuing to stroke in the brilliant magenta color on the pictured bougainvillea spray, Rebecca shook her head. "I don't think I'll go, Jed."

"There's times, Becky, when you kin be downright irritatin'. Best you stop actin' like a durn female and git yourself purtied up. Cap'n ain't a patient man, and you got a way of rilin' him even when you ain't bein' stubborn like y' are now. Jest cause he's a mite late in gittin' back to port don't mean he stayed away deliberate. This war ain't exactly run by a clock, and I reckon he 'uz detained by somethin' he couldn't git shut of."

Unwilling to admit that Jed's criticism was deserved and upset by the painful agitation replacing the emotional void that had numbed her for weeks, Rebecca dawdled through the bath Akhoi had drawn for her and donned the pretty brown linen dress slowly. When she finally settled beside Jed at the tiller of the gig bearing the last of the seamen permitted to leave the fort, her calm expression belied the inner turmoil she felt. Akhoi's insistence that she look her best had increased her tension to the point of demoralization, and she felt as unattractive as she had during her girlhood in Falmouth.

Arriving at Port-au-Prince just as the *Reine* was being towed into dockage, Rebecca watched from the fringe of the gathered crowd as the ship's lines were secured and its captain appeared on the bridge. Rebecca's heart was beating in an erratic rhythm as Philip stepped to the railing and looked out over the crowd with a conqueror's impatience; she'd forgotten that in addition to being a handsome man, her husband projected a dramatic intensity. Her heartbeat faltered a moment later as she experienced the dull stab of jealous defeat.

Walking up the lowered gangplank was the official greeting committee led by Jean Falconet; Jed identified the two gaudily dressed Frenchmen accompanying the aging privateer as the governor of Saint-Domingue and the mayor of Port-au-Prince. There was also a woman in the group whom Rebecca needed no help in identifying. Slender and elegantly poised, Madame Annette Gironde was wearing a gown Rebecca recognized instantly; it was one of those she'd had made in New London, a brilliant turquoise silk.

As instinctively as a wounded animal seeking the lonely shelter of its burrow, Rebecca moved swiftly away from Jed's side into the protective shadow of the stone warehouse. But her eyes never left the tall figure of her husband as he spoke to the men, nor did she miss the possessive hold the Gironde woman had on his arm. While Riccard's ship, *Mer Reynard*, claimed the attention of the crowd, Rebecca remained hidden until an abrupt fulminating fury drove her to a more complete escape in the small sailboat snugged to a dock several blocks away. Not until the gig reached the open water beyond the anchored ships did her mind begin to function logically. She knew of only two possible destinations— the hated Abrigo and the beach where she'd left Jean-Jacques Dessalines. In the end self-preservation prevailed; the half-savage slaves would have no use for a troublesome white woman, only for the boat. Resigned to the inevitable, she eased alongside the familiar stone pier at El Abrigo where Akhoi was waiting.

"Why didn't you warn me that Madame Gironde would be there?" Rebecca demanded harshly.

"I was hoping she wouldn't be, but I should have remembered that she was vicious enough to play her usual role. When Antoine was the fleet commander, his ship was always first in; and she would board with Jean Falconet

and put on a show of cousinly affection in full view of her
husband and me. Once Antoine became so angry he
shoved her from the gangplank into the water. She never
forgave him.''

"My husband just stood there like a besotted lump,"
Rebecca spat as she ran through the tunnel and up the
stairs to her apartment. She was tearing off her dress with
a vicious disregard for its delicately buttoned bodice when
Akhoi arrived to rescue the garment and to stand silently
by as her mistress stripped off the layers of dainty under-
wear and pulled on a paint-smeared blouse and skirt.

"You could be wrong about your husband, madame,"
the housekeeper announced judiciously. "Our lookout just
reported seeing a carriage being driven toward Abrigo at a
very reckless speed."

Jabbing her brush into a glob of magenta paint, Rebecca
snapped with a grim asperity, "Please don't ever call me
by that title again! One *madame* in my husband's life is
enough, and you're wrong about his coming here. More
likely he sent someone like Jesse Milford to make sure I
don't return to Port-au-Prince and interrupt his tender
reunion with that barracuda female he was bundling with
on deck."

Her dark eyes glinting with humor, Akhoi nodded.
"Very well, Rebecca, if you wish to act like a child, I'll
leave you alone with your childish thoughts. But if I were
you, I'd be preparing a greeting for a very angry man. The
one who is bellowing the gate open right now is definitely
not the craven Mr. Milford."

Rearranging the easel so that her back was toward the
door, Rebecca was concentrating on a second spray of
bougainvillea when Philip stormed into the room.

"You damned little fool," he shouted, "you bloody
damn fool! You could have killed yourself running away
like that."

Rebecca's shrug was stilled by the heavy hands which
landed on her shoulders and spun her around as if she had
no weight or substance. But those hands could not still the
cool words that issued from her lips.

"I didn't think you'd notice," she murmured.

"The whole bloody damn town noticed," he exploded again.

"With amusement, I'd imagine, especially after that charming scene with your current mistress."

"The hell she is! I didn't invite the bitch aboard; and if you'd had the sense to stay put, you'd have seen me push her down the gangplank as soon as Falconet and those damned officials got off my ship."

"Obviously the lady in question doesn't know that you've relegated her to the past. She was wearing a dress you gave her—one of mine that was in the trunk you so conveniently misplaced."

"I didn't give her a damn thing! She must have stolen it and then lied to me. I was only in time to save the black one."

"How very fortunate for me! Would you really have married her, Philip, if I hadn't come to Saint-Domingue?"

"God, no!"

"No," she gibed at him with a judicial sarcasm, "I don't suppose you would have. One wife had already proved a disaster for you, since you've always preferred less restricting arrangements."

"Cottontop, at the time I didn't think I'd ever see you again."

Meeting his glaring eyes with a cynical disbelief, Rebecca moved restlessly beneath his restraining hold. "You can let go of me now, Philip. I'm not going to jump off the balcony."

"I know you're not. You're going to put on that black dress and accompany me back to Port-au-Prince to attend the reception at the Riccards'. Only this time you're going to stop posing as a simpering ingenue and act like the acid-tongued shrew you are."

All of Rebecca's hard-won composure fled and she shrieked in angry defiance, "The devil I am, Philip Keane!"

"The devil you are, Rebecca Keane, even if I have to dress you from your pantalets out." Smiling with the sudden wolverine ferocity she knew all too well, he ran his hand boldly down her thinly clad body. "You were foolish to remove them when you knew I was coming," he taunted her, "or was that the reason you did?"

"No," she screamed with an abrupt realization of his intentions, "not after you've been with her as you were on the day I arrived, and not ever again under any circum—" Her voice dwindled away as his lips descended on hers.

Only in the bedroom did he release her long enough to ask, "Will you act as a civilized wife should and help me undress, or do I tumble you on the floor like some back-street doxy?"

"Neither!" she gasped, shoving him backward with a furious burst of strength.

Experienced in keeping his balance on a pitching deck, Philip laughed at her efforts, pinning her firmly against the clothespress with his legs as he removed his finely cut black coat and expensive ruffled shirt. Half-naked he cradled her head with his hands and stroked the softly ruffled curls, but his threats belied the gentleness of his caress.

"There are still the boots and britches, my defiant wife, and you're going to help me with them or lose a handful of your pretty witch's hair."

Rebecca squirmed only once as she pulled the polished boots off and tugged the fitted black pantaloons over his slim hips. Her jaw was set in stubborn lines and her eyes downcast in rebellion when she finished, but Philip only laughed as he unfastened her skirt and yanked the loose blouse over her head. For a moment he surveyed her unyielding body with a baffled anger before he shoved her roughly onto the ornate Spanish bed and followed her down. Kissing her with a pent-up hunger bedeviled into savagery by her resistance, he was oblivious to everything but his own fierce needs until he felt her arms around him and her lips respond with a tremulous pressure. Thrown emotionally off balance, he broke away to stare down at her flushed face.

"My God, Cottontop," he muttered thickly, "how could you think I'd ever forget your siren body or the fire it raises in me?"

But Rebecca was in no condition to respond verbally to

his perplexed bewilderment; she was too concerned with her own. How could she be experiencing such an overwhelming passion for a man she'd hated only a few moments ago? Where was her pride? Where was her logic? With a murmur of protest about the interrupted kiss, she pulled him impatiently back toward her.

Until her gesture of invitation, Philip's driving urgency had nothing to do with sentimental memories. It had evolved from a black fury so intense he'd had to restrain himself from striking her when he'd found her calmly working on one of her damned paintings as if she hadn't a care in the world. Until she blurted out the news about the stolen dress, he'd been the injured party, publicly embarrassed by the spectacle of a hoyden wife sailing away in his own boat with a skill he'd be hard pressed to match. It hadn't been his fault that the damned Gironde woman had accompanied her uncle aboard, and he'd gotten rid of her in a way that should have left no doubt in anyone's mind about his detestation of her. But to his continuing fury, his actions had not convinced the insolent Jed Daws or the officious Riccard or two dozen of the crew he'd left behind at El Abrigo!

Jed had been the first to flay him with a defense of Rebecca's insulting effrontery. "If you're durn fool enough not to go after her, Cap'n, you ain't goin' t' be seein' her agin. Becky's learned a whole heap about gittin' away since you 'uz gone."

There'd been a dozen volunteers waiting by one of the longboats, men whose faces reflected a partisanship as biased as Jed's. What the hell had she been doing to captivate these seasoned veterans? They'd glared at him with the same contemptuous distrust they'd have felt if he'd thrown their rum and whiskey rations overboard.

But the most incisive goad to his temper had come from the cursed Riccard, who'd rushed up and requested a word in private just as the longboat was being shoved off.

"Is it true what Madame Gironde told my wife, Philip?" the busybody had demanded, "That you'd be her partner tonight and that Rebecca would not attend? Such an arrangement is not acceptable, *mon ami,* not even in Port-au-Prince.''

Before Philip could sputter a denial, the Frenchman continued his paternalistic chiding. ''I did not see what happened aboard your ship, but my wife insists you welcomed Madame Gironde much too warmly, especially in front of a young wife. If your Rebecca were a timid *souris* or an *imbécile,* it would not matter so much that you are playing the fool, *mon ami.* Unfortunately, she is not a stupid mouse. She is a daring young woman who has made some most dangerous friends in Saint-Domingue.''

''Rebecca will be at your damned reception,'' Philip had rasped furiously, ''that is, if I have your permission to fetch the independent chit. As for the French bitch, the next time she boards my ship, she'll be heaved into the bay.''

Smiling with a satisfied complacency, the affable Frenchman insisted that Philip travel by land in the fastest of the Riccards' carriages. The drivers, he confided with a cynical wink, were accomplished smugglers who would understand the necessity for speed.

It was a ride Philip would not soon forget; while the drivers were excellent, the roadbed wasn't; and the passenger was jarred from one padded side of the cab to the other. His thoughts were equally unsettling, swinging erratically from anger to fear—anger that a towheaded girl he'd known for years could disturb his peace of mind even when they were apart, and fear that she might have succeeded in escaping from him this time. Furious at himself and at her, he'd been cruelly threatening to the point of rape until the unpredictable chameleon had capitulated without a word of explanation and returned his punishing kiss with a passion that destroyed the last remnants of his self-control.

Neither of them was a gentle lover during that reunion. In the hot, sultry room as the afternoon sun spread shifting pools of light about the walls, they were oblivious to everything but the primitive emotions of possession. Even after a mutually explosive climax that should have ended in a euphoric relief from tension, they clung wordlessly together in panting exhaustion until a rekindled desire obliterated all other awareness for a second time. Only after the drawn-out tremors of that violent ecstasy subsided did they separate enough to allow their perspiration-drenched bodies to relax; and only then did Philip's parting kiss reveal the tenderness their fierce passion had lacked.

"Don't go to sleep, Cottontop," he warned her softly. "We have to show up at the Riccards'; otherwise there'll be a dozen people coming here to find out whether or not I beat you senseless."

Rebecca giggled sleepily and burrowed her head deeper into the pillow, mumbling in protest when he reached over and shook her awake. He'd just remembered the second parts of the warnings Jed and Riccard had given him, the strong implications that his slim wife had developed some additional unfeminine skills. Only at the last moment did Philip remember the delicate state of their relationship and soften his customary direct approach to a more circuitous one.

"Sweetheart, the party tonight won't be so bad. At least twenty of the guests are going to be the officers from Matt Stoneham's and my ships, so it'll do you good to get away from this place. Riccard says that you haven't attended a social function since I left. What in the devil did you find to occupy your time here?"

Her pleasant drowsiness began to dissipate on the word *sweetheart*, and she was wide awake long before he finished talking. Whenever her Uncle Jonathan had overheard some gossip about her, he'd never ask her about it directly; instead, he'd begin his lecture with flattery and wheedling before he asked her any questions at all. Rebecca had never lied to him, but she'd developed a sharp facility in the art of evasion. Philip had just used the same approach as her uncle, and she knew that he'd been told something about Jean Dessalines.

Grinning at him with a deliberate impudence, she responded to his one question. "For one thing I learned to sail your gig. You'd never be able to overtake me again with a rowboat, no matter how many men were pulling the oars. And for another, I've become as good a fisherman as you are; almost every morning Jed and I fished along the beach. I played some cards and dice with the men, I did some scribbling about a few of the people I met, and I learned to like your *aguacates,* even though they're fattening.''

With an instant reflex Philip's hand swept down her body in a caressing appraisal. "Not for you, Cottontop," he murmured with satisfaction. "You're slimmer than when I left. Wear the black dress tonight, fondling. I want to show you off."

"In that case," Rebecca retorted lightly as she moved swiftly from the bed, "I'll go as I am. Since we're going to be providing the entertainment, we might as well do a thorough job of it."

Philip's short burst of laughter was quickly replaced by a frown of concern as he watched her enter the bathroom. She might be right, he reflected with a sudden distaste at the prospect of parading any more of his private life in front of the gossipy and vicious women on this island. Half an hour later his frown deepened to a scowl of disapproval as he emerged from his own brief bath to find his wife dressed, not in the black satin he'd requested, but in a much less enticing ivory gown.

Indulging in a number of silent recriminations about her wayward perversity, he continued to fret all the time he was grooming himself, until she turned around to face him. Almost the color of her hair, the shimmering pale satin made her tanned complexion glow; and the delicate lace that edged the modest neckline lent her vivid face a pristine look of untouched beauty. Philip's lips formed a soundless whistle of subdued approval.

"My Irish grandmother would have called you a changeling," he said softly.

"From the buff to satin in ten minutes?" she asked with the bubbling laughter of relief.

"From nymph to lady in even fewer," he murmured with a responsive grin.

Rebecca's expression sobered thoughtfully, and she wondered bleakly just how a lady was supposed to act when meeting her husband's mistress at a polite social function.

Not even her calm, disciplined mother had been able to restrain her bitterness completely. With an intuitive consideration he rarely displayed, Philip wrapped his arms around his wife and kissed her lightly on the tip of her finely boned nose.

"She won't be there, Cottontop," he assured her, "and I won't be leaving your side regardless of Madame Riccard's dining arrangements."

He was wrong on both counts! Driven into Port-au-Prince and deposited at the porte cochere of Patrice Riccard's impressive townhouse, the Keanes were intercepted by Matthew Stoneham. After leading the late arrivals deep into a lantern-lit garden park, Stoneham burst into animated speech.

"Sure didn't want you two to walk into that trap without warning. Some military official named Auxier has accused Riccard of helping eight dangerous slaves to escape. Seems our friend has been suspected of the same crime in the past, but this time one of the poor devils is reputed to be a black leader capable of inciting a revolution. Riccard isn't the only one implicated, Philip. Auxier is waiting for you in the library with the announcement that he believes some of the men we left behind at Abrigo are also involved."

"How do you know?" Philip demanded.

"Riccard invited me to stay at his home, so I was here when the colonel arrived. After I heard, I located Jed Daws aboard the *Reine* and asked a few questions. Best brace yourself, Philip. Our men *are* the guilty ones, not Riccard."

"How many of them?"

"Every damn one of them, except Milford. He's the jackass who stirred up the Frenchman's suspicions, but he denied knowing anything about it when I talked to him."

"Where's Jed now?"

"Stowed aboard my ship with as many of the others as he could locate."

"I'd better see him before I try to talk to this Colonel—"

"Auxier." Rebecca supplied the name in a flat voice. "You don't need Jed. I know as much about it as he does."

Neither man interrupted her concise monologue until she described the actual escape, and then Philip exploded in anger.

"You took the boat to Gonâve at night without a navigator?"

"Jed was there."

"Jed Daws couldn't find his way across a millpond."

"So I discovered on the way back. Do you want to hear the rest of the story, or do we argue about my recklessness?" she asked in exasperation. "I wasn't going to let that pompous tin soldier murder Jean Dessalines."

"So you hid the lot of them in your bedroom and entertained the Frenchman while they got away."

"It was the only place Auxier didn't dare search. Jean Dessalines isn't any more of a criminal than you and Matthew are. He's a revolutionary with more reasons to fight the French than you have the British. And he will never attack Americans because he wants us to be his allies. What do you plan to say to Colonel Auxier?"

Having spent many of his own shore leaves in the colonial ports of America and the Caribbean keeping his men out of the local jails, Philip had learned a considerable number of successful tactics. "Did Auxier ever see the runaways?" he asked impatiently.

"Not at El Abrigo."

"Did Milford?"

"Of course. They were there when Silas leased the place, but he didn't know Silas hired them as extra protection."

"He'd better damn well not have! What made Auxier restrict all of you to quarters when he had no real proof?"

Rebecca hesitated only briefly; the colonel would undoubtedly inform Philip about the terrible mambo Silas had hired as the housekeeper. "He found out who and what Akhoi is," she admitted.

"What the hell is she besides a damn talkative servant?" he demanded.

"A voodoo priestess."

"My God! How the devil am I to explain my father hiring a witch doctor to take care of you?"

"That'll be very simple," she asserted primly. "Akhoi was employed to cure me of overindulging in alcohol. That's what Auxier already believes anyway."

Philip's voice had acquired a harsh edge. "Just why would a French army officer believe a thing like that?"

"My drinking wine with him was part of the entertainment on the day he was searching for Jean-Jacques."

"And the rest of the *entertainment*?" her husband rasped.

Rebecca sighed tiredly. "Drawing sketches of his men! Philip, why don't you stop wasting time and send Matthew inside to fetch Milford so you can tell that idiot prude what to say to Auxier."

Stoneham's laconic agreement barely disguised his repressed laughter. "That's a good idea, and I think you two had better show up for the party as soon as you've finished with Milford. I'll keep Becky out of trouble while you're getting the men and Riccard off the suspect list, Philip."

The only response the veteran mariner received when he turned to leave was a muttered, "Just lock her in the first available closet and throw the key away! Why the hell didn't you tell me all this when I asked you earlier?" he demanded of his lady-wife once they were alone.

"If I had, we'd still be arguing in that stifling bedroom. As far as I'm concerned, this garden is much more romantic. Philip, you'd have done exactly what I did had you been asked to help those poor, unlucky slaves; so don't lecture me anymore. You might even consider kissing me so that we don't go into that house looking like a pair of fighting cocks. Please remember that I've had a shock or two myself today."

Somewhat mollified by the truth of her claims and subtly reminded of his own imperfect past, Philip complied halfheartedly to her suggestion; but halfhearted was not Rebecca's intention. Wrapping her arms firmly around his neck, she persisted in the caressing kiss until he gripped her tightly to him and took the lead with an arousing intensity.

"Christ," he muttered as he pulled away from her with an abrupt urgency, "I'm taking you home until I can regain what little sense I have where you're concerned."

But he didn't! Not for another three dramatically divisive days did they reach the comparative seclusion of El Abrigo. The first impediment was the arrival in the garden of Jesse Milford. Nervously repentant, he willingly agreed to his captain's brusque demands for a drastically altered testimony. The second was the curt order that Philip and Milford received in the brilliantly lit foyer of the Riccard mansion to accompany the two French soldiers to the library. There they were met by the unbending demands of Colonel Auxier, whose black fury stemmed from a second raid on his Port-au-Prince garrison, a raid which was undetected until the weekly musket count proved to be short by thirty weapons. Auxier's ultimatum to the Captains Keane and Riccard gave them a choice of naming Jean Dessalines' hiding place or of facing public accusation. However, after two hours of futile argument and circumvented interrogation, the French commandant agreed to drop all charges in return for the gift of forty muskets from the Falconet et Keane warehouse, guns that had been reserved for sale to the worried plantation owners. Neither of the captains protested; both were cynically familiar with the colony's system of purchased justice.

"Why the devil were you charged, Riccard?" Philip demanded after Auxier had departed.

"It is a game, *mon ami*, but this time I was most happy to play. When I was last here, I allowed Auxier to believe that I had once again broken the one law that keeps these white *imbéciles* from being murdered in their sleep—instant execution of disobedient slaves. Since he knows that I have smuggled hundreds of them to safer places, he was in an excellent bargaining position. I would be spared a public trial in return for the privilege of his buying this home for a third of its worth. I hope he lives long enough to enjoy it; the revolution of Jacques Dessalines will be much bloodier than your American one. *Mon Dieu*, I will be glad to live in a country where the insanity is only temporary! But now, *mon ami*, I suggest we rescue our wives. I promised poor Leoné that I would not leave her alone to face our American guests, and I imagine you promised Rebecca much the same."

Actually, both Leoné and Rebecca had met the unexpected challenges of the unique evening with surprising equanimity. Although the buffet supper and dancing arrangements suggested by her husband were much less formal than the usual Port-au-Prince dinner parties, Madame Riccard had anticipated no great change in the demeanor and activities of her guests. Her first shock was the early arrival of the younger American officers, whose plain suits lacked any hint of sartorial elegance but whose bold and mischievous eagerness soon made the properly mannered young French girls—the three Riccard daughters included—forget all semblance of dignified reticence. Lacking her husband's command of English, Leoné made no effort to curb the youthful exuberance, concentrating her efforts instead on the older Americans and the carefully selected French guests. Since no untoward incident had marred the general felicity of the first two hours, she was able to greet the late-arriving Rebecca Keane and Matthew Stoneham with relaxed graciousness in spite of a momentary suspicion that the young Captain Keane might have once again strayed from the path of matrimonial propriety.

Having been told nothing about the reason for Colonel Auxier's untimely demand to speak with Captain Riccard, Leoné listened without alarm to Matthew's halting explanation that Philip had joined Auxier and Riccard in the library. The evening, she reflected with satisfaction, would not be spoiled by scandal; and she would not be an instrument in hurting the young American artist she'd come to admire. Because she'd also developed a fondness for the unpretentious Matthew Stoneham, who'd been a houseguest on several occasions, Leoné decided to eat her own delayed supper with the two Americans on the festively lighted terrace. They would, after all, be her neighbors in Baltimore and very necessary for her social survival in the foreign America. Thirty minutes later she bitterly regretted deserting her position of hostess, and she was witness to a scene that she would remember with renewed mortification for a goodly number of years.

During Leoné's absence from the drawing room, the names of four additional guests were announced by the

Riccards' majordomo; unfortunately, only the mayor and his wife and a minor chargé d'affaires from the governor's office had been invited. At the insistence of her husband earlier in the day, Leoné had expressly requested Annette Gironde to ignore the prior invitation and remain at home. It had been an embarrassing experience for Madame Riccard to deny hospitality to a woman who for years had been an accepted leader of the elite clique of wealthy Saint-Dominguans.

The sudden disapproving scowl on Matthew's face and the stunned look of disbelief on Leoné's were the silent alarms that alerted Rebecca to the approach of a woman who'd destroyed her peace of mind for two months, but whom she'd seen only once from a distance. She'd known that the confrontation was inevitable from the day Akhoi had told her about Annette Gironde, but for a moment Rebecca felt only a hot fury that her erring husband wasn't here to do his own fighting. Ironically, it was a fleeting memory of the savage fierceness mirrored on the black face of Jean-Jacques Dessalines as he'd stood beside her in the crowded bathroom at El Abrigo that cooled her anger and allowed her to rise with a fair degree of grace to face her adversary. If a beaten and hunted slave could find the courage to fight a hated enemy, so could she!

In the final moments of Annette Gironde's smiling approach, Rebecca had her first opportunity to study her rival at close range. She'd expected a duplication of Paulette Burnell's softly feminine appeal, but this woman's face was dramatically angular, with a hard strength that Paulette's had lacked. And despite the expertly applied powder and rouge, the darkly olive complexion appeared sallow in contrast to the ornate powdered wig. But Rebecca gave full credit to the choice of gown; it was another of her own New London ones—a pale green silk embroidered with tiny frosty-white flowers.

Intent on remembering how costly the fabric had been and how many yards of it the full panniered skirt had required, Rebecca almost missed the significance of Annette Gironde's use of the English language in a question addressed to a French-speaking, nervous hostess.

"Leoné, have you seen Philip Keane? He and I arranged to meet here tonight, but I haven't been able to locate him."

It was a performance worthy of the theater, Rebecca reflected cynically as her pulse beat increased in tempo; and it had been intended for her, not for the disconcerted Leoné, whose stammered reply in French Rebecca understood readily enough, since her own name was mentioned. She braced herself mentally as the vivid, smiling face was turned toward her, and a volume of lightly accented words issued from the faintly carmined lips of Madame Gironde.

"So you're the reason Philip is in hiding! I didn't think you'd have the courage to appear in public after your amusing retreat today. But then, I was surprised several months ago that you chose to remain in Saint-Domingue at all after you'd learned that Philip and I had made other plans while you were cavorting with your former fiancé."

Sensing the tension in the protective arm Matthew had placed around her shoulders, Rebecca hastened to articulate the speech she'd rehearsed on the drive into town despite Philip's insistence that it would not be necessary.

"Philip has told me all about your kindness to him when he first arrived in Port-au-Prince, Madame Gironde."

Momentarily taken aback by the composure of the younger woman whom she'd been told was flighty and trouble prone, Annette's tone of voice sharpened into challenge.

"Then you know he agreed to an annulment so that he'd be free to marry me. That's what Philip and I were going to discuss tonight, how best to tell you that you'll be returning to America without him."

Matthew's laconic denial broke the strained silence that followed the Frenchwoman's bold claim. "She's gulling you, Becky. You know better than to believe the trash a woman like her spouts when she's been beaten at her own dirty game."

Rebecca smiled briefly at the man who'd been her protector in more dangerous situations than this one, before she returned her attention to the woman facing her. "I wasn't sure when I first heard the rumors about you,

Madame Gironde, not until I learned the details of your second husband's murder. Then, of course, I knew that Philip was too cautious a man to risk a similar fate. I will admit that I was disappointed this morning when he didn't push you into the water as Antoine Falconet had several years ago. But I promise you that if you ever again publicly remind my husband of your—your brief liaison with him, I'll push you in myself."

Annette Gironde's face was now a coldly controlled mask, and her voice had lost its charming lightness. "No wonder your husband hides from you at parties, Rebecca Keane; you have the tongue of an asp and the manners of a *cochon*."

Only with difficulty did the younger woman contain her anger long enough to reply to the stinging insult. "As you say, I may be a shrew, but at least I'm a generous one. You may keep the dresses you *borrowed* from me, including the expensive one you're wearing; and you may consider them full payment for the services you rendered."

Although Leoné Riccard understood only a few words of the acrimonious exchange, she knew the tension was explosive. Her plump face reflecting an angry disapproval, she gripped Annette Gironde's arm and propelled her down the terrace steps and into the garden, leaving a shaken Rebecca and a relieved Matthew behind.

"Never met anyone yet who could best you in a battle of words," he affirmed good-naturedly as he reseated her at the small table. "Best forget about her, Becky; you've got nothing to worry about as far as Philip is concerned. I doubt she'd have had the courage to say those things to him."

"Of course she wouldn't! They were intended for me exclusively because she thought I'd act like a ninny again and go running home to Silas. And she'd have the revenge she wanted by breaking up our marriage, which might even survive another few months if I ever see my husband again. Why did Auxier demand to see Philip and Patrice rather than Jed and me? He can't really charge them with anything."

"He won't, Becky. These French officials are a rum lot

who make most of their money through bribery. I imagine Patrice has paid a pretty price for the right to get away from this colony with most of his possessions intact. But Auxier won't be so hard on Philip since the governor wants Abrigo defended as long as possible. Only one thing; does Milford know where those friends of yours are hiding?"

"No, only eight of us know, nine including Philip."

"Good, you'll never need to worry about Philip telling anyone. He's as closemouthed as a tick when it comes to revealing any information."

"Not always. He seems to tell the Falconets everything. Will Edmond Falconet be going with you to New Providence?"

Matthew's eyes narrowed appreciably. "How'd you find out about Nassau?"

"From Silas. Will Edmond be going?"

"He'll be a part of the fleet for the duration, Becky. While Philip and I were cooling our heels in Washington's camp, Falconet went to Philadelphia and wheedled letters of marque from our Congress there."

"Matthew, if America hires scoundrels like that, we're no better than the English."

"I know a dozen respected American merchants who're every bit as unscrupulous as Edmond Falconet. To give the devil his due, he's cooperated with us so far, and he's almost as daring a ship's captain as Philip. During a raid on land, he's even better."

"But he's still dangerous. Everything Philip tells him, he'll tell Madame Gironde; and according to Akhoi, she has friends on both sides. Now that she can't get her hands on Philip's money, do you really think she'll care how she compensates for her *broken heart*? From what I heard in Falmouth, the British will pay very well for information about the Keane fleet. Paulette Burnell had a lovely home at no expense and the best-looking carriage in town."

"I know what the people there thought, Becky; but I don't believe the Burnell woman was guilty of anything other than letting that so-called servant live in her home."

"I know she wasn't, Matthew. She couldn't learn anything from Philip. Except for people like the Falconets, he could be in a drunken sleep and still not talk. But Annette Gironde is not Paulette! Akhoi believes that she helped her first husband murder Emile Gironde and Antoine Falconet. And she could have been the person who warned the British that the entire fleet was anchored in Port-au-Prince harbor two months ago.''

''Relax, Becky. Silas blistered Philip's ears for two days on that same subject. Very unnecessarily as it turns out. This time, Philip won't be announcing any particulars until the night before we leave. In the meantime we have four weeks to train the three hundred raw marines the Massachusetts congress assigned to this mission.''

''Is the raid scheduled for a month from now?''

Matthew smiled ruefully and thanked his lucky providence that he'd remained a bachelor. He'd hate to live with a woman as sharp-minded as this one, who rarely missed a careless slip. ''You ask too many questions I can't answer, young lady,'' he scolded.

''All right,'' she agreed readily, ''I'll ask some you can answer. Did you see my father while you were in General Washington's camp?''

''Jeremy wasn't there, Becky.''

''Where is he? The last I heard, he was with General Philip Schuyler at the Canadian border.''

''Schuyler's been temporarily retired because of illness and his command taken over by someone named Arnold—odd first name I can't remember. He was supposed to have served with our colonial militia at Ticonderoga.''

''That'll be Benedict Arnold, Matthew, but he wasn't a member of the Massachusetts militia. He's a Rhode Island merchant captain; and according to Mr. Cooper, he was a greater hero than Ethan Allen. Do you know where Arnold is now?''

''He was sent with an army to capture Quebec.''

''You mean General Washington sent an army to Canada instead of trying to retake Boston?'' Rebecca demanded in disbelief.

''No, he still has sixteen thousand men besieging Boston.

Arnold's force numbered only seven hundred because Washington expects the Candians to join the revolution.''

'Well, they won't! Canadians don't hate the British; they have too many problems with the French settlers there. Besides, they have better sense than to fight against the thousands of English soldiers in Montreal and Quebec. Did Arnold's men follow the Kennebec River from Falmouth?''

"As a matter of fact, they did.''

"Then Jeremy will be with that army. He knows the route all the way to Canada. Was there a battle, Matthew?''

"I don't know, Becky. The expedition was still under way when Philip and I left, but don't worry about Jeremy. He's had years of experience in frontier warfare.''

"So did Ethan Allen!'' she rejoined glumly. "And he's a prisoner-of-war!''

"Becky, those of us who fought in the last war don't have any illusions about the risk. I'll wager that Jeremy would be among the làst to call foul if he's unlucky, so let's stow the gloom and enjoy ourselves. I for one would like another glass of Leoné's syllabub; it's got a right tasty bite to it.''

Rebecca smothered a faint smile. "That frothy punch isn't just wine and milk curd, Matthew. It's what Jed made to celebrate when Auxier finally left Abrigo, and he called it 'white lightning.' You'll find out why if you drink too much of it. Jed mixed bowls full of rum and champagne and whipped egg whites and then told Jesse Milford it was a cure for seaman's clap. Milford ordered every one of the men to drink two mugs of it, and even sneaked out a portion for himself.''

"Best you never mention that particular disease in polite society, young lady,'' Matthew chided her before he burst into a rumbling laughter. "By God, I'll wager that's the first time those men ever took any medicine without grumbling.''

Had Matthew known that his desire for a second glass of champagne punch would precipitate a second minor crisis, he'd have gone without and kept Rebecca isolated on the terrace until Philip could join them. Unknown to him, the

caustic attack and counterattack between Rebecca and
Annette Gironde had not escaped notice as he'd hoped; it
had been witnessed by a young couple with distinctly
divided loyalties. While Leoné Riccard had barred the
older Falconets from her party, she'd seen no need to deny
her own daughters the pleasure of having the younger of
the Falconet girls as an overnight guest. And the seventeen-
year-old Charlotte Falconet was most prejudicially aware
that the unexpected arrival of the pale blonde *Américaine,*
Rebecca Keane, in Saint-Domingue had cheated her much
admired cousin Annette of an advantageous marriage.

When she'd seen Annette hurriedly cross the ballroom
floor and exit onto the terrace, Charlotte had maneuvered
her American dance partner into the garden and behind
some shrubbery from where she could overhear her cousin
without being detected. To her chagrin the conversation
between Annette and the detested *Américaine* had been in
English, a language the French girl understood not at all;
but she'd been furious when her hostess had virtually
dragged Annette rather than the offensive Madame Keane
into the garden.

In contrast, the young Bostonian who'd accompanied her
had been a student at Harvard until he'd joined the revolution as an officer in the Massachusetts marines; and he was
expert in both languages. Moreover, he'd been on the
Reine deck that morning when the overbearing Frenchwoman
had accosted his captain; and like many of his shipmates,
he'd watched the small sailboat in the distance and learned
from the older hands that the sailor was Mrs. Philip
Keane. He'd learned other things as well, so much so that
he understood fully the import of the English dialogue and
the subsequent French one delivered in sharp, strident
whispers as Madame Riccard pushed Annette Gironde
along the garden path.

Being a Bostonian who shared his community's distrust
of foreigners, even potential French allies, the young
lieutenant's sympathies and admiration were completely in
favor of his captain's wife. Minutes later after he'd returned
his partner to the ballroom, he was delighted that he'd had
the foresight not to reveal his knowledge of French to the

rather unattractive girl. As he stood next to her, hiding behind a vapid smile of incomprehension, he listened to the vindictive Charlotte regale a small bevy of her friends with a highly colored account of the incident, an outraged gush of words that labeled Rebecca Keane as a villainess and her cousin as the offended heroine. When one of the girls gave a warning hiss about the Bostonian overhearing, Charlotte responded airily with an insulting shrug, *"Le stupide ne comprends pas!"*

Without a flicker of shame, he listened to the entire report and to the giggling responses it received, many of them unflattering commentaries about himself and his companions. His moment of revenge came as the music started up and Charlotte reached possessively for his arm. In accurate French he called her a maliciously dishonest child and her cousin something substantially worse before he left her standing in the middle of the floor with her mouth unattractively open. Walking swiftly away, he was in time to intercept four of his fellow officers and to turn them back toward the refreshment table where he gave them an edited account of both incidents. Since he wanted no trouble with the fierce-eyed commander whom they shared in common, he omitted all mention of Captain Keane's affair with the Frenchwoman.

As a result of his efforts, a partisan cadre of five Americans was waiting to greet Captain Stoneham and Mrs. Keane when they arrived at the punch bowl. From that moment on, as the young men discovered that she was as articulate and lively as she was comely, and no more adept in formal ballroom dancing than they were, they began a game of dancing a travesty of the stately minuet three at a time with her.

Such was the sorry condition of her carefully planned reception when Leoné Riccard returned from the onerous task of summoning the chargé d'affaires and ordering the startled man to escort Madame Gironde to her own home. Met with a chorus of complaints from the deserted girls, Leoné listened patiently until she heard the word *égoïste* used to describe Rebecca Keane and *sots stupides* applied to the American officers. Although Leoné was a tolerant and tractable wife, she was a stern mother with a sharp eye to the social future of her daughters. Demanding that her oldest one tell the entire story, she listened with narrowed eyes before she turned toward the culprit who'd started the trouble.

"Charlotte, ta cousine Annette fus à faute ce soir; et tu es une enfant ignorante."

Having delivered the sharp reprimand, the plump Frenchwoman walked determinedly onto the dance floor and scolded the five young Americans with equal asperity. While a chastened Rebecca attempted to apologize, it was the Bostonian who explained to his hostess some of the causes of the misunderstanding. As Leoné listened to him with growing admiration, she speculated shrewdly that he'd make a splendid husband for her middle daughter who, like Leoné herself, needed a domineering man. But, alas for her incipient plans, while the young man advised his companions to reclaim the French girls as dance partners, he escorted Rebecca to Captain Stoneham's secluded terrace table and remained.

Irritably hungry after eighteen hours without food during what had been an exhaustingly tense day, Philip delayed the search for his wife until after he'd joined his host in consuming a plateful of sustaining supper delicacies. Still unsatisfied, he enthusiastically agreed with Riccard that they'd earned a tumbler full of champagne punch as well. Thus it was the decision to visit the refreshment table in the ballroom that crashed their improving moods back into angry vexation. A young woman accosted them with an emotionally delivered complaint about the insulting actions of one of the American officers. Philip's scowl of concern deepened when Riccard identified the girl as the youngest of the Falconets. He didn't need the additional problem of an *affaire d'honneur* threatening the already strained relations between the Keanes and Falconets. Jean and Edmond would be angry enough when they learned that they'd be losing forty rifles.

Riccard and Philip reacted characteristically to Charlotte's charges. More knowledgeable about the emotional exaggerations of young females, the Frenchman left to find his wife and a more reasonable explanation, while Philip, whose own officer was the accused man, agreed to accompany the girl in search of the lieutenant in question. Had he not been so preoccupied with his own anger, Philip would have noticed that his young guide led the way with a purposeful step and that her thin, waspish face mirrored a vindictive anticipation.

Unlike Philip, Rebecca had no trouble recognizing a Falconet, even an immature one wearing a ridiculously overcurled wig; she also correctly identified the expression on the girl's face. It held a malicious intensity of purpose that was leveled squarely at her rather than at Matthew or the lieutenant. Rebecca listened with keen interest to Philip ask the Bostonian if his insults to Miss Falconet had been intentional or merely the unfortunate result of a language difficulty.

Having risen abruptly to stand at rigid attention, the lieutenant responded tersely, "Intentional, sir. At the time she didn't realize that I understood her language. When I overheard her telling the other French girls some ugly lies about—about a friend of mine, I merely called her what she was."

In a flash of understanding, Rebecca realized that she was the friend and that the lies concerned her meeting with Annette Gironde. Hastily she pushed her chair back and stood up.

"Philip, you're about to scold the wrong person," she warned him sharply. "Lieutenant Haskins was merely trying to protect my reputation. He and Miss Falconet evidently witnessed an unpleasant scene that took place some time ago here on the terrace, and she is upset because our hostess asked her relative to leave rather than me."

Rebecca watched the dull flush of comprehension darken her husband's face and heard his muttered curse, but her smile of gratitude was focused on the blunt young lieutenant standing beside her. He'd rushed to the defense of his captain's wife even before he'd met her, and he'd been willing to accept punishment without exposing her. His captain, on the other hand, seemed intent only on charming a spoiled, vicious seventeen-year-old simply because she was French and a member of the unscrupulous family that had dominated his life for too long.

CHAPTER
11

AWAKENING sluggishly late the following morning, Rebecca glanced at the man beside her who was still heavily asleep and then turned her head away to gaze without enthusiasm at the sun-dappled interior of the cabin aboard the *Reine*. Only at the last minute the night before had Philip informed her casually that they wouldn't be returning to Abrigo until the crew had completed its promised leave. His only response to her protest that she had no replacement clothing had been a skewed grin and a confiding whisper that she wouldn't be needing any.

But then, she remembered dismally, the entire evening had been a disaster. Before she and Lieutenant Haskins could reseat themselves while Philip solicitously tucked the smirking Charlotte Falconet into a chair, Matthew laconically suggested they fetch another pitcher of Leoné's syllabub. Contrarily, Rebecca had not rushed to fulfill the request, deciding instead that she and her equally maligned companion had already paid for their truancy and could take the time out for a lively contredanse. Upon arriving back at the table, they'd found the size of the gathering increased by the addition of the Riccards and another

French couple. Smiling with a pleasant, well-simulated composure, Rebecca had adroitly avoided taking the vacant chair next to Philip's and chosen instead a shadowed location near Matthew. She'd listened with a grudging admiration to her husband's eloquent and mendacious assurance that no American at Abrigo had aided in the escape of the dangerous band of slaves. She'd also listened with a sharp twinge of conscience to the unknown Frenchman's faltering English as he described the fear and tension among plantation owners in the remote areas. They were almost as imprisoned as the slaves they feared!

Of more trivial interest was Riccard's solution to the problem of Charlotte Falconet. Rebecca had been amused to see the wily privateer joking with the girl much as he had with Rebecca herself at the Falconet party. He would make a very popular politician, she mused with a fleeting humor. As other guests drifted by, she'd noticed how often the women greeted Philip with arch familiarity and how he responded with an automatic charm that heightened the dramatic appeal of his lean good looks. Rebecca's sense of detachment had been threatened only once, when one of the more roguish of the women had murmured something in French. Instantly Philip had looked in Rebecca's direction, and their eyes had met for the first time since they'd parted in the Riccards' foyer hours before. She had withdrawn farther into the shadow after that brief clash; he was very sure of his appeal to her, she'd thought tiredly.

In the privacy of their cabin aboard the *Reine,* though, he hadn't been sure of anything—he'd been quietly drunk, and she'd had to help him out of his clothes and into bed. His helplessness had shocked her and made her forget her own light-headed unsteadiness. She'd never before considered him vulnerable. This morning she noted other changes in him as well. Even in deep sleep he was restless, and his face was lined with fatigue.

Thoughtfully Rebecca slipped out of bed and rummaged through her husband's sea chest until she located a pair of canvas breeches and a jersey. Dressing hurriedly, she went in search of Louis or Leon and hopefully of a pot of hot, black coffee; but instead of the soft-spoken mulattoes, she found only a cantankerous Jed Daws in the galley.

"What're you doing here?" she asked in surprise. "You're supposed to be hiding in Matthew Stoneham's ship."

"I 'uz there only long enough to see the others stayed put. Ain't no way that fancy-steppin' Frenchie kin outtalk the cap'n. Good thing I come back here too. The water-front scum the cap'n hired as cooks took off whin they hit this port and ain't been heard of since."

"What happened to Leon and Louis?"

"Stayed with the old cap'n in Baltimore, near as I kin figure. Heered tell they took care of him when they 'uz on the raid in Tobago. Reckon you'll be needing coffee, Becky. Seen you and the cap'n stumble around some when you come aboard last night. Reckon the cap'n's still asleep; ain't never seen him drunk afore. You two still feudin'?"

Irritated by the cook's blunt curiosity, Rebecca inquired sharply, "What about the coffee, Jed?"

"Ain't ready yet. Only jest now got this place clean enough fer cookin'. What crew is still aboard made do with watered grog and sea biscuits fer breakfast. Was the Frenchie woman there last night?"

Laughing helplessly at his unabashed persistence, Rebecca replied, "She was, but the captain didn't see her."

"Then what're you so all-fired glum about?"

"Because the captain decided he was the appointed champion of still another Falconet woman, this one a nasty girl."

"What would she be to the Frenchie cap'n of *L'Aventure*?"

"Baby sister, I suppose."

"Then the cap'n only done what 'uz best if what I heered 'uz true. Seems like the Frenchie saved the cap'n's ship from being smashed by a limey ship-of-line. Course I ain't believin' what I 'uz told until I know the straight of it. Only the cap'n and the officers kin really see what goes on once the fightin' begins. They git t' stand on the quarterdeck and kin see both to starboard and larboard."

"Doesn't the captain usually remain in the cockpit?" Rebecca demanded with a nagging fear.

"S'posed to, but the cap'n ain't like the others. He races all around so's he'll know what's going wrong, and he ain't above usin' a long gun hisself."

"When did this battle take place, Jed?"

"Jest after the fleet 'uz leaving French waters early on the first morning out. Two limey privateers 'uz waiting, and the *Reine* took a poundin' afore she knocked one of the devils out. But it 'uz a skulkin' ship-of-line waitin' in ambush that almost sank her. S'posedly that's when the Frenchie ran *L'Aventure* with all her cannon primed twixt the *Reine* and the limey. Reckon if the story's true, Becky, we 'uz wrong about the Frenchie. If you 'uz to read the Cap'n's log while you 'uz havin' your coffee, might be we'd both find out. Leastwise we'd know a thing or two more 'n we do now."

Rebecca needed no urging to open the heavy volume that chronicled the most recent part of her husband's life at sea. Written in the plain language of a man preoccupied with accuracy, it was a terse record of a ship and its crew; and the pages that described the encounter with the two privateers and the British ship-of-line were unemotional and factual. As the lead ship when the fleet emerged from protected Saint-Domingue waters at dawn the morning after they sailed from Port-au-Prince, the *Reine* had been first attacked; and the battle had progressed much as Jed had thought. However, Philip had been more thorough than Jed's informants about the action of *L'Aventure*. Edmond Falconet had risked his ship when the man-of-war moved in to attack while the *Reine* was still engaged with the second privateer.

Rebecca continued to read the carefully dated pages of the log with a gripping fascination, understanding for the first time something of the strain of command. The bleak sentences beginning with the words, "I ordered the marines aloft"; "I read the services for the twelve shipmates lost in the battle"; and "I ordered a dozen lashes for the marine who threatened the life of a rigger when one of the rat lines gave way" were revelations to a young woman who'd seen only one person die in her twenty-one years. She wondered if she'd ever have the courage to face the danger her husband did or the strength to order other men to risk their lives. Yet men like Jed Daws and John Sugs gave Philip their complete loyalty and trust—men who'd been sailors more years than he was old. Rebecca jerked at the sound of her husband's voice.

"What are you reading with such concentration that you didn't hear me calling you, Cottontop?" he asked with the peevish irritability of a headache-ridden man. "I hope that there's more coffee in the pot and that you had the sense to order something for this damned head of mine," he added less aggressively.

Rebecca surveyed his disheveled appearance with a tolerant giggle. "I ordered the medicine for myself, but there's enough of it left for you. And the coffee's still hot."

"Good," he mumbled as he lowered himself gingerly into a chair. Blinking owlishly, he peered over at the book in front of her and demanded querulously, "Why the devil are you reading the ship's log?"

"Something Jed said made me curious."

"Is that old reprobate aboard?"

"Yes, he was certain you'd be able to charm away Colonel Auxier's suspicions. Did you?"

"They weren't suspicions, Cottontop, they were certainties; but he settled for the gift of forty rifles to replace the ones your friend stole. Milford's delivering them this morning. Did you find what you wanted to know in the log?"

"Yes. Charlotte Falconet is a beautiful, charming girl."

"She's a pampered twit, but that doesn't change the fact that her brother risked his ship to save mine. It shouldn't take long, Cottontop, but I do have to see the Falconets today; and I'd appreciate your remaining inside the cabin while I'm gone. There's a hundred and fifty raw recruits aboard, and I don't need any more trouble with them at the moment."

Resisting the impulse to say, "Aye, aye, Captain," Rebecca protested mildly, "It's too hot to remain inside this box all day, Philip."

"It's your own fault. If you hadn't caused me this extra work, we'd be able to spend the day together. But now that pleasure will have to wait, and you'll have to spend the afternoon alone."

Resentful of being forced to shoulder all the blame for his present ill-humor, Rebecca asked abruptly, "Will we be returning to Baltimore on schedule?"

"Within four months, if we're lucky."

"Did you know that Patrice Riccard has already bought a home there?"

"That's right. Only it's more of an estate than a town house."

"Did you think to acquire one for us?"

"No, I didn't, Cottontop. My father expects you to live with him while I'm away, and he's promised to keep you busy."

"Do you really think he'll enjoy being resident grandfather to our children?"

"My God, you're not—"

"No, I'm not, but it is quite possible in the future."

"Not until after the war, I hope."

"I didn't know it was a matter of choice; I thought I was just lucky. You can stop frowning, Philip; I've decided I much prefer our current life to motherhood and housekeeping. And as long as we're going to be here for another four months, I might even buy myself a wig and one of those intriguing mask fans."

"Why don't you stop talking nonsense and go get us another pot of coffee while I finish dressing. And don't bother Jed any more than you have to today; he has work to do."

Nothing short of a tropical hurricane could have broken Jed Daws's concentration on his beloved galley as he ordered six unlucky helpers to scour and rescour until he was satisfied. But for once, Rebecca didn't need his cheerful companionship to break the monotony of a lonely exile. As soon as Philip left the ship, she located paper, ink, and an earlier log. In the two volumes before her was the authentic background for a story that could be as grimly exciting as "Mama Mambo." Without hesitation she wrote the title "Captain King" and began copying whole paragraphs from the journals. Gradually from her copious notes, the character of the hero emerged, a man she was just beginning to know, a master whose word was law once his ship cleared port. By dating the story 1756, she used another war and a different enemy; but the battles were the same and the action remained faithful to Philip's descriptions.

The cabin was almost in darkness when she finally laid down the quill pen and straightened her cramped fingers. Strewn over the table were pages of messy writing, but Rebecca was supremely satisfied with her day-long efforts. In writing a story about her husband, she'd come to accept the limitations of her marriage. Too much of his emotional intensity was expended in his battles on and with the sea for him to cope willingly with a complicated wife or with a family. During wartime a privateer captain could not afford the luxury of a sentimental attachment to land; his was the lonely job of command, and it required his total concentration.

In her haste to gather the pages together, Rebecca knocked over the tray of untouched food that had been delivered hours earlier. Writing was also an absorbing occupation, she reflected with a wry humor; she could barely remember the frightened young cabin boy who'd made the delivery. But she couldn't ignore Jed's demanding knock on the door or his scolding voice as he pushed his way into the cabin.

"What in tarnation are you settin' around in the dark fer? The lad I sent with your supper says you didn't even answer him. And whin I couldn't locate you on the deck, I 'uz worried you might've took off agin on account of the cap'n ain't come back yet. Well, he ain't coming until he finishes the business of sellin' cargoes. The lads were durned upset yesterday when the cap'n warn't there to pertect our share."

"I thought that was Mr. Milford's responsibility."

"Old Milford's worse than a squawkin' jaybird when it

comes to sellin'. Only the Cap'n kin git top price if the buyers git skittish, and even the Dutchies' are goin' t' dicker a long time afore they buy the two limey merchantmen we took twixt Baltimore and here. Usually the Dutchies ain't pertickular as long as a ship'll make it around the Horn and 'cross the Pacific to them East Indian islands they own. Heered tell some of them're bigger 'n Maine, with enough spices to fill a thousand ships. But now I reckon the Dutchies are as scairt as we are of bein' caught in a brig too slow to outrun the limeys.''

The most bearable aspects of a conversation with the garrulous cook, Rebecca mused as she prepared for bed two hours later, was that she was seldom required to participate and that eventually his ramblings yielded the information she wanted. Because the entire crew, even those men who'd remained behind during the last voyage, shared in the proceeds from the sale of captured ships and cargoes, Captain Keane had been under the eager surveillance of his own crew the entire day. Rebecca smiled with relief; her newfound tolerance did not extend to clandestine rendezvous with mistresses, old or new.

Hours later, long after she'd concluded that her relief had been premature, she heard sounds in the outer cabin—a pair of muted thuds and a hastily repressed curse. Her first dismal thought was that her husband was as drunk as he'd been the night before; but when he entered the darkened bedroom, his movements were efficiently surefooted.

"You can use a lantern, Philip," she called out.

"Don't need one, Cottontop, and why aren't you asleep? It's after midnight."

"I know," she replied neutrally. "You've been gone a long time."

"Couldn't be helped, sweetheart, I've been busy."

Vaguely resentful of the exuberance in his tone of voice, she asked the expected question, "Doing what?" and flinched at the sound of his laughter.

"Selling ships, Cottontop! We sold both prizes in a single day to the Dutch East Indies Company. There won't be a sober sailor in town tonight, but you and I will be doing our celebrating tomorrow."

For the second time she asked the question, "Doing what?"

"Oh, I'll think of something! Good night, Cottontop."

Rebecca was still seething with indignant curiosity minutes after her invincible Captain King had fallen asleep with the ease of a blameless child. She was far more annoyed with him when she awoke the following morning to find him gone. As usual, she reflected with a scornful resentment, she learned more of her husband's business from the ship's cook than she did from her husband.

"Is the captain aboard?" she asked Jed as he served her breakfast.

"Reckon not, Becky. Him and two of the Dutchies left ship an hour ago. Reckon they got some more dickerin' t' do 'bout the sale of them limey merchantmen. Dutchies are as demandin' as hometown Yankees whin it comes t' gettin' what they bargained fer. Cap'n says you 'uz t' be ready by the time he gits back."

"Ready for what?" she asked in exasperation.

"A party, I reckon. Cap'n 'most a'ways gives one afore he clears port. Heerd tell the Hotel Royale is jest 'bout the fanciest in the whole Caribbean. S'posed t' be a dead ringer fer the one in France where the durn Frenchie gents do their playin'."

"Has my husband hosted other parties at this Hotel Royale, Jed?"

"Reckon this'll be his third; folks hereabouts don't cotton much t' shipboard dinners."

Stiffly refraining from asking her old friend if Madame Gironde had played the hostess at the earlier two affairs, Rebecca turned her attention to more practical considerations.

"Did he make any arrangements for me to return to Abrigo, Jed? I only have one dress here, and I don't imagine he'd appreciate my wearing these breeches in public."

"Cap'n says you 'uz to look inside these chests he had lugged aboard last night. Reckon it's his way of payin' back them fancies of yourn what got stole. One of the sail makers is waitin' t' see if you'll be needin' a stitch or two to make 'em fit. Used t' be a tailor's apprentice in Boston, so he's right handy with a needle.''

"It won't be necessary, Jed. I'll wear my own dress."

"Cap'n reckoned you'd git mulish onct he 'uz gone, so he sent it back to the fort with the lads who 'uz returnin' t' duty. What in tarnation are you complainin' about, Becky? Best you start choosin' the purtiest dress in them chests and stop fussin'. Cap'n's parties gener'ly start in the afternoon.''

In spite of her reluctance to acquire any more clothing that had been intended for other women, Rebecca was pleased that one of the chests contained garments suitable for American winters. She was less than thrilled about the color her husband had chosen, however; everything from the fur-lined cloak to the exquisitely tailored petticoats was black. As she closed the lid of the chest, Rebecca experienced a momentary chill; black was her favorite color, but it was also the symbol of mourning and death. She had no desire to tempt fate by wearing either of the two somber dresses.

Ironically, she was even more repelled by the brilliant magnificence of the gown that occupied most of the space in the second sea chest. She recognized the style as a Pompadour, the dress her New London seamstresses insisted had been the favorite of Paris aristocrats ever since the old king's favorite mistress had made it famous. Rebecca had laughed at the ridiculous excess of a six-foot-wide skirt and refused to consider even a modified version. But now she was faced with the prospect of wearing one so opulent it seemed more like a costume for a royal princess than a party dress for an American privateer's wife. The heavy ivory silk of the skirt and bodice was stiffened with small pink and coral flowers woven into the fabric while the wide front panel of the skirt was encrusted with tiny pearls. That the gown required only an hour of the sail maker's skill to make the waist two inches smaller was a tribute to Philip's memory, Rebecca mused with a sharp pang of jealousy as she wondered if he'd been as accurate about his mistresses' measurements.

As she practiced walking in the confines of the cabin,

forcing herself to move gracefully despite the encumbrance
of the heavy belled-out skirt, Rebecca's dour mood lightened to one of reckless humor. Since her heroic husband
wanted a wife who'd be little more than an available
bedmate and a woman he could display in public, she
decided that on this occasion at least, she'd be very much
on display. She giggled as she glanced downward at the
square-cut neckline of her Pompadour, which revealed two
inches more of breast than the most daring of her other
dresses. Her lively sense of comic irony remained intact
even though Matthew Stoneham and Lieutenant Haskins,
rather than her husband, escorted her to the palatial Hotel
Royale.

In the small, mirrored ballroom, one of the several the
establishment maintained for private parties, some thirty of
the assembled guests were already celebrating. For a
moment Rebecca did not recognize her husband among the
participants of the dignified quadrille under way on the
dance floor until she remembered the gold satin suit she'd
seen in the closet of the Émeraude cottage. Although the
flamboyant style and the powdered wig altered his appearance considerably, she admitted silently that he still looked
handsomely masculine. Quite obviously his slender young
partner was equally impressed, and Rebecca felt some of
her lightheartedness dim as she watched Philip smile down
at the expensively garbed woman with the practiced charm
his wife had begun to hate.

But when a sympathetically observant Matthew guided
her toward a group of people standing near the refreshment
table, Rebecca's own smile reflected none of her momentary insecurity. Both Patrice Riccard and Edmond Falconet
greeted her with compliments about her own exotic appearance, and she was gratified by the flash of envy that
sharpened Charlotte Falconet's avid features. However, it
was the bold look of speculation on the sanguine face of a
stranger, introduced to Rebecca as Captain du Kuyper of
the Dutch East Indies Company, that refired her earlier
reckless mood. With small regard for propriety she accepted the Dutchman's invitation to join the dancers; and thus,
during one of the traverses of the patterned dance, she

faced her startled husband for the first time in more than a day. Instantly his pleasant expression was replaced by one of disapproval as his narrowed eyes measured the expanse of her exposed bosom, and his color reddened with anger as he noted her challenging smile. That anger increased considerably when she accepted the invitation of another Dutch captain before her outraged husband could rid himself of his own partner.

Unlike the dark-skinned Captain du Kuyper, the middle-aged Hals Van Rickstaad was as comfortably blonde as the Holland mariners who'd been Jonathan Langley's longtime friends. His blue eyes twinkled as he led her with surprising skill for an overplump gentleman through the unrestrained gallop of a contredanse.

As Philip had discovered throughout his two days with the indefatigable Dutchman, Rickstaad was far more than an accomplished dancer. With England now challenged by a rebellious group of thirteen American colonies, Rickstaad had been among the Dutch agents commissioned to determine the capability of those colonies to sustain a revolution. His particular assignment had been to evaluate the patriotism of American privateers. If he determined that these sea captains had pledged themselves to fight their enemy at sea, Rickstaad would recommend that the powerful Dutch merchants group he represented help finance the American revolution. There would be little of altruism in the offer; Holland wanted the British naval power concentrated in the North Atlantic rather than in the Caribbean Sea and the Indian Ocean where the Dutch plied their trade.

It was no accident that Rickstaad had arrived in Port-au-Prince before the return of the Keane fleet. During the two months he spent on the Dutch island of Aruba, he'd learned a good deal about the privateers operating in the Caribbean, and how successful the Keanes had been. The only finding that had distressed him was the partnership with the French Falconets. Like most of his countrymen, Rickstaad distrusted the French as much as he did the English. However, he admitted with an innate honesty, the Dutch privateers operating under the auspices of the West

Indies Company had committed as many acts of piracy as
had the French. In the past two days he'd withheld judgment on Edmond Falconet but approved heartily of Philip
Keane's intentions about the war and those of the older
American captain. It'd been Matthew Stoneham who'd
recommended that Rickstaad talk to Mistress Keane about
colonial military strength.

As a careful husband who'd protected his own wife
from all political realities for a quarter of a century, the
Dutchman had been amused by the suggestion; moreover,
he'd expected an older, plainer woman than the vivid girl
who danced with him at the party. Convinced that any
woman as young as this one would prove woefully ignorant, Rickstaad had been cautious about meeting her, so
cautious, in fact, that a man he detested had reached her
first.

Dirk du Kuyper was one of the thousands of half-breeds
hired by the East Indies Company to man the vast merchant fleet—the product of a marriage between a Dutch
company employee and a native woman. In this case the
father had been the director of the Java office and the
mother a Batak princess, one of the hundreds of daughters
produced by the numerous political chieftains. Like his
older brothers, who worked for the company in lower-
echelon positions, Dirk had been well educated in Holland;
but unlike his brothers, he'd chosen the sea and had
become the most daring of the company privateers, amassing
by the time he was thirty a fortune reputed to be one of the
largest in Sumatra. Had the bounder not been so damnably
arrogant, Rickstaad reflected bitterly, he might have gained
some degree of acceptance with the white colonists. Certainly the fact that he was the finest navigator in the
company made him a valued employee, and Rickstaad
himself always requested du Kuyper's services as fleet
commander when he traveled abroad. But the charlatan
had refused to accept the prevailing Dutch mores; he'd
defied the company order to convert to Lutheranism,
clinging instead to his mother's heathenish religion that
had been introduced to the natives centuries before by the
Arab traders. Du Kuyper was a Muslim with a Muslim's

attitude toward marriage; and he'd possessed enough of the devil's own charm to persuade two attractive Dutch women to join what amounted to a cursed harem. Moreover, he maintained a native mistress aboard his ship.

Yesterday when Philip Keane had extended the invitation for this party, Rickstaad had subtly warned the American not to include du Kuyper; but his advice had gone unheeded. And now it was Rickstaad's unpleasant duty to alert his host's reckless young wife about the danger of enticing such a man. East Indies Company officials were paid handsomely to prevent trouble whenever possible. As soon as his own dance with her concluded, he guided her swiftly to a corner table and seated her with authoritative courtesy.

Beaming with a paternalistic concern, Rickstaad leaned across the table. "Mistress Keane," he began with the patronizing assurance of a wealthy man, "this morning your husband and I concluded a business arrangement far more important than the mere purchase of two ships. He has agreed to supply the company with all the ships he and his father acquire which are too slow for their wartime activity. It is therefore important that no one in my company offers you an insult that might interfere with that agreement. But before I explain, there is another matter that concerns me, and Captain Stoneham informed me that you might be of some help."

Thoroughly bored with his fatherly condescension, Rebecca looked across the room hoping to catch Philip's eye and signal her need for a timely rescue. But as he had been all evening, her Captain King was solicitously engaged in being gallant to the pair of young ladies he'd danced with alternately for the past hour. Resignedly, she returned her attention back toward her unsought companion and discovered to her amazement that the Dutch merchant was talking avidly about the American revolt, and he was asking her for specific information.

Before she'd worked for Eldin Cooper, Rebecca had been relatively disinterested in such details; but the New London editor had been a zealot about facts and figures and the names and individual accomplishments of the colonial patriots. Thus she was able to answer the probing questions with a fair degree of remembered accuracy—the outcome of the battles, the relative strength and training of the colonial militia, and the determination of its leaders. It was his penetrating questions about the character of New Englanders that finally aroused her anger.

Glaring at the plumply pink face opposite her and at the sparkling pin adorning his white silk tie, she lashed back, "Mister Rickstaad, few of my countrymen will ever earn a tenth of the money your lovely diamond cost, but thousands of them are risking their lives for the illusion of freedom. Men like my father and Simon Parrish and William Prescott consider what you called a 'disorganized rebellion' a holy crusade. They may retreat from battle but they'll never surrender; my father-in-law will fight to his last ship, and my husband is reckless enough to challenge a ship-of-line. I don't approve of this war, but *they* do and they're determined to win it."

Smiling broadly now, the Dutchman reached over and patted her clenched hands. "I thank you, Mistress Keane," he intoned sententiously. "You have helped me make a difficult decision."

"What decision?" she asked cautiously, already regretting her outburst.

"To assure Holland businessmen that it would be to their best interests to invest in your revolution. England is as much our enemy as yours. Now, about that other problem we were discussing. Tell me, mistress, have you ever heard the expression *pukka sahib*? It's an Indian term—from India, mistress, not from your American savages—and it means *gentleman*. It is the reason I came to your assistance tonight. I regret having to speak ill of a company employee, but I'm afraid Captain du Kuyper is unfortunately not a *pukka sahib*."

Rebecca's modest expression concealed an inner mirth; it was the word *unfortunately* that had triggered one of her fonder memories of a popular minister in Falmouth. Often praised for his Christian charity and tolerance, Reverend Pitkins had persistently called Indians, Negroes, and all non-English-speaking immigrants "the unfortunates of the

earth'' and described Quakers, Catholics, and Jews as
"unfortunately misguided."

Without a hint of a smile, she leaned toward Rickstaad
and asked confidentially, "You mean Captain du Kuyper is
not a gentleman because he is half Malaysian?"

"How did you learn that, mistress?"

"He asked about my antecedents, so I asked about his.
Are the Malaysians savages?"

"Not precisely savages, mistress; some of them do have
a crude form of culture. Unfortunately many of them,
especially the Bataks, have adopted a heathen religion. I
believe you Americans refer to it as Mohammedanism."

Enjoying herself for the first time during the lengthy
conversation, Rebecca nodded alertly. "I've read about it
in stories of the medieval crusades." And from Jonathan,
she added silently, remembering the Islamic Turk who'd
been her uncle's finest sail maker until he'd left America
to rejoin his four wives in Ankara.

"A young lady such as yourself," Rickstaad continued,
"would have no way of knowing about the degradation of
such a religion. Suffice to say, men like du Kuyper are not
safe companions for decent women, especially a pretty
blonde one. He has a penchant for blonde women, perhaps
to compensate for his own dark blood. Mind you, he's not
a savage, and I do appreciate his numerous talents; but—"

Resisting the impulse to bat her eyelashes with pretended innocence, Rebecca prompted gently, "But?"

"He has strange habits, mistress."

"Such as?"

"He—Bluntly, mistress, he has several wives whom he
leaves at his various homes while he travels with some
native woman who is not a wife. There now, I've told you
the brutal truth, so you take care, young Mistress Keane,
and forgive an old man for meddling in your life. I'll bid
you good night, mistress, and see to the welfare of my
own daughters before I retire. I'm afraid that they've been
monopolizing your husband's time today and yesterday;
but then, he's the only man here I could trust with the
assignment. They're young and naive yet, and somewhat

restless with the confinement of travel. I was happy to allow them this opportunity for a little recreation.''

Rebecca's slight smile did not waver as she gazed once again at her husband and his two companions. Neither girl appeared naive to her prejudiced eyes. Although the short blonde one had inherited her father's complacency, she still clung to Philip's arm with a possessive tenacity. However, it was the slender brunette whom Rebecca studied the most carefully, concluding cynically that the cloistered Holland school must have had very low walls. She looked like a younger version of Paulette Burnell with all of Paulette's sensual confidence, and she was managing quite successfully to keep Philip's attention focused on her to the exclusion of her sister.

Absorbed by the disturbing spectacle, Rebecca jerked imperceptibly when Hals Van Rickstaad delayed his departure with yet another question.

"Mistress Keane, something you said still bothers me. Why is it you do not approve of the war your father and husband are fighting?"

Discarding all trace of pretended innocence, Rebecca countered with another question, "Mr. Rickstaad, are your daughters free to marry whom they will or will you choose for them?"

"I've arranged for them to meet their husbands-to-be for the first time when we reach Sumatra. I am a careful father, mistress, as I'm certain yours was when he planned your marriage."

"Then the answer to your question as to why I dislike war is obvious. Just as in the case of your daughters, a woman does not care who rules the country since her obedience is expected to be exclusively to her father and her husband. I can only hope that your daughters find the husbands you have chosen for them as attractive as they have found mine."

Rickstaad's beaming smile returned, and he nodded with a complacent assurance. "They will, mistress, they most assuredly will!"

Rebecca watched with a stoic composure as he strode across the dance floor with a dancer's balance and spoke briefly to Philip before he kissed his daughters and departed from the room. Carefully she avoided meeting Philip's eyes, but she knew that his face was tense with concern— not with solicitude for her, but with worry about Rickstaad's approval. Almost fervently Rebecca welcomed the pleasantly accented voice of Captain du Kuyper.

"May I join you, Madame Keane; or do you now consider me a social outcast? Before you answer, I must warn you that everything the good Hals Rickstaad said about me is true, except the implication that I intended to add you to my harem. As beautiful and desirable as you are, I would never contemplate such an insanity. I insist on domestic tranquility in my home; and you, my lovely firebrand, are not a tranquil woman."

Returning the charmingly cynical smile that had accompanied the blunt declaration, Rebecca bantered lightly, "Not that I had requested such an invitation, Captain du Kuyper, but you might have phrased your refusal a little more diplomatically, especially since I've already been discarded enough for the past two days. However, I'd be delighted with your company for the remainder of this unusual party. As outcasts I thought we might contrive some special entertainment for the others."

Laughing openly as he seated himself at the small table, du Kuyper asked appreciatively, "How old are you, Madame Keane?"

"My husband would probably tell you twenty, but I'm actually twenty-one and three months. And I'd prefer you call me Rebecca. I hate the word *madame* and at the moment I'm not too fond of the name of Keane."

"So young to be such an accomplished rebel! Philip Keane was not your father's choice, was he?"

"No, I made that mistake all by myself. How long have you known my husband, Captain du Kuyper?"

"We met several years ago when he was first learning the trade. We were racing for the same fat Spanish prize and I won; but since I was currently in trouble with both English and Holland authorities, I allowed him to sell the cargo in Nassau. Afterward we met to divide the spoils. Today the result of such a race might be very different. He has gained a reputation that might well compensate for my greater experience.''

"You don't look so much older than he is, except around the eyes," she murmured candidly.

Again he laughed unrestrainedly and shook his head in mock condemnation. "You must learn to look more intrigued if our little charade is to be successful, Rebecca. It is a game we're playing, is it not? To make a neglectful husband aware of his stupidity?''

Heedless of the consequence, Rebecca grinned with enthusiastic agreement as du Kuyper continued his perceptive interrogation.

"Is your Philip susceptible to nubile young brunettes?''

"Three days ago I would have said that he preferred older ones, but Miss Van Rickstaad seems to have altered his pattern.''

"He strays often then, your foolish husband?''

Unhappy about the changed direction of the conversation, Rebecca avoided a direct answer. "Our marriage has been unusual," she hedged.

"I don't think you have to worry about him this time," du Kuyper assured her hastily. "Yesterday he was most irritated when Papa suggested he escort his daughters on a shopping tour of the warehouse.''

"But he didn't refuse the assignment," Rebecca countered sharply.

Her companion shrugged philosophically. "Yesterday he had two ships to sell, and today Papa offered him an even bigger carrot.''

"He could have suggested that Papa choose someone else.''

"Van Rickstaad is a most careful papa, Rebecca. He distrusts Frenchmen as much as he does me; and then too, he knows his daughters. They would not have been so content with someone less handsome and less—less agreeable than your husband. But I believe your Philip needs a lesson in good manners, and I propose we administer one. This time when we dance, I suggest you watch me instead of him and allow me to set the mood.''

Even though Rebecca was confident that her companion

was only pretending an interest in her, she was nonetheless disturbed by the intensity of his dark, exotic eyes and by his sinuous grace throughout the slow, hypnotic minuet. Nor was his smile completely reassuring when he led her back to the table and seated her with the lingering hands of a confident pursuer. His words, however, were triumphantly conspiratorial.

"I trust your husband's temper does not extend to dueling, Rebecca. When he is angry, his Indian blood makes him appear quite savage."

Surprised by the revelation, Rebecca gasped, "He told you?"

"It was one of the things that bound us together during our first encounter. Your American Indians must be Oriental, I think. He reminds me of one of my older brothers at the moment." A sudden smile rippled across du Kuyper's sanguine face as his voice softened to a confiding murmur.

"We have been even more successful than I anticipated. It would seem that your husband's partners are just as determined as he is that Holland merchants help finance your revolution. The Captains Falconet and Riccard have just offered themselves as substitute partners to the Misses Rickstaad. No, do not turn around, Rebecca," he interrupted himself with another smile. "It is an interesting drama, but I think our own farce will be more convincing if you do not watch. The offers of Falconet and Riccard were refused, and most ungraciously, so your husband remains a captive, but most unwillingly now. It is time, however, that we visit the supper table together, unless you wish to be rescued by your American escorts. Captain Stoneham is smiling, but the young one is scowling at me as if I were the devil incarnate."

"That will be Lieutenant Haskins," Rebecca admitted as she rose hastily. "He would most definitely agree with Mr. Rickstaad that you're not a *pukka sahib*. After supper I'll dance with him and assure him that I'm still a Bostonian puritan."

But supper proved another fascinating experience for the young American woman. While she'd heaped her plate with samples of all the tempting delicacies, her partner had served himself only small portions of curried rice, lobster, and fruit; and he'd refused all alcohol.

"In my childhood home in Jakarta my father ordered our cook to serve him *flash un kas* with his afternoon beer. My mother wouldn't allow us children to eat the heavy meat and cheese pastry or any of the other rich foods my father craved. He died when he was forty while my mother is still a slender, healthy woman at seventy."

To her continuing shock, Rebecca learned that the youthful-looking du Kuyper was a year older than Van Rickstaad and the father of eighteen children. However, when a frustrated Philip brought the Van Rickstaad daughters to the table, neither girl revealed an iota of their father's hatred for the Dutch-Malaysian, clinging to him with the same adoration they'd previously lavished on the American.

The "charade," as du Kuyper had called his performance, ended with good-humored masculine banter as other of the men drifted over to the table and remained until a beaming Van Rickstaad returned to retrieve his daughters. As Rebecca listened to the pompous man explain to Philip that he'd decided to endorse the "colonial revolt" because of the facts Madame Keane had given him despite her disapproval of war, she shuddered with anticipation. Philip would not appreciate her meddling nor would he ignore her more flagrant behavior. But the contrary imp of mischief that had ruled much of her life nudged her conscience now with the fleeting regret that she'd not been allowed one more dance with the dangerously charming du Kuyper who spoke eight languages, the most eloquent of which was his wordless communication with a woman. Philip, she decided judiciously, was merely a self-centered, insensitive man by comparison.

That he could also be a violent one, she discovered quickly as he shoved her roughly into a carriage after the other guests had departed from the Hotel Royale. Despite an aching arm which was already turning livid where his fingers had gripped it, she regarded him with a calm composure as he took the seat opposite hers.

"What the hell did you think you were doing tonight,

acting like a cheap harlot with a man who collects women as a hobby?"

"Don't be melodramatic, Philip," she retorted with a provoking candor, adding lightly, "Like a demimondaine perhaps, or a *jolie fille de joie*, but certainly not like a common *lorette*—not in this dress or with a gallant escort who took pity on a deserted wife."

Ignoring the final words of her flippant admission, Philip pounced, "Where the devil did you learn those words?"

"What difference does it make? You understand them. And while we're on the subject, the older of your Dutch tabby cats could have taught me a thing or two about flirting. Or did you believe her flattering invitations were merely a girlish fondness for a favorite uncle?"

"Matt Stoneham was supposed to have explained the damn situation to you before he brought you to the hotel."

"Matthew knows me a good deal better than you do. Had I realized that you'd been entertaining two pretty girls while I was relegated to a ship's cabin for two days, I'd have refused to come. I estimate it would have taken me only three hours to have walked to El Abrigo."

"So instead you played the fool with a man old enough to—"

"A very intriguing man, Philip Keane, who showed me that our on-again, off-again marriage of the past thirteen months is too one-sided for me."

Aboard the *Reine* a stonily silent Philip shoved her ungently into the cabin before he ordered the blue-peter muster flag hoisted. Equally estranged, Rebecca removed the complicated Pompadour dress with a violent distaste and donned the hideous seaman's garb. It was when she was returning the finery to its chest that she discovered the other gifts Philip had given her. Beneath the muslin wrapping was a matching jewel-encrusted cap, a beautifully cobbled pair of spool-heeled shoes, and a jeweler's box containing a perfectly matched strand of luminous pearls. Rebecca wept for the first time since New London, but her tears remained a private expression of her unhappiness; Philip did not return to the cabin that night nor come to her apartment at El Abrigo for the following five days. Instead he remained aboard ship and directed the marine training from there.

On one of her lonely walks away from the now crowded facility, Rebecca encountered Lieutenant Haskins. Despite his inexperience as a marine, he was a thorough scholar. On all the previous landings of the Keane fleet on the British-held Caribbean islands, the American losses had been greater than the French, he told Rebecca worriedly. At the next landing, the largest and most ambitious one, he'd estimated that fifty marines would die unless he could discover the reason for the disparity.

"I've tried to reach Captain Keane, but he won't listen to any complaints these days. Could you tell him that the new marines are edgy about this extra danger?"

"I'm afraid he won't talk to me either, Lieutenant," she admitted ruefully and resumed her walk along the deserted, rock-strewn beach. Fifty feet away she stopped in abrupt consternation; she'd just remembered the night she'd sailed Jean Dessalines to Gonâve Island. In the partial moonlight, he and his men had been invisible while she and Jed had seemed to glow almost incandescently. She remembered something else as well, something Jed had told her on the way back from that frightening voyage. Four Americans had accompanied Dessalines on the first raid of Colonel Auxier's barracks, but the wily Negro leader had made those men wear black clothing and smear their skin and hair with a black paste. Captain Falconet's crew were all darker skinned than the New Englanders, a third of them mulatto, and all of them in drab dark uniforms.

Turning around, Rebecca raced back, only to see Lieutenant Haskins in the vague distance, striding toward the fort. She was breathless by the time she reached him and was forced to grip his arm until she could blurt out her discovery.

"Go aboard the *Reine* right now," she ordered, "and even if you have to break every military rule of protocol, force him to listen. Once he knows you're right, he'll stop glaring at you and hear you out. Remember, you're charged with the responsibility of protecting your men as well as leading them.''

Rebecca watched sympathetically as a smile of self-contempt spread across his pleasant-featured face. "I feel so stupid," he confessed. "Such a simple solution while I was wasting my time with complicated formulas."

"Think how the captain will feel when he hears it," she countered lightly and turned to leave, only to be stopped by a hesitant hand on her arm.

"Mrs. Keane, may I talk to you sometime before we leave? You're one of the few educated people here."

"Of course, Lieutenant, but if it's someone educated you want, you should meet my housekeeper."

"Akhoi? I talk to her every chance I get, but she says that you're the one with the ideas. Mrs. Keane, don't you think you should tell your husband about this one yourself? I mean—wouldn't he appreciate it more coming from you?"

Rebecca shook her head blindly and fled back toward the beach, her heart pounding with a sick realization of her own cowardice. She'd been afraid to answer the probing question, to admit to an outsider or even to herself that she didn't dare put the challenge to a test. In six days of tortuous argument with herself, she'd reinforced her conviction that her marriage was a failure, but as yet she couldn't bring herself to admit that it was over. If she went to Philip and he refused to see her, even that faint hope would be destroyed. She was still unprepared to answer the question three hours later when she arrived back at her apartment to find her husband furiously pacing the floor.

"Why the hell didn't you have the sense to come to me yourself instead of sending that impudent pup to relay your message?" he shouted.

"I didn't think he'd mention my name."

"Mention it! He bounced it off the bulkheads right in the middle of a captains' meeting after he'd shoved his way past the sentry. And he had the damned temerity to tell me that the men were nervous enough without having to contend with my temper."

Smothering a wayward impulse to giggle, Rebecca asked,

"What did the other captains think about the first suggestion?"

"Matthew blamed himself for not remembering the oldest trick in smuggling, and I was made to feel like a fool for the second time by a wet-eared college boy. I didn't particularly enjoy being excluded by the pair of you at the Riccards' party."

"Goodness, I thought you and Charlotte Falconet were having too good a time to notice, not that Charlotte was any real competition for the Dutch brunette you saved from boredom during her stay in Port-au-Prince."

"There were two girls, remember?"

"Blondes aren't your weakness, Philip. Did you continue your escort service during the first two days of our current separation?"

"I went into town to complete the business transaction and to make certain Van Rickstaad's letter of recommendation was put aboard Cort Luden's ship for a direct voyage to Amsterdam. Unlike you, I want America to win this war. And if Van Rickstaad's say-so will gain monetary support for our military, my so-called escort service was a small price for me to pay."

Rebecca's face was stiff with tension, but she still retained an impersonal tone of voice. "Well, it seems you accomplished your purpose. Was there anything else you came to see me about, Philip?"

For a moment he stared moodily out over the balcony's balustrade. As usual, he'd failed to dent her iron self-control, and as usual the fault for their estrangement lay with him. He'd been vaguely irritated with her on the morning after the Riccards' party. She'd displayed no contrition at all for arousing the French colonel's anger or for publicly displaying a preference for that damned lieutenant's company over his own. He hadn't relished Van Rickstaad's subtle insistence that he squire the two girls around that first day; but in the end he'd begun to enjoy their flattering admiration for him. And Rebecca was quite correct in her assumption; he'd found the not-so-innocent brunette more than a little tempting until he'd seen Rebecca with du Kuyper. The look of awakening radiance on her face throughout the second dance had stunned him, and in the carriage her flippant admission of interest in the man had infuriated him to the point of violence. He'd fed his anger throughout the following two days, reminding himself that she was the one who'd denounced their marriage and recalling the caustic insults she'd flung at him during their frequent and bitter fights.

In the late afternoon of the second day after Cort Luden's departure with the critical letter, and after the sale monies had been carefully banked, Philip had accepted Van Rickstaad's invitation to dine aboard ship. The meal had been a dreary enough affair, and shortly after, he'd taken his leave, only to find himself accosted in the dim companionway by the brunette sister whose bold kiss startled him. In retrospect, Philip was certain that he would have refused had any additional intimacy been offered; but he was spared the necessity by a softly sardonic order issued by Dirk du Kuyper.

"Go to your cabin, Katryn, Captain Keane is leaving." When she made no move to obey, clinging instead to Philip, du Kuyper's quiet voice was no longer indulgent.

"Go quickly, Katryn, or Tamud's father will be assigned as your personal steward."

During the initial moments of the interruption, Philip's emotions had swung rapidly from incipient desire to embarrassment to a contemptuous conviction that the Dutch-Malaysian wanted the girl himself. But the final words had contained a cold threat that held no hint of jealousy. Belatedly galvanized into action, Philip had disentangled himself from her restraining arms and walked rapidly onto the deck and down the gangplank. Du Kuyper overtook him ten paces along the stone embarcadero.

"Had you accepted her invitation, Philip, you might have discovered that Mynheer Van Rickstaad is not the jolly fat man he appears to be. On the voyage from Holland he found a young Malaysian cabin boy in Katryn's bed. As ship's owner he ordered Tamud keelhauled in heavy seas and made quite certain there were no witnesses to his charge of rape. At Aruba I was forced to replace most of the crew to prevent a mutiny."

"I had no designs upon her, Captain," Philip muttered tersely.

"I'm not the one who needs convincing, but I think you would have gone with her. Five years ago you were adamant in your declaration that you'd never shackle yourself with a wife. Naturally I was curious when I learned you had, so I watched you and asked your fleet captains about the woman you'd married. Falconet was most informative, the other two most defensive; but it was you, my friend, who told me what I wanted to know. You made quite certain that Rebecca would see you with another adoring woman in your arms—a spoiled, self-centered young woman who meant nothing to you, but whom you'd deliberately charmed by dancing attendance upon her adolescent whims.

"When I met Rebecca, I understood the reason for your obvious neglect. She does not cringe or shriek with jealousy; she smiles and conquers. Oh, yes, my friend, it was a charade she and I played for your benefit; but had she not been in love with you, I might have been tempted to play the game in earnest. She is a rare woman, with the wit and humor to make that elfin beauty of hers seem unimportant. It was for her sake I remained aboard tonight until you were safely removed from the temptation of proving yourself once again the irresistible man.

"It is not merely idle mischief that I involve myself in your affairs. I thought perhaps you might yet salvage your happiness before it is destroyed by bitterness. Twenty years ago I married an Englishwoman with the courage and intelligence to be a companion as well as a lover. Had she not died giving birth to my oldest son, I would never have needed or wanted another woman. Rebecca is very like my long-dead Eleanor. For a few moments the other night, I recaptured a small part of that long-ago magic. But you, my reckless friend, will never experience a shred of it unless you take care. I said that your Rebecca loves you, but it is not a happy love nor a secure one."

On the boat trip back to the *Reine*, Philip could find no satisfactory explanation for the silence he'd maintained throughout du Kuyper's lengthy castigation. But he'd not been able to sleep that night or the next because the recurring words had continued to prod his conscience with a relentless persistence. Nor did the intermittent days of driving work bring the relief he sought; instead, for the first time in ten years of command, he failed as a leader. His orders to the inexperienced marines lacked logical consistency, and his anger at their failure was uncontrolled until Matthew Stoneham called a temporary halt to the training and dismissed the men for a three-day leave.

Relieved that Philip had not countermanded his order, Matthew had joined the two French captains aboard Falconet's *L'Aventure* for a hurried conference. Some time later the three men invaded Philip's cabin armed with two demands designed to circumvent the growing crisis. Despite New England prejudice against taking orders from a Frenchman, Edmond would complete the marines' training, and Matthew would take over the job of planning the logistics for the coming strike. Neither demand was ever voiced. Just as the four captains had settled around the table, uneasily sipping from their ample portions of brandy, a flushed Lieutenant Haskins had burst into the cabin, and his stridently shouted words had indeed bounced off the bulkheads.

Mercifully for the other occupants, Haskins had quickly settled to a more normal delivery; and he'd gained both the approval he sought and the order to carry out the suggestion. His departure ended the meeting because Patrice Riccard had finally found the courage to articulate the one demand that none had dared to make before.

"Mon Dieu, Philip, see to your wife before you drive the entire camp insane!" Reluctantly, the beleaguered man agreed.

When Philip failed to respond to her question about the reason for his visit, Rebecca nervously studied his tense hands gripping the railing. He doesn't know how to end this torture any more than I do, she thought with an odd relief that somehow eased her own unhappiness. Forgetting her windblown hair and her sand-encrusted feet, she joined him by the balustrade to stare out at the ruby-tinged sky of darkening sunset.

"Are you going to stay and have supper with me?" she asked without warning, adding quickly before he could refuse, "Before you say no, I think you should know, if you don't already, that everyone at El Abrigo would like to dump us headfirst into a deep channel of water. I've refused to speak to anybody, and you've been shrieking nautical orders at seventeen-year-old farm boys who don't know a gunnel from a scupper."

"You talked to your protective lieutenant!"

"Because I thought his question important."

"He said you chased him a half mile down the beach, but you couldn't find the time to come to me."

"Nor could you come to me, Philip."

"Did du Kuyper come to see you before he sailed?"

Although Rebecca's hesitation was infinitesimal, Philip's eyes still glinted dangerously.

"No, he didn't,'² she asserted, "but he did send me a gift."

"What was it?"

"It's a native house robe that he called a *kaftan*."

Again Philip's voice was deceptively mild. "Have you worn it?"

"Several times. Why did you ask?"

"You wear something a man you met only once gave you, but you refused to wear my pearls."

Rebecca flinched in self-condemnation; she'd forgotten all about the pearls. "I didn't find them until I was putting the dress away," she admitted defensively. "I would have thanked you for them then if you hadn't been angry enough to throw me overboard."

"I thought I had good reason."

"According to the letter Captain du Kuyper sent me, you found out four nights ago that you didn't. I'd have been more impressed if you'd come to see me then. They were just silly games."

"Why did you play them, Rebecca?"

"I had some foolish notion that you might stop playing yours until I discovered that we use different sets of rules. You look tired, Philip. While I'm seeing Akhoi about supper, why don't you relax in the bathtub before the water in the cistern cools off?''

Without waiting for a reply, Rebecca scurried from the room and from the oppressive presence of a husband whose mood seemed so oddly different. But instead of Akhoi, she found Jed Daws waiting for her at the bottom of the stairs leading to the fort's kitchens.

''Cap'n still with you, Becky?''

Something about the pinched look of concern on the weather-beaten old face gave Rebecca pause, and she sat down next to the cook.

''He's still upstairs, but at the moment he's very much against me. What's wrong with him, Jed?''

''Reckon he's packin' a load of guilt he don't know how t' put down. Never could admit he 'uz wrong, not even to his paw, and it's worse with you. Only, he ain't all that guilty this time.''

''How would you know that, Jed?''

''I heard it straight from the half-breed Dutchie cap'n. Fust two days you and the cap'n 'uz feudin', I 'uz in the warehouse checkin' ship's stores when I seen the cap'n with the Dutchie women and their fat paw what bought the limey prizes. Cap'n 'uz tryin' to stick to business, Becky, but the dark-haired one of them pussies sure had other ideas whenever her paw had his back turned.

''Knowed right off that she 'uz the reason you 'uz sulkin', and I 'uz danged mad at the cap'n fer bein' a durned fool agin. But that 'uz afore I larnt about your shenanigans at the Frenchies' party and then agin at the fancy hotel. Seems you jest got to rile him, Becky, by runnin' away every chance you git and then by playactin' fust with a smart-mouthed lieutenant and then with the half-breed Dutchie.''

Having learned long ago that Jed Daws had ways of gathering information that surpassed those of the most inquisitive journalist, Rebecca sighed in resignation. ''What happened, Jed?''

''Second night cap'n went aboard the fat Dutchie's ship—fer dinner I reckon—and I 'uz waitin' by the cap'n's gig when he and the half-breed Dutchie came down the

gangplank and stood talkin' near the warehouse where I
'uz settin'. The Dutchie told the cap'n he 'uz plain durned
lucky the Dutchie'd been there. Said the fat paw had
already kilt a cabin boy fer messin' with his daughter.

"Cap'n claimed he 'uz innocent, but I reckon the
Dutchie had the right of it. I ain't excusin' the cap'n,
Becky, jest tellin' you. But that 'uz the fust time he larnt
you 'uz jest playactin' with the Dutchie. Reckon he larnt a
whole lot 'bout hisself too because the Dutchie knowed
you a heap better 'n he did. Since then the cap'n's been
worse 'n he 'uz when you 'uz missin'. He ain't been eatin'
or sleepin' right, and them greenie marines are scairt out
of their wits. Heered tell this raid ain't goin' t' be like the
others; and unless the cap'n gits hisself straightened out, it
won't be none too safe fer the rest of us."

The only part of Jed's sermonizing narrative that had
shocked Rebecca was the accurate accounting of her own
culpability. She hadn't been surprised by the abortive
incident aboard the "fat Dutchie's" ship; she'd expected far
worse. When she'd denounced their marriage as too one-
sided, she'd given Philip tacit permission to return to his
old, less restrictive life. And Lord knows, the Dutch girl
had issued a blatant enough invitation to tempt him to do
so, while Rebecca had played the fool even after her
emotional experience with the ship's log and her determination to accept her limited marriage. But three times during
their few months together she'd tried to run away from it;
and because she'd been so defensive of her own freedom,
she'd never once considered the strain her outbursts had
laid upon the shoulders of a man already overburdened by
a vicious type of warfare. She'd never even relaxed her
vigilance enough to admit she loved him.

Impatiently, she returned her attention to Jed still seated
glumly by her side. "Tell Akhoi to bring us a light supper
in two hours," she ordered crisply, "and in the meantime
I'll try to talk some sense into the big boobie."

But Rebecca planned only one sentence of that promised
talk as she raced up the stairs and through the apartment
toward the sound of water still being drawn into the tub.
Pausing long enough in the bedroom to brush her hair and

wipe the dried sand from her feet, she waited until she heard the tap being turned off before she walked into the necessaries room, stripped off her blouse and skirt, and joined her startled husband in the blue-tiled tub.

"As Jed would say," she announced lightly, "it's about time that one of us showed enough gumption to stop acting like a durn fool."

Almost instantly the questioning look on Philip's face was replaced by a predatory smile of appreciation as he watched his slender wife lower herself into the water. Even as she settled at the opposite end of the tiled tub, his hands reached out to pull her astride his lap before he leaned forward to kiss her breasts in an eager acceptance of her invitation. Nothing—neither the intensity of their reunion a week earlier nor their frequently uninhibited lovemaking on the isolated little island—had prepared Rebecca for the silken sensuality of the sun-warmed rainwater that made their joining languorously effortless. Perhaps it was the emotional relief they were both experiencing that increased the poignancy of their passion and lengthened the moment of ecstasy far beyond the usual shuddering violence of climax.

When they finally separated to complete the more ordinary task of bathing, they remained as silent as they'd been throughout, as though a thoughtless word might destroy the momentary peace of their fragile unity. But while they were toweling each other dry, Philip wrapped his arms exuberantly around her, chuckling softly as he looked down at her flushed face.

"Don't ever change, Cottontop. I'll need that gumption of yours for the rest of my life. And just in case I've forgotten to tell you, you're everything else I'll need as well. That is, providing you remembered to order our supper."

CHAPTER
12

PHILIP's exuberance lasted throughout the weeks of grueling training until even the rawest recruit mirrored some of his ebullient confidence. While the other captains prepared the ships for warfare at sea, Philip concentrated on the intricate job of coordinating the landing of four hundred marines on a distant island where the reception might be a bloody resistance by British regulars and the Negro troop they'd trained for island defense. More often than not Rebecca was conscripted to act as spotter—to point out the men who still floundered in the water when a boat was deliberately capsized, to watch for marines who exposed themselves needlessly once they reached land, and to report those men who handled their weapons carelessly. She smiled ruefully as she remembered her training for this latter task; her father had often requested she perform the same service for his militia.

During the final two landing drills scheduled in the predawn hours, Rebecca watched with Matthew Stoneham as the marines, now dressed in the brown uniforms Lieutenant Haskins had devised and liberally bedaubed with burnt cork, clambered down the rope netting into the waiting boats. Despite the warmth of the tropical night air, she shivered with an increasing apprehension she had never experienced before any of Philip's earlier departures.

"This is no place for a woman, Becky."

"It's no place for a man either, Matthew."

"Aye, but we chose this path, girl, you didn't."

"I think I did when I married Philip."

"You've come to terms with his life, have you?"

"Not with his life, but with him? Yes."

"And he with you, Becky. I've never known him to be so happy."

Rebecca giggled faintly. "He's learning to relax," she murmured softly, grateful for the darkness that concealed the blush staining her face as she remembered the source of that relaxation. Each night since the first one, Philip had cajoled her into joining him in the blue-tiled tub, where they'd loved each other with unrestrained passion. On the night she'd finally found the courage to admit she loved him, the water had become cold before either of them noticed.

Embarrassed by the untimely recall of such memories, Rebecca refocused her attention on the almost invisible boats straining toward shore.

"Lieutenant Haskins did a remarkable job disguising the men," she commented.

"He's a fine lad, Becky. Had me worried for a while, though, until you had the sense to turn his infatuation for you into admiration."

"It's never even been admiration, Matthew; he just likes to argue politics with me."

Rebecca never saw the smile that softened Stoneham's craggy features or guessed at the thoughts that triggered it. He was remembering the comments of the four young marines she'd taught to swim when they'd failed to learn from veteran seamen, flattering comments he'd ordered them to belay. She still hadn't learned the potency of the personality that was slowly enslaving even a spoiled sophisticate like Philip Keane. He was also recalling a remark made by Edmond Falconet, a man who had small cause to appreciate her interference. "She is a danger to any man because she does not think like a woman. Unfortunately she is too beautiful to ignore."

Matthew's smile broadened into a chuckle as he listened to her next excited exclamation. "Matthew, when you see Philip, will you tell him to instruct some of those ridiculous officers to whisper their orders to the men? Three of those older marines act as if they're on the parade ground in the town square, and one of them forgot to blacken his sword.'' Matthew didn't agree with Falconet that she thought like a man, but he was quite certain that few men could match the shrewdness of her observations. He himself had frowned at the loud voices, but he'd missed the gleam of the drawn sword completely.

Her final commentary, though, was a poignant reminder that she was a young wife about to see her husband off for yet another uncertain battle.

"It's the waiting I hate, Matthew, not knowing if he's safe or even still alive."

"This will be the last of the landings, Becky," he consoled her. "From now on we'll be at sea, tackling merchantmen who rarely show much fight."

But the kindly reassurance was of little help to Rebecca, watching from the stone rampart as the four ships sailed on the evening tide, their decks stripped for action and their canvas billowing in the westward wind. Despite the smile still lingering on her face as she waved her hand, she felt a foreboding no amount of logic could dispel.

Five weeks later she was standing on the same rampart as the four ships returned, seemingly unscathed but for the terrifying yellow flags flying on their forward masts. Only once had Rebecca seen a plague ship enter Falmouth harbor, but she'd never forgotten the unreasoning panic of the townspeople. There'd been only twenty Basque whalers afflicted by smallpox on that first grim occasion, but all sixty of the crew were quarantined together aboard the unlucky ship. In a town that had survived earlier epidemics, a few courageous Samaritans volunteered to go aboard. A month later when the quarantine was lifted, only half of those Samaritans and five of the crew were still alive on a derelict ship no one would ever sail again.

Rebecca watched in mute horror as Captain Riccard's smaller brig was pulled alongside the dock. She wasn't aware of the thirty Americans and the fort workers also staring outward with the same terror in their eyes; she was aware only of that cruel square of yellow canvas flapping listlessly now on the *Reine*. Her mind dulled by fatalistic despair, she didn't turn around when Akhoi spoke to her.

"It is yellow fever, Rebecca; have you ever heard of it?"

Paralyzed with fear, Rebecca remembered the death of her mother's first family and could only nod her answer.

"Plague ships are always frightening," Akhoi continued, "but the French are very civilized about them. I imagine port doctors are already aboard and in charge."

The words trembled on Rebecca's lips. "Will we be allowed to see the—"

"Not you or any Americans, I think. But there are many of my people who will help if they're asked and if the ships' owners agree to pay them in advance. *La fièvre jaune* is a fact of life in slave compounds, and those of us who survive the disease are immune."

"Have you ever—?"

"Done the actual nursing? No. Antoine would not permit me even when his own ship was struck six years ago. But I have friends who earn their living that way— some of the people you saw during your first day in Port-au-Prince. They will be expensive, Rebecca. Will your Mr. Milford agree to hire them?"

Released from the hypnotic immobilization by a flash of anger and the need to make certain that Jesse Milford dare not refuse, Rebecca pushed her way past the silent cannoneers to confront the second mate, who once again had been left in command during Philip's absence. At Milford's cautious disclaimer that he must wait for proper authorization before releasing any funds, Rebecca lost the last remnant of her civilized control.

"If my husband is already dead, then I am half owner of the Keane fleet. Whatever funds are left in the strongboxes are at my disposal. Any refusal on your part will be regarded as mutiny, and I will order you taken to Gonâve Island, where friends of mine will gladly roast you for their dinner."

With a half dozen of the cannoneers listening avidly to her grim words and nodding a grimmer approval, Milford's furiously begun protest became an inarticulate bluster of agreement.

"Then we must leave immediately, Mr. Milford," Akhoi

urged the discomfited man, "before the soldiers arrive to include all of you in the quarantine."

Startled out of his sullen anger by fear, he demanded, "Why would they detain us? We aren't the ones who brought the cursed disease here."

"Fear, Mister Milford," Akhoi murmured ironically, "of the same kind you're feeling. The townspeople won't know whether or not you were aboard; there are those who would shoot on sight anyone suspected of escaping from a plague ship."

A timely interruption by Captain Riccard spared Milford the additional indignity of a public admission of cowardice. Shouting in English from the railing of his ship, Riccard ordered the men onshore to evacuate the fortress and establish a camp five hundred feet farther along the beach. Monsieur Milford was to supervise the evacuation and make certain none of the men left the area. The only part of El Abrigo that would be available to them would be the cannon ramparts.

Singling out Akhoi next, the worried captain spoke in rapid French for several minutes, ending with the order that she take Rebecca with her.

Having understood that part of Riccard's instructions to the housekeeper, Rebecca screamed out her question, "Patrice, is my husband all right?"

"He is sick, Rebecca; but he is in good hands. In Baltimore when we were first quarantined, Louis and Leon came aboard the *Reine* to help out. When Philip became ill, they remained with him."

"Rebecca," Akhoi interrupted sharply, "we must be away from here before the soldiers arrive and quarantine us. There is still much to be done in town."

Dressed alike with their distinctively different colored hair covered by identical kerchiefs, the two women spent an exhausting five hours in a section of the island city Rebecca had only glimpsed before—the crowded, shanty-filled, all-Negro ghetto. While Akhoi and a calm-faced voodoo hungan hired the workers and assigned the Negro merchants who volunteered to deliver wagons of food, medical supplies, and the caustic lye soap that would be used for laundry and sterilization, Rebecca doled out money without questioning the sums demanded. When one of Jesse Milford's hoarded money boxes was emptied, she opened another and still another until Akhoi signaled a return to the fortress that had now become a prison, with French soldiers forming a cordon around it and the camp housing its fifty former inmates. While Akhoi and Rebecca watched, the procession of sixty immune blacks laden with bundles filed into the forbidding structure while the less courageous merchants unloaded their wagons hurriedly outside the gates.

To a numb and despairing Rebecca, the next fortnight seemed an oppressive eternity of silence as she and four of the cannoneers kept vigilance over the only sources of news available to them. Each day they watched the burial details drive two wagons from the fort and deposit the dead into newly dug pits before they sprinkled sacks of lime over the sheet-wrapped forms and replaced the dirt. From the ramparts Rebecca and her companions kept a grim tally as the total reached and passed a hundred.

Back in her cubicle at the camp, made somewhat private by stacked trunks and the blue counterpane from her bed, Rebecca suffered agonizing hours from the desperation of helplessness. Each day, from Akhoi mainly, she learned the known facts about the disease no one could understand or cure. Some people survived the violence of vomiting and burning fever while others died; there was no predicting the outcome for any one individual. What simple nursing could be done seemed the only efficacious treatment possible—fresh bed linens, cool water dripped past parched lips, fevered bodies washed, and the delirious victims tied to their beds to keep them from harming themselves further.

"French doctors are more advanced than anyone else about the disease," Akhoi explained patiently. "They save more than half of their patients; and with their quarantine system, they keep the disease from spreading."

"I hate their hideous quarantine. I don't even know if my husband is still alive."

"They don't inform the public for good reason. People often become violent in their demands to bury their own dead. Rebecca, it might ease your self-pity if you'd just think about the men who weren't sick when the ships arrived here. Yet they're forced to remain inside to learn whether or not they're next.''

"Aren't any of them immune?''

"Probably a hundred or more of them, especially among the French crews. But until the doctors are certain, no one will be released.''

"How much longer?''

"Who knows? It was six weeks before they released Antoine and his surviving crew.''

"I only wish there were something I could do to help.''

Four nights later Rebecca's forlorn wish was granted in a terrifying manner. Just before midnight on the eighteenth day of the quarantine, Akhoi awakened Rebecca with an urgent whisper.

"Jean Dessalines and his men are here. They came to warn us about the four ships that were anchored all day off Gonâve Island. Three of those ships were being readied for action when Jean and his men began rowing double time to warn us. He isn't an expert about ships; but he says they're a little smaller than your husband's, and they're armed with twenty cannon each. They weren't flying any flags, but he says the language he overheard sounded something like yours. One more thing; one of his men insists he saw a woman aboard the lead ship. It's my guess the woman is Annette Gironde, and those ships are the same English privateers that attacked Antoine in Havana. Someone must have told them that the Keane ships were anchored here and defenseless.''

Rebecca's heart and mind were racing together with a frenzied speed as she remembered what four other English ships had done to Falmouth. But these English privateers and Annette Gironde were not motivated by revenge, as Captain Henry Mowat had been as he sank twenty American vessels and burned the town. These privateering pirates planned to steal the Antilles fleet just as they had in Havana. Galvanized into action by the determination that her husband's ships would not be taken without a fight, Rebecca recalled Silas Keane's words about the cannons he'd installed at Abrigo: "The British aren't going to burn me out again.'' He'd said those cannons could outdistance any except the ones aboard the deadly frigates of the Royal Navy. So could the cannons aboard the Antilles fleet, she reminded herself with a vindictive satisfaction. If those ships were anchored parallel to shore, at least half of their cannon could be used to repel the intruders.

Clad once again in her seaman's garb and sandals, Rebecca raced to warn the sentinel cannoneers on the ramparts and to explain her plan of action. Mr. Williams, the yeoman in charge, shook his head in rejection even as he sent one of his men to arouse the entire camp.

"Not enough of us to man these cannon and those aboard the ships too, Miz Keane. And we don't have the marines to fight off the prize crews the limeys will send over in their longboats—that is, if you're guessin' right. But we sure as hell—excuse me, ma'am—we can and will shoot any of those boarding boats out of the water."

"No, you won't, Mr. Williams," Rebecca contradicted sharply. "If you did that, the British privateers would try to sink our ships at anchor. I think we have to wait until the enemy is anchored itself and within our cannon range before we open fire. And we have to let their prize crews board before we deal with those men. That will be Mr. Dessalines' job. We have to worry only about the cannon."

"We still don't have enough men," the yeoman insisted.

A youthful voice, still cracking into childish treble with excitement, interrupted shrilly, "We do too. My brother says a whole passel of the gun crews inside are as right as rain. Warn't them what got the cussed yellow jack. It 'uz the marines what cotched it when they 'uz fightin' the limeys on some island."

"Willy, you're a durn crackbrain! You don't know if your brother's even alive," the older man scoffed.

"Do too! I talk to him every night and that's a fact. Reckon I could git inside without anyone findin' out."

Instantly, Rebecca forgot about Jean Dessalines' warning and about the dearth of cannoneers. Here was someone who might know about Philip's fate.

"Willy, do you know if Captain Keane is still—?" Her voice broke before she could articulate the final word.

"Not fer certain, Miz Keane, but I reckon he must be. Leastwise my brother says them two 'latto guards of his are still workin' like slaveys, and they wouldn't do that for

anyone 'ceptin' the cap'n. But about my gittin' enough
gun crews out to give them limeys a real Yankee welcome—"

Shaken by the first positive words she'd had in weeks
about Philip, Rebecca had to force her attention back to
the immediate problem. "No, Willy, not you. You'll be
too valuable out here. If you tell me how to get in, I'll—"

"If any of you go in," Akhoi interrupted calmly,
"you'll extend the quarantine another month. I won't since
I've already had the disease. But there is another matter
that must be settled first. Jean Dessalines will order his
men to take the place of your marines—but for a price. He
wants another hundred muskets and ten cannons. He also
wants two cannoneers to go to Gonâve Island afterward to
instruct some of his men. He promises to return them here
three nights later. There is one additional request. None of
you are to tell the French authorities that he took any part
in this battle or that he was even here. Mrs. Keane, Jean
said that your agreement will be sufficient guarantee."

"If I survive the night, I'll go to Gonâve," the Yeoman
Williams volunteered heavily.

Once again Akhoi assumed abrupt command. "No, Mr.
Williams, you must remain here to explain your actions to
the French. But since Jean Dessalines will be saving all
your lives tonight as well as your ships, I imagine there are
others who—" Allowing her voice to trail off suggestively,
Akhoi waited stoically until four men stepped forward
before she reminded Rebecca of the need for haste.

Knowing that her promise was merely a formality, since
the wily Negro leader could take whatever he wanted
anyway from the unguarded ships, Rebecca nodded impatiently and added in a voice that the assembled men could
hear that she'd guarantee that all of Dessalines' requests
would be met. The only audible reaction she heard was
Jesse Milford's sharply inhaled breath; however, even the
wary second mate understood the gravity of the situation
and offered to command the detail volunteering to reanchor
the ships.

Three hours later the miracle of preparation had been
completed. Akhoi had led a hundred gunners from the
compound through Willy Beckworth's hidden entrance,

and the seaward cannons on all four ships were manned. Also positioned aboard each vessel were twenty almost invisible black men armed with the bayonets they'd stolen from French arsenals.

Rebecca's companion throughout the frantic hours had been Jean-Jacques Dessalines himself, and what small authority she'd exerted earlier had been usurped by the slave leader, who seemed to have no difficulty in understanding the intricacies of modern naval warfare. Even the hard-bitten Yankee cannoneers sensed the Negro leader's ruthless control as he stationed himself and the pale-haired woman in the lookout tower of the stone rampart.

Another half hour inched by with a silence Rebecca found almost unendurable as she struggled to control the panic that churned her insides and rendered her incapable of logical thought. When Jean-Jacques gripped her arm suddenly, she reacted with a palsied quivering until she saw what her tense companion was pointing out. Like giant ghosts, the white sails of three ships were barely visible in the dim light of a fading moon, appearing to float free of their masts and rigging. She watched with hypnotic fascination as the intruders glided past the fortress far out of cannon range. Her physical terror was momentarily replaced by a consuming anxiety that the marauders might escape the trap set for them; but as the ships were tacked into a return run in front of their targeted prey, this time much closer to shore, she gasped in relief. Not until the third pass, though, did she note any change in the appearance of those graceful sails. Exactly opposite El Abrigo, those great white blobs of canvas were being partially reefed; and the faint sound of anchor chains echoed across the water, followed quickly by the creaking of davit lines lowering boats onto the calm surface.

The minutes it took those boats, loaded with determined human cargo, to clear the protective darkness of the mother ships that launched them seemed more like hours to the young woman who was experiencing her first dread anticipation of battle. But when she glimpsed the telltale white of seamen's britches in the lead boat, it was she who grabbed her companion's arm and pointed. The confident

British privateers had scorned the use of protective coloring! Stretched out across the open water were twenty boats, each carrying a dozen men. Breathlessly, Rebecca watched as the longboats bunched into four groups headed toward the target ships. Beside her, Jean-Jacques cupped his hands around his mouth and emitted the plaintively guttural call of the sea loon as the enemy was hidden from view by the seaward sides of the American and French ships. The only sounds that followed were the dull thuds of grappling hooks biting deep into wooden decks.

Only much later did Rebecca learn the details of the fierce reception that awaited those English prize crews, a reception that lasted only a short time before the answering calls of loons coming from the four ships signaled the exploding violence of eighty cannon sending their message of death toward the waterlines of the enemy privateers. Although there was a smattering of answering volleys, the contest was uneven from the start. The Americans and French had forty minutes' warning time to adjust their cannon range while the English gunners had relaxed their vigilance. In the gray light of breaking dawn, Rebecca watched the debacle with a concentration so intense she failed to hear the sounds of arousal erupting from within the fort or to note the fires that flamed into existence along the cordon lines of the French soldiers.

Dessalines, however, had remained alert to all sounds and movements, not merely to the drama of one English privateer engulfed in flames and the other two sinking sluggishly into the water. Once again he sounded his signaling cry and waited briefly for the scattered responses. Without a word he took Rebecca's arm and guided her swiftly down the stone steps leading to the docks, where an armada of small boats was already waiting. In the center of ten of those boats, carefully tied down, was a cannon; and in the largest longboat, seated next to four Americans, was Akhoi. While the Negro leader barked terse orders to his followers and checked the piles of muskets, Akhoi spoke with a calm remoteness to the young American woman she'd served for tension-filled months.

"When you see Silas Keane," Akhoi said softly, "tell him that I have paid my debt to him and that the guns and cannons that paid for Jean-Jacques's services were taken from the Falconet ship as the inheritance the Falconets owe me. Tell him that I also paid my debt to Antoine. The names of these privateer ships were the same as those that attacked in Havana."

"What will you do now, Akhoi?" Rebecca asked sadly.

"I will fight with Jean-Jacques until my people are free. In your country I would have been only a servant in spite of your offer of friendship. Now go, Rebecca, and explain to the French officers with your innocent duplicity. When Colonel Auxier returns, protect Jean-Jacques if you can."

"Auxier will come after you too, Akhoi."

"No, the workers inside will tell him that I died of the fever and was buried with the other victims. *Au revoir*, my unusual young friend, you can stop worrying now. Last night Leon told me that your husband is recovering."

The conspiracy to protect the runaway slave army was carried on in both the fortress and the camp. Within minutes of achieving victory, the quarantined gunners had left their posts and filed silently back into their prison, mingling with the other obliging sailors. Outside, the other cannoneers rounded up the terrified survivors of the English boarding parties and calmly claimed responsibility for the entire defense. Even Jesse Milford maintained the fiction that forty men alone had achieved the overwhelming victory; for once his moral scruples were overruled by the harsh economic truth that without Dessalines' help, the four ships would most certainly have been commandeered by the enemy. One final action, however, that the heroic cannoneers refused to take was the rescue of English sailors clinging to bits of flotsam from their destroyed ships. That task was left to the French soldiers who'd arrived too late to take part in the brief battle. Awkwardly, the soldiers manned the few remaining of the English longboats—Jean Dessalines had left only five behind—and rowed unevenly toward the dots of floating debris. In all, more than a hundred prisoners were taken into custody, but

Rebecca never learned whether or not a Frenchwoman was among that number; nor did she ever ask.

For the ten days following, an atmosphere of celebration endured in the camp. There'd been no burials since two days before the invasion, and the doctors had relaxed their discipline enough to allow immune Frenchmen to return to their ships. Thus it was Patrice Riccard who chronicled the fleet news to the Americans who'd remained at El Abrigo.

During the voyage to New Providence two months earlier, the fleet had captured three English merchantmen leaving the Nassau harbor, ships that were sent to Baltimore with Americans at the helm and the original crews locked in the hold. The raid on the Nassau arsenal beginning on the last day of February and concluding five days later had been successful, and the eight American ships under the command of Commodore Esek Hopkins had taken enough hostages to put the colonials in a bargaining position for prisoner exchange.

The Keane fleet had not been as fortunate; although the ships were undamaged, the marines ashore had been pushed back into mangrove swamps by territorial militiamen defending their island. While the fighting had been only sporadic during most of the eight days, there'd been several brief battles; seventeen Americans and twenty-eight Falconet men had been killed and others wounded. On the trip to Baltimore the fleet had captured only one additional ship because a heavy winter storm had prevented any further searching. Their reception at the Keane docks had been a dismal one of quarantine for yellow fever. Among the crews of the enemy ships delivered there earlier, the plague had already taken a toll; and the cautious citizens of that American city wanted no epidemic among their own. One of the smaller Keane ships had already been requisitioned as a hospital and holding ship; but when dozens of the Massachusetts marines aboard the newly arrived Antilles fleet sickened with the disease, a second small brig had been commandeered. At the request of Maryland authorities, Philip Keane had agreed to return his small fleet to Saint-Domingue. Two days out of port all four ships were forced to raise plague flags, and by the time they reached Port-au-Prince, the disease was wide-spread, especially among the marines and older seamen. Captain Matthew Stoneham had succumbed on the first day at the fortress, and more than a hundred others had died within two weeks.

Riccard's narrative ended with a touch of sardonic praise for the medical advances of quarantine. "Twenty years ago in a Martinique harbor when I had the plague, anyone who tried to leave ship was shot. But *mon Dieu*, I'd almost prefer a bullet to the lye soap these good doctors made us use. It removes the skin and leaves one looking like an overboiled lobster."

On the thirty-third day of the ordeal Rebecca was reunited with her husband under the most unpleasant of circumstances. Colonel Auxier had chosen the previous day to exercise his authority. Having returned from an arduous campaign of pursuing runaway slaves entrenched in established strongholds situated on the interior mountains, the French commandant was confronted with the news that three English ships had been sunk by shore batteries at El Abrigo. Unlike his underling officers who'd accepted the fiction of a forty-man defense, Auxier had not forgotten Jean Dessalines' escape or the Americans who'd aided him. A thorough investigator, he'd questioned the English prisoners first and learned that the boarders had been attacked by an army of "bloody knife-wielding blokes" and that their ships had been sunk by more cannon than forty gunners could operate.

Convinced that Dessalines was responsible and fearful that the savage runaways had become expert cannoneers, Auxier began a careful interrogation of his own men first and then the Americans. The inconsistencies only confirmed his suspicions, and he did not believe that the mambo Akhoi had died of *fièvre jaune*. Although not a superstitious man, Auxier respected the educated mambo's powers; her death seemed much too convenient for a logical man to accept. It was, he reasoned, time for a more judicial inquiry inside a courtroom, especially for the evasive Americans. Although he held no particular antipathy for Americans, the idea of a slave army led by Dessalines and a mambo priestess horrified him.

After choosing the potential witnesses carefully—four American seamen he judged less capable of lying under oath, the officer Milford, and of course Madame Keane, whom the colonel had not forgotten—Auxier ordered them and their personal belongings brought to Port-au-Prince. In the city itself, however, the officials proved to be more politician than policeman. Despite their collective fear of a slave rebellion, they felt obliged to follow their home government's edict of complete cooperation with American colonials. Thus they settled for an informal interrogation on the following day in the private chambers of a judge whose excellent command of English was more than exceeded by his astute awareness of political realities.

Housed in a suite of rooms in a comfortable hostelry which the judge had insisted on, Rebecca spent hours in a succession of baths, rinsing away the accumulation of camp grime. She dined alone in her rooms, savoring a meal excellent enough to blunt the memory of unappetizing camp food; and only then did she contemplate the potential dangers of her present predicament. Colonel Auxier had chosen the other witnesses shrewdly; Willy Beckworth was a youthful braggart without the maturity to edit his words, and Jesse Milford was a moral prude already regretting his part in the conspiracy. Of her own loyalties, Rebecca had no doubts; Akhoi and her Negro plague experts had saved American lives, and Jean Dessalines had saved the fleet. Her reaction to Auxier's accusation that arming outlaw slaves was tantamount to murder was equally uncomplicated: slavery itself was the worse crime.

Her problem would be to persuade the interrogator that she should be the first one questioned; not even Milford would have the courage to contradict her testimony. To this end Rebecca made thorough preparation, but only the delicate green dress and a frightened expression of innocence proved necessary. Judge Raoul Gautier had a keen appreciation for pretty women and a well-preserved reputation as a gallant. The young woman smiling faintly at him from the entrance to his chambers was more than merely pretty. She had the unawakened look of a fawn, he thought sentimentally as he escorted her gently to a chair.

Ignoring the motley five men already seated, Judge Gautier addressed his opening remarks to the intriguing girl whose large brown eyes met his with such a trusting faith. After concluding his brief speech on the unstable and often savage character of Negro slaves, he addressed his first question to Rebecca with kindly solicitude.

"Did you know that the woman hired as your house-keeper might well be a voodoo sorceress?"

Even as her eyes widened in spurious shock, Rebecca noted the use of the present verb tense and shook her head in disbelief before she launched into a lengthy description of Akhoi's heroism. She ended her fervent testimonial with a poignant regret that the housekeeper had nobly sacrificed her own life to save the plague victims.

Having endured the excessive loquacity with a patient consideration for the speaker's youth, but fully cognizant of his own superior grasp of precise points of law, Gautier asked more specifically, "Did you actually see this woman Akhoi enter the fortress with the other plague workers?"

Aware of the pitfalls of an outright lie, Rebecca shook her head vaguely and offered a lengthy explanation of the confusion engendered by so many supply wagons being unloaded simultaneously. Without pause and with the same fluttery disregard for logical order, she detailed the hardships of camp life where she had no one to take care of her, the loneliness of missing her housekeeper's companionship, the terror of not knowing whether or not her husband was alive or dead, and the sadness upon hearing that Akhoi had died.

In the process of altering his evaluation of this witness—instead of being fawnlike, she was rapidly assuming the character of a magpie—Gautier asked abruptly, "You are convinced then that your housekeeper is dead?"

"I am now," Rebecca responded promptly with a directness her earlier ramblings lacked. "If she weren't, Colonel Auxier would have located her when the workers were allowed to leave Abrigo. She was too distinctive in appearance for him to overlook."

Nodding his approval of the first logical answer he'd received, Gautier plunged into the more important matter of the privateer raid itself. To his annoyed confusion, he was forced to listen first to a description of another English raid on some American town named Falmouth before the witness recited a remarkably believable account of a small garrison of gunners who'd been warned by Captain Silas Keane to expect a similar raid on El Abrigo. The men had responded with vigorous preparation and around-the-clock vigilance.

"Did you watch the actual battle, Madame Keane?" he demanded impatiently.

"Some of it."

"Colonel Auxier believes that a slave army led by Jean Dessalines may have assisted your Americans. Be careful how you answer, Madame Keane. The colonel's claim seems to be borne out by the testimony of the English prisoners."

"I wasn't the only watcher, Judge Gautier. There were hundreds of French soldiers. Did any of them report seeing Colonel Auxier's phantom army?"

Gautier studied the witness more carefully; she had been quick to point out the one major flaw in Auxier's theory. None of the French soldiers had seen any sign of a Negro army that night. There was, however, one further question that needed clarification.

"According to Colonel Auxier, there were cannons and muskets missing from Captain Falconet's ship. Can you explain what happened to them?"

"My wife cannot, Monsieur Gautier, but I can," a voice rang out from the doorway; and Rebecca rose shakily to her feet to confront a husband she expected to appear gaunt and emaciated. Instead, he looked much the same as he always did whenever he greeted her after a separation. He was scowling in anger, but this time his attention seemed to be directed at someone other than herself.

Philip Keane was glaring at the judge as he strode across the room. "Before I give you the explanation," he declared, "I want my wife and my men released from custody and out of here."

"They're not in custody, Captain Keane; they were merely brought here to help us clarify some confusion about the unfortunate attack on your ships. Except for this one point, your wife has done so most convincingly." Gautier smiled with a politician's powerful instinct for survival; let Auxier risk his own future in this quixotic hunt for black witches.

"All of them are perfectly free to leave my chambers," he added graciously.

As brusquely as he'd thanked the judge, Philip ordered Jesse Milford to conduct the men to the ship and supervise the storage of new supplies. His command to Rebecca was even more obligatory; she was to return to the inn and await his arrival.

Regarding her unsmiling husband for a brief moment, Rebecca changed her mind about his anger. It was, at least in part, focused squarely on her, she decided with a rising temper of her own. Silently she walked unsteadily from the chambers, tears of outrage blinding her eyes. But those tears changed magically to sentimental ones of relief when she heard Jed Daws's greeting.

"What in tarnation you cryin' fer, Becky?"

In spite of the odds against older people, he'd escaped the plague completely with his rolling walk intact and his love of gossip unabated.

"Don't you be worryin' none about the cap'n. No furrin jedge is gon' t' trap him up on-account of what he's got t' say is purt'n near the truth anyways."

"How will he explain the missing guns, Jed?"

"That they 'uz lost on that bloody durn island. It 'uz the Frenchies what got cut down the most; even the Frenchie cap'n took a bayonet wound in the head that left him talkin' gibberish until last week when he come to. Reckon now he'll be able t' go t' France with the rest of us."

Rebecca took a deep breath when she heard the casually delivered announcement; she already knew what the answer would be, but she still felt compelled to ask the question.

"Am I included in that 'rest of us,' Jed?"

"Reckon not, Becky."

"I won't stay here alone."

"Don't have to. You'll be goin' to Baltimore with the Riccards."

"Why France? Philip's never even crossed the Atlantic before."

"S'posed t' deliver a passel of papers t' some American over there. Would have gone a long time ago 'ceptin' for old yellow jack. But mainly it's on account of the ships; they ain't been dry-docked since they 'uz launched, and the bottom seams are gittin' ready to bust open."

"I didn't think there'd be enough crew left for such a long voyage."

"Not many of the gunners and crew went ashore, Becky, and it 'uz that blasted island what held the plague."

"Then how did Captain Stoneham—?"

"Soon's he knowed we 'uz in trouble, he come in with the reserves."

"How bad was it, Jed?"

"The redcoats 'uz easy t' spot; it 'uz the durned territorials sneakin' in at night. Jest like the limeys'll be usin' Injuns up to home, it 'uz the blacks they put t' fightin' down here. Don't envy the Frenchies none onct Jean Dessalines gits goin'. Them blacks on that durned island jest kept comin'."

"Why were you in the fight, Jed?"

"Went along t' cook, wound up shootin' like everyone else."

"Why didn't you get yellow fever like the others?"

"Reckon I'm jest too ornery 'n old, Becky, but it 'uz a bad run of yellow jack this time. Seems like we walked straight into an epidemic of it, leastwise some of the prisoners we took already had it. So don't you be hard on the cap'n 'til he gits completely over it. Last night he 'uz fit t' be tied when he heered that durn fool Auxier had took you. Worked hisself into a real stew gittin' the ship over here this mornin'."

"But he looked so good, Jed."

"Yep, but he's still as shaky as a new-borned colt. That don't mean he'll let on 'bout the help Jean Dessalines give us. When he heered, he 'uz durned grateful; and fer onct he ain't mad that you 'uz mixed up in it. He jest ain't one t' say 'thank you' polite-like. But this time he's changed a whole heap, Becky. Even afore he 'uz took sick, he 'uz actin' peculiar—like he'd got something stuck in his craw. Reckon it 'uz jest old yellow jack and losin' men from it; but in Baltimore, he 'uz downright upset about a heap of things. So don't you be expectin' too much from him—not yet anyways.''

Still shaken by the brief glimpse she'd had of Philip in the small courtroom, Rebecca listened to Jed's advice with a heavy heart. Her old friend might be illiterate, she reflected gloomily, but most of his observations were uncannily accurate. When Philip arrived an hour later, though, he seemed in excellent spirits as he hugged her and sent Jed to order the best wine and food the hostelry had to offer. Even after the veteran cook had left the room, Philip's good humor never wavered as he regaled Rebecca with a lively account of Judge Gautier's apology.

"He didn't have any choice, Cottontop, after I told him that while the resident gunners fought from the ramparts, I ordered a hundred others to break quarantine and man the ships. I explained that none of you knew anything about those men because they'd returned to the fort as soon as the enemy craft were destroyed."

"And he believed that?"

"Why not? He knew that someone had fired those ships' cannons. He doesn't believe that Akhoi is dead, though; and he suggested very politely that I take you back to America."

Although her tone of voice remained light, Rebecca tensed uncomfortably when she asked her next question. "Why not take me to France instead?"

Even as he pulled her closer to him, she sensed his withdrawal and knew that his words would be a refusal.

"Too dangerous, sweetheart."

"I'd be safer on the *Reine* than I'll be on Riccard's small brig."

"The *Reine*'s still a warship, but the *Mer Reynard* will be nothing but an unarmed merchantman during its voyage to Baltimore."

"Philip, I don't want to be separated from you again."

"You won't be for long, Cottontop. Once I return from France, I'll be in Baltimore most of the time, and any future action will be limited to a few weeks in coastal waters. I don't want to be separated from you either, but the Antilles have to be repaired and refitted. The doctors at the fort ordered them stripped of everything that might be contagious, and the replacements we get here will be only makeshift."

"That could take a whole year."

"I hope no more than six months, but you're not going to have time to miss me. You'll be too busy."

"Doing what, Philip? Your father doesn't need me to work for him."

"No, but I do, Cottontop. While I was sick, I thought about our future together; and I decided that I wanted both a family and a home. During the next six months, you'll be buying that home, a big enough one for children and servants; and you'll be furnishing it. That *is* what you wanted, isn't it, sweetheart?"

While she'd been listening to him and hearing the words she'd longed to hear throughout the months of their marriage, Rebecca felt only an odd sense of make-believe. Three months ago he hadn't wanted either a home or a family, and he'd certainly been cavalier enough about his infidelities then. She hadn't forgotten his two mistresses or the aggressive Dutch girl. Nor had she ever found any proof for the old adage that illness changes people. Hannah Tupton had been just as unpleasant after she'd spent a month in bed as before; and the only difference smallpox had made to a Falmouth blacksmith was to pockmark his homely face; it had done nothing to eliminate his temper.

Recalled abruptly to her present dilemma by Philip's repetition of the question, "Isn't it?" Rebecca noted the lines of fatigue on his face and the tense concentration of his eyes.

"I thought you wanted to wait until after the war," she murmured lightly, smiling with relief at the sound of Jed's voice outside the door.

The concierge himself arranged the table for the dinner

the two waiters carried into the room; and Rebecca was once again reminded that even on a benighted, feudal island like Saint-Domingue, men considered themselves the more important of the species. Yesterday when she'd moved into these rooms, that same concierge had scowled in disapproval at the invasion by an unescorted woman.

Philip lasted through one glass of wine, a guanabana fruit compote, and a small bowl of delicate shrimp bisque before he rose shakily to his feet and asked Jed to help him into bed. At the door to the bedroom he turned his head, and in a querulous voice Rebecca scarcely recognized, he said, "You too, Cottontop."

Believing that he needed her help in undressing, she hurried forward and took his other side, only to be rebuked.

"Jed can take care of me, Cottontop. I just want you with me."

Thus began the three weeks of his convalescence. He did indeed want her by his side both night and day; and from his small servant's room next door, Jed Daws did yeoman duty as valet and messenger. Each morning Philip insisted on dressing and receiving the ship's officers he'd summoned, mainly Jesse Milford. Grudgingly Rebecca developed an admiration for the bulldog tenacity of the dour second mate. In the task of procurement he had no equal; he accepted the assignment of equipping three ships without complaint, and he was meticulous in his accounting. Since Philip had recruited her as secretary, she was usually the one who reviewed the lists; and although Milford's respect for her was more grudging than her admiration for his work, he did occasionally mutter, "Very comprehensive," without adding the words "for a woman."

During those morning work sessions, Rebecca learned that her husband was a thorough organizer who left nothing to chance. Even before the quarantine had been lifted, he'd dispatched Patrice Riccard to Baltimore for equipment and crew replacements and for Luke Stoneham to take over as captain on the *Belle Dame*. The arrival of the two captains signaled a switch in Philip's concentration from ships to sea-lanes, ocean currents, and port customs in France. For Rebecca, these were pleasant hours because her husband's attention was not focused on her, or on himself either for that matter. He was once again the efficient sea captain he'd been during the early months of their marriage.

By contrast, the afternoons and evenings were oppressive. Philip was not an easy convalescent to tend. He was a restless sleeper unless Rebecca remained with him; he consumed more wine than was good for him and ate only sparingly; and he was moodily silent much of the time. Rebecca could understand some of the reasons for his depression. He'd been desperately ill for weeks, and he'd lost more than a hundred men assigned to his command. Had the ships' records and rosters survived the sterilization ordered by the French doctors, Philip might have eased his burden of responsibility by writing letters of condolence to the surviving wives and parents of the dead men.

"I don't even remember the names of some of those young marines," he admitted gloomily. "God knows if their families will ever learn what happened to them."

Suppressing the bitter impulse to remind him that such was the usual fate for sailors' widows—that when ships went down at sea, there were few, if any, survivors left to carry the tale home—Rebecca was bluntly factual in her reassurance.

"Two-thirds of them are still alive, Philip; so I expect Massachusetts has heard all about the plague by this time. And not even Samuel Adams is going to accuse the British of starting this epidemic of yellow fever deliberately."

"I wish you weren't so cynical, Cottontop."

"I'm not!"

"Then why have you been evading my question about starting a family?"

Rebecca sighed in frustration; it was his curious persistency about the subject, not the question itself, that puzzled her.

"As I've told you, Philip, I have no choice in the matter."

"You did last night."

"Only because I didn't think you were well enough."

"The doctors wouldn't have released me if I weren't,"

he countered swiftly with a petulant logic that defeated her.

Responding with a laughter that was her first since the day the stricken fleet had arrived at El Abrigo, she put her arms around him and kissed him unrestrainedly. "Believe me, I won't refuse you tonight, sweetheart," she promised.

Whether it was the term of endearment she'd never used before or the kiss itself, Philip's reflex was instantaneous and his smile reflected some of the predatory playfulness it had in the halcyon days before the New Providence mission.

"What's wrong with right now, Cottontop?"

There hadn't been anything really wrong, she reasoned afterward as she attempted to ease herself away from his perspiration-soaked body without awakening him. Nothing that wasn't to be expected from a man still recuperating from the delirium of yellow fever. He'd been slow to climax because he hadn't as yet regained much of the weight he'd lost or his normal vigorous strength. Even his clinging to her as if he doubted her willingness she could accept as another unpleasant aspect of convalescence, but the words he'd mumbled just before he fell asleep puzzled her.

"I promise I'll make it up to you, Cottontop," he'd said tiredly. Since her own physical needs had been satisfied overwhelmingly, she had no idea what it was he felt obliged to make up.

His words of farewell two weeks later were even more enigmatic, although by that time she'd learned that his preoccupation had nothing to do with the dangers of privateering. At the first captains' meeting aboard the *Reine*, Philip announced that the fleet would avoid all contact with the enemy until its return to Baltimore. Since the Antilles ships could outrun the British, there'd be little chance for a battle at sea. As relieved as she was for that mercy, Philip's avoidance of an explanation as to why she could not accompany him to France annoyed and worried her.

"Why all the questions this time, Rebecca?" he asked.

"Personal curiosity, Philip," she retorted bluntly. "Since

this mission isn't going to be as dangerous as you said, why can't I go?"

He ended the brief flare-up with the defensive finality she was beginning to hate. "Because you're going to Baltimore."

That afternoon in their suite of rooms at the inn, she defiantly donned the flowing kaftan Dirk du Kuyper had given her, its voluminous folds of peacock-blue silk concealing every trace of feminine curves. Philip's reaction had not been what she'd intended. He'd made love to her with virility that overrode her initial reluctance, and afterward he informed her fervently that he expected her to be big enough with a child to fill the peacock robe by the time he returned. Just as fervently, Rebecca hoped she wouldn't be.

But his parting words at the dock before he took over the helm of the *Reine* destroyed the fragile defenses she'd erected against the crushing desolation of another separation from him.

"Whatever happens, Cottontop," he said heavily, "remember that you're my wife and that I love you."

Never before had he made such an open avowal of love, but her momentary joy was dimmed by his tone of voice and by the words "whatever happens." These were the words she remembered as she watched the *Reine* join its sister ships in the wide harbor waters. Had she known that another watcher concealed inside a curtained carriage a hundred yards away was viewing Philip's departure with emotions as deep-rooted as her own, Rebecca's tears would have been replaced by corrosive jealousy.

CHAPTER
13

A S she walked toward the rented equipage waiting for her on the embarcadero, Rebecca's gloom was lightened by Patrice Riccard, who was cheerfully unsympathetic. "*Quelle tristesse*, Rebecca; it is not like you to weep. But no matter, it will not be for long. In two weeks you will be installed in your beautiful home in Baltimore."

"I don't have a home there or anyplace else, Patrice."

A look of astonishment replaced his smile. "Philip did not tell you that he commissioned me to locate one for you?"

"He didn't tell me that or anything else," she declared resentfully.

"*Mon Dieu*, he is a fool! But the home will be beautiful anyway; since by the time we arrive, Leoné will have located the best one—"

"Leoné is already there?"

"But of course she is, ever since my last voyage. Philip did not tell you that either?"

"No."

"Or that he instructed me to act as your guardian until we reach Baltimore? But no, he would not have told you that. Even *he* is too much of a coward to tell such a formidable rebel she needs a guardian."

Riccard chuckled as he watched her face. "Do not scowl so fiercely, Rebecca, I am a bigger coward than your husband. But since we're both exiled in the same hotel, perhaps we can share our loneliness at dinner tonight on the terrace.''

Thus it was Patrice Riccard that Rebecca was expecting when she brashly opened the door in response to a persistent knocking late in the afternoon. Instead of the short, plump Frenchman, however, a heavily veiled woman swept into the room. Only after her uninvited guest had removed the concealing lace did Rebecca recognize Paulette Burnell, and then just barely. In Falmouth, Philip's longtime mistress had been a frivolously pretty woman who had worn her lavishly expensive gowns with a confident bravado that had alienated the sober wives of that town even more than the brazenness of her social status. The woman who now faced an unwilling hostess was dressed in a somber brown cloak which emphasized the taut expression on a face that had lost much of its youthful beauty.

"Have I changed so much you do not know me, Rebecca?" she asked in the cultured, musical voice the younger woman remembered all too well.

"Not that much, Madame Burnell," Rebecca replied warily.

"There was a time when you were the only woman in that *cochon* town who called me Paulette. We were both outsiders there—me because I was—what I was, you because you dared to be *différent*.''

"Philip isn't here, Paulette," Rebecca murmured evenly, wanting no exchange of intimacies with a woman who'd threatened her own peace of mind so often.

"Philip has already given me my *congé*; it is your help I need, Rebecca.''

"Then you've wasted your time coming here, Paulette, because I won't help you. I was in Falmouth when your English friends destroyed it.''

"You know too much about the *politique* of that town to believe that I had anything to do with that, Rebecca. Falmouth had been a *problème* for the *Anglais* long before I arrived. Your *cochon* Sons of Liberty had victimized hundreds of loyalists before they drove them away and stole their homes.''

"It was your servant who kept Henry Mowat informed!" Rebecca accused hotly.

"I do not deny that charge, Rebecca, but I knew nothing about his activities until my last day there when he informed me that I'd be the one the *autorités* would blame in the event of an *Anglais* attack. Before that, he'd told me only when Philip's ship was due to arrive. And Philip himself told me nothing of his business, so what could I possibly have reported to anyone?"

Despite her recognition of the probable truth of the older woman's claim, Rebecca was still driven to ask, "Did Philip pay for your expenses while you were in Falmouth?"

A bittersweet smile briefly softened Paulette's expression. "Philip had been supporting me for a number of years, but in Falmouth he paid only my personal expenses. The Tory whose home it had been gave us permission for its use, and the *Anglais* colonel—my servant—paid for the maintenance. But this is unimportant *histoire*, Rebecca; my current *problème* is far more urgent."

"I am still not interested, Paulette."

"Not even *curieux*? Particularly since you already know that your husband reported to my bed on several occasions after he'd married you? The first time was only weeks after he had so gallantly rescued you from the *avide* Tuptons, but I was jealous of you even then. I knew that if he ever realized that you were not a *gauche* innocent, I would lose him. When he returned the second time, I was desperate enough to gamble. In Baltimore I learned how much of a fool I'd been."

"You saw Philip the last time he was in Baltimore," Rebecca stated with a flat certainty.

"The last time was an impossibility because of the quarantine, but the time before? *Oui*, I saw him—for fifteen minutes while I listened to his hypocritical abuse before he strode from my hotel without hearing what I'd come a long distance to tell him—that I'd borne him a son. That was my gamble, Rebecca," she added more gently to the girl who seemed frozen with shock. "I had considered Philip my property for so long I could not accept the fact that it was you he now loved."

Rebecca didn't hear the explanation; the words "borne him a son" had destroyed her mental control, leaving only a tumult of violent emotion behind. Philip's son! The child she'd not been able to produce, but that another woman had! The child that explained her husband's enigmatic words of farewell, "whatever happens." Her unwilling lips formed the question with painful difficulty. "How did he learn his son was in France?"

"A foolish revenge on my part. I wrote Philip a letter telling him that I'd sent his son to Lyon to be raised by my sister. Men being what they are—even men like Philip, who always said he wanted no children—cannot resist the idea of having a son."

Remembering the withdrawn look on her husband's face when he'd begun his abrupt insistence on a family, Rebecca felt the gorge of bitterness welling in her throat. He didn't need her or any child she might have conceived; he already had his son!

"Will your sister give him up to Philip?" she asked dully.

"I have no sister in Lyon or anywhere else. I wanted Philip to suffer as I had. Michel is here in Port-au-Prince with me—and my new husband."

Too preoccupied with her own seething jealousy to be polite to the woman who'd caused it, Rebecca asked the expected question with a biting candor, "What happened to your first husband?"

"Charles Burnell died five years ago. Had his *cochon* heirs notified me, I would have married Philip Keane. At that time he was still—manageable. Ironic, *n'est-ce pas?*"

"Under the present circumstances, very ironic! What is it you want of me?"

"To listen to me as Philip would not. When he left me in Baltimore, I was *désespéré*, desperate as you say in *Anglais*. I had no one to turn to except Henri Dupris, a business *associé* of my late husband. He had taken care of me during all those terrible months when I looked so—so grotesque. In Baltimore he offered to marry me, but at a price—he will not allow me to keep my son. That is why I am here, Rebecca; I want you to adopt Michel. Is it too much to ask?"

Shocked to the core of her being, Rebecca could only stare at the other woman in disbelief. As she floundered for words, she knew she sounded like a mindless parrot. "You ask me to—?" she stammered.

"Who else could I ask? I want him to have a better home than the one Henri has located here in Saint-Domingue."

"Then you should have left him with his father and grandfather in Baltimore," Rebecca blurted.

"*Non*, I could not take the chance of your hating him. It must be your *décision*, not Philip's. If you resent him, you would not be a good mother for him."

"And if I refuse, you're going to leave Philip's son here on this damnable island?" Rebecca demanded hotly.

"I will have no other choice. Henri has decided that—"

"I don't care what your husband has decided. How can you give a child away to someone you don't know?"

"That is why I am here," Paulette responded tensely. "You are *not* a stranger. You were the only person in Falmouth who had the courage to befriend me."

"Only because I was as much an outcast as you were!"

Paulette's strained face relaxed into the semblance of a smile. "*Non, ma jeune amie,* you broke only the little rules; I defied the *sacré* taboos of those hypocrites. Rebecca, I dislike reminding you that I have known your husband for many years. It is a *nécessité* that you think carefully before you refuse his son. Philip can be vindictive if he believes he has been wronged. He would not forgive you if you made such an *erreur* in *jugement*. I lost him because I was frivolous and foolish. It would be *dangereux* for you to make the same mistake."

For Rebecca, what began as resentment of Paulette's subtle manipulation subsided slowly into agreement. The Frenchwoman spoke the bleak truth. Philip would never forget or forgive her cowardice or her jealous envy. As much as the prospect of mothering another woman's child alienated her, she knew that a refusal to do so would eventually destroy her marriage. It would also destroy her own self-respect. She could not abandon a child, especially not Philip's child, to the mercy of the violent society of Saint-Domingue.

"How old is *Michael*?" she asked finally, unaware she had anglicized his name.

"He will be five months old in two days; and he looks like Philip except for his brown eyes." Pausing to study Rebecca's set face, she added with the cynical candor the younger woman had once admired, "It should not prove *difficile* to convince people that he is your son. With your brown eyes and that look of such fierce *détermination*—"

Unable to exchange pleasantries even after she'd made her commitment, Rebecca interrupted Paulette coldly, "I will need some time to make arrangements."

"I'm sorry, Rebecca, there is no time. That is why I was so *désespéré* to see you today. Henri has made arrangements for us to leave this island on a ship that is sailing tomorrow *après-midi*. We have been delayed for weeks already by the *fièvre jaune*, and he is anxious to return to Martinique."

Aghast at the immediate need to take responsibility for a strange child, Rebecca cried out in distress, her rigid composure shattered, "Paulette, I don't know how to take care of a young babe. I'll have to find someone to help me."

"That will not be a *problème*. Michel already has a nurse, the same one who has been with him since he was born. Dena's own *enfant* died at birth, so Henri purchased her from the Philadelphia blacksmith who owned her."

"A slave woman?" Rebecca gasped.

"There was no other kind available, but Dena is well trained and very intelligent. She'll be an excellent *domestique* for you as well as Michel's nurse. Of course," Paulette paused and shrugged her shoulders delicately, "Henri will expect payment for her."

"From me?" Rebecca asked in sharp amazement.

"It is the way of the world, *chère*; why should the idea disturb you? Henri is not a *riche* man, but Philip is; and you have a fortune of your own."

"My inheritance is in a London bank," Rebecca snapped defensively. "How much money does your husband want for—for Michael's nurse?"

"Three hundred pounds, a mere *bagatelle* to a man with Philip's wealth."

Shocked by the amount and by Paulette's vindictive greed, Rebecca realized that she was being asked to pay for the child as well as for his nurse. Not one of the household servants sold by Edmond Falconet had earned even half that sum, and Silas had paid only two hundred pounds for Akhoi. Unwilling to place herself in a pauper's position by using most of the money she'd earned through her paintings, Rebecca asserted flatly, "Philip did not provide me with any funds before he left."

Her face tightened now in speculation, Paulette murmured lightly, "You were foolish not to insist; but perhaps money will not be so *nécessaire*. Perhaps one of the *bijoux* he has given you—a bracelet or a *broche* or a necklace—will be *suffisant*."

It was then that Rebecca noticed the strand of pearls around Paulette's neck and remembered the almost identical one hidden in her trunk. She'd worn it only once during a simple dinner with Philip at El Abrigo the night before his departure for New Providence Island. For a long moment Rebecca hesitated, but in the end practicality triumphed over sentiment. In the months ahead before Philip returned from France, she'd have more use for her money than she would for the pearls.

"I do have a necklace similar to the one you're wearing," she admitted. As she watched the avid look of satisfaction on Paulette's face during the subsequent examination of the perfectly matched strand of lustrous pearls, Rebecca knew that Philip was paying dearly for the son he'd never seen.

"This will be most adequate," Paulette acknowledged graciously. "Even Henri will be *agréable* tomorrow morning when he brings Michel and Dena to your hotel. There is just one more *bagatelle* to complete before I leave, Rebecca. When I arrived in Saint-Domingue, I had papers prepared naming you as Michel's new mother. I will leave them with you, as well as the sale contract for Dena."

"Were you that certain I would agree, Paulette?"

"*Oui*, Rebecca, I was that certain. Henri was not, but then he does not know you. Michel will have a happier life with you than with me. Your luck has been better than mine."

"I will try to give Michael a good home," Rebecca promised awkwardly.

"I was thinking of Philip. *Au revoir*, Madame Keane."

For a few minutes after Paulette's departure, Rebecca stared at one of the pieces of parchment which would change her life, without attempting to read the flowing script written on it. Not until she focused her eyes did she discover the words were French.

Exploding from her rooms in a frantic burst of energy, she located the harried concierge, who viewed her with a veiled suspicion when she demanded he send Captain Riccard to her suite. She was pacing her sitting room in an agitated extremity when Riccard arrived minutes later. Silently she shoved the documents into his hands and continued to pace.

His first words were muttered imprecations which changed gradually to a prayerful *"Bon Dieu."*

"You have agreed to this insanity, Rebecca?"

"I had no choice."

"Without seeing the child first?"

"How would my seeing him change his existence?"

"Are you certain he is Philip's child?"

"As certain as Philip himself is. Yes, I'm sure, Patrice. She was his mistress for eight years."

"But she produced this child long after he married you. A woman like that could have many—friends."

"Paulette had no other friends in Falmouth."

"Did you realize that she has given you exclusive custody of the child without any mention of the father?"

"I think that is why she is giving him to me rather than to Philip."

"It does not terrify you, this responsibility?"

"I'd feel much worse if I'd refused. Is the adoption paper legal?"

"I'm not an expert in such matters, but usually it is the husband who is held accountable. Perhaps tomorrow we can consult a lawyer."

"Tomorrow will be too late; it must be done tonight. What does the second paper say?"

His shrug was one of eloquent distaste. "That you're the new owner of a slave woman named Dena. *Mon Dieu,* she is but a sixteen-year-old girl."

"No, not even for one night will I agree to that. Can a lawyer prepare her freedom papers?"

"Easily. The difficulty will be to find an English-speaking one who is willing to work at night. *Les avocats* are not notable for accommodating cooperation.''

"The one Silas hired was. Do you know him?"

Riccard smiled cynically in surrender; with such a woman, it was best not to waste time in futile argument. Of necessity, dinner would have to be postponed. It took three hours for the meticulous lawyer, who still remembered the fee Silas Keane had paid him with gratitude, to translate the documents into English, explain their contents to the intelligently inquisitive *Américaine,* and prepare the requested freedom papers—a request he secretly thought foolishly idealistic. But he was well pleased with the gold coins Madame Keane paid him for the simple chore of assuring her that the adoption papers were entirely legal.

At the hostelry, however, the concierge was anything but pleased at having to produce two dinners an hour after the cook had retired for the night. He was even more disturbed the following day when a small platoon of footmen carried an infant bed and piles more of luggage into Madame Keane's rooms. In his agitation he overlooked a plump young Negress who hugged a small bundle to her ample bosom as she placidly followed the carters.

Dena was Rebecca's first introduction to the mysteries of motherhood and to the unfathomable illogic of contented slavery. After she'd tucked the sleeping infant into his bed, the Negro girl listened complacently to her new mistress explain that she was now a free woman, and shook her head. Smiling good-naturedly, her strong white teeth contrasting vividly with the brown skin of her broad face, she responded in the melodious vernacular common among the slaves of the American South.

"Lawsy, Miz Keane, that chile's gonna need me a heap more years. He ain't been nothin' but good luck for me, jest lak the conjur woman done said. So's long as I's workin' at som'thin' I likes, that paper don' mean nothin'."

"Someday you'll want a family of your own, Dena."

"Conjur woman tole me my chile 'ud be a spirit chile before I borned him. She say I don' need nothin' lak a fam'bly of my own."

"Were you married to your child's father, Dena?"

"Lawsy no, Miz Keane! Misser Jim done loan me to a white-trash neighbor to hep with a new-borned chile, and that no-count Misser Bundy done use me for a week 'til my pappy and Misser Jim come for me. When I tole them, my pappy hit ole Misser Bundy 'til he's gonna be chompin' on gums the rest of his life, lessen he grows new teeth."

"Mister Jim was your owner?"

"More lak fam'bly, and he done take care of his own. When the sheriff come for my pappy about hittin' that white trash, Misser Jim say he done the hittin', not my pappy. Conjur woman say Misser Jim be a good man."

"Were you sold at a slave market, Dena?"

The girl's dark eyes moved heavenward in protest against the ignorance of some white folk. "Misser Jim don' stand for nothin' lak that. He make sure Miz Paulette treat me right before he sold me."

"But he still sold you for money, Dena."

"Course he done sold me, but he kep me 'til I's full-growed when he was jest poor folk hisself. Conjur woman say he done his best by me."

Shaking her head in amused resignation, Rebecca wondered what Akhoi would have said about a rival "conjur woman" who counseled such tolerance of slavery or about a girl who'd so obviously admired her owner. Rebecca's introduction to the second addition of her new "fam'bly" was a squalling bellow of impatient rage erupting from the bedroom. Immobilized by a heart-pounding terror, she listened helplessly to the steadily increasing outrage and to Dena's quiet chuckle.

"That chile sure do let a body know when it's eatin' time, and he eats 'til he's fit to bust. But don' you pay no nebermind to his squallin', Miz Keane; he ain't been sick a speck since he 'uz borned."

For an hour Rebecca watched the well-practiced routine of nursing with awe, a strangely touching spectacle she'd never witnessed before, not even with Abigail and her nephew Willy. Before Dena picked him up, Michael had stopped crying; and throughout the vigorous changing and washing process, he'd gurgled and smiled at his young nurse, his sturdy little legs beating a busy tattoo in the warm air. As Rebecca looked on, Dena washed both of her large brown breasts with yet another soft linen cleaning cloth.

"Neber knowed a body as pertick'ler 'bout washing as Miz Paulette," the girl explained good-naturedly, "Onct a day, I's got to wash eber'thin' Michel wears and eber'thin' I wears."

"His name is Michael now," Rebecca interrupted, "Michael—Michael Philip."

"'Spect I laks that a heap better, Miz Keane; it sounds more lak the folk in Phil'delphie where he was borned anyways."

"Dena, why do you call Michael's mother Miss Paulette and me Mrs. Keane?"

"'Cause conjur woman say I's got to be ast before I uses given names."

"Then I'm asking you to call me Miss Rebecca."

"Yas 'um, Miz Rebecca, it do make us more fam'bly, but you got to 'member that Michael is your chile now, not Miz Paulette's."

In a stunned silence Rebecca stared over at the sturdy infant lustily sucking his dinner; it was the first time she realized the enormity of the responsibility she'd assumed so impulsively. She was now the legal mother of a five-month-old despot whose cherubic smile reminded her sharply of Philip's even more than his demanding squall for attention had. Two hours later, when the sitting room was festooned with infant and nursing garments and three of her own white blouses, she knew with a sobering certainty that her own carelessly adventuresome youth was over. No more treks through a Connecticut forest with Simon Parrish, no more dangerous sailboat rides with a rebel Jean Dessalines, and most repressive of all, no more escapist dreams about independence. Her future was now tied irrevocably to Philip Keane's; she desperately hoped that he would feel equally bound.

Patrice Riccard's reaction at the sight of the lines of wash was a heartfelt groan. "*Mon Dieu, le pauvre Reynard* will be nothing more than a floating *chambre d'enfants*. Such cleanliness is not possible aboard a ship, Rebecca."

"I'm afraid we'll have to manage, Patrice. Dena insists on washing every day."

Ironically, thirteen unlucky days later on the Atlantic Ocean, that same infant clothing flapping from the aft rigging of the *Mer Reynard* saved the unarmed brigantine from being fired upon by a British ship-of-line prowling the seas due north of the Florida Straits.

Almost from the moment the *Reynard* ventured beyond the protection of Saint-Domingue waters, the voyage was plagued with trouble, beginning with a desperate two-day flight from an English privateer. Standing with Captain Riccard on the quarterdeck when the warning was shouted by the lookout on the crow's nest, Rebecca knew with an abrupt terror what ship it was.

"The fourth ship!" she gasped. "Jean Dessalines said there were four ships, but only three attacked at El Abrigo."

"*Mon Dieu!* You told Philip of this?"

"No, I just remembered it now."

All trace of joviality vanished as Riccard ordered her to remain belowdecks; his face had become that of a hardened buccaneer who'd won twenty-five years of battles on and against the sea and did not intend to lose this one. He was shouting orders even as Rebecca made her way cautiously to her cabin. Six harrowing days later after he anchored his storm-battered *Reynard* in the protective lee of one of the hundred uninhabited islands north of Cuba and slept for sixteen hours in a state of exhaustion, Riccard summoned his young American passenger to his cabin.

"My steward tells me *le petit* weathered the chase and the storm better than anyone aboard. You're still convinced he is Philip's son?"

"I never had any doubts. Why do you ask?"

"I'm not sure, Rebecca; but it is possible that *cochon* privateer was after more than my ship and cargo. When I ask myself why he persisted for two days before the storm mercifully stopped him, I can only answer that he wanted information and perhaps hostages. How much did your husband tell you about his mission to France?"

"Besides ship repairs, only that he would avoid contact with the enemy."

"Then I will tell you the rest, and afterward we will make a decision. On their return to Baltimore all three ships will be loaded with guns and ammunition that France is donating to the American forces. The British must, of course, try to stop all such shipments any way they can. In the case of the Keane fleet, they have other causes for revenge as well, including the fact that they do not know the fleet's home port. For such information the British would pay heavily; and if they had the means of forcing your husband and Silas to stop operations entirely, they would pay even more."

"Patrice, what would have happened if they'd boarded your ship?"

"For myself and my crew? Who can tell with *criminels* like those? But Madame Philip Keane and *le petit* Michael might have been held for ransom, a regrettable practice pirates have used for centuries. *Mon Dieu*, I wish this *malchanceux* voyage were over!"

"What name would you suggest I use, Patrice?"

"Another name is a simple matter of changing the ship's log, but the explanation of an American woman aboard a Saint-Domingue ship—that is what worries me. Perhaps in the two days we will be making repairs, you can create some more of those nonsense stories you send to your uncles in New York, *un petit déguisement*."

A gallant man who believed sincerely in the protection of women, Riccard did not tell Rebecca of his multiple other worries. With a crew only half its normal size, since many of his men had elected to remain with their families in Port-au-Prince, he'd been unable to reef the sails quickly enough during the storm to avoid damage to both masts. His *Mer Reynard* would be reduced to half its normal speed, and it had yet three hundred miles of English-controlled waters to traverse. A realist more than a fatalist, Riccard breathed a sigh of relief that both his family and his fortune were already safe in Baltimore.

Rebecca, too, was busily considering the realities of the altered situation; but the creation of a believable new identity eluded her until an illiterate sixteen-year-old Negro girl supplied the inspiration. Throughout the five days of imprisonment in the small cabin, Rebecca had recited stories to the frightened nurse, both those she'd read and others she'd written. Just how enthralled Dena had been, the white woman learned on the second night of the anchorage at a time when she was still casting about for a solution to her own immediate problem.

"That story you tole me about the mambo, Miz Rebecca, how come you knowed som'thin' lak that? Most white folks jest makes fun of conjurin'."

"No white folk will ever make fun of Akhoi again," Rebecca promised grimly.

"And you done writ all that down?" an admiring Dena persisted.

"I did better than that, I sent the story to my uncles in New York; and if they publish it—" Rebecca stopped talking abruptly; she'd just eliminated her own dilemma by becoming a widow—the widow of Eb Burns, a Connecticut journalist who'd joined the Keane fleet and died in the yellow fever epidemic. When Captain Riccard challenged her decision with a sharp reminder to her that the informant in Saint-Domingue might have given the English privateers a description of Philip Keane's wife, Rebecca dismissed his objections with a confident shrug.

"I merely posed as Captain Keane's wife on a few public occasions to help him keep his mistresses in check. Our families had been good friends in Falmouth."

"And this Monsieur Burns, you have some proof of his existence?"

"A trunk full of writing signed Eb Burns. And as soon as I decide what he looked like, I'll have a sketch of him. If you're asked, you can say that when you were introduced to me in New London, my name was Rebecca Burns but that you never saw my husband."

"*Et le petit?*"

"Born last January at El Abrigo."

"Your servant girl understands all this?"

"Dena has a very flexible mind. It seems her 'conjur woman' instructed her not to contradict white folk; and 'Misser Jim' taught her to distrust all 'red-coated varmints.'"

"Then I agree, it is most convincing except for the costume."

Rebecca looked down at her brightly colored skirt and giggled. Already laid out across her bunk were a black cloak and dress, black gloves, and for good measure, a black veil fashioned from a lace-trimmed petticoat. "My costume," she retorted lightly, "will be depressing enough to discourage even King George himself."

"Even an absurd king, Rebecca, is a gentleman compared to the scum he released from prisons to serve on his cursed privateers. Hide your money if you can, and your jewelry."

"I have to hide my wedding ring in any case, since it has Philip's initials on it, unless of course you know someone who can change *PK* to *EB*."

"You're not sentimental about this ring?"

"The only thing I'm sentimental about is getting Philip's son safely to America and being there myself when my husband returns."

"*Bien,* then I will see to it. One of my men has learned something of the art—a professional necessity in my business if one hopes to sell contraband jewelry."

Two hours later when Rebecca reclaimed her ring, the initial *P* had been changed to *R*; an *E* had been inserted into the space the original silversmith had failed to fill with Philip's middle initial; the *K* had become a *B* and Eb Burns had acquired the first name of Robin. Within two weeks a gold band which had cost her only five pounds three shillings assured her safety for the second time.

The capture of the storm-damaged *Mer Reynard* by a British ship-of-line had been a prayed-for blessing by a desperate captain and crew. Just as the ship reached the Florida Straits, the lookouts spotted the same privateer that had dogged the smaller craft earlier. This time there'd been no doubts about the intentions of the enemy; all of its gun ports were in operational readiness. Jettisoning cargo and equipment alike, Riccard ordered full sail despite the weakened masts and pushed the *Reynard* dangerously close to shore. When the powerful frigate-of-line first appeared on the northern horizon, moving swiftly south under four masts of billowing sail, but still an hour's time farther away than the pursuing privateer, Riccard ordered one final reckless gamble—an outsized jib attached to the bowsprit which drove the shuddering ship forward at a racing speed. Long before the sixty-gun Royal Navy vessel accepted the surrender, the white Bourbon flag was lowered on the *Reynard*'s mast. Even so, the English privateer attempted a perilous interception and fired a broadside at the stricken craft. The abortive battle ended with a dramatic flourish when the ship-of-line fired a warning shot across the bow of the English privateer and took the French ship under tow into Charles Town harbor.

It was there that Rebecca learned a harsh truth about British justice. Despite his merciful rescue of the unarmed *Reynard*, the naval captain proved as much an enemy as the privateer. He declared the *Reynard* a forfeit of war and Patrice Riccard a captured prisoner subject to a maritime trial. Within hours the appointed board of inquiry condemned the Frenchman and his crew for illegal acts of plunder against the English. While Riccard and his officers were remanded to a Charles Town jail, the hapless crewmen were sentenced to spend two years as impressed seamen aboard English merchantmen whose own crews had been reduced by desertion.

Still shaken by the terrifying experience at sea, Rebecca knew nothing of these proceedings until a British army officer arrived at the inn where she and her family had been placed under guard. Responding to a staccato, authoritative knocking, Rebecca opened the door cautiously, only to stumble awkwardly backward as two men strode into the room.

The shorter of the intruders, a ranking officer whose uniform and boots were too exquisitely pristine ever to have been subjected to the rigors of a battlefield, surveyed the sitting room with expressionless gray eyes before he moved over to the dining table and spread out a sheaf of papers with the precision of a surgeon about to perform an operation.

"We are here, mistress," he announced in a voice as coldly impersonal as his ferret-sharp features, "to search your luggage and to ask you some questions. According to our records, you were traveling with a Negro woman and a child. Where are they?''

''My son is asleep in the adjoining room, and his nurse is attending to the laundry.'' Rebecca's heart was pounding uncomfortably as she remembered that concealed in Michael's small crib were the three hundred pounds in gold coins she'd earned in Port-au-Prince, and wrapped in a belt around Dena's ample waist were the only documents bearing the name of Rebecca Keane—Dena's own freedom papers and Michael's adoption records.

''Is this the extent of your luggage, mistress?'' the man asked crisply, indicating the five trunks stacked against one wall.

''No, there are two others in the bedroom containing the clothing for our immediate needs.'' Perversely, she almost hoped that her arrogant inquisitor would begin his search there. When Michael was aroused unwillingly from a nap, his screams could be piercingly loud. But this policeman seemed knowledgeable even about children as he ordered his sergeant to perform his duty quietly in the sitting room only.

''We'll check the other ones later,'' he added and returned his attention to Rebecca. ''Please be seated, mistress.''

''Not until I know who you are,'' she retorted stiffly, ''and why my possessions are being searched.''

''Colonel Crane, mistress, of His Royal Majesty's governmental services. It is my assignment to locate and punish traitors, and I am the one who ordered you held in protective custody.''

''Why? What treason have I committed?''

''You? Perhaps none. It is the Captains Silas and Philip Keane who are my immediate targets, them and all seamen foolish enough to have been in their service, your friend Captain Riccard, for example.''

''On this voyage he was nothing but a merchant,'' she declared hotly.

''True, but on previous missions he performed as the pirate he has been convicted of being. However, at my intervention he has been spared the gallows and placed on parole in exchange for his ship and a sufficient sum of ransom. His men will pay their debts with two years of service in His Majesty's merchant marine."

Rebecca gasped with shock. "I have often heard the word *impressment*," she accused bitingly, "but I never thought the Royal Navy would stoop to the level of Turkish and Moroccan pirates. Tell me, Colonel Crane, was the so-called privateer who attacked our unarmed ship condemned with an equal harshness?"

"He was merely following orders, mistress. But now if you've vented your spleen sufficiently, we will proceed to your particular case. Although Captain Riccard obligingly identified you as the widow of one Robin Eben Burns, my records list you as the wife of Philip Keane. Before you perjure yourself with a denial, you should know that the description I received of you is undeniably accurate. Last November you arrived in Port-au-Prince in the company of Silas Keane, who introduced you as his daughter-in-law, and you were subsequently known in that city as Mrs. Philip Keane."

Relieved that his information had most probably been supplied by the vindictive Annette Gironde, who knew very little of her previous life, Rebecca began her own defense with a glib fluency. "Had you consulted your colleague in Falmouth whose information to Henry Mowat led to the destruction of that town, Colonel Crane, you'd have learned that I posed as Philip Keane's wife there too. It was a mutual defense pact to discourage the ambitions of Philip's two French mistresses and, in my case, the unwanted attention of Roger Tupton. If you'll check your lists, I'm certain you'll find all three names listed. You'll also find the name of Captain Brian Sinclair, who could tell you that during my stay in New Bedford I was most definitely *not* married to Philip Keane. Like you, he researched my relatives very carefully. He knew all about my father, Jeremy Rayburn; my uncle, Jonathan Langley; and my two New York uncles, Samuel and Joshua Rayburn. If you had similar access to Connecticut records, you would know that I was Miss Rebecca Rayburn during my stay in that colony until my marriage in Hartford to Eben Burns, a reporter for Thomas Green's *Hartford Courant*. My New York uncles also knew my late husband, since they published two volumes of his stories. You'll find the copies of those stories in the trunk your sergeant is now searching.''

Without pause Rebecca continued her memorized narrative until the mythical character of Eben Burns became almost as real to her as it seemed to be to the English colonel who studied the contents of the carefully arranged trunk with precise attention. When he'd completed his perusal, his questions were less accusatory; and he appeared to accept her responses without suspicion. even when she denied all knowledge of the whereabouts of Philip and Silas Keane. However, her announced intention of returning to Connecticut met with a frown.

''As you said, mistress, we no longer have contact in that colony; therefore, I have decided to conduct you and your family to New York. As you undoubtedly know already, your uncles there are staunch loyalists. If they agree to take custody of you, your future destination will be at their discretion, and I will cease having any professional interest in your activities. When your servant returns, she will complete your packing; and I will escort you to a merchant ship which sails tomorrow for that city.''

''May I see Captain Riccard before I leave?'' Rebecca asked shakily.

Colonel Crane smiled for the first time and shook his head. ''I cannot permit that, mistress. Suffice to say, he will be detained until this colonial hostility ends. Now, mistress, I advise you to prepare for departure.''

After five interminable days restricted to a dark cabin aboard a heavily armed cargo ship, Rebecca was summoned deckside by Colonel Crane, who greeted her gasped question of ''Boston?'' with another of his cold, humorless smiles.

With a negligent wave of his hand, he indicated the vast fleet of British naval ships riding at anchor in the harbor and shook his head. ''It's New York, mistress,'' he affirmed smugly. ''Admiral Lord Richard Howe has secured both the inner and outer ports of the city and the Hudson and East rivers, while his brother, General William Howe, has already landed his army on Staten Island.''

''I thought they were in Boston,'' she demurred with the dull realization that once again she'd been led into a trap.

''Not since April, when we decided that Boston was no longer a threat.''

''What happened to the Continental army?''

''Seventeen thousand undisciplined, untrained rabble are trapped on Long Island with the renegade George Washington. Within months the fool will be forced to surrender, and the rebellion will be finished. But in the meantime, mistress, we have your problem to consider.''

''What problem, Colonel Crane?'' Having spent five days in anxious contemplation of the reception she'd receive from two old men who might not even recognize her claim to relationship, Rebecca was more aware than the Englishman of the precariousness of her current position.

''The test of your remarkable story, mistress! According to my records, the men you claim as uncles are related only to the Enderlys of England. It seems unlikely to me that they could be brothers to a journalistic propagandist like your father, who has now committed the ultimate in treason by taking up arms against his king. Would you care to change your story before you're further embarrassed by a public denouncement?''

For a moment Rebecca was too angry to reply. It was true that her father had never mentioned his older brothers, but her mother and her Uncle Jonathan had in great detail. And to be called a picaresque liar by this arrogantly sly Englishman infuriated her.

''Do you know my uncles, Colonel Crane?'' she asked with a spurious innocence.

''Not yet, mistress, but I intend to know them well. I have requested quartering at their estate once our forces occupy the city.''

''What happened to your promise that I was to be a free woman if they claimed me as a niece, Colonel?''

''I reconsidered, mistress. Despite the evidence you presented to the contrary, I'm still not certain about you.

But we shall learn the truth soon after we're taken ashore; my sergeant left the ship three hours ago to bring one or both of the Rayburns to the military headquarters on Staten Island.''

Throughout the interminable period of waiting, Rebecca maintained a determined calm, reassuring a frightened Dena and holding a wriggling Michael tightly in her arms as she walked down the swaying gangplank onto the busy dock. When she heard Colonel Crane's autocratic voice above the din of the crowd, she was tempted to walk in the opposite direction until she realized that he'd called her Mistress Burns for the first time. However, it was the voice of the older man standing next to the uniformed colonel that sent familiar shivers down her spine; it sounded like her father's when he was being most pompous and insufferable.

"Come along, Rebecca," Samuel Rayburn ordered her peremptorily. "This is no place for a family discussion."

Neither, it seemed, was the three-hour-long trip on the Hudson River to a private dock near the upland end of Manhattan Island. In the starkly furnished cabin of an armed riverboat manned by British seamen, Samuel paid no attention to Michael or his nurse, and his occasional comments to Rebecca were caustically statistical. The island was nothing but a huge granite outcropping, he told her, fourteen miles long and less than two and a half wide; and its teeming population of thirty thousand was the least disciplined, most heterogeneous people in the world. There were Swedes, French, Germans, Walloon Dutch, Irish rabble, refugee scum from other colonies, Scots who hated the English, and freed Negroes who hated everyone.

Amused that Englishmen had been omitted from her uncle's list of undesirables, Rebecca asked pointedly about indentured immigrants, and quickly learned that Samuel Rayburn detested them far more than the others.

"Criminals and fortune hunters," he rasped. "Once they've served their terms, they join the hoodlums terrorizing the street. Half of the freedom-shouting Sons of Liberty are nothing but thugs and thieves. When they took possession of the city in April of 'seventy-five, they made a mockery of government until Manhattan has become the most lawless city in the colonies."

There was no hint of lawlessness, however, when the boat docked at a well-maintained stone pier where a dozen workmen waited to carry Rebecca's trunks along rock-lined walks and through landscaped gardens. As the small procession came into sight of the large white stone-and-wood house, Rebecca exclaimed with involuntary delight:

"What a beautiful old home!"

"It is that," Samuel agreed, "not that many people have the sense to agree with you. It was built a hundred and twenty years ago by one of Peter Stuyvesant's Walloon ministers."

"How long have the Rayburns owned it?"

"Since 1670 when the first Samuel Rayburn purchased it. It has a history, Rebecca, that you will appreciate after you've lived here for a time."

Diplomatically deciding not to tell him that she intended leaving as soon as possible, Rebecca rushed through the now familiar routine of settling Michael and Dena in yet another place unprepared for the emergencies of infancy. Not daring to refuse her uncle's invitation to join him and his brother for a traditional English tea, she limited her own grooming to a hurried sponge bath and a change into a more flattering black dress. But even these improvements did little to ease her nervous perplexity about Samuel Rayburn. Why had he claimed her so readily? And how had he convinced the skeptical English colonel that she was a widow rather than a suspect wife?

Once inside the gracious library, however, Rebecca relaxed some of her stiff vigilance; her Uncle Joshua proved far less intimidating than his brother, greeting her with a warm smile as he poured her a cup of tea almost as black in color as uncut rum. Having tasted the controversial beverage on only a few occasions and never a brew this strong and bitter, Rebecca wondered dismally what insanity had inspired the Boston Tea Party. She flushed guiltily when she looked up to find Samuel regarding her sardonically.

"Are you as rebel in all of your opinions as you are

about tea?" he asked with a glint of humor in his sharp blue eyes. "From now on, you'll be served your heathenish coffee," he added offhandedly, without waiting for a response.

Resisting the impulse to tell him that she'd prefer her coffee laced with rum and that her rebellion was not limited to Englishmen, Rebecca sipped her tea stoically and studied the faces of the two men who resembled Jeremy Rayburn only vaguely. While her father's lean face was darkly dramatic, his older brothers' were lighter skinned and too aristocratically aesthetic to be considered handsome. But she did not make the mistake of underestimating their intelligence.

When Samuel casually asked her how long she'd been widowed, she responded promptly, "I'm not! My husband is very much alive, only his name is not one you'd mention to an English policeman bent on locating candidates for the hangman's noose."

Samuel was the first to chuckle. "We wondered if you were going to repeat the balderdash you told that gullible martinet."

"He wasn't ready to believe me until you talked to him."

"Bullies like the suspicious colonel are quite easy to convince if a lie is told with sufficient authority. As soon as I learned you'd taken the name of Burns, I assured him that I was the one responsible for your marrying a writer instead of a notorious privateer or a villainous turncoat. You see, Rebecca, Josh and I have been kept very well informed about you, not by your father, of course, but by your mother and her brother. We knew both of them when they lived in New York. Now it's time you learned about the other skeletons in the Rayburn closet. Perhaps then you'll trust us enough to drop that defensive shell you hide behind."

Given no choice but to follow Samuel as he strode from the library into an adjoining wing of the spread-out house, Rebecca fumed silently. For three hours on an uncomfortable boat, he'd been as impersonal as a museum curator, yet he accused her of being secretive!

"Samuel doesn't mean to be unkind," Joshua whispered softly as he ushered her into a newspaper office ten times the size of Jeremy's, its untidy walls cluttered with the yellowing memorabilia of a century of turbulent colonial history.

"Over there, Rebecca," Samuel called out imperiously and pointed to a small framed portrait hanging amid a welter of newspaper clippings taken from long-ago copies of the *Falmouth Clarion*.

"As you can see, I had no problem recognizing you today, although I'll admit that you turned out prettier than I expected. You were a fierce-looking printer's devil when your mother drew that picture of you."

Rebecca stared at the painting and nodded in agreement; both the nose and the brown eyes were too large for the small, intense face, and the ink-stained hands clutching the handle of the press were anything but daintily feminine. Only the pale curls cascading messily from beneath a lopsided mobcap had remained unchanged until her marriage.

"Remind me to be tolerant while my own children are growing up," she murmured ruefully. "I was certainly ugly enough."

"Oh, your mother sent us others of you and that pretty little nothing of an older sister, but this one is our favorite. It convinced us that perhaps you'd really written what Audrey claimed you had. When you finally sent us those first stories, we had no doubt," Samuel declared brusquely.

"They were really my mother's stories," Rebecca admitted. "That's why I used a pseudonym."

"We'd already read the parts that were your mother's," Joshua explained gently. "About eight months before her death, she came to New York—for medical and legal advice primarily—but also to find out if her literary efforts were publishable. Because she'd had such a miserable life with your father, we thought perhaps— But she was too shrewd to accept even well-meant lies. It was then that she presented us with your portrait and the samples of your childish attempts at humor and asked us to look after you, should the need arise. But it never did. Despite his indifference as a father, Jeremy provided you with an

excellent opportunity to develop. The additions you wrote
to your mother's stories were what made them marketable.
And the ones you sent from the Caribbean will sell even
better, particularly in England. Because thousands of the
fortunes there were built on slavery, your 'Mama Mambo'
might well become very popular, if for no other reason
than scandal. Since your character was biographical in
part, there'll be hundreds who'll wonder if other Mama
Mambos aren't a part of their own ancestry.''

Before Rebecca could respond to Joshua's praise, the
less effusive Samuel demanded to know how many additional stories she had ready for publication.

"People on both sides of the ocean could use a little
comic relief from this bloody damn war," he insisted.

Remembering her own recent experiences with the "bloody
damn war," Rebecca shook her head. At the moment there
was nothing remotely humorous in her life, and Samuel's
next casually delivered remarks threatened what little philosophical equilibrium she'd retained.

"Well, no matter," he disclaimed. "You'll be writing
on a daily basis now that you're here."

"I won't be here that long, Uncle. As soon as possible,
I'll rejoin my husband."

"No, my dear, you won't! Like everyone else in this
captive city, you're a prisoner. And your Captain Keane's
life will be forfeit if he tries to rescue you."

"How did you learn my husband's name?" she demanded.

"From your father's current family. According to them,
it was you who suggested they seek our help after Falmouth
was burned."

"Was Sidney Tupton the one who told you that?"

"Sidney brought his mother and daughter here, yes. Seemed
to think that since your mother had not seen fit to finance your
father's subsequent family, you were somehow responsible for
the support of two women and three children. He was highly
critical of your refusal and requested that we assume the burden."

"Fire or no fire in Falmouth," Rebecca denounced
hotly, "Sidney Tupton is a wealthy man."

Samuel Rayburn's laughter was more a snort of contempt. "We're as familiar with Sidney Tupton's sly ways

as you are. Since your father married the first of his
Tupton wives, we've had occasion to investigate every
member of that acquisitive clan, including the dangerous
hypocrite your father chose for you.''

"Jeremy didn't know Roger was a loyalist," Rebecca
defended her father wearily.

"Roger Tupton is nothing but a turncoat opportunist! When
he posed as a Son of Liberty, he persecuted the peaceful
loyalists of your town for financial gain as greedily as his
father and uncles did. Now, according to our information, he
is being paid by the English to help Iroquois Indians murder
frontier settlers. And that, my dear, is something every New
Yorker has reason to fear regardless of his political sympathies.
None of us want to see those savages take the warpath again
any more than we want another Negro uprising.''

Surprised by Samuel's allusions to an earlier slave
rebellion, Rebecca demurred sharply. "According to the
letters of correspondence I've read, New York doesn't
have a slave problem.''

"According to a few of those rebel propagandists, the
colony doesn't have a loyalist problem either. There are
twenty thousand Negroes scattered throughout the colony,
twelve percent of the people in an area where they were
never needed economically. More than half of the poor
devils have been freed to shift as best they can in the worst
of our slums. During the past seventy years, they've
staged two bloody insurrections. The one in 1740 cost
your great-grandfather his life, Rebecca.''

Stunned by the implication that she had Negro blood,
she blurted the dread question, "Is that why my father and
I are dark skinned?''

"Good Lord, no," Joshua assured her. "Lloyd Glynns was
a Welshman. Didn't your father ever talk about his family?''

"No, my mother is the one who told me he had two
brothers.''

"Half brothers," Samuel corrected her pointedly. "Our
father was a foolish old man when he married the seventeen-
year-old daughter of Lloyd Glynns who had been an
indentured Welsh revolutionary deported to America in
1725 for political crimes against the crown, and your

grandmother Gwenna was as outspoken a rebel as he was.''

"She was a well-educated, beautiful woman," Joshua interceded hastily. "Except for your hair, you look very much like her."

"Was she an indentured criminal too?" Rebecca asked bluntly.

Joshua hesitated before he nodded. "It's a cruel system, but yes, she was condemned as an accessory to her father. They were indentured to the Rayburn-Enderly publishers because Lloyd Glynns was an excellent printer and journalist."

"How was he killed?"

"He was shot in a Negro street riot he helped organize," Samuel volunteered caustically. "Had he lived, he would have been hanged as an insurrectionist."

"What happened to my grandmother?"

"Instead of accepting the restraints of marriage and motherhood, she defied all social convention and carried on her father's mischief among the dregs of Manhattan's slum people. During a smallpox epidemic, she insisted on working in the affected area, and both she and our father died of the disease. At the time, Joshua and I were in England, where we'd been most of the preceding fifteen years. Upon our return to America we found the Rayburn fortune badly depleted. It seemed the beautiful Gwenna had persuaded our elderly father to invest heavily in charity, a wasted effort among people too undisciplined to be reliable workers. It took us ten years to rebuild the business and our family's reputation."

"And my father?"

"He was a rebellious sixteen-year-old when his mother died. At his insistence we sent him to Harvard College, where unfortunately he acquired additional revolutionary attitudes rather than a sound education. Shortly after his nineteenth birthday he married Jobina Tupton and promptly demanded his share of our father's estate to establish the *Falmouth Clarion*. Until he married your mother six years later, we supplied him with money. But that's enough of ancient history, Rebecca; at the moment your problems are far more urgent."

"My problems are not your concern, Uncle Samuel,"

she disclaimed swiftly. "I appreciate your hospitality, but I won't impose on you. Unlike my father, I am not a pauper. Tomorrow I will make arrangements to leave the city."

"I've already told you that you'll do nothing of the kind, young lady. At the moment no one is able to escape from the city. You were allowed to leave Staten Island only because we agreed to assume responsibility for you and your child. As for your living elsewhere, there are no other accommodations available; and within a month a large English army will be occupying the city."

"Colonel Crane predicted that the war would be over when General Washington's army falls," Rebecca admitted, oddly disturbed by the prospect. Samuel's reaction, however, was not the confident reaction she'd expected from a man who'd been labeled a staunch loyalist.

"Crane is wrong," he snapped. "He underestimates the depth of American resentment and the unpopularity of this war in England. The British will win this battle, but not the war. There are almost four million colonials, more than half of them rebel, who'll raise army after army until they eventually win. At sea the two thousand privateers like your husband will wreak havoc with British shipping. In the end the Americans will have won the sorry independence the idealistic politicians in Philadelphia have just declared.

"In the meantime," he insisted cheerfully, "you'll remain here under our protection and continue being the Widow Burns. It won't involve any charity, my dear; in addition to your own writing, you'll help us produce the *Observer* as long as our supplies and equipment last."

During this autocratic rearrangement of her life, Rebecca maintained an expressionless face; but beneath the superficial calm, she was seething with rebellion. Of all the men who'd attempted to regiment her attitudes and activities to suit their own purposes, Samuel Rayburn was the most openly dictatorial. For the first time she understood the forces that had driven her father to defy his brothers and seek a faraway independence.

In a voice as devoid of expression as her face, she asserted quietly, "Unless your readers are interested in the antics of my infant son, I won't be of any help to you. I can write only about the people I meet and the things I see for myself.''

''You're wrong about that too, Rebecca. You have an excellent journalist's imagination, just as I have. Josh and I rarely leave these premises, but we have hundreds of friends on both sides who supply us with enough news to produce an unbiased and comprehensive newspaper. This next year will be the most exciting of your young life. And you'll have an additional challenge as well. You are to help us redirect the interests of your two young half brothers. We sent your sister Tamara and the two Tupton women to live with a family in New Jersey, but we accepted the tacit guardianship of Sidney Lloyd and Jeremy John.''

Rebecca was still speechless with a frustrating rage when she reached the privacy of her bedroom. Collapsing on the bed, she buried her face in the pillow and wept for the first time since her husband had kissed her good-bye on the dock in Port-au-Prince. She had survived the trauma of adopting his child and the terror of being captured at sea. But the threat of a year-long separation from Philip and from the freedom she'd fought for all of her life momentarily overwhelmed her.

CHAPTER
14

AFTER what seemed an endless night of broken sleep, Rebecca left her uncles' home early the following morning. Unwilling to accept Samuel Rayburn's autocratic pronouncement that there was no escape from Manhattan Island, she began a search along the banks of the Hudson River bordering the Rayburn estate. If she could find a boat large enough to take Michael, Dena, and a small amount of essential baggage to the far shore of the wide river, she might be able to send a message to her father-in-law. The bleak realization that Silas already believed her dead after the *Mer Reynard* failed to arrive in Baltimore added desperation to her search. Once the British were in control of the island as Colonel Crane had confidentially predicted, escape would be impossible; and she'd have no way then of notifying anyone that she was still alive.

Like trapped rats, her thoughts raced frantically around in frustrating circles. She had to be in Baltimore when Philip returned from France; otherwise he might become suicidally reckless if he thought he'd lost his wife as well as the infant son he hadn't found in France. But if she couldn't escape, she reminded herself hopelessly, it would be safer for him not to know where she was. After she'd been kidnapped in New London, he'd risked the safety of his fleet in a search for her. This time all of his ships would be destroyed if he dared enter New York Harbor.

Moodily depressed by the time she abandoned her futile search, Rebecca returned to the Rayburn dock only to find her Uncle Samuel waiting for her.

"Did you find what you were looking for, Rebecca?" he asked sardonically.

"No."

"Had you listened to me last night, you'd have known that there were no boats available on the island. What the loyalists didn't take when they left, your General Washington did, including every ferryboat and barge. And before you ask that impudent question you're considering as to why my brother and I didn't leave with the other loyalists, I'm going to tell you something that even Joshua doesn't know.

"While he is a loyalist because of his inordinate fondness for our English relatives, I am one simply as the lesser of two evils. I am an American, young lady, and I'll remain an American no matter which side wins this ill-advised conflict. I intend to continue writing an unbiased account of the war both in the *Observer* and in a private history book. Last night I offered you an opportunity to assist me in the endeavor, but I gather from your actions this morning you are refusing."

Goaded by the brusque candor of his accusation and by a dismal sense of failure, Rebecca's temper flared in response. "Last night you weren't offering, you were ordering! I heard everything you said, including your claim that you were supplied with news from both sides. Well, unless your messengers can walk on water, there must be a boat somewhere."

"My messengers from the outside supply their own transportation across the river."

"Will you let me hire the next one who makes a delivery?"

"To go where, Rebecca? Long Island will soon be turned into a bloody battleground, and that stretch of New Jersey you're staring at is under the control of six loyalist battalions. You would be endangering your own life and that of your son if, by chance, you could reach either place. There is another danger you seemed to have forgotten; any flight on your part would reaffirm Colonel Crane's suspicions as to your identity. If he were to apprehend you again, I doubt that his disposition of you would be as merciful."

Defeated by the harsh logic of her uncle's argument, Rebecca surrendered to the inevitable. "I'm sorry I was rude to you, Uncle Samuel," she apologized. "I wasn't thinking very clearly this morning."

"On the contrary, my dear, you revealed a good deal more initiative than most women in your predicament. On one point at least, I can relieve your anxiety. Within weeks your husband's family should learn that you survived the capture of the *Mer Reynard*."

"How?" Rebecca asked warily.

"Very simply. Yesterday afternoon I added the story to this week's issue of the *Observer*, stating that all passengers were taken safely into British custody. Copies of the paper will eventually be distributed to the major colonial newspapers. You can stop frowning now, Rebecca. I did not reveal your name or your present location. After the elaborate lie you invented to protect your husband, I'm certain you wouldn't want him killed in a quixotic effort to run the British blockade in New York Harbor. Now, young woman, shall we stop this nonsense and get to work?"

"I'll have to take care of my family first," she protested.

"That will not be necessary. I've already interviewed your servant and found her eminently qualified and quite willing to undertake the physical care of your brothers as well as the infant. My staff will see that she is not burdened with drudgery. Since she seems remarkably intelligent for her race, I have granted her request to remain with my nephews during their tutorial hours. It would seem that you have inspired the girl with enough incentive to earn the freedom you generously granted her."

"There was nothing generous about it. I don't believe in slavery."

"Nor do I, but I expect our reasons are quite different. Slaves are not allowed to develop ambition or initiative, the two qualities needed for a productive society. Now, about the work I expect you to perform and your demeanor while you're performing it. As far as the public is concerned, you are a widow; and henceforth you will dress like one. I have already instructed the seamstress to make you some appropriate attire."

"I have my own black dresses, thank you!"

"The one you wore last night was frivolous enough to distract the most reliable of my clerks, to say nothing of the more susceptible men who visit the editorial office. I want your hair covered and your deportment above reproach during working hours. Until you're properly prepared, you'll work alone in the library."

Exasperated by his presumptuous orders, Rebecca asked with a barely controlled insolence, "Doing what?"

Samuel's eyebrow flicked upward in annoyance, but his

further directives were precise and unemotional. "You will study the back issues of the *Observer,* and you will become conversant with the available reference books. You have a certain facility for writing fiction, Rebecca; but you display little respect for objectivity or facts. Until you develop such respect, you will never utilize your talents properly."

Thus began Rebecca's formal education in journalism. During those first repressive weeks of her exile in the library when her moods vacillated between despondency and bravado, Samuel Rayburn regulated her activities with an impervious control. He dictated her daily reading and writing assignments, merciless in his censorship of her comprehension in the former and of her wordiness in the latter. He presented her with a succession of research exercises and monitored the speed with which she located a book or chapter. Nor did he limit his control to professional matters. On the second day he informed her at breakfast that she was to be in sole charge of her son for two hours a day while Dena attended class.

"This will give you an opportunity to become a practicing mother for a change, my dear. So far you've relegated most of your maternal duties to a servant, and you've ignored your brothers."

To her dismay, Rebecca realized that she'd never before been alone with the active infant, who was no longer content with the confinement of bed. Seeking escape herself from the smothering closeness of an airless library, she carried Michael down to a grassy spot near the river's edge and sat him on a blanket. At first her thoughts were silent memories of the man who'd sired this alert, adventuresome child already attempting to crawl. But gradually she began to speak aloud and to unite the father with his son.

"You might as well get used to the sight of water, Michael; your papa is a sailor, and I imagine he'll want you with him. Before that time, though, he'll teach you to swim and fish and sail a small boat around Baltimore Harbor. He's so tall, he'll seem like a giant to you at first;

but you'll love him. Do you know that he went all the way to France just to find you? Won't he be surprised when he first sees you at our beautiful home in Baltimore.''

Impulsively Rebecca hugged the small, warm body next to her own and laughed in response to his delighted smile. ''It's only a pretend game, sweetheart,'' she murmured; but somehow that pretend game eliminated part of her own gloom. It wasn't really pretense, she assured herself; by the time Philip returned to America, the war could be over, and she and Michael and Dena would be allowed to leave New York.

That dream of freedom, however, was sharply curtailed on the day Samuel ordered her to report to the workroom at seven o'clock the following morning. Sedately clad in the loose-fitting black dress her stern uncle deemed appropriate and with all of her hair and much of her face concealed beneath a black-banded mobcap, she was installed at a desk uncomfortably close to Samuel's own. For a month she wrote the routine stories he assigned her, rewrote them an hour later after he'd slashed her original work with corrections, and at his insistence, read the longer articles and editorials he'd written so effortlessly. Gradually, she learned to imitate the precision of his vocabulary and to use the reference books and lexicons without embarrassment. But the instruction that humbled her the most effectively had been her study of the five preceding years of the *Observer*. Compared to their scholarly thoroughness, the *Falmouth Clarion* had contained only fragmentary reports, many of them more rumor than fact.

Challenged by the excitement Samuel Rayburn generated in the workroom, Rebecca worked hard to win his approval; but until a predawn summons in mid-August, she had no inkling that she'd succeeded. In the company of both of her uncles, she was driven to the Rayburn print shop in the center of the shabby commercial district near the lower tip of Manhattan Island, where a group of burly workmen were already dismantling the massive press. Without explanation Joshua escorted her up three flights of stairs to an attic room whose open windows overlooked the harbor. Anchored to a table covered with an assortment of maps, paper, and writing equipment was a large telescope.

"Before the British fleet arrived," Joshua informed her, "we obtained much of the shipping news with that thing, but you'll be watching for something quite different. As soon as it becomes light enough, you're to take notes of what you observe in the harbor. I'm sorry I can't leave the lamp with you, but a light at this time might be dangerous."

Remembering the terror she'd experienced during the shelling of Falmouth, Rebecca asked shakily, "Are the British attacking Long Island today?"

Joshua nodded heavily and sighed. "According to the information we received last night, it is very probable. In these uncertain times, Samuel and I deemed it prudent to remove our equipment and supplies to our home. Because you've already witnessed another British naval attack, Samuel thought you were experienced enough to handle this assignment."

"Have the Americans on Long Island been warned, Uncle Joshua?"

"Our informant was a rebel friend, so I imagine they've been thoroughly alerted."

"Is my father there with them?"

"No, he's not, Rebecca. When last we heard in late April, Jeremy was still with Benedict Arnold in the northern Champlain Valley. I'll leave you now; but if you should become frightened, just use that rope pull. It's connected to a bell in the press room."

"Aren't you afraid, Uncle Joshua?"

"All of us are, Rebecca," he admitted softly.

The reverberating footfalls of Joshua descending the uncarpeted stairs were the last sounds Rebecca heard for the following three hours. In the eerie silence of the loft she adjusted the controls of the telescope to focus it on the expanse of the East River that separated Manhattan from Long Island. As the first streaks of light illuminated the summer calm of the water, she counted the number of towering ships-of-line under sail, their massive, squarish hulls being jockeyed into attack position midriver. Repressing the fear that urged her to flee and hide as she had in

Falmouth, she forced herself to study each ship as it passed within range of her telescope.

With the passing of the third frigate, the meaning of the several oddities she'd observed became clear. Admiral Richard Howe had no intention of bombarding Manhattan! While the gun ports were open, the cannon barrels had not been shoved forward into firing position, nor were there any marines stationed in the rigging or on the decks, and the fore and aft davits which normally held the longboats were empty. What appeared to be an assault fleet was an empty threat; those mighty vessels of destruction would be used only to prevent any escape of the American army from Long Island.

In the increasing light of dawning day, she readjusted the telescope to the harbor waters beyond the fleet now being anchored, and sucked in her breath sharply as she focused on the second drama taking place. Along the shores of Staten Island hundreds of boats looking like awesome marine centipedes were being launched—longboats with oarsmen pulling relentlessly toward the southern reach of Long Island; barges weighted with brass cannon being towed; sailing boats loaded with red-jacketed soldiers, their bayonets glinting in the sunlight, being steered swiftly over the crowded expanse of water.

Recalling Samuel's caustic exhortation to report only the facts, Rebecca marked the targeted bay on the map and began to write: "On August 22, 1776, the British forces under the command of General William Howe landed at Gravesend Bay on Long Island." Counting the numbers of boats as accurately as she could and estimating the staggering size of Howe's army at twenty thousand, she continued to record what she observed methodically, suppressing the vicarious fear she felt for the "farm boys and overage veterans" awaiting the onslaught amid the thick stands of trees covering the slopes of Brooklyn Heights.

Engrossed in the hypnotic drama of watching the lines of soldiers forming on the landing beaches and climbing up the low bluffs, Rebecca didn't hear Samuel enter the room. Silently he scanned the pages she had already completed. She jerked nervously at the sound of his voice without hearing the brusque praise his words expressed. "It's printable," he rasped, "especially the part about the ships, and Admiral Howe's intentions. But now train the telescope down on the Manhattan waterfront and record the reactions of the people gathering there."

Obediently Rebecca followed the tensely given orders and shivered in sympathy at the uncontrolled fear mirrored on the faces of the men standing paralyzed along the embarcadero, staring hopelessly at the threatening line of ships. At the extremity of the telescope's range Rebecca focused on a church her uncle identified as the Anglican Trinity and watched the people filing silently into the century-old structure.

Rebecca didn't have to guess at their probable state of mind. She'd experienced the same desperate entrapment during the hours she waited with Jean-Jacques Dessalines in the Abrigo watchtower. These frightened city dwellers were even more hopelessly imprisoned than the Abrigo defenders, without any means of crossing the swift rivers which isolated them. There was nothing objective or factual about the description she wrote of the dread apprehension of a city awaiting the outcome of a pending battle that would decide its fate.

After he'd read the final pages, Samuel's only reaction was a gruff announcement that it was time to leave. But on the trip back to the estate, Rebecca's intent concentration on the stunned people lining the streets would inspire her to add even more poignant details to her stark description of the prelude to battle violence.

By the time she and Samuel arrived in the workroom, the press was already reassembled and operational. Nostalgically, Rebecca watched the two printers prepare to set the type for her story that Samuel handed them without comment. It had taken Ezra Jenkins days to fill the uneven pages of the *Falmouth Clarion,* but this crew completed the four ten-by-fifteen-inch pages in hours. By late afternoon, under the letterhead *Observer* and a simple dateline, her account of the invasion of Long Island filled the first two pages of the neat stacks of newspapers awaiting distribution to an anxious city.

Numbed by the fear and tension she'd experienced, Rebecca left the workroom and walked alone to the river's edge. At dawn when she'd watched the mighty frigates form into their deadly cordon, she'd trained the telescope briefly on the British officers in the cockpits, relieved that none of them had resembled Brian Sinclair. Arrogant faces, she'd thought at the time, uncaring that the people they were threatening were only unarmed civilians in a captive city! And their ships? The deadliest floating fortresses in the world, invincible to attack once they massed together into fleet formation.

The enemy, she thought dully, the enemy that Philip and the other American privateers might have to face! Please God, no, she prayed, not Philip. Gazing hopelessly down the wide expanse of the Hudson River, she whispered a plea she knew would never be heard nor heeded. "Stay in France, Philip. Michael and I will survive the separation, but your death would leave us without hope." The pretend game she'd played for weeks was finished! For her, there'd be no miraculous release from this prison; for her husband there'd be no reprieve from the threat of battle until this war was finished one way or the other.

For the five days following the British invasion of Long Island, the voices of the men, both loyalist and rebel, were hushed as they talked to Joshua and Samuel in the workroom. Even the brief battle of Brooklyn Heights that left three thousand Americans dead or prisoner brought no jubilation to either side. And the news two days later that George Washington had succeeded in ferrying twelve thousand of his men across the East River, past the warships stationed there, and onto Manhattan Island aroused only the fear of being trapped in the midst of battle.

After Rebecca completed her work on that historic day, Samuel escorted her silently toward the rear door of the workroom. Once outside he informed her tersely that henceforth she'd be living in a small cottage at the rear of the manor house.

"Your servant has already moved in with your son and your brothers," he explained. "You'll be safer there too. At the moment Josh and I are in no position to help you;

there's talk that all loyalists may be taken into custody and confined. But you'll be safe enough in the cottage if you follow my instructions to the letter. Since the water pump and washroom are in a connected lean-to, there'll be no need for any of you to go outside. And you are not to light a fire under any circumstances. The servants have already been instructed to bring you hot food twice a day whether I'm here or not.''

"I'm not afraid of American soldiers," Rebecca protested.

"Use your head, girl! This is war, not your father's minuteman practice! There's already looting, not only by deserters but by the criminals and human scum that infest this city. You're to keep the doors barred and the windows shuttered inside and out, and at night you will not light either lanterns or candles. For the sake of the children, I trust you will have the sense to curb your own reckless curiosity."

Standing inside the walled front yard of the small stone cottage, Rebecca watched her uncle disappear among the trees and shrubs that all but obscured her view of the big house. Whatever brief, quixotic hope she may have entertained of asking the American soldiers to help her leave the island had been crushed by Samuel's harsh warning. Behind the heavy oak door of the cottage were four young and vulnerable human beings whose immediate future depended upon her. Opening the door, she smiled at the brown-eyed faces regarding her tensely.

"Do Misser Rayburn say true, Miz Rebecca?" Dena demanded.

"Every word, Dena. The five of us are going to pretend to be hibernating bears until he tells us otherwise. Now, while Dena takes care of Michael, you older children will show me around our new home."

It took Rebecca only a few moments in the downstairs rooms to learn that a home was exactly what Samuel Rayburn had intended it to be, not merely an emergency stopgap. The cupboards in the kitchen half of the large main room were freshly stocked with dishes, pots, and food staples while the open shelves in the remaining area contained schoolbooks, slates, boxes of sharpened quills and chalk, and a supply of trimmed lamps. In the one adjoining bedroom, Rebecca's trunks were stacked in a storage closet and her clothing hung in the clothespress.

By the time the lower tour of inspection was completed and the one through the second-floor loft begun, Rebecca had lost all of the aversion she'd developed for her two small brothers. When she'd first met them, the seven-year-old Sidney Lloyd had resembled the Tuptons too vividly for her peace of mind, while six-year-old Jeremy John had glared distrustfully at her with eyes identical to her own. During their infrequent meetings in the company of one or the other of their uncles, there'd been few attempts at communication and only one brief glimmer of interest on the part of the older child after Joshua had told the story of her capture at sea.

Looking very much like his suspicious Tupton grandfather, Sidney Lloyd had demanded, "How come the lobsterbacks didn't keelhaul you?"

To Rebecca's slight amusement, Joshua had delivered a very sharp, Samuel-like reprimand to his young nephew. "The English do not make war on women and children, Lloyd."

"They do too! Grandpa said they 'uz out to kill everyone the day they burnt our town."

"Your grandfather wasn't even in Falmouth that morning, and neither were you," Rebecca had reminded the child. "You were all safe on your Uncle Myles's farm miles away."

"Well, we heard them!"

"But I watched them, little brother, and they didn't kill anyone." For a brief second of time a reluctant admiration had enlivened his small, sober face. Remembering that momentary approbation as she climbed the narrow stairway, Rebecca experienced an abrupt flash of shame at her earlier aversion. The war had been more traumatic for them than for herself. They'd been deserted first by their father and then by their mother, who'd callously left them with a pair of elderly, autocratic uncles. Even before the war, she reflected, their childhood had been blighted. While she'd had an educated mother and a generous uncle to compensate for an absentee father, her brothers had lived with two ignorant Tupton women and a miserly grandfather.

Seated with them on a dormered window box in their half of the rough-beamed loft, she explained the rules they would have to obey during the next few weeks; and she told them about the days she'd spent with the Purdy children in Saco. It was this lighthearted story that broke through the suspicious reserve of her brothers.

"Reckon we could do that too," Sidney Lloyd declared.

But it was the perceptive response of the younger child that surprised and delighted his sister.

"Don't have to," he said quietly. "We've got us a hidey-hole."

"Where?" his brother challenged.

For an answer, Jeremy John reached shyly for Rebecca's hand and led her over toward the stairs where the slanted walls had been replaced by a vertical partition. Between the wall and the roof was a long, narrow space accessible through a well-concealed opening that Rebecca had not noticed but that the observant six-year-old had. And at sometime in his young life, he'd learned the grim purpose for such a hiding place.

"Can't no one find us here," he announced with satisfaction.

"Reckon not," his brother agreed. "Not Dena or Michael or 'Becca either."

Hearing the slurred version of her own name, Rebecca was reminded of one of the reasons for her earlier avoidance of these two small lads now watching her intently. She'd hated the fact that they'd been named after the two men who'd done very little to deserve namesakes.

"Our names are all too long," she said matter-of-factly. "So you're to call me Becky, and I'll call you Lloyd and Johnny. Lloyd was the name of our great-grandfather who was a real hero, and Johnny is my favorite uncle's name. Someday soon I'll tell you all about them."

As imperceptibly as her love for Michael had developed during their afternoons together on the grassy riverbank, so did her affection grow for her brothers and for the sixteen-

year-old Negro girl in the dim interior of a stone cottage.
Welded into a family by necessity, they quickly became
one in spirit. Resolved to make the hours pass as agreeably
as possible, Rebecca resorted to the gentle techniques
her mother had used in teaching Abigail and herself.
Art, reading, and games were mingled together on an
undemanding schedule, alternated with what had become
an absorbing pastime during the first week. Samuel had
been quite accurate in his claim of looting both official and
unofficial. During the brightest daylight hours, Yankee
supply wagons carted away sacks of grain, bales of hay,
and barrels of rendered pork from the well-stocked Rayburn
barn.

Late in the afternoon, however, the five watchers in the
cottage were more cautious as they peered out of a small
dormer window in the loft. The thieves who visited the
barn during these hours were furtive groups of men, some
rebel soldiers and some motley-garbed civilians who stole
not merely food, but equipment and tools as well. One pair
of men, as frightening as the runaway slaves Rebecca had
seen on Gonâve Island, left the remote barn area and
reached the low stone wall in front of the cabin before they
turned and ran off. Rebecca slept very little that night, and
what dreams she had were ones about her frightening walk
back to New London after she'd escaped from the Tuptons.
Shivering in fear after she awoke, she remembered sadly
that because of that one night she'd been separated from
Philip for five long months.

The only outside news Rebecca and the others received
for two weeks came from the tight-lipped servants who
brought their meals twice a day. Half the family linen had
been requisitioned for bandages, the *Observer* was not
being published, and both Misters Rayburn had been
visited frequently by rebel officers. On the morning of the
fourteenth day of isolation, September 15, however, the
distant sound of cannon ended the period of waiting. All
day long the firing continued, and Rebecca didn't need
Joshua's late night visit to know that the British had
invaded Manhattan.

"They began landing at Kips Bay before dawn," he told

her, "and already the lower half of Manhattan is under their control."

"Where is the American army now, Uncle Joshua?"

"Too close for comfort, Rebecca. One-half is entrenched at Harlem Heights under General Putnam, but we don't know where General Washington will make his stand. Pray God it isn't in our front yard!"

During the first five days of battle, Rebecca struggled to keep the others entertained and busy. She told them stories; and to her slight amusement, Dena insisted she repeat every one she'd recited aboard the *Mer Reynard*. On the sixth day still another danger threatened to destroy what small degree of calm she'd established. Acrid smoke began to permeate the air within the cottage, and toward evening the red glow of fire could be seen toward the southeast, an inferno that quickly enveloped the lower half of the city.

"They're going to burn us like they did Falmouth," Lloyd whispered in terror.

"No, they're not, little brother," Rebecca reassured him with a confidence she was far from feeling. "We have the whole Hudson River to protect us." But no one except Michael slept peacefully that night. At dawn a haggard Joshua visited the cottage again.

"It started on the waterfront," he told Rebecca privately. "Trinity Church was burned to the ground along with hundreds of businesses, our own included, and as many as a thousand homes. God help us, but a third of the people are without shelter. Be doubly cautious now, Rebecca," he warned briefly before he returned to the manor house. It's been harder on him than it has on us, Rebecca reflected sadly as she watched him walk with the tired gait of a very old man.

The ordeal ended during the first week in October, and Rebecca did not need Samuel's exuberant announcement to know that the battle for Manhattan had been won by the British. All of the previous night she'd listened to the rumble of caissons on a distant street, and she knew by the cadence of marching feet that the soldiers were the trained professionals from England.

"Don't look so glum, Rebecca," Samuel chided her. "Your General Washington did it again; he escaped across the Harlem River with more than ten thousand of his men. And now, my dear, I'll need your help in producing the first issue of the *Observer* in more than a month, the longest interruption in over thirty years."

"I'd rather not, Uncle Samuel."

"Nonsense, the emergency is over; and it's time to get on with your education and to allow your brothers to do the same."

"I can tutor my brothers as I've been doing, Uncle."

"You have been entertaining them, Rebecca, and doing a fine job of maintaining their morale. But you're not equipped to teach Latin, Greek, mathematics, or science; Reverend Stebbins is. He was the assistant pastor of old Trinity, and until his church is rebuilt, he needs to supplement his income. Now, about practicalities . . ."

As always after a confrontation with this uncle, Rebecca wondered why she'd bothered to disagree with him; he paid her protest not the slightest attention, and in the end he proved to be so insufferably right. He'd already told Dena that she was now to do the cooking for the cottage residents and informed Lloyd and Johnny that they were to feed and milk the two nanny goats that had escaped Yankee notice. To her slight annoyance, Rebecca found her brothers already milking the patient creatures under Dena's supervision, and Dena herself delighted about the cooking chore.

"Lawsy, Miz Rebecca, I's glad ole Misser Samuel done fin' me som'thin' else t' do. Michael's gittin' restless 'bout nursin', an' he's already squallin' fer what t'other git t' eat."

"Michael's not even a year old yet, Dena."

"I knows an' you knows, but Michael's got a min' of his own. 'Sides, Misser Samuel say best we keep away from those red-coated varmints who done shove their way into his house las' night."

"My uncle never used the expression 'red-coated varmints' in his life," Rebecca scolded mildly.

"No, mam, he don't; he jest say that ole Colonel Crane done move in with a passel of polecats and took over."

Rebecca's heart plummeted. She'd forgotten Crane's promise to apply for quarter at the Rayburn estate. It was irritating enough to have her Uncle Samuel dictating her life without the added danger of a watchful policeman like Weldon Crane monitoring her activities.

Within the week Samuel Rayburn's opinion of Colonel Crane was in complete agreement with Dena's. While the officers under his command left the estate each day with orders to apprehend and imprison American deserters, suspected traitors, and activist rebels, Crane himself remained on the premises. Except for weekly conferences with the city's military governors, General William Howe and General Sir Henry Clinton, the humorless colonel commuted from his converted office, the rarely used drawing room of the manor, to the *Observer* workroom where he established himself as censor of what was and what was not publishable news.

Highly critical of the *Observer*'s policy of unbiased coverage, Crane insisted that the stories of the additional American defeats in outer New York be highly embellished with praise for British superiority. Just as autocratically a month later, he denied Samuel permission to report General Washington's New Jersey victories at Trenton and Princeton. "Unimportant skirmishes," Crane called them. He also banned Samuel's editorial criticizing King George for hiring twenty-two thousand German Hessians to fight England's war. "The King does not believe in wasting English lives for such a rag-tag enemy," Crane affirmed sententiously.

Ironically, Colonel Crane wanted the other American colonies to learn about the brutal housing of American prisoners-of-war in New York. "The sooner the undisciplined scum still fighting know what will happen to them when they're captured," he boasted, "the sooner they'll desert their traitorous leaders." His reason for insisting that wide coverage be given to the deplorable conditions of the city's civilian population was equally cynical. "Once the other rebel cities learn the fate of this one, they'll refuse to harbor the criminal soldiers.''

On the occasion of this particular pronouncement, Samuel asked with deceptive mildness, "Tell me, Colonel, why aren't Generals Howe and Clinton equally concerned about the real criminals on New York City streets?"

With a coldly contemptuous smile, Crane responded harshly, "They believe, as I do, that those criminals aid us in keeping the rebels under control.''

That week the issue of the *Observer* was burned in the workroom's Franklin stove at the colonel's furious order before it could be distributed to the city. Samuel had begun the lead story with the words, "According to Col. Weldon Crane, General William Howe and General Henry Clinton approve of the criminal violence on New York streets.'' Watching the flames consume a week's work, Samuel smiled sardonically. The preceding night he'd dispatched a dozen copies each to the Enderly Publishers in London, the *Massachusetts Spy* in Worcester, and the *Pennsylvania Gazette* in Philadelphia.

Throughout those repressive winter months, Rebecca had been spared any unpleasant notice largely because Samuel kept Colonel Crane's disapproval focused on himself. Each day she had completed the noncontroversial stories assigned to her as unobtrusively as possible before she left the workroom and rejoined her family in the cottage. Except on the stormiest days, she'd accompanied her brothers on a wild romp across the estate, releasing her own pent-up tension with the strenuous exercise of snow fights and footraces. On occasion, she'd bundled Michael into her arms and walked apart from Lloyd and Johnny. Only with this youngest, least aware child could she talk about the man who bound them together.

One day in late March, Rebecca's luck deserted her. Seated at her workroom desk, she heard the British officer demand of Samuel, "Where the devil did you get these ridiculous statistics, Rayburn?"

"An unimpeachable source, Colonel," the editor responded smoothly. "The Enderly Publishers of London, who consulted Lloyd's insurance records. More than one-fourth of the merchant ships bound for the western colonies are captured by American privateers.''

"What's your source for this next story about the French-built ships operating off Long Island?''

"One of my reporters talked to the English crews which had been sent ashore in longboats after their ships were taken at sea. They described those particular three privateers as the French Antilles line, almost as long as royal frigates and much swifter.''

"The goddamned Keane pirates!" Crane muttered. "Would to God they'd dare stick their bows into port.''

Instantly aware of the Pandora's box he'd inadvertently opened, Samuel hastily added, "Those three are only a small fraction of the enemy privateers in Long Island waters.''

Refusing to be sidetracked from his central interest, Crane turned his attention toward Rebecca. "Mistress Burns, can you think of any reason Captain Keane might be attempting to rescue you?''

From the moment Samuel had mentioned the Antilles ships, Rebecca had been physically paralyzed with shock— her jaw clenched, her hands gripped motionless in her lap, and her thoughts in a chaotic turmoil. After ten months of an emotional void, she felt again the sharp pangs of returning life, like chilblained feet before a fire. She didn't respond to Colonel Crane's taunt because her mind was focused on a daring sea captain driving his ship through the waters with a reckless courage.

His voice sharpened by an accelerated interest in the silent woman, Crane tried a second, more provocative gibe. "Could it be that Philip Keane considered you more than just a make-believe wife? Perhaps after your husband's convenient death, he made you another of his mistresses. And if he thought you were being held hostage on his account rather than your treasonable father's, he might—''

Rebecca heard the baiting jeer, and her mind stopped whirling. "My father would be very flattered to know that you rank him important enough for hostages, Colonel,'' she declared softly. "But Philip Keane would have no

reason to know or care where I was being held. His only
interest besides the complete collapse of the British Empire
is the money to be made from captured merchantmen and
their cargoes. And under the present circumstances, I
imagine that the best place to find English merchant ships
is offshore New York. So you can blame the British
occupation for Philip Keane's presence there, not me.
Uncle Samuel, I've completed my work for the day; if you
and Colonel Crane will excuse me, I'll leave you to
continue your discussion alone.''

The twenty feet that separated her desk from the rear
door seemed endless; but for once the heavy oak swung
open easily, and Rebecca reached the safety of the garden
before her knees began to shake. Without conscious volition, she walked toward the riverbank, unmindful of the
light rain that was falling. Halfway there, the exultation
that had begun in the workroom burst through its bounds,
and her tears of joy mingled with the rain. Philip had not
forgotten her, not even after all those empty months; and
he'd chosen the only way possible of letting her know that
he still cared.

CHAPTER
15

IN the weeks following the unpleasant scene with
Colonel Crane in the workroom, Rebecca experienced
an increasing anxiety. Her daily questions about additional news of the Antilles ships elicited only gruff denials

from her Uncle Samuel; and to her sensitive ears, his voice sounded unnecessarily irritated. Had she known that her uncle was more anxious than she was, her distress would have turned into terror.

When two of his Long Island reporters first sent him the message about the extent of privateering action off the Atlantic coast of Long Island, Samuel had considered the story an excellent one for publication. Not only were the American ships attacking merchantmen, some of them were raiding coastal settlements. But the most exciting news item was the description of armed marines from the distinctive French-built ships coming ashore in what sounded like a small invasion. Always a cautious man, and doubly so after the advent of Colonel Crane into his home and his life, Samuel had shown the British officer only fragments of the two stories. When he'd learned that the three Antilles ships belonged to Philip Keane, Samuel cursed his own shortsighted stupidity. He'd been proud of Rebecca's composed response to Crane's insults; but the publisher knew that if Philip Keane were captured, no one in the Rayburn family would be spared from an ugly investigation. In this case, the investigator would be the only man Samuel Rayburn had ever detested personally, and with excellent reason.

As a member of a small branch of the British military that was accountable only to the king, Colonel Weldon Crane worked apart from other high-ranking officers, coordinating his actions to theirs at his own discretion. Samuel's investigation had revealed that the man had been given wide powers that exempted him only from battlefield leadership. Reflecting sourly on King George's simplistic conviction that all American rebels were personal traitors to the crown, Samuel realized that Colonel Crane could justify any cruelty in the name of treason, including hostages, ransom, and blackmail.

For a tense month after that disastrous arousal of the policeman's suspicions, Samuel had burned every communication he received from his Long Island agents. The one that signaled an end to his worry he burned with particular relish in the colonel's presence without revealing a word of the contents. The marines had rejoined their ships, and the Antilles fleet had left New York waters! It was time, Samuel thought tiredly, to tell Rebecca.

He found her where he expected her to be, by the river's edge, watching her brothers fish and her son toddle around near her. Samuel wondered if she was watching the river too and hoping. It wasn't like her to daydream, but lately he'd noticed the difference in her—her eyes vulnerable and glowing instead of guarded and defensive, and a soft smile curving her lips when she thought she was unobserved. Well, the nonsense was finished, and like everyone else caught up in this insane war, she had to face reality!

"He won't be coming, Rebecca," he announced abruptly, ignoring her startled glance and the sudden rush of understanding that flooded her eyes as she stood up to face him.

"I didn't think he would be, not really," she mumbled softly.

"Well, he tried; and if he'd succeeded, he'd have found Colonel Crane here waiting for him with a hangman's noose."

"Philip wouldn't have been that foolish," she protested. "Tell me what happened, Uncle Samuel."

"Not much to tell. He anchored his ships off an empty stretch of Long Island and brought his marines ashore twice. Had he reached the East River either time, he'd have encountered the troops waiting to intercept him. The second time he returned to his ships, he hoisted sail and left. We were all fortunate this time, Rebecca. Our ubiquitous colonel seems to hold a special enmity for your husband."

"I'm sorry I ever invented that lie and pushed Philip's and my problems off on you and Uncle Joshua."

"Nonsense. You probably spared yourself and your husband an unpleasant hostage situation, but it's my opinion that Crane now prefers that remarkable theory he proposed the other day. I suspect his experience with mourning widows is very limited. And now back to practicalities. I hope you intend to continue these fishing expeditions. They'll keep you from moping, and they'll give your brothers something to think about. There are good-sized fish out there if you use the right bait. Josh and I spent our childhood with our lines dangling from this same spot—kept Josh from becoming a social wastrel and taught me to think clearly.''

As always, Samuel's gruff advice accomplished its purpose, not that Rebecca would have had much to say even had she hated the sport. Lloyd, Johnny, and Dena quickly developed both skill and a passionate enthusiasm for fishing. Since Michael had learned to walk a few months earlier, he too had developed an obsession; he insisted with outraged screams, if necessary, on accompanying his young uncles on any and every occasion remotely resembling an outing. Restrained by a short length of rope anchored to his mother's waist, Michael scampered as close to the water's edge and as far into the screening shrubbery as he could reach, laughing with the awakening abandon of childhood at every insect and acorn he carried back to his mother. With her own fishing limited to the technique Philip had taught her during their brief sojourn on the barren Caribbean outcropping, Rebecca watched her line bobbing gently in the water and learned to accept the limitations of her present life as she once had the limitations of her marriage. Nothing could ever rob her of the healing knowledge that Philip had risked his life and his ships in an effort to reach her. No longer were her memories clouded by jealousy; she'd won her gamble of marrying a man as elusive and handsome as Philip Keane.

Those warm spring weeks spent by the Hudson River passed quickly in undisturbed succession until the day in late May when a British patrol boat deposited two men and four impressively expensive trunks on the Rayburn dock. Instantly, John and Lloyd rushed to her side as alertly quiet as they'd been during the early days in the cottage, and Rebecca noted with an emotional warmth that John placed a protective arm around Michael.

It was the captain of the boat who called attention to the children by shouting to the younger man standing on the dock, ''Better find out who they are, Captain Enderly. We don't like trespassers, especially along the river.''

"We're not trespassers," Rebecca shouted back. "We live here."

"In what capacity, mistress?" the young army officer in the exquisitely tailored uniform asked as he walked toward the small cove.

Tempted to answer flippantly, "As poor relatives," until she remembered that the Enderlys and the Rayburns were connected by family and business ties, Rebecca remained silent.

"Are you the nursemaid, mistress?" he persisted.

Amused now, she shook her head. "No, Captain, these are my children."

Studying each child in turn and then Rebecca with an arrogant appraisal, he concluded crisply, "You look too young to be the mother of these older lads."

"And you, sir, look too immature to judge a woman's age accurately," she retorted.

Stung by what he considered raw impudence from an inferior, he snapped out the next question with a military arrogance. "Just what kind of work do you do for my uncles? It isn't like them to employ young women or to allow children on the premises."

Rebecca's smile broadened. "I'm sure it isn't," she murmured. "Gather up the fishing poles, Lloyd, I don't think Captain Enderly wants us to use his river."

"I asked you a question, mistress," the Englishman reminded her sharply.

No longer smiling, Rebecca shrugged indifferently. "Since I consider your curiosity impertinent, I suggest you ask your uncles the same question."

With a defensive brother on each side of her and Michael in her arms, Rebecca turned to walk toward the cottage, only to find the path blocked by the persistent captain. Returning his rude stare, Rebecca resorted to the same kind of impudent challenge she'd often hurled at her father and Philip.

"You're very brave, Captain, accosting a woman who might be a leper for all you know, or something a good deal worse for a well-bred gentleman like yourself to be seen with."

With her own humor restored, Rebecca watched the flush of anger that disfigured his pleasant young face before he turned and strode stiffly back to the dock where his servant waited.

"What in the world were you thinking of, Rebecca?" Joshua scolded her several hours later, still flushed from running the distance between the manor and the cottage. "I'm afraid you've stirred up a hornet's nest. Colonel Crane no longer believes you're our niece, and he's insisting—"

"You mean that pretty toy captain reported to the colonel instead of you?"

"He is a soldier, Rebecca, and I daresay a good one despite his tendency to be overbearing when he's angered. Kent has never been particularly tolerant of—"

"He is your nephew then?"

"One of our Enderly nephews, yes, but no blood relative of yours, Rebecca. He's the son of my mother's daughter by a previous marriage. Kent's father is Lord Enderly. Kent is the youngest child—a little pampered, as late-in-life children frequently are, but a capable lad in spite of his youth."

"An interesting family history, Uncle Joshua; but what did your spoiled nephew say to arouse Colonel Crane's suspicions? Surely when you explained to him that I really am your niece—"

"Unfortunately, Kent's mother would never permit us to tell him about our younger brother or his children, so Kent quite naturally informed the colonel that he had no American cousins. And your rather unwise conversation led him to believe—something very far from the truth. As a result, the colonel wants you in the library for additional questioning."

"Right now?"

Joshua surveyed his casually disheveled niece with a critical appraisal. "Perhaps if you wore the dress you did your first night here—"

He's ashamed of me, Rebecca realized with a swift stab of understanding. Compared to the Enderlys of England, the Rayburns of Falmouth, Maine, are only unimportant commoners.

"I'll change, Uncle, and I'll brush my hair. It wouldn't do for Captain Enderly to be ashamed of his colonial cousin."

After months of ugly dresses and careless grooming, Rebecca grinned lightheartedly throughout the meticulous process of transformation. Looking much as she had on the only other occasion she'd worn this particular black dress— at the dinner party Philip had hosted aboard the *Reine* in New London—she swept into the cottage living room and curtsied mockingly before her startled uncle. Pausing only long enough to wink at her wide-eyed brothers and a smiling Dena, she continued her regal progress out the door before Joshua could voice the disapproval that trembled on his lips. Of the three men waiting impatiently in the library, only Samuel regarded her with amusement. Kent Enderly stared at her with a stunned fascination, and Colonel Crane stopped being a policeman long enough to escort her to a chair.

Without waiting for the subdued colonel to begin his threatened inquisition, Rebecca quietly reaffirmed her identity as the widow of Eben Burns. "And I'm quite certain," she continued, "that my Uncle Samuel has convinced Captain Enderly that I am a legitimate Rayburn niece regardless of our unconventional introduction earlier today. To my uncle's reassurance, I would like to add that I am dependent on his charity only momentarily, until I can gain access to my own funds in London. Is there anything else you wish to know, Colonel?"

"No, there isn't, Mistress Burns," Captain Enderly volunteered before the higher ranking officer could respond. "This awkward situation is my fault, and I apologize for my rudeness at the dock. Colonel Crane was only acting on my behalf because I made some foolish accusations. Will you accept my apology, cousin?"

He spoke, Rebecca reflected, with concealed amusement, with the subtle assurance of a man who'd never had to earn authority or respect. Whimsically, she wondered what her great-grandfather, the Welsh revolutionary Lloyd

Glynns, would have thought about a caste-proud English aristocrat asking pardon of a hybrid colonial like herself. She hoped he would not have groveled as obviously as Colonel Crane, who added his apology to the younger man's. Even Crane's subsequent questions, delivered over small ceremonial glasses of Madeira wine, were friendlier in tone, as if her nebulous relationship with a titled English family had increased her credibility. He nodded approvingly when she told him about her distrust of Samuel Adams and the Sons of Liberty, and he actually smiled when she described the conditions of her brief friendship with Brian Sinclair.

Despite the general pleasantness of the hour-long gathering, Rebecca was relieved when Samuel signaled an end and escorted her back to the cottage. Had she realized that her already complicated life was to become much more so, her relief would have changed to exasperation.

While only two years her senior, Kent Enderly was a tenaciously determined man. The following morning in the workroom during her five-hour daily stint, he virtually besieged her with attention despite Samuel's annoyance. While she'd always been sternly repressed by the oldest Rayburn brother, Kent seemed impervious to censure; and he had a firm ally in Joshua, who was indulgent to the point of doting on this charming, irrepressible nephew. Just how fond Rebecca discovered three days after Kent's arrival, when she refused to accompany him to a ball that same night.

"I think, Rebecca, that it would be entirely appropriate for you to attend," Joshua urged her gently. "Colonel Crane and I will go along as chaperons, and perhaps you can convince Samuel that a little society news would not be amiss in the *Observer*."

"Hogwash!" Samuel exclaimed disgustedly from his desk. "Ever since our nearsighted governor declared the war over, the fools have declared a Roman holiday. Josh, this one will be the sixth victory party you've attended, and you're beginning to sound as optimistic as the others. However, since a story about our governors might be of interest, you have my permission to attend. But mind you,

Kent, this young woman works for me. I don't want her daydreaming at her desk tomorrow.''

The morning following, Samuel solemnly handed Rebecca's article to Colonel Crane and watched expressionlessly as the officer nodded his approval. Thus the descriptions of the women's lavish gowns, the plentiful bowls of champagne punch, and the overflowing platters of chicken, ham, and lobster were read with varying degrees of shock by middle-class New Yorkers whose diets and wardrobes were equally depleted.

That ball was the first in a rapid succession of six that Rebecca attended in the month of June, and not until the sixth party did Joshua take his chaperonage seriously. On the afternoon before that occasion, he reported to the cottage to make certain that Rebecca would again wear black, despite Kent's constant urging to the contrary.

''The continued pretense of widowhood is your only protection against those persistent young officers who seem to be competing for your attention, Rebecca; and I'm very afraid that Kent is the most eager. I was hoping he'd be recalled to Canada.''

''For his sake or mine, Uncle?'' Rebecca asked lightly.

''Don't be frivolous! Two years in the army has made him an intense young man, and I'm no longer certain he's being merely flirtatious. As for you, I don't propose to know how felicitous your marriage was; but I trust you're wise enough not to encourage my nephew to act even more recklessly.''

Annoyed by the subtle reprimand, Rebecca retorted sharply, ''My marriage *was* and *is* most felicitous, Uncle Joshua, and that's how I mean to keep it. As for your nephew, I've already told him that I'll never remarry.''

''Dear God! He proposed marriage?''

''A week after he arrived, and in the workroom, where I look as attractive as a chimney sweep.''

''You must be tolerant of his impetuosity, Rebecca. Like all young men caught up in this terrible war, I imagine he feels rushed for time. Did he tell you that he fought at Bunker Hill under General Johnny Burgoyne?''

"No, he didn't. Did you know that there were fifteen hundred young men who didn't survive that battle?"

"Rebecca, you must be careful of exposing your rebel sympathies under your present—"

"More of them were English than American, Uncle."

"Unfortunately, yes. But you still must be careful."

"I agree, so if you'll convey my apologies to your nephew, I won't be attending the party tonight."

Instantly, Joshua's worry turned into concern. "I'm afraid I promised our hostess that you would, Rebecca. There's a shortage of young ladies available, and she would like—"

"I know. She's one of the wealthy loyalists who sent their daughters to England in order to avoid the 'unpleasantness' here. And tonight I don't feel much like being the available substitute."

"Just this one last time, Rebecca, as a favor to me and to Kent. He's been working under considerable pressure these past few weeks."

"When does he do all this work, Uncle? Most mornings the only thing he does is sit on my desk and bother me."

"But he spends his afternoons at headquarters. His courier duties are of a very sensitive nature." Joshua glanced at his niece and sighed. "I'm sorry if you've been annoyed, Rebecca. I hope tonight will be a happier time for you. You will remember to wear black, won't you?"

"Yes, Uncle, if you'll remember that this is my last party."

"I promise, my dear."

Rebecca's reluctance to attend any more of these celebrations was not merely the result of her ingrained hatred for social inequality, as it had been in Port-au-Prince; it was also due to a personal uneasiness. She did not want anything to disturb the emotional serenity she'd finally achieved. Since the day Samuel had told her about Philip's desperate attempt to find her, all doubts about her marriage had vanished; and her love for her husband had lost its last lingering shadow. His son was now hers, and their future together as a family could be destroyed only by an unkind providence.

Secure in her own private world of dreams and memories, Rebecca had resented the brash intrusion of an arrogant young Englishman into her life. At first she'd considered him little more than a youthful libertine seeking release from the boredom of war. But gradually she'd realized that his boldness was only superficial and that his avowals of love were entirely sincere. Unable to reveal the truth about herself—Colonel Crane was still an ever-present danger—Rebecca had failed miserably in her attempts to establish an impersonal relationship. Kent Enderly had optimistically ignored her protests and refusals. How could she tell him that compared to the man she loved, he seemed only an immature youth? Barely two inches taller than herself and almost as slender, he lacked any hint of Philip's masculine handsomeness and magnetism. In contrast, Kent's light coloring and pleasant good looks were unimpressive.

That he was extremely likable Rebecca readily admitted; he was charming, elegantly mannered, and as irrepressible in temperament as Michael. But he was also as vulnerable, and she didn't want to hurt him. Relieved that this would be the last night she would be forced to fend him off, she donned one of her more modest black dresses and brushed her hair.

Ironically, in mid-July it was not Joshua who insisted she attend still another reception, but Samuel, who informed her that this would be the first such "claptrap nonsense" he'd been unable to refuse.

"A personal insistence by General Henry Clinton himself," Samuel complained, but Rebecca noted the gleam of anticipation in his shrewd eyes that belied his protest.

"Why do I have to go, Uncle?" she asked casually.

"News, young lady, real news, not the balderdash about a pack of fools swilling wine and food while half the city starves. If my speculations are right, we'll be back in the business of printing war news by tomorrow. Not a word about this to my nephew."

During the crosstown ride in the sedate Rayburn carriage, Kent maintained a glum silence. Not only had his Uncle Samuel usurped the seat next to Rebecca's, he'd lectured everyone like a fussy schoolmaster. He'd cautioned his brother to forgo the wine, warned Kent to guard his temper, and told Rebecca to limit her dancing. "I don't expect any of us to be there for long," he'd announced cryptically.

"Why not?" Kent demanded.

"Better ask Colonel Crane; he'll be waiting for us."

Inside the entry of the huge estate house Sir Clinton had appropriated as his temporary headquarters, there was no mistaking the mood of victory as small groups of celebrants, predominantly uniformed officers, toasted each other and the crown with enthusiastic lack of formality. Breaking away from one such group, Colonel Crane greeted the newcomers with a jubilant smile.

"Ready to retract your gloomy predictions yet, editor?" he demanded of Samuel with a malicious delight. "The war will be past history by October. Johnny Burgoyne will have finished the job of splitting the colonies in two, and General Howe will be in control of Philadelphia."

"General Howe is supposed to join Burgoyne at Albany," Kent protested sharply.

"That won't be necessary now, Captain Enderly," Crane declared. "Burgoyne retook Fort Ticonderoga on July eighth and turned the Yankee defenders into a rabble of frightened rabbits running for cover."

"Is that what this premature celebration is all about?" Samuel asked dryly. "A minor victory of nine thousand against three?"

"Burgoyne took Crown Point a week earlier and scattered those rebels to hell and gone, and now he's in hot pursuit of the remnants of Philip Schuyler's vaunted Continental army," Crane countered proudly.

"Your news is eight days old, Colonel," Samuel affirmed sardonically. "The report I received three hours ago is five days newer. John Burgoyne has been slowed to a mile a day by General Schuyler. That Yankee rabble, as you call it, has laid waste the entire countryside, and our British troops have to send back to Canada for food."

"You were warned to ignore all war news, Rayburn," Crane blurted with an abrupt anger.

"I was ordered not to publish any, and I haven't; but I still keep abreast of the critical events. For your information, Burgoyne has a second problem as serious as the shortage of food; our Indian allies are killing as many Tories as Whigs."

"Burgoyne doesn't need those Indians now; he has twelve thousand regulars in his command."

"He has fewer than nine thousand," Samuel countered brusquely, "and half of those are Germans. The colonial secretary promised him the twelve thousand, but the Canadian high command claimed Canada needed them for defense and reduced the number. The Secretary also promised that Howe's army would join Burgoyne's. Just why has that plan been changed?"

"George Germain considers the Philadelphia campaign of equal importance and has left the choice to General Howe."

"Good God, what idiocy! Does Sir Clinton agree with his superior?"

"No," Crane responded curtly, "he agrees with you. He'll remain in New York with troops ready to sail up the Hudson if the need arises. Now, sir, I demand to know how you receive news in advance of official communiqués."

"It's no mystery, Colonel. When I first learned about the great three-prong plan—"

Looking directly at Kent Enderly, Crane asked the question with a deceptive mildness, "From whom did you learn the details of that plan?"

"You can stop glaring at my nephew, Crane. I received the information a month before he arrived in Manhattan."

"From where?"

"Direct from England. You're welcome to inspect my files."

"At the moment I'm more interested in your other sources of news."

"Rivermen the *Observer* has employed for twenty years."

"Loyalists?"

"I presume so, since your General Clinton has used them on several occasions."

All of Crane's earlier jubilance had been replaced by his

more habitual suspicion. "Rayburn, you and your brother will accompany me to General Clinton's office. We'll let him decide whether or not you've breached security. Captain Enderly, you will keep yourself in readiness for a subsequent summons."

Left alone with a grim-faced Kent Enderly, Rebecca was silent. How could she offer any consolation to a man who was fighting on the opposite side from her husband and father?

"The damn war would have been finished if they'd followed the plan," he muttered.

"No, it wouldn't," she contradicted him sadly. "The Americans won't surrender. They'll just retreat as they're doing now until they can re-form into smaller armies to fight another battle, and another until there's no one left on either side."

With an abrupt change of thought that confused her, Kent demanded, "Where would you like to live if you had your choice, Rebecca?"

"By the time this war is finally over, I may be too old to care."

"I mean right now. Could you stand living in England? You and your family both?"

Belatedly aware of the purpose behind his question, Rebecca retreated hastily into a denial. "I'm an American, Kent; this is where I belong."

"That settles it then. I'm resigning my commission and accepting Uncle Joshua's offer."

Cautiously, Rebecca phrased the question, "What offer?"

"Josh wants to return to England, so I'd be taking over the job of managing the company here."

"You're not a journalist."

"No, but you and Uncle Samuel are. You wouldn't have to work if you didn't want to, but I think you're too talented a writer to be merely a wife and mother. Now will you marry me, Rebecca?"

Shaken by the realization that this proud Englishman was offering to adjust his life to hers, Rebecca tried vainly to lighten her refusal.

"Kent, our countries are at war, and neither of us knows the future well enough to predict the outcome."

"What has the war to do with us?" he demanded hotly. "I don't believe in it any more than you do; and once I've resigned my commission, I won't care who wins as long as we're together."

Knowing that any further evasion would only prolong the ordeal for both of them, Rebecca shook her head. "I don't want to argue with you, Kent, but I can't marry you now or ever."

"Then I'll keep right on asking until you can," he promised stubbornly. But Rebecca felt a hundred years older as she noted the vulnerable hurt mirrored in his transparent blue-gray eyes.

From a distance of five feet away, a hard-striding Samuel interrupted irritably, "Save those questions until later, Kent. Right now she and I have a paper to produce, and you're wanted in the office of your new commander. You've been transferred to General Clinton's staff."

For three wearisome hours that night and seven the next day, Rebecca transcribed Samuel's copious notes into story form, increasingly heartsick at the gloomy news. The Americans had lost battle after battle in a long line of retreat from Fort Ticonderoga. Try as she might, she could find no basis for Samuel's earlier prediction that the English would lose this decisive campaign. Outnumbered three to one, six to one, sometimes ten to one, the Americans could fight only briefly before they were forced to scatter and retreat.

Rebecca was emotionally and physically exhausted when she submitted the finished story to her uncle. Seemingly tireless himself, he scanned the pages briefly before he submitted the lengthy article to Colonel Crane for censoring. But for once Crane was uncritical.

"I read most of it while Mistress Burns was working. If you ask me, she's a better writer than her husband was."

More alert than Rebecca to the pitfalls inherent in that casually delivered comment, Samuel disclaimed brusquely, "Hardly. Most of this is a copy of my own work. My niece is merely a promising beginner, but a very tired one right now. And I think in view of the potentially critical situation of the next few weeks, it would be advisable for her to remain away from the workroom. Don't you agree, Colonel?''

Startled by the unexpected question, Crane frowned briefly before he acquiesced; but so ingrained were his suspicions, he could not resist an insulting qualification. "I'm not sure that her work isn't more unbiased than yours, Rayburn." Rebecca fled from the room.

Hot and uncomfortable in the sultry heat of midsummer, she walked listlessly toward her home, frowning slightly at the unaccustomed shrieks of childish laughter coming from the cottage. Inside on the floor, a game was in vigorous progress. While Lloyd and John crawled wildly from one spot to another, a joyously shrill Michael rode on Kent Enderly's back, clumsily brandishing a crude wooden sword.

"Saint George and the dragon," a disheveled and sunburned Kent explained, grinning broadly at the tired woman. "Uncle Josh suggested that I take over while you were working. Why don't you remove that smoldering witch's dress and get ready for dinner. We're having Dutch slaw and fish."

"And molasses cake," John shouted eagerly.

"Where in the world did Dena find molasses?"

"She didn't," Lloyd volunteered. "Kent brought it here before he took us fishing."

"Pilfering from army supplies, Captain Enderly?" Rebecca asked lightly.

"Just one of my many talents, Widow Burns."

Alone in her bedroom, Rebecca removed her clothing, nonplussed to discover that Kent Enderly did indeed have many talents. He'd quite easily captured the affection of three children who'd never exhibited such exuberance before, and he'd been expert in his handling of them. Irritated with herself for absentmindedly donning one of the brightly colored skirts she usually wore in the privacy of the cottage, she hastily changed into a drab black one and controlled her curls with a sedate snood. It was much easier to discourage an impetuous suitor in a formal ballroom, but considerably more difficult in a family cottage.

Yet still more evidence of Kent's unexpected talents awaited her in the front yard. While she'd dawdled over dressing, he'd washed the children at the pump and moved the kitchen table and benches outside. Rebecca sucked in her breath sharply at the sight of Dena tending the dozen fish spitted through the tails, roasting over a small campfire. An odd pain gripped her heart as she remembered the last time she'd cooked fish, when the spit had been the ramrod of a long-barreled American rifle. For a moment she felt only a fierce resentment that it wasn't Philip who was holding his son and winning the rapt admiration of her brothers.

Throughout the meal Rebecca listened guardedly to Michael's shrill excitement and to her brothers' unrestrained laughter. It was most probably Lloyd's and Johnny's first experience with a man who wasn't sternly disapproving or callously indifferent, she thought sadly; and it was the first time Michael had ever been held by a man at all. When he fell asleep before the others had finished the festive dinner, his small head dropped trustingly on this stranger's shoulder. Rising slowly, without disturbing the sleeping toddler, Kent whispered softly, "Come on, Mama, let's put your son to bed." Turning toward the Negro girl, he smiled companionably. "Just for tonight, Dena, let me take care of him."

Silently Rebecca led the way to the loft and watched as the aristocratic Englishman deftly tucked Michael into his crib and gently covered him with a sheet. "He needs a father, and so does Johnny," Kent murmured as he led Rebecca down the darkened stairs to the picnic table and the firelight and the enthusiastic boasting of her young brothers. "Kent taught us to clean fish today."

"We got to use minnows as bait."

"Tomorrow he's going to teach us to swim."

Only this last juvenile boast caught her wandering attention. "The river current is too swift for swimming," she admonished quickly. "I'm sure you misunderstood."

"No, they didn't, Rebecca," Kent retorted with a smiling impudence. "Years ago the family next door dug out a part of the riverbank for a safe swimming hole. I used it during my summer visits, and it's still in excellent shape. The owners gave us permission to use it and donated the cabbage for our dinner. It's only sensible to know how to swim when you live near a river. If you like, I can teach you too."

"That won't be necessary," she declined the invitation stiffly. "I already know how."

"You learned in icy Maine waters?"

"They're not that cold in summer."

"They are too. The Atlantic Ocean is arctic-cold north of the Cape Cod peninsula."

"You know a great deal about my country, Captain."

"I warned you, Cousin, that I expect to live here."

Although his voice was softly humorous, Rebecca recoiled from the challenge of his words; but she didn't forbid him to return for the promised swimming lesson. That night she rummaged through the shabbiest of her trunks and dragged out the sailor breeches she'd worn in Port-au-Prince. With scissors, needle, and thread, she refashioned the wide-legged garment so that it would provide her with more secure protection in the water. Kent might be a magnificent swimmer, but she wasn't going to trust her brothers' or Michael's lives to anyone but herself. A troubled Dena joined her before the task was complete.

"You sho' 'nuff knows how to swim, Miz Rebecca?" she asked doubtfully.

Rebecca nodded shortly.

"Michael's gonna be howling mad effen he's left behind."

"Michael and you are both going, Dena. I thought we might take along a picnic lunch to eat after the swimming lesson."

"Miz Rebecca, that man be powerful good 'round chil'run. I 'spect they minds him better 'n they does me, an' he neber onct scold them. He jest laughs liken he 'uz a chile hisself. But, Miz Rebecca—"

"Yes, Dena?"

"That man's courtin' you, Miz Rebecca, and you ain't 'xactly free. Conjur woman say a courtin' man kin be mule stubborn when his mind's made up, and Misser Kent done made up his mind to marry you. Best you tell him the truf 'fore you gits t' temptin' the devil.''

Despite her long-established respect for Dena's conjure woman, Rebecca shook her head. "I can't take that chance, Dena. Kent is still a British soldier, and his commanding officer is still Colonel Crane. But you needn't worry about my tempting the devil; when you meet my husband, you'll understand why.''

Fortunately for Rebecca's and Dena's peace of mind, the question of courtship did not arise through the remainder of that summer holiday. The afternoons dedicated to introducing three enthralled children to the excitement of water sport was not conducive to adult conversation on any level. Each day after Lloyd and Johnny had been dismissed by their tutor, Kent arrived in time to escort everyone to the rustic swimming pool on the neighboring estate. Gradually, Rebecca relaxed her vigilance enough to participate in water fights and to pace her brothers in their first thrashing attempts at staying afloat and later during their successful swims across the shallow pool. Only on the long walks home, as Kent remained by her side with Michael riding happily on his shoulders, did Rebecca's uneasiness recur.

The pleasant idyll ended with jarring abruptness on the thirteenth day when a stiffly correct soldier greeted Kent on the cottage porch with the order to report immediately to General Clinton.

"Emergency or routine, Sergeant?" Kent asked crisply; and Rebecca watched in dismay as her good-natured companion of the past days changed instantly into an alert military officer in spite of the oddity of his attire.

"I'm not at liberty to say, sir," the man responded woodenly, "not in front of territorials.''

Watching the angry flush stain Kent's fair complexion, Rebecca intervened hastily, "The sergeant's quite right. Official army business is none of my affair.''

Ironically, it was Colonel Crane who revealed the entirety of this particular official business to Rebecca the day after Kent had left with the sergeant. Exhausted after a long afternoon of readjusting the children to a routine that lacked the excitement Kent had infused into their limited lives, she was engaged in the drudgery of washing the supper dishes when Dena nervously admitted Crane into the cottage. Alarmed by the unexpected visit, Rebecca braced herself for expected trouble; but for once the usually decisive man seemed at a loss for words.

"I would appreciate your help, mistress," he admitted brusquely after pacing the length of the living room with restless strides before seating himself in one of the chairs flanking the fireplace.

Nodding a cautious compliance, Rebecca took the opposite chair and waited.

"What do you know about a man named Herkimer?" he demanded abruptly.

"What's he accused of, Colonel?" she asked cautiously.

"Of exaggerated heroics! Do you know him, mistress?"

"I've heard of a Nickolas Herkimer."

"In what capacity?"

"One of the militia leaders in western New York."

"Have you ever heard of a group of religious zealots called Palatines?"

"They were German colonists who settled in the Shoharie and Mohawk valleys, but they're not religious zealots like the Quakers and Mennonites. Uncle Samuel said they could be fierce fighters. Why are you asking me these questions, Colonel? My uncle knows far more than—"

"Your uncle knows too damn much for his own good. Last night one of his cursed rivermen reported a battle in the Mohawk Valley and claimed that a few hundred Palatine farmers under your Nickolas Herkimer defeated the whole of our army from Fort Oswego—sixteen hundred men and God knows how many Indians. A damned impossibility!"

"Perhaps your Indians deserted their white leaders as they did General Burgoyne," Rebecca suggested with suppressed malice.

"And perhaps pigs can fly," Crane snapped. "Those Mohawks were led by Chief Joseph Brant, a great warrior and a Christian missionary as well. He thinks like a white man, not like one of those murdering savages with Burgoyne. And he's not as barbaric as the bloody rebel minutemen who whistle up their damned armies in an hour's time like skulking Indians bent on massacre.''

"You forget, Colonel, that American militia leaders learned their skill in the last war, when they helped England fight against the Indians the French hired,'' Rebecca murmured.

"Did your father?"

"For seven years, Colonel.''

"Well, their tactics won't work against General Burgoyne, mistress.''

Colonel Crane's confident optimism was again shaken nine days later when two other armies of "whistled-up'' militia defeated and captured thirteen hundred of Burgoyne's own men. Almost simultaneously General Howe demoralized the loyalists in New York by moving his vast army into New Jersey to begin the march on Philadelphia. For captive New York, war was no longer the central concern. Both Tories and Whigs faced winter starvation if western harvests were not allowed to reach the beleaguered city. In response to loyalist outrage, General Clinton began his long-delayed departure to relieve Burgoyne's forces in early October, one day before a frustrated Kent Enderly was allowed to return to his uncle's estate.

Privately, he informed Samuel and Joshua that he'd been detained in Staten Island for six weeks, forbidden to attempt a courier mission up the Hudson to warn Burgoyne.

"Where's Colonel Crane?'' he demanded abruptly.

"He left the city at the same time as Clinton,'' Samuel responded.

"Damn!''

"What does Crane have to do with you, Kent?''

"Everything. I was transferred to his command, and he's ordered me on a tour of courier duty among the Seneca Indians on the frontier.''

"Dear God!''

"Don't say what you're thinking, Uncle Samuel. He's the one who has to approve my resignation.''

"Did he say he would?''

"Only after I put in six additional months of courier work between New York and Philadelphia. I've already made arrangements to take Rebecca and her family there as soon as I return from the west. They'll be better off there, where the food's plentiful."

While Joshua appeared only helplessly distressed, Samuel's face was stony with shock. "Has she agreed to this insanity?" he rasped.

Kent smiled for the first time since entering the library. "No, she hasn't," he admitted, "and she hasn't agreed to marry me either, but she will."

"Your parents will never approve," Joshua protested weakly.

"Since I plan to remain in America with Rebecca, their approval isn't important. Where is she anyway? She wasn't at the cottage or near her usual fishing spot when I looked a few—"

"Never mind where she is," Samuel interrupted harshly. "I want to know precisely what you're supposed to do on the frontier."

"I'm to make contact with the remnants of our Indian and loyalist allies there. Now if you'll excuse me, I'm on a short chain as far as time is concerned, and I want to see Rebecca."

"We'll help you find her," Samuel volunteered, but Kent was already racing through the doorway. Skillfully, Samuel prevented his brother following.

"I know where she is," he explained hastily. "I've been sending two guards along with her and the children ever since we spotted those poachers a week ago. You delay the young fool as long as you can while I warn Rebecca what she's in for. How the devil did this mess happen?"

"Kent proposed marriage a week after he met her."

"Why the devil didn't you tell me?"

"I thought he'd have the sense to accept her refusal. I couldn't very well tell him the truth about her, could I? It's not merely her safety that's at risk; it's our own reputation as well. If you hadn't agreed to her lie that first day, we wouldn't be in this unfortunate position. Now Kent is going to be damnably upset when she tells him."

"If I reach her first, she's not going to tell him. Unless I miss my guess, that damned bounder Crane deliberately placed our nephew in a dangerous position; and Kent will need all the wits he possesses just to survive. I doubt if he's met more than a handful of tame Indians since he's been in this country. There he is at the dock; and thank God, he's turning in the wrong direction. You intercept him and keep him away for ten minutes. But no confessions, Josh. If you remember, he can be as hotheaded as our sister."

The hurried conversation Samuel had with Rebecca in the small shrub-enclosed cove was a revelation to the sixty-five-year-old editor. As it had throughout the fifteen months he'd known this oddly reserved niece, her speed of comprehension delighted him. She was, he reflected, an unusually perceptive female, fortunately lacking in the hysterical sentimentalism most women affected during emotional emergencies. When he'd told her bluntly that he didn't want Kent hurt unnecessarily before departing on a dangerous assignment, she'd smiled faintly, but not before he'd seen the flash of anger in her expressive brown eyes.

"I never encouraged him, Uncle Samuel."

"I'm sure you didn't, my dear."

"What happens when he returns?"

"I'll tell him about your marriage."

"And if he proposes to ignore my marriage, what will you and Uncle Joshua say then?"

Shocked into a belated realization that this middle daughter of a scorned half brother was a sophisticated woman, Samuel sputtered his reply. "That decision will be entirely yours."

"Then I'll warn you now, that decision will be *no*, even at the risk of our safety."

Samuel's nod of approval was terminated abruptly when Kent burst through the shrubbery and swept Rebecca into his arms. Almost simultaneously, Joshua arrived on the scene as did Dena and the three children.

"I warned you what would happen when you stopped

wearing black,'' Kent mumbled indistinctly as he kissed her in complete disregard of two uncles, three children, and a disapproving Dena. Ruefully, Rebecca remembered that the only black she was wearing this day was the disfiguring smears of river mud on the hem of her brightly flowered skirt.

Her awareness of reality, however, had not deserted her. She smiled sardonically at the older uncle when Kent announced exultantly that the wedding would take place the day after he returned and that Samuel was to take care of the official notification and Joshua, the arrangements. His instructions to the nonplussed bride-to-be about burning every black garment in her wardrobe, though, were terminated by a maternal shriek of alarm.

Having taken instant advantage of the momentary lack of supervision, Michael had pulled himself away from the restraint of Dena's hand and was running as fast as his chubby legs could carry him toward the water's edge. As Rebecca stumbled toward the gleeful toddler in numbing fear, Kent shoved her aside to race the twenty feet with the skill of a conditioned athlete, grabbing the small fugitive's shirttail with enough force to send them both tumbling into the soft mud of the tiny beach.

''Remind me,'' he reprimanded his uncles after surveying the ruins of his once immaculate uniform, ''never to employ you two as guardians for my family. As for you, young imp,'' he addressed unrepentant, giggling Michael, ''from now on you'll be tied to a tree whenever your mother brings you near the water.''

Wisely, Kent refrained from scolding Dena, whose plump face was still frozen with terror; instead he suggested she take the subdued older children back to the cottage. On the pathway leading toward the manor house with the muddied culprit perched on his shoulder and his arm around Rebecca's waist, Kent was quietly exuberant.

''If I hadn't taken you by surprise, my reluctant love, you'd still be thinking up new ways to refuse. But never again; you and Michael and the others all need me. Besides, with our mutual uncles as witnesses, you haven't a prayer of escaping.''

Thirty paces behind, two elderly bachelors regarded their niece and nephew in puffing silence until the older one articulated what they were both thinking.

"Even when he learns the truth, I don't think he'll let her go."

CHAPTER
16

AS disturbing as Kent's declaration had been to Rebecca and her uncles, their preoccupation with personal problems was of short duration. Four days after Kent's departure, one of Samuel's rivermen arrived with the news of General Burgoyne's unconditional surrender to a jubilant American army. But even while the type was being set for the *Observer*'s account of that disaster, reports began trickling into the office about a contrived catastrophe that would adversely affect hostage New Yorkers far more than the military defeat.

Traveling slowly up the Hudson River, General Clinton was destroying all rebel towns and burning all farms. Determined to prevent any American threat to retake British-held territory, Clinton was laying waste the countryside which had traditionally supplied the teeming population of New York City with food, firewood, and fodder for animals. With the existing supply of these essential commodities already critically low, people rushed to buy whatever they could at whatever prices the merchants charged before the winter snows began.

Although neither Samuel nor Joshua engaged in the actual haggling with shopkeepers or barge captains, their wagon was frequently first in line on the waterfront or in the small commercial district that had survived the holocaust of the September fire. Since the Rayburn servants had been instructed to outbid all but the most extravagant of potential customers, sufficient quantities of the necessary food staples, wood, coal, and fodder were eventually obtained and stored on the estate. Even the winter boots and coats needed for the three young children were purchased without complaint despite their exorbitant cost.

Throughout the purchasing ordeal, Samuel Rayburn had maintained a stoic calm, allowing nothing controversial or critical to be published in the *Observer*. He refused to print the story that a thousand city residents had been impressed into the British Navy against their will. He ignored the frequent visitors who urged him to censure General Clinton for endangering the food supply. Most inexplicably of all, he minimized General Burgoyne's defeat and defended General Howe's decision to invade Philadelphia.

Not until the afternoon Weldon Crane returned unexpectedly did Rebecca learn the reason for her uncle's uncharacteristic tolerance for both governmental blundering and merchant cheating. Summoned to the Rayburn library, she arrived in time to hear her uncle demand sardonically, "Now that you have made a journalistic liar out of me, are you or are you not going to recall my nephew from that suicide mission you sent him on?"

"Come now, Rayburn," Crane protested, "Captain Enderly is a trained courier."

"Captain Enderly," Samuel snapped, "doesn't know a word of any of the five Indian languages; he hasn't the foggiest idea about the geography of that savage battleground; and he hasn't had enough experience with American militia to know the difference between loyalist and rebel."

"I daresay he's intelligent enough to learn," Crane

interposed blandly, "and I did arrange for him to have an experienced guide. But enough for the moment about your nephew's future; I have a commission that I want you and Mistress Burns to undertake. You're to be part of a civilian delegation to conduct a prisoner exchange. If both of you agree to follow my instructions in this matter, I will reassign Captain Enderly to his more customary duty."

"Is this prisoner exchange under your or General Clinton's jurisdiction?" Samuel asked casually.

"Mine. It is an assignment I have been empowered to carry out independent of command. General Clinton is not aware of this mission, nor do I propose that he learn of it."

"How did you make the arrangements without his knowledge?"

"For the past weeks my officers and I have been operating in enemy territory under a flag of truce, dealing privately with rebel authorities. Since the numerical figures are in their favor, I had little trouble gaining their cooperation. You will be exchanging two hundred of the enemy prisoners presently under my control for a hundred British officers wounded in the recent battle."

Samuel was silent for a moment before he responded; when he finally did speak, his voice held an angry rasp. "Colonel Crane, I submitted to your earlier blackmail and followed your dictation about my newspaper to insure my nephew's safety. But now you're asking me to endanger my niece. The answer is *no*. I will accept the commission, but she will not accompany me."

"Mistress Burns was *not* my idea. Her attendance was requested by the other side, by her father to be precise."

Having remained silent during the earlier discussion, more from a repugnance for Crane's callousness than from fear, Rebecca was abruptly galvanized into speech by the odd emphasis he'd placed on her name. "How did my father know that I was in New York?"

"If you recall, Mistress Burns, I asked you a similar

question last March about your Captain Keane, and you pleaded ignorance. Well, mistress, I am not as devious as you; I informed your father that I have been responsible for your safety ever since your unfortunate capture at sea."

Gasping at the effrontery, Rebecca lost her temper. "Did you tell him that his sons are also under your—protection?"

"No, Mistress Burns, that I did not see fit to tell him."

"May I take them and my own son with me?"

"No. They'll be held here as security for your safe return. I will personally see to their welfare."

"Under those circumstances, I refuse to go, Colonel!" Rebecca declared defiantly.

"That would be a foolish decision. Half of the boats on the return trip will be empty, and I understand Albany has a large surplus of food. You might also care to consider an additional exingency; your cousin's transfer is as much dependent upon your cooperation as upon your uncle's. As I implied earlier, your father has made your attendance a mandatory contingency."

"Rebecca will go," Samuel promised heavily.

"Good. Now about the arrangements. The American prisoners have been selected by the other members of the committee—the pastor of the Trinity congregation and the head of the Quaker church in Brooklyn. The members of that church will take care of all the nursing chores both going and returning. You, Mr. Rayburn, will be responsible for the final negotiations in Albany with a man named Dietrich de Witt. He claimed to be a friend of yours. Is he?"

"A friendly rival, Colonel. Will my brother Jeremy be present at the final exchange point?"

Crane's eyes narrowed and his lips pursed with a remembered anger. "So he said."

"You met him?"

"Yes."

"I'm surprised my brother allowed you to select British officers to be exchanged rather than common soldiers."

"That point was not negotiable."

"I imagine not. The families of officers are more politically important in England. One more question, Colonel. How do we prevent the boat crews from deserting once they reach—enemy territory?"

There was a satisfied smugness about the colonel's words and the smile that accompanied them. "Like Mistress Burns, these men all have families here."

Those were the callous words that haunted Rebecca during the three-day voyage to Albany. Even though she'd paid Reverend Stebbins, her brothers' humorless tutor, to remain full-time at the cottage until her return, she still feared Crane's vindictive cruelty—especially now that he'd met her father and knew the truth about her! She wondered dismally what special punishment he would devise. Bitterly, she reflected that if only Philip and his ships were available now, she would help organize the raid to rescue three helpless children and a frightened Negro girl. Even more fancifully, Rebecca dreamed of capturing Colonel Crane himself and transporting him to Gonâve Island and into the custody of men more savagely inhuman than he was. Smiling ruefully at her sour humor, she welcomed the cold wind that brought stinging tears to her eyes. Even here on the open deck of a lowly riverboat, she could remember Philip so much more clearly than on land—how blue his eyes were as he scanned the water ahead, how easily he'd controlled the small captain's gig he loved. Other, more poignant memories crowded into her consciousness, and she wondered how much longer she was to be forced into the emotional limbo of emptiness.

Briefly, she thought about the young Englishman who'd offered so impulsively to fill that void, and she frowned with regret. She was sorry that she hadn't blurted the truth to Kent on the day of his arrival. Even if he'd told Colonel Crane, she'd be no worse off than she was now; and he'd be spared unnecessary hurt. She would have liked to have kept his friendship for her own sake as well as for Michael's and her brothers'. In spite of the uniform he wore, he'd been a good friend to all of them.

Seated at the chart table inside the unheated cabin of the

boat, Samuel Rayburn was also preoccupied by his own thoughts; but they held none of Rebecca's sentimentality or regret. He was thinking about the horror he'd witnessed on the morning of departure from New York Harbor—and of the men responsible for the outrageous inhumanity. He'd watched as two hundred American prisoners-of-war had been carried in litters down the swaying gangplank leading from the rotting hulk of the old battleship *Jersey*, now grounded in the mud flats off Long Island. Those pathetic, emaciated, skeletal men were not suffering from battle wounds; they'd been starved almost to death.

Turning to the man who'd been standing indifferently beside him, Samuel had demanded, "How many more men do you have penned aboard that abomination of a prison, Colonel Crane?"

"Fewer than two thousand with these gone."

"Whose decision was it to starve them to death?"

"One of the exigencies of war, Mr. Rayburn. I believe you know the King's opinion about traitors."

"What do you think will happen, Colonel, when these released prisoners tell their stories to the American authorities?"

"No doubt your editor friends will spout fire and brimstone, but I'll wager there'll be fewer volunteers for the rebel armies."

"Is General Clinton in agreement with you?"

"With regard to prisoners, absolutely."

Writing with dispassionate accuracy at the makeshift desk inside the crude cabin, Samuel filled page after page with carefully marshaled facts. Of the seventeen thousand American soldiers on Long Island fifteen months ago, only six thousand had reached New Jersey. Of the others, fewer than four thousand had been killed and more than seven thousand taken prisoner. Samuel's quill paused in midair, and he hesitated to write what he knew must be a certainty. Thousands of those prisoners had already died of starvation! And the world must be told, Samuel reflected dismally, especially the unawakened, uncaring mother country of England.

Samuel frowned in a furious concentration. Colonel Crane now inspected every Rayburn message sent to the Enderly Publishers and every private letter as well. He would never allow this damning evidence to pass his censor. While Crane and the other leaders responsible for the cold savagery wanted the colonials to know, they did not dare risk exposure at home. Smiling with an abrupt, vindictive inspiration, Samuel reached for the list of the hundred British officers being exchanged for the half-dead Americans. These men had real reason for hating General Howe and General Clinton, the military opportunists who'd betrayed the Burgoyne expedition. Most, if not all, of them might welcome a chance for revenge. A few of them, Samuel reasoned, might have sufficient political influence to demand that the remaining prisoners aboard the *Jersey* be given food—providing such an amount of food was made available by the citizens of Albany.

When the flotilla of twenty riverboats reached the thriving Dutch-American city, only Samuel went ashore; three hours later he returned with Dietrich de Witt, a journalist Samuel had known and respected for twenty years, a decisive man who'd read Samuel's conclusions about American prisoners and immediately summoned the town's leaders to his office. Angrily shocked by the revelation, but cautiously practical, these Dutch-Americans had voted to supply the food, demanding only that Dietrich de Witt be certain the British officers could be trusted.

Early the following morning on an isolated beach south of Bemis Heights, Dietrich de Witt and Samuel Rayburn waded ashore together and met with the grim-faced Americans awaiting them. While these officials supervised the transfer of the pathetic human cargo from the boats to the waiting Conestoga wagons, the two editors approached the British prisoners at the far end of the beach. Although some thirty of these men were confined to litters, most were ambulatory and in reasonably good health. Ironically, Samuel needed to exert very little persuasion to win support for both of his requests; his standing as a loyalist had been established by none other than Colonel Crane, and his position as a member of the elite class was quickly accepted through his relationship to one of their own—Kent Enderly. Moreover, Samuel had correctly gauged the extent of their anger at Howe and Clinton and the degree of their gentlemen's distaste for unsportsmanlike conduct in war. With the overwhelming evidence of starving men being paraded before them, the officers voted to deliver the copies of Samuel's letter to various recipients in England and to force Colonel Crane's cooperation in regard to the food. Impulsively, they even offered to pay for part of that food, and an impassive Dietrich de Witt collected their contributions.

Privately, however, as he and Samuel were returning to the American side of the beach, de Witt was still doubtful about the success of the project. "Those men sounded sincere enough, and no doubt they'll do as they promised. But once they've sailed for England, what guarantee do we have that your Colonel Crane will carry out their orders?"

"Those men," Samuel retorted with a burst of sardonic laughter, "are the sons of some of the most powerful men in England. No mere army colonel would dare risk incurring their collective anger—particularly not one as ambitious as Colonel Crane. Return to Albany, Dietrich, and start collecting that food, enough for six months if possible. Perhaps by that time Parliament will force General Clinton to reverse his policy."

"Will you and your niece be returning with me?"

"No, I'll have to remain here until the job is finished; and Rebecca has an appointment with her father. You wouldn't know where Colonel Jeremy Rayburn is hiding, would you?"

"He's waiting for her in a cabin just beyond that stand of trees at the end of the beach. But your brother isn't hiding, Samuel. This exchange was arranged independently from army command; we have some bastards among our generals too."

"Do you know my brother?"

"Yes, he's one of Philip Schuyler's most trusted officers. He was the one who insisted that you head the committee from your end."

"I'll be damned! I wondered what I was doing here, since the Quakers have done all the real work."

"None of us trust the Quakers all that much, Samuel; they're loyalist to a fault—you're not."

Samuel was still pondering that odd evaluation of his political views when he located Rebecca. For hours she'd been working with the Quaker women near the Conestoga wagons; and her face reflected the horror she'd witnessed among the American prisoners.

"Your father's waiting for us, Rebecca," he insisted quietly.

"Did the American army starve its prisoners?" she asked as they walked away.

"No, it did not!"

"Uncle Samuel, I want to get back to the children as quickly as possible."

"Don't create foolish bugbears, young lady. Colonel Crane has no reason to harm any of the children. There's your father standing in the doorway. I'll say this for him, he hasn't changed much in appearance; and I'll wager his temper is the same too."

Frowning heavily, Jeremy Rayburn greeted the older brother he hadn't seen in thirty years with a brusque nod of recognition; but he appeared merely irritated as he glanced at his daughter. "Well, Rebecca, I see Colonel Crane has some sense of honor. He said he would convince his superiors to let you leave regardless of the difficulty. It would seem that you caused as much trouble for the enemy as you did for our friends in Falmouth. But no matter; now that you're here, I won't allow you to return."

"I have to go back," Rebecca said breathily, staring at the changes three years had wrought in her father. Still handsome at fifty-two despite the gray now streaking his dark hair, he was whipcord lean with an expression of hard, uncompromising authority etched on his face that reminded her distressingly of Colonel Crane's.

"As always you seem to take delight in disobeying me,

Rebecca. As soon as I'd left Falmouth, you went against my express wishes and married a scandalous libertine who maintained the most notorious woman in town. And then, instead of settling down to the discipline of marriage, you conducted yourself like a picaresque adventuress, using a variety of names before you returned to Falmouth without a husband or an explanation."

"Who kept you so well informed about my marriage to Philip Keane?"

"Sidney Tupton came to see me after Ticonderoga, and I've talked to Stanton several times since he settled in a home near Albany. Incidentally, Roger is still very much interested in you, Rebecca. Had you been a dutiful daughter in Falmouth, you would now be—"

Interrupting her father's castigation with a cool insolence, Rebecca completed his unfinished sentence, "I'd now be married to the most notorious traitor in America! Roger was the agent I couldn't identify in that drawing I made."

"That's a preposterous allegation! I've known Roger—"

"Roger was and still is a traitor. Ask Eldin Cooper in New London about the day he kidnapped me from the newspaper office, allowed one of his thugs to render me unconscious, and then threatened to turn me over to one of the other British agents I had sketched."

"Did Sidney know?"

"Sidney and Stanton both knew. They were waiting for us aboard a ship. When I convinced them that I was already married, they sent me ashore alone at night in open country. It was an interesting experience walking twenty miles in the dark, but at least I was rid of Roger."

"It would seem that I may have been misinformed. Stanton told me that Roger was bitterly disappointed when you eloped with another man, and Sidney informed me about your conduct in Connecticut."

"Your Sidney Tupton is an accomplished liar, Jeremy," Samuel affirmed quietly. "Did you, by any chance, make him the official guardian of your other children?"

"As a matter of fact, I did, and I've sent him money regularly for their support."

"More fool you, Jeremy; they never received a shilling of it. Two months after the burning of Falmouth, Sidney arrived in New York and complained that he could no longer support the family you'd left in his care. Without a backward glance, he deposited his mother and his daughter and your three children on Joshua's and my doorstep and departed in great haste. Your sons have been with us ever since."

"And the others?"

"We kept them for a month until that old harridan all but destroyed the serenity of our home. Since your daughter preferred to remain with her mother, we moved the three females into a boardinghouse in New Brunswick and paid their expenses. The old woman died the following April."

"What happened to my wife?"

"According to the landlord, she formed an alliance with a loyalist merchant and accompanied him to London a year ago. As far as I know, she and your daughter are still there."

Hearing the story for the first time, Rebecca gasped with shock—not at Jane Rayburn's infidelity but at Hannah's death. Somehow the indomitable old despot had seemed as immortal as the witches she resembled. A quick glance at her father's face assured her that the flush staining his tanned complexion was the expression of anger rather than heartbreak.

"You're well rid of her," Samuel counseled blandly. "She was expensive baggage. I know since I paid the bills she accumulated in the wine and clothing shops in New Brunswick."

"I'll pay you back every shilling," the younger man blustered.

"That won't be necessary, but something else is. Before your wife left America, she sent a message insisting that your sons be returned to her father. In that letter she named Roger Tupton as their temporary guardian. But there was no way in hell that I'd turn Lloyd and John—"

"Who?"

"Your sons, Jeremy—their middle names seemed more

appropriate somehow. As I was about to say, there is no way I would entrust young children into the care of a man like Roger Tupton who boasted about his work in recruiting Indians for the dirtiest kind of warfare. Nor will I ever consider turning them over to any other of that sorry lot of thieving land grabbers. Therefore, I suggest you rescind the guardianship agreement you made with Sidney Tupton and name—''

Jeremy's reaction was a violent slamming of his fists on the hand-hewn table while his shout resounded against the log timbers in the ceiling.

''No! I wouldn't name a lickspittle loyalist like you as their guardian if my life depended on it. I'd rather they be dead than become the slavering lackeys of a depraved and murderous king.''

Samuel smiled cynically and shook his head. ''You haven't changed in thirty years, Jeremy. You still spout exaggerations without regard for truth or for the meaning of words. I was going to suggest that you make Rebecca their legal guardian. For the past year she has been a better mother to them than Jane Rayburn ever was or could be. As for Rebecca's politics, I'd hate to be the one to order her to bend that stubborn head in respect to any man, much less to a king she considers a pathetic incompetent at best.''

Stunned by praise from the uncle who'd bedeviled her through months of demanding work, Rebecca stared dazedly at the scarred boards of the tabletop, prouder of that hard-won accolade than she'd ever been of any earlier success. Dimly she heard her father ask to speak alone with her, and she watched Samuel stride stiffly from the room.

How could she ever have been so self-centered, she asked herself remorsefully, as to have misjudged a man so completely? The warmth with which she answered Jeremy's stern questions about his sons' education had nothing to do with filial devotion; it was inspired by the old man she imagined to be shivering in the cold November wind just outside the cabin. But upon Samuel's reentry into the room, she greeted him with laughter. Old he might be and grudgingly sentimental beneath a gruff exterior, but he was still the most organized man she'd ever known. He'd walked to the boat and back, returning with a roll of parchment, two quill pens, and a tightly capped bottle of ink. Stuffed into the pockets of his greatcoat were a bottle of Madeira wine and three small pewter mugs.

The signing of the document that Samuel had already prepared was stiffly formal, despite the civilizing warmth of wine; but when the older man asked his brother for an eyewitness account of the two Saratoga battles, Jeremy exploded into speech. Halfway through the intensely expert description, Rebecca knew that her father had finally found his destined vocation. The harsh, unyielding militancy which had destroyed him as a journalist had made him into a relentless, unwavering army officer. Even his personal farewell to her, Rebecca reflected with an amused cynicism, was a stern, moralistic lecture rather than an expression of gratitude to a daughter who'd just assumed guardianship of her brothers.

"Now that you have a worthwhile goal in your life, Rebecca, I trust you will not allow your past mistakes to influence your future. When you finally do settle down, I trust you will choose a man strong enough to control your impulsive nature."

Fifty feet from the cabin, Samuel asked dryly, "Did you tell him about your own child?"

"He never asked. You know something, Uncle Samuel, I don't think he really believes that Philip Keane ever married me. I'm not sure he even believes what we told him about Roger."

"Rebecca, why didn't you ever tell me about that scoundrel's brutality to you?"

"He was past history by the time I reached New York."

"Did he ever tell you which Indian tribes he was working with?"

"Senecas, I think. At least he was enthusiastic about some young Seneca chieftain. Why?"

"Just curious, my dear. Did you ever mention Roger's name to Colonel Crane?"

"I'm sure I did, probably on several occasions. Why all this sudden interest in Roger Tupton?"

"I distrust coincidences as much as I do Colonel Crane and the entire Tupton tribe," Samuel murmured cryptically. It was those coincidences that were worrying him. Why had Stanton Tupton moved to Albany, and why had Kent been sent into Seneca territory? And what the devil had Jeremy been talking about when he referred to Rebecca's marriage? Samuel frowned in irritation; none of the explanations he devised silenced the vague suspicions that were forming in his mind. A hundred feet farther along the trail, part of the mystery was solved when Jeremy Rayburn shouted imperiously from the cabin.

"Wait a moment, Rebecca!" When he caught up to them, his speech lacked its earlier harshness and he sounded almost apologetic.

"It suddenly occurred to me that you might not have heard; but since Colonel Crane knew, I naturally assumed you did too—especially in view of the widow weeds you're wearing. Now I'm not so sure, and regardless of the failure of your marriage, you still have a right to know. Philip Keane is dead, Rebecca. During a battle in the English Channel, two of his ships were sunk by enemy privateers, and he was not among the survivors. At the time the three ships were on their way home with a consignment of French arms—their second such delivery. Luke Stoneham was the one who brought the news."

Rebecca stared at her father in stunned disbelief before she turned and ran blindly toward the beach.

Throughout the return passage to Albany and the two-day layover there, Samuel did not intrude into Rebecca's lonely world of grief. Unlike Jeremy, who'd been easily reassured by his daughter's lack of tears, Samuel knew that she'd loved her husband deeply. Although she was still somewhat of an enigma to him, this bright, talented woman who confided in no one and who invited no sympathy, he knew that her self-control was only superficial. She'd sustained two bitter blows—the tragic news

itself and Colonel Crane's vicious revenge in allowing that
news to be announced by her insensitive father. Samuel
was determined that she not be hurt further, but his
journalistic instinct warned him that the drama was far
from finished. At the land recorder's office in Albany, one
of the most incorruptible of such public establishments in
the colonies, he located the answers to one of his more
pressing questions. And at de Witt's newspaper office he
located the Philadelphia paper that had carried the story of
the Keane disaster. No wonder Crane knew about it; the
paper was loyalist and the account biased. Samuel did not
mention the findings of either of his investigations to
Rebecca.

Not until Rebecca opened the door of the cottage did
she feel any emotion other than the draining emptiness
of loss; and not until a shrieking Michael hurled himself
into her arms did her pent-up tears begin. Kneeling on
the stone floor with her arms enfolding Michael and
Johnny, she felt the first pangs of returning life.
From a few feet away, Lloyd stared at her with eyes
that were suspiciously bright for the usually self-confident
child.

"Old Crane said you wouldn't come back, Becky," he
accused her. "He said you wouldn't want to."

"Colonel Crane was wrong, Lloyd. You're my family
and I won't leave you ever again."

"That's not what he said. He said we got to go where
the law says."

"Well, the law says you stay with me. I am your legal,
permanent guardian, and no one can ever take you from
me."

Rebecca's heart was beating with a painful fear as she
turned her head to stare at Dena, who appeared as terrified
as Johnny had been.

"What's this all about, Dena?"

"Reckon ole Misser Joshua say best he tell you."

"Best he tell me what?"

"We done have a visitor while you 'uz gone."

"Who?"

"A white-trash polecat I 'spects you knows. Lloyd and Johnny done hid the minute they sees him."

"It was old Roger, Becky," Lloyd exploded with pent-up anxiety, "and he said we got to go with him."

"Well, he's as wrong as Colonel Crane. Dena, where's Reverend Stebbins?"

"Best you ast Misser Joshua 'bout that, Miz Rebecca."

"Ask him about what, young woman?" Joshua Rayburn demanded from the doorway.

"Jest things," a startled Dena replied evasively.

"As a matter of fact, there are several things you should be told, Rebecca," Joshua announced sternly. "But I prefer that the children not be subjected to adult problems. Lloyd, take your brother and—and the younger one upstairs please."

"There is no need," Rebecca protested.

"There is every need. Lloyd, do as I tell you."

Helplessly, Rebecca watched the three chastised children file from the room; only when Dena started to follow them did she protest again. "Dena may stay, Uncle Joshua. She is quite old enough to understand *adult* problems."

"As you wish. First, perhaps you should tell Klaus and the other groundskeeper where to put all the parcels you left on the dock. Samuel said they were presents for the children. I would say that you were recklessly extravagant in view of your situation."

"Uncle Samuel must have purchased them; I didn't. I didn't even leave the boat in Albany."

"Then Samuel acted foolishly. Where do you want them?"

Indicating the empty corner of the room, Rebecca watched as the two husky workers deposited a dozen heavy packages on the floor. She hadn't remembered to buy the children a thing; for days she'd hardly remembered the children at all. But her Uncle Samuel had, just as he'd remembered everything else on that torturous river trip from the prisoner exchange beach to Manhattan Island.

"Where is Uncle Samuel?" she asked after the men had gone.

"He remained aboard to complete the journey to Long Island; he said you'd understand. I trust his meddling won't get us into any more trouble with the authorities. Our home has already been turned into a camp for frontier rabble, and I'm afraid much of that punishment is your fault, Rebecca."

"Is Roger Tupton the leader of those men?" she asked dully.

"Yes. Did the children tell you that they were rude to him when he tried to talk to them?"

"I know they hid because they were frightened."

"Well, your brothers had best get over that fear; he'll be taking them to England in the next few weeks."

"That white trash don' have no right," Dena exploded into an angry defense. "Miz Rebecca done say Lloyd and Johnny b'long to her."

"Your mistress is wrong! Major Tupton has a letter from their mother instructing him to bring them to her home in Liverpool."

"Their mother is too late, Uncle Joshua," Rebecca said harshly. "In both England and America the father is the one who controls his children's lives; and Jeremy Rayburn has made me their official guardian. Is Roger at your home now?"

"No, both he and Colonel Crane are presently in Long Island. Did Jeremy actually turn his sons over to you?"

"Very legally. Why?"

Joshua shook his head, his lips pursed together in disapproval. "Did he know that you were never married to the man you called your husband? And that you played fast and loose with other men as well?"

Shaken to the core of her being by the brutal questions, Rebecca stared hopelessly out the window, knowing that her uncle would never believe her protestations of innocence. She could even predict what his next accusation would be.

"You duped my brother Samuel into supporting your lies, and you artfully deceived my nephew into believing you a helpless widow. I am grateful to Roger Tupton for bringing Kent away from the dangerous frontier and for curing him of his foolish infatuation."

"I'm glad Kent is safe, Uncle," Rebecca asserted leadenly. "I also appreciate your bluntness; it does set the record straight, doesn't it? As to my relationship with Philip Keane, you can forget your moral outrage. The relationship—whatever it was—is over—ended permanently. Philip was killed in early August during a battle at sea."

It was the first time Rebecca had articulated the dread words and the first time her composure had failed her. Blinded by tears, she fled into the cold emptiness of her bedroom, which could offer only a momentary sanctuary. The needs of three frightened and confused children must take precedence over her own. They were too young and too vulnerable to understand her grief, much less to share it. In the ten days of her absence, much of the happy security she'd established for them had been destroyed; she dared not delay even for an hour the task of reestablishing their confidence in her. And until Samuel returned from Long Island, she was also responsible for their physical safety. Rebecca's hands were shaking as she removed two pistols from a trunk in her closet, the pistols Philip had given her for protection in Saint-Domingue. Ironically, it was Manhattan Island in America that was proving to be the more dangerous place. Rebecca had no illusions about the frontier criminals that Joshua had called "rabble" and that her father had considered more savage than Indians. If those were the type of men Roger Tupton had brought to the estate, she might very well need these weapons.

When she returned to the living quarters, Dena and the children were alone. Her uncle, Rebecca reflected cynically, had not even waited to determine whether or not she might need his help. But Joshua Rayburn was no longer important in her life; she'd lost his friendship a month ago when Kent Enderly's life had been placed in jeopardy.

Smiling at her two sober-faced brothers, she held up the paper her father had signed. "Before we open Uncle

Samuel's gifts, Lloyd and Johnny, I want you to see this document that makes me your guardian.''

Always the literal realist, the oldest child demanded, ''Does it say Roger can't take us away?''

''No one can take you away from me.''

Still apprehensive, Johnny stared at the paper. ''Does it say that no one can take Michael too?''

Rebecca took a deep, painful breath; more than the other two, Michael was now hers and hers alone. ''Michael too,'' she said softly.

''And Dena?'' Johnny persisted.

Smiling at the young girl who'd had the courage to defy a threatening Roger Tupton and a disapproving Joshua Rayburn, Rebecca nodded. ''Especially Dena. Now let's open those gifts!''

Before the first crate had been unpacked, Rebecca knew that her Uncle Samuel had turned the job of purchasing over to an expert who understood children. There were balls and bells and an ornate hobbyhorse; there were a barrel of apples, a sack of raisins, and a box of butter-rich Dutch cookies. Of a more practical nature, there were a tub of butter, a wheel of cheese, a barrel of molasses, a crate of eggs cradled in hay, and a huge crock of berry jam. Like Uncle Samuel, Rebecca mused wryly, I would probably have bought them books and mittens and a new slate; and they would have said, ''Thank you,'' without uttering a single shriek of joy.

Those gifts and the icy winter weather that began the next day made the two weeks of imprisonment within the small cottage bearable for the inmates. Only twice a day did they venture out the back door to tend the two goats tethered in a small shed a few feet away. While the others did the work, Rebecca stood guard with loaded and primed pistols. On one occasion only did she glimpse two bearded men slouched behind a sparse stand of shrubbery in the distance. ''White-trash polecats,'' Dena muttered angrily. Rebecca nodded in agreement as she watched the men leave their post in a hurried retreat.

Despite the frequent rewarding moments of those house-bound days, Rebecca spent the restless nights of interrupted sleep fighting against despair. She had only the memories of a few tempestuous months of marriage to ease the pain; and the only thing she possessed of the man she'd loved was the half-finished manuscript of *Captain King*. Seated at the kitchen table, she reread the blunt, impersonal paragraphs she'd copied from the ship's log of the *Reine*, and she remembered the passionate man who'd written them. Try as she might, she could write only a sentence or two of the story that had once fired her imagination. The tears that clouded her eyes also dulled her mind.

When Samuel Rayburn returned from Long Island and summoned her to the library of the big house, Rebecca reacted with a desperate relief. Leaving Klaus, the burliest of the groundskeepers, to guard the cottage, Rebecca hurried toward the manor, her hands nervously gripping the butts of the pistols concealed in the pockets of her black cloak. Characteristically, Samuel's greeting was a peremptory order.

"Kindly remove your veil, Rebecca; I want to see your face, and I want you to meet Chief Sagoyewatha, the Seneca chief we were discussing the other day."

When she'd entered the fire-lit library, Rebecca had thought her uncle alone. She hadn't seen the dark-skinned man standing in the shadows. Now as he stepped forward with a fluid grace, she gasped with the shock of near recognition. He projected the same expression of fierce authority as Jean-Jacques Dessalines, the same proud intelligence. His voice startled her still more, possessing a soft, musical cadence rather than the guttural breathiness of most Indians.

"My people would call you a moon woman, Mistress Keane. Hair the color of yours has great significance in our religion."

"A young Abenaki brave once called me *ne-oma*," she admitted.

"I have heard the story of York around many campfires, but I wasn't certain is was true until I saw you just now."

Rebecca's slight smile of pleasure faded when she

remembered that this charming and poised Indian might well be Roger Tupton's special friend.

"Chief Sagoyewatha," she asked shakily, "are you also known as Red Jacket?"

"When I am with my English brothers, I wear the coat they gave me. They call me Red Jacket because they cannot remember my Indian name."

"Then you're Roger Tupton's friend," she responded dully.

"Major Tupton is a blood brother to the Seneca, but I am no longer certain he is a friend."

"Chief Sagoyewatha is here at my request, Rebecca," Samuel interrupted. "I believe he will be of help in solving the problems Major Tupton has created for all of us. You may put your veil back on, my dear. Since you will not be a performer at this meeting, I see no reason to expose you to Colonel Crane's ungallant sarcasm. You have my permission to ignore my nephew as well. Against my advice, Kent asked to hear what Major Tupton has to say about the lies he told my foolish brother concerning your reputation."

Raising his voice to a sardonic pitch, Samuel called out abruptly, "You may come in now, gentlemen. The others are already present."

Grateful for the veil that hid her set and haggard face, Rebecca watched as four men strode silently into the room. Her Uncle Joshua, she thought with contempt, appeared uncomfortably embarrassed, as if he had no real interest in the proceedings; and Colonel Crane looked as blandly indifferent as a sheriff watching the hanging of a criminal he'd apprehended. But Roger Tupton stared at her with a rude appraisal, his handsome face marred by a vicious arrogance and a calculating speculation.

Turning her head to study the face of the fourth man, Rebecca shivered with regret. Kent Enderly's brooding blue eyes projected only misery as he gazed reproachfully at her. But he hadn't hesitated in believing the story Roger had told her, Rebecca reflected defensively. A bittersweet smile touched her lips briefly. Even though Philip Keane had accepted the lies another man had told about the Indian boy, he'd still married her.

Rebecca's wondering thoughts were terminated by Samuel's crisp order. "Be seated, gentlemen. I want this unpleasantness terminated as quickly as possible. Colonel Crane, during the exchange of prisoners after my brother had expressed doubts about Rebecca's marriage, I asked one of the Bostonians present to check the records in his city, and I asked him to address his reply to you. It arrived here yesterday. Have you had time to read it yet?"

"Yes," Crane snapped, "but then I never did have any real doubts about the identity of Mistress Keane's husband. It was her unnecessary lies that disturbed me."

"Those lies were very necessary at the time, Colonel. You forget that she was threatened with capture by one of our less noble privateers. Because of her husband's profession, her life and that of her infant son could have been forfeit. But now that she is a widow in reality, her defensive lie is no longer necessary or important. However, the myriad falsehoods that Major Tupton told to the people here present are of utmost importance. That is one of the reasons I invited Chief Sagoyewatha to attend this meeting. He has some information which I believe will prove pertinent."

Since Sagoyewatha had once again been standing in the shadows, the newcomers all leaned forward with a nervous tension when he stepped forward and spoke in his quietly resonant voice.

"When I first heard my white brother speak of this woman he called an adventuress harlot, I did not realize that she was the *ne-oma* the Abenaki tribe regards as an honored member. He said that she had taken an Indian lover when she was young, and he named the white village of York as the place."

"That story was common gossip in Falmouth," Roger defended himself hotly. "It was reported by the white man who survived the massacre."

"The white man lied," Sagoyewatha disclaimed calmly. "But there were Indians who did not. They watched as this moon maiden buried the warrior grandson of their chief. Captain Enderly and Joshua Rayburn would do well to question everything else my white brother told them about Mistress Keane.''

Rising to his feet with the agility of a man alerted to danger, Roger Tupton smiled at Sagoyewatha. ''I ask my brother's indulgence for any harm I may have done Mistress Keane's reputation. The truth is that she was my promised wife, and I was jealous. Even now her father wishes me to become her husband.''

''Sit down, Tupton,'' Samuel interposed swiftly. ''Jeremy Rayburn no longer believes what your father told him. But now to another matter. May I see the letter you showed Joshua concerning the disposition of my nephews, Sidney Lloyd and Jeremy John Rayburn?''

''I don't have it with me,'' Roger retorted warily.

''What's this all about, Rayburn?'' Colonel Crane demanded. ''I read the letter and found it a reasonable request from Major Tupton's sister, asking him to bring her sons to England.''

''It might have seemed reasonable, Colonel, but the truth is that Major Tupton is only a cousin to Jane Rayburn and that Jane herself is an illiterate whom her miserly father did not see fit to educate. I imagine Major Tupton has forged other letters which he intended to present to the London bank where Rebecca's fortune is being held, requesting that her money be used to support her brothers. And I imagine that he intended to extort money from me to pay for their return to America.''

''That's a lie,'' Roger snapped. ''Jane made the request; I merely wrote the letter.''

''A very interesting defense, Major, considering the two thousand miles of ocean and the fact that your request to go to England had been denied until you invented this plausible reason. Is anyone here interested in the reason Major Tupton wished to leave his native land and move to our mother country?''

Smiling cynically at Colonel Crane, whose interest was no longer negligent, Samuel addressed his next casual question to Chief Sagoyewatha.

"How many rebel farms have you and Major Tupton confiscated during the past two years?"

"What the devil is this, Rayburn?" Colonel Crane demanded. "That was the military assignment the Senecas and Tupton were hired to accomplish, and they'd done a damned good job of it."

"I've no doubt. How many farms, Chief Sagoyewatha?"

The Indian's response was thoughtfully slow. "I have counted only those farms which were stolen from Seneca tribal lands. There are forty-two which will now be returned to my people."

"I think not, Chief Sagoyewatha," Samuel disclaimed as he unrolled a scroll of paper across the table. "This map was prepared for me by the city clerk in Albany. The Seneca complaint about these disputed lands was well-known to the officials there. Two years ago when Major Tupton first visited my home, presumably as an emissary for my nephews' mother, I was curious about the reasons why a man who had long been a member of the Falmouth Sons of Liberty would suddenly become a loyalist Indian agent. At that time—long before the declaration of war, Colonel Crane—I corresponded with the Albany authorities, and they remained vigilant on my behalf. From the beginning of its history, New York has never permitted the blatant theft of Indian lands; but Massachusetts did. For a hundred years the Tupton family has gained its wealth through just such thefts. I was interested, therefore, when I learned that thirty of the farms Chief Sagoyewatha claims as Seneca land are now registered to Stanton Tupton, Major Tupton's father, a man who loudly proclaims himself a patriot to the rebel cause."

The silence which followed Samuel's dramatic announcement was ended by Colonel Crane, who belatedly realized that his earlier support of Roger Tupton had led him into an embarrassing trap. "We will correct any injustice done to your people, Red Jacket," he blustered.

"You cannot fulfill such a promise," the Indian stated flatly with implacable logic. "You do not control the enemy to whom my false brother gave these lands. As for you, my false brother, I advise you not to return to my people. Perhaps the Mohawk Joseph Brant will better understand your sense of honor. Being Christian, he is no longer as Indian as the Seneca.''

On feet as silent as the conversational void he left behind him, Sagoyewatha walked out of the library; and only one of the white men felt any need to follow. Colonel Crane was faced with the dilemma of choosing one or the other of Britain's allies in the only war still possible in New York—the frontier terrorism being waged by loyalists and Indians. That he chose to support the brashly arrogant young chief was simply a matter of numbers. Whether or not he represented the Seneca nation as he claimed, Red Jacket would have to be pacified and flattered back into the British fold.

Realizing that he'd been sacrificed in favor of a shrewdly political savage, Roger Tupton rose swiftly and walked toward the door, only to find his path blocked by Kent Enderly. Taller by inches and heavier by forty pounds, Roger smiled with a mocking confidence as his hands grasped the hilts of his hunting knives concealed beneath his coat.

"I see I'm not the only one Rebecca made a fool of," he confided companionably. "Somehow she always locates some man to champion her cause. I may have been wrong about the pirate she married, but what about the others? Have you asked her yet how long she lived with this Eben Burns whose name she took when she came to New York? I wonder which one of them fathered her child. To tell you the truth, I wondered if I might not be the lucky man. Rebecca and I spent some time together in Connect—'' Roger's mocking tones ended midsentence and his voice sharpened into a warning. "Don't reach for your sword, Captain Enderly; you'd be dead before you cleared the scabbard.''

"Not as dead as you'll be, Roger, if you don't remove your hands from those knives,'' Rebecca called out stridently from across the room. Swiftly Tupton spun around to face his new threat, only to raise empty hands in surrender. This was not the irritating girl he'd once kidnapped; this was a determined woman who held two cocked pistols trained on him without a tremor.

"Let him leave, Kent," she ordered sharply. "He doesn't know how to fight like a gentleman any more than he knows how to act like one. There is no Eben Burns, Roger; it is the name I used for the stories my Uncle Samuel published. Don't move, Major. If you recall, my father trained me to be an excellent shot. What is more, I'd have no compunction against killing you; and if you ever threaten my brothers again, I will. Now get yourself and those mercenary cutthroats you call *scouts* off of my uncles' property."

Returning to the library in time to hear Rebecca's denunciation, Colonel Crane rasped out a sharp command. "Put those weapons away, Mistress Keane, or I'll charge you with threatening the life of a loyal British subject. Major Tupton, you and your men will prepare to leave Manhattan within the hour to await reassignment orders on Long Island."

CHAPTER 17

AS ignominious as Roger Tupton's expulsion from the Rayburn estate had been, the revenge he took against the five people who had condemned him more than compensated for his temporary embarrassment. With the paid cooperation of an impecunious Brooklyn printer, whose scruples were as depleted as his purse,

Roger prepared a multiple indictment that blended truth
and fiction into a believable whole. For the four men, his
accusations were only slight exaggerations of fact. Red
Jacket was described as a savage marauder who made little
distinction between rebel and loyalist farms. Colonel Weldon
Crane, Captain Kent Enderly, and publisher Samuel Rayburn
were accused of concealing the identity of the infamous
rebel agent, Rebecca Rayburn, whose treasonable activities had begun long before the declaration of war.

Identifying himself as a loyalist agent who'd failed in
his own attempt to capture this spy three years earlier,
Roger wrote a starkly convincing account of a seductive
woman who'd traded sex for official British secrets. The
daughter of the avowed rebel Colonel Jeremy Rayburn,
and the surviving mistress of the late pirate-privateer Philip
Keane, Rebecca Rayburn was credited with beginning her
espionage career as a girl by sleeping with the British
naval officers who visited her loyalist uncle in Falmouth.
The information she collected had been turned over to her
father. In New Bedford she had seduced the captain of a
British ship-of-line, and in Connecticut she had lured an
undercover British major to his death. Taken by her pirate
lover to the French colony of Saint-Domingue, she'd
become a voodoo mambo and the scandalous mistress of a
black revolutionary. After her expulsion from that dissolute
colony, she'd inveigled Colonel Crane into bringing her to
New York, where she'd seduced at least one more British
officer.

Supported liberally with twisted quotations from Rebecca's
published stories, the completed document was a masterpiece of vilification. As he emerged for the last time from
the printer's dingy office, Roger was smiling with satisfaction. There was no way the albino bitch could escape
punishment this time! He was still smiling when he issued
his last command to the frontier mercenaries who'd served
as his scouts for three years. They were ordered to deliver
the six separate packets of the newspaper to the various
military headquarters on the three islands and to the
leading booksellers of Manhattan. Four nights later, after a
hundred-mile horseback ride to the unguarded northern

reaches of Long Island, Major Tupton sailed to New Haven, Connecticut, aboard a colonial fishing boat. Within a month he was reunited with his father. His only mistake was in choosing northwestern New York as his refuge. The six tribes of Iroquois Indians were united into a nation; and the individual members, whether Tuscarora or Mohawk or Seneca, never forgave or forgot a white brother who'd played any one of them false.

Had Roger not included the name of Colonel Crane in his accusation, his revenge might have succeeded completely. But Weldon Crane was too experienced a professional to be trapped by an amateur. By claiming that he'd sent Samuel and Rebecca to Albany to investigate the treasonable theft of Seneca lands by the renegade Tupton, Crane succeeded in reversing the charge of treason. Because of his need to clear his own name of any hint of misconduct in office, he convinced the other military leaders that Rebecca Keane had never engaged in espionage against the crown. However, he refused Samuel's request that he denounce the other lies Roger had printed.

"Why not?" Samuel demanded.

"Because I don't know which ones are true and which are false. She lied to me about her marriage; and long before she learned that she was a widow in reality, she promised to marry your nephew."

"That was a private family matter. How did you hear of it?"

"As soon as Captain Enderly requested permission to move her to Philadelphia, I reopened my investigation of your inventively mendacious niece by sending for Philadelphia newspapers. When I read about Keane's death, I remembered her mention of Roger Tupton and communicated with him to learn the rest of her story."

"You believed what that scoundrel told you?"

"Not entirely. Her father was equally informative. I decided then to let him tell her of Keane's death, and I decided that it would be more effective if Tupton told your nephew about her."

"So you sent Kent into that deadly situation."

"I didn't know about the Seneca land problem then.

Tupton was reputed to be one of our finest loyalist agents until—''

"Until he revealed his true colors and deserted!''

"As you say, Rayburn, he was a scoundrel, but he did expose your niece as a potential problem. General Clinton wants her removed from your newspaper and from this estate. He's worried about her easy access to the river and to any possible contact with the enemy. I did persuade him that she didn't require actual detention, but he's adamant that she be moved into the central city.''

"Is there any way you can return her to colonial-held territory?''

"Don't be a fool! She's had better access to your unique information files than I have.''

"How long before you force her to leave my home?''

"A few weeks at the most, but I advise you to get her out of here as soon as possible—and without telling Captain Enderly where you've located her.''

"Why?''

"I'm afraid your nephew does not learn from experience. He'll be killed if he persists in his current insanity of attempting to clear Mistress Keane's name by force. So far he's been fortunate that the men he's challenged have been gentlemen, but—''

"Duels?'' Samuel sputtered. "Kent's been fighting duels over that damned article?''

"Several of them that I know of. After he failed to locate Tupton and force a public retraction, he—''

"Thank God he didn't find that villain!''

"Agreed, but he could be in even greater danger now. These are English gentlemen he's fighting, not colonial rabble.''

While Colonel Crane's warning may have been well intended, his claim that Kent's dueling opponents had all been gentlemen was erroneous. One of them at least was a gentleman in name only. A brash lieutenant—whose arrogance, bad manners, and uncontrolled temper stemmed from expectations of wealth and a prestigious title—had been forced to make a public apology to a victorious Kent Enderly after only minutes of dueling. Never having learned to accept discipline or punishment, the Honorable William Ramsden decided on a revenge that would make Kent Enderly the laughingstock.

Inviting a fellow officer equally lacking in moral restraint to accompany him on what he promised would be a merry romp, Ramsden paid a visit to the notorious Rebecca Rayburn for the purpose of proving her the available courtesan the article had claimed. So specific were Roger Tupton's directions to her home, the two half-drunk officers had no trouble avoiding the loyalist recruits who guarded the estate's entrance at night or locating the cottage. Although Ramsden's primary interest was the restoration of his own prestige, he was intrigued by the prospect of a night's bed play with a woman he'd heard described as uncommonly beautiful. An experienced rakehell, he was prepared to pay whatever she asked. During his year-long tour of duty in the imprisoned city, he'd found few women who could resist the lure of a sufficiently large number of gold sovereigns.

Inside the cottage Rebecca was attempting to concentrate on a goal she'd set for herself immediately after the disagreeable scene in her uncles' library. She was organizing the notes she'd taken from the log aboard the *Reine* and adding to them all she remembered of her husband's life other than her own intimate memories. The record was not for publication, but for Michael when he was old enough to be told about his father. Although her own grief had dulled into a poignant realization that she'd never again experience the wild, sweet excitement of Philip's love, she still found the task emotionally shattering—enough to keep her awake each lonely night of her self-appointed vigil. Not until early morning, when Reverend Stebbins arrived to tutor her brothers, did she dare sleep for a few hours.

It had been the minister who'd brought her a copy of the damning newspaper and a brief note from Samuel stating that there would be no official action taken. Perhaps in atonement for his earlier gullibility, Stebbins had accepted Samuel's fierce declaration of her innocence and had become a friend to the young woman whose grief was so obviously sincere.

The only other visitor Rebecca had seen during those tense weeks had been Kent Enderly. He had been broodingly protective during each visit, mentioning neither her impending eviction nor his own dangerous preoccupation in her defense. But his attempts to convince her that she was no longer in any danger fell on deaf ears. Rebecca had too many bitter experiences with the social ostracism of her youth and with Roger Tupton's persecution to be easily reassured.

On this night, her first awareness of another unpleasant intrusion into her life was the noise of scuffling on the front porch and Klaus's warning shout. There was no mistaking the gardener's voice; even after a century of British rule, uneducated Walloon-Americans reverted to the Dutch language in moments of stress. Curses in English quickly followed the first outcry, and then came the sounds that galvanized Rebecca into terrified action. Gripping one of her pistols, she fumbled with the latching of the door, opening it in time to hear Klaus's agonizing scream of pain as the arm that had held only a shovel as a weapon was mercilessly slashed by a sword.

Only one man followed Rebecca as she backed into the room; the other Englishman leaned weakly against the door frame, his pale face streaked with blood from a wound on his head. Klaus had landed at least one blow before he'd been incapacitated. Holding a pistol pointing steadily at the threatening intruder, Rebecca reached for the second gun lying in readiness on the kitchen table. Slowly a smoldering anger replaced her earlier terror.

In the room only dimly illuminated by a small whale-oil lamp on the table, Rebecca kept her eyes unswervingly on the figure of the British officer facing her from twelve feet away. Her only response to his angry, officious command that she put the weapons down was a tightening of her hands around the polished wood of the pistol butts. But when he took a tentative step in her direction, her voice rasped out harshly, "Move back. At this distance I won't miss."

Straining to hear the faint sounds of awakening coming from upstairs, Rebecca was only dimly aware when the second man lost his hold on consciousness and slipped heavily to the floor.

"For God's sake, mistress," William Ramsden blustered, "we have to get help for my friend. Your cursed man attacked us without warning, and we were forced to defend ourselves."

Rebecca's frozen expression didn't change as her eyes flickered briefly downward to the bloodstained saber still gripped in Ramsden's hand, but her only words were a relentless "Don't move"; and the muzzles of both pistols remained directly aimed at the expanse of white breeches covering the man's plump midsection.

Suddenly aware of a shaking Dena standing mutely in the entrance to the rear hallway, Rebecca ordered sharply, "Use the back door, Dena, and fetch Colonel Crane and my uncles. You'd better tell them to send for a doctor."

As if this longer speech on the woman's part had relaxed his own vocal cords, the Honorable William Ramsden began to talk, pleadingly at times, boastfully at others—a rambling monologue about the importance of his family, the pride in possessing a five-hundred-year-old name, the social jungle that was the American colonies, and the dearth of entertainment in the dreary city of Manhattan. But beneath the lightness of his words, delivered with the speed of upper-class Englishmen, Rebecca sensed his underlying fury at being trapped in so humiliating a situation.

"Let's sit down, mistress, and act like civilized people," he wheedled. "We intended you no harm; it was a purely pleasurable visit to while away a winter's evening. And you would have benefited in the end. It can't be easy for someone like yourself to be away from your own kind, trapped among conquerors who have been cruel perhaps."

She watched the parody of a smile that spread across his perspiring face; she could almost have predicted his predictable next words.

"You're a woman of the world, mistress, and a young and pretty one." She heard the wavering in his voice over the word *pretty* and knew she looked as grim as an avenging Fury of Greek mythology. But William Ramsden was not a sensitive man or one who could admit gracefully to failure. He didn't know who the devil this Crane was, but he didn't relish being set down by any superior. With a recklessness rooted equally in alcohol and desperation, he moved forward, unconscious as he did so that he'd raised his sword to an operable position.

With a soft moan, Rebecca retreated until her back was against the stone wall of the fireplace. She hated this arrogant, immature cockerel of a man enough to wish him dead, but she didn't have the courage or the will to kill him. She listened to his high-pitched, braying laughter with a sick despair.

"Never met a woman yet who couldn't be bluffed," he gloated. "Now put those pistols down if you value that smooth skin of yours. And when that colonel of yours arrives, you're to tell him that my friend and I were invited here."

With a fatalistic desperation she raised one pistol and discharged it at an unseen target a foot to the right of his leering face. His slow advance stopped as if he'd been sledgehammered.

"You goddamned bitch," he shrilled, "you might have killed me!"

"Too bad she didn't, Ramsden," Kent Enderly shouted from the open front doorway. "But I'll have no trouble finishing the job I began the other day."

"Don't bother, Kent," Rebecca mumbled dully. "Just get him out of here and see to Klaus. I think they killed him."

Without a backward glance she walked unsteadily from the room, replaced the useless pistols in her trunk, and climbed the stairs to rescue three frightened, shivering children from the cold hidey-hole.

"There's nothing to be afraid of anymore," she assured them flatly. "Kent's downstairs now, and I'll stay right here with you all night long."

"Was it those men Roger brought here with him?" Lloyd asked.

"No, sweetheart, these men were different."

"They were lobsterbacks," Johnny whispered, "lobsterbacks like old Colonel Crane, weren't they, Becky?"

"Yes, sweetheart, they were lobsterbacks!"

Tucking them all into the one large bed, Rebecca wrapped a blanket around herself and sat wearily down in Dena's rocking chair to think. By morning she'd decided on a plan of action.

"We have to move," she announced abruptly to the Negro girl the next morning as they prepared breakfast.

"I knows we do. Misser Kent done already told me t' start packin'. He say he's gonna take care of us jest lak he al'ays planned."

"When did he tell you that?" Rebecca demanded irritably.

"Las' night after that no-count colonel done take that redcoat trash away. Misser Kent say it 'uz his fault they 'uz here 'cause he done already whup the one who come after you."

"In a fight, Dena?"

"Sometimes, Miz Rebecca, you acts lak you don't know nothin' 'bout what goes on 'round here. Misser Kent done been fightin' duels."

"Oh, my God! So that was what that fool was talking about last night. Do you know where Kent is right now, Dena?"

" 'Spect I does."

"Where?"

"Jest where he done planned t' be—in your bed."

"The devil he is!"

"Ain't no use fussin', Miz Rebecca. Misser Kent done say he's gonna take care of us. An' that ole colonel done say we got t' git out of here anyways. We needs a man t' take care of us 'cause them chil'run's been scairt a long time."

"What happened after I went upstairs?"

"Time I got here wif Misser Joshua and Misser Samuel, that loud-moufed scalawag was tied to a chair and Klaus was gittin' his arm tended by the doctor."

"I thought he was—"

"He 'uz cut up and bleedin', but he 'uz better off than

that one he done bashed with a shovel. Doctor say that one—''

"That one deserved what he got. Dena, what did my uncles say when Kent told them about his taking care of us?''

"Old Joshua sputtered some, but Misser Samuel say it 'uz for the best, 'specially when I tells him you 'uz stayin' up at night 'cause we 'uz all scairt. Misser Samuel jest nodded his head to Misser Kent. So I 'spect it's all settled.''

"The devil it is! We'll locate our own home with people who need money more than they do respectable boarders.''

"You knows better, Miz Rebecca. This town done already burn half down. 'Sides, nobody 'ud care 'bout us lak Misser Kent, an' don' you be forgittin' 'bout food. Poor folk goes hungry; an' lessen we lives here, Misser Samuel don' have 'nuff to give us.''

Rebecca stared at the Negro girl in dismay; her own plans had included none of these practicalities. Nor had she taken into consideration the limited amount of money she possessed. If Colonel Crane insists I leave here, she thought dismally, I may be forced to accept Kent's charity. Dena's right; from now on, I have to consider the children first. When Rebecca knocked on the bedroom door, she felt as helpless as she had eight years earlier after she'd buried her mother.

"Wake up, Kent,'' she called out. "I want to talk to you.''

Startled by the strange voice that responded to her demand, she pushed the door open and stared in shock at the scene which greeted her. Kent was stretched out on the bed in obvious pain while the man Rebecca recognized as his self-effacing valet was rebandaging his young master's bloody shoulder and arm. No stranger to battle wounds after her stay at El Abrigo, she waited silently until the critical task was completed—quite expertly, she reflected, by a man who'd had considerable experience in such matters.

"He reopened both wounds last night when he rushed to your defense,'' Malcolm Garner explained quietly. "I would appreciate your encouraging him to remain in bed for a few days, Madam Keane. The master tends to be reckless about his own safety.''

Studying the beads of perspiration that dampened the ''master's'' pale face, Rebecca nodded grimly and held the door open for the valet, whose arms were laden with stained linens and a tray of medicines.

''He won't leave that bed until he's completely healed,'' she promised as she gazed at the wounded man, more than a little upset that she'd been the cause of his injuries.

''I didn't want you to know,'' Kent muttered, meeting her eyes with a feeble attempt at a smile.

''Why did you do it?''

''It was the only means I had of protecting you.''

''Was it the *honorable* William Ramsden who cut you?''

''No, but someone just as much a scoundrel. Why didn't you just shoot the drunken braggart, Rebecca?''

''I didn't wish to become the main performer at a public hanging,'' she retorted defensively. ''If only half of his boasts were true, his family would have made quite certain that I was properly punished. Besides, I couldn't, Kent— not in cold blood—no more than you could have killed him during the duel.''

''Did you know that Colonel Crane wouldn't even allow Uncle Samuel to charge him with trespassing?''

''The colonel has a peculiar weakness for men whose fathers have impressive titles.''

''I know. That's why he promised you'd be safe with me.''

''Kent, is it true that he's going to force me to leave here?''

''For once, Crane is not the villain. It's General Clinton who insists.''

Rebecca sucked in her breath slowly. ''Will you help me locate some home where the children will be safe?''

''I already have, and as soon as the doctor will allow me up—''

''When did you?''

''Right after that damned liar—right after that day in Uncle Samuel's library, I told Malcolm to start looking. A week ago I bought the town house he and Uncle Samuel located. It's a small home on a quiet street with six resident soldiers quartered in the carriage house and a dozen neighbors close enough to discourage intruders.''

Disconcerted by the thoroughness of his planning, Rebecca mumbled, ''I can't accept your charity, Kent.''

Sensitive to her reluctance, Kent continued his recital of particulars with a subtle change of emphasis. ''The children will be much happier there, Rebecca, because there'll be more for them to do. One of the soldiers has promised to teach them ice skating, and there's enough slope on the street for sledding. As for their education, Uncle Samuel said that the Stebbins fellow will be delighted to have a shorter distance to travel.''

''How long has Uncle Samuel known about these plans of yours, Kent?''

''When he found out how many officers believed what they'd read.''

''You mean when he found out you were risking your life! Kent, you can't change people's minds by force. That's why I don't think idiots like the one last night are going to respect me any more in a town house than they do here.''

''There is a way, Rebecca,'' Kent said slowly.

Her response was instant and negative. ''No, there isn't, Kent, not now—perhaps not ever. I can't marry you.'' Rising swiftly from the edge of the bed, Rebecca fled from the room.

The following week her independence was even more subtly undermined. Even though he remained bedridden at the doctor's insistence, Kent began to exert a skillful domination over the family. Exhausted by months of strain, Rebecca relaxed enough to sleep most of that first day in the loft; and before two days had passed, Dena discovered the magic words of discipline, ''Misser Kent say so!'' Lloyd and Johnny lost the pinched, guarded expressions that had become habitual since Rebecca's return from Albany. And Michael found his soul mate—a grown-up who answered his infantile, garbled questions with serious consideration.

Repressing the twinge of jealousy that troubled her, Rebecca complimented the man who'd so quickly become a part of her family. "You're better with children than anyone I've ever known—except my mother."

Kent's laughter was warmly unrestrained. "My one small claim to success! Whenever my older brothers and sisters dumped their children at the family's country estate—and that was just about every time I was home from school, even my mother departed hastily for London. So I had absolutely no competition in winning their affection or in learning how to keep them on the hop and out of trouble. But none of them really needed me—not like Johnny or Michael. Lloyd's already acquired enough independence to survive, but Johnny needs reassurance—and I plan to give it to him unless you object."

"No, not really."

"Then what *are* you objecting to? I've told you that Malcolm and I will be living in rented rooms two houses away. So there'll be no scandal."

"That's just it, Kent. It's your home, and you've refused to let me pay any of the expenses."

"Uncle Samuel's paying Reverend Stebbins; and since we're taking all of the supplies from here, there won't be many other costs."

"I do have money in England; and if you'll trust me, I could pay for the house. I dislike the idea of being dependent on your father's money."

"You won't be; my money's quite separate from the family's—a legacy from a great-uncle no one else would talk to, and one my mother believed was a penniless old reprobate. When he died a year ago, he left me a bundle slightly larger than my father's fortune and a rambling estate in Wales that I've never seen. Now, will you stop worrying and start packing; tomorrow's moving day."

It was also Rebecca's second wedding day!

Three hours after she'd left Kent in the bedroom, she was summoned by an imperious shout from the loft where she'd been supervising the packing. Downstairs she found an agitated Samuel pacing the floor, and her heartbeat increased with dread anticipation. Not once in fourteen months had he ever visited her in the cottage unless there was an emergency. Silently he handed her a folded letter.

"It's a directive from General Clinton," he rasped angrily as Rebecca scanned the brief paragraphs.

"It's blunt enough," she murmured without inflection.

"Nothing but cursed meddling interference!" he blustered.

"Whose?"

"Colonel Crane suffers from the delusion that Kent's father will be grateful, and Joshua is afraid Kent will become involved again. My God, as if he ever stopped!"

"You'd better take the letter in to him, Uncle Samuel. He'll have to obey those orders."

"Where are the children?"

"Upstairs with Dena."

"Tell them to remain there, and then you wait right here."

Seconds after Samuel had reached the bedroom, Dena flounced down the bottom two stairs, her arms akimbo and her broad face rigid with curiosity.

"What 'uz writ on that paper, Miz Rebecca?"

"It seems there's an army regulation that prohibits officers in His Majesty's service from associating with undesirable enemy civilians during an occupation."

"What's that t' do with Misser Kent?"

"It means he can't have anything to do with us—with me."

"Misser Kent don' stan' for nothin' lak that."

"He has no choice, Dena."

"You jest wait, Miz Rebecca. Ain't no way that ole redcoat colonel kin—"

"This time it was a redcoat general."

Both women jerked at the sound of a softly articulated imperative issuing from the bedroom, and Dena broke the tense silence with a chuckle.

"Misser Kent don' ever shout, but he sho do make hisself heard."

"Get upstairs, Dena, and keep the others from knowing as long as you can."

"Yes 'um, but you 'members t' listen t' what Misser Kent say."

As Rebecca headed reluctantly toward the bedroom, Samuel emerged to give her the same advice.

"At least listen to him, my dear. The only alternative you'll have will be a slum shanty that belongs to one of my printers. You know the conditions in that part of the city as well as I do, and you'd be risking your children's lives."

Rebecca shook her head. "I know what he wants, and I can't, Uncle Samuel."

"Just listen to what he has to say. I think he'll agree to whatever restrictions you place upon him."

Half an hour later Rebecca agreed to her second name-only marriage!

Early the following morning in the crowded bedroom, the brief ceremony proved to be remarkably similar to the one three years earlier in a crude log cabin with a disconcerted Reverend Stebbins instead of a dour Scot parson, Rebecca's three instead of the Purdy children, and hastily assembled servants instead of hastily summoned fishermen.

The similarities ended there, though. Samuel Rayburn and Malcolm Garner signed their names with a relieved flourish; and an hour later the bridegroom proudly announced the *fait accompli* to a peppery Colonel Crane and a disapproving Joshua Rayburn. Throughout that awkward meeting, Rebecca remained silent, her thoughts buried in the bittersweet past when a reluctant Philip Keane waited months to claim her publicly. In contrast, Kent sounded triumphant.

"My wife Rebecca, gentlemen."

Crane's mouth was grimly set and his words chipped out like bits of ice. "You defied a direct order, Captain Enderly."

With characteristic aplomb, Samuel intercepted the reprimand. "He never received it, Colonel. In the excitement I forgot all about General Clinton's letter labeling my niece an undesirable enemy civilian."

"This marriage does not change her status, Rayburn; it merely focuses attention on your nephew," Crane snapped.

Watching Kent's charming smile and listening to his subtle response to Crane's gibe, Rebecca was suddenly reminded that her new husband was an articulate aristocrat whose social rank took precedence over the older officer's military superiority.

"That's where it should be, Colonel, and I hope you're friend enough to help me protect her privacy in the future." Without waiting for a reply, Kent addressed Joshua Rayburn, whose lips were still held tightly pursed.

"Why the dour face, Uncle Joshua?"

"Rebecca knows that my objection is not personal, Kent," he replied stiffly, "but she has not been widowed long enough. And you know that your mother had very definite plans for you."

"I met that definite plan four years ago, Uncle. The girl in question had the rehearsed vocabulary of Johnny, but only half the intelligence. And now, gentlemen, if you'll excuse me, I'm moving my family to our new home, where all of you will be welcome, providing you come as friends."

Six weeks after moving into a home much more formal than the cottage, Rebecca still marveled at the easy transition her brothers had made to a more regimented and disciplined life. They'd adjusted to being tutored in a cloistered second-story schoolroom, to formal meals in a dining room under Kent's firmly benevolent control, and to afternoon sledding and skating sessions supervised by an athletic young soldier. Even the ebullient and heedless Michael seemed content to spend quiet hours with Kent in the fire-warmed parlor without shrieking to join his young uncles on every outing.

At first Rebecca had worried that Dena would resent Malcolm Garner's quietly efficient household management and the two taciturn Swedish maids who reported each morning to do the cleaning, washing, and basic food preparation. Rebecca had been especially concerned that the Negro girl would be hurt when she was excluded from eating with the family. But Dena had reacted cheerfully to the challenge of cooking for thirteen people instead of five, and she'd quickly decided that the six soldiers who complimented her increasing cooking skills were "quality folk" rather than "redcoat trash."

For Rebecca herself there'd been no easy adjustment; much of the time she felt like a guest rather than the mistress of the house. During the month of Kent's continuing convalescence, she spent hours each day in his company, reminding herself that even a name-only marriage needed to develop a cohesive unity. Because he honored the agreement they'd made, she gradually relaxed enough to accept the friendship he offered and the advice. He encouraged her to resume her artwork and sent Malcolm into the city to secure the oil paints and canvases. Rebecca had responded halfheartedly by beginning a portrait of Kent himself. To her surprise, she'd found him as easy a subject as Brian Sinclair had been three years earlier. He'd also been good company for her as she worked, keeping Michael entertained with quiet games and lively stories. Unavoidably, though, his adult conversation frequently wavered into sensitive areas despite her determination to keep it impersonal.

"How do you want yourself immortalized, Kent—glorified or realistic?" she'd asked jokingly.

"Just as I am, but a foot taller."

"You're tall enough."

"Am I, Rebecca?"

"Yes."

The subtlety of his reminders kept her aware that she wasn't really a wife—only another dependent he was supporting; and she hated the idea of surrendering her self-reliance. Always before she'd earned her own keep—with her father, with Silas, with her Uncle Samuel, and eventually with Philip. Toward the end of that marriage she'd finally become adult enough, she reflected sadly, to be an understanding wife. How she wished Philip had lived long enough to know that she'd adopted his child. That regret and an oppressive sense of betrayal had inhibited Rebecca's adjustment to the new marriage she'd accepted out of necessity. She even welcomed Kent's return to courier duty with relief, but that relief quickly turned into worry when another winter storm blanketed the entire American coast with icy drifts of snow. Everyone in the household was concerned about the man who'd become the pivotal stability in their lives, Michael most of all. The two-year-old would call out Kent's name at every sound of anyone entering or leaving the house, and he stood with his face pressing against a window overlooking the street much of the time.

During one of his infrequent visits, Samuel commented on the child's behavior. "Your son needs a father, Rebecca. Why not allow Kent to take over the job permanently?"

"He has already," she retorted defensively.

"No, my dear, Kent is very aware that you consider this marriage only a temporary stopgap in your life."

Rebecca hated her uncle's perceptive understanding, and she resented her own loneliness. Except for Dena and an occasional friendly greeting from one or another of the resident soldiers, she had little to keep her restless intellect alive. On her uncles' estate she'd had the stimulation of the *Observer* workroom, but here she was more isolated than she'd ever been in her life. Without Kent's attentive companionship and his shared interest in the children's problems, Rebecca no longer felt confident enough to raise them alone. She could not help her brothers with their Latin homework as Kent had done; she lacked the necessary training to continue their education in social graces at the table; and she was too depressed to entertain them as she had throughout the year on her uncles' estate.

By the time Kent returned after a six-day absence, she welcomed him as fervently as did the children, only to spoil the reunion by starting a quarrel. He'd brought back a sedate, middle-aged Shetland pony he'd located on a Long Island farm. As her brothers and Michael squealed in delight, she'd exclaimed in dismay, "They don't need any pets other than the goats, Kent."

"Every child needs a pony," he insisted, his own temper provoked by her sharp asperity.

"I don't want them to have expectations beyond my—"

"Since I'm now in charge of their futures as much as you—"

"You're not!"

"Yes, I am, Rebecca. Our marriage gives me that right

at least. Would you mind telling me why you're so angry?''

At his look of sensitive vulnerability, Rebecca's irrational resentment dissipated, and her complaint was only token. ''You're spoiling them, Kent; they didn't know what to do while you were gone.''

Kent's voice was casual, but his appraisal of her averted face was not. ''How about you, Rebecca?''

''I missed you too,'' she admitted.

Two days later Kent was again assigned the same courier duty, and within weeks he'd established a reputation as the swiftest messenger on General Clinton's staff. Each week he carried a pouch of orders from Clinton to his subordinates on Staten Island and Long Island, making the trip in three days largely at his own expense. Instead of relying on navel craft large enough to transport the courier's horse, Kent hired a pair of Long Island smugglers whose small, sturdy boat could travel under more adverse conditions; and he used the snowshoes he'd brought from Canada. Clad in wolf-skin boots, pants, and hooded coat with the fur on the inside, he was well enough insulated to travel under all but blizzard conditions. Because he was the most reliable courier on the island route, whose multiple stops covered more than two hundred miles of combined water and land, he avoided the longer assignments to Philadelphia.

With Kent in residence four days a week, the household quickly resettled to a lively routine. There were times when Rebecca considered herself the only adult family member; Kent seemed as tireless as the children in sledding, skating, and snowball fights, with occasional hours on the sunnier days devoted to teaching Lloyd and Johnny ponyback riding. During those lessons Michael was always in attendance; but his pony was Kent's shoulders, a favorite roost he had appropriated six months earlier on the first of the swimming parties. Usually Rebecca accompanied them to the various recreation spots, frequently occupying herself with graphite sketches of the four participants. Ironically, it was the least active of these sports that almost ended in tragedy.

Always less adventuresome than his older brother, Johnny was astride the staid pony, proceeding at a cautious pace on the small meadow near the skating pond. No one saw the hard-packed snowball that struck the pony's head, only the horrifying result when the startled animal bolted toward the pond with a terrified child clinging to its back. Instantly, Kent shoved Michael into Rebecca's arms and started running, reaching the pond just after sharp hooves had broken through the ice. Rebecca arrived in time to comfort the sobbing child and help Kent extricate the shuddering pony from the broken ice at the shallow edge of the pond. If the pony had crashed through the ice at the center of the pond where the water was deeper, the small accident might have become a deadly one. Even so, Kent was thoroughly soaked by the time the subdued family headed home with all three children on the pony's back and with Kent swaddled in Rebecca's long cloak.

Because her bedroom was the only fire-warmed room upstairs, Rebecca insisted that Malcolm put his half-frozen young master there while she herded the children into the kitchen.

"Is the coffee hot, Dena?" she demanded.

"Yes 'um. What happened to Misser Kent?"

"Johnny will tell you all about it while Lloyd takes care of the pony. Michael, you sit right here and mind what Dena tells you. I'm going upstairs."

Kent was still being disrobed when she arrived in the room, but she ignored his embarrassed protests. Setting the coffeepot on the mantel of the small Franklin stove, she removed a long-hoarded bottle of rum from her trunk and poured a liberal portion into the steaming coffee.

"I told you a month ago that we didn't need that damned pony," she scolded as she held a cup of the pungent brew to Kent's blue lips.

"How is Johnny?" he sputtered.

"He's bragging his head off to Dena; Lloyd is rubbing that idiot pony down; and Michael is stuffing himself with gingerbread. Now, let's talk about you. How is he, Malcolm?"

"He'll be all right, Mrs. Enderly, as soon as he gets warm."

"Then I'll tend to him while you supervise the children's supper. In an hour you can bring Kent's and my dinner here."

"You don't have to take care of me, Rebecca," Kent protested after Malcolm had left the room, burdened with an armful of wet clothing.

"No, but I'm going to anyway. That was my brother you rushed to save today."

"It wasn't very dangerous."

"You'd have gone after him regardless of the danger. Can you hold your own cup yet?"

"I can if you get my robe. It's in the dressing room opposite yours."

"I know where it is, Kent. In case you haven't noticed, our rooms are connected." Rebecca didn't wait to hear his rejoinder; she was intent on rehearsing a speech that had been forming in her mind for a week or more. In the man's dressing room that was twin to her own, she absently noted the precision neatness of the twenty uniforms, an equal number of other suits, and the array of boots, shoes, and hats. Momentarily, this discreet reminder of Kent's wealth made her pause; despite his youthful enthusiasms, he was a sophisticated and educated man. Just how permanent, she wondered, would his interest in an unconventional colonial widow prove to be? Picking up his elegantly furred brown robe, she retreated into her own dressing room, removed the drab clothing she was wearing, and donned the plainest of her own robes, a modest green wool she'd purchased the previous winter. Pausing only long enough to wash her face and brush her hair, she returned resolutely to her bedroom.

"Kent," she blurted before she lost her courage, "the agreement we made when you married me isn't working."

Instantly on guard, he disclaimed swiftly, "I've no complaints. I know you consented out of desperation, Rebecca, and that you're still in mourning for Philip Keane; but I think you need me anyway."

"I know I do, Kent, and that's why we should make our marriage permanent." –

"It's already permanent to me."

"It's a sham and you know it. I would like it to become real, Kent—that is, if you haven't changed your mind."

"Because you're grateful to me, Rebecca?"

"Partly, but there's more."

"What about your feelings for your late husband?"

Rebecca took a deep, ragged breath. "I loved Philip very much; and I still don't know exactly how I feel about you, except that I miss you when you're not here. I think we'd both be happier if you shared my room and my bed. You room's as cold as an ice house anyway, so at least you wouldn't have chilblained feet in here. Have you thawed out yet, or do you need some more hot bricks?"

Kent's laughter was softly triumphant. "I feel warmer than I ever have in my life. How soon can we put Michael and your brothers to bed?"

Two hours later, though, after he'd helped her tuck the three tired boys into their beds—something he hadn't done since the one time he'd carried Michael upstairs at the cottage—Kent seemed oddly nervous as Rebecca joined him in their own bed.

Perplexed after his earlier warm humor, she murmured, "I won't break, Kent."

"You're thinner than you were last summer," he mumbled.

"You've a good memory, Kent Enderly."

"Where you're concerned, I do. Someday, Rebecca, I hope you'll be as much in love with me as I am with you. Then maybe I'll be able to tell you how much you mean to me without feeling like a fool."

Sobered by the depth of his avowal, Rebecca put her arms around him. "Love isn't an exact science, Kent. I don't think anyone knows what it is or why it's so unpredictable. But at least we have an advantage in the physical part; we can teach each other." She'd added this last sentence cautiously since he seemed to need reminding that she wasn't an inexperienced girl facing an unknown ordeal. His hesitant response to her blunt admission brought the warm laughter of relief bubbling to her lips. It wasn't her inexperience that had been worrying him; it was his own. Never had she considered the possibility that a twenty-five-year-old man could be virginal or almost so, especially not a man with Kent's charm or self-assurance at social functions.

"You'll have to do most of the teaching," he blurted. "My education ended after one initiation at Oxford. It just wasn't something I wanted to share with a woman I didn't know or much like. Until you came along, I was never tempted; but now I wish I were so expert you couldn't resist me."

Touched by his blunt honesty and by the memory of her own raw ignorance years before, Rebecca took the lead with a gently caressing kiss. When his arms gripped her body, she shook her head and guided his hand to her breast, relieved that she felt no embarrassment and pleased by his ardent reception of her gesture. Whatever the limitations of his past indulgence, his innate sensitivity to her needs kept pace with his passion. Only when her questing hand moved caressingly down his muscular abdomen did he restrain her.

"Better not, my beloved Circe," he cautioned her with a rueful laugh, "unless you're just as ready. I feel like a volcano about to erupt."

That thread of humor woven early into the fabric of their relationship established a rapport which eliminated the remainder of their inhibitions.

"In that case," she murmured judicially as she moved sinuously against him, "you're ready for the next set of instructions."

"That part I remember," he whispered with an exuberant chuckle, and accepted her invitation. Contrary to her expectations, his trembling eagerness did not signify a lack of control. He entered her slowly and waited for her to set the pace, and Rebecca soon lost all awareness of his inexperience as her responding passion swept her swiftly toward the physical narcotic of ecstasy.

Afterward as their bodies cooled and their breathing slowed, she reflected with a sleepy satisfaction that both of them had reached fulfillment. Kent had outlasted her with a strength of will that overrode his own tumultuous passion. But the greater part of her contentment was the awareness that he hadn't lied to her—he wasn't an experienced lover! There'd be no shadowy ghosts of other women to haunt her, to make her doubt his love for her. During his moment of release, he'd cried out her name and mumbled nothing but praise for her alone; and his ingenuous exclamation immediately after held the warm humor she loved.

Propping himself up on his elbows, he grinned down at her. "I don't want to leave you, because this is one of those skills that needs frequent practice. I hope you weren't planning on any sleep tonight."

Rebecca's laughter was muted as she pushed him away and snuggled deeper into the warm bed. "You don't need any more practice, Kent Enderly, so you can stop boasting. If you aren't as tired as I am, you should be."

His echoing chuckle was the last sound she heard before she fell asleep, but his playful boast had not been an empty one. Twice again during the night he awakened her with gentle caresses and made increasingly competent love to her. His sustained virility was still another unexpected surprise to the young woman who'd stopped being his name-only wife.

CHAPTER
18

SCHEDULED for another courier circuit the next morning, Kent kissed Rebecca good-bye without asking any probing questions or referring sentimentally to the night just past. Once again she was left alone with her troubled thoughts and a vague uneasiness. The decision to end the awkward, two-month probation to this new marriage had seemed so morally right when she'd made it; but in the cheerless light of another wintry day without her new husband himself to reassure her, Rebecca experienced the sinking sensation that, as always, she'd acted in haste. Despite her fondness for Kent and the physical satisfaction of their lovemaking, she knew that part of their future life together would be blighted by her need to pretend. She could never feel for this man the wild surge of overwhelming love she'd felt for Philip Keane. And Kent was too sensitive to her emotions to be persuaded easily that she did. She would need a constant source of creative diversions to keep herself content and her husband as happy as he'd been this morning.

Late in the afternoon, after a day with Michael and her restless brothers pent up inside the house by a drizzling rain, Rebecca's exasperation turned into wry humor. Once Kent was released from the army, he'd be there to help her cope with the three children, who were no longer satisfied without the excitement he'd infused into their lives. That night she began her first really creative writing since her early days at El Abrigo when she'd survived another separation from another husband.

With only her memories and imagination for inspiration, she devised a lighthearted tale about a cabin boy whose leprechaun heritage enabled him to locate buried pirate treasure. Part Willy Beckworth and part Kent Enderly, the boy hero was both comically brash and charmingly persuasive; and his adventures were nothing more than childish fantasies that ended happily in fifteen pages. While Michael played with his hobbyhorse the following morning, Rebecca wrote a second Willikin story. As she worked, she paused occasionally to read what she'd written out loud; and occasionally Michael listened. To her delight, when Johnny and Lloyd joined them for lunch, the two-year-old shouted the word *Willikin* in greeting. During the afternoon Johnny became her second audience, an intent listener whose eyes gleamed with comprehension and whose usually sober young face was wrinkled by quiet laughter.

Looking at this brother who resembled her so closely, Rebecca asked impulsively, "Would you like to help me write these stories, Johnny?"

"I don't know," he responded doubtfully. "I don't know all the words yet."

"But you can help me with ideas. If you had your choice, what would you like a story to be about?"

"About yesterday, about how Prince didn't hurt me and how he couldn't see where he was running because the snow was in his eyes."

"Is Prince the name of your pony, Johnny?"

Johnny's eyes were defensive as he noticed his older brother glaring at him. "It's my name for him," he declared defiantly.

"But his real name is Leatherback, Becky," Lloyd explained with the lofty superiority of one year seniority. "Prince was an old mule on Uncle Myles's farm that nobody liked except Johnny. And old Prince was just as slow and stubborn as old Leatherback too."

Rebecca smiled at the older brother; Lloyd was the absolute realist, she reflected; their Uncle Samuel would have a difficult time turning him into an imaginative journalist.

"Do you mind if Johnny and I change Leatherback's name to Prince in a story?"

"It won't be a true story," Lloyd persisted.

"Stories rarely are. Do you mind?"

"Guess not, but you can't change my goat's name, even in a story."

"What is your goat's name, Lloyd?"

"It's Nanny and that's what it stays. Johnny calls his Flower 'cause he thinks goats are beautiful," Lloyd sniggered.

"Well, my goat is, even if she does smell funny sometimes," Johnny persisted.

Rebecca regarded the younger child with a warm affection; Johnny was learning to accept the realities of life without losing his childish idealism. Suddenly she remembered her mother's favorite advice, "You accept what you can't change, young lady; and you learn to appreciate what you have in life." Compared to her mother's unhappy marriage, Rebecca's relationship with Kent was without any real problem.

During the next two months, that relationship deepened into a serenely warm unity that included the entire family. Kent was delighted with the fanciful stories Rebecca wrote so effortlessly, and he frequently added his own lightly humorous touches. But he never invaded her other private thoughts as she'd feared. There were moments when she still wept for Philip, when she still held Michael lightly to her and whispered to him about the father he'd never known. On the whole, though, those two months were the happiest Rebecca had known since the moment she'd arrived in New York. Lavishly generous as always, Kent always returned from his courier journeys with gifts; and Rebecca had stopped complaining. She even accepted the exquisite fur cloak and the pretty, colorful dresses that arrived from England. Although he had not insisted, she'd packed all of her worn black clothing into trunks; she had no need to remind Kent that she remembered her first husband.

On occasion, his own oblique comments revealed the depth of that awareness. Once after he'd just made ardent love to her, he'd said unexpectedly, "If we'd met five years ago, my sweetest wife, you'd have been spared all of the ugliness of this war and all of your unhappiness."

"We're happy now," she murmured sleepily, "and we have the rest of our lives together."

That happiness, however, was all but shattered in late April when Kent arrived home and announced gloomily that his next courier mission would take three weeks. "I have to travel overland through coastal New Jersey to reach Philadelphia," he complained. "There'll be three of us traveling together for safety."

This bleak reminder about the war was the first Rebecca had heard since November, and she regretted the passing of the long winter that had held all fighting in abeyance.

But her personal concern now was for her English husband who hated the war as much as she did and who seemed so uncharacteristically preoccupied as he stared out of their bedroom window. That night after supper she discovered that this preoccupation had little to do with his pending trip to Philadelphia.

Having remained behind in the dining room to help Dena remove the dishes from the table, Rebecca was late in joining Kent and the children for the traditional hour they spent in the parlor whenever Kent was home. Her entry interrupted his glowing description of the fine horses in the green pastures of his Welsh estate. Having forgotten the details of Kent's inheritance from his Welsh great-uncle, Rebecca interrupted the conversation, "I thought your family's country place was in Essex."

"My father's is," he responded promptly, "but mine is in the heart of the finest land in southern Wales, and it's also close to Pembrokeshire, where your great-grandfather lived."

"Who told you about Lloyd Glynns?" she demanded.

"Uncle Joshua. Why?"

"Did Uncle Joshua tell you that he was an indentured criminal?" she demanded.

"Uncle Samuel said he was a revolutionary like your father and a popular hero in Wales before he was deported to America."

"Kent, that was over fifty years ago, and it's no longer of any importance to my brothers and me, since we'll never be going there."

"We are too, Becky," Lloyd declared hotly. "He was our grandfather too; and I'm named after him, and Uncle Samuel says Johnny looks like him."

"Lloyd, we're fourth-generation American, and the people there would treat us just as the Sons of Liberty treated the lobsterbacks in Falmouth."

"No, they wouldn't, Becky," Lloyd contradicted her again. "We'd be Kent's family like we are here, and he wouldn't let anyone hurt us."

Only an insensitive fool could miss the longing in Lloyd's voice or the anxiety on John's face, Rebecca realized contritely, regretting her momentary anger. Kent had provided the only real security and excitement the three children in her charge had ever known; and by comparison, politics and social censure had little meaning. Acutely aware of the brooding expression of hurt which had replaced Kent's earlier enthusiasm, Rebecca hastily reassured her brothers.

"Kent will always be a part of our family, wherever we live. Anyway, it's bedtime, Lloyd. We had a late supper, and tomorrow will be another day. You and Johnny help Michael into his nightclothes, and Kent and I'll be up to tuck you in."

Rebecca waited stiffly as the three reluctant children filed out of the parlor before she exploded into angry speech. "Kent, you have no right to make promises I'm not going to let you keep."

"Who has a better right? I love them as much as you do, and your father hasn't tried to see them in three years."

"He's still our father, and he's fighting a war to make certain that we will have more freedom than he did. So is Michael's grandfather."

"The children need a secure home now, Rebecca, not five years in the future when your relatives stop fighting this war."

"You're fighting the same war, Kent, and who knows where you'll be five weeks from now, much less five years."

"By mid-June, I'll be out of the army and finished with both of my missions in Philadelphia. That's when we'll all be leaving for Wales."

"What happened to your promise to become an American, Kent? You can't just order us to leave our country just because you—"

"We'll return after the war to visit your father and Michael's grandfather, but right now there's more at stake than national loyalty. When were you planning to tell me about the child you're carrying?"

"I'm not carrying any child," she flashed angrily in denial.

"Dena said you are."

"Dena talks too much."

"She also claimed you insist you're barren. How could you possibly believe that after Michael? Or is it just because this time I'm the father?"

Silently cursing her presumptuous servant, Rebecca turned away in frustration. Until a few days ago when Dena had reminded her sharply that her flux was two weeks overdue, she'd sincerely believed that she was barren. During her intermittent months with Philip, there'd been no sign of a child, not even after she'd fervently begun to want one. Tempted now to blurt out the truth about Michael, she turned to face her current inquisitor, only to sag in defeat at his expression.

"It isn't you, Kent," she admitted dully. "It's just the wrong time and the wrong place."

"Since when do children ever wait for the right time? Is Dena right about your condition, Rebecca?"

Rebecca's heart was thudding in sick defeat when she answered, "I suppose she is. Kent, I don't want to meet your family looking like a breeding sow. They're going to be shocked enough when they learn that you married a colonial widow with three children already here and a fourth one on the way."

"We won't be seeing my family. The only reminder they'll have of me will be that portrait you're painting, provided you finish it by the time we sail in June."

"Kent, why can't we stay in New York?"

His voice was more explosively sharp than she'd ever remembered it being before. "Because I want you out of this damned plague city, and I want our child to be born in a place where he'll survive." Abruptly his temper subsided and he smiled sheepishly. "Sorry about being a crosspatch tonight, Rebecca, but I've had a beastly three days of it. Let's tuck Michael in and then go to bed ourselves."

Later in the bedroom, as she was preparing the coffee and rum which had become a ritual on each of Kent's homecoming nights, Rebecca asked curiously, "When did Dena mention the possibility of a child?"

"Just before I left the last time."

"Did you tell her we were going to Wales then?"

"No. I decided later."

"You know she will have to go with us, don't you; that is, if we do go?"

"I'm counting on her going; we'll need her help with the children aboard ship."

"Suppose there isn't to be a child, Kent?"

"We'll still be going to Wales. This city's no place for children at any age."

"Have you told Uncle Samuel yet?"

"Yes, and he agreed."

"About the child?"

"No, about Wales. He doesn't know about the child yet. Why this sudden inquisition, Rebecca?"

"You've just rearranged my life, and I don't know whether or not I like the idea."

His voice had sharpened again when he demanded, "The idea of me or the changes?"

"You are a crosspatch tonight. I just thought we should wait before we decide."

"It's already decided. I've arranged for us to leave in mid-June aboard an armed merchantman traveling in a convoy. Don't look so glum! Wales isn't the end of the world, and I want the voyage over with long before it becomes dangerous for you. Sweetheart, it's a large estate, and you'll have the freedom to do anything you want. Please humor me this one time, Rebecca; I just want you and the children safe."

Smiling faintly as she joined him in bed, Rebecca surrendered to the inevitable. "All right, Kent, I don't suppose there's really any alternative."

But emotionally she was still far from being convinced. During the weeks Kent was on his first courier assignment to Philadelphia, she struggled to overcome her reluctance to leave America—even the America of a plague-infested, captive city. Although the hard core of prudential logic that had sustained her through earlier crises in her life dictated that she had no choice, she could still not come to terms with a decision that irrevocably severed all connections with her own past. Nor did she have any illusions about the life on an English country estate; she remembered Akhoi's description all too vividly. However, the knowledge that cut the deepest into her conscience was the immutable fact that her own child, the one whose existence was just beginning, would be English without any legal claim to American citizenship.

Those weeks of Kent's absences were rendered even more upsetting by the quiet man who'd managed the town house so unobtrusively for five months. Malcolm Garner had assumed control, not just of the house, but of the people in it. He limited the children's outdoor play to the back yard, and he denied entry to all visitors except Samuel Rayburn. Not even the two neighborhood mothers Rebecca had met during the winter sports on the pond were admitted.

"The master does not want the family endangered by any possible contact with disease," Malcolm explained apologetically.

Samuel, too, had been adamant that there be no contact with outsiders.

"Manhattan is a plague city, Rebecca. The death rate has tripled since the spring thaw."

Startled by the frightening statistic, she demanded, "Why hasn't the public been notified?"

"Censorship! General Clinton has forbidden us to publish any statistics about the plagues ravaging the lower half of the city."

"Is yellow fever one of them?" Rebecca asked with remembered terror.

"Quite probably since Clinton doesn't enforce any quarantine restrictions. Neither does he believe in the smallpox inoculations George Washington ordered Dr. Nathaniel Bond to use on the Continental army a year ago. Like all benighted aristocrats, Clinton is convinced that diseases such as plague, smallpox, and dysentery can be restricted to the slums by enforced isolation."

On the morning of Kent's return, Samuel visited her once again, and this time his conversation was considerably more explicit and considerably more revealing.

"Kent's arriving by ship this afternoon, and he asked

me to talk to you before he gets home. I would have, for my own peace of mind at any rate. Are you still reluctant to go to Wales?''

''Yes.''

''Have you any idea how many officials Kent has bribed to win your release from this cursed city?''

Rebecca stared at her uncle. ''Why would anyone object now that I'm his wife?''

''People like Colonel Crane have long memories. But now that Kent has secured permission, I want you to forget your personal objections and leave without any more arguments. I want you and my nephews alive when this war is finished.''

''Uncle Samuel, we've survived here for almost two years. Why—?''

''You've been lucky and you've had a very careful maid,'' he snapped. ''Was it your idea or hers to scrub everything in sight?''

Momentarily nonplussed by the oddity of Samuel's question, she shrugged lightly. ''Neither. It was the Frenchwoman who owned her before I—'' Rebecca paused with the abrupt realization that she owed Paulette a debt of gratitude beyond the existence of Michael for training an ignorant girl to use standards of cleanliness far exceeding those of most servants. Suddenly she remembered that Akhoi, too, had insisted that everyone in camp use an abrasive lye soap during the yellow fever epidemic. She was about to ask Samuel the significance of such extremes in cleanliness when his own question drove all such trivialities from her mind.

''Would that be the Frenchwoman who was Michael's natural mother? Don't look so shocked, Rebecca. I've known for more than a year—something your cook said, although she didn't realize what she was revealing. It was then I decided you were a fine young woman, far more like your mother than your father—although God knows, you've enough of his defiant stubbornness to make you irritating at times.''

''Does Kent know?'' she gasped.

''No, but I imagine he'd be delighted to learn the child

you're carrying will be your first. In answer to that furious question you're about to ask, Kent didn't tell me—not directly. But I assumed as much from his protective attitude and from questioning your servant."

"I'm glad you know, Uncle Samuel, but I prefer you not to tell your brother until after Kent and I have left the city."

"Then you've decided to go."

"Yes, I told Kent I would."

"He wasn't sure; he's not as self-confident as he pretends. Would you mind answering several more questions just to satisfy an old man's curiosity, Rebecca?"

Ignoring her abrupt wariness, he continued without giving her a chance to respond verbally. "When did you first learn of Michael's existence?"

"Just after Philip had sailed for France the first time when Paulette came to my hotel room."

"Had you known before of your husband's infidelity?"

"Yes, but—"

"So had I, my dear. Sidney Tupton took delight in revealing all the sordid details of that affair. According to him, the Frenchwoman was responsible for the betrayal of Falmouth."

Rebecca sighed wearily. "No, she wasn't. Paulette was just a survivor, very similar to what I've become. She was just—vindictive in the way she turned Michael over to me without Philip's knowledge."

"Then your husband didn't know you'd adopted his son?"

"No, and I regret that more than anything else about his death."

"Tell me, Rebecca, had conditions been reversed, would he have adopted your child?"

"Philip is dead, and there's no purpose to any of this conversation."

"Would he have?" Samuel persisted relentlessly.

"I don't think so," she responded heavily. "Have you finished with your questions yet?"

"Not quite. I know you loved Philip Keane, but I'm not sure about your feelings for Kent."

"I love him—in a different way."

"Enough for a lifetime?"

Rebecca hesitated before she answered the blunt, intrusive question; but eventually her response was affirmative enough to satisfy her unrelenting inquisitor. "Yes, I miss him very much when he's not here."

"Then tell him so tonight, and wear something more attractive than that puritanical cover-up you have on now. He'll need cheering up for the next ten days because his final mission to Philadelphia is going to be a strenuous one. He'll be going there with General Clinton, who's replacing William Howe as commander-in-chief of the British forces in America. And to make matters gloomier for Kent, Colonel Crane will accompany them. While Clinton is evacuating that city and Admiral Howe is returning to New York with the fleet, Kent will come overland with the main force under General Cornwallis. That's privileged information, Rebecca, so don't be bothering Kent for details. He wasn't my source, but he could be court-martialed if anyone accused him of revealing official secrets."

With Kent's exuberant return that afternoon, Rebecca's troubled world became peaceful again; and long before she and Kent retired to her bedroom, she found herself resenting the one final mission of his military career.

Throughout the afternoon and evening the laughter of reunion reverberated from the kitchen to the parlor as the children stuffed themselves on the boxes of confections Kent had brought from a butter-rich Philadelphia. Despite the warmth of the late spring weather, they tried on their new wool suits without complaint while Lloyd and John enthusiastically recited all they'd learned about Wales. Bedtime was particularly chaotic, because Michael artfully required three tuck-ins until Rebecca took over from Kent with a disciplinary finality.

When at last she entered the bedroom and secured the door, she found Kent already there, standing before his finished portrait.

"You've made me look like a bloody hero," he accused her with a wide grin.

Returning his smile, she bantered lightly, "Wait until you see the second one I'm working on. You look like a bloody Saint Nicholas in that one."

"Where is it?"

"Under the drop cloth on the other easel, but I promise you it's the last time I ever use oil paints. There're too many critics in this family."

After studying the four faces informally grouped on the unfinished canvas, Kent said quietly, "You used the sketches you drew on the day Michael almost fell into the river. It's a beautiful piece of work, Rebecca."

"Not according to my brothers. Johnny claims I made his eyes too big, and realistic Lloyd insists it didn't happen that way."

"What about Michael?"

"He just jumps up and down and shrieks your name over and over."

"You know I consider him mine, don't you, darling?"

"Michael would be the last person to disagree with you, but you do tend to spoil him."

"I want ten more just like him to spoil."

"I'm not even sure you're going to get one yet. I feel wonderful, and my dresses still fit."

"That's because you lost weight while I was gone. Was it that hard for you to decide whether or not to go to Wales with me?"

"I'd already decided before you left."

"No, you hadn't. Your eyes were still glinting fire. Would you really have insisted I go without you?"

"No, I wouldn't have, and you know it," she murmured. Kent's relieved chuckle tickled her ear as he embraced her triumphantly, but there was nothing lighthearted about his kiss. It was the passionate one of possession—urgent and demanding, and his arms tightened into steel bands as he propelled her toward the bed, releasing his hold only long enough to inform her, "You won't be needing a gown tonight, and your hair is going to look like your Viking ancestors' by morning. It's been a long, empty month without you."

Pushing him away long enough to remove the Caribbean

clothing she'd donned earlier in deference to the heat, she barely had time enough to kick off her sandals before Kent pulled her down on top of him without bothering to remove the counterpane on the bed. While she tried to adjust emotionally to the novelty of the position, she gasped helplessly as his hands and lips combined in an unhampered exploration of her body, slowly awakening her quiescent passion to a quivering intensity. Her last coherent thought before he gripped her hips and entered her with a gentle strength was that he'd learned techniques far beyond her teaching. Then all thought stopped except the primitive one of fulfillment as her body obeyed its instinctive urges without conscious volition and with an unrestrained freedom. The moment of release for both of them was a sweet, trembling ecstasy that obliterated all memory of their earlier tensions.

Exhausted, she lay draped over him until he broke the spell of enchantment with humor. "The colonial doctor I talked to in Philadelphia said this position was one way to avoid hurting you and our child with my weight. He advised me not to give you any warning because he thought you might be too horrified by the innovation to permit it."

Noting his impudent smile, Rebecca laughed and rolled to one side, only to be told that she was now in the correct position for the second recommended method.

"Your doctor friend must lead an exciting life," she murmured with a jesting amusement.

"I imagine he does, since his wife has produced thirteen children in an equal number of years."

"If I ever prove that fertile," she warned him half-seriously, "there's going to be an additional innovation practiced in our bed."

Kent grinned at her and rumpled her already tousled hair playfully. "Dr. Marlowe told me about that one too. We'll use it when you reach the never-again stage."

"Seriously, why did you consult a doctor?"

"I didn't want you to be hurt by my ignorance."

Rebecca kissed him then, the brooding doubts of the previous weeks vanquished; with Kent there would always be security and tenderness. There would also be children, she reflected with a humorous resignation when he responded to her kiss with an eager readiness and proceeded to demonstrate the earthy Dr. Marlowe's additional instructions, which were far more comprehensive than a mere change of position. As uninhibited as he'd been since their first intimacy, he aroused her skillfully with drawn-out caresses; but he restrained her hips from responding when he consummated their union.

Laughing at her efforts to break free of his hold, he chided her lightly. "The doctor said this was supposed to be a minuet instead of an athletic contest. You're to keep our child from being seasick, and I'm to prevent you from becoming bored."

With her senses already throbbing for the second time that night, Rebecca relaxed and let the languorous mindlessness of sensuality dominate her consciousness. Afterward though, she made the first complete commitment in her defensively emotional life—a pledge she'd extended to Philip only conditionally because her feelings for him had been too heavily tinged with jealous distrust.

"I love you, Kent," she murmured quietly.

"It's about time, my darling wife. I've loved you since the day we met, but I was beginning to wonder if I'd ever really win you over. Not that you ever had a chance of escaping from me; only that now when you have a headache, I won't think I gave it to you."

When Sir Henry Clinton announced that he would leave for Philadelphia two days ahead of schedule and that his staff officers would be prepared with full dress as well as regimental uniforms, Samuel Rayburn commented sourly to Kent, "He delayed going to Johnny Burgoyne's aid for two months. But when his own glorification is at stake, he's as eager as a politician in search of graft; and he expects the pomp and glitter of a coronation. Does the uniform mean that Malcolm goes with you?"

Kent nodded morosely. "Malcolm and three horses. Damn it, Rebecca can't be alone right now."

"Don't worry about her; I'll take over the task of fending off the busybodies—official and otherwise."

"Even Uncle Josh?"

"Especially my brother. He's been chomping at the bit since he received that letter from your mother. Have you warned Rebecca yet about the reception she's likely to receive from that part of your family?"

"No, but I'll make certain that Wales is on the other side of the world as far as my mother is concerned. Don't worry about Rebecca, Uncle Samuel; she's my first concern and always will be." Kent paused awkwardly and peered more closely at the older man. "You know about the child, don't you?"

"Yes, that's why I'm willing to keep the vultures away until you return."

"Are you sure you can?"

"With Colonel Crane gone, it shouldn't prove too difficult."

"I'm grateful to you, Uncle Samuel."

"Not doing it entirely for you, Kent. With you and Rebecca permanently in England, the future of the *Observer* most probably rests on Lloyd and John; so I'll want them back after the war. I don't know how Josh feels, but I'm making them my heirs."

"I've already made Rebecca mine."

"Your mother's not going to appreciate that gesture; she seems to consider the estate that old reprobate adventurer left you a communal part of the family fortune."

"She wouldn't even stay in the same room with him when he visited us. Anyway, it's Rebecca and the children who are important now. God, I'll be glad when all of this is over and I have them safe in Wales."

Long before mid-June, when Samuel's three weeks of custodial residency at the town house ended, Rebecca was sorely tempted to use her fighting skills against this uncle she loved and admired. From her retreat in her bedroom where she'd spent as many hours as she dared avoiding him, she fumed in a silent annoyance as she daubed the finishing paint on Kent's portraits. Samuel Rayburn was the most dictatorial, arbitrary, and interfering man she'd ever known. Within days of his arrival, Reverend Stebbins had requested an early termination of his tutorial duties; and Samuel himself had taken over the classroom. The six resident soldiers who'd become a congenial part of the family now ate their meals with silent speed before they left the main house in relief, and the two usually taciturn Swedish maids rushed through their work with muttered protests. Dena kept relentlessly busy; and for the first time in the town house, Lloyd and John performed their assigned chores of fetching the wood and tending the animals slowly enough to do a thorough job.

The only household member who relished his great-uncle's tenure was Michael. With the exuberant two-year-old, Samuel was unfailingly tolerant, submitting occasionally to the indignity of holding the active child on his lap. Puzzled at first by the difference in her uncle's varying attitudes toward the children and remembering the stern demands he'd made on her when she'd worked on the *Observer*, Rebecca finally concluded that he expected superior performances only from those related to him by blood. A curious man, she thought as she hugged Michael defensively close.

Had she not deliberately taken refuge in her room as often as possible, she would have been puzzled by another of Samuel's odd departures from his normal habits. He monitored the front door himself and explained to each of the dozen visitors that his niece was too ill to see anyone. Congratulating himself that even the three rival newspapermen had accepted the lie without challenge, Samuel was preparing for his morning stint of teaching his nephews on the twenty-first day of Kent's absence when two additional visitors arrived. Scowling at his brother Joshua, Samuel greeted the second man with disapproving familiarity and ushered the pair into the parlor. Ten minutes later he emerged, sent Lloyd and John into the back yard to ride their pony, and ordered Dena to summon her mistress.

"Misser Samuel say you is to fetch down that picture of Misser Kent. 'Spect he wants old Misser Joshua to see it."

"You take it down for me, Dena, while Michael and I finish packing this trunk."

"No, mam, it's you who is wanted. An' Miz Rebecca, I thinks you best brush your hair and wear som'thin' pretty. Misser Samuel done act a heap more upset than usual."

Irritably, Rebecca yanked off her soiled housedress and pulled on one of the loveliest of the summer gowns she had worn in Saint-Domingue. She was halfway across the room before she remembered to brush her hair. Silently as she walked down the stairs, she addressed the painted face in the picture she was carrying. "As fond as I am of our uncle, my lovely Englishman, he is not an easy man to live with. Even shipboard life with three children is beginning to sound like paradise compared to being at his beck and call."

Samuel was waiting for her at the foot of the stairs. Brusquely he removed the painting from her hands and told her to make certain that Michael was safely in the back yard with the older children.

"Dena will watch out for him," she protested.

Older and more tired than she'd ever seen him look before, he responded heavily, "Just do as I say, Rebecca. Your servant has been given other duties to perform. Join me as soon as you've finished with your son."

It was a measure of her impatience with the slow passage of the past weeks and her anxiety about the future that Rebecca entered the parlor without any expectations other than an awkward visit with her Uncle Joshua, who had avoided her company for months. Bracing herself for his ill-concealed disapproval, Rebecca was greeted instead by the unexpected third man in the room whose voice was more autocratic than Samuel's. It was also distinctly British.

"Young woman, I would like to purchase this portrait. I'm Kent's father."

Although her heart had begun an agitated pounding as soon as her eyes had focused on the face of the man whose resemblance to his son was unmistakable, she retained enough composure to respond with a reckless arrogance of her own.

"It's not for sale, Lord Enderly. But since it was intended as a gift for you and your wife, you may take it with you when you leave." She almost smiled at the familiar signs of anger on his face; like his son, the eyes were narrowed and the nostrils flared. Also like his son, anger did not render him speechless.

"I insist on a more businesslike arrangement, and I'm certain you'll agree once you've heard what I've come a long way to tell you. Be seated, mistress. I suggest we make this discussion as painless as possible under the circumstances."

With impeccable manners that reminded her poignantly of Kent's he seated her in the chair next to Samuel's before he took the one some ten feet removed.

"Before I must become the harsh parent, mistress, I would like to speak to you professionally. Samuel informs me that he paid you only a few pounds for your first volume of stories and nothing so far for the second. They earned considerable money in England, and I am prepared to pay you the due amount. I also want your permission to publish the last series of stories you submitted to your uncle. I read them last night after my arrival here in New York. I particularly liked your stories about the animals."

"My brother Johnny helped me with those, and Kent helped me with the other ones."

"However you achieved them, they are quite excellent; I would like to produce them. If, however, your animosity toward me is such that you prefer another publisher, I will negotiate the sale."

"Stop playing the fool, Brandon," Samuel rasped angrily, "and get on with your cursed interference in my niece's life."

"In due time, Samuel," Lord Enderly retorted calmly. "I'm certain she has already guessed that purpose of my mission. In the meantime I want her to be aware of the financial arrangements I have made for her future. The monies that your books have earned have already been deposited in a Boston bank that still does business with England through reliable though unofficial channels. In addition, the substantial funds you inherited from your mother have been likewise deposited at the insistence of Jonathan Langley."

Aroused to a burning anger by the sheer effrontery of

this man, Rebecca demanded hotly, "What gives you or my Uncle Jonathan the right to determine the disposition of my money under any circumstances?"

"My official position, Mistress Keane. I have been given the assignment of relocating problem colonials. This afternoon you and your family will be placed aboard a British ship which sails on the evening tide bound for Casco Bay. Once there, you will be transferred to an American fishing vessel for the trip to Boston. In that city you will contact a representative of the designated bank, who will escort you to a home in Roxbury, where I imagine your family will feel more comfortable since it is a smaller town."

"I don't care what you imagine, Lord Enderly. I refuse to leave New York until I have spoken with Kent."

"You have no choice in the matter. I've already told your maid to complete the packing and prepare your children for the journey."

Goaded beyond caution, Rebecca stood up defiantly. "You're a fool, Lord Enderly, unless you *want* your son killed. Kent will try to follow me to Boston regardless of the danger he would face in enemy territory. Even if he's no longer a British soldier, he would still be—"

"I have no illusions about my son," the Englishman interrupted heavily, "or about the sincerity of his love for you. I was quite certain that the young fool would attempt the insanity you described, so I gave him no more choice than I'm giving you. He is already on the high seas aboard a ship-of-line bound for Gibraltar. Since the acceptance of his resignation was delayed for two years, he will continue to serve as a military courier in that embattled colony, from where there is no easy return to America. Two years is a long time in the life of a young man."

With Samuel's awkward help, Rebecca sank into her chair, finally accepting the totality of her defeat. Two years will be an even longer time in the life of a fatherless infant, she despaired. Aloud she articulated the one bitter word, "Why?"

Regretting the vulnerable hurt mirrored on the young face, Enderly spoke more softly. "Not for the reasons you

are attributing to me, mistress. It is my wife, not I, who
has a fetish for titled in-laws. As a result of her matchmaking,
I have three extravagant and impractical daughters-in-law
and one son-in-law whose only accomplishment is gentleman horse racing. Among them, they have presented me
with fourteen untalented, self-centered grandchildren. When
Kent notified me that he was marrying the Rayburn niece,
whose background and accomplishments I already knew
from Samuel, I was delighted.''

Convinced of his sincerity despite her ingrained distrust
of aristocrats, Rebecca listened with an increasing sense of
foreboding. She was familiar enough with the journalistic
technique of building suspense to realize that Lord Enderly's
monologue was far from complete.

''What happened to change your mind?'' she asked
warily.

''Your husband happened, mistress, your only husband.
Philip Keane is very much alive.''

Rebecca's emotions remained frozen for a moment in
deep shock until her heart began to beat with a painful
rush. Oh, God, she should have known that Philip was still
alive, that he had mastered the sea for too many years to
become its victim. But his resurrection was too late to save
their marriage or to save her! He would never forgive her
inconstancy, not now when she was carrying another man's
child. A man she'd learned to love as she had Philip—as
much as she loved Philip still. She couldn't deny her
pounding heart any more than she could the awareness of
defeat that was slowly draining her last reserve of courage.
She had two husbands who loved her, but she could claim
neither of them!

Clutching her hands tightly in her lap, she asked shakily,
''How did you meet Phil—my husband, Lord Enderly?''

''I interviewed him at the request of Jonathan Langley. I
learned then that Captain Keane was a determined man
who'd twice risked his own life and the lives of his
marines to remove you from New York, and that he—''

''Rebecca knows all about those unsuccessful raids on
Long Island, Brandon,'' Samuel interrupted angrily.

''Then she knows he is the type of man who will

continue to search until he finds her. At that meeting I decided that my son's impetuous marriage could never succeed even if I could arrange the annulment he desperately requested in a letter I received just before I sailed from England. Belatedly, I decided that Kent had no moral right to happiness at the expense of a man who'd been fighting a war without pause for three years. But most importantly, I decided I did not want him killed by a jealous husband some years down the road.''

At those final words, Rebecca's dread increased. ''Where did this interview take place, Lord Enderly?''

But instead of responding directly, the Englishman glanced meaningfully at Samuel. ''An hour after my ship docked last evening, Joshua revealed that his brother and my son had conspired for several months to keep you in ignorance of the fact that your husband had been captured and placed on trial before an admiralty court on the charges of piracy on the high seas, in Jamaica, and ashore on Guernsey Island.''

Letting her breath out slowly, Rebecca turned to face her uncle accusingly. Never at a loss for words, especially in his own defense, Samuel answered her unasked question stiffly.

''Last February when I first heard the news, the evidence against him seemed so overwhelming I expected his immediate execution. I saw no need to put you through the ordeal of his death a second time, and I didn't want Kent to lose you because of that New England conscience of yours in the event it proved unnecessary to tell you at all. In late April when we learned his life had been spared, I was at a loss, my dear, to know which course was best.''

Rebecca nodded mutely; by that time it was already too late. No wonder both Kent and Samuel had acted so oddly during those weeks.

''Before you condemn your protectors too harshly, Mistress Keane,'' Lord Enderly interrupted her thought, 'I think you should read the letters they sent in February requesting my help.''

Woodenly she accepted the proffered letters and read them, knowing in advance the probable contents. Samuel's was a brusque demand that Lord Enderly monitor the trial and prevent Philip Keane from being convicted on false charges. Of a more personal nature, Kent's letter was a plea that his father save Philip's life if he could. "I don't want to live with the guilty thought that I might have wanted him dead."

Repressing the desolate sense of loss she experienced as she read Kent's letter, Rebecca forced herself to ask about Philip's capture and trial.

"A month before your husband was put on trial, one of his partners, a Frenchman named Edmond Falconet, had raided the Guernsey Island town of St. Peter Port, killing some eight civilians and taking ten hostages, six of them children. Your husband was unaware of that raid until Falconet returned to the French port of Cherbourg. According to witnesses, Philip Keane demanded that the hostages be returned without ransom; and two days later his and Falconet's ships left Cherbourg. Off the eastern shore of Guernsey Island, the two ships anchored at night, and Captain Keane and a Lieutenant Haskins took the hostages ashore in a sailing gig. Onshore they were met by the island constabulary, and both of the Americans were injured before the hostages could inform the authorities that these men were not the villains who'd done the kidnapping. Your husband and the lieutenant were taken to the estate of one of the hostages and given medical treatment for three weeks.

"It had been a Guernsey fisherman who'd witnessed Falconet's raid three nights earlier and notified the large privateer community on the island. Those privateer captains were the ones who organized the trap that sank both of the enemy ships. Within days, Cherbourg port authorities learned that Philip Keane had not been among the survivors rescued at sea. Soon after, the third Keane ship left for America with the news.

"As in all such cases, the British Admiralty took over the trial and charged the men who had survived with piracy. Even after Guernsey citizens testified that the marauders had been French, the Admiralty made no distinction between the French and American crews. When

Philip Keane heard about the pending trial, he surrendered himself in an effort to save his men from hanging. It was then that the admiralty produced the extensive dossiers they had accumulated on both Keane and Falconet. They dredged up the additional charge of piracy pertaining to a Jamaican raid in which eight Kingston citizens were murdered and more than two hundred household servants stolen.''

Rebecca shuddered at the memory of the slave sale she'd witnessed in Port-au-Prince, and protested helplessly, ''Philip never went into Kingston during that raid.''

''So he and members of his crew contended, but they admitted that the public sale of those stolen servants was conducted on the embarcadero in front of the warehouses owned in common by the Falconets and the Keanes. But far more damning than these charges were the ones leveled against your husband only. Captain Keane was accused of attacking and capturing three English privateers on the open sea off the coast of Delaware in April of 1775, more than a year before the American Congress officially declared war. That was when Jonathan Langley contacted me and aroused my interest in the case, long before I received Samuel's and Kent's letters.

''Almost two years before, Langley had registered an official protest with the British Admiralty over that same incident and submitted a copy of the official findings of a Connecticut board of inquiry. Your uncle was protesting the murder of one of his former captains at the hands of the English privateer. At his insistence, the admiralty agreed to summon Captain Brian Sinclair from his post in Gibraltar. Under oath, Sinclair revealed far more than the Connecticut officials had learned. As a preventive measure sometime in 1774, the British Navy had adopted an unofficial policy of paying English privateers substantial rewards for destroying prominent American and French fleets of privateers. Both the Falconet and Keane fleets were targeted. Sinclair admitted that he had cooperated in the planned destruction of the Keane fleet and that the English privateers had attacked first.

''The trial should have ended with Sinclair's testimony, but it required another month of additional deliberation before the board rendered its verdicts, which proved to be too lenient for the Frenchmen and too harsh for the Americans. Ten of the French crew were hanged for the murder of Guernsey citizens, and the rest sentenced to ten years of hard labor on Jamaica. Falconet was given the same term, to be served in a British prison. The American crew and officers, excluding your husband, were extended a choice of two years in prison or two years of service aboard English ships deployed in Mediterranean waters rather than American ones. Most of them sensibly chose shipboard duty. Your husband, however, was sentenced to two years in prison, and the prison specified was the *Jersey* in New York Harbor."

While Rebecca remained seated in benumbed silence, Samuel exploded into speech. "Hanging would have been a more merciful death than starvation aboard that damned abomination of a prison ship."

"I'm as aware as you are of that particular cruelty," Enderly countered dryly. "God knows I've condemned it often enough in print. It was the unnecessary viciousness of that added punishment that forced me to apply for the official position I now hold. In that capacity I have decided to relocate Captain Keane in less deadly quarters of confinement, but only under the condition that his wife remain in the Boston area and make no effort to contact my son. Do you so agree, Mistress Keane?"

For a tense moment Rebecca stared at the English aristocrat with a stunned blankness, her thoughts too tangled with conflicting emotions for coherence. A gentle nudge from Samuel, though, focused her anger with a shattering finality.

"I would not endanger Kent's life any more than I would Philip's. If you have finished your instructions concerning my future conduct, I will explain your decision to my family."

"When I release your husband, should I tell him how to locate you?"

Visibly shaken by the question, she shook her head. "I don't think so, Lord Enderly," she murmured slowly and allowed her voice to trail off. "Perhaps when the war is' over." She'd almost reached the door when the now familiar English voice halted her progress.

"I still want to purchase this portrait, mistress."

Experiencing a shadowy flash of tolerance for the man who'd proved to be both friend and foe, Rebecca turned to face him.

"Several years ago when I was stranded without funds in a strange town, I earned my living by drawing the faces of gentlemen in a public inn. I charged them two gold sovereigns a sketch. You may pay the same amount if you like."

Her reward for the softening grace of generosity was an apologetic smile and a more pleasant dismissal. "I wish we could have met under more pleasant circumstances. It may be that my interference in your life will prove to be a mistake, but I had to act according to my conscience."

"Perhaps I should have followed mine, Lord Enderly," she replied. "But when you see Kent, tell him I have no regrets for the happiness we shared." With the briefest of nods to each of the three men, she left the silent room swiftly.

CHAPTER 19

In retrospect some hectic weeks later, Rebecca concluded that her return trip to freedom had contained more elements of desperation than heartbreak. At the hurried dockside farewell to her uncles, discreetly monitored

by Brandon Enderly from a short distance away, Samuel
had been gruffly unsentimental, shoving a small packet of
hastily written letters into her hands with the admonition
that she memorize the contents and deliver them to the
designated recipients personally.

Joshua limited his farewell to a moralistic warning.
"Rebecca, a woman in your peculiar position must be
circumspect in her actions both public and private. I'm
very sorry about your present unhappiness, but I beg you
not to endanger your reputation with any more impulsive
mistakes."

Reminded of the child that was yet to come, she'd
smiled with a cynical irony. "Don't worry, Uncle Joshua,
I'll be well chaperoned by children." Only Samuel returned
her smile.

Once aboard the armed British merchantman with three
confused and tired young children tucked hugger-mugger
into one of the bunks in the crowded cabin, Dena reminded
Rebecca sharply of future realities.

"Jest what is we s'posed to do in this here Roxbury
without Misser Kent, I asks you?"

Having already read the first of Samuel's letters, this
one addressed to Isaiah Thomas, editor and founder of the
Massachusetts Spy in Worcester, Rebecca had explained,
"According to my inventive uncle, we're going to become
respectable enough to satisfy even Bostonians and psalm-
singing Congregationalists."

"And how is we gonna do that, you jest tells me how,
onct folks there knows there's a chile in your belly whose
pappy ain't your husband and ain't about to be?"

"Uncle Samuel knew about the child when he wrote this
letter. As far as the Massachusetts public is concerned, I
conceived the child in England, where I was allowed to
live with my war-hero husband while he was on trial. Read
the letter, Dena, so you'll know what you're to say in case
anyone becomes curious."

As the girl settled to the slow process of reading four
pages of Samuel's incisive handwriting, Rebecca studied
the young Negress. Despite the privations of two years in
Manhattan, Dena had added twenty pounds to her broad,

muscular figure; and she'd developed a self-assured sense of her own worth. Although she still had trouble with verbs and still clung to the vernacular of her southern patois, she was no longer illiterate. She could write simple directives and read with excellent comprehension. As impressive as these outward manifestations of improvement were, Dena's inner changes were the more remarkable. Always a friendly, outgoing person, she'd gradually become an emotional mainstay for the children and for Rebecca herself. During the traumatic months in the cottage when her mistress had been dominated by Samuel and the *Observer*, Dena had supplied much of the love and security the children needed.

Always reluctant to admit her own need for other people, Rebecca had been slow to recognize the opposite quality in her servant friend. But aboard ship on the way to an uncertain future, the older woman desperately hoped the eighteen-year-old Dena would remain with her. Not that either or both of them could replace Kent entirely, especially with Michael. Michael, with his exuberance, his mercurial temper, and his restless energy, had needed the loving reassurance that Kent had given him. Reflecting for the first time how completely the physical child of one man had become the spiritual child of another, Rebecca felt the hot sting of tears flood her eyes. Kent was gone, and Philip might never know his own wonderful son. Rebecca let her tears fall unchecked, unsure which man she was weeping for. The brief thrill of joy she'd felt when she'd learned Philip was alive had vanished, leaving only the empty conviction that she'd lost him as surely as she'd lost Kent.

How she dreaded the necessity of explaining to her brothers that the dream of a carefree life in Wales had ended with Kent's mandated transfer to a distant colony in Europe. For herself, she admitted with a sad finality that only Kent's love had made the prospect of living abroad bearable; and deep in that part of her awareness ruled by conscience, she knew that she was too American to have become a peaceful English wife to a wealthy aristocrat. Like her Grandmother Gwenna, she would eventually have become an embarrassing troublemaker in a land dominated by social inequality.

Rebecca's moody introspection was interrupted by Dena's blunt condemnation of Samuel's letter of introduction to Isaiah Thomas. "This here ain't nothin' but a passel of lies. I 'us outside the door when that old man 'uz talkin' an' he don' say one word 'bout redcoats bein' gen'mun. He say they treat your Cap'n Keane lak a polecat."

"I know," Rebecca admitted, "but it'll be safer for Philip if people believe that he was treated decently in England. Only then will they accept the story that I was allowed to live with him for three months. My child is going to need a name, Dena, even if it's the wrong one."

"And what's gonna happen when this Cap'n Keane gits to Roxbury?"

"I'll have to tell him the truth."

"You thought on what to say if Misser Kent come callin' instead?"

"His father made very certain Kent would be unable to return to America—at least for years. Anyway, neither of them will be calling on us for a long time, and life will be more bearable if I'm not labeled a woman of loose morals. Dena, I have to ask you—are you willing to put up with all the problems this next year will bring?"

Balefully, the black eyes glared at Rebecca. "Sometimes you ain't got no more sense than Michael. Ain't no way you kin git 'long without me. Who's gonna b'lieve the lies Misser Samuel tole lessen I says they's true. And them tired-out, scrambled-up chil'run gonna need me much as they need you. What's more, Miz Rebecca, you ain't got the least notion 'bout bornin' a chile. I 'spect when the time comes, you is gonna need me worse 'n the chilrun. An' I plans t' be right there 'cause I ain't forgot what the conjur woman taught me when both mammy an' me 'uz birthin'. So don't you be wastin' my time again wif questions that don't make good sense. I's fam'bly, Miz Rebecca, long as you needs me."

Only after Dena had finished her impassioned declaration, did Rebecca realize how much of her emotional reaction to the day's events had been fear. Until Kent's

protective shield had been snatched away, she had given
little thought to the dangers of childbirth itself or to public
opinion. But now she was being returned to her native
New England, whose citizens rarely forgave human frailty.
And for the first time in her life she lacked the inner
assurance of innocence. The only protections against public censure she possessed now were the loyalty of a servant
girl and the four letters Samuel had written at considerable
expense to his own integrity. With a renewed sense of
survival, she turned her attention to the remaining documents.

The letter addressed to John Adams that began with the
salutation "Dear John" was a slashing indictment against
Roger Tupton's persecution of Rebecca and a request that
Sidney Tupton be restrained from interfering in the lives of
his grandsons, Lloyd and John Rayburn. He asked that the
paper naming their sister, Rebecca Rayburn Keane, be
recorded in Massachusetts courts as insurance against any
spurious Tupton claim that she was unfit. The concluding
paragraphs dealt with Lord Brandon Enderly's part in
saving the life of Captain Philip Keane and in getting his
wife and family out of plague-threatened Manhattan.

Rebecca was thoughtful as she set the letter aside. She
was remembering that Samuel had often described John
Adams as the one New England lawyer with enough
bone-hard common sense to admit that both Whigs and
Tories could live peacefully together in America. But even
a lawyer as courageous as Adams wouldn't be able to stem
the tide of public outrage if the Tuptons ever learned of her
bigamous marriage to an Englishman.

Frightened by the thought that she could lose the custody of her brothers, Rebecca read the third letter without
the resentment she might otherwise have felt. Addressed
simply to the unnamed minister of the Roxbury Congregationalist Church, it repeated the lie about her stay in
England and announced that she was now in a delicate
"family way" and would need the understanding friendship of a minister to help her during the difficult months
ahead. In some detail, Samuel had written about her
hardships in New York, her shock over the imprisonment
of her husband, and her constant worry that her guardianship

of her brothers might be wrested from her by a hypocritical grandfather whose interest in his grandsons was entirely mercenary.

Rebecca's momentary resentment at her uncle for revealing her condition to strangers quickly subsided when she recalled the influence wielded by Congregational pastors in New England towns. If she played the role Samuel had outlined for her, she could gain the sponsorship of a townsman whose authority no one would challenge; and she would achieve acceptance and respectability without any effort except church attendance. She read the remainder of the letter with a growing respect for her uncle's knowledge of human nature. He'd asked that the minister locate household help—Christian women with their own homes to tend, a doctor who could be relied upon during any emergency in childbirth, and a young scholar in need of tutorial work. Since the child was not yet three years old and tended to be extremely active, Samuel explained, the candidate would also need to be somewhat athletic.

As she'd concluded on the day Samuel had maneuvered her father into accepting her as a substitute guardian, her uncle was a thorough organizer. He left nothing to chance or to an unhappy, demoralized niece, not even her brothers' education. The fourth letter was a polite request—if Samuel's precise demands could be considered polite—for the immediate admittance to the Roxbury Latin School for Boys of Lloyd and John Rayburn, nephews and heirs to the Rayburn Publishers of New York and sons of Colonel Jeremy Rayburn, Massachusetts patriot serving with the Continental army. Rebecca could understand the inclusion of Jeremy's name in the petition—Massachusetts could claim few ranking officers despite its enormous contribution in fighting men. However, she considered Samuel's curriculum requests highly prejudiced. He asked that his nephews be taught oral and written rhetoric, mathematics, history, Latin, a smattering of law, and only a minimum of religious dogma. "Journalism," he'd written, "requires a clear mind, uncluttered by trivia."

Fervently, Rebecca hoped the Roxbury headmaster might have a sense of humor; but it was a long, painful month before she even met the man or any of the other recipients of Samuel's letters. When she and her family arrived in Boston, she did not need to pretend the feminine frailty her uncle had recommended. She'd been feverish and seasick throughout most of the six-day voyage, and the fear expressed in Dena's and the children's eyes had intensified her misery. Her strength and conscious self-control lasted until she'd established her identity to the satisfaction of the bank manager before she collapsed.

For a week Rebecca alternated between feverish insensibility and lethargic stupor, rarely alert enough to realize that the gray-haired man who forced her to drink drafts of evil-tasting medicine was the doctor summoned by the worried Congregationalist minister of Roxbury. On rare occasions Rebecca mumbled unintelligible words to Dena, who bustled in and out of the sickroom with a worried vigilance. Midmorning of the eighth day, with her fever broken and her thoughts lucid, she awakened in a strange bed without any memory of how she'd arrived there. Her first futile attempt to arise was halted by the smiling command of a strange woman who introduced herself as a neighbor.

"You stay put, Mrs. Keane, while I fetch Mrs. George and let her know you've returned to the land of the living. A heap of folks are going to be mighty relieved."

Rebecca's confusion about the identity of Mrs. George ended when Dena entered the room, grinning broadly in relieved triumph.

"'Bout time, Miz Rebecca, 'bout time you come to."

"What's wrong with me?"

"Doctor say it 'uz common fever an' that you 'uz hit harder than most 'cause of your chile and the mountain of misery you 'uz totin'."

"Then I'm still—"

Dena's chuckle interrupted her mistress's sigh. "'Spect this child's gonna be the most famous borned 'round these parts. Las' Sunday Reverend Elliott done ask his congregation to pray that you gits better, an' he tells them all 'bout your troubles jest lak Misser Samuel says."

"How did he receive the letter?"

"Banker feller say he'd deliver them when I tells him 'bout Misser Samuel wantin' folks here t' take care of us. Then he done bring us to this house an' fetch the reverend. Well, the reverend he kept old Jemmy hoppin' 'til we 'uz settled in."

"Who is Jemmy?"

"He 'uz left here by the las' folks an' he lives in the cottage at the rear jest lak we done at Misser Samuel's. Next morning the reverend come back with two women and now they works for us ebery morning 'ceptin' Sunday. 'Member that money you tole me I 'us t' use iffen there 'uz need? Well, the reverend showed me how to count out what I 'uz to pay them so's they could git the food they need for their own chil'run. An' then the reverend hisself walked me to the market so's I could git our food. Miz Rebecca, they got food here I ain't neber seed before, and ebery day they gits more of it."

"Dena, what about the children?"

"Johnny and Lloyd's at that school old Misser Samuel say. Benn took them there third day we 'uz here. Then Benn, he takes on Michael and who-ee, you neber heered such a ruckus! But Benn pays no nebermind to Michael's caterwaulin' t' be toted on his shoulder lak Misser Kent done. He makes that chile do his own walkin' an' his own pickin' up, an' that child done mind him better 'n he do me."

Rebecca sighed and waited for the inevitable explanations; she knew from experience that Dena was a thorough, if disorganized, reporter. However, Dena had also become a thorough housekeeper, so the interruptions in her narrative were frequent. But gradually during another week of convalescence Rebecca learned about the people who'd taken over the management of her life while she'd been incapacitated. The lawyer—not the mighty John Adams, who was presently in France on a diplomatic mission, but a Roxbury colleague—had responded to Samuel's letter with a businesslike promptness. Without meeting his client, he'd filed the guardianship documents Jeremy had signed, and written letters announcing the fact to the various Tuptons residing in the Boston area. He'd also registered

Dena's freedom papers and condescendingly suggested that as a free woman, she'd need a last name. He was among the first in Roxbury to learn that the young Negress possessed little of the trait that characterized most of her racial compatriots in America; she possessed no sense of inferiority. Her answer was prompt and comprehensive.

"Yes, sir, I knows; so I done chose *George* after the one that old Misser Samuel call 'the sly fox.' 'Spect you knows him as *Washington*, but I 'uz in Manhattan when he done keep those polecat redcoats on the jump, so I reckon I knows him a heap better. An' you jest put the word *Miz* down too, 'cause I's Miz Rebecca's housekeeper and I's the one in charge 'til she gits well."

The second person to underestimate Mrs. Dena George was the reporter who covered the Boston area for the *Massachusetts Spy*. Five days into Dena's stewardship, he arrived at the house and asked to speak to the mistress. Within minutes he discovered that he was doing just that. At least the black woman who greeted him was highly articulate and knowledgeable; and her concurrence with the information contained in Samuel Rayburn's letter was complete to the last detail, but without a single factual extention. Thus it was the Reverend Elliott who gave the reporter the inspiration for the final paragraph of his article, a statement that the expected child of Mrs. Philip Keane would have a proud heritage of bravery from both a father and a grandfather.

Reverend Elliott himself had gained an immediate appreciation of Dena's organizing talents as he'd watched her during the early days after the family's arrival in Roxbury. She'd managed the sick woman, the confused children, and himself with a relentless efficiency. He still smiled whenever he remembered that she'd inveigled him to escort her to the food stalls on Market Street and to help her carry home the baskets of food—a homely task he'd never performed before. Her interrogation of Benn Maddock, though, ended any doubt he may have had of her abilities.

Benn was an eighteen-year-old survivor of Bunker Hill whose left arm had been permanently disabled by a British bayonet, but whose fleet legs had prevented him from becoming a prisoner-of-war. Of a scholarly bent, he'd spent the postbattle years studying religion under the reverend's supervision and earning his living with occasional odd-jobs employment. In response to Samuel Rayburn's request, Elliott had presented Benn as a candidate for the position of tutor. Dena's questions had been merciless; he'd had to prove he could read, write, total sums, and more important, run with a speed that would outdistance a nimble little boy. In the end the youthful housekeeper had hired Benn and installed him in the loft of Jemmy's cottage.

The Sunday following, she and Benn had brought the three children to church, a gesture that had touched the heartstrings of the reverend. Richard Elliott was not an interfering busybody by nature. When he'd been appointed to the Roxbury church thirty years earlier, he'd been forced to overcome what amounted to an aversion for extending his ministry beyond the pulpit. But fortunately for his eventual success, Roxbury was not another Salem, where pulpit oratory was the chief measure of excellence in a religious leader. The parishioners had expected a seven-day-a-week tender of the flock, and gradually Richard Elliott had blended into their lives, reaping a rich harvest of trust. Thus his response to Samuel Rayburn's letter had not been a quixotic impulse, but a genuine concern for Rebecca's plight. And on that Sunday when Dena and the children had come to his church, he'd led the congregation in a prayer for the recovery of a young woman who, like many of them, had been victimized by the war.

Having taken no part in any of these activities that had thrust her into public notice, Rebecca delayed her convalescence, dreading the prospect of meeting her new benefactors. With her emotions in a state of gloomy confusion as her slim figure disappeared behind a telltale bulge, she brooded about the circumstances that had brought her to a strange town to bear a fatherless child. Her only protection, and that of her child, was to live the lie Samuel had invented, that of a distraught wife awaiting her husband's release from a British prison. Uneasily, Rebecca thought of the two men that lie affected, both of whom were capable of violence. Despite Lord Enderly's optimism, she was certain Kent would never forget her or their child; and Philip had already demonstrated his resolve to find her. She had a two-year reprieve before either man would be free to search, two years of an indecisive social limbo to endure.

On the day the doctor pronounced her well, he unintentionally reminded her that she had far more than her own unhappiness to consider.

"I'm relieved, Mrs. Keane, that this will be your second child; otherwise I might be concerned about your slender build and lack of appetite."

"Will you be here when my child is born, Doctor?"

"As a favor to your uncle, I will be available in the event of a medical emergency; but of course, the actual birth is the responsibility of the midwife. As I told you before, though, mistress, second births are never as dangerous or as difficult as first ones."

Rebecca turned sharply away from the smiling doctor in consternation; she'd forgotten the first lie that she'd already borne a son! In four or slightly more months, she would be bringing forth her first child; and she remembered with dread the number of Falmouth wives who'd died in tragic attempts to produce their firstborn. With a stoic composure Rebecca paid the doctor his fee and then spent an hour in intense concentration on the practical considerations involved in providing for the children already under her care and for the possibility of her own infant surviving her. The following morning she ordered the caretaker, Jemmy, to hire a rig and drive her to the bank in Boston where she learned that her accumulated wealth was, in the manager's cautious words, "a heavy responsibility for a woman who lacks a man's guidance, however temporarily."

Refraining from informing him that the money in question had been earned by her mother and herself without any help from a man, she asked to see the accounting and was shocked by the amount. No wonder Stanton Tupton had hoped his son would marry her! And among the papers the discreet banker handed her was a second surprise. Lord

Enderly had paid her well for relinquishing his son; he had placed the deed to the Roxbury home in her name.

On the way home Rebecca ordered Jemmy to make a second stop at the office of the Roxbury lawyer who'd handled the Tupton problems so promptly. James Price was a pleasant surprise, an astute man who'd already done his homework about this client he'd never seen. In Boston he'd researched the Rayburns, the Keanes, and the Langleys; and he knew more about the young woman now seated in his office than she suspected. Quite readily he agreed that the will she dictated was entirely sensible under the circumstances. A political realist about the horrors suffered by American prisoners-of-war at the hands of the British in New York, he was fully aware that a martinet such as the Colonel Crane whom Rebecca had described might prove more than a match for Lord Enderly in the disposition of Philip Keane. Thus Rebecca's will made no mention of her husband's name, only of the existing children and the one not yet born. With a blunt candor that equalled hers, he suggested himself, the Boston banker, and Reverend Elliott as the administrator-guardians in the event of her death.

Smiling for the first time in weeks, Rebecca murmured appreciatively, "You remind me of my Uncle Samuel; he never minces words either."

Having also researched the influential Rayburn Publishers, Price nodded thoughtfully. This new client was no ordinary housewife; she was, in the parlance of the trade, a potential channel to powerful people on both sides of the political schism.

Rebecca's final stop that afternoon was at the white clapboard parsonage next to the Roxbury Congregationalist Church. Having declined Reverend Elliott's offer of spiritual guidance during her final weeks of convalescence, Rebecca half hoped that he'd not be home today. She couldn't deny that he had already proved to be a good friend to her family; Dena's praise for him had been unstinting. He'd been the one older man in Rebecca's memory whose name her loyal servant had not prefaced with the adjective *ole*. In New York it had been *ole* Misser

Samuel, *ole* Colonel Crane, and *ole* Misser Stebbins. Dena had not even deigned to call the Anglican minister *reverend*; but this Congregationalist one she quoted with respect and quoted often. Gradually, Rebecca had developed a vague antipathy. After two years of having been dominated by older men in New York, she wanted no more interference in her life, especially not from a man who sounded as perceptively observant as this one.

But not only was Reverend Elliott home, he was expecting her, answering the door himself and escorting her into his study with pleased alacrity.

"When I called at your home today," he explained briskly, "Mrs. George said you'd be by to see me when you returned from Boston. I'm delighted to meet you, Mrs. Keane, and I can't tell you how relieved we all were when the doctor reported you completely recovered from your recent illness. Now, how can I help you with any of your additional problems?"

As he'd talked, Rebecca had studied the man who was prattling so knowledgeably about her private business. Immediately she retreated into the shell of composure her Uncle Samuel had criticized so often. Not that she found anything physically repugnant about Reverend Elliott. Late middle-aged in years, he was a pleasant-looking man with an amiable manner and a genuine interest in her problems. But Rebecca had recognized the strength of character expressed in his steady gray eyes, and she'd shuddered inwardly. Like her Uncle Samuel, he was a man with an unwavering purpose.

With a businesslike brevity she told him about James Price's suggestion of guardianship and asked if he would be willing to serve in that capacity should the need arise.

"What about your husband, Mrs. Keane?" he asked promptly.

"Philip will not be released for another two years, and then he may return to his father in Baltimore to acquire a new ship."

"Was there some reason you did not return to Baltimore, Mrs. Keane?"

Rebecca repressed her inner agitation; she'd been right in her estimation of this man—he was perceptively sharp!

"An excellent one, Reverend Elliott. I was released from New York through the kindly intervention of an Englishman who arranged for me to live here. At present the English have no access to Baltimore."

"But surely your husband knows where you are?"

"The English do not pamper their prisoners, Reverend."

"Are you allowed to correspond with him?"

'No, I don't even know what prisoner-of-war camp he's in, and I haven't heard from him since I last saw him in his English prison months ago. He knows nothing about the child I am expecting."

"It must be a lonely life for you," Elliott commiserated.

"It is for most sailors' wives and families, but I don't intend for it to be so for my children. I want them accepted here in Roxbury."

"What about you?"

After a slight hesitation, she responded with an unenthusiastic firmness, "The same for me."

"In that case, Mrs. Keane, I'll be delighted to serve as your children's guardian. And now, shall we take care of that other matter Mrs. George mentioned this morning about your need for a part-time cook? I have arranged for you to meet two candidates; and since you have a carriage and driver, I suggest we get started."

For two months after that first afternoon when she had readily hired one of his needier parishioners as her cook, Reverend Elliott had attempted in vain to win the trust of the composed Mrs. Keane. She attended church regularly and contributed generously to his various charities, but she remained aloof and withdrawn from anyone outside her own family. At first Elliott had thought she might have resented her husband because of the unborn child—during his years of ministry he'd learned that many women did; but her fondness for her brothers and son quickly dispelled that explanation. Because she was both a writer and artist of some merit, he suspected that she might be one of those dangerously self-centered women who were ambitious only for their own glorification. But just when he finally decided that Rebecca Keane really was the coldly efficient woman she seemed to be, the minister received a second letter from Samuel Rayburn.

The messenger arrived at Elliott's study early on a mid-October morning and announced that he would have to rejoin the ship waiting outside Boston Harbor by nightfall, and that Mr. Rayburn expected a reply from his niece. Since the letter was addressed as the first one had been, to the minister of the Roxbury Congregationalist Church, Elliott tore open the sealed envelope. Inside the pages of the one missive was a second sealed envelope addressed to Rebecca Rayburn Keane. Tucking that letter into his pocket, he began to read the first one. Essentially a man of God whose interest lay with people rather than with the progress of a tragic war, he was confused by what seemed to be a journalistic account of the Battle of Monmouth Court that had been fought outside the New Jersey village in late June.

Elliott recalled the accounts he'd read of the clash between Washington's and Cornwallis's armies, in which the rumored treachery of General Charles Lee had ruined the American chances for a decisive American victory.

"It was Lee's unexplained retreat," Samuel had written, "that caused the personal tragedy to my own family. Captain Kent Enderly, youngest son of Lord Brandon Enderly, was trapped with his small group of couriers by the retreating Americans, but his body was not among those returned to New York. Since neither his father nor I had expected him to follow General Clinton, who remained safely inside Monmouth Court during the battle, we were not alarmed until we received a letter from Malcolm Garner. For reasons of his own, my nephew had left the ship he was supposed to have taken to his new assignment in Gibraltar and rejoined his old command. With the permission of the American military, I was allowed to visit the battle site in New Jersey, and there I learned that the Americans had buried two hundred and fifty additional British dead. Among the effects of those dead that had been saved for future identification, I found my nephew's courier bag. Inside it were his personal papers, one of which involved my niece and her family.

"Kent was a special person in their lives; he was the only real father Rebecca's brothers and her son ever had. Although he was only a cousin, he offered all of them his protection when my brother and I were powerless during a troubled period of time. Rebecca and her brothers will be badly shaken by this news, and I am hoping you will be able to soften the blow somehow."

Rushing over to Rebecca's home, Reverend Elliott silently handed her the two letters and watched sympathetically as she read them. Merciful in his knowledge about human frailty, he realized intuitively that the relationship between the dead man and this grief-stricken woman had been more than a platonic love between cousins. But he passed no moral judgment on her; how could he understand what pressures she'd been under as a captive in a captive city? Compassionately, he remained with her throughout the hours it took her grief to subside into resigned composure, and waited without censure as she wrote two brief letters of reply.

Elliott's vague suspicions were blunted a few minutes before he left, however, by the usually cheerful Mrs. George, whose grief was almost as intense as her mistress's.

"Misser Kent done save our lives," Dena mourned, "an' he done love our chil'run lak his own. Now Miz Rebecca got this misery on top of all her others, an' she ain't as strong as she pretend. She done already mourn a long time on account of her husband an' on account of the las' two years of nothin' but worry 'bout all of us. An' she is still got t' git through bornin' that new chile in her belly 'fore she kin get better."

Audrey Gwenna was born in the evening of November 22 after sixteen hours of intermittent labor on the part of her mother. Throughout the second half of the ordeal the puzzled midwife had frequently consulted the doctor who'd arrived in the early afternoon with Reverend Elliott. As the two men sat comfortably in the fire-warmed sitting room after finishing the excellent dinner Mrs. Wymer had served them, their desultory conversation was once again interrupted by the midwife.

"She isn't any nearer delivery than she was hours ago," the frustrated woman complained. "It isn't like a second child to take so long, but her pains aren't strong enough even yet to get this child birthed proper."

Inviting the midwife to sit down and join them in a glass of Madeira, the doctor asked a few cursory medical questions, nodded gravely at the answers he received, and settled back to enjoy his own wine.

Not as immune to suffering as his companions, and certainly not about this particular patient, Reverend Elliott inquired sharply, "Is Mrs. George with her mistress?"

"That meddlesome savage has barely left the room all day," the midwife rasped angrily. "If I believed in such nonsense, I'd say she's cast some spell over her mistr—"

"You're not from Roxbury, are you?" Elliott interrupted sternly.

"Certainly not. My practice is in Boston, where servants have the good sense to know their place."

"Mrs. George isn't a servant; she's—"

"She's an ignorant Negro who talks incessantly about some higgledy-piggledy conjure woman. And she's in my way! Doctor—"

Smiling his reassurance at the angry woman, the doctor murmured, "I'll examine your patient in due time, mistress. Meanwhile let us enjoy this excellent Madeira."

Upstairs in the master bedroom, the target of the midwife's anger was massaging Rebecca's distended belly in the time-honored method the conjure woman had taught her. Since early morning Dena had distrusted the white woman who'd demanded her own breakfast before she'd even met her patient. That mild distrust had turned into something akin to suspicious vigilance when the New England martinet had shaken Rebecca's shoulder impatiently and told the suffering woman to stop acting like a silly chicken with a rock stuck in its craw. Displaying an implacable stubbornness, Dena had gradually taken over the supervision with her mistress's groaning approval and begun the massaging late in the afternoon during the midwife's dinner hour, continuing the strong, soothing strokes to the rhythm of a murmured encouragement. Twice again the frustrated professional had left the room to consult the doctor, leaving her day-long adversary in charge. It was during the last of these consultations that Rebecca's infant daughter was born. Dena's broad face was split into a jubilant grin of victory as she laid the tiny creature on her mother's perspiration-soaked body before she turned her attention to the aftermath of birth.

As alert as she'd been since the first racking pain, Rebecca responded to her faithful friend's smile with a tremulous one of her own, unable to voice the overpowering emotions she felt. Her sense of fulfillment was complete when she recalled the words her mother had written about Rebecca's own birth: "A new life, a new hope! There can be no greater creation on earth!"

It was the piercing shriek uttered by the midwife as she reentered the room that roused the doctor and brought him pounding up the stairs.

"The savage hasn't even washed the child," the midwife rasped furiously as she tried to push the black woman away.

Resisting the violence with an obstinate strength, Dena declared with an unshakable conviction, "Conjur woman say mama comes first lessen you wants an orphan on your hands. This chile knows her mama, an' right now she don' care a mite whether she's spanking clean or not."

Intervening between the two women with a sharp authority, the doctor handed the small, perfect infant to the midwife before he turned his attention to Dena. "Where did you learn the craft, Mrs. George?" he asked with a grudging approval.

As Rebecca heard the familiar words "Conjur woman say," she drifted into exhausted sleep. Outside in the hall Reverend Elliott smiled with an inner satisfaction.

Late the following morning when she was awakened in a darkened room, Rebecca's thoughts were as peaceful as her dreams had been, and the last of her fears had been exorcised. Ever since the day she'd learned of Kent's death, her spirit had been rebuilding. All of her earlier resentment had been replaced by the fierce realization that the one thing left alive of her passionate, protective lover was the unborn child stirring in her womb. Eliminated too had been the abrasive shame that, despite the ill-considered wedding, she was no better than the Paulettes of the world. Kent deserved a more fitting memorial than regret. The love he'd lavished on her, a love she'd eventually returned, had not been illicit by intent, only through an accident of fate. In the make-believe world they had created together, it had been a beautiful, unifying force.

On that terrible day of reckoning, however, as she'd read of his death, her customary disguise of stoic composure had been shattered, and she'd wept brokenly in front of Reverend Elliott. Had he asked any penetrating questions during those bitter hours, more than likely she'd have blurted the truth. At his quiet insistence, she'd written the reply to her uncle's personal letter to her, and she'd returned the enclosed will with the brief message that she didn't need Kent's money to remember him with love. "Please inform Lord Enderly that when Kent's child is old enough to understand, I will tell him about his English father and how much that wonderful father had wanted him."

Now as she held that tiny beautiful child in her arms, she experienced anew the disconsolate pain of grief that Kent was not here to welcome this blue-eyed infant daughter with his exuberant smile and his boundless love.

Exhibiting again the warm empathy that had helped Rebecca through the difficult months, Dena eased the bitterness of the moment. "I believes this angel chile has got her pappy's sweetness, Miz Rebecca, and she's gonna bring nothin' but love into the fam'bly."

Three days later, after Audrey Gwenna had mastered the art of nursing and lost her disfiguring wrinkles, Dena's prophecy seemed to come true during the infant's introduction to her young uncles and her brother. Realistic as always, Lloyd's reaction was a shrewd appraisal. "She's too little even for a girl, and she doesn't look like us; but we'll take care of her anyway."

"She does too," Johnny disclaimed hotly. "She's got Becky's hair so everyone will know she belongs to us."

Michael's approach was physically direct. He reached out to touch his sister's hand and giggled with delight as the tiny fingers curled around one of his. "She likes me, Mama," he chortled in glee.

Looking down on the shining face of the irrepressible child who'd become her son as completely as Audrey Gwenna was her daughter, Rebecca experienced a faint hope that the divided halves of her own life might someday be blended together as easily as these two children's. She thought of Kent and his generous, untainted love for Michael, and she remembered that Philip had risked his life to save the children of enemy strangers. Perhaps in the vague future, he might extend that grace to this small *ne-oma* whose petallike hand was gripping his son's fingers.

CHAPTER
20

MERCURIAL in their speed of passage, the winter, spring, and summer months of 1779 had been busy ones of adjustment for Rebecca's family. For Dena the transition to freedom had seemed effortless from her first day in Roxbury. She was born a free soul, Rebecca marveled with envy as she watched her youthful housekeeper manage the small staff with a firm friendliness, deal with shopkeepers who quickly learned to be colorblind in Mrs. George's case, and gain the respect of the townspeople without ever stepping over that invisible line of propriety. Her only explanation to Rebecca about her understanding of such a complex social concept was the cryptic statement "Misser Malcolm done 's'plain t' me 'bout what folks b'lieves."

Lloyd Rayburn, too, seemed to have absorbed the magic formula for success in a school attended by the disciplined sons of Puritan aristocrats. The sturdy ten-year-old was competitive enough to hold his own even in Latin and mathematics despite the brevity of Reverend Stebbins's tutoring.

"He's not really a great scholar, Mrs. Keane," Benn Maddock reported, "but he learns what he has to, and he knows how to impress his teachers." Lloyd will be the first honest Tupton in Massachusetts history, Rebecca reflected with amused admiration; and eventually he'll turn Rayburn Publishers into the most successful business in New York.

"What about Johnny?" she asked the young tutor.

"He's the bright one, Mrs. Keane, even though he doesn't play the school game as well as his brother does. He learns more by himself than he does from the teachers."

Even though she received a daily report about Michael's activities, Rebecca still had no inkling of her son's academic potential. "And Michael?" she inquired with trepidation.

Benn's eyes rolled heavenward and he laughed. "I'll let you know in a year from now after I've caught my breath. So far I've learned more from him than he has from me."

Rebecca smiled in understanding; Michael was as restless as the wind and just as unpredictable. But thank God, he had survived all of the traumatic changes in his brief life without losing a jot of his wild enthusiasm for adventure. Occasionally, Rebecca paused in the middle of her own hectic schedule of activities and wished she could experience again even a fraction of Michael's excitement.

Not that her own life was dull, only regimented and predictable. In the early months of Audrey Gwenna's life, Dena's "angel chile" had kept her mother housebound with six contentedly slow nursings a day. To keep her own impatience in check during those repetitive sessions,

Rebecca had begun reading aloud to her infant daughter. Eventually, at Dena's suggestion, she'd suspended the tiny girl in a sling anchored around her own neck and resumed her writing career, this time as a contributor to Isaiah Thomas's *Massachusetts Spy*.

The invitation to do so had been prompted by a letter Thomas had received from Samuel Rayburn stating that his niece was a skilled journalist who'd witnessed three separate invasions by the British. Since Massachusetts had suffered two military disasters the summer before—the destruction of New Bedford with the burning of seventy privateer ships anchored in the harbor and the futile attempt to expel the British from Rhode Island—Rebecca's eyewitness accounts of the British naval attacks she'd seen were well received. So were her subsequent descriptions of the decadent life in the slave colony of Saint-Domingue and of the brutal deprivations suffered by the poor people on captive Manhattan Island.

Rebecca had enjoyed writing those biweekly assignments, but she'd had decidedly mixed feelings about the second major disruption in her life. Reverend Elliott had not allowed her to backslide into isolated withdrawal after childbirth. Requesting her permission to use the locked-up drawing room wing of her overly large house, he scheduled meetings for those activities he deemed inappropriate for his church. Thus Rebecca had become the unwilling hostess for the patriotic women engaged in providing uniforms for the Massachusetts militia during two afternoons a week and for the war-relief committee of church members every Wednesday night.

Nor did the reverend's efforts on her behalf end with those weekly intrusions into her life. He urged her to host an occasional dinner party, and he supplied the guests, usually two or three couples from among the town's leaders. He fulfilled his commitment as prospective guardian by a monthly visit to talk to the three older children and to Benn. And he frequently recruited Rebecca's help in keeping up with church correspondence.

In early summer during the first hot weather, her routine was changed again when Audrey stopped nursing, and

Dena took over the chore of feeding the alert infant. To her dismay, Rebecca quickly discovered that Reverend Elliott was as pleased about her new freedom as she was.

On a warm September afternoon she was completing a story-reading session with Michael, extended this day because he'd been receptive beyond the usual half hour, when Dena burst into the library, her sturdy arms akimbo and her expression disapproving.

"Miz Rebecca, you knows what time it is?" she demanded. "You and Michael's been lolligaggin' for an hour 'stead of gittin' yourselves ready."

At her mistress's blank look of inquiry, Dena shook her head resignedly. "Miz Rebecca, you is gettin' forgetful. Las' night Misser Elliott done say he be by for you in twenty minutes in the church hay wagon, an' you knows he's gonna 'spect you to hep him lak you been doin' all summer at the fish fries an' clambakes."

Rebecca groaned in irritation at herself and at the omnipresent minister who had appointed her willy-nilly as his unofficial hostess at all church social functions. And it wasn't a task she enjoyed, particularly during outdoor parties when only the men and boys were allowed the excitement of fishing and clam digging. She would have preferred joining Benn Maddock and her three children at the water's edge. Her resentment abated somewhat when she looked down at her son's face; as it always had at the prospect of an adventuresome outing, it was glowing with an incandescent joy. Resigning herself to a tiresome five hours of the late afternoon and evening, she rushed to her room to change into a summer frock modest enough to be acceptable for a churchgoing matron of twenty-four mature years.

Hours later on the homeward-bound trip, with a sound asleep Michael sprawled across her lap, her reflections about the evening were only slightly less gloomy. There'd been small gracious moments of pride in her brothers; both of them had retained the polite good manners Kent had taught them. When Lloyd had won the footrace against a score of other lads, she'd been excited and proud, but prouder still when he'd earned a prized arrowhead for reciting a Bible passage more accurately than the others. Even more rewarding to her had been Johnny's thoughtful play with Michael, racing with the shrieking three-and-a-half-year-old along the hard-packed sandy beach. And later Johnny's thorough report about the available food had delighted Rebecca.

"You can eat the bread," he'd whispered to her and Benn. "It's all right because Mrs. Wymer baked it and Dena packed it. But the corn from Mrs. Williams's garden has worms in it, and there were flies in Mrs. Horton's pudding until she fished them out." Her youngest brother, Rebecca realized with satisfaction, was developing a journalist's sharp eye for detail and an accurate brevity in reporting it. Samuel Rayburn's heir apparent was unconsciously preparing himself for his destined future.

Rebecca's own participation in the festivities, though, had been more than vaguely frustrating. For two hours she'd accompanied Reverend Elliott on his round of greeting, adding a few perfunctory words to his at each stop. Dutifully, she'd remained by his side at the serving table, grudgingly admitting that he earned his popularity with his parishioners. He remembered the names of every child, even those still swaddled in their mothers' arms, and he invariably slipped an extra piece of ginger cake on each child's plate. Cheerfully interested in the small confidings of the old and young alike, he was a splendid minister, Rebecca reminded herself sharply; but she was relieved when he finally left her alone as he organized the communal singing. Seated apart on the warm sand, she listened without much interest to the ragged music, her pretty green muslin dress a pale blur in the wasted moonlight. But as she quickly discovered when a young militia officer sat down next to her, Richard Elliott had not forgotten his self-imposed duty as guardian. Unobtrusively, he'd instructed Michael and Benn to join her and the lonely militiaman.

For a moment Rebecca had fumed mutinously at the minister's interference. She might be matron-aged with a family to tend, but she hadn't entirely forgotten the thrill of harmless flirting. With a reluctant honesty, she admitted that he had good cause to monitor her deportment—she hadn't forgotten the wild excitement of physical love either. Submissively, she accepted the subtle warning and waited patiently until Elliott signaled an end to the evening's entertainment before she and Benn loaded the tired children aboard the wagon. It was a peaceful and trouble-free life, she reminded herself, regardless of its limitations; and she owed Richard Elliott a debt of gratitude for helping her establish it. She bid him a pleasant good night as she stood with her sleep-dazed children on the walkway of her home. Halfway to the front door, she stopped short. Even in the dim lamplight Dena's white apron was as visible as the moon in a black sky, and the housekeeper's sibilant hiss was clearly audible.

"Benn, you takes all three chil'run to the cottage. I done ruint their room with slop water, so's old Jemmy and I done already moved their bedding."

Rousing herself to semi-understanding, Rebecca protested, "That's ridiculous! There's plenty of other rooms in the big house."

"No, there ain't," Dena snapped sharply. "Now all of you do as I says."

Alerted by the urgent undertone in Dena's voice, Rebecca hastily undressed Michael and tucked him into one of the pallets on the stone floor of the cottage, kissed her brothers, and told Benn to hear their prayers. Outside the door she turned apprehensively toward her friend.

"What's happened?"

"He's here, Miz Rebecca, that's what's happened!"

"Who is?"

"Your husband, that's who—leastwise that's who he say he 'uz. An' he say it mighty positive."

"Dear God!" Rebecca gasped. "When?"

"'Bout four hours ago jest after Miz Wymer left. When he asked where you 'uz, I tells him at church; but I don' tells him which one. Then I cooks him a dinner and fix him the bathwater he asks for. He sure be a take-over man, Miz Rebecca."

"Which room did you put him in?"

"'Ain't nothin' I done; he puts himself in your room and say he'd wait for you there."

"Did he see Audrey?"

"No, mam! I 'uz givin' her supper in the kitchen when he done pound on the door and asks where to put his horse. I sent him round to see old Jemmy, and I puts her in my room an' she 'uz blessed quiet jest lak she knows there 'uz trouble. Miz Rebecca, he sure ain't one you kin keep hid long, an' he knows a heap 'bout orderin' folk around. He acts jest lak he done own eber'thin' in this house, an' he warn't s'posed t' know where we is. I done heered old Misser Enderly say he wouldn't tell, leastways not for a long time."

"Some people always think they know what's best for others," Rebecca whispered tensely, her mind swimming with apprehension. The vague tomorrow she'd worried about for almost a year and a half had materialized months before she'd believed it could.

"You best tell him tonight 'bout our four chil'run 'cause they ain't gonna stay hid much b'yond tomorrow mornin'."

Rebecca nodded stiffly and started up the stairs, walking on the inside of the treads to avoid the familiar squeaks. Steadying her shaking hands, she turned the knob of her bedroom door and eased herself inside. The windows were wide open and the curtains pulled back, and she noted with a prayerful relief that there was sufficient moonlight to avoid the necessity of lighting a candle. Her heart was hammering with a painful speed as she looked at the man sleeping in her bed. For a moment he seemed a complete stranger until he turned restlessly and she saw the hawklike profile and the shock of dark hair tumbled over his forehead. She'd never been able to draw that face for some reason, she remembered irrelevantly, but it had been imprinted into her memory anyway. When he turned again more fitfully than before, she walked swiftly into the dressing room and closed the door.

Standing shakily in the darkness and breathing as if she'd run an uphill country mile, Rebecca contemplated her options. She could wake him now and blurt out the truth before she lost the last shreds of her courage, or she could go to bed in one of the guest rooms and inform him more casually tomorrow. She smiled in self-contempt! There'd never been a time when informing Philip Keane of anything had been casual; he could explode into biting anger over trivialities much less over something as major as the news that she'd acquired four children during his absence.

Marshaling her wavering resolution, she turned to reenter the bedroom, recalling only at the last second some other half-forgotten facts about her temperamental husband. He'd hated to see her hair unkempt, and he'd always expected her to be smartly gowned. Feeling the grit of sand in her shoes and the flyaway curls on her head, she groped for the candle and lighted it as quickly as her perspiring hands would permit. Swiftly then, she stripped off her rumpled clothing and washed herself briefly with the tepid water in her basin before she donned a fresh summer-weight nightgown and the most concealing bedcoat in her wardrobe.

Seated before the silvered mirror, she brushed her hair with nervous, absentminded strokes as she organized her defenses. She tried to recall her own devastating emotions when she'd learned of Philip's infidelities early in their marriage. Instead, she remembered his unreasoning jealousy of Dirk du Kuyper, which had resulted from a few hours of a public flirtation. Dear God, how would he react to her admission that had Kent not been killed, she would most probably have gone to Wales and taken Philip's son with her? How could she explain that her love for Kent had not replaced or destroyed the love she'd borne Philip even during those long, empty months of separation? Perhaps if I'd proved as barren with Kent as I had with Philip, she thought desperately, he might have forgiven me more easily. But there was no way to soften the blow, no way to make the truth palatable except by more lies; and Rebecca would countenance no slur to Kent's memory. Engrossed in her own thoughts, she did not hear the door open or see the man who entered until his strong arms lifted her from the bench and swung her around to face him.

"Were you planning to take all night, Cottontop, before

you worked up enough courage to come to bed?'' he demanded.

Her lips formed his name, but her vocal cords were too paralyzed to produce any sound. He kissed her then and kept on kissing her until she managed to pull away with a desperate burst of strength.

Out of breath, she could only gasp the words. ''We need to talk, Philip.''

''No, Cottontop, we don't and won't. I told you a long time ago that we'd never again spoil a reunion with an argument. Are you coming to bed willingly or do I carry you there?'' The question was purely rhetorical because he gave her no time to answer. He began kissing her again with a draining strength as he propelled her from the small room to the large moonlit one without releasing her lips or her body. At the bedside she ceased struggling to free herself as a wildly sweet, barely remembered passion obliterated all logic and she responded with an urgency that matched his own. At some point during their unrestrained caresses and swift undressing, she felt transported back in time to their days together on a rocky, barren Caribbean island, and the pounding of her painfully awakening heart sounded like the pounding surf that had accompanied their lovemaking there.

There was no prolonging, no holding back. They joined together with a fierce compulsion that answered a need in both of their intense, passionate natures; and her responses were as uninhibited as his advances. They lay in exhausted silence after the fiery explosion of emotion had ceased racking their bodies, a silence as primitive as their union had been, a silence without thought other than the drugging need for sleep.

As if attuned to a mutual time clock, they awakened sometime during the dark predawn hours and came together again in the same compelling ritual of repossession. Lulled into abeyance by a sense of inevitability, Rebecca's conscience remained quiescent; but the inner, guarded core of her being that had seemed frozen since the day she'd learned of Kent's death was pulsing now with a rebuilding warmth that had little to do with physical passion. Her laughter was softly exultant when Philip's hands restrained her own uninhibited caresses, and his voice was raggedly breathless as he whispered the well-remembered advice into her ear, "Relax, Cottontop, we have all night," before he added the more alluring promise, "We have the rest of our lives."

Of the two partners, Philip was more aware of the unique poignancy of their union because he alone had spent long, empty hours anticipating it. Although he'd never analyzed why his attachment to this mercurial woman had become the mainstay of his sanity throughout the long, desperate months, he was experiencing a joyful relief at finding her still passionately responsive—at finding her at all. During the first year of their separation when he'd learned of her unlucky capture, he'd burned with a determined fury to rescue her—to prove that despite his earlier failures to protect her, she was the most important person in his life. But New York had proved impregnable, and that bitter defeat following the frustration of not finding his son in France had increased his hatred for the British to an incautious recklessness. Thereafter his small fleet had earned the epitaph of devil ships before two of them had been destroyed near Guernsey Island.

At the time of his surrender to the admiralty, such was his cynical distrust of the Royal British Navy, he'd had no hope for his own life; he'd fought only to save his crew. Ironically, it'd been the citizens of Guernsey who'd saved their lives and an English aristocrat who'd saved his. It'd been after the trial, during the interminable months of imprisonment that Rebecca had become again the magnetic lodestar of his thoughts, and gradually he'd accepted her domination. No longer did he strain against the invisible bonds that such a surrender placed upon him; no longer did his often feverish dreams swirl around the unhampered freedom of command at sea. Instead they concentrated on the slender, spirited girl he'd never fully possessed or conquered. And last night after one startled look of recognition and a momentary attempt at evasion, she'd capitulated more willingly than he'd ever expected, even in his most sanguine dreams.

For him their earlier physical reunion had been his first real act of freedom, his first assurance that he hadn't merely exchanged one miserable existence for another. But his memory hadn't played him false; her body was as pliantly muscular as he'd remembered and her responses just as unrestrained. If anything, she was even more alive and more excitingly bold. For a moment that small mental control he'd maintained stumbled over the ancient pitfall of jealousy until she'd laughed; and he'd taken his own advice and relaxed, allowing the sensual subjugation of ecstasy to take over his consciousness. Long after she'd fallen asleep, he still held her close to him, reluctant to break the contact that had brought him peace.

Glaring sunlight and Audrey's peevish cry brought reality crashing back into Rebecca's consciousness. Regretfully, she eased herself away from the man sleeping heavily beside her, noticing in the harsh light the gaunt tiredness etched on his features and hating the prospect of adding to the misery he'd already suffered. But there were others in her life now, more vulnerable even than a husband returned from the war, whose needs must be considered first. Praying that Philip would sleep another two hours, Rebecca rushed through her morning schedule of seeing her brothers off to school for their Saturday morning classes and Michael settled into his routine of outdoor play with Benn in watchful attendance. As casually as she could, she paid Mrs. Wymer and the two maids their wages and dismissed them for the day with the flimsy excuse that her house guest was too exhausted to be disturbed.

"You didn't tell him," Dena accused her mistress with a flat disapproval as she and Rebecca bathed and fed the happily gurgling infant whose existence would soon turn the "house guest's" exhaustion into a black fury.

"I will right after he's had breakfast. Mrs. Wymer said she'd baked fresh bread this morning and put a ham in the oven."

"You wants the dining table set?"

Rebecca shook her head and smiled ruefully. "No, we'll use the small table in the sitting room."

"He's gonna tear out of there lak a burnt cat soon's he

sees that picture you done hang over the mantel. You wants me t' take it down?"

"No, it stays right where it is. Can you manage Audrey while I carry some hot water upstairs and wake him up?"

Dena's note of derision was eloquent. "What you thinks I been doin' since he come? An' I plans t' keep right on doin' it. Ain't nobody gonna hurt this angel chile. You jest worries 'bout gittin' him up and gittin' him tole, Miz Rebecca, b'fore our other chil'runs gits home."

Half an hour later when Rebecca led her husband into the informal living room, she smothered a nervous giggle as she surveyed Dena's artful placement of the small table and chairs. Only if Philip twisted completely around would he be able to see the fireplace; and only after he'd devoured the ample array of ham and eggs, Rebecca decided, would she show him the revealing picture above that fireplace. Her nervousness increased steadily as she noted the small portion he ate and the growing determination of his expression. When he refused a second cup of coffee and pushed his chair back, she plunged into speech.

"Tell me about your release, Philip. I thought you were supposed to be detained for another six months."

"I was, but three weeks ago Enderly showed up ten days early for his regular monthly visit and—"

"Where were you imprisoned?"

"In two back rooms in a warehouse in New Port— luxurious quarters compared to what I had in England—a dungeon cell with rats and filthy straw. But for some reason I still don't understand, Enderly made certain I was comfortable in New Port. He kept me supplied with books, and he allowed my jailers to visit me. They weren't regular navy or army, but three merchant seamen he paid himself. On the night of my release, he finally told me why. Did you ever hear of a Colonel Crane while you were in New York, Cottontop?"

Rebecca sucked in her breath. "I knew him when he lived at my uncles' home," she admitted. "When did you meet him?"

"I didn't, but according to Enderly, he's the reason I was given an early release."

"You were lucky, Philip. Colonel Crane believed that all American prisoners should be hanged or starved to death—especially privateers. And even more especially *you*."

"So I was told. The day after this Colonel Crane was transferred to New Port, Enderly came to my quarters and ordered me into common seaman's clothing identical to my jailers' and the five of us waded out to a longboat anchored off the waterfront. It was then Enderly told me about the persistent colonel who'd been searching for me since the day my name didn't appear on the roster of the *Jersey*."

"Lord Enderly kept his promise," Rebecca murmured softly.

"So he did, Cottontop, and according to him, you're to tell me why."

"Did he tell you where to find me?"

"No, all he would say about you was that you were in New England and safe."

"Then how—?"

"How did I locate you? The merchantman the five of us boarded in New Port headed south into Long Island Sound. A mile out from New London the next morning, I was put into a small boat and told to row ashore with the tide. It was a damned long haul and foggy as hell, but when I got there I discovered that the packet Lord Enderly gave me contained enough money for some decent clothing and for overland travel."

"I would have thought you'd have preferred going by ship."

"I'm on parole, Cottontop, a very harsh parole until the end of the war. If I'm taken prisoner again aboard a ship or in a battle on land, I'll be hanged without a trial. The English court ruled me a privateer, but the admiralty did not. I'm forbidden to join my father in Baltimore or to have anything to do with his remaining privateers. About the only thing the British didn't know about me was my connection with the Massachusetts navy. Two days ago in Boston I signed up with Colonel Paul Revere to train marines for the planned assault on Bagaduce. After the fiasco in Rhode Island, the state plans to use its own navy and army for any future defense or attack.''

"Did you know I was living in Roxbury when you came to Boston?''

"I knew you were here somewhere because your gallant English lord gave me a letter to deliver to a Boston bank. But in New London I'd already learned a good deal else about you from Mr. Cooper. Why didn't you ever tell me that you'd had some of your scribblings published under the name of Eb Burns?''

Irritated by the slur, Rebecca shrugged. "I didn't think you'd be interested.''

"I was interested; I even liked some of the stories. Enderly made sure I read both your books while I was in prison, but he neglected to mention that my wife was the author. I also read your articles in the *Massachusetts Spy*. Mr. Cooper was the one who told me about those and let me read his copies. There were a number of things you neglected to tell me, weren't there, Cottontop?''

Philip's voice was still light, but its undertone held the sarcastic bite Rebecca remembered all too well. With a resigned self-control, she ignored the gibe and postponed the inevitable with still another question.

"Did Jed Daws survive the trial, Philip?''

"Jed Daws wasn't even there; I'd beached him after our first return from France. He's in Baltimore with my father; and when I last heard, they were both surviving as landlubbers. Any more questions, Cottontop?''

"No.''

"Then suppose you answer some of mine.''

Rebecca's heart was thudding with a painful heaviness as she shook her head. "I told you we should have talked last night, Philip.''

"Are you sorry we didn't?''

"No.''

"I'd have called you a liar if you'd said *yes*, Cottontop. Now about Lord Enderly. Just why did he work so hard on my behalf? And why is he so protective about you?''

Taking a deep breath, Rebecca moved stiffly away from the table to stand in front of the fireplace. When she finally spoke, her voice was tightly controlled. "Lord Enderly is the brother-in-law of my New York uncles, and he's the one who published my stories in England." She paused tensely before she added the blunt declaration, "He's also the grandfather of my ten-month-old daughter."

She heard his muttered rasp, "You goddamned whore!" with a shock that turned her crippling sense of guilt into a cold anger. Not waiting for him to articulate other epitaphs, she announced defiantly, "You might as well know the rest, Philip Keane. Since you left me in Saint-Domingue, I have acquired three other children as well. If you'd care to turn around instead of brooding on your God-given right to murder an unfaithful wife, you might be interested in the portrait I painted of them last year."

As she heard his derisive question and watched his eyes narrow as he stared at the offending picture, she felt a detachment that bordered on contempt.

"Is that the man?"

"Yes, that's the man, Philip. British Captain Kent Enderly, killed at Monmouth Court five months before his daughter was born."

"And now enshrined forever over your marble mantel! How touching that he left behind such a complete family."

"The family was mine before I met Kent."

"At least part of them were, Mrs. Keane. The oldest two are your brothers. I lived in Falmouth too, remember? That leaves only the youngest one seated so trustingly on your lover's shoulders. I gather he's the product of one of your earlier infidelities."

The smile that twisted her lips as she walked toward the door was one of hopeless resignation. He was glaring at her with a brooding anger that offered her no quarter, no escape from the bleak truth. As she turned to face him, her own defensive anger slipped its tight leash and she exploded into speech.

"No, Philip. Michael is yours. Paulette Burnell sold him and his nurse to me for a string of pearls just before I sailed from Port-au-Prince. It was the necklace you'd given me, and I will say it matched the one she was wearing almost perfectly."

Rebecca closed the door behind her with a shaking hand and shrugged in cynical defeat. "Well, I told him and you heard his answer," she hissed at Dena, who'd been hovering in the hallway. Plucking Audrey from the housekeeper's arms, she headed toward the library, muttering an irreverent paraphrase of Reverend Elliott's favorite scripture. "In my mansion there are many rooms suitable for hiding. Dena, you'd better send Jemmy to the church to tell the women's committee that I won't be able to attend. I'll take care of Audrey for the rest of the day."

The housekeeper snorted impatiently, "Jest what you 'spect me t' do when Benn gits home with Michael?"

"Tell Benn to introduce Michael to his father."

"Sometimes you tempts the devil, Miz Rebecca. S'pose that riled-up man in there done take a notion to tote his son off somewheres."

Rebecca paused and shook her head. "Philip wouldn't do that."

"Jest what make you so all-fired certain? 'Pears t' me this one's as hoppin' mad as that polecat Roger Tupton."

"Philip isn't anything like Roger, Dena. He has a temper and a sharp tongue, but he's not cruel. Besides"— Rebecca smiled suddenly with an impulsive malice—"How far do you think he'd get in Roxbury with Michael screaming like a banshee?"

Reluctantly, Dena returned the smile, but there was a speculative look in her eyes as she stared at the closed door of the sitting room. Waiting only until her mistress disappeared into the library, the black housekeeper took a deep breath and turned the doorknob. She was talking before she'd completed her entry.

"Cap'n Keane, you best set still 'til I speaks my mind. There's a whole heap you don' know nothin' bout, startin' with the fact that Miz Rebecca done got herself into all this trouble on account of you. She done lie to old Colonel Crane 'cause she 'uz pertectin' you an' your pappy."

In the library Rebecca was on the floor playing an unbalanced game of catch ball with her gleeful daughter when Philip slammed his way into the room and demanded,

"Why the hell didn't you tell me that you married the man after you heard I was dead?"

"Since the marriage turned out to be bigamous, what difference does it make?"

"When did you learn it was?"

"Just before Lord Enderly sent us out of New York."

"Did the man know?"

"Yes, he and my Uncle Samuel learned about your capture two months after Kent and I were married."

Philip's lips curled with contempt. "But they didn't think you had a right to know."

"My uncle believed you'd be executed, and he wanted to spare me another—"

"Another what?"

"Another—bad time."

"What excuse did the man—?"

"His name was Kent, and I never saw him again after his father told me."

"Did he know about—about her?" Philip jerked his head in Audrey's direction.

"Yes, he knew."

"How long had you known him before you married him?"

"About six months. Did Dena tell you that I posed as a widow in order to—"

"She told me. Is it true that Enderly saved my son from drowning?"

Rebecca glanced up at the tall man who'd seated himself stiffly at her desk. "Kent did much more for Michael than saving him from a dunking in the Hudson."

"So your servant told me. Does she always listen behind doors?"

"Dena isn't a servant. She's my housekeeper and the best friend I've ever had. And yes, she listens behind doors whenever she's suspicious of the people inside the room."

"Is what she tells me about your life in New York true?"

"She was there the whole time, and she's an intelligent woman."

"She said this Enderly was the one who saved your life."

"Kent protected and supported us after Roger Tupton told the newspaper my real name, among other things, and we were no longer safe on my uncles' estate. Even if Kent hadn't offered to marry me, I would have . . . accepted his hospitality and posed as his housekeeper. We were cousins of a sort."

Again Philip's glaring eyes sought out the fluff-haired infant sitting on the floor. "Blood relative?" he demanded.

Rebecca smiled faintly. "No, we merely had uncles in common."

After relaxing only momentarily, he returned to the attack. 'Your housekeeper said you married him because you had to. Had you been lovers?"

Rebecca took a deep, painful breath and her voice shook. "You ask that question as if you had the right to judge me."

"Were you lovers?" he persisted relentlessly.

"Were *you*, Philip?" she countered sharply. "Were you lovers with all those Frenchwomen who consoled you when you couldn't find Michael on your first trip to France?"

"You know damn well it's different with a man."

"You've answered my question; now I'll answer yours. Kent proposed to me a week after he'd met me in June, but he didn't become my—my lover until the following February."

"Did you love him?"

"Not at first," she admitted slowly, "but eventually I learned to love him very deeply."

"For these past three years I was under the delusion that you'd *learned* to love me before I left Port-au-Prince."

With her temper rising in response to his, her answer was defensively tense. "I loved you a long time before Port-au-Prince, Philip Keane, and I've never stopped loving you; but nothing can change the fact that I loved Kent too." No longer calm, her voice rose to a strident asperity. "You were right, though; it is different for a man. You men can walk out, or in your case, sail away, while women are left to raise—what did you call them?——the 'products of infidelity.' Well, I'll continue to raise my *product* just as I will the *product* you produced.''

Her anger subsided as quickly as it had flared, but not in time to prevent Audrey's wail of desolation. Instantly Rebecca was on her knees, cuddling her infant daughter and looking accusingly at her husband, who remained motionless in his chair, staring at the pair of females on the floor. His face reflected the indecision of a man whose last defenses had been snatched away.

''Where's my son, Rebecca?''

''He's with Benn.''

''And who is Benn? Another of your special friends?''

''Very special! He's a gangling young man of nineteen who's bright enough to tutor my brothers and fast enough on his feet to keep up with Michael. Eventually he'll become a Congregationalist minister.''

''He sounds very useful, but I propose to take over my son's care.''

''Before you become too possessive about Michael, I suggest you read his adoption papers. I laid them out for you on the desk.''

''They're in French!''

''Your mistress was French, remember?''

Philip glared at Rebecca for a moment before he turned his attention to the pages of neatly scripted legalities. His reaction when it came was a muttered curse.

''I hope you have a good explanation for this insulting nonsense,'' he rasped.

''Paulette dictated the terms; my only contribution was to change Michel Henri to Michael Philip. It was Paulette who omitted your name completely and signed her own as Madame Henri Dupris. So you see, Philip, Michael may be your natural son, but he's my legal one. I kept those papers to prevent Paulette's ever demanding more money or Michael's return, but I've never shown them to anyone before.''

''What a bitch she was!''

''A very bitter woman, at any rate.''

''What about his last name?''

"He was christened with your name at the same time my daughter was. If you object, I can have them both changed to Rayburn."

"The devil you can! Just as a matter of interest, how did you convince the minister that I could possibly be the father of—of *her*?"

"She has a name, Philip. It's Audrey Gwenna after my mother and my Welsh grandmother. And it was very simple to convince everybody in the state. My Uncle Samuel wrote a letter to Isaiah Thomas saying that I'd spent three months in England during your trial and that my journey there and back had been sponsored by Lord Enderly, who was fighting to save your life. Mr. Thomas printed the letter and the lie that I was carrying your child in his *Massachusetts Spy*."

Rebecca was tensely nervous by the time she finished speaking; and never had any interruption been as welcome as the childish shriek of "Mama" coming from the rear hallway, followed instantly by the clatter of small feet pounding on the wooden floorboards. Philip's first glimpse of his son was of a small, muscular whirlwind erupting into the library and throwing himself into his mother's arms. His voice was lowered to an excited shout as he tugged at Rebecca's sleeve.

"Come on, Mama, it's fishing day!"

"Sweetheart, Mama can't go today."

"Can Auggie?"

"Your sister's still too little to play near the water, and I don't think you'll want to go either when you hear—"

"Johnny's going, and Benn and Lloyd."

"Please don't interrupt me, Michael. There's someone very important I want you to meet. This gentleman is your father, sweetheart."

For the first time since Michael had entered the room, he had nothing to say as he stared with the uncompromising appraisal of childhood at the stranger who returned the look with a very similar degree of calculation. If Rebecca had ever had any doubts about the relationship, they were forever obliterated during that moment of mutual scrutiny. The two vividly handsome faces were comically alike as

they reflected an identical degree of caution. When Philip
spoke finally, his voice lacked any emotional enthusiasm;
and Rebecca wondered if he hadn't been hoping Michael
would prove to be another man's son.

"I'm your father." It was a simple admission of what he
couldn't deny or ignore.

Immature as he was, the not-quite four-year-old proved
the more persistent negotiator, the more stubbornly resistant to suggestion. "Auggie's too?" he demanded intently.

Reacting to the unexpected question with shock, Rebecca
cursed herself for being stupid enough to allow Michael to
meet his father in Audrey's presence. Since the day he'd
met the sweetly placid infant, her son had developed a
protective affection for the little girl that had delighted her.
But now that childish attachment had driven his sensitive,
skittish father into a corner; and Rebecca knew from long
experience that Philip hated any kind of entrapment. With
a heavy dread she heard Philip's reluctant, unwilling
answer.

"I'm Audrey's father too."

At least he remembered her name, Rebecca reflected,
frantically seeking a diversion of some kind to ease the
tension. But Michael had no intention of overlooking a
second golden opportunity. Taking two steps toward his
father, he addressed the demoralized man with still another
peremptory demand.

"Can we go?"

"Go where?" Philip asked in confusion.

"Fishing!"

Rebecca was never to forget her husband's initiation
into fatherhood that Saturday afternoon along a shallow
fork of the Charles River. Lloyd and Johnny had returned
from school as excited as Michael, but not about fishing.
As he did frequently as part of his broader community
ministry, Reverend Elliott spoke to the assembled Roxbury
Latin School student body during prayer hour, but on this
Saturday his message had not been religious. He announced the arrival of the Massachusetts naval hero Captain Philip Keane, who would reside in Roxbury with his
family while he was engaged in training marine recruits. In

his short sermon about Christian mercy during wartime, the reverend told about Captain Keane's courageous rescue of six English children, a heroic action that led to his own capture.

Dumbfounded by Johnny's glowing-eyed report of the school meeting, Philip muttered, "How the devil did anyone know I was here?"

Rebecca smiled and murmured something vague about small-town gossip, but her respect and gratitude for the ubiquitous Reverend Elliott increased. He had undoubtedly learned of Philip's return from his Boston friends and was making very certain that the "naval hero" was well received both by the townspeople and by two young brothers-in-law who might otherwise have a difficult time adjusting to a new authority in their lives.

Throughout the half-mile walk to the fishing spot, Philip was besieged by questions from Lloyd and Johnny, who walked on either side of him and competed for his attention while Rebecca, Benn, and Michael followed in mute silence. Having been overruled by her husband in her decision to remain at home, Rebecca was experiencing a disturbing ambivalence over his brusque assumption of fatherhood. The steely look he'd bent on his son boded ill for any future harmony, since Michael possessed an equally strong willpower.

At the riverside Philip curtly announced that he'd watch his son while the others fished undisturbed. To Rebecca's amusement, Philip discovered with a painful speed that Michael was also an avid fisherman who splashed through the foot-deep water of the rocky shoal pursuing the wily creatures with his hands and catching enough of them to astonish his father. Twice Philip wound up sitting in the water as he tried to keep up with the child's swift, darting movements. Both times Philip's irritation was blunted by his son's valiant efforts to help him stand, but it was the "Massachusetts naval hero" who suggested an early termination to the outing.

"We have enough fish to feed an army," he announced as he pulled his boots on over soaking-wet breeches. Rebecca had to agree; in the past months she'd been unsuccessful in her attempts to land the evasive brook trout, but today she'd caught three, bringing the combined total to fifteen.

On the way home, still in the rear with Benn and Michael, Rebecca experienced only one bad moment when Michael pulled away from her hand and darted forward to squirm up his father's tall frame to anchor himself firmly on the broad shoulders. She felt the hot sting of tears as she remembered the same performance with another man and another river.

"Oh, Kent, my very dear love," she mourned silently. "You were the one who welded us into a family—even Philip—although he'll never know it."

Recalled to a practical consideration of the present by the sounds of agitation emanating from Benn's throat, she noted the bobbing Adam's apple and convulsive swallowings.

"Mrs. Keane," he finally blurted, "will I still be needed now that your husband is home?"

"Benn," she assured him with a wide grin, "after chasing Michael around today, Philip will be very grateful for your services as long as you choose to stay with us." The young New Englander's answering smile was one of relief.

That night in the privacy of the master bedroom, Philip echoed her response to Benn with a tired vehemence. "I'm damned glad you had the sense to tell young Maddock he still has a job."

Rebecca's shoulders stiffened defensively; Philip had been thirty feet away when she'd talked to Benn. "You have good ears," she murmured.

"I'll be needing them here as much as I did aboard ship."

"Why would you?"

"Because it seems you didn't quite tell me everything during your confessions this morning. You didn't mention a word about your plans to take your brothers and my son to your lover's estate in Wales."

Shrugging her shoulders in a hopeless defeat, Rebecca struck back angrily. "You must have asked some interesting questions. It isn't like my brothers to confide in strangers.''

''I'm no stranger. Did you plan to go to Wales?''

''Yes, I would have taken all three of them to the ends of the earth to get them out of what had become a plague city.''

''So that's why Lord Enderly was so anxious to keep me alive. He didn't want the scandal dumped on his own doorstep.''

''You're wrong about Lord Enderly, Philip Keane. Before he knew you were still alive, he approved of me as his son's wife. And he didn't know about the expected child until long after he sent me to Boston.''

''What would he have done if he'd known? Secure an annulment for you so his grandchild would be legitimate?''

''I don't know what he would have done. I don't even know what I would ha—''

Ignoring the interrupted second part of her response, Philip continued his relentless castigation. ''It wouldn't have done any good under any circumstances. You're my wife and you're going to remain my wife.''

''You make it sound like a punishment.''

''It needn't be as long as you don't expect me to compete against a dead lover. Why didn't you tell me that he'd taught my son and your brothers to swim and to ride horseback and to ice-skate and God only knows what else? I felt like a fool today, thinking I was keeping that wild Indian of mine from drowning, and all the time he was taking care of me. What's there left for me to do for him?''

Rebecca was laughing with relief by the time he'd finished his complaint. ''You won't have to do anything but be his father. Michael has already decided that you belong to him. And you've given my brothers something they badly needed—a pride in being American. Before today the only decent people they'd ever known were two old loyalist uncles and a young Englishman.''

''What about their parents?''

''They hardly know Jeremy, and their mother left them with my uncles and never tried to see them, not even before she sailed to England. Instead, she sent Roger to keep an eye on them.''

''Did you know that they're still afraid of that blackguard?''

''Roger has become a very frightening man.''

''Then it's a good thing I'm here. I have a score to settle with all of the Tuptons. But you're wrong about the lack of decent people in their lives. They have you, and you're as possessive of them as you are of Michael and—and his sister. Why did you ever accept him as your own, Cottontop? You must have hated that damned Frenchwoman.''

''I was jealous that he wasn't mine in reality, Philip. As soon as Paulette told me about the letter she'd sent you, I knew that you'd gone to France to find him; so I adopted him before I'd ever seen him.''

''Was it difficult for you?''

''For months I was an absolute failure as a mother, but now I can't imagine life without him.''

''One more question, Cottontop. Is Lord Enderly supporting you?''

Angered anew by this abrupt return to an earlier antagonism, Rebecca responded with a blunt thoroughness. ''No. Except for this house, which he deeded over to me, I'm supporting my family. My Uncle Jonathan won't be returning to America because of Abigail, so he asked Lord Enderly to transfer the money my mother left me to a Boston bank. It's a considerable amount, Philip, enough for all of our needs; but you might as well know the whole story. Kent named me as his sole heir to an even larger estate. I returned the will and my refusal to his father; but by that time Lord Enderly knew there was to be a child, and he insisted that Audrey would inherit her full share. I'm sorry if it displeases you, but I accepted his offer in her name.''

''It doesn't displease me in the least, Cottontop; it merely explains why he made me promise to bring my whole family to visit him in England after the war. As for your money, I'm delighted. It may be months or years before I can retrieve my own fortune or what's left of it from Baltimore and France. In the meantime, I'll let you support me; and I warn you that for a few months, I'll be expensive. I ruined one of my two suits during that idiot display today.''

For a moment before she burst into laughter Rebecca stared at the complacent man relaxing comfortably in bed. He was exactly what Dena had called him, ''a take-over man.'' But even now she wasn't given any time to reply to his outrageous tyranny. With an impatient complaint, he ordered her to join him in bed.

''You've been brushing your hair for a half hour, Cottontop, while I've been waiting; and you might as well remove those shrouds you're wearing. I've spent almost two years thinking about the process of begetting children, not about taking care of those already here.''

Her opportunity for revenge came, however, with his final admonition. ''One more rule I expect you to follow, Cottontop. You'd better damn well be at my side tomorrow and every other morning when I wake up.''

With a boldness that lacked any trace of subservience Rebecca climbed into bed and reached her hand out in a caress that was both forward and expert.

''Tomorrow morning,'' she murmured piously into his ear, ''you'll arise promptly and put on your one good suit, because you're going to be on display at the Roxbury Congregationalist Church as its newest member.''

''We'll decide about that in the morning, Cottontop. Right now I'm not feeling one bit religious, only impatient for you to stop talking.''

Repressing a giggle at the ease with which he ignored his own day-long marathon of inquisition, Rebecca burrowed into the shelter of his arms, relaxing her taut vigilance for the first time since early morning. For a moment she lay quiescently content, savoring the comfortable sensation of a strong man's body next to her own. But more than the physical gratification, she welcomed the inner warmth of the emotional security he had offered her, however ungraciously. As if he, too, were experiencing the same sense of homecoming, he greeted her with a gently prolonged kiss that was more a pledge of permanency than the violent passion of the preceding night. And his quiet words when he did begin the ritual of love, she would remember the rest of her life. "It's been a rough voyage without you, Cottontop. If I hadn't been able to find you, I don't think I'd have cared what happened to me."

Rebecca closed her eyes in a different kind of ecstasy and kissed him. She didn't need the stimulation of long drawn-out caresses to receive him with a bottled-up hunger; she felt only the sweet tumult of exultation as she pulled him to her. Afterward, as they held each other in sleepy contentment, even his mumbled comment sounded like a benediction to her.

"I haven't been inside a church in twenty years. Are you sure you want me to go with you, Cottontop?"

"I want you with me," she murmured, "in church and every place else."

A hundred feet away from their home the next morning after Philip had smiled broadly at another couple headed for the same church service, he reached over and removed the tiny bonnet perched over Audrey's curls, fluffed the silky hair into a soft halo, and pronounced judiciously, "She looks prettier that way, and I'm happy to see that she didn't inherit your disposition or your stubbornness."

Rebecca was mute with astonishment when he removed the gurgling, happy infant from her arms, cradled her comfortably with one of his, and gripped Michael's hand tightly. His relaxed humor, though, astonished her still more, and she was glad that Dena and her brothers were not within hearing distance.

"Since I let you talk me into this public display, we might as well put on a good show. I'll even tolerate that pretty Puritan disguise you're wearing, provided you remember that I'll expect the real Cottontop to emerge the minute our bedroom door is closed. And that reminds me; we're converting the room next to ours into a bathroom with a tiled tub. A man about to become a churchgoing pillar of society will need at least some of the basic creature comforts to keep him human. As I remember, you were just mastering the art of scrubbing my back among other things when—"

"Philip!" Rebecca protested with a meaningful glance at Michael.

Looking down at the glum little boy whose face bore none of its fishing-day sparkle, Philip remembered how he'd hated the hours he'd been forced to sit with his mother in bored silence on the uncomfortable pews of his boyhood church. But he doubted very much that his own son would prove as tractable or as patient. Already, in the short time he'd known this boisterous and active little boy, Philip had noted Michael's stubborn and resourceful resistance to discipline. He obeyed good-naturedly enough, but only after his artful repertoire of distractions had failed or when Rebecca smiled at him and shook her head.

As Philip glanced over the small blonde head resting trustingly against his shoulder, he met his wife's eyes and smiled involuntarily. She glowed with a warm radiance, but her expression held more than a little of challenging humor. With a perverse admiration for her, Philip acknowledged her right to that humor. Despite his anger and hurt, he'd accepted her terms because the prospect of a future without her was untenable. In two nights she'd almost erased the memory of his bitter loneliness that had been three years in the making, and she'd salvaged his pride without surrendering a jot of her own by welcoming him into the family she'd already bound together with love. Nor had she made any demands about the degree of his participation in that family other than his appearance at church. Philip's smile broadened; he had no intention of becoming a mere figurehead father. This morning his son would learn that his impulsive whims were now under firmer control.

Aware that he was the center of considerable interest among the members of the congregation already gathered, Philip responded with the poise of a man accustomed to public attention. Unfortunately, he did not notice that his small son was equally alert. As they passed a pew belonging to another family, Michael had reached out with his one free hand and appropriated a prayer book. Before Philip could react with anything other than embarrassment, a watchful Johnny had returned the book to its owners.

Repressing his chagrin, Philip seated his son firmly next to Audrey and cautioned him to be quiet with a stern look and a steady finger touching the small curling lips. But twice during the introductory prayers, Michael's delighted shout of "*Auggie*" had mingled with the *hallelujah*s of the responsive congregation.

Moving his son judiciously to his other side, Philip reached into his pocket and removed the compact Gowin-Knight compass the British merchant captain had given him to steer the small boat safely through the fog into New London Harbor. For a few minutes Michael watched the shimmering needle in hypnotized silence, and Philip relaxed his taut vigilance. His wandering attention was again focused on his son, however, when he heard a victorious intake of breath. To his consternation, his son's busy fingers had loosened the center cap of the card compass and the needle was in dire jeopardy until the agitated father hastily repaired the damage and returned the valuable instrument to his pocket. Thoughtfully, Philip shook his head; he doubted that even his most dextrous navigator could have unscrewed that firmly set pivot cap so easily.

Throughout the remainder of the service, mercifully shortened to two hours in deference to the summer heat, Philip struggled to retain control of his temper and his restless son, whose wiry body seemed incapable of quiescent repose for intervals exceeding a minute or two. Even before the stirring words of the benediction stopped reverberating through the cathedraled timbers, Philip herded his family outside and sighed with relief as Michael darted off in a mad dash for freedom to join the other children exploding from the church.

"I lost what little religion I had, trying to keep him quiet," Philip grumbled.

Rebecca giggled as she handed her drowsy daughter to a Sunday-clad Dena. "When maple candy failed," she murmured, "I sent him outside with Johnny."

Smiling up at the tall husband she'd never expected to recapture so easily, she hugged his arm. "I'm glad you decided to stay with us," she whispered.

"What would you have done if I hadn't, Cottontop?" he

asked softly, tempted to break the remainder of the church rules pertaining to propriety and prudery by kissing her.

Sure of her hold on him for the first time throughout a turbulent, often interrupted marriage, Rebecca grinned triumphantly.

"Oh, I'd have sent Michael to keep you company until you came to your senses," she admitted airily.

Philip was still laughing when a beaming Reverend Richard Elliott approached them, his hand outstretched in greeting, his missionary zeal bent upon welcoming still another imperfect member into his growing congregation.

The Best Of
Warner Romances

___**BOLD BREATHLESS LOVE**   *(D30-849, $3.95, U.S.A.)*
by Valerie Sherwood   *(D30-838, $4.95, Canada)*

The surging saga of Imogene, a goddess of grace with riotous golden curls—and Verholst Van Rappard, her elegant idolator. They marry and he carries her off to America—not knowing that Imogene pines for a copper-haired Englishman who made her his on a distant isle and promised to return to her on the wings of love.

___**LOVE, CHERISH ME**   *(D30-039, $3.95, U.S.A.)*
by Rebecca Brandewyne   *(D32-135, $4.95, Canada)*

"Set in Texas, it may well have been the only locale big enough to hold this story that one does, not so much read, as revel in. From the first chapter, the reader is enthralled with a story so powerful it defies description and a love so absolute it can never be forgotten. LOVE, CHERISH ME is a blend of character development, sensuous love and historic panorama that makes a work of art a masterpiece."
              —*Affaire De Coeur*

___**FORGET-ME-NOT**   *(D30-715, $3.50, U.S.A.)*
by Janet Louise Roberts   *(D30-716, $4.50, Canada)*

Unhappy in the civilized cities, Laurel Winfield was born to bloom in the Alaskan wilds of the wide tundras, along the free-flowing rivers. She was as beautiful as the land when she met the Koenig brothers and lost her heart to the strong-willed, green-eyed Thor. But in Alaska violence and greed underlie the awesome beauty, and Laurel would find danger here as well as love.